Admirals and Generals

Admirals and Generals

Dan Ryan

AuthorHouse™
1663 Liberty Drive
Bloomington, IN 47403
www.authorhouse.com
Phone: 1-800-839-8640

First published by AuthorHouse   2/23/2010

ISBN: 978-1-4490-7096-0 (sc)
ISBN: 978-1-4490-7098-4 (e)
ISBN: 978-1-4490-7097-7 (hc)

Library of Congress Control Number: 2010901863

Printed in the United States of America
Bloomington, Indiana

This book is printed on acid-free paper.

Prelude

On June 26, 1877, I would celebrate my 60th birthday. After my retirement from the Naval Academy, we moved to Seneca Hill, Pennsylvania, and started to plan a giant, retirement, graduation and birthday party with family and friends. For a week people had been arriving in Oil City by train. The first to arrive was Monty Blair with the news that Bell's air cooled telephone lines had been successfully strung and tested in Boston. Sam and Rachael Mason had come up from Annapolis and had moved into their old living quarters for the week. Rachael's mother had not lived long after her father's death and they had sold the house in Arlington. They then moved onto the grounds of the Naval Academy so that Sam could be closer to his position as Superintendent of the Naval Institute. My parents were both gone also; my mother first and then my father. They had died in their Beaufort home while helping Robbie, their Grandson, restore his dream. They were both buried in St. Helena's Church yard beside my brother and sister who had died in infancy. My brother, Robert, and his wife, Mariann, had sold all their property in Bermuda and moved back to South Carolina. Robert and Mariann had come for our son's graduation and then came north with us to Pennsylvania. Robert's twin daughters, Karen and Sharon, were both married, one lived in Virginia and the other in Maryland with their families. Louise had sent invitations, but they had not responded. Our immediate family was home. James, known as JJ, had graduated from the Naval Academy on June 2nd and was scheduled to begin his two year tour of sea duty, shortly. He was hoping for a stop in Norway, no doubt! Ruth was home from Harvard with the "nice young man" she had met, a Mr. Theodore Roosevelt. She told her mother that it was not serious, but I had seen them mooning over each other. Carol had finished her last year of preparatory school before entering Columbia University. Soon the house would be empty and Louise and I could finally begin retirement.

Hotel rooms in Franklin, Oil City and as far away as Titusville were reserved for last minute guests who would arrive on the day before the celebration. There was a definite pecking order. You could not ask the President of the United States, his Secretary of the Navy or the Commandant of the Marine Corps to stay in a hotel. I had become one of President Hayes' closest confidants. We had bounced ideas off of each other by telephone since March 4th. If he stayed in the house, then several rooms were taken by the White House core. When the President saw this, he had a funeral parlor in Titusville donate several large tents for use at Seneca Hill and he moved everyone but himself, Ben Hagood and Chris Merryweather, into the tents for the week. He wanted bedrooms set aside for "special guests" that were coming from long distances. The President personally helped welcome the train from Hannibal, Missouri, which carried Samuel Clemens, but he neglected to a meet another train a few hours later from Louisville, Kentucky, which carried Jerome Lewis and his family. Jerome was retired from the navy and was now the Chief of Police for Louisville.

Brigadier General Tom Schneider and his wife, Beth, arrived without children and checked into the hotel in Oil City in order to have a place to sleep, but spent all their time at Seneca Hill. Hop Sing would have loved the celebration had he lived to see it, but his son ,Won Sing, was there. Won Sing was the vice president of Seneca Oil and followed the president around trying to anticipate his every need. The president was Peter Clivestone, who had dropped his British accent, and left Seneca Hill long enough to study for a degree in business administration from Penn College. He would remind Won Sing that his father never liked him and he was a terrible cook. Won would bow low and reply, "Most honorable president of world's smallest oil company, you wery good person at hart. But Admiral will fire your ass, if he ever hear you say that about honorable father."

The train from Nevada caused the most stir, when several men with ten gallon cowboy hats and side arms stepped off the train in Oil City. David Dewayne Wilson and Corene were still childless but she made quite a stir dressed as a native American Indian. Mathew James and his wife, Connie, and their three children got off next, followed by Marshal and Karen Peters with their young child and new infant. They were on their way to Pittsburgh so the grandparents could see the new grandchild. Herman Schussler, his wife and thirteen children and grandchildren filled the empty places on the platform.

The last arriving guests were from Bermuda. The Cold Harbor brought anyone who could come aboard for the voyage to the Port of Philadelphia. From there they took a train to Oil City. They filled the remaining hotel rooms and the celebration could finally begin. My wife was a former first lady in the White House and a gathering this size did not affect her. She was the commanding general of the "house on the hill" between Oil City and Titusville, Pennsylvania. It was built while we both worked in the White House under the Buchanan Administration and it had over a 135 rooms, because that is what Louise wanted.

"You are the chairman of Caldwell International, Jason. You will be entertaining US Presidents and foreign heads of state. We need something as impressive as my 'brother's house'".

"You mean, The White House?" I was stunned.

"That is exactly what I mean. You are an Admiral in the United States Navy and you are the National Affairs Advisor to the President of the United States."

And so the building began and it became a corporate headquarters for the company I had founded many years before in Port Royal, South Carolina, called Caldwell Shipping and Trading. Today, June 24, 1877, the house was full. Every bedroom was taken. Louise had hired more household staff for the week. The first evening meal was not unlike those she organized in the White House. The main table held all the Admirals and Generals in the house. President Hayes, a former brigadier general, and now the commander-in-chief, and Mrs. Hayes sat beside Louise and I. Admiral Ben Hagood and his side kick, General Chris Merryweather, sat next to General and Mrs. Tom Schneider. They were seated next to the Chief of Police and his wife from Louisville Kentucky. Next to them sat Colonel Sam Mason, Superintendent of the Naval Institute, and his wife from Annapolis, Maryland. They were seated next to General John Butler and his wife, Sally from Bermuda. The tables forming the dining hall were arranged so that they contained smaller groups. The tables had a theme to them, the rapid response marines and their families were grouped together. The Nevada group of tables was placed next to them. The South Carolina relatives were grouped together with our children and their mates. The original Caldwell Shipping group was headed by Captain Jacobs and his family. The original Caldwell Trading and Banking group was headed by Robert Whitehall and his family. The ATT table was headed by Monty Blair. And so the dining room looked like a gathering of family and friends from the last forty years.

After dinner, Louise said, "Welcome everyone to our home. I have asked Jason to tell you a story of his life. It involves everyone in this room. As you know, Jason, is a talker and it may not be finished after this meal. He will continue each night until he is finished. He has promised me that he will not be offended if you find his story boring and want to excuse yourselves to retire early or put little children to bed. Jason, you have the floor." Louise sat back down on her dining room chair and I stood.

"I suppose my story begins with the acceptance to the United States Military Academy.........."

1

Acceptance to the Academy
Spring 1832

My father, Robert Caldwell, was a wealthy planter. He was also the South Carolina State Chairman of the Democratic Party. He had helped convince John C. Calhoun to accept the nomination for Vice President in 1825, as running mate to President John Q. Adams and again in 1829, as running mate to Andrew Jackson. We lived in a large white house on Bay Street, Beaufort, South Carolina, that overlooked the intercoastal waterway. We had the normal house servants, and a carriage house with horses and a couple of men who lived above the carriage house. They drove my family wherever we needed to go in the county. At any early age, I remember my father taking me and my one year older brother , to Port Royal. In addition to the family plantation beside Datha Island, he ran a small shipping company that hauled goods as far east as Bermuda and as far south as Amelia Island, Florida. I was fascinated by the people I met on the docks there. Especially the workers who came early in the morning to work hard all day, just off shore, to harvest the shrimp and sea food sold on the docks. That is where I met Christopher Merryweather. His father owned a fleet of fishing boats and my father said Mr. Merryweather was an up and coming young business man. They did not live in a large house with servants. They lived close to the docks in Port Royal. Christopher's parents had five children and they did all the household tasks themselves. His mother cooked, cleaned and ran the house. His father kept his own horses, drove his own wagon to work and town. Naturally, Christopher and I became best friends.

Before I met Christopher, the best friend I had was the banker's son, Robert Whitehall. My father approved of Robert and he tolerated Christopher. When I begged my father to join Christopher on the shrimp boats one summer, my father said, "If you and Christopher want to spend time on ships, I will hire the two of you to sail with the captains back and forth to Amelia Island. They never leave sight of the coast and you should be safe."

Christopher's father thought that this was the perfect way to teach his son how to earn money on his own and how to manage it for his college education. My father was a college graduate, Christopher's was not. We spent our summers together aboard the Westwind, a schooner, the Oracle, a cutter, and the Spritewell, a galley. All three Caldwell merchant ships were just large enough to make us yearn for the large transatlantic vessels that we saw in many of the harbors that we visited. During the school year, I did not see Christopher much because he attended the Port Royal elementary and secondary school there. Robert Whitehall and I attended the Beaufort Academy. The year before we finished our school years, Robert applied to South Carolina College in Columbia. My father had sent my brother ,Robert, there a year ago. He looked at me and said, "I suppose you do not want to go to college, Jason." He was surprised to hear, "I want very much to make application to West Point, but I do not know how that is done."

"Leave it to me, Jason. Should I also include Christopher in my letter of inquiry to John Calhoun?"

"We have talked about going together, either to West Point or the USMA prep school in Bamberg, South Carolina.

"Governor Richardson has asked the State legislature to form a Military College of South Carolina. It would be located at the Citadel building on Marion Square in downtown Charleston. The Citadel would be army, Jason, you could not qualify for sea duty from there."

"Chris needs a way to enter the United States Marine Corps, and I need a way to enter the United States Navy as an officer."

During the next few months we waited to see what, if any, influence my father might have with the Vice President of the United States, the honorable John C. Calhoun. In the Spring, I was rejected by both the Carlisle Military Academy in Bamberg and the newly formed Military College of South Carolina. A week later I was accepted by the United States Military Academy. Christopher was accepted at Carlisle. My father said, "Now, boys, we have to visit West Point so you can see what you have chosen and what type of institution has granted you acceptance. What do you know about West Point, Christopher?"

"I know what I have studied in school. It is the site of the United States Military Academy, as well as a military post. The entire post comprises 2300 acres of property, 2100 acres were purchased in 1790 and the remainder in 1826. I know it was an important military position during the American Revolution (1775-80). It is 1500 hundred feet above the Hudson and this was fortified at a total cost of $3,000,000 by the Polish patriot, Kosciuszko, who was an army engineer. The fort at West Point defenses comprise a curious and massive iron chain stretched across the channel from the Point to Constitution Island. At the disbandment of the army at the close of the war, West Point was designated as the depot for the storage of military property. In 1794, it was garrisoned by the Corps of Engineers. In 1802, it became a military academy to train army engineers and in 1826 two hundred acres were set aside for the training of general officers to serve in our military."

"You are absolutely correct, Christopher. You know that Carlisle will prepare you for West Point and that transfer there will depend upon openings available at that time."

"Yes, Sir."

"Good, I have arranged for you and Jason to visit the 200 acres that you described as the campus. We will see the cadet barracks, academic buildings, library, superintendent's office, mess hall, hospital and riding hall. We have an appointment to meet with the Superintendent, a Captain Sylvanus Thayer. I must warn you boys that my letters from Vice President Calhoun do not sound hopeful. It seems that President Jackson is not pleased with the progress made by Superintendent Thayer to integrate other branches of the service into the academic curriculum or military training. He has ignored the Navy requests, for instance. He may be replaced before you get there, Jason, and he will surely be gone when you report a year later, Christopher. You boys understand?"

"Yes, Sir." We both said.

My father arranged with my headmaster at Beaufort and Chris's teachers in Port Royal for us to be gone from school to visit West Point. We drove to Port Royal, picked up Chris, and boarded the Westwind. We spent several days at sea, mostly close to shore as we hugged the North Carolina outer banks, Virginia's and Maryland's eastern shores. We sailed across Delaware Bay and passed Atlantic City and Newark, New Jersey. We entered New York Harbor and were within 50 miles of West Point. We kept to the right bank of the Hudson River and saw the Point in all its picturesqueness. The Hudson River was breaking through the highlands in a winding gap. The buildings were grouped upon a plateau of 200 acres at an elevation of 175 feet above the water.

We got permission to dock at the "Point" and asked for directions to the Superintendent's office. We waited a few minutes before being asked to enter his office and he began his remarks. " I want you to understand what you are about to see. Many young men, some famous, come to West Point and leave after just a short time. The most famous, I can think of is Edgar Allan Poe, who lasted only a few months. Last year, '31, saw 35 cadets leave the Point. A graduation class is less than 55 per year. So far this year, 24 cadets have called it quits."

My father asked us, " Do you two boys remember J. J. McMahan's boy from Sumter, South Carolina? He quit, it may not be for you, boys. Write to me each month and let me know if I need to bring the Westwind up for you."

"Your son's letter of acceptance is based on the fact that he will leave here as a second lieutenant in the United States Corps of Engineers. After his graduation he may apply for acceptance into the United States Navy. This acceptance into the Navy will be based on how well he does in the summer cruises. He will still have a civil engineering degree and a position in the United States Army Corps of Engineers, no matter what the Navy decides."

"He understands that." My father replied.

"If I pass the first summer cruise, father, I will travel with my class from Annapolis to West Point and you will not have to bring the schooner up for me."

"Christopher, do you understand that your acceptance here at West Point is dependent upon how well you perform at Carlisle?"

"Yes, Sir."

"Good, I have assigned your tour to a member of my staff, I hope to see both of you here at the Point."

2
Summer Cruise
Annapolis, 1833

I remember that summer like it was yesterday. Robert Whitehall stayed in Beaufort and worked at his father's bank, waiting for the fall term to begin in Columbia. Chris stayed in Port Royal and worked his last summer on my father's three cargo ships before reporting to Bamberg and Carlisle. My father and I went to Port Royal to catch one of his packet ships to Baltimore, Maryland. He had bought me a ticket on a new mode of transportation called a railroad which consisted of two parallel tracks and a Baltimore and Ohio steam engine that pulled a series of box like cars into Annapolis, Maryland. I was already accepted at West Point and if I passed my summer cruise duties, I was on my way to the United States Navy. My entire belongings were stuffed in a sea bag that I had used on my father's ships. I thought I looked very seaworthy. The train pulled into the Baltimore station, my father shook my hand and said, "Jason, write to your mother as often as you can."

I was trying to get my sea bag into the seat beside me when I met other cadets going to Annapolis. Their names were John Campbell, Alexander Bowman and Benjamin Hagood. Ben was from Savannah, Georgia. My father and I had been to Savannah many times over the last couple of years for his shipping business and we struck up a conversation.

"What does you father do?" Asked Ben.

"He owns a small shipping business, just three ships. I think he started it because it was difficult to get goods to and from our plantation."

"My, lord. Your family owns a plantation? You must be filthy rich!"

"No, my friend, Robert Whitehall, is filthy rich. My father gave me a hundred dollars before I got on the train and said it had to last me until next term."

"At least your father gave you money, mine gave me advice!"

The conversation lasted just long enough for the train to enter a platform like structure with a sign over it which read, "Naval Training Depot." We got off the train with our bags and stood on the train platform in Annapolis. We were two wide eyed southern boys nominated by our home US senators to serve our country as Naval Cadets, US Military Academy. We were standing around waiting for someone to meet us and take us to the US Naval Depot.

5

A sergeant of some kind and an officer, we did not know ranks in the Navy at that time, came striding up to us. The officer was stern looking and yelled at the top of his voice, "All you men that have arrived as first year cadets will come to attention!" None of us had ever been in the service of our country before, so we stopped talking and paid attention to him.

"What the hell is this?" The sergeant yelled. "I am Master Chief Gunnerman! When a United States Naval Officer commands you to come to attention, you will place whatever is in your hands two inches from your right ankle, you will suck in that flabby excuse for a gut, square your shoulders and stare two inches above his head. You will then cause your right arm to extend upward, bent at the elbow and give your best imitation of a boy scout salute."

Master Chief Gunnerman scared the shit out us. We jumped into a straight line and attempted to come to attention. Ben screamed, "Yeas, Sir." in his best southern drawl.

"You do not, 'Yeas, Sir me,' you dumb ass. I am not an officer. The proper response is aye, aye."

"Aye, aye, Sir!" We all yelled at the top of our voices.

Master Chief Gunnerman turned to his officer and said, "Sir, they are hopeless, I will throw their ass's back on the train and send them back to where they came from."

"Let me have a crack that them, Chief."

"Aye, aye, Sir"

"Gentlemen, in just four short years you may be standing where I am, a graduate of the United States Military Academy, looking at a bunch of shave tails. Shaking your head and wondering how they are ever going to make Naval officers and gentlemen. The Chief, here, will get all of you onto the depot grounds and be with you through your processing. That will be all."

He turned on his heel and marched away. The Master Chief smiled and said, "The pleasantries are over, you bunch of maggots. Hoist you gear and fall in a straight line."

We fumbled around for our belongings, clutched them to our chests and tried to form a line. "What the hell is this? Hoist your gear, means throw it on your shoulder, I am not going to show you babies how to do things. I am NOT your mother! Form a line of three abreast." He shouted. We marched, sort of, off the train platform and down a brick covered street. I had never seen bricks on a street before. There were cobble stones on the streets of Savannah, but Beaufort had hard packed, red clay streets that became very slippery when it rained. We marched down side streets until we came to a rough collection of wooden buildings at the water's edge. We took our gear into a building that looked like it was a hundred years old. It was. It was built in 1730. The floors were dirty, windows broken out in places and completely bare of any furnishings.

"Drop your bags, maggots!"

We piled them into a corner and stood waiting for instructions. "You need to follow me to the supply warehouse. Line up single file. Step forward as I call your name." The master chief had produced from somewhere, a hand full of paper name tags and he began calling the names of the 1833 cadets assigned to the "summer cruise".

A summer cruise sounds like you might be headed for a nice sail down the Chesapeake and into the Atlantic Ocean. This summer cruise was "boot camp". We each had a name tag and followed Master Chief Gunnerman to the supply warehouse. He turned us over to the Navy personnel for processing. First we stripped off every bit of clothing that was on our bodies. The thirty-three boys and men stood around trying not to be self-conscious, until we were called to pickup our Navy underwear. It was an odd shade of gray and had the following stamped on the back of each piece. "US Navy Depot, 1812."

"Jason, these things are older than we are." Ben whispered.

"Only by five years." I replied straight faced. We pulled them over our heads and up over our legs and waited.

"Step forward, go behind the curtain so the doctor can examine you."

We each passed the doctor's probe and were issued sailcloth shirts, pants and a real sailor's white cap. We were will still barefooted. We were issued 1812 socks and white canvas shoes that were stiff as boards. We were now fully dressed and we filed through another line to pick up a second issue of everything we had on our bodies. By this time, Master Chief Gunnerman was back with a smile on his face. "You will take your second set of Navy issues back to your barracks and place them inside your bags." The empty warehouse with the broken windows was the "barracks". When we had done this the Master Chief said we should clean out the barracks so that our cots could be brought over from "supply". He handed us each a bucket, a bar of soap and a stiff brush. "Now the object of this exercise is make the ceiling, walls and floor so clean you can eat off them. Walk down to the water, dip your bucket and get your water. Return here and begin scrubbing."

We did. The rest of that day, that night and part of the next day. None of us had slept. We were getting punchy and light headed. We needed food and water. Master Chief Gunnerman, finally appeared for inspection and said. "You maggots are going to make some women very happy in later life. This is the cleanest barracks I have ever seen. Fall out for showers, take your second set of utilities and get ready to go over to mess. We are short two members, maggots. Where are they?"

"Over on the pile of bags in the corner, Chief."

"You thirty-one awake ones head for the showers and get into clean utilities, you stink!"

I had never tasted anything so good in my life. "What is this we are eating?" Asked Ben.

"Mystery meat cutup in gravy over some sort of dried bread." I replied. The Chief showed up minus the two sleepers and we never saw them again. Supply showed up with folding cots so we could arrange them along the outside walls and get some much needed sleep. A cot had never felt so good, I slept soundly until 5 am the next morning when the Chief returned banging a metal garbage can and screaming something none of us could understand. When he finally calmed down he explained that we should be up every morning at 5 am ready for inspection. What he was going to inspect, we did not know until he showed us. Where we had taken our showers was a mess. We spent most of the day cleaning the latrines and shower heads, removing mold and mildew. We passed through mess again, ate the same stuff, whatever it was. Everyone was afraid to ask until someone dubbed it, "shit on a shingle."

That afternoon we were taken on a march around the Naval Depot, we ran down the docks and back as fast as we could. We saw six ships that looked like they had been moth balled since the American Revolution. We were not far off. They were decomissioned in 1813. A decomissioned ship is removed from the list of ships available to the Secretary of the Navy and placed on "ready reserve". Ready reserve can mean everything from men stationed aboard to keep the ship fit or what we saw at the ends of the docks at the naval training depot in the summer of 1833. Congress had decided, after the American Revolution, that the United States did not need an Army or a Navy. Army equipment, of all types, was stored at West Point and Navy ships were stored at naval depots all along the eastern seaboard. The War of 1812, with England, pointed out the errors of our ways and we kept the Army and let the Navy sit on ready reserve. Thirty-one hands came aboard the USS Spitfire, built in 1797 as a brig and used heavily during the War of 1812. Since 1812, she had seen little attention.

"You will report every day to Commander Jensen until the Spitfire is made sea worthy, maggots." The Chief turned and left us with the oldest looking man we had ever seen.

"Hello, how many of you have served on a merchant marine ship of this class?" He waited and all of us raised our hands. "What would be the first thing you would do to make this ship sea worthy?" He asked Ben Hagood.

"I would ask for volunteers to swim under the hull and check for sea worm damage and breaks in the planking, Sir!"

"Very good, seaman." He walked over and read Ben's name tag. "Cadet Hagood, pick two volunteers to go with you and go under this excuse for a war ship."

"Sir?"

"Strip down to your birthday suits and get in the water." He motioned for me and John Campbell to "volunteer" with Ben. We did.

"Take breathing hoses with you, cadets, the water is not clear enough to see everything, use your fingers and hands to find weak spots."

We spent the next hour or two inspecting the hull of the Spitfire. Unknown to us, the rest of the cadets were under the hulls of the rest of the ships at Annapolis, USS New Haven, USS Trumbull, USS Providence, USS Nelson and USS Somerset. Not a single ship had a solid hull, yet they floated on the water like they were in ready reserve.

"You thirty-one volunteers are going to learn how to pack off worm holes, mend broken planks from the inside of the holds, and make each of these vessels ready to sail. The first man here on my right is a ship's carpenter, on his right is a naval architect, on his right is a ship's wright. You will get detailed instructions on how to fill worm holes, boil pitch, saw timbers and make metal fittings of all types."

We all slept soundly that night and at 5 am we were up out of our cots, dressed and ready for inspection. "Good morning, maggots. Today, I am to bring you thirty-one down to the docks for your lesson on ship careening. Get over to mess and down to the docks by 0600." Master Chief left us standing at attention. We finished mess and walked down to where the USS New Haven was docked. Commander Jensen was waiting for us.

"Good morning, cadets. The New Haven is the smallest of the Annapolis fleet and in the worst shape. If we can get her sea worthy, the others will follow. Who were the swimmers who went under her yesterday?"

"We were, sir." Answered Alex Bowman and Tom Gibson.

"Did you notice the temporary repairs to the hull?"

"We noticed that pieces of canvas were lowered under the hull and tied with ropes. The canvas appeared to be smeared with tar."

"That is correct, Cadet Gibson, the process is called 'fothering' and it is a poor excuse for proper repair. We need to make repairs to the hull by careening this vessel. I need a volunteer to climb the main mast with this rope and pulley set."

Several cadets stepped forward and Commander Jensen sent one up the mast to attach one end of the pulley system to a metal hook. He stood below bellowing orders on how to attach the pulley so that he could carry the other end of the block and tackle to a hook inset into the surface of the repair dock. Once this was done, he grabbed the middle rope of the pulley and walked over to a capstan and fastened the rope in place. "I need four large volunteers or eight small fry to turn this capstan."

Four of us got on each of the capstan bars and began to push. Slowly the two pulleys began to come toward each other and the New Haven began to list until it was 45 degrees from the surface of the water and the left hull was fully exposed.

"Now the fun begins." The commander was smiling. Not like the Master Chief, but with a knowing smile when he said, "Today, I will show you cadets some very useful techniques that you can use later in life to make a lot of money."

The commander spent the day showing us how to brace the masts with six inch diameter poles tied to the mast and wedged into the port side gunwales. Our crew was divided into two work parties. One worked from long boats from the surface of the water as high as a man could scrape, drill out worm holes and pound in an oak plugs. The other party worked on wooden planks lowered over the side by ropes and did the repairs from the top water line to meet the surface party work areas. In a matter of days, the starboard side was completely repaired and we thought we would now do the same thing on the port side. The commander surprised us by saying, "So far all you cadets have done is what a common workman could do for you. Today the ship's wright will show you how to cut and install copper sheeting. A coppered bottom will be free of the barnacles and marine growth that you have all been working so hard to scape off. Remember, the more shit that grows on your bottom, the slower your vessel passes through the water. You will be using a punch and copper screws for fastening the sheets. If you find any flat head iron bolts, do not copper over them. The galvanic action between the two metals will cause a hole in the sheeting. Tell the ship's wright and he will place a patch over the bolt for you."

The commander looked at us and said, "I know you are all looking forward to getting the New Haven out into the Chesapeake. We are ahead of schedule and we will meet our goal of sailing the USS New Haven before the end of summer. Each of these vessels will be repaired by each of the incoming cadet classes."

We all had good intentions and we all pledged to do our best, but as the weeks turned into months the number of cadets kept getting smaller. They disappeared like the two who slept through our first day, until we had twenty-four members who had finally managed to get the USS New Haven, a ketch, away from Annapolis for a shake down sail in the Chesapeake.

After our summer was over, whenever Ben saw me, he yelled, "I am NOT your mother! I am not going to show you babies how to do things."

3
Plebe Year
West Point, 1833-34

Ben and I were each others built-in support for surviving that first summer cruise and we left Annapolis with twenty-two other survivors to help create, the 1833 Plebe Class at West Point. One of the first things that Superintendent Rene DeRussy said to all incoming plebes was, "Under Superintendent Thayer, USMA was a training institution for the Army Corps of Engineers. It was not a place where he encouraged you to join other branches of the Army or Navy. You left here prepared to do what your military fathers did before you. Many examples of this father/son relationship exist. The first to come to mind is a graduate of '29. Robert Edward Lee, son of 'Light Horse Harry Lee' a cavalry hero of the War of Independence. Robert's appointment was supported by General, now President, Andrew Jackson, just like many of you sitting here today. Robert graduated second in his class and is now a Army Corps of Engineers, second Lieutenant serving in Washington City."

Ben whispered to me, "Was your father in the American Revolution?"

I whispered back, "No, my grandfather. My father was born during the Revolution. So was Robert Lee's, I would bet."

Superintendent DeRussy replaced a living legend at West Point, Sylvanus Thayer. Captain Thayer was from the class of 1808, was a military engineer and thought everyone else should be, also. He came to the Point in 1818 and stayed until he was dismissed by President Jackson for failure to provide additional areas of study and military options. "Under my supervision, we will provide a civil engineering degree immediately. You may select from the following options of military science: Infantry, Artillery, Signals, Cavalry or Naval Division. The new superintendent continued, "I have written to President Jackson asking him to consider a separate academy for the Navy, which will contain, Marine Corps, Ordnance, Signal Corps and Fleet assignments. Until that time, however, we have one military academy in the United States with fifty plebes committed to the US Army and twenty-four plebes committed to the Navy."

We sat together with the incoming naval cadets that we had met that summer. John Campbell-Alexander Bowman were from Pennsylvania, William Dewey - Tom Gibson were from Indiana, Walter Crane - George

Thomas were from New Jersey, Andrew Battey had come with Ben from Georgia, Frank Ogden - Charley Oliver were from Louisiana, William Church - Charles Vandeventer were from New York, Thomas Ash - Paul Bullock had come from North Carolina, Harry Martin - John Spurgin were from Kentucky, Billy Cox - Abe Eustis had come from Mississippi, Tony Rogers - William Israel were from Maine, Donald Sprague - Robert Watson were from Rhode Island, and John Rich had come with me from South Carolina.

We had not met the Army cadets from Ohio, Alabama, Vermont, Maryland, Virginia, Michigan, Massachusetts, Connecticut, Delaware, Florida, New Hampshire, North Carolina, Tennessee, Illinois, Missouri and Arkansas. Therefore, we were unaware of the following plebes that would graduate with us:

Henry "Hank" Benham, was the smartest person I ever met. When I first met him, I thought, "How can anyone be this intelligent?" He and I would be life long acquaintances until his death. He was a model cadet from the first day he sat foot on the "Point." He graduated with us in '37, and became an engineer with the corps. He was connected with various Government works until we met again at the start of the Mexican War in '47. From 1849 to 1852 he was superintending engineer of the seawall for the protection of Great Brewster Island, Boston. In 1852, he became the superintendent of the Potomac Dockyards and we saw each other on a regular basis after I was promoted to Naval Intelligence. In 1861, when the great national storm began, he was promoted to brigadier general in charge of volunteers in the engineering brigade for the Army of the Potomac. He was mustered out after the war, as were many others who served in the Army of the Potomac, and was reduced in rank to Colonel and was put in charge of the Boston Harbor seawall until 1873. In 1873, he was transferred to New York Harbor. When he was age 60, he retired from military life. He lived two years in retirement and I talked to him a few months before he died and he was happy and content.

Braxton Bragg, was never on time for anything. What I remember most about Plebe Bragg was that he was late for everything and very proud he was born in North Carolina. He was usually the last plebe to arrive at everything except mess. He had more demerits for late assignments and delay in following orders than any other plebe in our class, I was amazed that he graduated at all, let alone, fifth from the top. He saw action immediately after graduation when he served in the Seminole War from 1837 to 1842. I met him again during the Mexican War when he served under General Taylor. He was decorated for "Gallant and distinguished conduct" at Fort Brown, Monterey and Buena Vista. After Fort Brown he was promoted to, Captain, after Monterey, major, and then lieutenant colonel after Buena Vista. We lost track of each other after the Mexican War, when he left the military to become a sugar planter in Louisiana. He joined the Confederate Army at the outbreak of the national storm. He was a brigadier general in 1861 and was placed in command at Pensacola, Florida, to capture Fort Pickens. He was promoted to major general in February, 1862, and placed in command of the Army of Mississippi. At the battle of Shiloh, he replaced A.S. Johnston when he was killed and assumed command of Johnston's Army. He replaced General Beauregard as commander of the Western Division of the Army of the Confederacy on June 20, 1862. That made Braxton my opposite, he for the south, me for the north. In August, I predicted that he would lead an army of 45,000 into Kentucky. Here he met General Buell of the Union Army, at Perrysville, Kentucky, on October 8. Bragg was defeated and he withdrew back into Tennessee. Here he regrouped his forces and met General Rosecrans at Stone River, Tennessee. He was again defeated and retreated to Tullahoma. His army received reinforcements and he marched against Union General Rosecrans and defeated him at Chickamauga, September 19 and 20th. This was a much needed victory for the south. By the end of November, however, he had to face General Grant at Chattanooga. Here, he lost half his army and was replaced by Confederate General Hardee. He was recalled to Richmond by President Davis and given the assignment of trying to stop Union General Sherman's march to the sea. In February, 1865, he was assigned to General J. E. Johnston, and remained with him until the surrender to Grant. After the war, I found him in Alabama serving as the state's chief engineer trying to repair the war damage in Mobile Bay. He died in 1876, at age 59, one year before my retirement from the US Naval Academy.

Alexander "Brydie" Dyer, went by the name of Brydie Dyer and was from Richmond, Virginia. He never tired of telling anyone who would listen to him, that he was the next George Washington of the United States military establishment. He was the leading scholar in our class until the third year when he spent several weeks in the infirmary trying to get over a bad case of German measles. The disease left him with a slight hearing loss. He said it did not matter, because he was an officer in the army artillery and would soon lose what hearing he now had. He graduated sixth instead of first in 1837, and was assigned to the Third United States Artillery serving in the Florida War, 1837-38, with Braxton Bragg. I met him again when he was a Lieutenant of Ordnance in the War with Mexico from 1846 to '48. He was promoted to captain for gallant conduct at the same time as Bragg.

When the Civil War began he remained loyal to the Union and did not return to Virginia. He served as chief of ordinance for the Army of the Potomac in Washington City and I saw him often when I was serving in the Army Navy Building and later in the White House. He retired as a Brigadier

General but was brought back as a Major General in charge of the Springfield Armory until his death in 1874.

William "Wham" Mackall, was called "Wild Bill" or "Wham" Mackall and he came to the Point from Maryland. He was the first of our graduating class to be severely wounded in war. In February, 1839, he was serving in Florida and was caught in an ambush at New Inlet, Florida. He recovered from his wounds and was sent to Plattsburg, New York, during the Canada border disturbance in 1840. He then was promoted and served on the Maine frontier until the Mexican War. He was promoted to captain after the battle of Monterey, major after Contreeas, and lieutenant colonel after the battle of Churbusco. He was promoted to adjutant general to serve under General Butler and then General Worth until the end of the Mexican War. Between the Mexican War and the Civil War he was adjutant general of the Western division of the Third Military Department. In May 1861, he resigned to join the Confederate Army where he was adjutant general on the staff of General Albert Sidney Johnston. He was promoted to Brigadier General in 1862, and assigned to the command of the forces at Madrid Bend and Island No.10, where he was captured with a large number of his men. Union General Pope arranged for his exchange back to the Confederacy for Union troops held by Confederate General Beauregard. President Davis did not recommend that "Wild Bill" be given another command and he finished the war as an adjutant to Generals Bragg, Herbert, Polk, Johnston, Smith and Cobb. He retired from military life and lived quietly until his death.

Eliakim "Parker" Scammon, graduated ninth in our class and he was considered the most likely to be a President of the United States before he was fifty years old. He entered the "Point" from Whitefield, Maine. He remained at West Point after graduation in 1837, serving as Assistant Professor of Mathematics. He was selected as one of the original officers in the newly created US Army Corps of Topographic Engineers in 1838. He served in the Seminole Wars and the Mexican War, serving under Winfield Scott in the Army of Occupation. He was promoted to captain in 1853 and assigned to various surveying assignments, but he was dismissed from the service on June 4, 1856, as unfit for command. He moved to Ohio and became Professor of Mathematics at Mount Saint Mary's College. With the outbreak of the Civil War, he offered his services to the governor of Ohio. He was appointed Colonel of the 23rd Ohio Infantry and commanded two men who would later become President's, Rutherford Hayes and William McKinley.

Lewis "Cap'n G" Arnold, graduated tenth in our class and was the first member not to survive the Civil War due to natural causes. He progressed through the normal promotions by serving in the wars of Florida and Mexico with the 2nd US Artillery. He was a second lieutenant in Florida, 1837. He was promoted to first lieutenant with the same regiment, on the Canada frontier, at Detroit, in 1839. He accompanied his regiment to Mexico, and was engaged on the southern line of operations under General Scott, being present with me at the siege of Veracruz, in which he was wounded. In the battles of Cerro Gordo and Amozoque his artillery saved an entire company within the battalion of Navy Marines. The company was led by Captain Christopher Merryweather also of the class of 1837. Chris later told me that he ordered artillery fire ahead of his advancing marines and good old Cap'n G delivered. He became a Brigadier General in 1861 and served the entire war in the gulf, first in Florida and later in New Orleans. In February of 1864, he collapsed from a stroke in Algiers, Louisiana.

Isarel Vodges, came to the Point from Chester, Pennsylvania and graduated with us as a second lieutenant in the 1st US Artillery. He also stayed at the Point with Parker Scammon to teach mathematics. Unlike Parker, he stayed until he was promoted to full professor in September, 1849. He missed the Florida and Mexican Wars, but was called to active duty to serve in the Civil War. Promoted to Major, he was stationed at Forts Monore and Pickens. He was taken prisoner with the fall of Fort Pickens, exchanged in August, 1862. He commanded the forces at Folly Island and participated in the Battle of Olustee. He commanded X Corps in the Military District of Florida in 1864. After the war, he was reduced in rank and retired from the army in 1876 with the rank of colonel, at the age of 65.

Thomas Williams, and I did not spend much time together as plebes. He joined the Point from the regular army after the Black Hawk War and was older than some of us. He graduated as a lieutenant of the 4th US Artillery and was sent to Florida and Mexico with me. After the Mexican War he was assigned to Mackinac Island, Michigan in 1847. He served at Fort Mackinac until he was sent to Utah Territory with Colonel Albert Sidney Johnson to put down a Mormon insurrection in October, 1857. I met him again in Fort Bridger and asked for his help in clearing a Mormon blockage of the roads into Utah Territory. President Buchanan had sent me and a detachment of Marines to meet with Brigham Young and grant him a Presidential Pardon.

Thomas was the first of our graduation class to be killed in the Civil War. He was a Brigadier General commanding Union troops when he was killed, August 5, 1862, at the Battle of Baton Rouge, Louisiana.

Jubal Anderson Early, graduated 18th in our class. He entered the Point from Virginia. He also served in the Seminole War, but resigned from the army in late 1838 to practice law. He passed the bar in Virginia and lived in Rocky Mount, Virginia. He entered Virginia politics and was elected to the Virginia House of Representatives in 1841. He served there until 1847, when he joined the volunteers from Virginia to serve as a major in the Mexican War.

At the outbreak of the Civil War he joined the Confederate Army as a colonel. He commanded a brigade at the first battle of Manassas and was promoted to Brigadier General immediately after this battle. He was the most successful general in the Confederacy with victories at Williamsburg, second battle of Manassas, Fredericksburg, Lynchburg, Winchester, Hagerstown, Monocacy Junction and Chambersburg. He was ranked the third highest Confederate General at the end of the war. He refused the oath of loyalty and moved to Canada for a time before returning to Virginia where he practiced law until his death.

William Henry French, was a friend of Thomas Williams, both coming to the Point directly from the Black Hawk War. He graduated with us, fought in the Florida War and then served as an aide to General Franklin Pierce in the Mexican War. At the time of the Texas secession of 1861, he refused to surrender his troops to the state. Instead, he requested naval evacuation and marched his troops to the gulf coast and was met there by Benjamin Hagood for transport to Key West, Florida. On September 28, 1861, he was appointed a Brigadier General under Major General McClellan and commanded VIII Corps during the Peninsula Campaign, Seven Day's Campaign, and Antietam. He was promoted to Major General and fought in the battles of Fredericksburg, Chancellorsville and Gettysburg. After the war he remained on active duty and died in Washington City, while on garrison duty.

John Sedgwick, was the perfect example of Superintendent Thayer's ideal cadet. His grandfather was General Theodore Sedgwick, an American Revolutionary member of George Washington's general staff. He was from Cornwall, Connecticut, and wanted very much to be an army engineer. He was ranked 24th out of the 50 of us who graduated in 1837. He got out of the idea to be an engineer when he was stationed in the swamps of Florida trying to defeat the Seminole Indians. He transferred to the Artillery for the Mexican War. He transferred to the Cavalry after the Mexican War so that he could qualify for western territory duty in the Indian Wars which were fought in Utah, Colorado and Kansas. In the summer of 1860 he commanded an expedition to establish a new fort on the Platte River in Nebraska Territory. He was greatly handicapped with the non-delivery of expected supplies and materials which had to be forwarded from the nearest Fort in Kansas. There were no railroads west of the Missouri River and communication with St. Louis was by river boat. He was the second of our class to be killed in action, on May 9, 1864, he was shot by a sniper at the beginning of the battle of Spotsylvania Court House.

John Clifford Pemberton, came to the Point from Philadelphia as a twenty year old cadet. He was older than most of us except Tom Williams and Bill French. He left the Point with the 4th US Artillery, fought against the Seminoles in 1837 and '38. He was wounded at the battle of Locha Hatchee on January 24, 1838. He was assigned to Camp Instruction until his wounds healed and then he was sent to the northern frontier during the Canada border disagreements. He was stationed in Michigan at Fort Mackinac with Thomas Williams in 1840 and '41. He was stationed at the following forts before the Mexican War; Bradyin, Buffalo, Monroe and the Cavalry School at Carlisle Barracks, Pennsylvania. His actions in the Mexican War found him at the siege of Veracruz in March, the battle of Cerro Gordo in April, the skirmish of Amazoque in May, the capture of San Antonio and Churubusco in August and, most notably, in the battle of Molino del Rey on September 8.

His Civil War duty was with the Confederacy, despite his northern birth. He was assigned to the Army of South Carolina and was stationed in Charleston. The governor of South Carolina did not trust his commitment to the Confederacy and petitioned for his removal by President Davis. Davis sent him to defend Vicksburg on the Mississippi. He surrendered after 45 days of siege and was a prisoner of war until his release in 1864. He ended the war in the defense of Richmond when he was captured a second time. There is no record of his parole or release from prison.

Joseph "handsome Joe" Hooker, came to the Point from Massachusetts as a twenty year old. He was mature beyond his years and every cadet wanted to be seen with him whenever we were given leave in New York City, our third and fourth years at the Academy. Ben Hagood said he left a trail of broken hearts in his wake. He served in Florida and Mexico in campaigns with both Zachary Taylor and Winfield Scott. He was promoted to Captain after Monterrey, Major after National Bridge and Lieutenant Colonel after Chapultepee. He left the serve after the Mexican War and moved to California to become a farmer and land developer. At the start of the Civil War he joined the California Militia as a colonel. The California volunteers were not called to war, and after Manassas he wrote a letter to President Lincoln and offered his services in the defense of Washington City. He was commissioned directly by Lincoln, as a Brigadier General in charge of troop training for the Army of the Potomac. He would be best remembered for his stunning defeat by Confederate General Lee at the Battle of Chancellorsville in 1863. He became 'fighting Joe" Hooker after that defeat.

Arnold Jones Elzey, graduated with us ranked 33rd. He dropped his middle name, or else the Point did it for him as a mistake and he went by Arnold Elzey the rest of his military career. He was sent to Florida to fight in the second Seminole War before being assigned to duty at Detroit, Michigan, during the border dispute with Canada. During the Mexican War he was cited for bravery during the battles of Contreras and Churubusco. He was promoted to Captain. He fought with me at the battle of Veracruz. He resigned his commission on April 25, 1861, and surrendered the arsenal to the Confederates in Augusta, George. He was one of the few officers to receive an on-the-field promotion to general by President Davis.

John Blair Todd, I remember John Todd because his first cousin was Mary Todd Lincoln. He was assigned in Florida, fought with Chris Merryweather at the battle of Veracruz, and was an Indian fighter in the western United States. He resigned his commission in September, 1856, settling at Fort Randall, Dakota Territory. He was admitted to the bar and practiced law in Yankton. When the Civil War began, he was recalled to active duty as a brigadier of volunteers. He died in 1872.

William Henry Talbot Walker, went by his initials WHT most of the time at West Point. He was from Georgia and he arrived at the Point with Chris Merryweather. Walker was wounded in every theater of war in which he served; Florida, Mexico, Western Indian Wars and was finally killed at the battle of Atlanta, as a major General of the CSA. WHT loved to tell stories to anyone who would listen. He met his wife, Mary Townsend, at a story telling session and married her a year later when he was home on leave. They had two sons and two daughters.

Robert Hall Chilton, graduated last in 1837 and we all assumed that he would pass into history as a footnote. He did not and proved that the last place in the class at Annapolis or the Point could be first in the class at other military academies. He served as Chief of Staff for the Army of Northern Virginia under Robert E. Lee. He is alive and well living with his wife, Laura Ann in Laudoun County, Virginia.

4
Summer Cruise
Annapolis, 1834

After our experiences with a summer cruise in 1833, we did not know what to expect when we arrived by train from West Point to Annapolis in June, 1834. We stepped off the train and saw a group of boys huddled together on the platform. We heard,

"What the hell is this? I am Master Chief Gunnerman! When a United States Naval Officer commands you to come to attention, you will place whatever is in your hands two inches from your right ankle, you will suck in that flabby excuse for a gut, square your shoulders and stare two inches above his head. You will then cause your right arm to extend upward, bent at the elbow and give your best imitation of a boy scout salute."

Master Chief Gunnerman scared them, just as he had us. They jumped into a straight line and attempted to come to attention. Someone screamed, "Yeas, Sir."

"You do not, 'Yeas, Sir me,' you dumb ass. I am not an officer. The proper response is, aye, aye."

"Aye, aye, Sir!" They all yelled at the top of their voices. Master Chief Gunnerman turned to his officer and said, "Sir, they are hopeless, I will throw their ass's back on the train and send them back to where they came from."

"Let me talk to them, Chief."

"Aye, aye, Sir"

"Gentlemen, in just four short years you may be standing where I am, a graduate of the United States Military Academy, looking at a bunch of shave tails. Shaking your head and wondering how you are ever going to make Naval officers and gentlemen out of them."

He pointed directly at the group of us who had come from West Point and said, "Watch this." He strode over to us, winked, then screamed, "Attention in the ranks, cadets!"

We placed our sea bags beside our right feet and came to attention and presented him with the proper salute. He smiled and said, "Welcome back for your summer cruise to Bermuda, gentlemen. If you will wait just a moment I shall get these plebes off with Mr. Gunnerman, you remember the Chief, I am sure." He walked slowly back to the group of plebes and said, "The Chief, here, will get all of you onto the depot grounds and be with you through your processing. That will be all."

He turned on his heel and marched toward us. The Master Chief smiled and left with his group shouting, "I am not going to show you babies how to do things!"

The LT stopped before us again and said, "You all know what is in store for them. They will start where you left off on the weeks of hell designed to divide the "want-a-bees from the real Navy men I see before me. Thanks to your efforts, the USS New Haven and Spitfire are ready to sail this summer." He unfolded a map and held it up in front of him. "You can all see where you will be sailing this year. You will leave Annapolis and sail for Bermuda. You will have shore leave there to inspect the Royal Naval Dockyards. Remember, you are invited guests there. I expect professional conduct from everyone who expects to return to the Point. You will see the Canary Islands and the coast of Africa before returning through the middle Atlantic Ocean. At the end of the summer, you will return here to tell me all about your adventure. Hoist your gear and I will take you to see your ship's captains and wave goodbye."

We followed him to the docks and found the USS New Haven and Spitfire waiting for us. Beside each, sat a steamboat tug ready to push us out of the harbor. "Would you look at that, Jason?"

"Steam engines are being added to every ship of the fleet as fast as they can be retrofitted." the LT explained. "We already have small dispatch steamboats, tugs and transport sidewheelers in service this year. By next year every utility vessel in the Navy will be steam powered."

"When will we have steam engines on war ships?" I asked.

"We already have steam engines available to turn the capstans and windlasses aboard all the primary ships on ready reserve. The next thing will be the raising and lowering of yard arms, power lifts and powered halyards, all by steam engines. This will reduce the number of seamen required to sail ships in the Navy. By the time you men graduate, we should have our first steam driven screw propeller."

"What is a screw propeller, LT?"

"It looks like a fan blade that turns underwater and drives the ship forward. They are mounted at the stern."

"They? There are more than one?"

"As many as you like, smaller ships will have one, larger two or more iron propellers."

"Why is the Navy doing this?"

"Because the steam driven side wheelers can not have side mounted ordnance, they fire only from the stern and bow. A screw propeller allows you to mount guns along the sides for broadsides. I believe that the paddle-steamer warship is a dead end for the Navy. You cadets may be the last to sail a real ship of the last century. These seven, that you see here will be a part of the training at Annapolis for years to come."

Ben and I were assigned to the USS Spitfire. We asked for permission to come aboard, saluted the first officer and asked where we could put our sea bags.

"You two are sharing the warrant officer's space. Do you know where that is?"

"Yes, Sir. We were all over this ship last summer getting it ready for service. It is below the lower cabins aft. Correct?"

"That is correct, store your gear and report back to me, Lieutenant Carlson."

"Yes. Sir." We both said in unison. We hoisted our bags and walked toward the stern gangway. We went down three sets of ship's ladders until we came to a small, cramped space located just above the aft magazine.

"I wonder if we are carrying any shot and powder on this cruise, Jason. We will be sleeping right on top of it."

"We must be the only cadets with cabin space, Ben. The captain and his first officer are in the upper cabins, the crew have all the lower cabins. The ship's doctor and the infirmary are located in the forecastle. If the cadets are to sleep anywhere, they are probably in hammocks strung in one of the holds."

"I wonder how we got so lucky?" Ben was trying to lie down in one of the bunks that swung down from the bulkhead of the cabin. With both bunks swung down, there was barely room to slide our legs through to the cabin door. Just then one of the tugs began pushing us away from the docks.

"We better get top side and report to the LT." Ben was smiling. We found the first officer at the wheel located just aft of the mizzen mast.

"Reporting for duty, Sir."

"Good, take the wheel Cadet Hagood and follow my hand signals that I will relay from the pilot in the tug." He ran up the ship's ladder to the poop deck so he could get a clear view of the tug. He wig wagged his instructions and Ben followed them like an old pro. When the tug left us, the LT returned to talk to us.

"I have read both your files. You two are the most experienced seamen of the cadets who reported to us on the Spitfire. The USS Trumbull has a couple of experienced cadets as well, you two will be promoted to midshipmen so that you can relay orders to the cadets that will report to you. Next year, all of you will be midshipmen, so do not let that go to your heads, you are still teenaged school boys as far as the regular Navy seamen on this ship will see you. If a

Navy seaman gives you an order, you follow it to the letter, they know what they are doing and you are just learning. Do you understand?"

"Yes, Sir."

"I know you have just spent nine months in an army environment and you 'yes, sired' a lot there. But you are in the Navy now and we 'Aye, aye. Sir', here." He was smiling.

"Aye, aye. Sir." We both said.

"Good, get down to the galley and get some chow, one of you two will be on the first watch as we head for Bermuda."

It took us five days to sail the 880 nautical miles from Annapolis to the Royal Naval Dockyards in Bermuda. That meant that we traveled at the speed of 7.33 miles per hour. Not a killer pace, more like the track and field runners at the Point. When I asked Lieutenant Carlson about the slow pace, he just said, "We barely move at night, just enough steerage to keep us on course. These are old wooden ships, Mr. Caldwell, the New Haven could sail away from us, because she is much faster than the Spitfire. The Spitfire carries most of our supplies. There are twenty-four of you cadets plus the captains and crews of the two ships. If either ship develops serious problems, we can all make it to a friendly port on either ship. We are short handed in order for this safety measure. Therefore, we creep at night and sail as fast as the Spitfire can during the day."

"Thank you, that explains a lot. I have never been to Bermuda before. What was all that talk about coming across the 'Brackish Pond Flats'?"

"Bermuda is a series of islands and reefs situated roughly latitude 32 degrees, 14 minutes and longitude 64 degrees, 40 minutes. I say roughly because there are over 300 islands spread from 32, 14' to 32, 22' by 64, 30' to 64, 60' on a chart. All of these islands are protected by coral reefs and these reefs will tear the bottoms out of wooden ships. Only 20 islands have safe approaches and places to dock small or large craft. I gave you the coordinates for St. George's harbor on the east end. We are headed for the Royal Naval Dockyards on the west end on Ireland, Island. We have to cross several coral beds called 'Flats'. The Dockyards are surrounded by Cow Ground Flats, Green Flats, Brackish Pond Flats and the Great Sound. I think this is why the British selected this location. British maps and charts, still call it Somers Islands instead of Bermuda. A Spanish captain, Juan Bermudez, discovered the chain of islands in 1522. Because the islands contained no fresh water, they were never claimed until Sir George Somers was swept ashore by a hurricane in 1609."

A steam tug met us between Green Flats and Brackish Pond and piloted us into our dockage here. "How long will we stay in Bermuda, LT?"

"Long enough for you and Ben to ride the street cars from one end to the other and take several side trips if you like. People either love or hate Bermuda. I will be interested in what you think, Mr. Caldwell. You can tell me all about it on our trip to the Canary Islands." He walked away from Ben and I to join the Captain who was leaving the ship to visit with the commander of the Royal Naval Dockyards.

"We better get this sight-seeing under way, Jason. We have the third watch and we need to get back here in plenty of time to eat and take a nap."

We asked for permission to leave the Spitfire and walked down the pier taking in all the stone buildings that make up the Dockyards. "Do you think this is coral cut into building blocks, Ben?"

"It sure looks like it. Remember what St. Augustine looks like in Florida? This reminds me of that, also."

"We need to find the street car station. There is a sign that says St. George's Ferry. Should we take that? I have no Bermuda pounds, do you?"

We talked to the ticket master and bought round trip tickets to St. George's with a gold eagle and got British change in the form of paper money with King William's picture on them. I had never seen foreign currency before and I kept a six pence as a good luck charm, refusing to spend it. We got off the ferry an hour later at the terminal in St. George's. I was amazed at what we saw. It looked older than St. Augustine.

"We should start our tour at King's Square, known variously since its founding in 1609, as King's Parade and the Market Square." I told Ben.

"Where did you learn that?"

"From the LT, this is the hub of St. George's life and most days everyone passes through it at least once. The Lt said to look for the visitor's center on the water side of the square. There it is over there. We need to stop and get a map."

"You are not going to go 'tourist' on me, are you ,Jason?"

"No, we need to be able to find our way around, that is all." We entered a small shop front and asked for a map.

"You fellows, Americans?" Asked the man behind the counter.

"Yes, will we need a map in order to find our way around?" asked Ben.

"Depends on what you want to see. This is the second oldest English town to be established in the New World, and it continues with its own lively way of life while the first town, Jamestown in America, has long since been abandoned. Here in St. George's, you are surrounded by nearly two hundred and twenty-five years of history, two and a quarter centuries of lusty human habitation, foolish follies and high virtues of which our species is capable."

"I would be interested in that 'lusty lifestyle' you mentioned, Sir." Ben had a big grin on his face.

"Then you do not need a map, son. Go to the White Horse Tavern on the corner of Water Street and King's Square. Now, the other gentleman needs a map." He handed me a printed map.

"What places do I need to stop and see on this map, Sir."

"Let me mark them as I find them. The first thing everyone sees in St. George's is the 'Deliverance'. It is across the bridge on Ordnance Island. It is a replica of the ship built after the hurricane of 1609 to carry survivors of the shipwrecked company of the Sea Venture to Virginia. A second ship was built, called the Patience, in 1610 and it led to the colonization of Bermuda in 1612."

"I would like to see that, how about you, Ben?"

"Look across Ordnance Island and you can see the statue of Sir George Somers who was the admiral of the Sea Venture. Later, on your walking tour, you can visit the gardens named after him, where his heart is buried."

"His heart? Not his body?"

"That is correct, he always said he would be buried in England along with his ancestors, but his heart belonged to Bermuda."

"Bring your map and so we can find the White House, Jason."

"Hold on a minute, he has not marked the rest of the places that I want to see." He circled the Town Hall, Bridge House, State House, Featherbed Alley, St. Peter's Church, Tucker House Museum and Fort St. Catherine.

We left the visitor's center and headed for the White Horse across the square. I dropped Ben off to have a drink at the bar and visit with the bar tender while I took the walking tour of St. George's. I went first to St. Peter's Church on the Duke of York Street, two blocks from the White Horse. I visited the churchyard in order to get a feel for the history. Many headstones dated back over 200 years. To the west of the church, behind a wall, I found the graves of many slaves. Most of the tombs were small, oblong blocks of limestone or coral, I could not tell which, with the initials of the dead scratched into the rock. Notable graves included that of Midshipman Dale and Governor Sir Richard Sharples. Next to the back of the entrance of the church was a giant cedar tree nearly five feet in diameter. A bronze plaque indicated that the tree was estimated to be 500 years old and that the church bell used to hang from one of its branches.

I walked inside the church, which I found out was the oldest Anglican Church in the Western Hemisphere. Since I was raised in the Anglican Faith, this meant something to me. I learned that the original church was built in 1612, it had a palmetto thatch roof and cedar walls. The Palmetto tree grew in South Carolina and was used there in the 1600's also. I read that, until the building of the State House, this was the meeting place for the Bermuda Parliament. I walked down the front steps and paused for a minute at the bottom to see St. Peter's from the street level. I then turned right on Duke of York and thought, most of the streets here are named after King George the III's sons or relatives. I stopped at Barber's Alley. The alley commemorates a runaway slave from South Carolina called Joseph Haynes who was a stow away on a ship bound for Bermuda. Here he changed his name and lived as a freeman and had a son he named, Joseph Rainey.

I continued down Barber's alley to Water Street beside the Tucker house which contained a memorial room to Mr. Haynes, the barber, who had his barber's shop in the alley. I was at the White Horse, so stopped and picked up Ben so that we could see the Town Hall across the square. From King's square we walked up King Street. On the left of the little triangular walled lawn, we saw a bust of Tom Moore. On the right was Bridge House, built shortly after 1698, it is the home of the governors of Bermuda appointed by the British Crown.

"Why is it called Bridge House, Jason?"

"It says here that in the early 1600's, much of the town square was an arm of the sea, and into it ran a muddy creek from a marsh where the Somers' garden is now. The creek was bridged hereabouts, and so the house was dubbed Bridge House."

"Where is this State House, that you want to see?"

"At the top of King Street, see it? It is the oldest building in Bermuda. It was built by Governor Nathaniel Butler in 1620. St. George's is the capital of Bermuda and the parliament meets here."

We came to Princess Street, walked down to the end to see where the public hangings are held. Ben was getting restless and said, "How many more buildings are you going to see?"

"Just one. It is the St. George's hotel on Rose Street. The man at the visitor's center said it was for sale."

"You want to buy a hotel?"

"No, I want to see how much a hotel sells for. If the Navy ever stops interesting me, I would like to own several hotels."

"You would?"

"Come on, we will go back to the ferry terminal just as soon as we find out the selling price."

The agent representing the hotel was not on the premises, but the desk clerk indicated that he thought the management wanted 20,000 pounds for the hotel and the attached golf course. We thanked him and hurried back to the ferry terminal so that we could get back to the Spitfire in time to assume the third watch.

When we came on board, Lieutenant Carlson was waiting for us. "Where did you two go today?"

"We took a ferry to St. George's and went to the visitor's center as you suggested." I said.

"The White Horse Tavern is the first English Pub that I have ever seen." said Ben.

"Tomorrow, you need to catch the ferry into Hamilton and see what a modern harbor and dockyards can do for the growth of a small city. The Crown Colony is in the process of building a new parliament and government houses to replace the historical buildings in St. George's. They should be all completed by 1838. You two are lucky to see both Bermudas, the original capital and the new capital under construction."

The next day we took the ferry into Hamilton and Ben liked what he saw, 'progress', he called it. I felt sad. We needed several more days to really see Bermuda, but that would have to wait until next summer, because the next morning we were being piloted away from the Royal Naval Dockyards to resume your cruise to the Canary Islands.

I do not remember how many days it took us to dock in Santa Cruz de Teneriffe, the capital of the Canaries. Unlike Bermuda, which are ancient volcano remains, the Canaries are more recent inactive volcanoes that spread from latitude 27 degrees, 40 minutes to 29, 25' and from longitude 13 degrees, 25 minutes to 18,16'. This means that the Canaries cover an area of 2808 square miles. In this area are seven large inhabited islands, Teneriffe being the largest at 782 square miles and Ferro being the smallest at 107 square miles. You can see Teneriffe from a long distance at sea. Pico de Teyde volcano rises 12,000 feet above sea level and is easy to spot with its steaming top.

Like Bermuda, the Canaries are a colony of a European power. Spanish is spoken, instead of English and it was hard for Ben and I to talk to people that we met ashore. The climates are similar, generally mild, the average temperature is about 65 degrees. Precipitation is very scant on the Canaries and it falls mainly in winter. The hot east and southeast winds blowing from Africa dry up the vegetation at sea level. There are several zones of vegetation depending upon the altitude, however. The vegetation of the lower zone, up to about 1300 feet is African and includes the date palm, sugar cane, and dragon's-blood tree for example. The second highest zone resembles that of southern Europe and comprises grape vines, orange trees and several kinds of grain. The third zone consists mainly of trees and resembles northen Europe with many types of pine trees. Ben and I took many side trips the days we spent on Tenneriffe.

In a few days we were on our way to northwestern Africa and the port of Tangier. The captains called the two groups of twelve cadets together and talked to us about our conduct in a Moslem country. "You are about to set foot ashore in Morocco. Morocco is controlled by several Sultans or

Moslem Holy Leaders. The Sultan Abd-el-Kader controls the port of Tangier. Christians here are put to death or captured and sold as slaves. You are not welcome here. Do not leave the immediate port area and stay together as a group. Do not explore on your own in groups of two, like you have done in Bermuda and the Canaries. We leave in eight hours, we are here to resupply, not discover what the continent of Africa is like."

We all left the ship and walked down the gangway and milled around in sight of the ship. Someone said, "Well, we have set foot on African soil, I am going back on board." We all followed him back up the gangway and settled back into our routines for the return voyage to North America.

5

Yearlings Transfer
West Point, 1834-35

It was common practice for West Point to accept second year cadets from the other military colleges throughout the country to replace those cadets who left the academy for whatever reason. In 1833-34, thirty-six cadets left West Point. The most outstanding plebes from other schools were sent letters of request and Christopher Merryweather was at the top of his class at Carlisle Military Academy, Bamberg, South Carolina, and he accepted the appointment as a second year cadet at West Point. He accepted the position left by John Rich of South Carolina. Now, I saw Chris during the academic year, but not when I went on a summer cruise. We became friends again and "The Three Musketeers" began to appear everywhere around the "Point". We got the nickname because all three of us were on the fencing team.

The incoming members of the graduating class were called Plebes, the next year you become 'yearlings', the third year you become 'cows' and your final year you are known as 'firsties.' As yearlings we were given a few more freedoms than the plebes got the first year. The Point is located adjacent to the village of Highland Falls, New York, in Orange County. Last year, none of us had permission to enter Highland Falls. So naturally, Ben Hagood, Chris Merryweather, Alex Bowman (another member of the fencing team) and I talked "Handsome Joe" Hooker into walking into the village with us. Ben reasoned that we needed something to attract the local girls and Joe was it.

"West Point's motto is *Duty, Honor, Country*, men. It is our duty to make ourselves available to the young women of Highland Falls. It would be my honor is escort one of these local beauties to a local church supper. And if she cared anything for her country, she would make sure that a future Admiral, like myself, did not leave the Point as a virgin." Alex had a sharp wit.

This brought peals of laughter from "Handsome Joe" who claimed he lost his at age 13 with the daughter of his pastor at his church in Hadley, Massachusetts. He then followed this escapade with a school girl at the local Hopkins Academy. He was our idol, he was born in 1814, so he was three years older than the four of us. We were teenagers and he was a man of twenty-one. That first trip into Highland Falls was a great disappointment.

There were no local girls hanging around street corners saying, "Hey sailor, want to have a good time?"

We did find a local pharmacy that had a good lunch counter and we ordered vanilla sodas from the soda jerk working the lunch counter. "Where are all the local girls, today?" Ben asked the soda jerk.

"If I knew the answer to that I would be out chasing some of them." He said. "You cadets will find the going rough here in Highland Falls. You need to catch the steamboat into New York City. They have all kinds of painted women there. But take plenty of money, the women there are not cheap!"

We thanked him and walked around the village before starting the walk back to the Point. The conversation led to what team sports we were going to sign up for this year. The Black Knights of the Hudson played all sorts of field sports and had regular competitions with the other local colleges in New York State. I had tried rugby as a Plebe, but I did not make the traveling team, as Alex did, so I was not going to try that one again. "What is cricket like?" I asked.

"Just like 'one old cat', only you do not have to run the bases." Alex replied.

"I have never seen a cricket or a baseball game. There were never any playing fields at home."

"Jason, you need to go with me to the next 'town ball' game at the Olympic Club in Philadelphia."

As Joe and I decided what field sports to sign up for, Alex, Chris and Ben were having their usual banter.

"So, what are you going to do after you get your degree, Chris?"

"I am going to serve in the US Marine Corps and see what happens. If I make a career out of it, it will depend on how fast I can be promoted through the ranks."

"The ranks are the same as the army. So you plan to be a general, Chris?" Ben had that joking smile on his face.

"I will be a general before either you or Alex become an admiral or I will quit in disgrace." Chris always joked with a straight face.

"I bet you a hundred bucks that does not happen."

"You have a bet Mr. Hagood! What shall we do about interest on the money over the years?"

"What interest?"

"You put 50 dollars with my 50 dollars and let Jason invest it with his friend Whitehall, the banker, and the winner will collect the 100 plus interest. Earliest date of appointment wins!"

"And the bet is you will beat both of us?"

"Yes, one marine is worth two swabbies any day!"

"Even if the marine is a retread from the Citadel?"

"I did not attend the Citadel, you dummy. The Citadel is a storage facility in Charleston! I am a Carlisle man."

"Well, excuse me, Mr. Carlisle man, I bet that will scare the hell out of the enemy when you stand up and shout, 'I am a Carlisle man from Bamberg, South Carolina, so you better surrender right now!'"

And this closeness and friendly competing continued for the next three years.

6
Summer Cruise
Annapolis, 1835

After our experiences with the summer cruises in 1833 and '34, we were prepared for anything. Two groups of Navy Cadets arrived by train from West Point to Annapolis in June, 1835. We stepped off the train and saw another group of boys huddled together on the far end of the platform. We again heard the familiar,

"What the hell is this?"

From Master Chief Gunnerman as he continued to terrorize the newly arrived plebes. His Lieutenant continued to be the nice guy be saying,

"Gentlemen in just four short years you may be standing where I am, a graduate of the United States Military Academy, looking at a bunch of shave tails, shaking your head and wondering how they are ever going to make Naval officers and gentlemen."

He pointed directly at the two groups of us who had come from West Point and said, "Watch this."

He strode over to us, winked, then screamed, "Attention in the ranks, cadets!"

We placed our sea bags beside our right feet and came to attention and presented him with the proper salute. He smiled and said, "Welcome back for your summer cruise to the Gulf of Mexico, gentlemen. If you will wait just a moment I shall get these plebes off with Mr. Gunnerman, you remember the Chief, I am sure." He walked slowly back to the group of plebes and said, "The Chief, here, will get all of you onto the depot grounds and be with you through your processing. That will be all."

He turned on his heel and marched toward us. The Master Chief smiled and left with his group shouting, "I am not going to show you babies how to do things! I am not your mother!"

The LT stopped before us again and said, "You all remember what is in store for them. They will start where you left off on the weeks of hell designed to divide the "want-a-bees from the two groups of real Navy men I see before me. Thanks to your efforts in '33 and '34 the USS New Haven, Spitfire, Trumbull and Providence are again ready to sail this summer." He unfolded a map and held it up for us to see.

"Midshipman Hagood, you are in charge of second year cadets on the New Haven this summer. Caldwell you are cadet leader on the Trumbull and Campbell you will take charge on the Spitfire. That leaves us with the Providence and that assignment goes to the highest ranked naval cadet the last two years, Mr. Bowman." We all looked at Alex and gave him a thumbs up.

"Get your forty-nine bodies on your assigned ships and we can get the four ships bound for Bermuda underway."

I reported to the Trumbull and did not see Ben, Alex, or my other close shipmates until we docked in St. George's Harbor several days later. We met at the White Horse with Ben's crew from the New Haven and twenty-five of us tried to drink a barrel of beer before closing time. We had no idea where the cadet crews of the Providence or the Spitfire spent their first shore leaves. When I awoke in my hammock on the Trumbull, the first officer, Lieutenant Silverman, was looking down at me.

"Well, well. Midshipman Caldwell does have feet of clay. Your shipmates carried you back last night. Not a good example for you to set for the second year cadets under your command, Mr. Caldwell. If I have to speak to you again, I will assign a new cadet leader from the Spitfire and have you transferred off the Trumbull. Is that clear?"

"Aye, aye. Sir, it will not happen again."

I did not ask for shore leave again in Bermuda and spent my time getting familiar with a ketch. A ketch is a smaller sailing vessel than a brig, like the Spitfire. The New Haven was 150 tons and the Trumbull was 200 tons, therefore the New Haven was faster through the water. I wondered what we would have to do in order to keep up with the New Haven if we were ever required to run as fast as we could. Ketches have two masts, both square rigged; the main mast, very much higher than the after mast, is placed very nearly in the center of the vessel. This arrangement allows the great spread of after canvas to be balanced by large and numerous fore and aft sails forward. I walked around the Trumbull with my pocket notebook and sketched the profile of the Trumbull and the Spitfire. I continued my sketches as we left Bermuda and headed east across the Sargasso Sea before looping and heading for the Gulf of Mexico. I could see the USS Providence and the New Haven off our port side and I added their sketches to my pocket notebook.

By the time we reached the West Indies and San Juan, Puerto Rico, I felt maybe I had redeemed myself with Lieutenant Silverman and I asked for shore leave. I had written my father and Chris Merryweather. I would find a post office there. He said, "Stay away from the taverns and pubs, Mr. Caldwell and bring your cadets back to the ship early so that we can sail across the Caribbean to Jamaica."

I was a model leader in San Juan and Jamaica. All my charges were returned early, as promised. We sailed into the Gulf of Mexico through the Yucatan Channel and headed due west for the port of Veracruz, Mexico. The Captain called all of us together and asked who could sketch pictures, no one volunteered, so I showed him my sketches that I had made during the cruise. "Excellent Mr. Caldwell, the Secretary of the Navy would like to see the harbor defenses of Veracruz. Do you think you could get away with taking a large sketch pad and pencils with you and getting us some detailed sketches to show the Secretary?"

"Aye, aye. Sir, I will do my best. What do I say if someone asks me what I am doing?"

"Tell them you are a tourist and ask them if they would like you to sketch their picture."

"I do not speak Spanish, Captain."

"That could be an advantage, find someone who can translate. Do not try to hide the sketches, show them to everyone who will look at them and ask what these buildings are. That should throw any suspicion off of you. If it does not, there is a US Consul's office in Veracruz and we can get him to assist us."

"Assist us?"

"Yes, we do not want to have you spend a year in a Mexican prison, Mr. Caldwell."

I had a lump in my throat as I left the Trumbull with my sketching supplies tucked under my arm and a Spanish beret on my head. I had no idea where the beret had come from, but one of my shipmates said that all "real artists" wore one. The Trumbull had entered the harbor through a narrow channel with three openings. Only two were marked as passable for merchant ships and we left them for the Providence and the Spitfire, while the two ketches tried the third. The captain would report to the Secretary that a ketch can enter the harbor through any of the three passages. In an hour, the Trumbull had released us for "tourist" activities and I began to sketch what I saw. Veracruz was the most important gulf port for the Republic of Mexico, situated 193 miles from the capital on the Bay of Campeche. The city extends in a semicircle along the coast for nearly a mile, facing the fortress of San Juan de Ulua on a rocky islet a half mile from the shore. I made several sketches of the harbor approaches with the fortress in the background. Workmen were busy adding dock facilities and I sketched them at work. Various buildings were located adjacent to the docks and I made a quick sketch of these.

"Are you a visitor, Senor?"

I jumped because I had not seen the young woman looking over my shoulder at the sketches. "You speak beautiful English, Senorita. Yes, I enjoy sketching. Do you want to see what I have so far?" I flipped the sketch pad to the front and began to show her what I had done.

"These are not very good, Senor. Are you a painter and you plan on refinements later?"

"Why, yes, how did you know?"

"From your silly looking cap, Senor."

I pulled it from my head and stuffed it in my back pocket. "My name is Jason. Can you tell me what these old building are miss?"

"Si, my name is Juanita. The first building is the Fortress of Veracruz, built in 1582."

"It is that old?"

"Si, in 1519 Cortes established the city of Villa Nueva de la Vera Cruz and it took us eighty years to complete its construction. Would you like me to show you my city, Jason?"

"Only if you would let me sketch you in the foreground of some of them." I said.

"We will begin with the old walled city, it has beautiful architecture with stone streets, plazas with fountains, and villas, some two stories." She was smiling and I wondered if she was always this friendly with complete strangers. We walked several blocks, through brick and stone archways with variegated walls and a suggestion of Moorish styles. We stopped so I could sketch Juanita standing in front of the National School of Seamanship, the artillery school, public library and the hospital Gutierrez Zamora.

"It is very sad, Jason. My beautiful city is also known as the 'City of the Dead' because it is so unhealthy. Veracruz is surrounded by sand dunes and stagnant marshes. Yellow fever kills many each year."

"Tell me more of the history of Villa Nueva de la Vera Cruz, Juanita." She smiled at my attempt at Spanish.

"In 1599, the city was completed, only to be sacked by buccaneers, what you call pirates, in 1653. It was the only gulf port of New Spain and it came under attack often. It was nearly destroyed in 1712. Previous to 1810 it was the center for revolution and our fight for independence from Spain. The French have tried several times to invade Mexico through Veracruz."

"The French?"

"Si, the French are crazy, Napoleon has made them so."

I laughed and said, "Juanita, that is so true, the French sold us a part of our country in 1803, so that Napoleon could finance his army and try to conquer all of Europe. Now Napoleon II would like to do the same thing, only on the North American continent."

"Jason, I like the way you think!"

"Thank you, Juanita. Am I keeping you from something, do you have a job that you need to get to?"

"What time is it?"

"Almost ten o'clock."

"I am already late, but my father will forgive me, he owns the bank where I work. Come, it is in the next plaza. My father is old fashioned, he will not like it that you and I have been talking alone without an escort. You can meet him and tell him you asked me for directions to his bank to make a deposit."

"I can do that."

We hurried into the next plaza and entered the Banquo de la Vera Cruz and we were stopped by Juanita's brother, Simon. He glared at me and spoke in rushed Spanish directly in my face. I looked at Juanita for help in what he had said.

"He says he would like an explanation of why you are in my company, Jason."

"Tell him I am here to open a new business account and that you were kind enough to show me where the bank was located."

Simon glared at his sister and said in English, "Then how did you know his name is, Jason?"

"I introduced myself. I am a businessman from the United States and need to open a business account in a bank here in Vera Cruz, but I do not think that this is the right bank for me or my company. Perhaps you can suggest another bank that would like a considerable investment of, say a million pesos over the next year?" I did not realize that I had raised my voice until the president's office door swung open and a bass voice said, "Simon."

Juanita was smiling as she said, "Jason, let me introduce you to my father, the president of this bank." We left Simon standing in the lobby and entered her fathers office. "I will translate for you, Jason. I am sorry, I do not know your last name."

"It is Caldwell, Senor Jason Caldwell, from Beaufort, South Carolina, Vice President of Caldwell Shipping." She turned to her father and introduced me. We shook hands and he motioned for me to have a chair in front of his desk. He said something in Spanish and Juanita translated for me. I looked hard at her father and thought, he is an international businessman he understands English and probably French, do not underestimate this man. I turned to Juanita and said, "Tell your father that I am very honored to meet him and that I hope that our two business enterprises can be mutually profitable in the next year. I would like to invest capital in his bank from the profits of my business so that he can make wise use of the money." His eyes lit up and I knew then that he understood English perfectly. "You may tell him that if I had not stopped you and asked for directions to his bank, in my rude 'north americano' manner, I would not be sitting here in his office."

She translated and he gave no hint that he understood my rather rude approach to his daughter. My mind was searching how to get out of this situation and back to the ship, when Juanita turned to me and said, "My father thanks you for your deposit, how much shall I make it out for." She was smiling, thinking this poor starving artist does not have a peso to his name.

I reached into my front pocket and removed a leather pouch that the captain had given me so that I could pay bribes to the local police if I were detained for questioning. I had not looked inside it. She opened it and counted the double gold eagles inside. There were twenty, 400 dollars. "I will need to find out the exchange rate between dollars and pesos Mr. Caldwell."

Her father said, "The rate is 110 to one this morning." He then realized that he had spoken in English and said, "That will be a deposit of 44,000 pesos, Senor Caldwell."

"Thank you, Senor Simon Hernandez de la Veragua. A man of your position would not normally accept such a small deposit but it was all the money that I felt comfortable carrying through the streets of Veracruz." I wildly searched my history lessons from Beaufort Academy. Where had I heard this man's last name before, Veragua - Veragua. Then it came to me, the Duke of Veragua, the title borne by the successors of Columbus, bestowed originally on Luis Colon (the Spanish name for Columbus), the grandson of Christopher Columbus. The male line died out in 1600 something and the line was then continued through Luis Colon's sister. The Duke of Veragua had been received at the White House by President Jackson. I cleared my throat and said, "Senior Veragua you can trace your family to Christopher Columbus and you are a man of honor. I searched for you because my father, the President of Caldwell Shipping will not do business with anyone he can not completely trust. He also comes from a royal blood line, Ireland, not Spain. I will do something that I rarely do in business." I stood, took off my jacket and rolled up my left sleeve. Just above the left elbow, I showed him a tattoo. This is the mark of the Irish royal line.

Tears came into Veragua's eyes as he said to Juanita, "Please make out all the paper work for Senior Caldwell in English. If you are free for lunch senor, I would like to eat with you here at the bank in our executive suite."

Several hours later I returned to the USS Trumbull with my sketches, bank papers and a story that I was sure the captain would not believe. When I had finished telling him what I had done, he smiled and said, "Money well spent, Mr. Caldwell. Do you think you could keep this contact for us in Veracruz?"

"You mean you want me to keep the Navy's money in the Banquo de la Veracruz, Sir?"

"I will report all of this through channels to the Secretary, but I think, that money and some more will be deposited by you when you visit the Veragua's next time."

"Next time?"

"Yes, Mr. Caldwell, unless I miss my guess you will be dropped off here next summer while the USMA summer cruise passes through the gulf. You will spend the summer with the Veragua's, if invited, and continue to gather as much information as you can on what the Mexican Government is going to do to handle the French intentions of invading Mexico."

"Sir?"

"Yes, Midshipman."

"I am a college student, Sir. The Navy already has agents that should be doing this type of thing, correct?"

"No one who is as young as you Mr. Caldwell, with the family 'cover story' that you have developed with the Veragua's. How old are the son and daughter?"

"I have no idea."

"Why not write to the daughter and see if you two can start some communication."

"I would need permission from the father, to do that Captain."

"Then I suggest that you polish your writing skills, Mr. Caldwell and get that first letter off to the father before we leave the harbor."

"Today, Sir?

"Today, Mr. Caldwell."

We continued on our cruise around the Gulf of Mexico, but not before I had written and mailed a letter to Simon Veragua, asking for permission to write to his daughter, Juanita. I mailed it in Veracruz at the bank's address and indicated that my mailing address was 1121 Bay Street, Beaufort, South Carolina, USA. I also mailed my father and brought him up to date on my experiences on this summer cruise. I indicated that he would be getting bank statements, addressed to Jason Caldwell, Vice President of Caldwell Shipping and if I were lucky, letters from Juanita Veragua. He was welcome to open the letters from the bank, but the letters from Juanita were personal, and please forward them to West Point.

Our last stop on the summer cruise of 1835 was Key West. We approached the harbor dockyards and I noticed three of my father's ships in port. I reached for my pocket sketch book and sketched them.

7

Cows, The Point
West Point, 1835-36

Our third year at the Point gave us some freedom to explore our surroundings. We knew where West Point was, we got here in 1833. It was located on the right bank of the Hudson River, on the eastern edge of Orange County, New York, 50 miles from the city of New York. We got to West Point by train. The New York Central and Hudson River railroads provided connections into the city as well as a steamboat line. John Campbell, Alex Bowman, Bill Dewey, Tom Gibson and I got permission to visit New York Harbor the first break in the fall of 1835. We had our passes in hand and were ready to leave our barracks when a messenger from Superintendent DeRussy stopped us and told me, "Midshipman Caldwell, your leave has been cancelled. The rest of you may proceed."

I wondered what I had done. I followed the messenger back to the Superintendent's office. I was shown into the office and introduced to the Secretary of the Navy, Levi Woodbury from New Hampshire.

"Midshipman Caldwell, I have studied your sketches and diagrams from Veracruz. You are a remarkable young man."

"Thank you, Sir."

"I wanted to meet you to see if you would be willing to go back to Veracruz over your Christmas Holidays."

"I had planned on going to South Carolina, Sir. It is a family tradition and I would be missed."

"I have visited with your Mother and Father in Beaufort, Jason. They understand and approve of the mission that I would like you to undertake."

"Mission, Sir?"

"Yes, we have been trying to get basic information on what Mexico intends to do with their most northern State of Tejas. Our early information is that General Santa Anna is forming an army in Mexico to march north and put down the revolt in Tejas. It would be in our best interests if the revolt was successful and that a separate country be formed north of Mexico. President Jackson does not want to enter this war, but he wants to give as much aid as possible to men like Finlay Macnab and Zave Campbell who might make such a request."

"Mr. Secretary, General Santa Anna is known as El Salvador de Mexico. He was given this title after the rape of Zacatecas."

"I am sorry midshipman, I am not totally aware of what happened in the northern State of Zacatecas. Have you read what happened?"

"Yes, Sir. The silver rich State of Zacatecas had refused to recognize the dictatorship of Santa Anna and supported the Mexican Constitution of 1824. On May 11, 1835, Santa Anna led a large army up to the walls of the capital city, he then took a page from Napoleon's order of battle and swung around to the rear of the city for the actual attack. At the same time, he ordered several of his best officers to leave his ranks in apparent defection. They were to sneak into the city, and proclaim themselves 'defenders of the Constitution.' As trained soldiers, they were given command of Zacatecas troops, which they directed into certain slaughter when the fighting began.

It is what happened next, that you must communicate to your men Macnab and Campbell. Two thousand five hundred women and children who not participated the battle were lined up and slain in the public squares. Foreign diplomats became special targets, with English and American husbands bayoneted and their wives stripped naked and coursed through the streets and turned over to Santa Anna's troops who raped them to death. Not a single person survived inside the city."

"Are you sure about this, Mr. Caldwell?"

"It is a matter of record, newspaper reports were softened somewhat, but the city of Zacatecas is now a ruin. It has not been rebuilt, it is reminder to all who oppose Santa Anna."

"Santa Anna was born in Veracruz in 1794, someone must know something that can aid us, so the same thing does not befall the State of Tejas. Your mission will be to try and find Santa Anna's Achilles Heel. Can you try to do that for us, Mr. Caldwell?"

"Yes, Sir."

"Good. Your father will send the Westwind to the Point, the last week in November. Superintendent DeRussy will release you from your studies here, with full credit, until the next term begins. You will need to be back at the Point no later than January 26, 1836. Understood?"

"Yes, Sir."

"Any questions?"

"Yes, Sir. I will need traveling expenses."

"Already deposited in the Caldwell Shipping account in Beaufort. You are to stop there to pick up the funds and see your father and mother before sailing around Florida and into Veracruz. Jason, you are not required to do this as a part of your USMA education or training, the President of the United States thinks you have the best chance of hearing what the Mexican

Government plans to do. You have already brought us more useful intelligence from Veracruz than all of our intelligence agents in the vicinity."

"I have?"

"Yes, Jason, you have a natural talent for making people like you and for the gathering of information. The Captains of the USS Spitfire and the Trumbull have both written to me describing your talents and ability to lead the men under you. I wish you every success in this mission and in your studies here at West Point."

"Thank you, Mr. Secretary. How will I communicate with you while I am in Veracruz?"

"You will not. I repeat, you will not communicate with anyone at West Point or Washington City. You will send letters to the Caldwell Shipping Company in Beaufort and your father will forward them to me. We have a set of code words for you and your father. He will be sending my instructions to you in Veracruz, via the bank and Senor Veragua."

"Senor Veragua is aware of my mission?"

"No, Senor Veragua is a friend of the State Department, but he is unaware of your assignment. All he suspects is that his daughter maybe in love with you."

"She is?"

"That is the first unintelligent thing that you have said, Jason. Of course, her father thinks she is in love with an Irish Catholic from the United States. He would do anything not to see the two of you together if he knew you are an Irish Protestant. He has other plans for her."

"Oh."

"Jason, are you in love?"

"No, Sir."

"Good. Keep it that way. This is US government business not pleasure."

"Yes, Sir."

"I must get back to the White House and report to the President, I will leave you with Superintendent DeRussy to work out all the details as to why you are missing for a few weeks here at the Point." He rose from his chair and left the office.

"Jason, this is very unusual. The White House should never have asked you to do this. President Jackson is a striking figure. He is combative, obstinate to the last degree, an unrelenting hater of his enemies, and an unflinching ally and defender of his friends. By accepting this assignment, the Point and, more importantly, the formation of a separate Naval Academy is insured of his support. He will be elected to a third term, if he chooses to run again, and the congress will grant his request for the formation of a Naval

Academy at Annapolis. Come home safely, Jason, you are there to listen and report. Do not get yourself in any trouble with the Mexican authorities. Understood?"

"Aye, aye. Sir."

The Westwind arrived at the Point and the cover story of a family emergency was circulated by the Superintendent's office. I arrived in Port Royal a few days later and was met by my father's driver. We arrived at 1121 Bay Street and my father was not overjoyed to see me. "Jason, what kind of trouble have you gotten yourself into with this Santa Anna thing?"

"He was born in Veracruz, Father. I was in Veracruz, Mexico, a seaport on the gulf this summer. I wrote to you and gave you an update, remember?"

"Oh, yes. I got the bank statement. Where did the 44,000 dollars come from?"

"Pesos, Father, not dollars. It is 400 dollars from the Navy."

"Oh. Do they want it back? What is the 9,009 dollars for that the Secretary of the Navy left with me?"

"Nine thousand dollars is a million pesos, I am to deposit it in the Banquo de la Veracruz, posing as the Vice President of Caldwell Shipping."

My mother ended the grilling with the statement that as far as she was concerned, I was the Vice President. "I have told your father that he is not to touch the Navy's money in Mexico and he is to draw up the papers making you his vice president for international shipping. You will have them on your person when the Westwind leaves for Mexico the day after tomorrow."

"The day after tomorrow? I just got here."

"Yes, I know. But the sooner you get there, the sooner you can come back home for the holidays. We will wait to celebrate when the Westwind brings you back to Port Royal."

"Yes, Ma'am."

In two days the Westwind headed for Florida and then the Gulf of Mexico. It was December and the winds were raw until we reached the keys. We stopped at Key West and I sent my father a letter. I hoped that a letter would be waiting for me at the bank in Mexico when I arrived. It took several days to reach the port of Veracruz. After we docked, I dressed in my best business suit and caught a carriage to the bank. I entered the bank and asked to speak to Senorita or Senor Veragua. I was shown to Simon Perez de la Veragua's office, Juanita's brother. He was cordial and spoke in clear English. "What can the Banquo de la Veracruz do for you, Senor Caldwell?"

"I have a deposit to make. It is slightly over a million pesos in gold bullion aboard my ship docked in the harbor. I will need for you to accept the deposit on board and transfer it to your bank."

"I am sorry, Senor, you will have to bring it directly to the banquo. We can not be responsible for it until it enters the banquo."

"How unfortunate, Senor Veragua, please tell your father that I was here and that we could not find a way to get my gold to your bank." I rose from my chair and left his office. I was crossing the lobby when I heard my name called out.

"Jason, is that you?" It was Juanita beaming from ear to ear. "What are you doing here?"

"Trying to make a deposit, but your brother would not accept my deposit. I brought gold bullion on one of my father's ships and I need some help in bringing it to the bank."

"Come with me." We headed for her father's office. She did not knock, she flung open the door and let out a string of Spanish curses about her brother. Her father saw me behind her and said, "Senor Caldwell, we have been expecting you. Your father is already here and we have had a nice visit."

"My father is here?" I said as I stuck my head around the open door and saw a man whom I had never seen before. "Senor Veragua, that is not my father. I suggest that you summon the police and find out who he really is."

All the color drained from Simon Hernandez de la Veragua's face. He regained his composure and went behind his desk and removed a revolver. "I suggest that you tell me your real name before I shoot you and claim that you attempted a banquo robbery."

"I am Robert Caldwell from Beaufort, South Carolina, I have already shown you my identification."

"Did he sign his signature on any documents Senor Veragua?" I asked.

"Why, of course, on a withdrawal slip."

I reached into my suit pocket and withdrew my vice presidential papers and said, "Does the signature match the signature on this document?"

"It is not even close, Jason."

"Then, I suggest you shoot this man for attempted robbery." The revolver in Simon's hand barked and the man grabbed his right arm. His face became white as several bank employees rushed into the president's office. Simon went over to the man and said, "My next shot will be to the head if you do not tell me your name and who sent you here."

"My name is Adam Smith and I am from the United States, I work for the Caldwells in Beaufort and I heard of the gold shipment being delivered, I was trying to steal it."

"Who sent you here?" Simon repeated.

"Your son."

"You are a liar!" I shouted. "I know everyone who works for Caldwell Shipping and you do not. You are trying to smear the name of a noble family and its only son, you bastard."

Simon Perez Veragua was standing just inside the door and was looking very guilty. "Tell your father the truth, Simon." Adam Smith was pleading with him. "He hired me to withdraw the entire million right after it was deposited, our timing was off, that is why I was caught. I was supposed to be long gone before the Caldwell son appeared."

I found myself with my arm around Juanita because she was crying. Her father was beyond being calm, he turned to his assistant and said in Spanish, " Call the Federals, I want to get to the bottom of this. Someone is lying and I fear it is my son."

Several hours later, Adam Smith was arrested for attempted bank embezzlement at the hospital, Gutierrez Zamora. I was detained for questioning along with the two Simons and Juanita Veragua. I was sitting on a bench outside a police interview room when a woman walked up to me and said, "Senor Jason Caldwell?"

"Si."

"I am Juanita's mother. Our family attorney is with the police arranging for everyone's release. Simon is so sorry that he was taken in by the man posing as your father. He has written the Caldwell Offices in America and has explained what has happened. He has also invited your parents to Veracruz for the holidays. I think it is only fair that we meet the family of the man that Juanita is so intrigued by, nes pa!"

"Senora Veragua, I do not know what to say. My parents do not know about Juanita or that I have any interest in her."

"Well, do you?"

"I am not blind, Senora Veragua. Your daughter is the most beautiful young woman that I have met, but I am very young, not yet twenty-one, I am still attending college, and I am not looking for a wife."

She burst out laughing. "Juanita has no idea that you are so young, Jason. She is already past twenty-one and I do not know what her reaction to this will be. I am so glad to hear that you are not a man looking for a rich wife to support him. Her father and brother protect her too much and she will rebel unless they give her some freedom to choose her friends and acquaintances."

"I agree, when everyone is released, she should go to church and light a candle and say a prayer for the peaceful settlement of the troubles that have befallen our two families."

"An excellent suggestion, Jason." The bass voice was from Simon Hernandez, he had been released. "I have been informed that the man calling himself, Adam Smith, is to be released for prosecution in South Carolina. He is wanted there for a similar crime in Charleston, for withdrawing funds from a Caldwell Shipping account. The Veracruz police are happy to be rid of him. He will be taken into custody by the US Counselor's Office and sent back to South Carolina, probably on your ship, Jason."

"Then, your son was innocent as I indicated in your office?"

"Si, Jason, I will always be in your debt for defending him to the police."

"Nonsense, Simon, you are a man of honor. Your family is beyond question for such a petty crime as this."

"Thank you, Jason. Your deposit has been taken from the Westwind and placed in our vaults for safe keeping. When do you plan to return to South Carolina?"

"As I was explaining to your wife, I am a college student. I was last here on my summer break and I am home to South Carolina for the Christmas celebration only. I have never missed a midnight mass with my family on Christmas Eve, it is a tradition."

"Were you an altar boy, Jason?"

"Still am. I am not an adult, Senor Veragua. I am a college student trying to learn my father's shipping business. He has trusted me with this Mexican investment as a trial. If I am successful, he may give me other assignments, who knows? He will not be happy with what has happened here so far."

The relief on Simon Hernandez de la Veragua's face was evident, as soon as he realized that I was not a suitor for his daughter. "Jason, my family may have reacted somewhat prematurely when I invited your family here for Christmas."

"Not at all, Senor. I foresee a day when the Veragua family attends the midnight mass with the Caldwells in St. Helena's Church, Beaufort, South Carolina. I hope that the two families can remain friends over the years and exchange letters so that we can keep track of the grandchildren that Juanita and Simon will certainly have for you. It is important to you to have the Spanish line continue in Mexico, as it is for my father to hope that the Irish line will continue in America."

"Are you sure, you are not an adult, Jason? I wish Juanita was so mature as to think in this way." He was smiling and he had placed his arm around my shoulders.

"What has been going on, Father. Why are you hugging, Jason?" Juanita had given her statement to the police and had been released along with her brother.

"Because, we have a new friend of the family tonight. Jason has invited us to attend midnight mass on Christmas Eve in Beaufort, South Carolina, whenever we wish."

"You do realize that there are no Roman Catholic Churches in Beaufort, South Carolina, Father?"

"I do not care. The Church of Ireland says mass in Latin and Jason has known his church Latin since the age of ten. Latin is Latin and Church is Church. Did you know that when the English invaded Ireland in the 1600's, Jason, that the noblemen of Ireland fled to the Court of Spain for protection. Every one of them was a Church of Ireland member and they intermarried with the Roman Catholics."

As Simon Hernandez and I walked arm in arm out of the police station, I said, "Did you know that my family was Roman Catholic in Ireland when the English invaded in the 1600's and they fled to America. There were no Roman Catholic Churches in the entire Colony of South Carolina, so they intermarried with the French Protestants and joined the Anglican Churches so they could attend mass in Latin?"

Still standing inside the police station, Juanita said, "Do you think it will break Father's heart when I marry Jason and move to the United States, Mother?"

"Jason Caldwell is a man of honor, Juanita. If you marry Jason, he will move to Mexico, take over your father's bank, fire your brother and renew his forefather's Roman Catholic heritage!"

"Father would never allow such a thing to happen, Mother." Simon Perez was smiling.

"Son, your father has an announcement to make when we arrive home. He will inform you that he has purchased an officer's position in Generalissimo Santa Anna's army forming in Saltillo. You will be leaving after Christmas."

The time before the week of Christmas melted away, with Juanita at my side where ever I went. I slept on the Westwind, she at her parent's home but the rest of the time was like magic for me. Juanita was nearly two years older than me by age, but younger in life's experiences. She had not left home at an early age to enter a college a 1000 miles away, like I had. She was protected by her father and brother. "Jason, do you know that you are the first man that I have spent any time alone, without another person present."

"Boy."

"What?"

"I am a, boy, Juanita. I will be twenty-one in June of next year."

"You do not kiss like a boy, Jason." She was smiling and she laid her head on my shoulder as we sat on a park bench.

"Juanita?"

"Yes, Jason."

"We are just dear friends, you know that I am flattered by such a beautiful young woman showing me so much attention."

"Dearest Jason, you are my first real love. But you are not Spanish and we will never marry, it is not in my Karma. My brother will die in the military service to his country, as will you. The Veragua family line will fall to me to carry on. I will hold on to you as tight as I can until that moment of permanent separation comes, but until then I am yours completely and without reservation. I want to give you my virginity and bear your children but I will not marry you. The man I marry, must understand that my heart belongs to another. I will not bear his children. I hope to meet a man of noble birth who has lost his wife and already has small children for me to raise along with ours. He will understand my love for you, it will be the same as his love for his first wife."

"Juanita, if you feel this way next summer, we will live and love as man and wife when I return to Veracruz. Until that time, think about what you want to become and what you want your life to be. I will be gone on the Westwind in the morning and this kiss must last until then."

8
Summer Cruise
Annapolis, 1836

On January 26, 1836, Generalissimo Antonio Lopez de Santa Anna, attended by his aide, Captain Simon Perez de la Veragua, entered the State of Tejas in northern Mexico to put down the rebellion that was forming there. I would miss part of the USMA Summer Cruise of 1836 because I would be in Veracruz on assignment for the Secretary of the Navy. After my experience with the summer cruise of 1835, I was prepared for my detour to Veracruz. It began like a normal summer cruise with three groups of Navy Cadets and one group of Navy Marine Cadets arriving by train from West Point to Annapolis in June, 1836. We stepped off the train, but this year there was not another group of boys huddled together on the far end of the platform. We did not hear the familiar, *"What the hell is this?"* From Master Chief Gunnerman. His Lieutenant met us instead.

He strode over to us, screamed, "Attention in the ranks, cadets!"

We placed our sea bags beside our right feet and came to attention and presented him with the proper salute. He did not smile this year when he said, "Welcome back for your summer cruise to the Gulf of Mexico, gentlemen. This summer, US citizens are being killed in Mexico. The group of plebes that you normally see here on the platform reported three weeks ago to Chief Gunnerman." He walked slowly over to the group of marine cadets and said, "This is the first year that the Army and Navy have scheduled a joint exercise with the fleet cadets. You will be under the command of Captain Jermine and his detachment that have been sent here by the war department. It will be your duty to land somewhere in Northern Mexico. You may see action and some of you will certainly die, if you do. Because you are cadets at the United States Military Academy, this is a volunteer mission on your part. If you have not been told this, please step forward and you will be dismissed for your normal summer breaks. If you have been informed and have now changed your minds, please step forward and you will be dismissed for your normal summer breaks."

The army and marine cadets were still at attention and not a one moved forward. He turned on his heel and marched toward us. The LT stopped before us again and said, "Fleet naval cadets come to attention. You are also

here as volunteers. If you have changed your minds, please step forward."
No one moved. He continued by saying, "We have six ships ready for action
this summer. Action, not a cruise. The USS New Haven, Trumbull, Spitfire,
Providence, Somerset and Nelson are fully armed and if the Mexican army is
foolish enough to march along the shore line in the State of Tejas, northern
Mexico, the President of the United States has authorized the use of lethal
force. They will be fired upon and killed without warning." You could
hear the intake of breath from our ranks. He unfolded a map and held it
up for us to see. It was an enlargement of last year's map to show where the
marine landing would be taking place along the northern shores of Mexico.
"Because the Secretary of the Navy considers this summer's actions, active
Naval service, the following have been promoted. As I call your name please
step forward and receive your insignia.

1) Alexander Bowman, Ensign active duty,
2) John Campbell, Ensign active duty,
3) William Dewey, Ensign active duty,
4) Thomas Gibson, Ensign active duty,
5) Benjamin Hagood, Lieutenant JG active duty,
6) Jason Caldwell, Lieutenant active duty."

He then repeated the procedure in front of the marine cadets from the
Point. He then said, "Marines, you are released for boarding the ships. About
face, forward march!" Chris Merryweather was a Marine Lieutenant on
active duty, under the command of Captain Jermine when he marched off
the platform to board his ship. The LT returned to us. "Ensign Bowman,
you are in charge of all cadets and US Navy personnel under the rank of
Ensign, report to the USS Spitfire at this time. All those cadets assigned to
the Spitfire, hoist your gear and follow Ensign Bowman.

Ensign Campbell, you are in charge of all cadets and US Navy personnel
under the rank of Ensign, report to the USS Somerset at this time. All those
cadets assigned to the Somerset follow Ensign Campbell. Ensign Dewey,
you are in charge of all cadets and US Navy personnel under the rank of
Ensign, report to the USS Providence, cadets assigned to the Providence
please follow Ensign Dewey. Ensign Gibson, you are in charge of all cadets
and US Navy personnel under the rank of Ensign, proceed to the USS Nelson
for boarding."

Ben and I were left on the platform with the remaining cadets. "Lieutenant
JG Hagood, come to attention and return my salute. Congratulations,
Lieutenant, you are the first West Point cadet to be promoted to the rank
of Lieutenant JG on active duty, since the War of 1812. Ensigns Campbell,

Bowman, Dewey and Gibson will report to you whenever you are ashore. They are your responsibility, as well as all the cadets and US Navy personnel under the rank of Lieutenant JG. Do you understand and accept this assignment?"

"Aye, aye. Sir."

"Lieutenant Hagood, report to the USS New Haven. Cadets assigned to the New Haven follow your Lieutenant. Lieutenant Caldwell, come to attention and return my salute. Congratulations, Lieutenant, you are the first West Point cadet to be assigned behind enemy lines during a national emergency. You will remain in Mexico until the end of the summer, when the USS Trumbull or US Merchant Marine will return you to the Potomac Dockyards for your report to the Secretary of the Navy. Lieutenant Caldwell and all cadets assigned to the USS Trumbull, report for duty."

During the sail into the gulf, I reread all of the letters that Juanita had sent to me at the Point. They were not love letters, they were not business letters, they were not friendly letters - they were from one soul to another. She had the ability to cut through all the emotion that most girls I knew had to deal with on a day to day basis. She knew what she wanted from life and how to get it. Each letter was more mature and self-confident. I did not think I would have to be a surrogate husband this summer. I had removed all of the written portions of her letters that dealt with her brother's experiences with General Santa Anna on his campaign into northern Mexico and had given it to Superintendent De Russy to forward to Secretary Woodbury. Her brother had described in detail what had happened on their march north. On February 13, 1836, a "blue northerner" swept down upon the marching army of Santa Anna. The temperature dropped to thirty degrees and it began to snow, lots of snow. By midafternoon a full blown blizzard was upon them. Mules, horses and oxen struggled in the blinding storm, collapsed and were buried under huge snow drifts. Simon rode his horse up and down the marching lines of his men. They fell to the ground and huddled in groups of twos and threes to try to keep warm where they froze to death. He reported this to his General who rode at the front of the army. They came upon a mission and the army huddled inside the outer walls of the mission while General Santa Anna and his staff were warm inside for the night. The next morning, his general had lost half of his invading army. He now had an army of less than 2000 to march against the four Tejas locations that the Generalissimo was determined to treat as he had the City of Zacatecas. He marched north to the San Antonio mission.

At the Battle of San Antonio de Bejar, a hundred and eighty-two American citizens were killed at the small mission site, a hundred during the battle and eighty-two after they had surrendered and the battle was over. Simon Perez

49

de la Veragua could not understand his General's command to "eliminate all foreigners upon Mexican soil." He was not impressed that nearly two thousand soldaderas had been thrown against the handful of Americans defending the mission. And he was further horrified that the Americans had killed 900 of his troops in the attempt to take the mission. Eleven hundred marched toward Mission Goliad under the command of General Urrea while Santa Anna and his aides remained in San Antonio. Messengers were sent to Mexico City for a second army to invade the State of Tejas. This second army would be commanded by General Jose Juan Perez, known to his troops as the "Rock." It was now March and the weather should be better. By the middle of March, General Urrea, acting under Santa Anna's orders, had surrounded the Mission of Goliad and demanded its immediate surrender. Three hunderd and eighty Americans, under the command of Colonel Fannin, did so. The entire company was shot, placed in a large body pile and burned.

It was apparent from Simon's account, that the first Mexican army would sweep over the next mission at Tampico unless something was done to stop them. General Sam Houston was camped at Tampico and ordered a retreat toward Nacogdoches, near the US border. Before he reached there, however, more American volunteers met him halfway. Houston ordered a halt and waited for the two Mexican armies to join forces. He had no way of knowing that a series of events would keep the two armies from joining.

After rounding Key West the summer action fleet sailed toward the northern shore of Mexico at a place called, East Matagorda Bay on our charts. We sailed into Lavaca Bay less than 90 miles from Victoria Station. Here, we landed the US Marines, under the Command of Captain Jermine. It took us several hours to shuttle the marines from their ships to the shore in long boats. No enemy was encountered and Chris Merryweather led his marines inland to set up an interception of the second Mexician army marching toward Victoria Station, State of Tejas, Republic of Mexico. The President of the United States had ordered this action to aid in the retreat and evacuation of American citizens from the State of Tejas. The six ships left the Bay of Matagorda, and sailed south and entered San Antonio Bay, north of San Jose Island. San Antonio Bay was long and narrow and ran inland nearly a hundred miles. We anchored at the head of the bay and waited for the advancing Mexican army.

Each day, we sent the USS New Haven from San Antonio Bay back north into Lavaca Bay with messages for Captain Jermine. On the third day, we sighted the second Mexican army coming north along the Refugio Real, a stone covered roadway that made easy travel for the horses, carts and artillery pieces being pulled behind the main body. The captain of our group signaled the USS Providence and Nelson to concentrate its fire upon the wagons at the end of the column and for the USS Somerset and Spitfire to open fire on the marching troops after the bombardment of the artillery pieces. The Providence and Nelson opened fire and scattered the wagons and artillery pieces. The troops had left the roadway to seek cover, only to be routed by the Somerset and Spitfire. General Jose Perez was amazed to see six ships flying the flag of the Republic of Texas shelling his army. He ordered a retreat to find another road into Victoria Station. He kept well out of our gun's range and took several hours before he decided upon the safe route. He would march directly into the US Marines camped north of his position.

Captain Jermine knew that his small company stood no chance in a conventional engagement, so he ordered Lieutenant Merryweather to hide his troops until nightfall and then creep upon the Mexican army while they were asleep. He ordered his men to kill only the night pickets set up around the sleeping army. This would leave them totally unprotected and unaware that five ships of the fleet had moved from San Antonio into Lavaca Bay. The sixth ship, the USS Trumbull, had sailed for Veracruz. At midnight, the fleet again opened fire on the sleeping army and the commanding General Perez had to make another decision, he could not take the shoreline any longer, he would have to march inland and swing west several hundred miles and enter Victoria Station from that direction. He began his march at night. The marines followed taking the stragglers one by one. At sun rise, General Perez halted his forced march and sent a messenger into Victoria Station to the waiting Santa Anna. Perez informed Santa Anna that he was attacked by Tejas Republic ships outside the Bay of Lavaca. Santa Anna sent a simple reply.

"Jose, stay away from the sea. Continue through Victoria Station and meet me on the road to Nacogdoches at the San Jacinto River."

General Jose Juan Perez arrived at the river on June 23, 1836, to find the river sides covered with dead soldaderas by the hundreds. The "Rock" was shaken. He had his aide count the dead and it was obvious that the entire army had perished, but the body of Santa Anna and his aide, Captain Simon Perez de la Veragua, were not found. General Perez ordered the bodies of the dead to be piled and burned while he set up his camp. A Mexican Lancer with Santa Anna's colors rode into his camp with a hand written letter from the Generalissimo. The letter indicated that he and his aide were in route to the capital of the United States with General Houston to speak with President Jackson about the misunderstanding of the treatment of American citizens living in the State of Tejas. Jose Juan Perez, the rock of Mexico, was to return with his army to Mexico City and await the return of the El Salvador de Mexico, Antonio Lopez de Santa Anna, Generalissimo of the armies of Mexico.

I stood on the bridge of the USS Trumbull as it pulled away in the dark of night. The sky to the northeast was aglow from the bombardment of the sleeping Mexican army. I prayed that Chris Merryweather would remain safe and come back to the fleet and resume his "summer cruise". Two days later the USS Trumbull docked in Veracruz, Mexico without incident. I changed into my business suit in case the newspapers had reported the defeat of Santa Anna at San Jacinto. There were no newspaper reports of any of the battles in the Mexican State of Tejas. Juanita, translated a morning newspaper story for me. "It says the leader of Mexico had been invited to the White House in Washington City for discussions with United States Officials on the immigration problems in northern Mexico. Generalissimo Santa Anna and his aide Captain Simon Perez de la Veragua were trying to explain to the US Officials that the uncontrolled, mass immigration of northern Mexico by poor, uneducated, US citizens was not a wise course for either country. No date has been set for El Salvador's return to Mexico City."

I looked at Juanita and said, "It sounds like your brother is going to be a very important man in Mexico City."

Juanita folded the newspaper and laid it by her breakfast plate. "Jason, tomorrow is Sunday, are we going to church with my parents?"

"Of course."

"Have you been happy this summer, Jason?"

"Of course."

"Did you approve of my telling my parents that you are living with me in my apartment?"

"Of course."

"Are you going to make an honest woman of me and ask me to marry you when you graduate from the military academy of your country?"

"Of course."

"Can you say something other than, of course?"

"Of course." That is when she threw the folded newspaper at me.

9
Firsties, The Point
West Point, 1836-37

Our final year at the Point gave us even more freedom to explore our surroundings. For the first time in West Point history some students would graduate above a second lieutenant or the lieutenant JG grades. The national emergency in northern Mexico and the information gathered in Veracruz and reported to the Secretary of the Navy had resulted in many promotions before graduation. Secretary Woodbury had indicated that he would recommend that the new incoming Secretary continue the concept of Naval Intelligence gathering. In order to do this, the new secretary would have to identify and train naval personal to perform this mission. He asked if I was interested in such an assignment and I indicated that I would. He then said something that surprised me. "Jason, I would like you to become the head of this group of young men. It will be totally "out of sight". I would like to send you to the Naval War College in Newport, Rhode Island. From here I would like you to take command of the six ships that the cadets have brought to life at Annapolis. We need to find six more near wrecks that the next bunch of naval cadets can repair during hell weeks. I want you to bid at an auction to be held at Annapolis next year after graduation. You will use the money in the Bank of Veracruz to purchase these ships. You will tell everyone, including Lieutenant Hagood, that your father is giving you the money. Better yet, tell him that the Navy will not let anyone under the age of twenty-one bid at the auction and have him place the bids for you. You will move the ships to Port Royal Naval Training center or to Caldwell Shipping, if you like, and hold them for intelligence gathering. Do you think you could do that?"

"I would like to keep them in Port Royal at my father's docks and use them to haul heavy goods to nearby ports of call. In that way the "out of sight"would be certain. My father will not understand the use of Navy funds for this, let me ask for the funding directly from him. I will repay him directly from the Caldwell accounts in Mexico or the profits from heavy goods shipping."

"Agreed. Jason, we are going to have a national election this fall and I know for a fact, that President Jackson is going to retire and he wants to see Martin Van Buren, his secretary of state, elected president. Van Buren will keep Jackson's cabinet members, maybe not in the same slots but I will be here to advise my successor. We need Naval Intelligence and we need it badly."

"Thank you Mr. Secretary, I will serve you or the next secretary to the best of my ability."

"I know you will, Jason. Report to Superintendent DeRussy that I will be in touch with him shortly."

"Aye, aye. Sir."

I arrived a day late to start my final year at West Point. I was given twenty demerits to work off before the weekend. So far, I held the record for the most missed days of instruction, ever at West Point. Superintendent DeRussy said, "Jason, you and the other naval cadets, have set a record here for the most absences during a three year period. You, and the others, have been excused for each of them from President Jackson and his cabinet on down. I have looked the other way, when requests have come from the White House. I am trying to run an academic institution here at West Point and the White House thinks it is a training ground for spies and covert activities of all kinds. I have decided to write a letter and place copies in all naval files, I will let you read it. It will say that I do not recommend that any of you be given a Civil Engineering Degree and further that you would not be qualified to graduate as a member of the corps of engineers. What this will do, is insure that naval cadets will be restricted to service in the United States Navy. No one has ever graduated from the Point as a Lieutenant and I want that distinction to belong to the Navy, not the Army. Understood?"

"Understood, Sir. And thank you for allowing me to begin my Navy Service before my graduation."

"I had nothing to do with it, Jason. You have friends in high places. Be careful that it does not come back to haunt you."

10
Graduation Day
June,1837

The graduation of the United States Military Academy in June, 1837, was held at West Point for the army cadets and at Annapolis for the Navy midshipmen. A single military academy held both branches but the Army and Navy had separate missions and had separate summer courses. New Navy Cadets were taken by train to Annapolis for a summer cruise to see if they were qualified to become sea going officers in the USN (United States Navy). A soon to be graduate of the US Military Academy, sat at Annapolis and searched the spectators for his mother and father, Robert and Mary Elisabeth Caldwell. They should be sitting next to his brother, sister and Juanita Veragua's family. He could not find them among the crowd, but he knew they were there. He had welcomed them the day before. They had come all the way from Veracruz, Mexico, on one of his father's packet ships out of Port Royal, South Carolina. It was not until he walked across the platform and received his bachelors degree and commission as an OF - 2, officer second grade, that he heard a rebel yell from his brother , Robert and located where they were sitting.

His brother and sister, and especially Juanita, were curious what a second grade officer was. Jason explained to them that there were 10 grades for naval officers, called OF classes. OF - 1 had two divisions Ensign and Lieutenant, (JG), Junior Grade. OF - 2 was a Lieutenant while OF - 3 was a Lieutenant Commander. OF - 4 was a Commander and OF - 5 was a captain. OF - 6 through 10 were all called Admirals and had one through five stars on their shoulder boards. A one star was commonly called a Commodore but he could also be called a Rear (lower division), depending upon where he served. A Commodore was at sea and a Rear was serving in the rear (on land).

"So what were you the last four years?" Robert was still curious.

"I began as a midshipman, promoted to Ensign and then Lieutenant JG."

"And you are a Lieutenant now?"

"Yes."

"Did you skip over the Ensign and JG grades?" Carol asked.

"No, I worked hard and earned them, little sister. My instructors have recommended that I go directly to the Naval War College at Newport, Rhode Island."

"What are you going to do there?" She asked.

"I will study for my master's degree and that will allow me to teach at any college or at the Navy Training Centers like Port Royal, San Francisco or Goat Island."

"I never heard of Goat Island. What do they do there? Chase and capture goats?"

"No, Carol. It is a torpedo station located in Rhode Island."

"So, does the Navy send you someplace different every four years, Jason?"

"Pretty much."

"Will you write to me?"

"Yes, Carol."

My father was smiling while he stood and talked with Juanita's father and mother. "Has Jason told you he has a chance to purchase surplus ships from the US Navy?"

"He has told Juanita that he will be spending more time this summer at Port Royal rebuilding some of them so they can be used from South Carolina to Veracruz. He asked me to try to lease some dock space in the harbor at Veracruz so that he can pay some expenses directly from my bank. That, I think, is an important element in his international business plans."

"Senor Veragua, do you think Jason will be successful in Mexico?"

"Look at my daughter, Senor Caldwell, I have never seen her so happy."

"We love Juanita, like our own daughter. I never thought Jason would settle down, your daughter has been a calming influence on him and we wish them every happiness, Senor Veragua. I know Jason is not from a Spanish line, as you hoped Juanita would find. But I understand that the Irish intermarried with the Spanish in the early 1600's, do you suppose that Jason has Spanish blood somewhere in his background?"

"I have gotten over the Duke of Veragua, obsession, Robert, I want Juanita to be happy and have a dozen children."

"I understand that, Mary Elizabeth and I had five children and only three lived to see adulthood. I walk among our grave markers at St. Helena and wonder what their lives would have been like."

"You, also? Veronica and I brought six babies into the world and yellow fever claimed four of them. My son, Simon, is an aide to the monster, Santa Anna in Mexico City and we rarely see him. We do not want to lose Juanita. We understand that Jason can not spend every minute in Veracruz, but he is going to have to spend some time in order for Juanita to give us those grandchildren!" Both fathers broke into laughter as Juanita and I walked up to them to ask them where they wanted to go in Annapolis to eat our dinner.

"Where are we going to eat?" Asked by father.

"I want Chesapeake crab!" My mother had decided for us. She and Senora Veragua began walking towards the waterfront in search of a restaurant. The rest of us trailed along after them like a bunch of ducklings following their mothers to the water.

"Wait! We have to find Ben Hagood and his family so they can eat with us!"

While the Veragua, Hagood and Caldwell families ate their dinner, the Oval Office in the White House had an unusual meeting and the following conversation.

PRESIDENT: Did the first choices graduate today at Annapolis, Secretary Dickerson?

NAVY SECRETARY: Yes, Mr. President. President Jackson's plan is on schedule.

PRESIDENT: When I was elected and sat down with Andrew, I thought he was crazy for what he did in Mexico last year. Now, I see the brilliance of his plan. It was so simple, yet effective. Identify, in each of the Navy, USMA graduates, those that will serve our nation on the sea and those that will gather information and act on it to protect US interests at home and in the western hemisphere.

SECRETARY: The first are out this year, Jason Caldwell from South Carolina and Ben Hagood from Georgia.

PRESIDENT: Who are the replacements in case of capture or death?

SECRETARY: Alexander Bowman and John Campbell.

PRESIDENT: Who will graduate next year?

SECRETARY: Franklin Buchanan and Andre Du Pont.

PRESIDENT: Have any of the training vessels been transferred to South Carolina?

SECRETARY: Yes, Mr. President, the USS Philadelphia was decommissioned and sold to Caldwell International Shipping. It is in route to Port Royal Naval Training Center where all ordnance will be removed and returned to the Navy. Jason has plans to complete the renovations by the end of the year.

PRESIDENT: Renovations?

SECRETARY: Yes, he paid little for the vessel, but he and this father own a marine facility at Port Royal where he will tear most of the ship apart and rebuild it. It is presently rigged as a snow, he will add a third mast and lighten the gross weight. For example, he will rebuild the stern and replace the old galleries, cabins, galley and holds with modern equipment for business and intelligence gathering. The ship will be deceivingly fast, in fact, he will be able to sail from the Potomac Dockyards to Veracruz in less time that our new steam powered side wheelers.

PRESIDENT: How will he get his crews for these ships?

SECRETARY: Secretary Woodbury and I have identified, young, single men from the fleet to serve under Lieutenant Caldwell. They will all be transferred to the Port Royal Training Center and he can use them to crew any of the ships under his command.

PRESIDENT: What about the captains?

SECRETARY: Same thing.

PRESIDENT: I can not think of anything else. Can you General Scott?

GENERAL WINFIELD SCOTT: Yes, Mr. President, we will need US Marines to serve on them.

PRESIDENT: Marines, not army soldiers?

GENERAL: No, Sir, I have seen these new Marines, like Lieutenant Merryweather, in action. The army could not have done what the marines did in the Gulf last year.

PRESIDENT: Talk to this Lieutenant Merryweather and see if this is something that he would like to do as a career builder. We have twenty-year commitments from the others, right?

GENERAL: Thirty, Sir.

PRESIDENT: That brings us to the Superintendent of USMA. Why did he place letters of reprimand in all the files of the Naval Cadets graduating this year?

SECRETARY: Mr. President, this is the first year that Naval Cadets have been officially recognized in a separate location. The Navy really needs a separate academy at Annapolis, Sir.

PRESIDENT: Well, both of you should know, that I plan to appoint Major Richard Delafield as his assistant. DeRussy has another year only, I want him gone by the fall of 1838, clear?

SECRETARY: Yes, Mr. President.

PRESIDENT: I want the paperwork completed for submission to congress for the separation of the United States Military Academies into two separate units by the fall of 1838, also.

SECRETARY: Yes, Mr. President.

11

Monetary Panic: South Carolina
September, 1837

Unfortunately for President Martin Van Buren, he inherited the lack of a Federal Bank Policy from the Jackson Administration. When Jackson refused to renew the Federal Banking System a "wild cat" system of state banks sprang up across the country and caused a period of speculation the country had never seen before. The result of Jackson's fight with and final defeat of the United States Bank was the formation of hundreds of new state banks. Most of these printed their own bank notes, which became worthless in March and April, 1837. The failures in New York and New Orleans amounted to 150,000,000 dollars. Eight states were bankrupt, and the Federal Government could not pay the interest on its bonds. All this confusion and distress was the result of the fevered speculation and unbusiness-like methods which prevailed during the last part of Jackson's Administration.

The condition became so bad that President Van Buren recalled the congress on September 4, 1837, to consider again a new Federal Banking System which would give him emergency powers to issue federal bank notes up to a limit of ten million dollars. This, he used to prop up the eight bankrupt states, like South Carolina. The panic threatened to erase the "out of sight" navy that was under construction in Port Royal, South Carolina. When I went to the Bank of Beaufort where the Caldwell Shipping account was located, I found the bank closed on a Monday morning. I went to the home of Robert Whitehall and asked him what had happened. He had just graduated from college with a business degree and he explained the situation to me. I wrote the Secretary of the Navy and asked for his permission to remove most of the funds in Veracruz in order to save the funds now within the US Navy account in Beaufort. He wrote back that I should begin to purchase Bank of Beaufort stock at the lowest possible prices until the bank reopened. In this manner the "out of sight" navy would own its own bank. Robert and I went to his father's house and convinced him to reopen the bank that afternoon so the local people could either sell their shares of bank stock or they could begin withdrawing their funds. My father assured Robert's father that the accounts of the Caldwell enterprises could be used to purchase stock until the US Navy funds arrived from Washington City. Every dollar in the Veracruz account was used to purchase Bank of Beaufort stock.

By the end of the panic, Caldwell International owned a shipping business with ten ships, a bank in South Carolina and a huge financial commitment to its stock holders. The holders were my family members, and the US Navy. Without my father's trust in me and the support of the Secretary of the Navy, the doors of the Bank of Beaufort would have remained closed.

12
Navy Careers Begin
1837 - 1838

Each of the three musketeers went their separate ways the year after graduation. Ben and I spent a few weeks together on the USS Intrepid that summer a brand new steam powered sloop-of-war, classified as a "light cruiser" in the new naval handbooks printed that year. It was in the handbook that I read the announcement that the United States Military Academy would be auctioning their Annapolis based training ships built prior to 1800. I showed the announcement to Ben and said, "I have decided to place a bid on the USS Philadelphia in order to begin my own International Shipping Company."

"How are you going to do that, it says right here that you have to be twenty-one to do that."

"I will be twenty-one on the 26th of this month, I will wait until then."

"Let me be your silent partner and we will put the bid in both of our names and I will sign it."

"Are you sure about this, Ben?"

"Glad to help a brother in arms, Jason."

I told Ben. "These ships that we repaired during our summers at Annapolis were used in the War of 1812, but built on the later 1790's. Most of these were solid oak, no iron plating of any kind. The Point sees no use in keeping them around, so they offered to sell them as scrap to whomever will place a bid."

What I did not tell Ben was that the new Secretary of the Navy, Dickerson, would only accept bids submitted by us. It was true that Ben Hagood was already twenty-one years of age, so I had him write out a bid for $400.00 for the USS Philadelphia.

He said, "We will never get ir with such a low bid."

I smiled and said, "The Philadelphia, first saw action in 1791. No one else may even enter a bid."

So, Ben said, "Your family is filthy rich, why not write to your father and ask for a business loan."

I did. He sent me a thousand dollars, which I repaid from the Veracruz account. My father said not to bid over a hundred dollars on anything. Ben and I thought we could late least pay the four hundred that we owed and return the balance to my father. As a lark, Ben bid one hundred dollars on six more ships: two Brigs, called the Spitfire and Somerset; two Ketches, called the New Haven and Trumbull and two Snows called the Nelson and Providence. We got all six. So now, we had seven ships and no way to get them to Port Royal where I wanted to repair and work on them in order to start Caldwell International Shipping.

A Brig needed a crew of eight seamen and two officers. Ben and I were the officers, so we ran an advertisement in the newspapers asking for able bodied merchant seamen who wanted to relocate in South Carolina. As soon as we had 8 sailors ready to trade work for transport, I notified the Department of the Navy, that we could now begin the transfers to Port Royal Training Center. We started sailing the ships to Port Royal. Every few weeks we had eight more sailors and we again requested transfers to Port Royal.

When my father saw these ships arriving at the Port Royal Dock Yards, he became excited and understood my plan to create a company that shipped anywhere in the Atlantic Ocean. He had his attorneys make up the papers for the company and assigned me his assets from his coastal company for ten per cent of the new larger venture. We now had a fleet of ten ships and the capital to begin working the surplus ships. We turned them into merchant marine ships and renamed them for service in the Caldwell International Shipping and Holding Company. Even my brother got into the act of renaming them. And soon, all of them were renamed by the Caldwell men who loved them. My father named one of the Snows "Cold Harbor." It was an inside joke, so like my father and his puns! My brother, Robert, liked historical names so he picked name of English Admirals like Somers and Nelson.

While Ben and I were having so much fun that summer, Chris went to Norfolk, Virginia, to join a marine detachment stationed at Fort Story. Here he was supposed to recruit marines to serve in the "out of sight" navy being formed in the US Navy Port Royal Training Center. I was still required to make a summer cruise for the next two years. During the academic year I was stationed at the Naval War College, Newport, Rhode Island. I completed the course requirements for a Master's degree in Naval History in spite of the fact that I was sent back to Mexico to monitor the "Pastry War". In stead of the second summer cruise, I was released to write my thesis on the "Ships and Seamen of the American Revolution."

My thesis was read by Secretary Dickerson of the Navy, a close personal friend of the former Vice President John C. Calhoun from South Carolina and my personal mentor. He was following up on the cadets that Secretary Woodbury had recommended for "special duty" and who had graduated form the "Point". In his letter to me, he recommend that I seek another degree as soon as possible. He was a member of the board of visitors for Georgetown

College and would recommend me for the degree in business administration. I accepted and packed by bags for Georgetown. The year of 1838, was passing swiftly and Ben was now an officer on another ship stationed in the Baltic Sea. He made port stops and sent me notes from Russia, Prussia, Norway, Denmark, Finland and Sweden.

13

Guerra De Los Pasteles
Veracruz, Mexico 1838

The "War of the Pastries" was a direct result of the growing pains suffered after Mexico gained its independence from Spain in 1821. A succession of governments replaced one another, and the presidency changed hands about twenty times in the first twenty years of independence. In the presidential election of 1837, between Anastasio Bustamante and Vicente Saldana, the results were hotly contested and riots resulted on the streets of Mexico City and Veracruz. A French pastry shop, in Veracruz, owned by Monsieur Remontel, had been burned to the ground. He applied to the Mexican government for payment and he was ignored. He then appealed to his home country for relief. France's King Louis-Philippe assigned a value of 60,000 pesos and demanded that the Mexican Government pay their citizen this amount. The Mexican Government also ignored the King.

The King sent the French Ambassador, Baron Beffaudis, to visit with the Mexican President and demand that, with interest and additional damages reported by other French citizens living in Mexico City, the amount now due was 600.000 pesos. When President Bustamante refused payment, the King of France sent a naval fleet, under Admiral Charles Baudin, to perform a blockade of all Mexican ports from the Yucatan to the Rio Grande. The Texas navy assisted the French by blocking all ports from the Rio Grand to the US border.

President Van Buren asked his General-in-chief, Winfield Scott, to monitor the situation. He replied that his army was fully engaged in Florida trying to bring Chief Osceola under control. He further added that this seemed an ideal time to use his "out-of-sight" navy to monitor the situation. I was ordered to Veracruz in November, during my break in graduate studies at Georgetown. I arrived in Port Royal and told the captain of the New Haven that his crew would need to use the Texas Navy flags again in order to get me through the French Blockade and into either Veracruz or a nearby port in Mexico. Since the Republic of Texas was now an ally of France, this might be possible.

Chris Merryweather was now stationed in Port Royal Training Center and I met with him to discuss the Secretary of the Navy's request for information from Veracruz or nearby ports. "We will be taking the New Haven, Captain Wendell Miller is her skipper and he informed me that he has already been contacted by Dickerson. He also reminded me that he was the captain in charge of the New Haven and I was a lowly Lieutenant in charge of the mission details only. I am requesting that you choose a marine detail to go with us and that you lead them on a land mission, if that becomes necessary."

"I have several Spanish speaking marines, Jason. I do not have a single French speaking marine, however. If you are captured by the French, you will be without translation."

"I understand. Spanish translation will be what we need because we are not going to test any blockade vessels. I have been asked to find out how many ports are blocked and by which navy."

"What do you mean, which navy?"

"The Republic of Texas has furnished blocking vessels for the French, north of Carboneras, the last port before the mouth of the Rio Grand River. Can your detail be ready in two days?"

"Of course. Have Captain Miller stop here for us tomorrow, if you like."

"I like. Thank you, Chris. I can not order you or your marines to go with me, but I would feel much better with some firepower on board the New Haven. Every piece of ordnance has been removed and replaced with smoke making equipment."

"Smoke making?"

"Yes, it allows you to lay down a thick blanket of smoke that you can run around in and hide from an enemy ship."

"Does sound travel through the smoke? So I can shout, 'I am a Carlisle man from Bamberg, South Carolina, so you better surrender your ship!'"

I had forgotten Chris and Ben's running joke about the fearless leaders from Bamberg. I laughed and said we would pick up his troops at the discretion of Caption Miller.

At day break the following day, we loaded a marine detachment of eighteen men and their Lieutenant Merryweather and set sail for Veracruz. The fall weather was ideal and we reached the outer harbor of Veracruz flying the Republic of Texas flag. We were allowed to pass for docking. I had dressed in civilian clothes and warned Chris that only his Spanish speaking marines should be allowed off the New Haven, and then only in civilian dress. He said, "Yes, mother."

I gave the same warning to Captain Miller, "Captain we are now on mission status and I am giving you a direct command. Keep all your English speaking sailors below decks and only Spanish is to be spoken on deck while we are in port. I should not take more than a few hours and I will return so that we can make a survey of all the major ports close to Veracruz for French blocking vessels." I did not wait for a response and turned to leave.

"Lieutenant Caldwell, we are flying the Republic of Texas flag, an English speaking country. It might be wise to keep the Spanish below decks and the English speakers top side. Otherwise, the French might think we are Mexican blockade runners."

I stopped cold. "Thank you, Captain, thank you very much. I have already made a fool of myself with Lieutenant Merryweather. If you see him, tell him to keep his Spanish quiet, will you?"

I did not wait to hear his answer and climbed the ship's ladder onto the open deck and left the New Haven. I walked along the docks and past the harbor master's office as I thought. 'I am a fine one to gives orders to speak only Spanish, when I can not speak a single word.'

I managed to get out of the harbor and onto the streets leading to the Banquo de le Veracruz. I entered the bank and asked to speak with Senor Veragua. I waited until he was free and entered his office.

"Jason, my son to be. How good to see you again, it has been awhile. Have you seen Juanita?"

"No, I just docked at the harbor and walked here."

"How?"

"I brought one of my ships from Port Royal, flying the flag of the Republic of Texas."

"Let me go get her from her office in the back, she will want to hear all about your adventure, also." He left and returned with his daughter. She had an unusual look on her face when she said, "I did not know you were coming to Veracruz, Jason."

"Nor did I. The Secretary of the Navy sent me to see what the King of France, Louis-Philippe, has done to the Mexican gulf coast. I came here first before checking other ports."

"How did you get in the harbor?"

"Your father asked me that and I told him that I flew the flag of the Republic of Texas."

She turned and spat as she said, "That upstart Republic is a disgrace, helping the French!"

"I agree, Juanita, I am here to offer you and your family an escape from Veracruz."

"Why? It is a disagreement over 60,000 pesos, 600 of your dollars, Jason. Father can pay it directly to the French and the matter is resolved. There is no need to flee from our homes."

"It has progressed from a single bakery shop owner's complaint to include all of the French merchants in Mexico City as well as here in Veracruz." I replied.

"So what is the French demand?" She asked.

"600,000 pesos." I answered.

"This blockade is over 6,000 dollars? That is also a tiny amount, pay it, father, and the harbor will remain open for trade."

"Juanita, that is only an excuse." Her father replied. "The bank has already offered the amount in question to the French Admiral. He has responded that the entire Mexican debt to France must now be paid."

"What Mexican debt?" She was staring at her father.

"Mexico borrowed money from France in 1821, to help free us from the King of Spain. It is more money than the Banquo de le Veracruz has on deposit."

"Oh, my God. I thought this was a diplomatic problem. Why has President Bustamante not paid this to the French?"

"He has reinstated General Antonio Lopez Santa Anna and he is sending him to Veracruz to defend the port."

"Simon is coming home?"

"Yes."

"Sir." I asked. "What is the size of Santa Anna's army? I counted ten French Luggers outside the harbor. A French Lugger can transport anywhere from 800 to a 1000 troops. There may be 10,000 waiting to invade the city."

All the color drained from both the Veragua faces. "Simon says that he will march with the standard 4000 Mexican troops."

"That is a start, how many troops are inside the Fort of San Juan de Ulua?" I asked.

"I have no idea, but I know it is not 6000."

"So, the offer to evacuate the family still stands, I must leave at dusk before we are discovered by the French. You know the New Haven when you see it, Juanita. Come to the harbor with your mother and father before sun down and we will take your family to another port north or to Port Royal."

"Jason, we should not panic and leave the bank assets to an invading army. Allow me to convince President Bustamante to have the bank pay the first 600,000 pesos and for the French Ambassador to travel to Ciudad de Mexico so that payments can begin on the national debt to France." Simon Veragua was smiling as he put his arm around my shoulders and walked me from his office, into the lobby. "Go with Juanita to her office and set a date for your wedding. This wedding will cost me more than the amount that the bank pays to the stinking French."

We walked back to Juanita's office and I asked her if she was having second thoughts about our wedding. "How can you ask me that, Jason?"

"You had a very unusual look of surprise, mixed with guilt when you first saw me. You did not throw yourself into my arms as you usually do when we have been apart for months."

"That is just the point, Jason. We do not see each other for months."

"After we are married, we have all the time in the world."

"I fear not, Jason. You are married to the military, just like my brother. You will be gone all the time when you are forced to cruise to far away places. I will be left here in Veracruz or in Port Royal, waiting just as I do now."

"And this is not acceptable to you?"

"It is what I have now. Why get married?"

"Juanita, the marriage can wait a few months. What about us? What do we have to do for each other? Do I have to resign from the US Navy and move to Veracruz? I will if that is what it will take for us to start our family."

"I can not ask you to do that!"

"Juanita, you are the most important thing in my life. I owe the US Navy four years of service because they have provided five years of college education and two degrees for me. When I return to Washington City, I will meet with the Secretary of the Navy and the Secretary of State and ask to be transferred to Ciudad de Mexico as the military attache there. I know it is not Veracruz but it is less than 200 miles from your family."

Juanita was crying. When women I love cry, I am a basket case. I think that I must have said something terrible to upset them. "You are upset, what is wrong? Why are you crying?"

"Oh, Jason, you will never understand Spanish women. I am so happy, I could marry you this minute!"

"Do you want to go to confession, first?" She hit me as hard as she could, with her fist, directly on my chest. She was on her tip toes because there was a difference in our heights. I placed my arms around her and lifted her off the floor to stop her assault. I held her close and kissed her softly until she was through with her temper outburst.

"Tell father we have set the date on your way out of the bank, Jason." She was smiling.

"What date shall I say?"

"The day after the Secretary of State sends you to Ciudad de Mexico."

"Si, Senorita Juanita Perez de le Veragua!"

"Jason, that is your first sentence entirely in Spanish. Maybe there is hope for you that you will become civilized."

"Hasty bananas and bungus snow shoes to you too."

"Jason, stop being a child and go see my father and ask for my hand, before I change my mind."

The New Haven was waiting for me and we sailed at dusk toward the port of Tuxpan, 200 miles north, along the gulf coast. We approached the port and were turned back by two French patrol vessels. The New Haven swung around and headed for the next port north. Each of the ports had at least two patrol boats until we reached Carboneras. Carboneras was really a fishing village and not a commercial trading port. It was protected by a series of long narrow barrier islands and Captain Miller searched for an opening to enter the Laguna Madre, an inlet that would allow a shallow draft vessel, like the New Haven, to tie up to a dock. Captain Miller ordered the Republic of Texas flag lowered and the Stars and Stripes raised. We did not know what to expect as we slowly crept along side an old wooden dock. An old man saw us and walked over to us and shouted something in Spanish. Chris's marines that could speak Spanish talked to him and found out that we were welcome to stay the night for a fee of ten pesos.

The next day we set sail for Port Royal to return Chris and his marines so that I could continue on to the Potomac dockyards. I reported to the Army Navy Building, telling them what we had found in various ports along the gulf coast. I waited nearly an hour to see the Secretary of the Navy. He finally saw me and it was what I had feared. The French fleet had begun shelling the Fort of San Juan de Ulua, which guarded the entrance to the port of Veracruz. The US Consul in Veracruz had been ordered to Mexico City. All US Citizens had been advised to leave Veracruz. The New Haven was ordered to return to Port Royal and I was to report back to the graduate school of Georgetown.

I continued to check with the Army Navy Building for updates on the French invasion of Mexico. I learned that Mexico declared war on France and had asked for a national call to arms from its citizens. General Santa Anna had been wounded defending the fort and was evacuated with the body of his aide, Captain Simon Perez de le Veragua. They were both assumed dead when they were found in their offices inside the fort. The bodies were loaded onto a wagon for removal to Ciudad de Mexico for a military burial. During the trip, the General regained consciousness and screamed. "Where is my other leg?" He survived the ordeal. His aide and his leg were buried with full military honors.

The Fort of San Juan de Ulua was abandoned by its defenders and they retreated onto the streets of Veracruz. The French fleet now turned its attention to the harbor front streets of the city. The gunners were told to spare the docks and harbor buildings as they would be needed later by the fleet. They were told to concentrate upon the fleeing Mexican army. The shelling began at the Plaza del Norte where the Banquo de le Veracruz was leveled by repeated mortar rounds. The entire plaza was leveled and the shelling was advanced into residential neighborhoods along the rode to Mexico City. The residence of Simon Hernandez de le Veragua was leveled with no survivors. The Duke of Veragua's descendants in Mexico died within four hours and thirty-two minutes of each other. Simon, the son, died in the Fort. Simon the elder died with his daughter in the Banquo de le Veracruz. Veronica Perez Veragua died in her home watching the fleeing soldiers pass her villa.

14

Graduate School of Business
Georgetown, 1839

I returned to Georgetown in January of 1839, with incomplete grades for the fall term. I could not function after the death of Juanita and her family. I wrote to the Dean of Graduate Students and requested that my course work that fall be completed after my return and proper period of grieving had occurred. He agreed and said that I could report early for the spring term and use the time in the library to complete the required papers and assignments. I had left my rented apartment and was on my way to the library. It had snowed the night before and snow always surprised me. Beaufort, South Carolina, had winter rain, not snow. My head was down, my feet were wet and I was feeling miserable, when I walked head first into another student. We both fell backward with instant headaches, our butts in a snow drift along side the walkway.

"I am sorry, I was not looking where I was going. Are you alright? My head aches!" I looked over at my fellow student and saw a young girl rubbing her head and moaning something about getting to laboratory late.

"Let me help you to your class. I was just going to the library and I am not late." I began picking up her books, I was kneeling in front of her when I noticed a trickle of blood across her forehead. "You are bleeding. Let me help you to the student hospital."

She spoke for the first time. "I work part time there and I need to get to my medical lab. They can look at me there."

"You are not making any sense, maybe you have a concussion?"

"I am a medical student, I work part time at the Georgetown student clinic, I am alright. Help me to my lab and my instructor can look at my forehead."

I helped her to her feet and found that we were nearly the same height. I had never seen such a tall girl. "Why are they holding nursing classes before the term starts?"

"Are you hard of hearing? I told you, I am in medical school. I finished undergraduate school two years ago and I am in my second year of the medical program here. If I graduate, I will be the first woman doctor in Washington City."

71

"You must have come to Georgetown very young, what you have accomplished as a teenager is remarkable!"

"Are you really this dense? Or does that pickup line about being a 'teenager' work for you? I am twenty-four years old, probably older than you, or are you in graduate school, also."

I was smiling, no one had ever called me deaf and dense in the same minute. I liked this twenty-four year old woman who looked like a teenager. We reached her laboratory and we went inside and took off our outer winter coats and jackets. This was no teenage girl, she was a mature woman.

"Put your eyes back in your head and help me with my boots. What is your name, anyway?"

"It is Anyway Caldwell, but my friends call me, Jason."

She began laughing and said, "Alright, Anyway Caldwell, you can leave me now. I am safely here in a warm building. How long will you be in the library?"

"All morning and probably most of the afternoon, I have some incomplete course work to make up from the fall term."

"They do not give incomplete grades in graduate school."

"They do if you are here studying on a US Navy Scholarship and the Navy sends you into a war zone."

"War zone?"

"Yes, there is a war going on in Mexico."

"There is always a war going on in Mexico." She said as she walked to the instructor's desk and showed him her forehead.

I stood there, not wanting to leave before I knew her name and something about her. 'She may be married, you fool.' I thought as I put on my navy peacoat and left the medical school lab building and headed for the library. I had a pile of research materials piled around me as I worked at a library table, when someone sat down in the next chair. "Excuse me, that chair is taken for my friend who works part time at the Georgetown student clinic and has a giant gash across her forehead." I looked up to see the Dean of Graduate Students sitting next to me.

"Excuse me, Lieutenant."

"I am sorry, Dean, I thought you were someone else."

"Obviously. Are you making any progress on the business courses?"

"Yes, Sir. I should be done by mid February."

"Excellent, you know where my office is, if I can be of any help. I have never gotten a message from the White House about a student before."

"The White House? I do not understand?"

"The Secretary of the Navy wrote a nice note for the President to forward. Here I will let you read it. I want to keep it for your graduate file, so return it at your convenience."

THE WHITE HOUSE
Office of the President

January, 1839

Dr. Edward Scott, Dean of Graduate Students
Georgetown College
Washington City

Dear Dr. Scott:

The department of the Navy has informed me of the heroic actions of Lieutenant Jason Edwin Caldwell while on assignment in the Gulf of Mexico, November, 1838. He was asked by the Secretary of the Navy to perform a classified mission for the White House. We have encouraged the Lieutenant to continue his studies at Georgetown and realize that his absence from fall classes was not the best choice on our part. Until he completes his MBA, he will be released from active duty.

Martin Van Buren
Martin Van Buren
President of the United States
lst endorsement Department of the Navy

I read the note, looked up to ask the Dean a question and he was gone. Standing in his place was my "billy goat" friend from this morning.

"Hello." She whispered. "How is your head?"

"It still aches. How is yours?" I whispered back.

She pushed back her bangs that covered most of her forehead and said, "Look at this goose egg, you pack a punch, Anyway Caldwell." She sat down and said, "I am off to another lab session and then I have to report to the clinic. If your head does not get better, come and see me."

Our heads were together and the whispering seemed a more intimate form of conversation. "I will, you are so busy, that is probably the only way I will ever see you, get sick. You know my name, but I do not know yours."

"Names are overrated, Anyway. You can call me, Someday. Someday Earley, my friends call me Amelia Earley."

"What is your real name? You know I will find out, I am an officer in the US Navy working out of the Army Navy Building in charge of intelligence.

You know I will find out sooner or later." I handed her the note that the Dean had given me to read. She read it and said, "Wow, Anyway. You are, somebody. You can call me 'sooner or later' if you do not like Amelia Mary Earley."

"Are you fishing for a date, Sooner or Later, Amelia Earley?"

"God, No. I am a medical student seeking a MD degree not a teenager looking for her MRS degree. I do not have time for a boyfriend and it looks like you do not time for any kind of social life until you make up last semester courses because you were off being 'heroic' in the gulf. How does one become heroic in a gulf, Anyway?"

I looked at her and said, "You are going to be late for your lab." She pushed up her sleeve and looked at a watch she had strapped to her wrist. I had never seen a watch like that, mine was in my pocket.

"You are right, Anyway, I must go. Come to the clinic and see me."

I sat in my library chair and tried to analyze the last two minute conversation. She had used the words or phrases; see me, time for a boyfriend, MRS degree, call me sooner or later, call me someday, and come see me. The woman was either very lonely and did not know it, or she was fishing for a date. She had definitely put me out of the mood to finish my library research. I packed up my things and headed for the Dean's office. I gave the note from the White House back to his secretary and told him to thank the Dean for letting me read it. I asked, "Where is the Dean of Medicine's office?"

He gave me directions and I trudged through the snow a second time following his directions. I entered the office and spoke to another secretary. I asked her if she knew Amelia Earley's laboratory or clinic schedule. I showed her the bump on my head and said, "She wants to take a look at this bump."

"Amelia Earley is not a doctor, not even an intern, she is a student here and the daughter of the Dean of Medicine. How did you meet her?

"Oh, I just bumped into her today."

"It looks like it from the size of that goose egg. Let me go and see when she will be working in the clinic, you have to see a real doctor over there, not a student."

"I understand, ma'am."

She returned with her laboratory, lecture sessions and work schedule, handed them to me and said, "You know, young man, Amelia is a delightful young woman. She is very lonely, what with being the Dean's daughter, she never gets asked out and she has no social life. It is none of my business, but you look lonely, also. The two of you were made for each other!"

"If you see Amelia, tell her Anyway Caldwell, was looking for her to ask her to the winter dance this weekend."

"She will tell you she has too much studying to do, Mr. Caldwell. Do not take that for an answer, tell her she can bring the studying along with her!"

"Yes, ma'am."

As I walked to the clinic, I realized that Dean Earley's office secretary was right. What I needed more than anything else was a friend my own age that I could talk to. Ben was assigned to the Atlantic Fleet, Chris was drilling marines on an island south of Port Royal, South Carolina, Robert Whitehall was an officer in the Bank of Beaufort and I was a student at Georgetown. We could write letters once a month, but we could not talk to each other. Verbal communication was instant, written took a better part of a month for a question to be answered. Until I was returned to active duty, my time at Georgetown may be the only time left to me that was my own to spend as I saw fit. Someone would be giving me orders and commands for the next twenty years! I entered the clinic and said, "I want to see Doc Earley, the young pretty one, not the ugly old man who claims to be a Dean of Medicine." An older man turned to face me and said, "You must be Anyway Caldwell, my daughter has just told me she ran into you today." He was smiling and I was smiling.

15
Presidential Election
November 1840

The Washington Post had the following headline after the election for President, 1840.

WHIGS WIN, HARRISON ELECTED

	Popular Vote	Electoral Vote
Harrison	1,275,017	234
Van Buren	1,128,702	60
Birney	7,059	0

I had voted for Martin Van Buren, along with another million or so voters, but it fell short and the President Elect was General William Henry Harrison. His vice-president was John Tyler. I thought the campaign slogan, "Tippecanoe and Tyler too," was meaningless. I heard it hundreds of times during the campaign and wondered each time what it meant. I was just getting used to having a new President in the White House and a new Secretary of the Navy, when General Harrison died of pneumonia on April 4, 1841. I was still awaiting orders of transfer from the Navy, when President Tyler vetoed the National Bank bill that President Van Buren had worked so hard to get passed. The entire cabinet of Harrison/Tyler resigned in protest except for the Secretary of State, Daniel Webster. He was involved with the completion of the treaty with England over the long disputed northwestern boundary between the United States and Canada. Many of my classmates from the Point had served on the border dispute and they would be free to finally end the Seminole Wars in Florida.

Months went by and I was still in my rented rooms in Georgetown. I had completed my course work, written my thesis and attended graduation. There is a saying, "let sleeping dogs lie." I should have followed that sage advice. I am convinced that if I had, I would have remained in my college rooms until my retirement. Instead, I wrote John C. Calhoun who was selected by

President Tyler as a member of his cabinet. I got a quick response and found myself on a train back to West Point.

The Navy had now paid for two college degrees. It was 1841, and I was assigned to the United States Military Academy to write and develop business administration courses for army cadets and navy midshipmen. I was to be an instructional staff aide member at West Point for one tour of duty. I would leave after four years to be assigned to the Atlantic fleet for assignment aboard a ship of the line. I had no idea what an instructional aide did. And, it turned out, that neither did the instructors at the Point. I wrote several outlines for courses that were never approved. I went to staff meetings, but never attended a faculty meeting, the entire four years. I rode the train into Washington City, whenever I could get away to visit with Dr. Amelia Earley, Intern of childhood medicine. She was still at Georgetown, of course, completing her degree. She still helped in the student clinic and had applied for a visiting professor at the school of medicine. I was still a Navy Lieutenant. Chris was a captain in the marine corps, still at Paris Island, South Carolina, Ben was a Lieutenant Commander and first officer of the USS Bearing Sea, and now attached to the Pacific Fleet. My friends were moving forward with their careers and I was still at the Point.

A break in my routine came, when it was announced that the Congress had approved the formation of the USNA, United States Naval Academy. The first graduation would be in 1845. That meant that we needed students in the pipeline, ready to graduate in 1841, and buildings constructed in Annapolis. I was assigned the task of preparing the midshipmen presently at the Point and those from the fleet who would form that first class. This was an exciting task. I became the defacto Superintendent of Naval Cadets. I met with Superintendent Delafield to coordinate the separation of cadets into two distinct and separate groups, with separate courses of instruction.

"You were a cadet here in '33, Jason. What would be the first thing that you would change?"

"I would not let the regular Navy personnel run the first summer cruise, which is not a cruise, but a 'weeding out' exercise. Master Chief Gunnerman needs to be assigned to Paris Island, not Annapolis."

"I agree. You write to the new Secretary of the Navy and I will write to General Scott and we will get this done this week."

I was on my way to see "Doc" Earley one weekend when I met a man who changed my life. He was headed to Washington City and when he saw me in uniform he said, "Good morning, Lieutenant, are you on your way to the Army Navy Building?"

"No, I have a good friend at Georgetown."

"The College? I have a professor friend there, maybe you know him? He is in the school of business. Professor Wadsworth ,he teaches ...."

"Contracts and business communications, he was one of my professors in '39 and '40. If I see him this weekend I will say 'hello' for you. What is your name?"

"Professor Stephen Morse from Mass Tech."

"Oh, my gosh. Professor Wadsworth used to talk about you all the time. You invented Morse Code. I am very glad to meet you, professor. Did congress ever fund your request to build a telegraph line from Washington to Baltimore?"

"No, I am on my way to beg for funds to do that."

"What level of funding are we talking about? The Navy should be interested in a line from Potomac to Baltimore dockyards."

"The navy has already said no, they think 3000 dollars is a waste of money."

"Three thousands dollars for exactly what, professor?"

"That is the total cost, wire, poles, materials and labor for a telegraph line forty miles long."

"Would you consider using private investment?"

"Of course."

"Would you be willing to sign a contract that gives Caldwell International the rights to construct telegraph lines anywhere within the United States? I am thinking about forming a communications company, called American Telegraph. I will need to rent office space in Baltimore and Washington. As I understand your process, it is an electromagnetic transmission that is sent by electricity over copper wires. I have an interest in the copper being mined along Lake Superior and I think this would be an excellent outlet for the raw material."

"What is your name? You learned a lot from Professor Wadsworth, I was ready in 1832 to do just what you suggest, but nobody was interested."

"My name is Caldwell, Professor Morse and if you are ready now, we need to get started on building as many telegraph offices as we can. People will pour into these offices to send instant messages from place to place. No need to wait days or weeks for a letter. We will charge pennies a word and will be millionaires a year after we are in business together."

He shook my hand, gave me his business card and said, "Send me the contracts, Mr. Caldwell, and I will sign them. I would like you to add a profit sharing agreement which says, as long as I am alive, the net profits at the end of each year will be split 90 - 10 between us. Ninety for you and ten for me. After all, the venture capital required to do this will come from you and your company."

The first telegram ever sent in the United States was from Washington to Baltimore by Miss Annie Elsworth, the daughter of one of Professor Morse's close friends. It was May 24, 1844. It read "What hath God wrought?" My profit from the telegram was nine cents and Professor Morse made a single cent. Professor Morse died a millionaire and I continue to be amazed at the success of the American Telegraph and Telephone company. Today, in 1877, if the telegraph lines in the United States were joined end to end, they would girdle the earth more than thirty times.

16
The Pathfinder
1842-53

I did not meet John Fremonte until he made his last exploring expedition during the administration of President Pierce. He is alive and well, living in New York as we meet here tonight. I had, of course, heard of his achievements that gave him the name of "Pathfinder" and I would like to tell you what I remember about him. Fremonte's first expedition which, like the following two, were under the direction of the government. He left Kansas City, June 10, 1842. It included twenty-eight men, who followed the general line of the Kansas and Platte Rivers. The country before them was the home of the American Plain Indians, who were unusually hostile, and Fremonte had not gone far when he was advised by the government to turn back. He pushed on, however, to the Wind River Mountains, where, on the 15th of August, he climbed one of the peaks and unfurled the US flag.

His company returned to Kansas City in October. This venture, though it gained much valuable knowledge, took Fremonte only to the borders of the western territories. He was ordered by President Harrison to go farther and learn more. This time he took thirty-nine men with him, starting in the spring of 1843, and did not return until August of 1844. His orders from President Harrison were to complete the survey of the line of communication between the State of Missouri and the tide-water region of the Columbia River. He was to explore the country south of that river. The expedition accomplished much. It arrived in sight of the Great Salt Lake in September, visited Oregon and California, and many of the principle streams of the region. He brought back a complete set of maps for the region. His survey team suffered from the cold, hunger and hostile Indians. For his efforts, he was promoted to Captain, US Army Expeditionary Force.

His third expedition took its departure in the autumn of 1845, with orders from President Polk. The purpose was to complete the mapping of the Great Basin, extending the survey west and southwest towards Mexico. They suffered again from lack of food and severe weather, as well as from the Indians. Fremonte was told by the President that war with Mexico was possible and he would be in a position to aid in the capture of California.

During the Mexican War, General Kearny and Commodore Stockton had a quarrel over who was the supreme commander in the western theater of the war. It was clear that President Polk had appointed Stockton and Fremonte recognized him as the supreme commander. General Kearny preferred charges against Fremonte and he was tried by court-martial. Fremonte was censured, and he resigned his commission in the army, refusing to accept the censure from General Kearny. When President Polk offered to promote him to General and readmit him to the US Army Expeditionary Force, he also refused saying, "It is clear that the US military is in need of a strong hand from the top down." He undertook his fourth expedition in the fall of 1848, it being under his own direction and independent of the government. His objective this time was to discover the best route to California, by way of the upper waters of the Rio Grande and the conquered Mexican territories. On his previous expeditions his guide had been the famous mountaineer, Kit Carson, a man unrivaled in his knowledge of the country, but Fremonte could not afford to pay his fee. The hunter employed to replace him was ignorant of the country and caused the frightful disasters that followed.

Fremonte wanted to learn what obstacles had to be overcome during winter and he began in late fall. This was his first mistake. The route he selected led through Indian country controlled by the Apaches, Utahs, Navahoes, Comanches and Kiowas. The Apaches, Comanches and Kiowas were among the fiercest of Indian tribes and were continually at war with the government of the United States and with the Utahs and Navahoes. It was late November when the party of thirty men reached the base of the first mountain range. The snow was so deep that their animals could hardly flounder through, and when the men dismounted, the snow reached their waists.

When they finally reached the other side of the range, they found a broad and inviting valley. There was little snow underfoot and Fremont carefully scanned the country in front of him with his telescope. He saw a pass which he thought led through the mountains. His guide insisted that his leader was mistaken and that the pass led to a dead end. Fremonte was not convinced and he led his party into the pass. This was his second mistake. A day later the pass ended in a shear mountainside and the party began to scale the mountain chain. They had to hammer down the snow with mauls before their mules could walk over it. By exhausting labor they finally reached the summit, where they were met by a gale as if it came directly from the north pole. It was so terrible that neither man nor beast could withstand it. To stay where they were was to invite death and they started to retreat back to the valley below. The mules, more than a hundred in number, huddled together and refused to move. Every one of them froze to death the first night. Fremonte was now without the means to transport his supplies. He ordered two of the mules butchered and their meat carried down the mountain with as many of the supplies as the thirty men could pack on their backs. The second day they found protection from the wind and built a fire to warm themselves and dry out. The nearest settlement was thought to be some ten day's travel on foot. Some of the horses survived because they followed the men down the mountain and these were rounded up and Fremonte ordered his guide to take five men and ride to the settlement to purchase horses and supplies and return for him and the twenty-five men under his command, his third mistake.

He told the guide to return in ten days. After sixteen days he divided his party again and took the strongest men to walk to the settlement. He reasoned that they would meet the relief party on their return leg from the settlement. His fourth mistake, they found the party frozen to death after only two days march. They had not reached the settlement, nor found any supplies for them. He ordered the frozen horses butchered and he returned with the meat to his remaining party in the protected cove. All their animals were dead, and the weakest men began to die. The survivors butchered and ate the dead in order to survive. Some refused to eat a human and they chewed on leather boot laces to lessen the pangs of hunger. All were found unconscious by an Indian hunting in the mountains. He gave them his game and melted snow for them to drink. He rebuilt their fire and warmed their bodies until all but one could stand and follow him back to the settlement, which turned out to be less than a full days march.

Fremonte remained in the settlement of Taos until fully recovered, then he made his way to California in the summer, where he built a house to retire from exploring. He entered California politics and would have been happy to die there at an old age, if not for President Pierce's contact. I was in Europe when the fifth and final Fremonte Expedition was formed. President Pierce did not want the same outcome as the fourth and he sent me and my detachment to meet him at the sources of the Arkansas and Colorado Rivers. We left Washington on a train with summer gear and horses to ride between train depots. The horses were given three box cars and care between points of travel. By the time we reached Council Bluffs, there were no more train tracks west and we rode on horse back. General Dodge had provided us with additional supplies and equipment as we passed through the Mormon settlements and the Great Basin. We added to the maps that General Dodge had given us as we discovered a number of passes. We joined Fremonte and traveled with him until the survey was complete. Near the end, John Fremonte's horse stepped in a hole and threw him. His fall was bad and he was unconscious for two days. When he awoke, he asked me who I was and why I was in his camp. His behavior was odd and erratic, but his men never questioned any of his orders. I left him in California where a ship waited to take me and the detachment back to Washington and report our finding to President Pierce.

17

Presidential Election
November 1844

The democratic candidates in 1844 were James K. Polk and George M. Dallas. The Whigs nominated Henry Clay and Theodore Frelinghuysen. James G. Birney was also on the ballot as the "Liberty" or Abolition candidate. Polk received 170 electoral votes to 105 cast for Clay. Birney carried no states and received no electoral votes. A joint resolution annexing Texas was then introduced into congress during President Tyler's lame duck session. A heated debate followed, but the resolution passed the House, with the proviso that the newly elected president might act by treaty, if he thought best. The Senate concurred. President Tyler signed the bill, and Secretary of State, John C. Calhoun, immediately hurried a messenger, one Lieutenant Jason Caldwell, to Texas to bring in the State of Texas under joint resolution. President Tyler made a treaty of annexation with Texas, but the Senate refused to ratify it. The annexation was not completed until December 29, 1845 by President Polk. I was promoted to Lieutenant Commander and was at sea by then.

President Polk chose a strong cabinet composed of: James Buchanan (State), Robert Walker (Treasury), William Marcy (War), George Bancroft (Navy), Cave Johnson (Postmaster General), and John Mason (Attorney General). These cabinet members knew that the admission of Texas would cause a war with Mexico. The "Lone Star Republic" had gained its independence, and was recognized not only by the United States but several European countries. Mexico, it was thought, would never willingly consent to see it pass into the possession of the United States. Mexico had committed many wrongs against American citizens and commerce, but she was so distracted at home, that our government generously forbore to call her to account. Mexico believed that this forbearance was due to fear or lack of will. We had claimed six million dollars in damages done to the property of our citizens. Mexico thought one-third of that amount was just, but, after repeated promises to pay, she finally refused to do anything at all toward settlement. She offered to recognize the independence of Tejas as a separate Republic, provided Tejas did not join the Union of States. Texas replied by joining as soon as was possible.

When President Polk admitted Texas, the Mexican foreign minister, asked for his passport and went home, thus severing diplomatic relations. President

Herrera of Mexico issued a proclamation, declaring that the annexation of Tejas could not affect the rights of Mexico, which would be maintained by force of arms. Mexico further claimed that the border between Mexico and the Republic of Tejas was the Nueces River, not the Rio Grande. Therefore, she would send Mexican troops into the territory between the rivers to protect its citizens.

President Polk ordered General Taylor and his army to land his troops on the island of St. Joseph, where he later sailed to Corpus Christi, a small village on the mainland. This was near the mouth of the Nueces. In September, 1845, he formed a camp and remained there until the following spring. President Polk asked President Herrera if he would receive a minister from the United States. Herrera was anxious for peace and agreed. The people of Mexico City were clamoring for war and they turned their president out of office and elected General Perez, the hero at San Jacinto. War was underway when our minister reached Mexico City and Perez arrested him. The Mexicans were confident of driving the "northern barbarians" from their soil. General Taylor was ordered to take position on the left bank of the Rio Grande, opposite the Mexican City of Matamoras. Here, the Mexican troops were gathering to invade. Taylor used his naval forces, supplied by Commodore Conner and under the command of Benjamin Hagood, to land his troops at Point Isabel, about thirty miles form Matamoras. Here he formed a camp. Leaving a small portion of his force behind, he marched with the remainder to a point on the Rio Grande, opposite Matamoras. He then began to build a fort to be occupied by Major Brown and a small company of troops. Seeing the American General divide his troops, President Perez sent General Ampudia and his army to drive Taylor beyond the Nueces, back into Tejas where he belonged. Ampudia arrived April 12, 1846, and sent a message to Taylor demanding his withdrawal from all Mexican territory within twenty-four hours, saying that if he not, he would attack under the red flag of battle (no quarter). Taylor was there by order of his government and refused to leave. Ampudia hesitated, never expecting Taylor to refuse and he was replaced by General Arista and a second army.

Taylor now learned from Commander Hagood, that two vessels, with supplies for the second Mexican army were about to enter the Rio Grande. Taylor ordered the Rio Grand to be blockaded and Commander Hagood had a brig and a revenue cutter placed across the Rio. General Arista considered this an act of war and prepared to attack Fort Brown. Taylor's position was becoming perilous, for his army was smaller than the combined armies of northern Mexico. Taylor sent for his commander of the Cavalry, Captain Thornton and an artillery spotter, Lieutenant Braxton Bragg. He ordered Thornton to take his dragoons to reconnoitre and find the size of the enemy.

The company was attacked by a larger force and captured, except for Lieutenant Bragg who escaped by a leap of his horse over a thick hedge amid a storm of bullets. This took place April 24, 1846.

Taylor saw the danger to his split command and marched back toward Point Isabel, leaving Fort Brown to be defended by just 300 troops. He reached Point Isabel on May 1, 1846. The Mexican armies saw this as evidence of the American's cowardice toward battle. Arista sent a force across the river to attack Fort Brown. On May 5, 1846, the Mexicans opened fire on the fort with cannons. Major Brown was killed and Arista sent a message asking for the surrender of the fort. The fort refused because General Taylor had said if the fort was attacked, to fire its cannon as a signal to him. The cannon fire was heard at Point Isabel. Taylor now had 2000 troops under his command. They consisted of Texan volunteers, marines from Connor's fleet, and the troops left at Point Isabel. He marched back to Fort Brown. He met Arista at Palo Alto. Taylor attacked the superior numbers (6000) of Arista and the Mexicans were routed. Six hundred died around Arista, while only fifty-three were killed or wounded on the American side of action. The battle lasted only five hours and the Americans were again on the march toward Fort Brown. Toward evening, when they were within three miles of the fort, the Mexicans were again discovered, strongly posted in a wide ravine near Resaca de la Palma. The ravine was not deep, but it was nearly a hundred yards wide and was bordered with palmetto trees. Within this depression, the Mexicans had placed a battery, commanding the road over which the Americans would be marching. Taylor advanced cautiously and a part of his army became engaged. Then Braxton Bragg was ordered to charge the battery. The dragoons leaped over the parapet surrounding the battery and were among the gunners the next moment, swinging their sabers. Over a hundred artillery pieces were captured along with the Mexican troops firing them. They were taken back to the Americans. Bragg was told to take the captured ordnance to "Brydie" Dryer and become a second artillery force under his command.

This, however, was only an incident of the battle, which grew fiercer by the minute. From the palmettos, a hot fire was kept up by the Mexicans. Slowly, the Americans pushed them out of the trees and captured the headquarters of General Arista. The General was seen wading across the river to escape capture a second time.

Taylor now retreated to Point Isabel to consult with Commodore Connor. Connor informed Taylor that Arista was retreating toward Monterey where another Mexican army of 4000 awaited their General's return. This would give Arista a force of about 7000. Learning this, Taylor crossed the river and entered Mexico, marching toward Monterey. This caused Mexico to declare war on the United States for an invasion of its sovereign territory. On May 23rd the United States declared war on Mexico.

Now that war was declared, Secretary Marcy and General Winfield Scott, General-in-chief of the armies of the United States, together formed a plan for the invasion and conquest of Mexico. This was the plan: the army of the west, under General Stephen Kearney, was to cross the Rocky Mountains and invade the northern Mexican states west of Texas. An American fleet, under Commodore Connor, would sail around Cape Horn to join with Commodore Stockton to attack the Mexican states on the Pacific coast. Commodore Perry would assume command of Connor's blocking fleet in the Gulf of Mexico. General Scott would enter Mexico through Vera Cruz and capture Mexico City. General Taylor would capture Monterey and hold all the districts below the Rio Grande. General Wool in San Antonio, and General Worth in Dallas were to supply troops to Taylor and Scott as needed.

Old "rough and ready" Taylor waited at Matamoras until September for reinforcements. On September 19, 1846, he was joined by General Worth and they approached Monterey. Monterey was defended by General Ampudia with 9000 troops. The fighting in the streets was furious. From every adobe house, the Mexican troops poured musket fire into the Americans. The American troops battered down doors, chased Mexicans across roof tops and shot them before they could surrender. Ampudia asked for a truce so he could retreat, Taylor refused and the Army of Northern Mexico surrendered on September 24, 1846.

It was early in 1846, when I was assigned to the USS Saratoga. David Farragut was her captain and I met him as I came on board the sloop-of-war Saratoga as the first officer. The Saratoga and several other ships were being put together for Commodore Connor's fleet to serve in the Gulf of Mexico for the duration of the "troubles with Mexico".

The Saratoga was assigned to Commodore Perry's squadron which was assigned the blockade of the port of Tuxpan. Later we were assigned other ports as the war in northern Mexico dragged on under General Taylor and on the Pacific coast under Commodore Connor.

We would get scattered reports from the north, some were victories and some were defeats. It was not until December and the fall of Saltillo, Victoria, and Tampico that I felt that the war might now be under control. I was mistaken. News reached us that General Antonio Lopez Santa Anna had returned from Cuba and was given an army of twenty thousand. He was ordered to capture or "eliminate" the northern barbarians at a gorge in the mountains opposite Buena Vista. The one legged, Santa Anna, reached Buena Vista on February 22, 1847. He sent the following message to General Taylor:

"You are surrounded by 20,000 and can not avoid suffering a defeat. Because I hold you in esteem for your past victories, I wish to save you and your troops. For that purpose I give you notice, in order that you may retreat back into the State of Tejas and then the United States. You must surrender your weapons and march in peace, north to your homes. With this view, I assure you of my particular consideration. God and liberty!"

El Salvador de Mexico,

Antonio Lopez De Santa Anna

Santa Anna's messenger was given the following: "Sir - In reply to your note of this date, summoning me to surrender my forces and march north, I beg leave to say that I decline acceding to your request. With high respect, I am, Sir your obedient servant,   Z. Taylor

Santa Anna had his translator read Taylor's message to him and said, "What does this mean? He says he declines the offer to retreat but says he is my obedient servant. Does this mean he will retreat?"

"Time will tell, Mia Generalissimo."

Taylor waited the rest of the day for Santa Anna to begin the battle. At day break it began and raged furiously throughout the day. An attempt was made to turn the flank of the American right, but was defeated by the Illinois troops. An assault against the center was then repulsed by Brydie's and Bragg's artillery. A left flank attack was thrown back by an Indiana regiment combined with the Kentucky and Mississippi companies. General Taylor, standing near Captain Bragg's batteries was heard to say, "Give them a little more grape, captain." Bragg ordered every Mexican cannon that he captured poured full of grape shot.

"But, Sir, that will split the barrel and ruin the cannon."

"Do it anyway, they are Mexican cannon."

Every Mexican cannon on the line was destroyed, but not before the middle of Santa Anna's army was torn to bits.

The Americans slept beside their arms during the night, expecting the red flag of Santa Anna to appear with the morning sun. When the sun rose, the battlefield was empty. The Mexican side of the battlefield had 2500 dead and another 5000 dying of starvation. Taylor had lost 749 troops. Among the dead was Colonel Henry Clay, son of the Kentucky statesman. Colonel Jefferson Davis from Mississippi was carried from the battlefield, wounded, but not killed.

Taylor forwarded his report to General Scott and wrote, "Without reinforcements, I can not hope to hold out against another Santa Anna attack. He is rebuilding his army and is determined to throw us out of Mexico."

All that changed when General Winfield Scott arrived from the war department to oversee the Mexican War. Winfield Scott was the general-in-chief and the second highest ranking officer in the United States Military command. He made several changes. I was a first officer on the Saratoga one day and Commodore Farragut's Aide and a captain the next. David Farragut was promoted by Commodore Perry when he took command of the fleet from Commodore Connor. Perry reported directly to General-in-chief Winfield Scott who arrived off Veracruz, Mexico, in February, 1847. Commodore Farragut's ship, the USS Saratoga, was now the flagship for the squadron that he commanded and he followed the formations signaled from fleet Commander Perry. Scott needed to put ashore 4,000 army and 8,000 US Marines commanded by Major Christopher Merryweather at Veracruz. The seemly impregnable fortress, the castle of San Juan, still guarded the water-front of the city, just as it had against the French fleet in 1838. Veracruz and the castle were engaged by Perry's fleet and a bombardment from the fleet began. Perry ordered a line formation with bow cannon rounds, he then shifted to a double column with broadsides pumped into the town. This lasted for several days. The Mexicans in the city suffered so dreadfully, that overtures were made for a surrender, which took place on the 29th of the month. The battle of Veracruz began on the 9th and troops were landed on the 29th with no casualties, because of the seamanship shown by Commodore Perry and his fleet during these twenty days of conflict. I, however, was well on the way to losing a hundred dollars to Chris the next month as he was promoted to Coronel.

During these twenty days, I learned more about ship formations than I ever learned at West Point. I entered West Point as a naval cadet not an army plebe and I spent very little time at Annapolis, summers mostly. We learned our seamanship 'on the job' as junior officers serving for an experienced ship's captain. David Farragut was that captain for me. Every naval officer should have a 'David Farragut' in their lives.

The US Navy was also engaged on the Pacific coast of Mexico at Monterey south of San Francisco, Los Angles, and San Diego. All of California was now in US hands. General Kearney captured Santa Fe and marched to California to support Colonel John Fremonte and his California volunteers. The entire Mexican State of Chihuahua was surrendered to the advancing Americans. Now, what remained was the third and final campaign under General Scott who had taken Veracruz and was marching toward Mexico City. General Worth was left in charge of Veracruz, while General Twiggs and his army engineers, led the Scott advance toward Mexico City. Santa Anna had managed to bring together some 12,000 troops on the heights of Cerro Gordo, a mountain pass through the Cordillera range. A battle was fought and the Mexicans retreated toward Mexico City. A series of five battles were fought all the way to the gates of the capitol.

Mexico City was built upon a series of marshes and dried lake beds. Entrances to the city were by causeways at five different locations. Each of these causeways was defended by a large stone fortress containing thousands of defenders. Captain Robert Lee, an engineer, under the command of General Twiggs had the following suggestion:

"General, it will take weeks to break through each of these fortifications. I propose to take the captured Mexican prisoners and have them build earthworks around each of these. We will sweep around each, surround them and starve them into surrender. Fewer troops will be needed to lay siege than will certainly die with a frontal assault."

These five distinct victories had thus been gained, and the Mexican armies of thirty thousand defending Mexico City, had been defeated by an American force of less than 20,000. The invasion force of 12,000 had been reinforced by General Taylor and General Worth. General Scott rode into the center of the city with 1000 cavalry and accepted the surrender of the entire country from the President of Mexico. A peace treaty was signed at Guadaloupe Hidalgo and all Mexican territories, north of the Rio Grande and west of Texas, were given to the United States. These became the territories of New Mexico, Arizona, California, and Utah. California and Utah were the largest areas to be joined with the United States. Utah included all or parts of the later states of Utah, Nevada, Colorado, Idaho, Wyoming and Nebraska. While the State of Texas was immense in its size, the areas west were four times larger.

As I, and many others, look back on the accomplishments of President Polk's administration we tend to think in terms of the Mexican War. We tend to forget that Iowa was admitted into the Union, December 28, 1846. The United States graduated its first classes from the Naval Academy in 1845 and 1846. A huge federal bequest from a dual National, Swiss and English, James Smithson, was used to organize and form the Smithsonian Institution in April, 1846. Andrew Jackson died at this home, "The Hermitage," in Tennessee. Former President , John Q. Adams, collapsed in the House of Representatives and died the next day, February 23, 1848. A cabinet position, and the department of the Interior was formed. The boundary between Oregon and Canada was settled during the Polk term in office.

Then, all of that paled in comparison when Colonel Sutter, in command of Fort Sutter, decided to build a saw mill. The mill was to be located at Coloma, California, on the American branch of the Sacramento River. The discovery of Gold, in 1848, caused the "Gold Rush" of 1849. In one year, the population of northern California increased by a hundred thousand, mostly miners.

Wisconsin was admitted to the Union May 29, 1848, by act of congress. Attached to this bill was an amendment which stated that all territories conquered from Mexico would prohibit slavery. This was known as the Wilmot Proviso and it split the democratic party into two groups. The traditional party was led by the slave holding states and the "free soil" party nominated Martin Van Buren for President, June, 1848. The candidates that November were Zachary Taylor and Millard Fillmore on the Whig ticket. Lewis Cass and William Butler made up the Democratic ticket. When the election was over, Taylor had 163 electoral votes, 127 for Cass and 38 for Martin Van Buren.

18
Zachary Taylor Takes Office
March, 1849

The war ended in Mexico and the navy went on about its business. David Farragut and I were joined at the hip. When he was assigned to duty at the Norfolk Yard, I was assigned as his aide. This was 1848, President Polk was ending his administration so that General Taylor could assume the office. "Did you read the account of Taylor's election in the Norfolk Morning Herald? Jason, this is a very good illustration of the fact that success in military affairs is speedily followed by civic honors."

"No, what did the article say, Admiral?"

"In the Black Hawk War of 1812, he is a colonel. He commands at Okechobee, Florida, in 1837, when the Seminoles are defeated. He is victorious over the Mexicans at Palo Alto, Resaca de la Palma, and Buena Vista. He gains, from his soldiers, the sobriquet of 'being rough and ready'. His last fight at Buena Vista was February, 1847, and he is elected President in November 1848."

"Yes, Sir. It seems strange that Henry Clay or Daniel Webster was not nominated for the Presidency, while an uneducated man is. He had so little interest in politics that he had not cast a vote for forty years. And who, to use Webster's own expression was 'an ignorant frontier colonel', should have been selected for the office."

"Jason, always remember, it is the people who choose the President. The halo of Buena Vista circled the brow of old 'rough and ready', and gave him a popularity possessed by no other man, and so he was chosen. I know you voted for Martin Van Buren again, but his popularity has gone, the people will not choose him again."

"Admiral, you have a way of cutting to the heart of the matter. I wish I had that ability."

"Watch and learn, Captain Caldwell, you will not remain a Captain long. I see a faint halo beginning to appear around your brow." We both laughed, as President Taylor began to select his cabinet.

Having no experience in civil affairs, Zachary Taylor showed his wisdom by selecting an able cabinet. His Secretary of State was John Clayton, of Delaware. The Secretary of the Treasury was William Meredith, of Pennsylvania. The

Secretary of War was George Crawford, of Georgia. While the Navy slot was filled by William Preston, of Virginia. The Postmaster-General was Jacob Collamer, of Vermont and the Attorney-General was Reverdy Johnson, of Maryland. Thomas Ewing became the first Secretary of the Interior.

On February 13, 1850, President Taylor submitted to the federal congress, the State Constitution of California, with the recommendation that the territory become a state. In accordance with the Wilmot Proviso, the state constitution forbad slavery. This action precipitated one of the fiercest debates in congress. It was the question of slavery. The Missouri Compromise forbad slavery north of 36 degrees, 30 minutes within the United States. Most of the territory acquired from Mexico was south of that parallel, while California was both north and south. By the Missouri Compromise, Congress could not exclude slavery in the south, but by the Wilmot Proviso, congress could in the northern portion of California. If the Wilmot Proviso was followed, then the new territories west of the State of Texas could not allow slavery. New Mexico territory objected and Texas, whose State Constitution allowed slavery, threatened to annex the New Mexico territory. An amendment to prohibit slavery in the newly formed, District of Columbia, was attached to the bill for California Statehood.

Colonel Monroe, the military commander in New Mexico, called a convention of the people, who formed a state government. They immediately applied for statehood as a free state. Texas was incensed, and prepared to seize the territory by force. The southern members of congress supported Texas. The debates in congress were marked by heated discussions and drawn pistols.

Once more, and for the last time, Henry Clay poured oil upon the troubled waters. He submitted a compromise measure, including so many details that it was named the "Omnibus Bill." It was submitted to congress and provided for the admission of California as a state. It also provided for the establishment of territorial governments, without mention of slavery. It called for the abolishment of the traffic in slaves in the District of Columbia, but declaring it inexpedient to abolish slavery there without the consent of the citizens of Maryland, a slave holding state. Daniel Webster spoke in favor of the bill and John C. Calhoun spoke in opposition. Calhoun was ill, but he came to the floor to present the southern case and died a few days later. Thus, the most formidable obstacle to the measure was removed. The Omnibus Bill admitted California as a free state. Utah Territory was organized without the mention of slavery. New Mexico was made a territory and could do as she pleased concerning slavery. Texas was given ten million dollars for giving up her claim to New Mexico. The slave trade, but not slavery was abolished in the District of Columbia. The Omnibus Bill was almost never passed but in the first week of July, Daniel Webster announced that President Taylor was near death.

July 10, 1850, Millard Fillmore replaced all of Taylor's cabinet. State was given to Daniel Webster until his death in October , 1852. Treasury was given to Thomas Corwin, War was given to Charles Conrad, Navy was given to William Graham until his death, Interior was given to James Pierce until is death, Postmaster General was given to Nathan Hall until his death, and Attorney-General was given to John Crittenden of Kentucky who lived to serve his entire term of office. Fillmore was President for only two years and seven months, but experienced more cabinet deaths than any other president. Admirals serving in the Department of the Navy from 1849 to 1853, would begin under the leadership of Secretary Preston of Virginia until President Taylor's death in 1850. President Fillmore dismissed Preston and appointed William Graham who died and was replaced by John Kennedy of Maryland.

In 1850, Admiral Farragut was assigned duty in Washington City, Army Navy Building by Secretary Graham. Farragut would serve as an undersecretary in charge of Navy regulations. I was still his aide and he assigned me, and others working for him, the task of writing Navy manuals. I wrote the manual still used on ordnance regulations. I had rented a small, walk-up flat on Maryland Avenue. It was a brownstone building located on the main street car line, which ran directly into the Army Navy Building on Pennsylvania Avenue. My office was, therefore, adjacent to the White House. Admiral Farragut lived with his family in a much nicer home across the Potomac and was driven to work by his driver. I liked to walk to work when I had the time and the weather was nice, otherwise I took the horse drawn street cars anywhere I needed to go in Washington City. I did not own a horse or a carriage.

I do not remember why I did not like horses. As a child, I spent the first few years exploring the plantation where my brothers and sisters were all born. It was called Pollawana and it was an offshore, barrier sea island along the coast of South Carolina. These islands were famous for their "sea island cotton" and rice. South Carolina produced four million pounds of rice the year I was born. My older brother, Robert, was on his pony from sun up until sun down, following my father on his horse as he checked the cotton and rice dikes over the entire island. I awoke each morning, dressed in white cotton shirt and tan colored heavy twill pants and pulled a single suspender over my shoulder to keep them up. I wore no shoes, no underwear and no hat. I was in a hurry to get out of the farm house that we lived in and out back to the slave quarters to see if Tobias was awake and could sneak off without doing his chores. Tobias' Mammy would ask, "Masta Jason, has you et your breakfast?"

I would always answer, "Yes, Mammy."

Her reply was always the same, "Do not lie to your Mammy, child. Sit down here with Tobias and et some eggs and grits. I brought these down from the 'Big House' and they will go to waste unless you two et'em."

My mother always made sure that Mammy left after cooking breakfast with plenty to feed her own family in the 'cabins outback.' My mother never called them, "slave quarters." My mother hated the concept of slaves and my father would always tell her the same thing, "Rice requires a hundred hands to grow on a plantation this size, Mary Elizabeth. I truly wish that we could hire seasonal laborers for planting and bringing the rice to market."

Tobias and I had a daily ritual. We thanked the Lord for our daily bread, we ran from the cabin out back to the ferry crossing to Datha Island and asked the men working the ferry if we could ride with them. Sometimes they were not busy and let us come with them. Other times, when they had horses and wagons to move, they refused. In that case we ran into the woods along the shore line and pulled our homemade raft from the brush and searched for our paddles. "You boys stay between the islands!" Was the last thing we heard from the ferry men as we paddled off in search of that day's adventure. If we got caught on the east side of Pollawana, the ocean breakers would turn us over and soak us with salt water that stung our eyes. At low tide the breakers were smaller, but at high tide we always risked being "ship wreaked," as Tobias called it. The waters between the islands off the coast of Beaufort, South Carolina, were our playground, and we learned to navigate in good weather.

Once a month, we left our plantation to go to church in Beaufort. The entire plantation population left. The field hands had their Sunday best dress clothes packed carefully in oilskins to protect them on the journey into town. We usually left at daybreak in order to make a noon service. The field hands could not sit in the pews with white people, so they would crowd into the large loft that ran across the back of the entire church. I would always look for Tobias' face in the crowd. He would smile at me and I wondered why the slave owners chose to treat them like that. They were nearer to God in heaven where they worshiped.

The street car jerked to a stop and jolted me from my childhood memories. We were across from Lafayette Park and the Army Navy Building. It was Monday morning, another week of the same thing was beginning to be a familiar routine. Until I heard, "Jason, I need to talk to you." It was Amelia Earley standing there waiting to meet me before my daily routine began. "Can we walk in the park?"

"Sure, Doc. What is bothering you?"

"Jason, you can always read me like a book. I have a decision to make."

"You do? About what?"

"I have been offered a one year visiting professorship in the College of London's, School of Medicine."

"Are you going to accept it?"

"That depends on you, Jason."

"It does?"

"Quit being so dense, Jason. You know I would never move to England without you. I see you everyday. I do not think I could live without that."

I looked into her eyes and saw something I was not prepared for, she loved me. "Doc, you are the best friend that I have ever had, that was not a man. I will not do anything to lose your friendship. My assignment, here in Washington, will be over in another year and I will be assigned to San Francisco to develop a new Pacific Naval Base there. I did not know how I was going to tell you that. I was going to ask you to move there with me, to live with me so we could start our lives together."

"You were going to ask me to marry you?"

"Yes, I was afraid it would end our friendship, when you turned me down. I had no idea that you would ask me."

"I guess, I just did."

"Yes, you did. You have a wonderful career here in Washington and now an opportunity to teach in England. If you take that opportunity, we will be apart for that year, unless I come to see you, correct?"

She was crying. I had just turned down her offer of marriage. "Amelia Mary Earley, you are the best thing that has ever happened to me, I love you. And, I accept your offer of marriage. We will find a way to be together so that we can both practice our professions."

"How?"

"Come with me. I am going to ask for the day off from Admiral Farragut. He is the wisest man on the face of the earth. We will tell him our situation and he will help."

We waited to cross Pennsylvania until the traffic cleared and I asked her, "Is this an offer that you would have considered if your father had not died suddenly two years ago?"

"Probably not. The salary is twice what I make now at Georgetown. My father left a huge debt and I am trying to pay it off. But I will never get it paid, I am completely out of money."

"Amelia, why did you not tell me this before, at your father's funeral, I could have helped."

"You are taking a lot for granted, Captain. We had not known each other very long and I was not in love with you then. Besides, the Earleys pay their own debts." She turned to leave.

My feelings were hurt. I had made a rather clumsy attempt at condolence and it fell flat. I realized I loved her more than ever and said, "Amelia, I am sorry I put it that way. I am sure of many things in my life. One, I have more money than I can spend and I would like to help you. Two, my feelings for you are genuine, wholesome and I want to marry you, if you will have me. Three, I withdraw the offer to help pay your father's debt. Four, I want you to finish your education at Georgetown, not go to England. Five, I want ....." but I never finished my list because her mouth was on mine, kissing me like a drowning person. She clung to me and said, "Oh, Jason. I love you so much. But I was afraid that you wanted to be 'just friends.' I do not want to go to England or even finish here at Georgetown. I want to marry you and have babies and I can tell the baby doctors how to treat them." Tears were streaming down her face and she was not bothered by the fact that we were standing in the middle of a crowd waiting for a street car to pass.

19
Plans with Amelia
Georgetown, April 26, 1850

We walked across Pennsylvania Avenue hand in hand and into the Army Navy Building. We found Admiral Farragut sitting behind his desk. His feet were up on his desk, his hands folded behind his head. This was his favorite position for thinking. He saw us and immediately came back to his normal working position.

"Jason and Amelia, nice to see you both."

"Admiral, we are going to get married."

"It is about time, Jason. You were 20 years old when the French took Juanita from you. You were 30 years old when we leveled Veracruz for a second time. You and Amelia were made for each other. Do you need a thirty day leave so you can go home and buy a house?"

"Buy a house?" Amelia asked.

"Yes, you are going to be a Navy wife first and a doctor second, Amelia. The Navy tends to send us around the globe, a family needs a permanent base from which to operate. Mine is on the Hudson River not far from West Point. My wife and children call that home and I will as soon as my career is over. I was just thinking about that when you two walked in here."

"Why not buy a house here, across the Potomac near you, Admiral?" I asked. "That way Amelia can keep her position at Georgetown."

"You could. I do not own the house across the river, I rent it. Home is where you own. A rental is where you and your family are at the Navy's present assignment. I would never recommend that you own a house everywhere you are assigned. How would you know where 'home' is?"

"Home is where Jason is, Admiral." Amelia was smiling. Her face was a calm I had never seen before. She was not like Juanita, a short tempered, Latino aristocrat. She was tall, tender hearted and beautiful from the inside out. And, she was older and smarter than I would ever be.

"We will take the leave that you mentioned, Admiral. We will use it to transport family from South Carolina that want to see us get married here in Washington. We will buy a house here and return to it at the end of my career."

"What will you do next year when you and I are transferred to California?" The Admiral was smiling. He already knew my answer.

"Amelia and I are never going to be apart, we will rent the most expensive town house that we can find."

"We cannot afford that, Jason." Amelia looked worried.

"Jason, you need to have a talk with your bride-to- be. Amelia, you have no idea what Jason does when he is not being my aide, do you?"

"What do you mean, Admiral?"

"I mean, the business interests that Jason oversees."

"Business interests?"

"Jason, take Amelia into my outer office and have a talk with her. Send some telegrams and enjoy your leave." He reached for a set of leave forms, signed them, and handed them to me. "Process these before you leave on your honeymoon, Jason. See you in thirty days."

We left his office and stopped at my desk in the outer office. I reached for an American Telegraph pad and began to write. As I completed each, I handed them to her to read.

To: Robert Whitehall, Bank of Beaufort
From: Jason Caldwell, Chairman
Subject: Letter of credit, amount 20,000 dollars

Please send the letter to my bank in Georgetown, address and contact information are in my office there. Best to Laura and the children, will introduce you to Amelia when you arrive for our wedding. Please notify the office in Port Royal that the Cold Harbor should be ready to transport my family and yours when you get a final date from us.

Jason and Amelia

I was busy writing the second, when Amelia asked, "What is this?"

"It is a telegram, you have received and sent telegrams before."

"Not like this, it is too long, it will cost a fortune to send this."

"No, all my telegrams are free."

"What?"

"Well, not exactly free. In addition to the Chairman of the board for the Bank of Beaufort, I own a few companies."

"You own American Telegraph and a bank?"

"Yes."

"Why did you withhold this information from me?"

"Because, I did not want you marrying me for my money." I said with a big grin on my face.

"What is this reference to 'Cold Harbor'?"

"That is a ship that is part of the Caldwell Shipping and Trading Company's fleet."

"You own a fleet of ships?"

"Yes, with my father, he owns ten percent."

"What else do you own?"

"Part of a plantation south of Beaufort, South Carolina."

"What else?"

"That is all, I am afraid. I am not wealthy, like my father, Amelia. Every dollar that I have is out working for me. I could not lay my hands on a hundred dollars until payday from the Navy."

"What about the 20,000 that you just moved from the Bank of Beaufort?"

"What about it? It is a loan, a letter of credit."

"My head hurts!" She said with a smile on her face.

"I am writing another telegram to my bank here in Georgetown, Amelia. I am asking for the amount to pay your father's debt. Does the estate owe the debt and to whom?"

"I can NOT ask you to do this, Jason."

"I know how you feel, Amelia. But I believe the marriage vows are, 'for better or worse, richer or poorer'. We need to start our life together free of anything from our past lives."

"Good, tell me about Juanita."

20
Amelia Disappears
Georgetown, April 27, 1850

My explanation of Juanita, in its entirety, took several hours. I told her the story of how we met. "I was sketching port facilities for the Secretary of the Navy that year and she walked right up behind me. I was not much of a 'spy'. I never saw or heard a thing until she spoke to me."

"What did she say?"

"Something about me being a terrible artist and wearing such a ridiculous looking hat."

"Hat? You never wear a hat, unless you are in uniform."

"It was part of the disguise, let me finish telling you what happened in her father's bank." I continued telling her what happened.

"So, that is how you became a banker."

"No, that is how the US Navy deposited 400 dollars in a bank so that I could get back to my ship with the sketches before they summoned the police!" We both laughed. My years seeing Juanita every few months were explained away as best I could. I did not tell her we spent a summer together living in her apartment in Veracruz. I did tell her that our families had spent time together traveling back and forth on the Cold Harbor and that Juanita was at my graduation from the Point. I was up to the place in time where the French had blockaded the Veracruz harbor and I managed to get the New Haven into and out of the harbor. Amelia cried when I told her that the French fleet killed Juanita's brother in the fort, her father and her still inside the bank and her mother waiting at home for them.

"I was an emotional wreck when I returned to school that January and we collied in the snow storm. You were wonderful to me, Amelia. I will never forget how patient you were with me, trying to be my friend."

"Jason, I was on my way to being an old maid, daughter of the dean, when you showed up and swept me off my feet. I have loved you for years!"

"Why did we wait so long to do this, Amelia?"

"To get married?"

"Yes."

"It never came up. We were having too much fun being each others best friends - until my father died and I was without any family at all. My mother died when I was little and my father never remarried. He said he could not manage the heartache of losing another spouse. Now I understand, for the first time, what he was talking about."

"Well, that is the last telegram that needs to go out. My place or yours?"

"My place, I am cooking you a meal you will never forget!"

We rode the streetcar to her apartment, ate a meal and I stayed the night. That was the last time I ever saw Amelia. I had no way of knowing that, when I kissed her goodbye to return to my flat on Maryland Avenue, she would be gone. A few hours later, I returned to find the front door broken and ajar. Her apartment was a mess. A path of dried blood was smeared on the back of the door, as though someone had opened it hard into her face. I was shaking with anger as I walked through her apartment calling her name. How many hours had I been gone? I walked through the apartment a second time. I found all of her things, her purse, jewelry, everything except Amelia. I ran down the stairs and hailed a cab. I reported what I found to the police and returned with them to help investigate what might have happened.

"Captain Caldwell, I think you are right. It looks like this door gave her a bloody nose. We do not know if the door was stuck and she pulled it into herself or if someone threw it open into her as she was looking through the peep hole. Either way, she probably needed more medical attention than she could give herself. You said she is a doctor?"

"Yes, she worked at the Medical College of Georgetown."

"Do you think she would have gone there for assistance with a broken nose?"

"She might have. I would think that she would go to the nearest hospital or clinic here in Washington if the injury was serious."

"We will find her, Captain. That is our job. We will start with clinics or hospitals that are within a short walk and then spread out all the way to Georgetown. Why was she living in this neighborhood, instead of somewhere in Georgetown?"

"She was trying to pay off her father's debts after he died and this was what she could afford." I felt a wave of shame come over me. She needed money and I let her down.

"You said you were on leave from the Navy, Captain? Where can we find you when we have information on this case?"

I gave him my address, office number at the Army Navy Building and told him, " Send me a collect telegram if you can not reach me. I am good for the payment of the telegram. I will also look at all the clinics, hospitals and friends that she has in Georgetown."

"That is a good idea, Captain. The more people we have looking, the sooner we will find her." He left me standing in the middle of her apartment. I tried to gather my thoughts. What did I know about Amelia's neighborhood? Had she ever said anything about being afraid of anyone? How many months had she lived here? Did she move here right after her father's death? I needed to talk with her closest friend at Georgetown as soon as I checked all the closest places where she might have gone for help. I left the apartment and headed down the flight of steps to the sidewalk. I stopped the first person I met and asked where the closest doctor's office or clinic was located. Two blocks east turned out to be the office of Doctor Hellsworth. I entered and asked a young man if he was Dr. Hellsworth.

"No, I am his assistant and orderly for his office. Can I help you?"

"Yes, my friend broke her nose today. Is she here?"

"A woman was here this morning, Dr. Hellsworth set her nose and suggested that she have her head injury treated at the hospital over on 33rd and L."

"Head injury?"

"Yes, she was confused, could not recall her name, where she lived or what she did for a living. She had no way of identifying herself and no money to pay the doctor's fee."

"Was she tall, blond hair, looked like a teenager?"

"No, she was very short, dark hair probably about your age."

I thanked him and decided to check out the hospital that he had mentioned. Maybe he got two patients mixed up. I found that I was no longer walking, I was running towards the address he had given me. I reached the hospital out of breath and had to wait a minute before I could ask the admissions clerk if a woman had been admitted with a head injury or broken nose. He looked at me and said, "I am not allowed to give out any information of that nature, Sir."

"I will need your name, Sir, so that I may give it to the police officer I am working with and he can ask the question for me."

"Give me his name, badge number and precinct and I will forward whatever information that he requires." I did and was on my way to Georgetown. I got off the streetcar in front of the student clinic and went inside to see if Amelia had reported for work today. They had not seen her. She was late for her shift. I thanked them and said I would check with her friend that works in the Dean's Office. I ran to the Dean of Medicine's office and was out of breath again. Dean Earley's old secretary still worked there and I brought her up to date on what had happened.

"Where can I reach you, Jason, if I find her?"

I told her the same thing I had told the police officer and I left to check other locations on the Georgetown campus. The day ended with me back at Amelia's apartment. The door was still broken and I looked for the building superintendent. I told him that I was sleeping there tonight, in case Amelia returned after getting some help. He came with his tools and replaced the lock and door knob. I did not sleep much that night or the next. I spent the rest of my leave looking for Amelia. She had vanished. The police now had her case as a missing person, probable amnesia.

I returned to work in the Army Navy Building and sent out another batch of telegrams telling my family back in South Carolina that the police had not found her and I was back at work. The money to pay Dr. Earley's estate debt was never sent. The letter of credit to purchase a house near Admiral Farragut was never used. The months passed into 1851 and the Navy transferred us to San Francisco to oversee the building of the Mare Island Navy Yard.

21
Mare Island Naval Yard
San Francisco, 1851-53

Admiral and Mrs. Farragut could not have been kinder that first year that we were stationed in California. They invited me to their rental home and introduced me to several young women. None of them were Amelia and I never contacted any of them. Women who I fell in love with, vanished before my eyes and I did not want that curse to fall on anyone else. The Navy is an all men's club and I threw myself into my work. If I did not form any contacts with women, then they were safe and I was safe from the hurt that always occurred when they disappeared from my life.

We lived in San Francisco, because Mare Island was located in Solano County at the eastern end of the Bay of San Pablo. The island was opposite the city of Vallejo and housing was limited there because Navy housing was at the San Francisco base. After the Navy purchased the island and began building, a second ferry was added to Mare from San Francisco to accompany the ferry across the half mile strait from Vallejo. Construction workers rode the Vallejo ferry and Naval Personnel used the San Francisco ferry. We had orders to complete the construction of the Pacific Station of the United States Navy. It would contain a naval yard, arsenal, sectional floating docks, an observatory, a light house and a radio-meter station. Radio-meters were something brand new for the Navy. A separate building was to be built for the fragile instruments, invented by Crookes and improved by Pringsheim and E. F. Nichols under Navy contracts. Crookes had built and tested the first radio-meter which consisted of a glass bulb which had a central axis inside the bulb. The axis was a framework carrying one or more mica vanes mounted and free to turn around the axis inside the glass. The air was pumped out of the bulb and the bulb was then sealed at the top. One face of each vane was polished while the opposite was coated black. When heat was applied to the Crookes tube, the vanes turned like a miniature windmill and produced what Crookes called an "ether wave." It was not until Pringsheim modified the Crookes tube to receive ether waves, that the Navy got interested in the concept. A Crookes tube can send and a Pringsheim tube can receive. Pringsheim's tube did not have a windmill, the vanes could not turn freely, but were restricted to turn through a small angle. When the ether waves fell upon the vanes of a

Pringsheim tube, they were absorbed. The Navy wanted to use the concept to send messages from ship to ship and from ship to Mare Island. E. F. Nichols was under contract to produce a workable set of instruments.

My plan to avoid women by never leaving the Navy was fool proof, until I met Sara Nichols. She was the brains behind the work done by her husband Edward Nichols. She came to Mare Island to deliver a set of working drawings while Edward was aboard the USS Bearing Sea, now captained by Ben Hagood. She was still at Mare Island when the Bearing Sea docked in San Francisco and brought the news that her husband was lost at sea. The body was never discovered. She felt what I felt at the loss of a loved one. She stayed at Mare Island a another year until the contract for a communications station was to be completed in late 1852. We spent a lot of time together and she gave me many ideas to improve the transmission of signals over a telegraph wire. For example, she put together a combination of a thermopile and galvanometer with fixed magnets and movable coils. A loop of wire was suspended between the poles of a horseshoe magnet, with its plane parallel to the line joining the poles.

"Look what I have done here, Jason. If you send an electromagnetic pulse, like that of your American Telegraph signal through this, we should be able to send it on, through the air, without wires."

"My God, Sara, do you realize what you have done? There are gaps everywhere in the telegraph lines across this country. We can begin to close those gaps with this device. What are you going to call this?"

"Short wave transmission. It is designed to travel only short distances, less than a mile, but it would be another means to send morse code from ship to ship."

"I have never met anyone who was as smart as Hank Benham. You are a genius!" I gave her a big hug. I immediately realized what I had done. "I am so sorry, Sara. I should not have done that. Please, forgive me."

"Can we try that again? I was not ready." She gave me an embrace with her whole body. I was paralyzed with fear. She sensed this and drew back.

"Sara, I was not ready for that. On the count of three, we will try again. Agreed?"

"Jason, stand still and relax." She took a step towards me and held me close while she cried on my shoulder. "Jason, I have missed being this close to a man since Edward died. I know about you and Amelia from Admiral Farragut's wife, if this makes you uncomfortable, I understand."

"I am very uncomfortable around you, Sara. You are so intelligent and interesting to watch while you work on your experiments. I am a confirmed bachelor, committed to the Navy. I am not looking for a relationship."

"Nor am I, Jason. I have been married and it was not a very exciting experience for me. You excite me."

"I do?"

"Yes, you do. I feel like a moth flying into the candle's flame when I am around you. I want to be your friend, your very, very, good friend. But I do not want to be a wife again. Agreed?"

Admiral Farragut called me into his office the next day. I was sure someone had seen Sara and me in her lab.

"How is everything going on the ship to shore and ship to ship communications, Jason?"

"The ether waves work under a mile, Admiral.

We have been successful from the USS Bearing Sea to Mare Island when the ship was docked. We need a second ship, equipped like the Bearing Sea, to test ship to ship communications."

"I will see what is available to us in San Francisco, Jason."

"Yesterday, Sara showed me something else that I think should be classified top secret by the Navy, Sir."

"What is that?"

"Sara is working on how to receive an electromagnetic impulse from a telegraph line and convert it to be sent through the air. Something she calls a hertz wave."

"You better sit down, Jason, what I am about to tell you is already top secret. The Russians and the Austrians have already figured out how to do half of what you have just described. They are also working with Hertzian waves. Last summer, Louis Kossuth and others visited the White House from their homes in Hungry. They had just been crushed in their bid for independence by Austria and Russia. They managed to smuggle out some of the working drawings for what they call a 'vacuum tube'.

"They? Sir."

"Yes. Electricians and inventors named Martin Koszta and Stephen Szirom. Szirom came with Kossuth to deliver the plans for the tube, Koszta is still in the Mediterranean Sea running tests for the Austrian Navy."

"Do we need Koszta as well as Szirom? Admiral."

"The Secretary of the Navy says, yes. He will want to see Sara's idea as soon as we can get him out here. I will contact him and tell him to come or send someone in his place. I will also hire Sara for another year to work here. You and Sara will be in danger if anyone finds out what she has accomplished. I do not like the fact that she carries documents to and from work. Tell her to send them by armed courier. And, before I forget it, you no longer work for me."

"What?"

"The Department of the Navy has reassigned you to Navy Intelligence, Army Navy Building, Washington. I will ask for your deployment to Mare Island for the next year until you and Sara complete your work. Then I think you and Sara will continue to work from Washington."

The Navy hired Sara to continue her work for another year and assigned me to Mare Island for a year. It was October, 1852, and the country had nominated two more generals for its candidates for president. General Scott was on the Whig ticket and Franklin Pierce was on the Democratic. I did not remember that General Pierce served in the Mexican War. Sara and I were constantly together that fall. We worked eight to ten hours in the lab at Mare Island, spent an hour on the ferry each day and ate our evening meals together at our favorite restaurant, called the "Hungry Fork". Neither one of us liked to cook and this was a way of ending our day together in comfort. It was now winter and Sara had to deliver a set of plans in Vallejo. She told me that she and her bodyguard would take the ferry to Vallejo that afternoon and she would meet me at the Hungry Fork for a late supper.

I left work at the normal time, caught the ferry into San Francisco and waited at the café for her. It was already dark that night, but it was a safe neighborhood, so I was unarmed and without my bodyguard. I looked at my pocket watch and wondered where she was. I walked to the front door of the café and peered into the dimly lighted street. I saw her come around the corner and I was relieved until I saw a hand reach out of a doorway and grab her shoulder length document bag and pull her to the sidewalk. I did not hesitate. I burst out of the door and ran toward her. The man tried to cut the strap on her bag with a sharp knife and had slashed her neck as well. I let out a yell figuring this would scare him off and it did. He ran into an alley with Sara's bag and disappeared. I was shocked beyond belief when Sara nearly died in my arms because I could not stop the flow of blood. I held my handkerchief over the slash and pressed as hard as I dared until someone from the café came to assist me. He was a doctor and he stopped the flow of blood. I showed him my brand new Navy Intelligence identification card and said, "This is a matter of National Security, doctor. You will make out a death certificate for this woman. A Navy representative will pick it up from your office. Now summon the morgue and we will get this woman to the hospital."

While her newspaper reported murder went unsolved by the local authorities, the Navy determined that Sara was attacked for the documents that foreign agents thought she carried. It was now assumed that Edward Nichols had not had an accident at sea and that a crew member, or a foreign agent posing as a crew member, of the USS Bearing Sea had killed him also. Sara did not regain consciousness and was near death in the hospital when her device was ready for sea trials. I was assigned, by Navy Intelligence, to the ship that would house the special communication equipment required to send and receive wireless code. The USS St. Louis was available and assigned to accompany the USS Bearing Sea in the top secret mission of testing the Navy's revolutionary new communications equipment. It was assumed that the crew of the USS Bearing Sea still contained the agent or agents responsible for Edward Nichols disappearance. We therefore, could not trust both the sending and receiving equipment to that vessel and it was placed on the St. Louis under my watchful eye and protection. We left San Francisco and headed north towards Mare Island. We sent our first message from the St. Louis to Mare Island and got an instant reply, "God's speed to you and Sara!" We then sent a message to the Bearing Sea using the receiving equipment and got a flag signal reply.

I could not believe my eyes, Sara had done it! We had loaded several crates of equipment with double and triple sets of radio-meter tubes because we did not know how the fragile tubes would respond to rough sea weather or to the constant exposure to salt air. We sailed the entire length of the west coast and sent a message to San Diego and got a reply. In the reply, we got orders to bring the devices to Potomac dockyards in Washington for inspection. The St. Louis and the Bearing Sea would be ordered on to the port of Smyrna, Turkey. Several federal agents boarded the St. Louis and Bearing Sea at the Potomac dockyards to escort a set of demonstration gear to the Army Navy Building. Two Admirals remained on board to brief Captain Ingraham of the St. Louis and Ben Hagood of the Bearing Sea.

"Captain Caldwell, you are in charge of the mission. You will follow Captain Ingraham's commands while on board. We do not want the Russians or the Austrians to discover who you are or what communication equipment we may have developed. Therefore, you will assume another identity for the mission. You will be Commander Wilson, the executive officer of the St. Louis. The real Commander Wilson will also be on board to assist Captain Ingraham. We also have to assume that one or more agents are aboard the USS Bearing Sea and that they are aware of the ether wave equipment. We have no idea if they know, we know about there hertz wave at this time."

"Aye, aye, Sir." We both said together.

"The first person I will now introduce to you, is Stephen Szirom. He is an American Citizen of Austrian birth. His name should be familiar to you, if you remember Louis Kossuth's visit last summer to the White House. Mr. Szirom must locate Mr. Koszta. He was last reported in Smyrna, Turkey. You will leave within the hour."

He handed us our sealed orders in an envelope from the White House, not the Department of the Navy. We sailed thirty minutes later. I sat in my cabin with Stephen Szirom and opened the sealed orders. I had entered a new phase of my Navy career. The orders included a presidential warrant. It guaranteed the safe passage of Mr. Martin Koszta once he was on board the USS St. Louis. He had been granted US citizenship.

"Is this how you were granted US citizenship Mr. Szirom?"

"Yes, when we arrived in Washington with the plans for the Russian vacuum tube, the department of the Navy determined that the idea was revolutionary and that it could be used for ship to ship communications. I was asked to continue my research and develop the instruments needed to send and receive morse code signals. I will need to work with Martin in order to complete both the sending and receiving instruments."

"Have you any idea where Martin is in Turkey?"

"Yes, he is still aboard the 'Huzzar', a ship of the line."

"What is he doing on the Huzzar?"

"Testing the device that we built in Hungary."

"What does the device do?"

"When the Huzzar is in port, a telegraph line is connected to the ship and then the ship can receive a morse code signal and read it."

"Can the Huzzar send a reply to the message?"

"Of course, the hardwired line allows this. Once the line is disconnected then the Huzzar can listen but can not send a message."

"So if we could manage to get the Huzzar disconnected, away from its docking, it could listen but could not send messages."

"That is my understanding, Captain."

22
Cruise to Turkey
May 28, 1853

I met with Stephen Szirom every day of the cruise from Potomac dockyards to the port of Smyrna, Turkey. I also met Sergeant Tom Schneider and his band of commandos that were assigned to the USS St. Louis. Tom was a third generation Navy Marine. He stood well over six feet, six inches tall and weighed about twice my weight. He did not have an ounce of fat on his body and his unit was as fit as he was. They were young and came from various backgrounds, there were former members of the Potomac dockyard shore patrol, medics from Georgetown, USMC riflemen who were former snipers and sharp shooters, demolition experts, and others whose specialities I had not learned as yet. There were eighteen members of his detachment and I tried to understand how I would lead them in this mission. For exercise, Sergeant Schneider would remove a naval deck gun and carry it around while he had the others performing routine training exercises. I asked him about the gun and why he carried it.

"Sergeant, why are you carrying that piece of ordnance around with you?"

"This is a modified Dahlgren, model 1440 Naval deck gun, Sir."

"I can see that, Sergeant, why are you carrying it about?"

"I have one of these back at the dockyards, Sir. The detachment uses it to increase our firepower. Are you familiar with it, Sir." He handed it to me and I nearly dropped it at my feet. I had never tried to lift a deck mounted gun, my entire time in the Navy.

"Sir, the English Navy has had a weapon of this type for many years. They used eight barrels which rotated into position for firing, it was a musket, not a heavy caliber rifle like ours. They could get off eight shots and then it needed to be reloaded with musket balls, wadding and powder. It was not very effective in a fire fight. Hand that to me and walk with me to the rail, Sir." He hoisted the gun like it was a toy and let go with a burst from his weapon. I heard forty eight shots ring out and the sea was churned with the reports.

"If there had been a long boat out there, Sir, what do you think would be left of it?"

"Not much, Sergeant, stay close to me in a fight."

"Aye, aye. Sir. What does the office of Navy Intelligence do? When I was assigned by Lieutenant Lewis, he said to talk to you, he had never heard of it."

"It has always been there, Sergeant. I was assigned from Mare Island Naval Yard in California on March 4th. I guess the new Secretary of the Navy must have decided that he needed a full-time officer and a detachment. Can you introduce me to your men? Tell me a little about each one."

"They are your men, Sir. Lieutenant Lewis picked most of them for you, since you were not in Potomac Dock yards when the orders came down."

"Jerome Lewis is in charge of shore patrol for the dockyards, is that true? Did a policeman pick my detachment?"

"When you meet Mr. Lewis, I think you will find that he is more than a policeman, Sir."

"Good, can we meet the men now?" We walked along the deck and watched the detachment during the training that Tom Schneider had been instructing.

"Attention on deck! Captain Caldwell is the new skipper of this outfit, come to attention and salute your captain!"

"At ease, Gentlemen. I will start over here to my right and work my way around the detachment." I walked to the first man and shook his hand. "What is your name?"

"Corporal Sam Mason, Sir, USMC." I moved to the next man. "Private First Class, Dwayne Wilson, Sir, USMC." I managed to remember some of them, there were seventeen names and faces besides the Sergeant's. Mostly privates, but some corporals with names like Keets, Mathews, James, Peters, Mahoney, Russell, Dempsey, Cornell, Wendleson, Turnsbill, Grantham, Rivers, Alexander, Fryerson, and Miller. I had not learned, at this point in my career, not to memorize every face and name before a mission where some of them might not be coming home to family and friends. So we spent the first few days of the cruise learning from each other. For example, I had no idea what an EOD did for the Navy.

"You see, Cap'n Caldwell, a torpedo or a floating mine is a device waiting to make a big hole in your boat. The job of an Explosive Ordnance Disposal [EOD] is to make that device harmless to us or it can be turned on our enemy to make him pay for setting it."

"Thank you, corporal Miller, I had no idea that an enemies mine can be used against them."

"We should see some devices on this trip, Sir. Them foreigners are not to be trusted."

"Tell the lookouts to keep a sharp eye, Mr. Miller, we do not want a big hole in the St. Louis!"

"Aye, aye. Sir."

I talked with a former member of Lieutenant Jerome Lewis' command and he gave him high praise for his novel approach to problem solving. I made a mental note to call on Lt. Lewis as soon as we were back in the Potomac Dockyards. This was followed by a visit with "Doc" Rivers, a medic from Georgetown. I asked him if he ever got on campus or to the student clinic but he indicated that he was assigned to the care of veterans at the other hospital there. I got Tom Schneider to question Stephen Szirom about what Martin Koszta's physical appearance was like. Tom asked Stephen where Marin would most likely go on shore leave. Who might be assigned to guard him on shore leave. He asked him if Martin liked to read or due research in a library. Tom asked him several questions that I would not have thought to ask. Tom was a natural leader, I would have to write a promotion letter when we arrived back in the US.

"Captain Caldwell, we are going to be in Turkey, soon. It is the only country with a city in two continents. Constantinople is located on both sides of the Bosporus Strait. The Bosporus separates Europe from Asia. If we have to leave the St. Louis, for any reason, we are going to stand out like a sore thumb. I can not think of a way to make our white faces look like an someone on the street in Turkey."

"Natives of Turkey are not dark skinned like an Arab, Tom. They look like us. The problem will be the language. We have no one on board how can speak the street language. Lucky for us, there are many foreigners in Turkey. If we are careful we should be able to keep watch on those that need watching. We need to identify the source of the leak of information from the USS Bearing Sea. If anyone leaves the Bearing Sea and speaks the language we have identified the source. The Presidential Warrant states that these individuals are to be eliminated so that a message will be sent to foreign capitals, that if you send agents into our country, they will disappear. The bodies are not to be found by anyone in Turkey or the US, that means they are to disappear at sea. The trouble is, we have not identified anyone on the Bearing Sea to throw overboard."

"Give me the names and descriptions, Captain and I will make sure that no one finds their bodies in Turkey."

23

Port of Smyrna
June 1853

We were to enter port on June 29st. The Bearing Sea anchored outside the port and waited to hear from us by radio-meter. The Bearing Sea could read our messages, but could not send any. I had gone on board the Bearing Sea and talked with Ben Hagood before they anchored. "It is important to know which of the seamen seem agitated or request shore leave, Ben. These are probably the foreign agents or hired by them to do their dirty work."

"These? You think there is more than one agent?"

"Yes, I do. Have you checked all the service records for everyone aboard the Bearing Sea?"

"I have. Jason, I can not find anything in any of the paperwork that will help you."

"Grant shore leave to anyone who requests it, but not until you have sent a messenger to the St. Louis with the seaman's name and description. I want two of Tom Schneider's men to follow him and find out where he goes and what he does."

"What about deserters?"

"They are the agents, Ben. We can hope that this is the manner in which they leave the ship. Why would an American seaman desert to a Muslim country? It would mean instant death, unless he was an agent with a cover story."

"I will send you at least one message every day we are in port, Ben. If you do not get a message, I would start to look at the men you have assigned to your radio room."

"I wish we had a better idea of what we are up against here, Jason. There are too many variables."

"You have that much right, Ben! I will be in touch. I have to get back to the St. Louis before Captain Ingraham thinks I have deserted him."

I returned to the St. Louis and Captain Ingraham provided just enough steam to follow the pilot boat into our docking station beside the Austrian ship of war, the Huzzar. The Huzzar was the flag ship of Admiral Archduke John, brother of the Emperor of Austria. "This is not going to be easy for you, Captain Caldwell."

"You had better get used to calling me, Commander Wilson, Sir. We would not want Archduke John to get the idea that we are here to snatch his radio man." I was smiling but Ingraham was not. He was deep in thought.

"How are you going to get Koszta off that monster beside us?"

"It would be nice if they would give him to us for some reason and we could sail away. If the Archduke is waiting for us and knows of our plans, then we have already failed."

"Exactly! What if I ask for permission to talk to the Archduke? When we are face to face with him, I will simply ask him if he has received a telegram from his consul in Smyrna, informing him that Martin Koszta has applied for US citizenship and that it has been granted by President Pierce. The St. Louis has been sent by the President to take him back to the United States."

"There is no telegram, Captain."

"Of course, but think of the confusion and time delay that will cause. When the Admiral sees the Pierce Warrant, he will need to telegraph the Austrian Consul and get a reply. It establishes our right to claim an American citizen aboard a foreign ship, in a foreign harbor."

"What if the Huzzar suddenly gets ether wave transmissions from us to the Bearing Sea? They should not be able to read them, but they will know that we are in contact with one or more ships outside the harbor. That should add credit to what you present to the Archduke."

"Good idea, Jason. Do it now. I will have our signals contact the Huzzar and arrange for you and I to see the Archduke."

I sent the following message to Ben: *Ingraham to contact Huzzar this hour for permission to speak with them and present the Pierce Warrant.*

Signals sent the following message by flags to the Huzzar: *Captain Ingraham of the visiting fleet from the United States requests a meeting with the commander of the Austrian Ship of War, Huzzar.*

The Huzzar returned the following: *please repeat message in German.* Signals was standing beside Captain Ingraham and said, "They are stalling for time, Sir."

"I know. Send it again, in German. Jason, send another message to the Bearing Sea. This time in German, just in case they can read our transmissions."

"Aye, aye. Sir." I retreated to the radio room and found seaman Scherschel.

"Captain Ingraham thinks the Huzzar may be reading our transmissions. Let them chew on this for a while. Send the Bearing Sea the following message, 'Mary had a little lamb, its fleece was white as snow!'" Our German speaking radio man was chuckling as he sent, *Maria pret ein klien lamm, es flausch pre weibe als schnee!*

I returned to the captain and told him the message was sent. A long boat from the Bearing Sea was pulling along side the St. Louis. A message and documents from Captain Hagood were hand delivered to Captain Ingraham. He tore them open and read the message and handed it to me. He began reading the attached crewmen files.

"Jason, you had better get Sergeant Schneider's detail ready to take the messenger back to the Bearing Sea and get a good look at these two before Hagood sends them on shore leave." He handed me the rest of the files and I read them and said.

"These are both US citizens with relatives living in Smyrna. They are probably not the foreign agents or hired by them - but you never know." I looked up to see the Sergeant walking toward us in plain clothes.

"Is the action about to start, Captain?"

"I want you to take Captain Hagood's messenger back to the Bearing Sea. You and your men will then take the two who have requested shore leave with you. You will not talk to them or ask them any questions. Make it seem like a routine, five seamen on shore leave. Here are the addresses in the city that these seamen are supposed to visit. If they go anywhere else, they must be eliminated as possible agents. Make a full report when you return." I saluted and the four men climbed down into the long boat and headed for the Bearing Sea.

"Jason, you are now Commander Wilson. We are heading for the Huzzar to see the Archduke. We may not get to talk to him, but we will try." We walked down the gangway and onto the dock that separated the St. Louis from the Huzzar. We walked to the bottom of the gangway to the Huzzar and I shouted in English, "Permission to come aboard with a message for Archduke John."

"Permission granted," in English, was yelled back down to us. We walked up the gangway, found the Austrian flag on the top mast, saluted and turned to face the Captain of the Huzzar.

"You are from the USS St. Louis beside us, Yes?"

"Yes, we are. Commander Wilson and I are here to meet with Mr. Martin Koszta, a citizen of the United States. And to present a letter from President Pierce to the Emperor of Austria or his representative. Is the Archduke aboard? I think he could read it as the Emperor's representative."

"Of course, I will have the letter delivered to the Admiral's cabin." I reached into my mail pouch and handed the letter to the Captain.

"I regret to inform you, Captain, that Mr. Koszta has been arrested by local authorities while he was on shore leave. I have sent my representatives from the Huzzar to bring him aboard to be placed in irons and returned to Hungary as a traitor to his country."

"How unfortunate that you have arrested an American citizen, Captain. You are aware that Mr. Koszta is a hero in our country for his families' assistance during our war of independence from Great Britain. When I report this to our President, I fear that he will order Mr. Koszta's immediate release or my fleet will be ordered to take him by force."

All of the color drained from the Captain's face and he said, "Can you wait here, while I speak to my Admiral?"

"Of course, Captain." He hurried away to speak with Archduke John and we stood looking at each other. When he returned, he was shaken.

"I am instructed to inform you that if you try to interfere with the arrest and transport of the prisoner, then a state of war will exist between our two countries."

Before I could think of anything to say, Captain Ingraham said, "You may report back to the Admiral that the US fleet outside the harbor will be instructed to begin shelling the six Austrian ships within an hour. You have until then to leave in peace before the prisoner is brought on board."

"I have not been entirely truthful with you, Captain, the prisoner is already in irons and if you sink this ship you will kill an American citizen."

"I do not believe what you say, Captain. Allow me to see Mr. Koszta, if he is indeed aboard, or I will start the bombardment in one hour."

"Follow me, I will take you to him." We followed him and found Martin Koszta in irons unable to fully stand or sit down.

"This is inhuman treatment, Captain. Make him comfortable or the shelling will commence immediately upon my return to the St. Louis."

"Only if you return to the St. Louis and give those orders, Sir."

"Not quite, if we do not return in half an hour, the St. Louis is ordered to build steam and get underway. If you would bother to look next to you, the St. Louis is probably already making steam from fired boilers. Care to go up on deck and check with us?" We turned and walked up the ships ladder and onto the main deck. The St. Louis had drawn the gangway and was producing steam as a cloud of smoke was coming from the stacks.

We ran down the open gangway of the Huzzar as the gangway from the St. Louis was shoved down to us. We ran up and onto the deck of the St. Louis. "Clear the decks for action." I heard Captain Ingraham shout. "Prepare to fire a broadside into the Huzzar at my command. Commander Wilson, make sure the first volley kills the Captain and the Archduke."

The reaction on the Huzzar was total disbelief. Its captain grabbed a bull horn and shouted across to the St. Louis. "Hold your fire, the Archduke wants to talk with you, Captain."

The Archduke appeared from his cabin and stood beside the captain of the Huzzar waving his hands in wild circles. We could not understand or hear what he was asking his captain. Several minutes passes until the Archduke took the bull horn and said something in German.

"Get your radio man up here, Jason, so he can translate for us." It took me a few minutes to find and bring him back next to Captain Ingraham.

"Seaman Scherschel, hail the Huzzar and ask if they are preparing to release Martin Koszta."

"Aye, aye. Sir." He asked the question in German and got a reply. "The Archduke says he has no authority to release the prisoner at this time, he would like time to send a message of our demands to the Austrian Consul here in Smyrna."

"Seaman Scherschel, please translate the following for the Admiral. *Excellent suggestion we will send messengers to the United States consul as* well! Jason, get your detail off this ship and put your plan into action. As soon as you are gone, I will tell Commander Wilson to get us off this dock and into the mouth of the harbor before the rest of the Austrian fleet realizes what has happened. We will be cut to pieces if we remain tied up here. You and Mr. Scherschel get back to the radio room and send seven messages. One to the Bearing Sea, and one to the Vampire, Intrepid, San Jacinto, and any others that you think may be in the Med. I want the six fake messages sent in German. I want the message sent to the Bearing Sea to be in code, asking that they acknowledge seven separate transmissions. Use the USS ship's fleet designation number for each separate message."

I was smiling as I said, "You want the Archduke to think that he is out numbered."

"Out numbered and facing a crazy person! Get those messages sent, Mr. Scherschel."

"Aye, aye. Sir."

I found Corporal Mason and said, "Is the detail ready, Corporal?"

"We are ready, Captain. I would like to get off this sitting duck."

"I need to get my diplomatic pouch that has the letters for Consul Brown and the Turkey Charge de Affairs here in Smyrna. Assemble the men, on the dock, I will be with you shortly."

"Aye, aye. Sir."

We marched, the fifteen of us, like we were a conquering army into the center of Smyrna and located "Embassy Row" on my map. We stopped first at the Turkish Charge de Affairs' office and hand delivered a letter from President Pierce. I had read the letter. It explained that an American fleet was sent to the Port of Smyrna to rescue an American citizen being held against his will aboard the Austrian Ship of War, Huzzar. The secretary of the Navy, James C. Dobbin, had advised President Pierce that a show of force might be necessary to convince the Austrians to release Mr. Koszta. Captain Ingraham

117

had certainly shown a willingness to use force, now it was up to me and my detail to convince the Turks, Austrians and whoever else was involved in this incident to release Mr. Koszta, unharmed.

We left the Charge de Affairs office and headed for the US Embassy. We had passed several large houses that served as foreign embassies or foreign consul offices. We were approaching the US office, when Tom Schneider and his two men stepped out of the bushes and said, "Captain, we followed the two seamen from the Bearing Sea to this house. It is the Greek Embassy."

"Are you sure? I was positive that they would be inside the Austrian Embassy that we just passed."

"I do not think they are coming out, Sir. I think they have delivered information and asked for protection."

"But why the Greek Embassy? The Greeks and the Turks have been at war with each other, off and on, for a century."

"Well, it looks like the Greeks are sharing information with the Austrians and using Turkey to get the process complete. What do we do about the termination of these two American seamen, Sir?"

"If they return from shore leave, they will be 'lost at sea', do not harm them on Turkish soil."

"When do you want us back on board the Bearing Sea, Captain?"

"No more than twenty-four hours from now, Sergeant. The St. Louis is going to block the mouth of the harbor. I gave that letter to the Turkish Consul just now. We need to get Turkey to come to the aid of their good friends the Americans, and punish the Greeks for helping the Austrians."

"Where are you headed now, Captain?"

"My last stop is the Austrian Embassy, to hand deliver a letter from the President, explaining why it might be necessary to sink the Huzzar inside the Port of Smyrna. I do not plan to wait around for a reply. See you tomorrow on board the Bearing Sea."

"Aye, aye. Sir."

24
Washington City
June 1853

When the news was telegraphed through the country that Franklin Pierce had received the Democratic nomination for the Presidency, the general inquiry was, "Who is he?" Until his name was brought before the Baltimore convention, he was hardly known outside his native state of New Hampshire. Now, in June, after he was elected, his history was familiar to all, from one end of the land to the other. He was a general in the Mexican War and had served as a state representative in New Hampshire. He was elected to the US House of Representatives in 1833 and the US Senate in 1837. He chose the following cabinet:

State ------------ William Marcy of New York
War ------------ Jefferson Davis of Mississippi
Navy ----------- James Dobbin of North Carolina
Treasury ------- James Guthrie of Kentucky
Interior --------- Robert McCleland of Michigan
Attorney ------- Caleb Cushing of Massachusetts
Postmaster ---- James Campbell of Pennsylvania

He was meeting with this cabinet to discuss the events of Mare Island Naval Yard that had led to the Koszta Incident.

"When did we become aware of the foreign agents operating in San Francisco, Secretary Marcy?"

"When documents were stolen from Professor Nichols, Mr. President."

"How is she doing after her attack, Secretary Dobbin?"

"She did not regain consciousness in the hospital and has died, Mr. President."

"What was the reaction from Admiral Farragut on Mare Island? Has he notified Captain Caldwell?"

"He has written Captain Caldwell and expressed his personal grief at the senseless killing of such a bright and promising scientist as Sara Nichols."

"I understand that they were working on the new communication gear that you have in the Army Navy Building."

"Yes, we are holding it for Captain Caldwell's return. No one has been able to get it to work properly."

"Has Professor Morse been called in from American Telegraph?"

"No, Mr. President, the gear has been classified as 'top secret' by the Navy."

"Does Professor Morse have top secret clearance?"

"I do not know, Mr. President."

"Find out, get him cleared and onto this project."

"Yes, Mr. President."

"Secretary Davis, has our letter to Turkey been delivered, explaining under what conditions we might have to commit an act of war upon the Huzzar?"

"Mr. President, I assume that the plan given to Captain Caldwell is being carried out. I have no recent information on what has happened in the Port of Smyrna."

"There is no way to send a telegram to Europe, we need a transatlantic cable. When will the next mail packet ship reach Smyrna, Turkey, Postmaster Campbell?"

"July 1, Mr. President."

"We have to trust in our representatives overseas; there is no way to communicate with them in a timely manner. I am not familiar with Captain Caldwell's record, can you send me a copy, Secretary Dobbin."

"Of course, Mr. President, are you thinking of giving him the task of improving our civilian and military communications?"

"You read my mind, Mr. Secretary."

25

Rescue of Ingraham
Off the Coast of Turkey

Sergeant Schneider reported back aboard the USS Bearing Sea the next day with Privates Mathew James and Marshal Peters. "What has happened in Port Smyrna, Captain?"

"Captain Ingraham has moved the St. Louis to block the entrance to the harbor. The Austrian Consul has visited the Huzzar in port and asked for them to reconsider taking Martin Koszta back to the closest sea port in Austria, probably the port of Castelinovo. That would be 400 miles closer than Trieste. The coast of the Austro-Hungarian Empire runs from Italy to Turkey in Europe. They could put in at any port along the coast once they sail from the port of Smyrna which is in Asia minor. The Bearing Sea is supposed to shadow the Huzzar, should she break out of Smyrna."

"What does the radio room report from the St. Louis, Sir?"

"Yesterday, the Huzzar and her escorts left the docks after the Turkish Charge de Affairs visited them and indicated that they were now 'Persona non-grata' and without permission to re-enter any Turkish port of call."

"Have they left the harbor?"

"No, the St. Louis stopped them and talked with them again. The radio messages from the St. Louis have asked the fleet to clear their decks for action and concentrate all their fire upon the Admiral's flag ship."

"What fleet?"

"Our Captain Ingraham has invented some ships to keep us company here, off the coast. He has sent radio messages to the USS Vampire, Intrepid, San Jacinto, Determination and Philadelphia."

"I never heard of the USS Vampire, Sir."

"Let us hope that the Archduke thinks he has heard of it and the others also. We keep sending messages to the St. Louis asking to come closer in support of them to complete the blockade and assist in the sinking of the Huzzar."

"Captain Hagood is going along with this, Sir?"

"He loves it, he wants to get close enough to send warning shots across the bow of the Huzzar."

"Two sloops of war can not stand against six Austrian ships of the line, Sir. It will be the shortest naval engagement in history."

"I know that, and you know that. But does the Archduke know how many ships are off the coast? That is the question, Sergeant. The Huzzar and her escorts are anchored in the middle of the harbor, unable to leave and unable to dock."

"Where does that leave us, Sir?"

"We have to wait and see what the Austrians will do when the next set of visitors come along side. This time it will be the Turkish Navy. The Turks have come up with an unusual solution to the matter. They will take the French Consul with them and place him on board the Huzzar, with the hopes that the US fleet will not sink a ship with a foreign consul on board. The French Consul will offer to take Martin Koszta off the Huzzar and give him protection inside the French Embassy until the matter can be resolved. We should have orders tomorrow or the next day from Washington and the War Department."

The next day the mail packet arrived along side the Bearing Sea, transferred a mail pouch and proceeded on toward the St. Louis. When it was along side the St. Louis, it transferred another mail pouch and proceeded into the docks to deliver mail along Embassy Row. Ben and I sat in his cabin and opened the messages from Secretary Davis. His letter of June 23rd stated that we were authorized to use lethal force in the removal of Martin Koszta from the Huzzar. He stated that President Pierce had indicated that he understood that the death of Martin Koszta would be the result of such action. The President thought, and Secretary Davis agreed, it would be better to stop the development of the Russian and Austrian Hertz wave transmission by any means necessary.

On board the St. Louis, Captain Ingraham was reading the same message. "Commander Wilson, send the Bearing Sea the following message in English: *send EOD detachment with high explosives to this location for the mining of the harbor entrance and the hulls of the Austrian fleet, set timers for four hours, I am tired of dealing with this mess.*"

"We will know if the Huzzar can read our messages, Sir."

"Yes, tell signals to be looking at the Admiral's flag ship for any immediate messages. Bring seaman Scherschel to the bridge so he can interpret for signals, Commander."

"Aye, aye. Sir."

"Mr. Scherschel, can you read flags?"

"Aye, aye. Sir. The Huzzar is sending a message to all ships in the fleet. 'Clear decks for action. Put small boats over the side from all ships with marines to shoot anyone coming within 100 meters of the Huzzar with mines.' End of message."

"That answers whether they can read our radio messages, Captain."

"Yes, that confirms that they read English messages sent from us and from the Bearing Sea. Send the following to all ships in the US fleet stationed outside harbor. *Austrians able to read radio messages, prepare to begin the bombardment of their fleet in four hours, do not stop until all vessels are sunk. Use special long range rockets developed at Mare Island Research Center for maximum effect. I do not want to see any Austrian ship afloat after the four hour deadline.*"

On board the Bearing Sea, the radio room was in turmoil. "We do not have enough mines or torpedoes on board to do anything like what Captain Ingraham has ordered, Captain Hagood."

"Wait, Mr. Nelson, that is probably meant for the Austrians, get Captain Caldwell down here so we can send a reply to the St. Louis."

"We have another message from the St. Louis, Sir. It says to prepare to begin the bombardment of the Huzzar in four hours with long range rockets. Do we have long range rockets, Sir?"

"No, we do not. But we have plenty of 'old fashioned rockets', it is nearly nightfall, we can get a lot closer and fire off a rocket and then immediately radio the St. Louis and say that one of the batteries aboard the Vampire has miss-fired and there will be no more firings until the four hour delay, or until the Austrians come to their senses. If all rockets are fired from all seven ships then the sinking should be immediate with little or no hope of survivors. Do you think you can do that for me?"

"Ben, what do you have planned? I am ordered back to the St. Louis to deliver a final message to the Huzzar."

"Jason, you need to indicate to Captain Ingraham that what I have planned will assist him in his charade."

Later that evening, Captain Ingraham sent me aboard the Huzzar with a note. His note formally demanded the release of Martin Koszta, and said that unless the prisoner was delivered aboard the St. Louis, we would take him by force. The Captain of the Huzzar was reading the note as a huge rocket came streaking across the night sky and splashed down, exploded and sent a column of water high into the air soaking both of us.

"What the hell was that?" Asked the surprised Captain of the Huzzar.

"I have no idea, Sir. Maybe we better take some cover, there may be more if the US fleet did not understand the four hour wait."

"Captain, I have a message for you from signals." An out of breath sailor had rushed up to us and stuck a piece of paper in his hand. He read it and gave it back to the sailor and said, "Get this to the Admiral and sound general quarters. It appears that the crew of the USS Vampire has no idea how to fire their new long range weapons."

I tried not to smile at what Ben had accomplished. The joy was short lived as the Captain said, "I do not have time for a formal reply to your Captain Ingraham, tell him we refuse and if he sends another messenger to us, we will place him along side Mr. Koszta. Do you understand?"

"I will give my captain your reply, Sir." I bowed and returned to the St. Louis as fast as the seamen could row us.

At sunrise, July 2nd, Captain Ingraham, again cleared his decks for action and sounded general quarters. The Austrian war ships cleared their decks and waited for the first rocket to come down out of the sky.

All this was happening with great excitement as the citizens of the port saw and heard these hostile acts, and began to crowd the shore line, eager to see the one sided battle. The Huzzar began signaling the St. Louis with flags, *to avoid the loss of life on both sides, we agree to release the prisoner to the French Consul.*

"It seems you have won, Captain Ingraham, congratulations."

"I will believe it when I see Koszta and the French minister leave that monster over there. I think that the firing of the rocket, last night, was the convincer. They assumed we would kill the French minister along with the Turkish representative. Tell Captain Hagood, when you are back on the Bearing Sea, how close we all came to being at the bottom of the harbor."

"Aye, aye. Sir."

"There are three people getting into a long boat, we need to know if they are Koszta, the Turk, and the French Minister."

"They are pulling for shore, Captain."

We waited about an hour and the long boat returned to the St. Louis with the French Minister. He asked to come aboard.

"Mr. Koszta is in the French Embassy in Smyrna. I will need proof that he is a United States citizen."

"Of course", and we handed him the Presidential warrant. He read it, smiled, and said, "Next time, gentlemen, please have a copy, En Francias." He bowed and turned to leave, under his breath he said, "As soon as the 'Bosch' leave the harbor, we will release Mr. Koszta. Viva La Fayette."

26

Return of Ingraham
Potomac Dockyards

For his intrepid and patriotic action, Captain Ambrose H. Ingraham received a gold medal and a vote of thanks from the Congress. He was taken from Washington to New York to receive another gold medal from the "Sons of Hungary" and other testimonials from several American organizations. The Secretary of the Navy gave him a fine, silver plated chronometer, with embossed lettering which stated that it was a gift from the long shore men of Smyrna, Turkey.

I was given an office in the Army Navy Building and put in charge of communications for the War Department and the Navy Department. My real assignment was in Navy Intelligence and we began running telegraph lines to every naval pier and army depot in the country. Whenever a ship left port, it was out of radio communication, but in port it could send and receive morse code like any other telegraph station. Professor Morse and I never got Sara's radio-meters to work over a mile away and that project was abandoned by the Navy. I often reread Admiral Farragut's letter about Sara's bright and inquisitive mind and what a shame it was that she died so young in the service of her country.

I would find myself thinking, *"Sara, I am not sure that you would have solved our radio transmission problems, but someone, somewhere, will and he or she will get the credit for the idea. A young child is living today in England, Austria or maybe Italy and that child will develop the radio for the world to use."*

Secretary Dobbin kept the detachment together after Turkey. He sent them to Lt. Jerome Lewis' office of shore patrol in the Potomac Dockyards. It was not long until they were at sea again, this time to Havana, Cuba.

On February 28, 1854, the American steamship, Black Warrior, was seized in Havana harbor. It was declared confiscated by the Spanish Government and the cargo was removed and sold. The charge was that the ship was aiding certain guerrilla, anti-government movements in Cuba.

President Pierce had enough, he ordered a blockade of the port of Havana by the Atlantic Fleet. He sent Colonel Christopher Merryweather and a company of US Marines from Port Royal, South Carolina. He was to remain with his troops on board until the president could get a letter to Madrid, Spain. In his letter to the King and Queen, he stated, "If the Court of Spain did not return the Black Warrior, then a state of war would exist between the United States and Spain. He would invade the port of Havana, capture it and make a secure landing area for the US Army of Occupation which would be under the direction of Secretary Jefferson Davis."

The Black Warrior was released within days of the letter arriving in Madrid and the situation was defused. I was called into the Oval Office to discuss what should be done with those US citizens who were giving aid to revolutionary movements in Cuba and throughout the Spanish territories in the western Hemisphere. A plan of action was decided upon when the next out break of "filibustering" occurred.

27
Black Warrior Seizure Reaction
California, 1854

The most violent reactions to Spain's seizure of American property came in the State of California. Those who opposed the peaceful settlement of the "Cuba Problem" were known as filibusters. The most famous of these was General William Walker. He was stationed in San Francisco and without orders of any kind, he asked for volunteers to invade Baja California, a State in Mexico. He landed at La Paz and tried to incite a revolution against the Mexican Government. Mexico City appealed to President Pierce and I was sent to remove General Walker from Mexico. I found him in Sonora, arrested him and released his volunteers. He was held in San Francisco for Court-Martial where he was acquitted of all charges, if he would resign his commission. He gladly resigned and as a private citizen, he recruited sixty men in order to invade Nicaragua in Central America. He landed and immediately attempted to capture the nearest town. He was soon driven out and escaped in a schooner. In September he came back with a much larger force and pushed his "freedom for all Nicaraguans" scheme with so much vigor that in the following month he seized Grenada, the capital. He then placed one of his Nicaraguan supporters in the presidential chair. This task was comparatively easy since Nicaragua never complained to the United States that a US citizen had started a revolution within their country.

Walker was not content with his success, and he appealed to other filibusters within the US to join him in Central America. Many responded and the governments of the isthmus between North and South America joined forces to defeat Walker. A huge battle was fought and the Walker forces were successful and formed the "Republic of Central America" with Walker as the Supreme Governor. He sent a Catholic Priest, Father Virgil, as his ambassador to Washington. President Pierce recognized Virgil over protests from the State Department and the Army Navy Building.

Walker ruled like a despot for two years. Eventually the alliance against him proved too strong and he was compelled to surrender his army. He was deported to the United States to be tried for violating the neutrality laws. He was acquitted. He sailed with his next attempt from Mobile to invade Honduras. At the port of Truxillo, a British Man- of- War captured his invading force and he was turned over to the President of Honduras who ordered his execution.

This was not the plan of action outcome that we had hoped for, but it ended the filibustering into Spanish territories in Central America and throughout the Carribean Sea. My detachment had become a fire brigade, in that we were sent to "hot spots" to settle disputes, arrest violators, and give assistance to local authority. President Pierce was reacting to situations rather than forming a federal policy for the orderly growth of the United States westward. He decided to begin to formulate that policy with Presidential Proclamations that set forth what the United States policies would be in regard to foreign nations, expansion into the western North American Continent and border disputes with other countries. I was sent to Ostend Belgium with his first attempt at a Presidential Proclamation.

28
The Ostend Circular
Belgium

The high handed act of the seizure of the Black Warrior caused great excitement in this country. It, therefore, was in consequence proposed in the House of Representatives to suspend the laws of neutrality between the United States and Spain. This made my trip to the Court of Spain and the demand for indemnity for the seizure of the ship easier. Chris never landed his Marines and the trouble subsided somewhat. The President issued a proclamation, on the first of June, that a special Presidential Commission would meet in Ostend, Belgium. The commission would consist of US members James Buchanan, Ambassador to Great Britain; Charles Mason, Ambassador to France and Marcel Soule, Ambassador to Spain. The Spanish representatives would be appointed by the Court of Spain.

I arrived in the Port of Ostend, Belgium, June 1, 1854, with President Pierce's letters of appointment for ministers Buchanan, Mason and Soule. Mason and Soule had not arrived from Paris or Madrid. I was met at the port by the undersecretary to Ambassador Buchanan and taken to the only four star hotel in Ostend. I was shown to his suite and met his family. His adopted daughter, Harriet Lane, was a cute teenaged girl and his sister, Louise Young Buchanan, was about my age. I wondered where Mrs. Buchanan was, until I realized that there was no, Mrs. Buchanan. Through conversation, I learned that Mr. Buchanan was born in a log cabin at Cove Gap, Pennsylvania, one of eleven children to be born to his father and three wives. His mother was Elizabeth Speer Buchanan. He was the second child born but was the oldest in the household, as the first born, Mary Buchanan died as an infant. The third born, a sister Maria, died in 1849. The fourth, a sister, died with Elizabeth Speer Buchanan during birth.

His father married again, and his half sister Harriet was born, she was the mother of Harriet Lane, who Mr. Buchanan adopted at his sister's death. His brother, John, was born in 1804, but died with his mother at birth. The third wife proved to be a wonderful mother to them all. She bore her husband two sons, named William and George, who died in 1826 and 1832. Louise was the last of eleven children and three farmsteads later.

James Buchanan was over twenty years older than his sister, Louise, and raised her after her mother died. James Buchanan was born at the last of the eighteenth century, served in the War of 1812, was an apprentice seaman in the US Navy and, after the war, was elected to the Pennsylvania House of Representatives. He served until 1821, when he was elected to the US House of Representatives. He was the 9th minister to Russia from January 4, 1832 until August 5, 1833. He was then elected to the US Senate and served until he was selected as the 17th Secretary of State under President Polk. He was now the 14th United States Minister to the Court of St. James and he looked like a President in waiting.

We waited four more days until all the representatives had arrived in Ostend. The Spanish representatives needed a translator even before introductions could be made. I handed three copies of President Pierce's Proclamation to the translators and the representatives from the Court of Spain handed me a document in Spanish from their King. I found a translator and he read it to me. I was amazed at what the document proposed. Cuba was for sale to the highest bidder.

This was in sharp contrast to what the Pierce Proclamation stated: "If Spain, actuated by stubborn pride and false sense of honor, should refuse to sell Cuba to the United States, then by every law, human and divine, we shall be justified in taking it from Spain by force of arms."

The Spanish representatives did not like the threat of war tone of the Pierce document and withdrew for ten days to consider their reply. During that time, I learned more about James Buchanan. He was engaged to Ann Caroline Coleman, the daughter of a wealthy iron manufacturer, while he was in the Pennsylvania House. He spent little time with her during the courtship, spending most of his time building his law practice and serving in the House of Representatives. He was a dashing young man, seen often in the company of attractive young women. And the rumors began to fly. Ann sent him a letter stating that his actions were an insult to her and her family. She ended the engagement and took a fatal overdose of laudanum.

His fiancee's death struck Buchanan hard and in a letter to her father, he stated, "It is not now time for explanation, but the time will come when you will discover that she, as well as, I have been much abused. God, forgive the authors of it .... I may sustain the shock of her death, but I feel that happiness has fled from me forever."

The Coleman family was very bitter and refused him attendance at Ann's funeral. He then vowed that he would never marry and spent his time with his brothers and sisters until their deaths.

Ten days later, the Spanish representatives indicated that they were now ready to begin the sale of Cuba. They produced letters of offers from Great

Britain, France, the Netherlands and the Grand Duchy of Luxemburg. The United States representatives were caught flat footed and they asked for a ten day recess until they could get an offer from Washington to place on the table. The Spanish representatives smiled and said, "Why not take as many days as is required to sail to America and back with your President's reply. We understand that a purchase of this magnitude, in excess of the Louisiana Purchase, will require congressional approval."

I looked at Mr. Buchanan and was about to speak when James Buchanan rose from his seat at the table. He cleared his throat and said, "What you have proposed is a very sensible solution to the problem that my government has always had with the island of Cuba. There is no need for a delay longer than ten days. I will forward all the letters of offer that you brought with you today and recommend that the United States offer at least ten per cent more than your highest offer."

"But, Minister Buchanan, that hardly seems fair. We will need your highest offer to lay before the courts of Great Britain, France, the Netherlands and Luxemburg to see if they would like to make a second higher offer." The translator said.

Mr. Buchanan cleared his voice a second time and spoke so softly that I had to strain to hear what he was saying. He leaned closer to the ear of the translator and said, "If I check with the courts of England, France, the Netherlands and Luxemburg and find out that these offers are not genuine, I will signal Washington to land the United States Marines that are anchored just outside the Havana harbor."

The translator's face became pale and he said, "Mr. Minister, I can not translate that to my representatives from Madrid."

"You translate it, just as I said it, or Captain Caldwell here is going to sail directly to the Atlantic Fleet and commence the invasion of Cuba."

"May I also add what you just said about Captain Caldwell sailing to Cuba?"

"Of course. You may also ask if Spain is ready for a war with the United States. Our time here is not unlimited."

"As you wish, Senior." And he began a rather long explanation of what Mr. Buchanan had said. It was longer than it needed to be. The representatives asked several questions of the interpreter and he asked them of the Americans present.

Question one: Do the other American representatives share Mr. Buchanan's opinions of how to purchase Cuba from Spain?

Answer: All three Americas agree.

Question two: Would the Americans like a brief recess to check the offers from Great Britain, France, the Netherlands and Luxemburg?

Answer: Yes, three days would be nice.

Question three: Why are the Americans so set on invading the island of Cuba?

Answer: It is our last resort. We seek a peaceful purchase of Cuba by the United States or any friendly nation.

Question four: Do you consider Spain a friendly nation?

Answer: Friendly nations do not seize property, steal the contents of ships and sell it for profit. We consider this the action of pirates.

Question five: Spain and the United States have signed the treaty which states that they will remain neutral in any conflicts involving European Nations. Would you not be breaking that treaty by invading Cuba?

Answer: No. The conflict is between Spain and the United States. If the conflict can not be settled by diplomacy then a state of military conflict may be the result of this dispute.

There were no more questions and the panel recessed for three days. James Buchanan was busy with his assistants checking the offers from England, France, the Netherlands and Luxemburg. I spent time with Louise and Harriet. Harriet was a typical young girl, wide eyed and enjoying being in a foreign country like Belgium. Louise was not a girl. She had lived in Russia, France and England with her brother and she had the grace and confidence of a woman of the world. She talked as we walked through a park near the hotel.

"Do you agree with what President Pierce has done the last three years?"

"He is my commander-in-chief, I do not question his decisions. I am allowed to question my direct superior, who is the Secretary of the Navy, but not the President."

"I noticed you said decisions and not orders!"

"That is correct, President Pierce has never given me a direct order. He would issue that order through the Secretary."

"Do you think Franklin Pierce is a 'dough face'?

"What is a 'dough face'? I have never heard that term before."

"It is someone born in the north, but supports the south in issues like states rights and the ownership of slaves."

"His actions in Turkey certainly would not fall in that classification, but his handling of General Walker and the Central American affair might."

"I understand you did not support Mr. Pierce in his handling of General Walker."

"I was sent to arrest him and return him for trial in San Francisco and stop the killing of innocent people."

"By invading Mexico?"

"Certainly not, I did not invade Mexico, we were invited into the country. Where do you get your information?"

"From my brother, he is considering running for president next year. He has many sources of information."

"Your brother is very well known within the Democratic Party, Miss Buchanan. My father is the state chairman for the Democratic Party in South Carolina. He has indicated to me that your brother has tried several times to get the Democratic nomination but has failed in his last several tries. Why does he think he has a chance this time?"

"He is not involved in the current turmoil involving the repeal of the Missouri Compromise or the Kansas-Nebraska Act. The party will turn to him as a compromise candidate. Franklin Pierce will not even be considered for a second term, everything he touches blows up in his face."

"I think that is a little harsh, Miss Buchanan."

"Please call me, Louise, Captain Caldwell. What is your first name?"

"It is, Jason, Miss Buchanan. I think we need to get Miss Harriet back to the hotel."

Louise Buchanan looked shocked. I do not think anyone had ever ended a conversation so suddenly with her.

"I am sorry if I offended you, Jason. I know I am a woman and you think I should be at home cooking and cleaning."

"Louise Buchanan, I do not think any such thing. A woman should be whatever she wants to be. I have known women who are considered the most advanced scientists in their fields of physics, medicine, business and political affairs."

"Name them."

"Dr. Sara Nichols, inventor of the radio meter. Dr. Amelia Early, Georgetown School of Medicine, Juanita de la Veragua, Vice President of the Bank of Veracruz and Queen Victoria of England."

"Jason, you could be just the man I have been looking for." She was smiling. Her ice blue eyes twinkled and a jet black lock of hair fell across her face and she brushed it aside. "Will you call on me again tomorrow? We need to talk without Harriet's big ears taking everything in." She whispered as she took my arm and pressed it against her side.

The next day I called at the hotel and we walked on the beach and found a washed up tree trunk to sit on. She carried a parasol to keep the July sun off her very pale skin.

"Jason?"

"Yes, Louise."

"Do you want to get married or are you married to the Navy?"

"Not today, I think we should wait until your brother is elected to the White House!"

"You rat! What a terrible thing to say. I was asking what you saw in your future. Would you like to have a wife and children some day?"

"That would be wonderful. What about you?"

"I dream of a large family, in a large white house on the top of a hill somewhere in Pennsylvania farm country. I see two boys and two girls. One boy is interested in becoming an Admiral like his father and the other wants to be President of the United States, just like his Uncle James Buchanan. One girl will marry a future President and end up as first lady in The White House, the other will remain single, become a doctor and find a cure for some dreadful disease."

"Without dreams, we are nothing, Miss Buchanan. You are really something. May I write to you when this conference is over?"

"I would be disappointed if you did not, here is my address in London. Come see me if you like."

"I would like that very much. Consider it a date to meet in London as soon as I can get leave."

"Really, you think the Navy would just send you to London?"

"Not on leave, I would have to check with my father to see if any of his ships are scheduled to arrive in South Hampton and when. I would use the leave to get to the nearest port so that his ship could pick me up."

"Do it. This conference will not last much longer." I was looking directly into her eyes and did not realize that our lips were touching until she pulled away and said, "Jason, I want to get to know you, come see me." She rose and we walked back to the hotel.

The six member conference was back in session the next day. The letters of offer proved to be one time offers and no bidding was intended by England, France, the Netherlands, or Luxemburg. James Buchanan offered ten percent above the offer from Luxemburg and the representatives from Spain said that they were pleased and that they would return to Madrid to place our offer before the King of Spain. They would return to Ostend with the response from their King. In the meantime, it would be a good idea if the Americans would produce a sum of fifty percent of the purchase price as a binder to the offer of purchase. James Buchanan nearly fainted. We are not in a position to raise that type of money in just a few days. He would contact Washington and have a reasonable amount transferred through the world bank to the court of Spain.

"Senior Buchanan, take as long as is necessary to raise the required fifty percent binder fee. We are instructed to wait here in Ostend until you provide us with your offer and binder's fee."

I then understood that Spain had no intention of selling Cuba to the United States or anyone else, as our bid was fifty times what the Louisiana Purchase cost the United States. But the dance would continue until August first when both sides were called home for further study. The representatives never returned to Belgium to finalize the sale of Cuba.

29
Civil War Begins
Kansas, March 20, 1856

If you ask anyone, now living, when the Civil War began in the United States, they would answer after Lincoln took office and the firing on Fort Sumter. I remember it differently because I was serving in the Army Navy Building during the Pierce Administration when it really began. It was March 20, 1856, when we received notice from General Lane that his headquarters had been sacked and burned. In his report, he noted that the skies were reddened at night by the flames of burning buildings. Incensed men belonging to both factions rode over the Kansas Territory. They hunted down their political opponents as if they were Seminoles or Apaches. Outrages of the most frightful nature were committed, while armed settlers, despite the trouble, continued to flock from both the slave and free states.

How had we gotten to this point? In January, 1853, Senator Stephen Douglas, of Illinois, chairman of the Senate Committee on Territories, brought forward a bill. It proposed to organize the immense area between Missouri, Iowa and Minnesota on the east, and the Pacific Territories on the west, into two new territories. The southern half was to include the lands lying south of the 40th parallel. It was to be called Kansas Territory. The lands north of the 40th parallel were to be called Nebraska Territory. The bill met instant opposition because slavery was to be allowed in both territories, this meant a repeal of the Missouri Compromise of 1821.

The bill passed the Senate by a vote of 37 to 14 and the House by 113 to 100. It was signed by President Pierce on May 31st. Kansas and Nebraska were left to do as they pleased with the question of slavery. Nebraska chose to be a free territory and stated so in their territorial constitution. Kansas allowed both. Hardly had the Kansas-Nebraska Act passed when associations were formed in the North and East, especially in New England, to send emigrants to Kansas. Churches furnished them with 'Bibles and rifles', and they went with the resolve to hold their ground and fight slavery.

The South, meanwhile, had become alarmed at those trying to settle Kansas with people from free states. Therefore, societies were formed under various names like, "Sons of the South", "Blue Lodges", and "Friends Society." Their purpose was to send enough men into Kansas to out-vote those forwarded by the "Emigrant Aid Society," of New England. The pro-slavery factions organized many companies in Missouri, who bound themselves to help their friends across the border in order to drive the free-state men from the territory. The roads to Kansas for northern settlers led across Missouri. People in the western part of Missouri tried to block them from entering Kansas. So soon, the settlers came through Iowa and entered Kansas from the north. The immigrants continued to gather from both the north and south. The feelings were so bitter that armed collisions took place. A. H. Reeder was sent into the territory as governor, in the fall of 1854. He ordered the election of a territorial legislature. The legislature would pass on the question of slavery. The Missourians came over with tents, artillery and rifles. They were prepared to vote as often as necessary to make sure Kansas was a slave holding territory. The whole number of legal voters in Kansas was 912. When the votes were counted after the election, they numbered more than 6000. The members of the legislature that were elected all supported slavery - not a single free man was elected. They began to write the laws of the territory supporting the right to hold slaves and the governor vetoed the laws. The legislature did not have the right to override a veto and they appealed to President Pierce for this right or the recall of Governor Reeder. The President recalled Reeder and appointed Wilson Shannon, of Ohio, to take his place.

The legislature held its sessions at the town of Shawnee, close to Missouri. The actual settlers met in convention in September, 1855, and decided not to recognize the Shawnee legislature. A delegate convention met at Topeka, on the 19th of October and framed a constitution, which was approved by the 912 voters of the territory. This make Kansas a free territory. Previous to this, the pro-slavery men came together at Lecompton, in March, and adopted a constitution permitting slavery. At this juncture, President Pierce sent a message to Congress, in which he declared that the formation of a free state government in Kansas was an act of rebellion. The violence in the territory was now so great that Congress, in March 1855, appointed a committee of three to go to Kansas and investigate. This committee reported in July, that neither election was valid and the territory should hold a valid election as soon as possible. Thus the civil war began. The free state men established a government at Lawrence, with retired General Nathan Lane at its head. On July 4th President Pierce sent federal troops under my command to arrest anyone still in the free-state legislature in Topeka.

Governor Shannon protested this action and resigned as territorial governor. President Pierce appointed John W. Geary of Pennsylvania. The new governor ordered both factions to disarm and had my federal troops enforce this order. The governor was vigorously supporting the concept of both free and slave holding within the territory. The President told him that the territory was to be slave holding only, and Geary resigned in protest. The President now appointed Robert J. Walker of Mississippi, his reasoning was that a southerner would certainly support the right to hold slaves. When Governor Walker saw the vote counts from the election, where 6000 had voted, he threw out the election and ordered a new one. President Pierce was livid! He sent a replacement for Walker, J. W. Denver. Denver ordered a new election and he was replaced by Samuel Medary. I met with Governor Medary and together we wrote a proposal to President Pierce.

TO: PRESIDENT FRANKLIN PIERCE
FROM: GOVERNOR SAMUEL MEDARY AND SPECIAL FORCES
COMMANDER CAPTAIN JASON CALDWELL
SUBJECT: ENDING THE CIVIL WAR IN KANSAS

THE FINDINGS OF THE CONGRESSIONAL SPECIAL COMMITTEE HAVE BEEN IGNORED. A NEW VALID ELECTION WILL BE HELD FOR THE CITIZENS OF THE TERRITORY ONLY. IF YOU CONTINUE TO APPOINT GOVERNORS, IT WILL PROLONG THE CONFLICT. FINALLY, NO ONE WILL ACCEPT YOUR APPOINTMENT AS GOVERNOR. IT IS OUR POSITION THAT OVER 5000 MEN FROM MISSOURI VOTED IN THE ELECTION THAT YOU SUPPORT. MISSOURI IS A SLAVE HOLDING STATE AND THEIR VOTES ARE NOT VALID IN A KANSAS ELECTION. EVERYONE BUT YOU, INCLUDING THE CONGRESS, SUPPORTS THE CONCEPT OF A ELECTION BY THE PEOPLE OF KANSAS. WE ARE FORWARDING THIS COMMUNICATION TO THE CHAIRMAN OF THE COMMITTEE, SENATOR SUMNER.

WE WILL NOT RESIGN OUR POSITIONS HERE IN KANSAS UNTIL WE HEAR FROM SENATOR SUMNER. IT IS YOUR RIGHT TO REPLACE US AT ANY TIME AND THE WAR WILL CONTINUE. THE LOSS OF LIFE IS UNNECESSARY AND TOTALLY AVOIDABLE. THE UNITED STATES IS A COUNTRY BASED UPON THE WILL OF THE PEOPLE - SO SHOULD THE TERRITORIES UNDER ITS PROTECTION.

Samuel Medar

Jason Edwin Caldwell

When this missive reached the White House and the Senate, the scenes of violence caused by the quarrel over slavery penetrated the halls of Congress.

Charles Sumner delivered a stinging speech on the "crime against Kansas." Senators Cass, Douglas, Mason and Butler all made violent replies, claiming that Sumner was miss-informed and ignorant of the situation in Kansas.

The next day Senator Sumner was approached by Representative Preston Brooks from South Carolina and assaulted so savagely with a cane that he fell unconscious to the Senate floor. Brooks was arrested awaiting the out come of Senator Sumner as he hovered between life and death. The House of Representatives voted to impeach Brooks and he was acquitted. Brooks became a hero in his home state and was re-elected to the house.

President Pierce replaced me, but left Governor Medary in place to oversee the election in Kansas. A letter of censure was placed in my files by President Pierce and a letter of commendation was placed along side it by the Secretary of the Navy.

30
English Recruitment
Washington City, 1856

England at this time was engaged in a war with Russia, and a number of recruits were enlisted in our country for service in the Crimean War. This was a violation of the neutrality laws, though it was sanctioned, or at least winked at, by the British minister to Washington. He and his English consuls at New York, Philadelphia and Cincinnati were dismissed by President Pierce.

President Pierce had met with James Buchanan shortly after the election and confided in him what must be done with Great Britain and Queen Victoria. We must capture a British Man-of-war upon the high seas and tow it to the nearest US friendly port. We must also remove all of the sea men aboard and then claim that we found the ship afloat, abandoned. After resupply, a US Navy crew will sail the ship to South Hampton and return it to the Queen.

In the eyes of the world, the United States would become an important ally of Great Britain. Britain still considered the United States a complaining little nation where the minister from England to Washington City had every right to contract American seamen. It did not matter that sometimes kidnaping and pressing them into service aboard HMS ships was a more common practice. The message to the Queen's Government was this - stop the unlawful pressing of seamen on our shores or we will make the entire British Navy disappear, one ship at a time.

I received the Warrant from President Pierce in the Oval Office nearly twenty years ago. I remember thinking, we can not do this, can we? The Warrant was clear. I and the Navy marines serving under me would not be punished in any court within the United States. It did not cover what would happen if we were captured and returned to England. The United States Navy was not involved with this action. This was funded from the War Department's special allocation funds and the Secretary of War was not aware of the Warrant. I was not to use Navy vessels, funds, or intelligence office personal. I would be granted a reassignment from my position as Captain in Naval Intelligence, Navy Building, Washington City, to the White House.

A Presidential Warrant is not a voluntary request. If you refuse, you are arrested and are detained until the mission described in the warrant is complete. Many warrants are open ended and therefore, you could remain in custody forever. I blinked when I read the warrant, returned it to President Pierce and said, "I will not fail you, Mr. President." I remember thinking, *"God help me. I will never see my home in South Carolina again.*

The mission, if you could call it that, began with my trying to find out where the pressed American seamen were being held. Sure, the Minister had been sent home, but his staff was still here using the British Embassy. If I could get myself and a few marines unnoticed into the bunch of held seamen, maybe there was hope. I left the Oval Office and walked to the Army Navy Building. Entering the side entrance across from the White House, I bumped into my aide, Sergeant Schneider. "Tom, what are you still doing here?"

"Waiting to talk to you, Sir. Your office is locked and a note says to go to the basement of the White House. What does that mean?"

"It means you and I have another mission, Sergeant! Go across to the Hay-Adams and see how many of our special attachment marines you can find. Then have them change into civilian clothes and search the docks for any activity, you know, men coming and going at all hours, into rented warehouses or buildings. We are looking for the Americans that have been kidnaped by the Brits."

"What do we do with them once we find them, Sir?" "Nothing, we are going to join them."

"Join them?"

"That is my plan, Sergeant, I will let you know more when you find your mates."

Tom Schneider was a third generation Navy Marine. He stood well over six feet, six inches tall and weighed about twice my weight. He always protected my blind side on a mission. I could not count the number of times that he had saved my operation by his shear will. He carried a modified weapon, first used by the English Navy, which had 8 barrels that rotated into position to fire so fast that it was like having eight marines instead of one at your side. A normal seaman could not operate such a weapon unless it was mounted on deck. Tom Schneider, on the other hand, was no normal seaman. I had seen him hoist the weapon off the mount and sweep the top sides of more than one ship. And later, he was bringing several of the weapons on land missions as well. He fired 48 rounds while another marine loaded a second weapon so it could be handed back to him.

Thomas Q. Schneider was a one man wrecking machine. The other marines in my special attachment used new Henry repeating rifles and carried extra cartridges in a special pack arrangement. This allowed them to be mobile aboard a ship or like ten times their number on a land mission. The detachment was small, designed to be covert.

The covert part was going to be tested on this mission. Two days later Sergeant Schneider and Corporal Mason walked into the White House basement and found the little office in the corner which was marked "Records and Receipts" and dropped down into two chairs opposite my desk.

"Sir, we think we have a handle on where the Brits are holding our seamen."

"Thank you, Sergeant. Here is what I want you to do."

Two more days had passed before the Sergeant and Corporal could put our plan into action. It was simple if they could get it to work. After four days of watching the docks they had identified what they thought was the boss man and the strong arms that were bringing seamen to a warehouse on the Potomac. Tom and Sam Mason had followed the boss man to a boarding house on Maryland Avenue and had visited his room late at night. Tom had knocked on his room door and then shoved his giant fist through the side panel and threw open the door. The man was so terrified that he did not move. Tom shouted, "You rotten limey son-of-a-whore, you have my brother locked up."

The man stammered, "Wait a minute your worship, you must have me mistaken for someone else."

"Not bloody likely. Get your ass out of that bed, so I can cut off your ears."

The man laid there frozen, so Tom grabbed the front of his night shirt and tore it from his body.

"Now listen, you English bastard, here is what I can do for you. I will give you twenty gold double eagles for my brother's release and I can tell you where you can press another ten seamen if you like. They are drunk nearly every night in a saloon near Lafayette Square. You can pick them up in the square when they pass out. What do you say to that, or do I have to kill you and go on to the next of you Brits?"

"Twenty double eagles? Who is this brother of yours? Why is he worth so much? Never mind, show me the gold!" "I will give you two tonight and the other eighteen when we pick up the ten seamen and drag them down to the docks for you. When do you want to do this?"

"Right away, tomorrow night, I have to deliver a shipment off shore to a waiting HMS for passage back to Bermuda."

"Good, we will see you tomorrow night at 12 o'clock in the square. Bring as many men as you like, chap, you are going to need them, because if my brother is not in that warehouse, then you are dead."

Tom handed him two gold eagles and fled out the door with Sam in tow. Out on the street, Tom laughed and said, "Never underestimate the greed of an Englishman."

"Yes, he did not even ask the name of your brother." "He has no plans to hand over a seaman to me, he thinks that we are coming tomorrow night with the gold and he and his friends will overpower and take it from us. Then he will deliver us along with the others to the waiting ship."

"Do you think he was telling the truth about taking American seamen to Bermuda, Sergeant?"

"It makes sense, the only ports that the British have are in Canada or Bermuda. If they sail from Bermuda on a set schedule to lay off shore a couple of miles, they could easily be met by a small boat. I think this is the information that the captain was looking for."

We had many items to get together before midnight of the next night. I had Sam Mason check the boarding house on Maryland Avenue to see if the man registered as Milton Black, Esquire had checked out. Tom checked the warehouse on the Potomac docks to see if the Americans were still there or if they had been moved. If our plans were correct, Milton Black would be waiting for us in La Fayette Square with men to take Tom's gold. At least two men would be left to guard the warehouse. So a coordinated attack was necessary, we had to capture or kill the men guarding the warehouse. At nearly the same time, we had to make sure Milton Black was taken alive in the square. I doubted that any of the hired thugs would know anything about where to meet a British Man-of-War in US territorial waters.

The detachment arrived in Lafayette Square around 11:40 and were singing and slapping each other on the back while staggering around in a tight little circle. Inside their cloaks each had a loaded pistol, and marine killing knife. No one showed at midnight. We waited another few minutes and I told Tom and Sam to walk through again and wait at the Jackson memorial. Milton Black and his men appeared out of the darkness and demanded the gold. That is when the real action began. In a matter of minutes, Black was lying on the ground with his hands tied behind him. Two of his companions were bleeding so badly we could not stop the flow of blood.

The other four were shocked at the speed of the attack. Black kept saying he was a British diplomat and demanded to be taken to the Embassy. I asked him for his credentials and when he could not produce them, I told him I thought he was a common criminal and should be turned over to the district police.

"Unless," I said, "we can come to some sort of agreement. I could take you offshore and release you to return to Bermuda."

He liked that idea. In less than an hour we had turned four bodies into St. Elizabeth morgue for special handling. Two were taken from the warehouse and two from the square. With my identification and past relationship with the hospital, the bodies would disappear, courtesy US Navy. The discovery of bodies left on the streets of Washington City would reach newspapers and the British Embassy and cause a different kind of stink.

Tom had a man to man talk with the seamen held in the warehouse and informed them that they would soon be taking a pleasure cruise from Washington to Nantucket. They would be released in Nantucket and provided passage back to Washington if they wished. For now, all they had to do was act like prisoners until the time necessary to take the British ship by force. Each was given a knife and told to hide it in his boot. Tom looked at a large sailor and asked him if he had ever fired a model 1440 US Naval deck gun. The look that Tom got was enough for Tom to know that he was talking to a loader, not a shooter. He broke the deck gun down and showed him how to load it, saying," If you do not do this right when we try to board, you will get us both killed."

By 2 o'clock we had the procession going. Milton Black was brought from a back room and told that we were taking over his operation and selling these seamen to the British. I explained that it was important to us that his boat be used to ferry the pressed seamen so that it would not to be fired upon by the man-of-war. If he used a password, he should use it. After docking with the ship and getting payment from the captain we would release him to return to Bermuda and we would return to Washington, richer for one night's work.

We all got on board from the docks and headed down the Potomac and into the Chesapeake as the sun was rising. We needed to hurry, Black said, because the captain of HMS *Resolute* had instructions to sail away at sunrise and return to international waters. My plans were not to approach a foreign ship in the dark of night - rather to catch her in a crew change as the sun rose and everything appeared normal. Alas, we were too late, we had indeed spent too much time on the Potomac and as the sun rose, the *Resolute* sailed away.

"Now what?" Black asked.

"Will she be back tomorrow night?"

"Yes, she lays out here every night for a week waiting for us."

"Good, then you can get some sleep, get below." A small steam powered ferryboat, overcrowded with seamen and US marines, waiting at the mouth of the Potomac was not a normal thing.

I decided to see what type of seamen the British had kidnaped. What a day at sea it turned out to be. Two of the men had never set foot on a large boat or ship and would be worthless on the sail to Nantucket. I asked them if they could cook, one shook his head and one said yes. The other said he worked on the docks and knew how to move supplies on and off ships. Not a total waste, we would need skills like that before we reached Madaket Harbor on Nantucket.

We slept or rested in shifts, got familiar with Black's ferryboat and waited for the *Resolute* to return. After the sun had set and the moon was high, we found the British Man-of-War drifting and not at anchor. I got Black up on deck and asked, " What is that man-of-war doing drifting in these waters? Have you met her like that or has she always been anchored.?"

"We always found her anchored, never adrift."

"You show yourself as we pull along side, Black. If you give the wrong password, I will cut your throat and throw you overboard."

We drew closer and Tom said in a low voice, "I do not like this, captain, they are waiting to cut us down."

"If they are, they are going about it all wrong. Look, the cannon are not moved forward, there is no activity on the forward deck, no one on the rails. Where the hell are they?"

We drew along side and reduced sail in order to keep pace. I ordered that we try to throw hooks and catch the starboard rails. Several hooks were thrown up towards the rails and several caught. My marines began to pull themselves on board. Several minutes passed and then Sam came back to the rail and shouted down to me on the ferry.

"Captain, the Brits only have a skeleton crew, they are sick and two are dead. The brig is full of American seamen."

"Are the Americans sick, too? Can they be released to help us sail to Nantucket? Let us all get on board and we can decide what to do next."

Within minutes our detachment had located two more dead and found the rest of a skeleton crew sick below decks. The Americans were hungry, but not sick. I decided to offload the sick onto the ferry and have two of the sailors we had rescued from the brig try to make it up the Potomac and into Washington City. I pulled Sam aside and said, " I hate to give this to you, Sam, but I don't know what made the crew sick, they might die before you reach Washington. If any do, bury them in the Chesapeake or the Potomac. The others need to be taken to St. Elizabeth for processing. Good luck, we have to get this ship to Madaket, clean it and resupply it so that the Navy can be the heros and return it to Queen Victoria."

"I can do this, Captain, I want to get off this death ship as soon as I can."

An hour later the British crew of the *Resolute* were sailing away from us towards the Potomac in the ferryboat with Sam Mason at the helm and a very angry Milton Black tied to the main mast. I watched until they disappeared into the night and reminded myself that this would be the last time that I would see Corporal Mason. Some of the paper work I processed in the "basement" before we left on this operation was for the promotion to Staff Sergeant for Sam and Master Gunnery Sergeant for Tom. Both these men served the nation without question and the least the nation could do was increase their pay by nine dollars a month.

The sun rose as we sailed down the Chesapeake towards the Atlantic. The crew's quarters were a foul place for anyone to enter. We were short handed, but I ordered buckets over the side to get some sea water to wash down the entire area. We had expected a bloody fight to happen that night and the aftermath of any naval engagement was the removal of human blood form the decks and gangways. The men did not seem to mind washing vomit instead of blood. I ordered everything that was not nailed down to be brought up on deck from the crew's quarters and thrown overboard. Sickness aboard a ship could be as simple as spoiled food or a dangerous as smallpox. Not knowing what caused the deaths of the four crew members would nag on all of us until we reached Nantucket and the whaler's harbor waiting there for us. I ordered that all food we did not need for the short sprint to Nantucket be thrown over board. We kept the barrels of fresh water, a potential source of sickness, but we had no choice. The hard tack was kept as well as a barrel of apples.

The next few days I spent in the ship's Captain quarters going through the ship's log and various papers. Nearly all would be intelligence on how the British were using their ports in Bermuda and eastern Canada. Tom and his marines unbolted, unlashed and otherwise stripped the ship of anything useful to a man-of-war. The Union Jack was pulled down and the black flag for sickness aboard was raised in case we met any other English ships.

When the *Resolute* entered Madaket Harbor it looked like a very large merchant marine, not a war ship. Her decks were covered with crates and boxes filled with stripped materials. Kegs of powder were stacked for offloading. Nothing was left on board. Boxes contained rope, pitch, soap and even uniforms. The plan was to return a "ghost ship". The ship's company to replace us on the voyage to England would bring aboard only the supplies to transport the *Resolute*. The US Navy would escort the *Resolute* in order to protect her and the men sailing on her and to return the US transport team home.

The transatlantic cable had been laid during the Buchanan Administration. Queen Victoria and President Buchanan were the first to exchange cablegrams. I wondered how the British High Command would react when the President cabled them that a British Merchant Marine called the *Resolute* had been found by an American Whaler, abandoned in the North Atlantic. He would also inform them that he would provide US Navy escort ships and an American crew to return HMS *Resolute* to a port of their choosing.

My mission was to end in Nantucket, but the Secretary of the Navy thought I should not miss out on the reaction in England at the return of the *Resolute*. Orders were handed to me by Captain Benjamin Hagood as I came on aboard the USS *Intrepid*. I had served with Ben on the *Intrepid* after we graduated from the academy.

I asked Ben, "Why did the Secretary send a light cruiser to escort the *Resolute*?"

He said, "The Secretary thought that a light cruiser would send the right message. You know all it takes to take care of a British Man-of-War is a US light cruiser. And besides, we do not know that HMS *Resolute* is anything other than a large merchant ship, thanks to you and your men."

"They did a good job in the short time that they had to work. The sea lanes have things floating in them from the Chesapeake to Nantucket, I am sure. Anything that we could use, we saved and there was this fellow that we rescued in Washington that was a dock hand, he was very useful. I wish he would join the Navy, I could use him."

"The seamen that you picked up in Washington and those aboard the *Resolute* are being sent home tomorrow. How did you manage to sail from the Chesapeake to here with that bunch?"

"They were so busy and glad to be set free, I do not think they minded a bit."

"What about your detachment of Marines? They are not ordered on to England are they?"

"No, they are not. Do you have room for them on the transport back to Washington City?"

"I will see to it. You can get some sleep in my cabin while I go ashore and cut some orders."

I went below opened the door marked 'Captain's Quarters' and fell into the bunk, I did not take off my boots and fell asleep.

31

Royal Naval Dockyards
Bermuda

Lieutenant A.J. Schmidts of the Royal Marines strode across the quadrangle and looked up at the twin clock towers of the Royal Naval Dockyards and noted the morning report for his commanding officer was going to be a tad late. He had spent more time doing his morning duties than he had thought. The conversation with the executive commander of the returning vessel HMS *Storch* had been most disturbing indeed. Each returning ship to the dockyards was met by Lieutenant Schmidts and his ever present notebook. He had already entered the time of docking, and was waiting to enter the number and names of the new recruits for the paymaster's list when the commander blurted out that HMS *Resolute* did not meet his ship at the half way point. The *Storch* waited a whole day and then steamed for the Chesapeake. They were several days late in returning to Bermuda because of the vast search network that they were forced to cover. He listed the items that they found floating on the surface of the ocean. There was no doubt that the items were from the *Resolute*. Wooden crates of food still had the markings of the Bermuda storehouse.

The *Resolute* would be listed as missing, whereabouts unknown. This meant that the daily report would certainly not be dull. A. J. could not remember in his thirteen months at the dockyards, of any ship listed as missing. Sure, there were vessels lost at sea due to storms, but the middle Atlantic had been calm for weeks. In time of war, vessels were captured, sunk, damaged during repair or simply ran aground somewhere on patrol. This was peacetime and weather had not been a factor. That left misadventure, such as fire aboard ship, a plague like sickness, or pirates.

Now he would have to fill out more forms for the daily report. A. J. was a slow typist and he did not like spending his day filling out forms. He was a Royal Marine, he should be on board one of the ships on patrol or on one of the supply ships going back and forth to South Hampton. He was small for his age, but he was a sharp shooter and would be ideal for the topside rigging of a war ship. Instead, he continued to type day after day.

"Lieutenant, front and centre." barked the officer of the day. "I need those report sheets, I am ready to report to the Admiral."

"Yes, Sir. Just finishing up the last one, Sir."

"I will file this missing while on patrol report and see what the old man wants to do about it."

The officer of the day grabbed the last sheet, stuffed it into his bundle and quick marched to the door and headed towards the quadrangle that Lieutenant Schmidts had just crossed.

The Royal Navy Dockyards had been expanded and almost rebuilt after the American Revolution. The Royal Navy was no longer free to dock and harbor in places like Boston, New York, or ports south of there. A major effort was now underway to make Bermuda the strong hold of the middle Atlantic. Now, Vice-Admiral, Lord Hornsby, waited and watched for any opportunities to establish new bases anywhere from Florida to New Brunswick, Canada. He had studied the port of Charleston in South Carolina. Fort Sumter would be the only trouble spot if he could somehow convince the State of South Carolina that they needed the Royal Navy to escort merchant ships from there to England. He had sent an envoy to Charleston and then to Columbia, the State Capital. Fort Sumter was a US Federal depot and not a state militia facility. State officials could do nothing about how the federal government used Fort Sumter.

"Yes, yes. What is it, Farnsworth?" The Vice Admiral was not pleased to see the officer of the day so early in the morning.

"Special report about the missing ship, *HMS Resolute*." Major Farnsworth was at rigid attention.

"As you were, Major"

Farnsworth went from rigid to one arm extended towards Admiral Hornsby and thought, " *I hope the old adage of shooting the messenger will not apply here.*"

The Admiral put on his reading glasses and scanned the sheets. "I know that Captain Swilling had a skeleton crew on his runs back and forth to the Chesapeake, but he is an excellent ship's commander. He would never have been taken by pirates, private or American sponsored. That only leaves an all out effort by the US Navy. That would mean that the *Resolute* must be in an American harbor. Send a packet of information to the British Counsel in Washington City. Indicate that I will need intelligence on US Naval activities during the last week. I need to have his agents check the Potomac Dockyards to see if our seamen recruiting efforts are still underway. Tell him to find Agent Milton Black and ship him to me here in Bermuda. The actions of the Americans will not be tolerated." Throwing the report back into Farnsworth's chest, he said, "That will be all, Major".

Major Farnsworth left the Admiral's office and walked back across the quadrangle and into his own office.

"Lieutenant, front and centre." he called out.

"Yes, Sir."

"Bring your notebook and come in here. I want to dispatch a message to the British Counsul in Washington. What is the fastest way to get that done?"

"We have a steam powered packet ship, bound for Washington scheduled to leave at the end of the week, Sir."

"Belay that and reschedule to this afternoon. Now take down and send the following:

> TO: Sir Lowell Crampton, British Minister
> British Embassy, 1412 Pennsylvania Ave.
> Washington City, USA
> FROM: Rupert V. Hornsby, Vice-admiral and commander
> Royal Naval Dockyards, Bermuda
> SUBJECT: HMS Resolute

A request for current information regarding the following:

(1) Status of seaman recruitment project currently underway your location,

(2) Location of Agent Milton Black - currently AWOL this location,

(3) Last known reported location for HMS Resolute - currently absent from this location, and

(4) Report of any unusual US Naval activities, late December.

Be advised that Agent Black is to report here as soon as possible, repeat as soon as possible. Also advise closure of temporary holding quarters Potomac Dockyards.

The packet ship would have diplomatic privilege, but Major Farnsworth had learned not to put anything into writing that could not be explained away as diplomatic communication. This was probably the best he could do to light a fire under Sir Thomas. He waited until his Lieutenant had typed it and then he signed with his name acting on behalf of the Admiral. It would be several days before any information would arrive from Washington and he would try to stay away from the Admiral's office until he had something in writing to show him. For now he would busy himself with other duties and hope for the best. Three days later the packet ship returned with the following information:

TO: HORATIO FARNSWORTH, ROYAL NAVAL DOCKYARDS
FROM: JOHN A. QUIGLEY, MILITARY ATTACHE BRITISH EMBASSY
SUBJECT: HMS RESOLUTE

PLEASE BE ADVISED THAT SIR CRAMPTON HAS BEEN CALLED TO LONDON REGARDING SUBJECT NAMED ABOVE. HMS RESOLUTE PRESENTLY UNDERWAY FROM NANTUCKET HARBOR TO SOUTH HAMPTON, MANNED BY US NAVY CREW. EXPECTED ARRIVAL JANUARY 5 THRU 7. QUEEN'S REPRESENTATIVE, LORD NAPIER TO ACCEPT RETURN OF HMS RESOLUTE AT THAT TIME AND PLACE.

NO INFORMATION ON PRESENT LOCATION OF AGENT MILTON BLACK - LAST REPORTED LOCATION ABOARD HMS RESOLUTE. NO INFORMATION ON PRESENT LOCATION OF TEMPORARY WORKERS ASSIGNED TO POTOMAC DOCKYARDS - LAST REPORTED LOCATION ON BOARD HMS RESOLUTE. NO INFORMATION ON PRESENT LOCATION OF CAPTAIN AND CREW. NO KNOWLEDGE OF UNUSUAL US NAVAL ACTIVITIES IN CHESAPEAKE, ALL VESSELS STILL IN POTOMAC DOCKYARDS.

RESPECTFULLY SUGGEST THAT YOU CONTACT OFFICE OF THE ADMIRALTY, LONDON. NO FURTHER COMMUNICATION ON THIS SUBJECT IS DESIRED FROM COMMANDER ROYAL NAVAL DOCKYARDS.

Major Farnsworth read the communique and smiled, the Admiral is not going to like this, he thought. He jumped from his desk, pulled on his tunic, grabbed his cover and started across to the Admiral's office. He waited nearly an hour for the Admiral to see him, but the Admiral was in a good mood when he greeted him.

"Come in, come in, Farnsworth. What was in the packet from Washington?" He began reading and his mood changed. "Major, we have a puzzle here, and I do not like puzzles. Black missing, captain and crew missing - but the ship is sailing back to England. The recruits that were supposed to be sent here are missing. Too many loose ends.

It is obvious what happened, HMS *Resolute* was taken inside the Chesapeake by the US Navy. How else could they be sailing it to England? The captain, crew, Agent Black and my recruits are all in an American prison somewhere."

"Yes, Sir."

"Well, there will be battle damage, Swilling would not have handed his ship over, he would have fought to the last man."

"Yes, Sir. Maybe that is exactly what happened. Maybe Agent Black, Captain Swilling, his crew and the recruits all are dead at the bottom of the Chesapeake."

"Good thinking, Farnsworth. Fire off a level 3 communique to the Admiralty, attention Lord Napier, telling him to look for any battle damage on HMS *Resolute*. You are good at writing those damn things - I am always too blunt. I am a sailor, not a diplomat, Farnsworth. I want our communique on the next steamer to South Hampton, can we make it before January 7th?"

"It will be close Admiral, I will do my best."

"You always do, Farnsworth, you always do - dismissed."

Back in his own office, the Major was busy putting into diplomatic language what his Admiral had said in his office. It was completed in just a few minutes, typed up by his Lieutenant and hurried down to the docks. It was placed on the next packet ship to South Hampton so that it could be handed to Lord Napier before he accepted the HMS *Resolute*.

Weeks had passed and Major Farnsworth had forgotten about his message to the Office of the Admiralty until a returning packet ship docked and brought a return. It was addressed to **Lieutenant** Farnsworth and not Vice-Admiral Hornsby. It was the front page of the London Times which carried the photographs and articles describing in gushing terms how Lord Napier and the Queen entertained the Captain and Crew of the returning HMS *Resolute*. One of the articles mentioned that a new era of cooperation was underway between the United Kingdom and the United States of America. The Queen had recalled four foreign ministers from America and the Admiralty was sending a new commander for the Royal Naval Dockyards. The Queen also announced that US Ships were now welcome to dock for emergency repairs in Bermuda. These repairs would be made without regard to cost in partial repayment of the kindness shown by the United States and President Pierce.

32

Potomac Dockyards
Washington City

Corporal Samuel Adam Mason of the US Marines stood at the helm of the little ferryboat and watched as the sick and dying were spread out over the deck. His two man crew had a gruesome job ahead of them. They had been given a bolt of linen sacking material with which to wrap the dead. Each body was wound, weighted and slipped overboard. Four hours into the trip back to the Potomac docks only four people were still alive on the ferryboat. Milton Black was still tied to the mast. Mason remained at the helm and two American sailors shoveled coal into the boiler.

One of the last things that his Captain had said was, " Be careful and approach the dockyards so that you can dock the ferry boat at the same pier and slip space that we left two days before. Sam, we have to hope that the British Embassy will not have agents already in place."

It was early morning when the tired little four man crew of the ferryboat tied up in the dockyards. There did not seem to be anyone around that should not be on the piers. They untied Black and walked to the closest guard house and asked for a Lieutenant Lewis.

"Lieutenant Lewis is in his office at shore patrol headquarters, Corporal," replied the shore patrolman. "Do you know where that is?"

"Thank you, that is no problem. Captain Caldwell has sent this man to Washington City for processing at St. Elizabeth. He said you would know how to get him there."

"Did the Captain give you any written orders, Corporal?"

"No, Sir. He told me to find Lieutenant Lewis and have you take charge of this man."

"Thank you, Corporal, I know Captain Caldwell and I will take charge of the prisoner.

"I am not a prisoner", shouted Black, "I am a member of the British Counsul here in Washington City."

"Please, show me your identification, Sir." replied the shore patrolman.

"I have no identification, these three took it from me", lied Black.

"Alright, everyone show me their identification, now."

The three Americans pulled US Navy papers and showed them. The patrolman glanced at the three sets of papers, winked at Sam Mason and said, "Look, whoever you are, would you like me to call you a carriage and have you taken to the British Embassy? No. wait, we can not do that, the Embassy has been closed."

"Would you like to go anywhere else?"

Black thought about it a few seconds before saying, "Just get me the cab. I will tell them where to take me."

"Good, do you have any money?"

Of course, Black had no money so a special horse drawn van with ST. ELIZABETH MORGUE printed on its sides pulled away from the shore patrol house about an hour later. Agent Black would not be pressing any more American seamen.

At about that same time, Corporal Mason was entering the shore patrol office and asking for Lieutenant Lewis. He noticed a young woman was sitting behind a desk marked *Shore Patrol Headquarters*.

"Excuse me, do you work here, Miss?"

"Yes, Corporal, Lieutenant Lewis was given permission to hire a civilian and he chose me!"

"Well, good for you. I was ordered to report to Lieutenant Lewis as soon as I docked."

"Let me see if he is busy, Corporal, who shall I say you are?"

"Tell him that Captain Caldwell's Corporal has returned from a secret mission."

She blushed and said, "I need your name, please."

"Oh, it is Sam, what is yours?"

She blushed again, turned on her heel and walked to the office door, knocked and stuck her head in and said, "Sir, there is a Corporal Sam out here. Says he is Captain Caldwell's Corporal."

"Thank you, Miss White, show him in, please."

"The Lieutenant will see you now, Corporal."

Sam filed away the fact that he knew her last name but not her first. He walked into the office and stopped 18 inches from the front of the Lieutenant's desk, and snapped a crisp salute. Lewis was busy with a pile of papers in front of him. "Mason, Mason, you must be here somewhere," he muttered, "Oh, yes, here it is, congratulations Corporal you are now a Staff Sergeant."

He glanced up and saw that Sam was still holding his salute. "Come on, Sergeant, you know that Marines do not salute indoors!"

Then he broke into a wide grin and said, "How the hell are you, Sam? You know when your Captain requested that you bunch of jar heads all be listed as SP, I had my doubts. But I am now proud to be a part of his operations. How did the OP go?"

"Fine, Sir, am I really a Sergeant or are you pulling my leg again?"

Lewis handed him the paperwork, he took it and read it. "Well, I will be damned, I never expected anything like this. I expected to die on that damn ship. The crew we took off was really sick, not a one made it back."

"Do you need to report to Sick Bay, Sergeant?"

"No, I never felt better."

"We had better get you over to the Navy building so that they can debrief you and put your summary report on Captain Caldwell's desk."

"Sir, can I ask a question out of school?"

"Sure, Sam, what is it?"

"What is your Miss White's first name?"

"So, you like what you see, Sergeant? Rachael is 19 years old, is unmarried and unattached, as far as I know. She lives with her parents over across the Potomac and rides a ferryboat to work every day. You could accidentally, on purpose, meet her again on the docks, whenever you like. But do not hang around here, she has work to do."

Good advice, that works, is indeed greater than gold. Sergeant Mason and Rachael White met accidentally-on purpose everyday for the next week. Whenever they were together, Sam could not take his eyes off her and she blushed at him until everyone working in the shore patrol office thought they might be a couple. Sam was invited to meet Rachael's parents and the 30 day leave that he was granted flew by. Tom and the rest of the detachment arrived about 5 days later from Nantucket. They each reported to Lieutenant Lewis's office.

Tom thanked Lieutenant Lewis for his promotion to Master Sergeant and then asked, "Has Corporal Mason reported in yet?"

"Corporal Mason is not here, but Staff Sergeant Mason reported in 5 days ago. He was shocked that Captain Caldwell processed his papers."

"Sam made Sergeant? He has only been in 4 years, Sir"

"I know, but these are difficult times and things move faster. He has even met a young lady!"

"Sam has a girlfriend? He is only a boy, Sir."

"I know, he enlisted when he was only 18 years old, but it looks serious with her, she is the one that works in the outer office. You met her as you came in."

Lieutenant Jerome B. Lewis was a lifer. He fully intended to make the Navy his career for as long as the Navy would have him. After all, his job was like any other Chief of Police in a major city of America. He dealt with drunken sailors on leave, sailors who reported late for assignments, and therefore listed as absent without leave and deserters. The real miss- fits would desert but were too stupid to leave the immediate area of Washington City. They would need to be arrested and held for court marshal. He dealt with the Navy's Judge Advocate General's Office on a routine basis and he liked the interaction with Naval Intelligence.

As long as Captain Caldwell's operations were on the Atlantic Ocean, Lieutenant Lewis was involved from an operation's start to finish. He provided warehousing, materials and small boats of all types. Whenever an operation started from Washington City and required over land transport he arranged for train berths. This allowed the detachment to sleep on long runs from Washington City to the western most terminal in Council Bluffs, Iowa. He would then turn the detachment over to General Dodge in Council Bluffs. General Dodge's office could provide barge or river boats up or down the Missouri River, or they could provide heavy wagons from the Army to haul men and supplies into the western territories. Army escort was provided from one western fort to another, and in this manner the detachment could leap frog from one protected area to another. The unsettled parts of the west were lawless in a sense that American Indians roamed freely and outlaw bands took anything of value anytime they liked.

The Pierce Administration began in March of '53 and was about to end with James Buchanan taking the oath of office in March '57. In the last four years, Captain Caldwell had reported to Secretary of the Navy, James C. Dobbin of North Carolina. The interaction with the Army on certain assignments had to be coordinated through the Secretary of War, Jefferson Davis of Mississippi. The Army Navy building in Washington City hummed with activity during these years. The boundary between Mexico and the United States was rectified in '54. A reciprocity treaty with England was made in '54 and opened the St. Lawrence River to American vessels.

33
Cruise of the Intrepid
Atlantic Ocean

Captains Benjamin Hagood and Jason Caldwell were standing on deck of the *USS Intrepid* looking out to sea and the silhouette of *HMS Resolute.* The *Intrepid* was a light cruiser, it was steam and sail powered. Two giant paddle wheels were driven by steam boilers with a single smoke stack near the center of the ship. There were large masts for sail both forward and aft. The fore and aft decks bristled with cannon, deck guns of all types, rocket launchers and mortars. "Jason, I can not believe that no shots were fired in the capture of that British Man-of-War. That has to be a first in recorded history!"

"Too bad no one will ever hear about it, Ben. We were very lucky that no blood was shed, but there was still loss of life. I do not even know if my squad leader, a Corporal Mason, is still alive or if he died of whatever was taking the British seamen's lives." "You will be home next month, Jason, relax and enjoy your time on *Intrepid.*"

"I am not like you, Ben, I am not a ship's captain anymore. I miss the action of Naval Intelligence and working directly for the Secretary of the Navy. My assignment was to end on Nantucket, I have no idea why the Secretary wants me in South Hampton or London, England. I will be like a fish out of water."

Ben smiled at my little pun, here we were in the middle of the Atlantic Ocean, talking like 1837 classmates again. Ben had entered the Naval Academy from Savannah, Georgia.. He took the same courses that I did, took the required summer cruises and signed on as an Ensign in the Atlantic fleet. He loved the long months at sea and was promoted up the ranks, until now he had his own ship. So far during this trip, I saw that his men loved him and would sail with him off the face of the earth if he asked them to.

"What are you smiling about, Jason?"

"Do you remember Master Chief Gunnerman?"

"Yes, Gunnerman scared the shit out of us. We jumped into a straight line and attempted to come to attention. I screamed, "Yeas, Sir." in my best southern drawl. He said, 'You do not 'Yeas, Sir, me,' you dumb ass. I am not an officer. The proper response is aye, aye.'"

"Then Gunnerman turned to his officer and said, "Sir, they are hopeless, I will throw their ass's back on the train and send them back to where they came from.""

"That is right, Jason. I remember the officer saying, 'Let me have a crack at them. Gentlemen, in just four short years you may be standing where I am, a graduate of the United States Military Academy, looking at a bunch of shave tails. You will be shaking your head and wondering how they are ever going to make Naval officers and gentlemen. The Chief here will get all of you onto the depot grounds and be with you through your processing. That will be all.'"

"We could never please Gunnerman, I remember him saying, 'What the hell is this? Hoist your gear, means throw it on your shoulder, I am not going to show you babies how to do things. I am not your mother!'"

"After our first year, whenever I saw you, I yelled, "I am not your mother! If that failed to get a laugh, I would scream, I am not going to show you babies how to do things!"

"We have good memories together, Ben. It has been one adventure after another. I wonder how this one will end?"

"I think the Secretary wants you to meet with Lord Napier. The Secretary thinks Lord Napier is going to want some answers. Just before we get to South Hampton, we are going to transfer you to HMS *Resolute* and you are to represent yourself as the captain assigned to return the ship to the Queen. You have read your orders that I handed you?" "Yes, Ben, they are not marked secret or eyes only. Did you read them?"

"No, they were sealed. What with you being the head 'cloak and dagger' captain in the Navy, I figured you would tell me if you could.""It says, I am to share everything with you and that you are in command of this operation, I am only along for the ride, it seems." "No, Jason, I think it is more than that. I think the president 'wants' you to sell the idea to the British Empire that we are no longer a colony and should be a full-fledged ally. In order to do that, the British have to know that we took their ship and we can do it again. It is 'put up or shut up' at this point."

"I can not tell them we took their ship. Besides, we were handed the ship by a crew that could not protect themselves."

"We know that, but the British are not aware of what happened. You have to keep them in the dark about how we took it. They will never see any of the hands that were on that ship. That is part of the punishment and cost that President Pierce has decided the British must pay for pressing American seamen. It is one thing to sail inside territorial waters whenever you like, it is another to walk on foreign soil and kidnap their citizens."

"You are right, Ben. My orders are clear. Keep the Brits in the dark. Act surprised if they tell us that the *Resolute* is a war ship. For every question that they ask, ask two in return."

"Well, you left them enough clues when you threw crates that will float overboard. Certainly she will miss her rendevous point and ships out of Bermuda will come looking for her."

"You can count on that. Also, the British Embassy will be alerted and send people looking for the ferryboat on the docks. I can only hope that my squad leader has put it back in place and covered his tracks well. We cleaned up the storehouse where the pressed American seamen were being held. The returning British seamen and Agent, known to us as Milton Black, will disappear. Either they will be buried in the Chesapeake if they die, or they will be taken to St. Elizabeth Hospital, for disposal." I continued.

"St. Elizabeth Hospital? Disposal?"

"You do not want to know about what goes on there, Ben. Let me just say, it will be easier on Agent Black if he rests on the bottom of the Chesapeake Bay."

We sailed on through winter weather in the North Atlantic. After a few days, we were ready to attempt the transfer to the *Resolute*. The two ships pulled along side each other and ropes were fired by small deck cannon across the space between both ships. A chair was attached to the ropes and I sat in it on the deck of the *Intrepid*. Ben walked up to me as I sat in my oil slicks and said, "We will send over your trunk with your dress uniforms if we get you safely across. No sense in sending your clothes if we drown you at sea by a broken rope. Besides, I am not your mother!"

"Thank you very much, Captain Hagood, you have a way with words."

"Remember, Captain Caldwell, *Resolute* is the man on a mission!"

"Oh, now you are really reaching, Ben."

He was about to say something clever again, but I never heard him as I was pulled up and over towards HMS *Resolute*. I dropped with a thud, in a heap, at the feet of sailors on the deck of the Resolute. I scrambled to my feet and waved at Ben across the way. I ordered the sailors to bring my trunk across. " I don't want to appear before the Queen dressed like a peasant," I said.

"Nice to have you on board, Captain"

"Commander Williams, you have done a splendid job of keeping the *Resolute* on course with the *Intrepid*. These old English tubs have six masts and a retrofit boiler but they do not have the speed of the *Intrepid*, do they?"

"No, Sir, many Royal Navy ships are old and slow," he replied.

My trunk made it across with only a splash of salt water and was taken to the captain's quarters below decks. I checked my belongings and hung a dress uniform on a hook so that some wrinkles would hang out on the rest of the voyage. I removed my waterproof slicks and removed a packet of letters that I had carefully wrapped in oil cloth and placed them for safe keeping in the Captain's safe. I wondered what was waiting for me on the docks of South Hampton.

If all went well, Lord Napier would meet the ship when we docked. We would have a short handing over ceremony. US Navy photographers boarded the *Resolute* in Nantucket and had managed to not get sea sick thus far. We were instructed in my orders to enter South Hampton with the Stars and Stripes flying proudly. The photographers would take a picture of the lowering of the Stars and Stripes and the raising of the Union Jack. So many pictures had been taken, we were sure that English newspapers would want copies for their front pages. It was unusual that a ship was returned to its home port. The neutrality act of 1854, called the Ostend Accord, said that the United States would remain neutral if France, Spain or Great Britain were involved in conflict anywhere in the world. It was under this act that President Pierce was returning HMS *Resolute*.

Lord Napier sat at his desk in the Admiralty and wondered what had happened to HMS *Resolute* assigned to the Royal Naval Dockyards, Bermuda. His thoughts were interrupted when the United States Ambassador and I were shown into his office.

"May I present Captain Jason Caldwell, of the United States Navy."said the ambassador to Great Britain. "He has returned HMS *Resolute* to Her Majesties Merchant Fleet", he continued with great flair.

I never thought I would ever hear those words spoken in a foreign capital. The official return of HMS *Resolute* was conducted in South Hampton. Lord Napier was photographed as the Queen's representative in the hour long ceremony. At the end, I was invited to come to London for unofficial meetings.

"Come, come, my Captain, it is an honor to meet you again," Lord Napier began. "Please, sit here by the fire and we can chat." The ambassador and I took chairs and I was glad for the presence and support provided by the American Embassy, London.

"Tell me what you can about the discovery of Her Majesties Merchant Marine."

Merchant Marine? Then we know how the diplomats are going to play this, I thought. "Well, Lord Napier, I did not discover the ship, I brought it to England."

"Call me Nevel, please Captain, you Americans are not a formal lot, are you? And what may I call you?"

"You may use my Christian name if you prefer. Can I ask you a question, Sir?"

"Of course, Jason, ask away."

"Well, on the voyage from Nantucket to South Hampton, I noticed that your merchant marine had once been a man-of-war, is that true?"

"Quite right, the older warships serving in the middle Atlantic without iron plating either had to be brought in for retrofit or turned into merchant ships. As you know, we have to supply the Royal Naval Dockyards, Bermuda from either Canada or here, and it is a long voyage either way."

"Yes, it is. What do you think happened to the crew? When it was found adrift by whalers from Nantucket, there was not a soul aboard."

"That was one of my questions for you, Captain."

Now we were back to, Captain and not, Jason. "When I came on board, the locals had stripped the ship bare - not even a bar of soap was left. I lodged complaints with the harbor master and he said the ship was sealed before it entered the harbor because it was flying the black sickness flag. The whaling vessels must have salvaged the contents. I then went back to the captain of the rescue vessel and talked to him. He said the ship was completely bare, he had never seen a ship at sea in that condition. For the record, Sir, I believe him."

"Why do say that, Captain?"

"Because on the voyage here it was very eerie aboard ship. I remember as a child going on a slave ship in Charleston Harbor. My crew got the same feeling. The brig was many times larger than it needed to be. I got the feeling that many men had been held there against their will. I know it is nonsense, but I was very happy to return it to your care and inspection yesterday during the ceremony at South Hampton."

"Yes, when the Stars and Stripes were lowered and the Union Jack was returned, I was overjoyed."

"I felt the same way, your Lordship."

"Queen Victoria has sent her cable of thanks to President Pierce and she has written a personal letter for you carry back to your President. I have read the letter before the Royal Seal was placed and I can tell you that Her Majesty is very grateful for the return of her ship. International Maritime Law states that ships abandoned on the high seas are to be salvaged by whoever finds them. It was truly a remarkable thing that your President has done for our Queen."

"Lord Napier, the US Navy stands ready to assist Great Britain upon the high seas and will return all ships to the Queen's fleet whenever we find them. In the future, you can rely on the United States to render aid as a full and important ally of Great Britain." I reached into my tunic and removed a letter, handed it to him and said, "From President Pierce to you, Lord Napier".

"I do not know what to say at your country's kindness, Jason. May I show this to the Queen?"

"Of course, Nevel."

After his guest left, Lord Napier opened the letter from President Pierce.

THE WHITE HOUSE
WASHINGTON, CITY

JANUARY 7, 1857

LORD NEVEL A. NAPIER
OFFICE OF THE ADMIRALTY
LONDON, ENGLAND

BY OFFICER COURIER

DEAR ADMIRAL NAPIER:

THIS IS TO INFORM YOUR GOVERNMENT THAT TODAY I HAVE SIGNED AN EXECUTIVE ORDER WHICH WILL STOP AND SEARCH ALL SUSPECT SHIPS WHICH MIGHT CARRY BONDED SLAVES BEFORE THEY REACH ANY SEAPORT OF THE UNITED STATES OF AMERICA. THIS ORDER WILL BE CARRIED OUT BY THE UNITED STATES NAVY.

YOUR GOVERNMENT'S ASSISTANCE IS REQUESTED IN THIS EFFORT. WE KNOW THAT MANY SUCH SHIPS STOP IN BERMUDA ON THEIR TRIPS TO AMERICA. IF YOU COULD REQUEST VICE-ADMIRAL HORNSBY TO ISSUE A SIMILAR BAN ON ALL SUCH SHIPS FROM DOCKING IN BERMUDA, OUR EFFORTS WILL BE AIDED AND APPRECIATED.

I TRUST THAT YOU MET WITH AND ACCEPTED FROM CAPTAIN JASON EDWIN CALDWELL, THE RETURN OF HMS RESOLUTE. THIS WILL BE THE FIRST OF MANY SUCH ACTIONS THAT I KNOW PRESIDENT- ELECT BUCHANAN SUPPORTS AND WILL CONTINUE UNDER HIS ADMINISTRATION.

Franklin Pierce

FRANKLIN PIERCE

The letter to the Prime Minister was less tactful:

THE WHITE HOUSE
WASHINGTON, CITY
JANUARY 7, 1857

PRIME MINISTER OF GREAT BRITAIN
OFFICE OF FOREIGN AFFAIRS
LONDON, ENGLAND

BY OFFICER COURIER

DEAR MISTER PRIME MINISTER:

THIS IS TO INFORM YOUR GOVERNMENT THAT TODAY I HAVE DISMISSED, FOR CAUSE, THE FOLLOWING foreign ministers TO THE UNITED STATES: WASHINGTON CITY, NEW YORK, PHILADELPHIA AND CINCINNATI.

YOUR GOVERNMENT MAY REPLACE THESE REPRESENTATIVES AT YOUR CONVENIENCE. WE ARE A NEUTRAL NATION IN THE PRESENT CRIMEAN WAR. AMERICAN CITIZENS HAVE BEEN TAKEN TO BERMUDA. IF YOU COULD REQUEST VICE-ADMIRAL HORNSBY TO ISSUE A BAN ON THE RECEIPT OF ALL FUTURE PERSONS TAKEN FROM THE UNITED STATES IT WOULD PROVE HELPFUL IN OUR REMAINING A NEUTRAL NATION.

I TRUST THAT YOU MET WITH AND ACCEPTED FROM CAPTAIN CALDWELL THIS COMMUNIQUE. THIS WILL BE THE FIRST OF MANY SUCH ACTIONS THAT I KNOW PRESIDENT ELECT BUCHANAN SUPPORTS AND WILL CONTINUE UNDER HIS ADMINISTRATION.

Franklin Pierce

PRESIDENT OF THE UNITED STATES
COMMANDER-IN-CHIEF OF THE ARMED FORCES

34
Officer Courier
London

I asked Lord Napier to make an appointment to see the Prime Minister at number 10, Downing Street, London. The Admiral said that it would be impossible for me to see the Prime Minister at his home. The current spat with the Russians and security and all that sort of thing, he said was the reason. He could, of course, set up an appointment at the Foreign Office without a problem. I told him he was very gracious, and that I would call upon the Prime Minister tomorrow.

I took a handsome cab the next day to the Foreign Office. I entered and was greeted by a rather sickly looking man who said he was the secretary for the Prime Minister and he would be meeting with me today.

"I am sorry, Sir. There must have been a misunderstanding. I am not to meet with you. I am an Officer Courier from The White House and I am ordered to place a communique directly in the hands of the Prime Minister."

"The Prime Minister does not meet with couriers. I would be happy to give you a signed receipt that you could take back with you."

"I will need your name, Sir, so when I return to the United States, I will tell President Pierce that the Prime Minister does not meet with couriers from the President of the United States. He will then place your name in his cable to your Queen, Lord Napier and the Commander of the Royal Naval Dockyards."

All the color drained from the poor fellow's face and he stammered, "Please wait here, I will fetch someone who can help you."

An hour later, another secretary for Foreign Affairs told me about the same thing in different words. They were very sorry but there was nothing that they could do.

"I have an audience with the Queen later today, She would like to thank me personally for returning HMS *Resolute* to the Royal Navy. I will mention that the Office of the Prime Minister refused acceptance of a personal communique from President Pierce."

"Oh, my, we can not have that."

"I thought not. Does the Prime Minister have an office in this building?"

"Yes, he does."

"Is he in that office at this moment?"

"Why, yes, he is."

"Can you inform him that a representative from the President of the United States wishes to place something on his desk?"

"Yes, of course."

"Please inform him that he does not have to touch the communique, I will not speak, I do not need a receipt, all I need is to see him sitting at his desk. I can then, in all honesty, say to my President, yes, I delivered his letter directly to the Prime Minister."

"I will ask the Prime Minister for his permission for you to do so."

He returned a shaken man, the Prime Minister has said and I quote, "Tell the courier that I am sorry he has made a trip for nothing, but threatening to go to the Queen is absurd."

"He will not see you, Sir"

Later that day at my audience with her Majesty, Queen Victoria, I handed her the communique from the President and said, "The Prime Minister would not accept this letter from the President of the United States, if you could share the contents with him I would be most grateful. The President wants to make certain that Great Britain understands the conditions under which we might enter the Crimean War in support of Russia."

A regal nod of the head was all I got from the Queen. She handed it to Lord Napier and said, "Nevel, please read this and respond for the Prime Minister. We wish that this response be in writing on Official Foreign Office Letterhead and signed by the Prime Minister. We also wish that this be handed to Captain Caldwell before he sails from South Hampton tomorrow."

"Yes, your Majesty."

She then turned to me and said, "Some of my cabinet members do not understand that they serve at the pleasure of the Queen."

She rose from the throne and left the room with a small group of diplomats in tow. I waited a few moments and left Buckingham Palace with Lord Napier. Nevel was smiling, "Our Queen will set things straight, I will see you in South Hampton before you sail."

The next afternoon about an hour before high tide a carriage pulled onto the docks at South Hampton A man stepped from the running boards and asked for his luggage to be handed down to him. Dock workers hoisted the luggage onto a cart and began pulling it towards the *Intrepid*.

The gentleman removed his hat and asked, " Lord Napier sends his regards, can I speak to Captain Jason Caldwell? Permission to come aboard?"

I hurried to the rail and shouted down, "I am Captain Caldwell, what brings you to this ship?"

"Lord Napier has sent a reply for President Pierce and says I must place it in his hands."

I laughed and said, "I will come ashore."

I hurried down the gang way because I knew Ben Hagood and he would want to sail on the tide. A packet of information was handed to me and I signed for the President.

"You will find a communique to you inside as well, Captain. My luggage is waiting to be loaded onto your ship so that I may personally hand the reply to your President."

"You will have to share a cabin with me, is that all right? What is your name?"

"Captain, my name is Lord Pittsmith, Prime Minister of England and I have the unpleasant position of making an apology to you, your President and to your country."

"Lord Pittsmith, I have already signed for the President, I have your apology and my country wishes to end this matter in a friendly manner. Can you return to Lord Napier with a message from me?"

"Of course, Sir."

"Tell Nevel to keep his powder dry and I will call upon him the next time I am in London."

"Oh, Sir, that would be most welcome, indeed. I am a diplomat not a sailor, I was not looking forward to the voyage."

35
Buchanan Takes Office
Washington City

The inauguration of James Buchanan in March, 1857, brought an entirely new cabinet to the White House. The incoming Secretary of the Navy, Isaac Toucey, was from Connecticut and he met with James Dobbin because President Buchanan had asked him to do so. "Secretary Dobbin, I appreciate you taking the time to meet with me."

"Come in Mr. Toucey, President Pierce has had me prepare several important files that you might want to review. I have summarized them on this single sheet and I will leave both with you as I depart today."

"As you may know, President Pierce has made excellent use of the Navy's Intelligence branch of this department. In particular, Captain Jason Caldwell, is from South Carolina. He understands the importance of dealing with slave holding states and how to deal with them. But his strength is his leadership and incredible amount of good fortune in carrying out his assignments. Here is a list of assignments that he was involved with during this administration." He placed a hand written note across the desk towards Toucey.

Koszta Incident - June, 1853
Rescue of Ingraham - July, 1853
Fremonte Expedition - 1854
Seizure of Black Warrior - 1854
Ostend Circular October, 1854
Capture of General Walker - 1855
Reciprocity Treaties of 1855, 1856
Civil War in Kansas - March, 1856
Resolute solution - December, 1856

"Summaries of after action reports can be found in the department files, if you are interested in seeing what type of career officer you will have in Captain Caldwell."

167

"Thank you, Secretary Dobbin, the good captain has just returned from his trip abroad and has shared his report with President Buchanan. Then President-Elect Buchanan was consulted by President Pierce before the operation began last December. They both agreed that something had to be done with regard to Great Britain's actions in this country. I think the right approach was taken and I might add that I would support such actions in the future."

"As you know, Mr. Toucey, President Buchanan will face many problems, not just what to do about slavery. I think the first step should be the limiting of slave holding to the present number of states allowed to do so. The next step has already been taken, and that is to choke off, or at least slow, the flow of slaves into this country. We, the United States Navy, were directed by President Pierce to stop and search all slave ships trying to enter US ports along the east coast. It is my hope that you and President Buchanan can be successful in this endeavor."

"I assume that this policy will continue with President Buchanan, but I do not know this for a fact. It will probably depend upon how the slave holding States react to this. Will they be happy with the slaves presently in the country? Will the birth rate keep up with the death rate among the slaves presently held? Or will they see the need to continue the purchase of slaves outside the United States?"

"I really do not have an answer to that, Isaac. The slave auctions will, of course, continue in places like Charleston because it is still legal to buy and sell property. We were trying to slow down the flow into the country by the United Kingdom, France, Spain and the Dutch Colonies in Africa. Slavery is banished in Europe, so the richest place left to sell Negroes is the United States. These same colonies in Africa, enslave their own people for profit, sell them to be transported by merchant mariners from England, France and the rest of Europe. As long as there is money in the sale of people, the practice will continue. If we can make it difficult, or impossible, to land in this country with slaves, the policy will work."

"This will have an effect on this country, we can expect to have problems with the European countries that do not take kindly to the US Navy's actions."

"Exactly, the first reaction, oddly enough, may come from Spain. You remember the troubles we had in Havana with the USS *Black Warrior*? Cuba still needs plantation field hands to work the sugar cane and will continue to bring in slaves. England will still capture and press able-bodied seamen wherever She can find them. But I predict that before the century ends we will be at War with Spain."

"You think there will be a national civil war similar to what happened in Kansas?" asked Isaac Toucey.

"I doubt that. Federal troops may have to put down uprisings in places like South Carolina, but I think it will be restricted to individual states like Kansas. The Federal Government is not able, or prepared, to put down an uprising from all the slave holding states at the same time. Speaking for the Navy, we do not have the ships or the manpower to control the coast lines of states like Virginia, North and South Carolina, Georgia or Florida. If Texas, Louisiana, Mississippi and Alabama were to join, then we would be required to control the Gulf of Mexico as well. We are not prepared for that, it would be a nightmare."

"Speaking of nightmares, what do you think would happen if the western territories joined into a national struggle?"

"That is a very good question. The Utah Territory, for example, is ready to explode. Brigham Young is now the head of the Mormon Church, after the death of Joseph Smith. President Buchanan will have trouble with the Mormons this year, I predict."

"In what way?"

"The population of Utah was upset and angry when Utah was refused admission to the Union last year. The bulk of the population is Mormon. They will follow Young's leadership because he is a zealot who few will dare to oppose or question."

Before the incoming Secretary of the Navy could respond, he was interrupted by a knock on the office door. "Come," said the outgoing Secretary. The door opened and Captain Jason Caldwell said, "You sent for me, Sir?"

"Yes, come in. Jason, I want you to witness something that I think is important. Secretary Isaac Toucey will assume command today and I want to change chairs with him."

I nodded and the two men walked around the desk in opposite directions. Having each reached the opposite chair, they extended their arms and shook hands. "Congratulations, Mr. Secretary."

"Thank you, Mr. Secretary." Both men smiled and sat down.

"Captain Caldwell, we have not met before today. But if Secretary Dobbin is correct, you are going to be a very busy man these next four years. What do you know about the Utah Territory?"

"I have been there, Sir, to meet with the Fremonte Expedition."

"How would you get there in a short time frame if President Buchanan asked you to go?"

"Lieutenant Lewis, of the Office of Shore Patrol, is in charge of the detachment's transportation, Sir. I think he would send us by train to Council Bluffs, Iowa, then by Army protection across country and into Utah."

"How many days to get there?"

"Only a few days to Council Bluffs, but after that weeks or months."

"Months?"

"Yes, Sir, it is slow going in the mountains. If it were winter, then months, if it were summer, then weeks. It would be much faster for a detachment stationed in the Oregon Territory."

Secretary Toucey turned to Secretary Dobbin and asked, "What do we have for Army or Naval Forces on the Pacific Coast?"

"We have a series of forts built by the army throughout the western territories, including Oregon. The Indian uprisings have made fort construction throughout the territories a matter of protection for settlers moving west. The Navy maintains depots at San Francisco, Portland and on the island of San Juan in Washington Territory. A naval detachment could be sent from Washington to San Francisco by ship, but it is a long cruise around the southern tip of South America, longer than a train ride to Council Bluffs and a wagon train into Utah."

"Captain Caldwell, give me a report that I can show the President in case Secretary Dobbin is correct and there is trouble in Utah. In this office, I want to be prepared for action, not be forced to plan, organize, and then react to a crisis."

"Yes, Sir. I will leave here and go directly to the Potomac Dockyards and speak to Lieutenant Lewis so that we can begin."

"Thank you, Captain, I look forward to seeing a plan of action in the next few days!"

I left the office in the Army Navy building, waved down a Washington City cab and told the driver that I needed to get to the Potomac Dockyards. I was wondering why the Navy would be called upon to do anything in Utah. Only the Great Salt Lake would be of any interest to a sailor. Maybe the new President was going to use my detachment as his means of getting letters and other important papers to points within the United States and around the world. The last President used us to gather information, conduct small covert operations and sometimes be his envoy to deliver critical documents.

I was still musing when the cab driver said, "Here we are, Sir." I looked up and we were at the docks. I paid him and walked over to Lewis's office. He was in, but someone was with him and I waited and talked to Rachael White. She and Sam were going to the Hay-Adams and she asked, "Captain, do you and your Lady from the White House want to meet us there?"

I was about to answer her when Lewis's office door opened. His guest and he were in the outer office.

"Captain Caldwell, good to see you."

"Jerome, can I talk to you for a few minutes?"

He turned to his guest and said, "JAG will get my report tomorrow." He walked him to the outside office door and said a few words in a low voice that I could not hear.

"Jason, what can I do for you?"

"Secretary Toucey has sent me to talk to you about making an OP plan for travel into the western territories."

"He does not waste any time getting into things, does he?"

"I just came from his office, both he and Secretary Dobbin were there putting their heads together. I think Toucey is going to use everything that has been passed on to him."

"He is already concerned about how long it takes for a federal force to get to a trouble spot west of the Mississippi. He is going to show President Buchanan a detailed plan for moving troops into these trouble spots. That means it will be your plan, approved by me, with his signature. In fact, I think he is going to send me and my detachment into Utah to see how long it takes and he will report this to the President. I would not be surprised if he sends us out within the week."

"Within the week?"

"I may be wrong, but I get the feeling that this Secretary is not going to sit around and wait for things to happen. He will be in a position to react to a crisis as it is happening, he will be able to give the President options."

"What do want from me, Jason?"

"We need to get busy on a practical estimate of how many days it will take my detachment to load our gear and be gone from the railhead here in Washington. Then estimate how long it will take General Dodge to get an Army escort together after he is given orders from the War Department. And most important of all, how many days it might take in winter and summer routes through the mountains and into remote places, like Utah."

"I assume speed is the most important element in the equation."

"Exactly. If we estimate that we can get out of the railhead in half a day and it takes four, then you and I will be looking for other jobs in the Navy."

"Let me ask you this. Why not travel as civilians, or better yet, as members of my SP from here to Council Bluffs?"

"How would that help?"

"O'ye of little faith, let me explain. You let me contact General Dodge in Council Bluffs by telegraph. I let him know that you, or the detachment, or both, are on your way. He can contact the Army for a copy of his orders by telegraph. Zero days involved."

"How do we get our gear there?"

"I will ask General Dodge if you can store some crates of materials on a permanent basis in his depot there. The wooden boxes will be marked **Property of US Government, RR tools.** That way anybody who sees them, will think they are railroad tools. In our coding within telegrams, RR will stand for Rapid Response Unit."

"I like that idea, Jerome! If we leave such items as weapons, uniforms (both winter and summer), maps and what not at the western most railhead on a permanent basis, this will work."

"Yes, and traveling with SP badges you can carry side arms onto the trains that you will be using to get from Washington. Remember, we use Baltimore & Ohio, Reading, and other rail lines to book passage."

"It would be nice if we could step on a train in Washington and step off in Utah."

"That will happen very shortly, Jason. President Buchanan has promised that he will persuade the railroads to build new lines into the unsettled territories. In fact, General Dodge is in charge of the western expansion from Council Bluffs. He will begin laying track from the east and a separate track will start from the west coast. They hope to meet somewhere in Utah."

"That is exactly what this country needs, ride a train from the Atlantic to the Pacific!"

"Did you know that General Dodge has built a home in Council Bluffs? He figures he will retire there after the transcontinental railroad is complete. The house sits atop a huge hill, I guess they call them bluffs there, and he can look down into the rail yards. He is a real modern thinker. He had his men run a telegraph line from the rail yard up his house. Because he can not read Morse Code, he has a machine that types out the code on a narrow paper strip. He can read messages in his home office."

"That means that I could send him messages from anywhere along the rail lines during our trip!"

"You should visit him at the house the next time you are there, Jason. Did you know that he had a large copper lined tank installed on the third floor of the house? It collects rain water from the roof, pipes run through the walls and a water tap is in every bedroom on the second floor and in the kitchen on the first floor. If someone wants to wash his hands, all he has to do is turn the tap and water runs into the wash basin."

"What will they think of next?"

"That is not all. He has a device installed in a little closet like room in every bedroom that has a tiny metal tank near the ceiling that also gets water from the huge tank on the third floor. A chain can be pulled letting water down into a chamber pot mounted on the floor. When you pull the chain your job goes down a larger pipe and into a cesspool. No more emptying chamber pots, now that is progress."

"I can report back to Secretary Toucey that we now have a plan called Rapid Response. We can indeed get from Washington to the end of the railroad in less than a week!"

"Jason, let me think out loud what we can do to make the trip with wagons a little faster. What if we can get the Army to improve the escort process?"

"I do not follow you, Jerome."

"Suppose you did not have to leap frog from one Army fort to another? The last time you went through Council Bluffs, you had to wait for more than one ferry to cross the Missouri to Omaha. With all your gear, this sometimes takes half a day. What if you had wagons, purchased by the US Navy and stored with General Dodge? You could get off the train, harness the horses to the wagons that were already loaded before your arrival, and start immediately. Zero days involved."

"How do I get across the Missouri and into Omaha?"

"You do not go to Omaha. You head straight north along the bluffs until you meet the Mormon trail. A shallow ford is there, remember Joseph Smith had oxen and humans pull his wagons from Indiana to Utah. The trail is clearly marked. Why not have the Army supply fresh horses along the trail? At the end of a hard day's travel, say ten to fifteen miles, you had to stop for the night and rest. With fresh horses and depending upon the condition of your men, you can continue for another ten or fifteen miles. I bet that in flat land you could cover at least three times the distance in a day."

"I like that. I will ask the Secretary to decide whether he wants to use Army horses and mules or if he wants the Navy to purchase draft animals to keep in Council Bluffs."

"How can that help, Jason."

"If we use twice as many animals as we normally would, a pair can be pulling while the other pair rest. We can switch several times a day if necessary."

"Yes, but it would be better to have stations along the Mormon trail with fresh horses, water and a place to sleep if you needed it. I do not know how travel at night would work."

"If the Army can not provide an escort, I will have to have Tom Schneider rig up a wagon that contains one of his deck guns. Indians or outlaws would get a real surprise if he let go with that."

"Sounds like you have enough information from me for the time being. What are you doing this evening?"

"Rachael asked me the same thing as I came in, what is up?"

"I think she and Sam Mason are going to announce their engagement!"

"I know, but the Army Navy building frowns on Officers and Enlisted mixing at social meetings."

"Well, she invited me as her boss and not a Lieutenant – so I am going to wear civilian clothes, not my uniform. This is important to Sam."

"You are right, Jerome, I will tell Rachael that I will join them at the Hay-Adams. That is the least I can do if the detachment is going into the West."

"Good, see you there!"

36
Utah Territory
October 1857

As predicted, President Buchanan had trouble with the Mormons in the first year of his administration. Disgusted over the refusal to admit Utah to the Union, Brigham Young ordered the records of the Federal Court House destroyed. The Federal judges were packed into wagons and driven to the boundary of the territory and released. The reason given by the Mormons for this action was that the personal character of the Federal officials was offensive (they were not of the Mormon faith). When news of this reached Washington City, President Buchanan thought the action intolerable and he ordered the following:

1. Alfred Cummings, superintendent of Indian Affairs on the upper Missouri was appointed to replace Brigham Young as territorial governor.
2. Judge Delana Eckels, of Indiana was appointed Chief Justice of the territory.
3. Colonel Albert Sidney Johnson was appointed as commander of 2500 Federal troops that would be stationed in Utah to protect Federal officials and uphold the laws of the territory.

The Mormons under Brigham Young reacted by publishing the following proclamations:

1. Colonel Johnson and his troops under territorial law constitute an armed mob and as such are forbidden from entering the territory. He reasoned that if Utah were a state then Federal troops could enter the State of Utah.
2. The Federal troops will be met at the territorial boarder with a territorial militia under his command consisting of 5000 troops.
3. If Federal troops enter the territory they will be arrested and held in the territorial prison located at Provo.

Colonel Johnson reached the Utah territory on October 6, 1857, and was attacked by the territorial militia and driven back. The Army supply train was captured. Eight hundred oxen were driven off and collected for use by Mormons living in the territory. Colonel Johnson and his battered troops marched into Fort Bridger near Black's Ford. Governor Cummings then declared the territory in a state of insurrection and appealed to Washington.

In Washington, the President met with his cabinet and said, "We tried your way, Mr. Floyd, and the Army is not the answer in Utah. I want Mr. Cass to try diplomacy, what can the State Department do?"

"Mr. President, we can send Mr. Thomas L. Kane who is serving in California. It has snowed on the western slopes of the mountains and passes are closed. He could get there in early spring." Replied Cass.

"Why not send someone from Washington now?"

"It is the same problem. California is much closer, Mr. President."

"Why do we have to wait until spring, I want something done this year."

"Mr. President, what about using our Rapid Response Unit?"

"Yes, Mr. Toucey, that would be fast but what can a handful of men do that Mr. Floyd's army was unable to do?"

"The RR force is covert, it is not a military unit. It gathers intelligence, can deliver messages by officer courier and sometimes can be creative and diplomatic in nature."

"What do you propose?" asked the President.

"We send Captain Jason Caldwell and his detachment on a fall mission with winter supplies into and out of Utah with the following mission:

1. Meet with Colonel Johnson in Fort Bridger and advise him to stay withdrawn from the Utah territory for the time being.
2. Carry letters of Presidential Pardons for Brigham Young and others that might be needed to stop all militia activities.
3. Carry a directive to governor Cummins.
4. Carry a Presidential directive to minister Kane, in case he is successful before spring."

"When can the Rapid Response Unit leave for Utah?"

"Tomorrow, Mr. President."

"Make it so, Mr. Toucey, I will write the necessary letters this morning and get them to your office this afternoon. Thank you, everyone, for attending this meeting."

As soon as Secretary Toucey returned to the Army Navy building across from the White House he summoned Captain Caldwell. "Captain, we have an ideal mission for you in Utah."

"When do we leave, Sir?"

"Tomorrow, follow the same procedure that you used this summer when I sent your detachment to Council Bluffs with equipment and supplies. I do not need to tell you that the President is counting on your success in this matter. I have contacted the SP office and have them working on straight through train connections. Your detachment will not have to stop and change trains. Thanks to the financial panic here in the east, the railroads will give priority status to your men. Lieutenant Lewis has already telegraphed General Dodge and told him that you are on your way."

"What about orders from Secretary Floyd for the Army, Sir?"

"The Army is not going to be used. It is up to the Navy and Postmaster General Brown to get the job done this time."

" How is the Postmaster involved, Sir?"

"Butterfield Overland Mail Service has built way stations for the US mail to be carried from St. Joseph, Missouri to Sacramento in just ten days! The postmaster will arrange for transportation from a place called, Hebron Station, in South Eastern Nebraska Territory. Here are your written orders which are listed in priority. We must meet with Colonel Johnson in Fort Bridger. Second, you must try to deliver the letters and communications from the President. Third, you must try to find State Department representative Kane, if he has arrived. If you are unable to do any of these, leave the letters with Butterfield Service who will deliver the letters. You are not to spend the winter in Utah! You have until tomorrow to take care of personal business that will not keep for a couple of months. Good luck, Captain."

I walked out of the Secretary's Office with a packet of papers. I left the Army Navy building and walked across to the White House basement. There, I found Master Gunnery Sergeant Schneider asleep in the corner of my office.

"Sorry, Sir, just catching a few winks before we have to shove off."

"How do you know we are going anywhere?"

"Master Sergeants have a special information network, you do not want to know, Captain."

"Have you told your wife we are leaving tomorrow?"

"I will tonight, Sir. She expects these last minute assignments."

"Have you found Sergeant Mason and Rachael? Oh, never mind, she already knows from her work in Lewis's office."

"Where are the rest of your Marines, Sergeant?"

"They are saying goodbye to loved ones and packing personal items that we found useful on our last trip west this summer."

"Very good, Sergeant, I am going home to grab some sleep – it may be many days before we see beds again. Send a messenger if you need me for anything."

I walked up and out of the White House and to the intersection of Pennsylvania and Lafayette Park. The street car stopped here and I caught a ride to my lodgings. I had a check list of items that I needed to take and letters to write. I sat at my writing desk and wrote a short note to my parents, saying I would not be in Washington for the next two months. My brother would read the letter to them, so I did not have to write more than one letter to South Carolina. I wrote a personal note to the White House in care of Louise Buchanan, I settled on the following:

Louise Buchanan
The White House
1600 Pennsylvania Ave.
Washington City

Dear Louise,

Your brother, the President of the United States, has sent me on another mission. I regret that I will be unable to attend the State Dinner for the Russian Ambassador. Do not sit next to him, he pinches. I will miss not seeing you for the time that I will be away from Washington.

Ask your brother about the mission details, as I am not permitted to say where we are going or how long it will take.

Fondly,

Jason

I slept like the dead and awoke when the sunlight came streaming through my bedroom window. I sat up and looked at my watch. I was already behind schedule. I dressed, grabbed my gear and hurried to the train station. The detachment, all eighteen of them, were ready to step aboard. I found a seat beside Tom and dropped down with a sigh.

"Long night, Captain?"

"Not long enough, I overslept and I will have to shave on this train."

"Life will be very comfortable on the train ride compared to this summer. Lieutenant Lewis said we stay in the same coaches all the way to Council Bluffs."

"That is right, Sergeant, and another surprise, we do not have to drag wagons this time. The Overland Stagecoach Line will provide space for us as passengers and the Butter field Mail Service will haul our gear. The problem is that the closest station is on the Oregon Trail."

"How do we get to the Oregon Trail, Sir?"

"While we are riding on this train, General Dodge's men are re-packing for 18 horse back riders and 12 pack horses. We have to cross the Missouri and find the trail at a place called Hebron. It seems that the Mail Service has built way stations along the Oregon Trail from St. Joseph all the way to California. We have to make it on our own from Council Bluffs to the trail, two days ride. We then take stagecoaches all the way into Fort Bridger, probably 10 to 12 more days on the coaches. The Postmaster General has already cleared that for us."

"You are only talking about a two week journey from Washington City to Utah!"

"Yes, if we do not stop to fight Indians, shoot game, and sleep 8 hours every night. Tell the men to get as much sleep as they can on the train."

"Aye, aye, Sir."

The train rumbled out of the railhead and headed for Pittsburgh. We stopped very late that first day to get on the line to Fort Wayne, Indiana. We slept the first night as we crossed the State of Ohio. When we awoke, we were leaving Akron and heading for the Indiana State line. We ate three meals in the dining car, played cards, told stories and caught up on family. We slept again the rest of Indiana and into Illinois. The train made stops along the way for fuel and water, picked up mail sacks and anything else that could be done in a matter of minutes. We arrived in Fort Wayne and I sent a telegram to General Dodge.

From Fort Wayne, we stopped in Joliet, Illinois, and made the run to Rock Island. We crossed the Mississippi River and pulled into Davenport, Iowa. Council Bluffs was due west one day. We had set a US Troop Travel time record. A detachment had traveled 1750 miles in just under 86 hours. That meant we had averaged twenty miles an hour, an amazing feat, I thought.

We were all glad to be this far. It was only October 13,'57, and we still needed to get into Utah and out again before the heavy winter snows blocked the eastern slopes of the Rocky Mountains. General Dodge telegraphed Secretary Toucey that we had left the Council Bluffs railhead and were heading into Nebraska Territory to find the Oregon trail.

"Did you double check every pack, Tom?"

"Yes, Sir. Let us hope and pray that the Butterfield Service Stations are alerted. We will not have enough food to make it all the way into Fort Bridger."

"Horses, food and lodging are critical, Sergeant. On the way home we can stop and sleep at every station after we pass the snow line. Pass the word to spare the horses until we find the Oregon trail."

We rode south and west, slept for 6 hours in a roadside inn near Lincoln. We showed our maps to the inn keeper the next morning and headed for a village called Crete. Townsfolk there said we would find the Oregon Trail at Hebron Station. We gave the station master, a Mister Steven Werner, our horses, I took some gold coins from my money belt and paid the Butterfield Agent for our freight bill. Werner had a pot of stew hanging over the fireplace and 18 hungry marines were fed.

"Here is a company map, Captain, I will mark the stations that have overnight lodging so your men can sleep."

"How many coaches have you reserved for my men?" I asked the station master.

"Two, Captain, it will be a squeeze, two of your men will have to ride on top with the driver."

"So, when we leave here today, there will be three coaches. One for freight and two for my men?"

"That is right, one of your men can ride shotgun up top with the driver and maybe one inside.".

"What is the time table, when do we leave?"

"As soon as your men help unload the pack horses and get everything loaded, you can go."

"I wish I could send a telegram to Council Bluffs."

"You can. It is not a continuous line. It stops and starts, but horse back riders go between the breaks. It will cost you, it has to go to St. Joseph and then to Council Bluffs."

"Very good, I will write it out for you to send as soon as we leave."

I walked over to Tom and motioned for Sam Mason to come over. "How is Private Keets doing? I noticed he has bowel troubles. He stopped every mile and voided himself coming here."

"I gave him something from the Medic Kit, Captain."

"The stagecoach is much faster than we can travel on horse back with sick men. If one is sick now others will follow. I have asked the station agent to telegraph General Dodge and give him an update. Here is what you two are to do. Separate the packs so that we can put some on top of the stagecoaches and the freight coach to Fort Bridger. Do not leave weapons, or other military gear in those packs. Put that equipment in infantry packs for each man. You can start as soon as the station master gets back from sending the telegram." I was interrupted by a smiling station agent.

"You must be the luckiest Captain in the Army."

"Navy, Mr. Werner, but you are close. Marines are the ground force of the Navy."

"I was about to key off your request, when I got an incoming. The company has sent a message to make whatever arrangements you need, the US Government is good for the charges."

"Can we get nonstop passenger coaches for my men and a freight coach for our equipment?"

"Yes, Sir. The passenger coaches will be nonstop, the freight stops for overnights on the map that I gave you." If some of your men ride on the freight coach, then they will arrive two days after the passenger coaches get into Fort Bridger."

"Sergeants, take Mr. Keets and a volunteer out to the freight coach and get their packs tied on top. I will sell the horses to Butterfield now, re-pack as we talked about." I turned back to Mr. Werner, our station master, and said, "Can you use our horses? I think we will take the Overland Stage all the way back to St. Joseph and we will not need horses to get back to Council Bluffs on our return."

"Horses are always welcome, let me make out a receipt for you, here is the payment you just gave me."

I found the Hebron telegraph office and sent another message to General Dodge which stated that I had found civilian transportation directly back to St. Joseph. And that we would be ahead of schedule if all went well. The next six to eight days would find the detachment divided into three groups. The freight group left first and we saw them that night in Chimney Rock.

"Sergeants, by the time we get to the Julesburg station we will be starting to go into the mountains. Give each man his winter gear and pick up all the summer utilities and put them on the freight coach, we may not see them again."

"Yes, Sir. Can I unpack the deck gun and keep it on top of my coach with me?"

"Feeling lonely without it, Tom?"

"I know that a coach load of Henry repeating rifles should be enough to discourage Indians and highway men, but the coach is moving forward and bouncing, I think a full magazine from me would discourage a small band from approaching the coaches."

"Better to be safe than sorry, Tom, you are right. Get that done before we continue on to Julesburg station."

Julesburg was the beginning of the Wild West and was known as the California Crossing. We followed the South Platte river from Julesburg towards Latham station. There, we saw Fort Sedgwick but did not stop. Latham was an important junction on the South Platte and we turned towards LaPorte to bypass Denver. Fort St.Vrain sat along the South Platte and so did Fort Vasquez, built in 1837 by Louis Vasquez. At Fort Morgan we rested for a few hours and changed drivers, horses and ate some food called Denver Stew.

Traveling at night was slower than daytime speeds. The drivers were afraid of their horses stepping in a hole and breaking a leg. But we kept rolling until we came to Namaqua station at the Big Thompson river. We forded the river at Mariano's Crossing in early daylight of the morning of October, Twenty-first. I heard Tom's booming voice beside the driver.

"Captain, we have got outriders coming from the North. Looks like about twelve or so, they are riding hard and headed straight for us."

"I see them, Sergeant. If they have rifles drawn from their saddle holsters, lay down one single burst ahead of them. Aim low, we do not kill anyone unless we have to."

Tom and I were riding in the first coach. Sam and Corporal Peters were riding in the second coach. Our driver slowed until the second coach was behind. I felt the coach come to a stop and immediately heard the sound of heavy gun fire. Forty-eight reports echoed off the hill sides. I strained to look out the coach window as both coach's doors flew open and my men were scrambling to set up a skirmish line in front of the two coaches. I was out of the coach in time to see the outriders pull to a stop. They were a couple hundred yards away.

"Sam, can you or Corporal Peters draw a bead on the last rider?"

"Got him in our sights, Captain." Corporal Peters was the best rifleman in the detachment.

"If they start towards us with weapons drawn, drop him. I know it is a long distance, wing him if you can."

"Aye, aye, Sir."

The leader of the band, shoved his rifle into his saddle holster. He raised both hands and slowly edged his horse closer to the coaches. I heard Tom loading his deck gun. He would cover the lone rider and the rest of the band unless they fanned out. Tom could drop the entire bunch if they tried an attack. The lone rider got closer and stopped within voice range.

"Hello, the coaches!"

I yelled back, "We do not want any trouble, who are you?"

"Just a group of hunters looking for deer."

"We are law enforcement. You do not look like deer hunters. Stay clear of the coaches or you will be shot."

"We will swing east and stay clear of you."

With that, he reined in his horse, tried to get a good look at what Tom was using and then slowly turned and rode away. We stayed put until the riders were out of sight.

" A very useful break," I said to the detachment. "We need to get to Virginia Dale station and report this."

We pulled into Virginia Dale and asked the station master if he knew of any way to report what had happened. He said, " No, I doubt that many riders were deer hunters. Deer skins are rare in these parts and Jim Bridger is paying top dollar for them down at his trading post. The band are probably rough necks out of Camp Floyd. Colonel Johnson has had a fair amount of deserters from there."

I thanked him and we pressed on along the old Cherokee trail and into Livermore station. We changed horses, drivers and ate again. Later that day, we pulled into Willow Springs station. We crossed the North Platte river at Big Laramie. We had a short layover in Fort Halleck the next day and the men got a few hours sleep. Before sunrise we were moving again, this time following the North Platte and into La Clede station. The last way station was built at a place called Big Pond. We changed from field utilities into winter uniforms so that we might make a presentable group when we entered Fort Bridger.

We saw Indians off in the distance but they did not attack the coaches. No more outlaw deserters were encountered and no snow fell on us all the way into Fort Bridger. It was October, Twenty-third.

37
Fort Bridger
Western Territories

It turned out that it was a waste of time to change into uniforms, as Fort Bridger was a converted trading post built by Jim Bridger in 1843. Before arriving, I had hoped that Fort Bridger would be a military outpost, similar to Fort Laramie. Instead, Fort Bridger was a crude collection of rough-hewn log buildings that greatly disappointed every man in the detachment.

"This is the famous, Fort Bridger? This is a shabby concern, built of poles dabbed with mud. Have we come to the right place, Captain?"

"Yes, Tom. I saw maybe 25 Indian lodges outside the main gates as we came in. Look, there is a blacksmith shop and a livery stable. Tom, you go and see what a couple of horses will cost us. We have got to get out to Camp Floyd as soon as we can."

"Sam, you and the Corporal see to unloading the top sides of the coaches." Tom ordered.

"Consider it done, Gunny."

"The rest of you men, start scouting around the area. There are about a thousand acres of flat land that surround this fort with some timber stands and a local saw mill. Meet back here in two hours."

I walked into the original trading post building and asked for directions to Camp Floyd. The woman behind the counter said, "Ya ain't from Camp Floyd?"

"No, ma'am. I have just arrived on the Overland Stage Coach. I am trying to find Colonel Johnson and I figured he would be out at Camp Floyd."

"Ya dun't have ta go out thar, Sir. He has sit up head quarters har. The troops is'a fixin ta sit up a winter camp down at Floyd. The soldiers are in pretty bad shape after running with thar tails atween their legs from them there Mormons."

"Yes, I was sent here from Washington to get an idea of what happened."

"They got the shit knocked out 'em, that's what happened!"

"Ma'am?"

"Pardon ma French. We dun't git many gentlemen officers from Washington in har."

"Yes, Ma'am. Where will I find Colonel Johnson's head quarters?"

"Walk three buildings over, turn right and ya cin't miss it."

Tom was coming out of the livery stable with a smile on his face. "Captain, you are going to love this. You and I can rent a horse, saddle and tack for as long as we will be here."

"Good, I found out that Colonel Johnson's headquarters are right here in Fort Bridger. Walk with me and we will drop off his orders."

We waded through the mud until we found a small shack like building at the end of a side street. We pulled the mud off our boots and opened the building's front door. It was a one room office space with Army privates at tiny tables along one side wall and a large desk in the opposite corner. Colonel Johnson, or what I took to be him, sat behind the desk. Tom and I walked to the desk, removed our hats and saluted, even though Marines do not salute indoors or without a head cover. The man looked up at us, waved his hand close to his temple and said, "Yes, what is it?"

"Captain Caldwell, Sir. This is Master Sergeant Schneider and we have just stepped off the Overland Stage with this for you." I handed him the packet marked *Colonel Johnson, Camp Floyd.*

"You what?"

"Colonel Johnson?"

"Yes, Captain. Where did you come from?"

"My detachment was sent here from Washington."

"Good, this must be orders from Secretary Floyd."

"No, Sir. President Buchanan has sent these. Would you care to sign for them?"

He looked at us in disbelief, pushed things around his desk and found an ink pen. He signed my receipt and said, "Why don't you wait, Captain, maybe this requires an answer."

We looked around the office and not finding a place to sit down, we stood until the Colonel had read the President's Directive.

"Good, God, Almighty! This set of orders was signed October Eighth! How in the hell did you get here that fast!"

"Master Sergeant Schneider is a troop movement specialist and I will let him explain it to you, Sir."

Tom spent the next several minutes describing what the Rapid Response Unit was and how it traveled at the request of the President. Because of that, the railroads in the east had given us a priority run from Washington to Pittsburgh. We had started on one rail line and then transferred to another for the run into Council Bluffs. We rode across Southeastern Nebraska on horse back to find the Butterfield Mail and Overland Express. Again, with White House support we rode nonstop from Hebron Station directly into Fort Bridger.

"My God, this has to be some kind of record!"

"Don't know about the Army, Sir, but that is normal travel speed for United States Marines." Tom said with a grin.

The Colonel started to laugh, got up out of his chair and said to one of the privates sitting along the wall, "These two United States Marines and I are going down to the Red Horse and have a drink."

The people at the Red Horse, knew the Colonel. They could not find us an out of the way table fast enough. The Colonel ordered a bottle and three glasses. When he had poured the drinks he said, "I will follow the President's Directive to the letter. You know, I have never seen the White House, let alone had orders from them."

"My boss is Secretary Toucey in the Army Navy building right across from the White House. Once you start working there, it gets normal. When the President sends an officer courier out onto the battlefield it is supposed to be impressive to the theater commander."

"It is. Have you read the Directive, Captain?"

"No, I was given my mission orders and told to deliver three packets."

"Three?"

"Yes, I am to find Brigham Young and a Mister Thomas Kane from Sacramento who is traveling to Utah."

"I can help you find Brigham Young, I can have an army cavalry escort take you out to him whenever you want to go."

"Do you have any extra mounts?"

"How ever many you need, Captain. What do have in mind?"

"I think that the Master Sergeant here has a little fire power demonstration that he would like to give for all the Mormon troops. Sort of show them what they are up against in the next round of confrontation."

"I will need a couple of wagons, Colonel." Tom said.

"The wagons have to be heavy enough to support two Navy deck mounted weapons, one on each wagon. My men will take about a day getting everything together for our little show of force." Tom added, "Is that alright with you, Colonel?"

"I would like to be there to see what you have planned."

"Are you willing to go disguised as a cavalry rider?" I asked.

"Yes, count me in on a little payback for that ambush on October sixth!"

We finished our plans with the Colonel and told him we needed to meet with our scouts. Depending upon what they found, we would need the wagons in the morning. He said to ask for whatever we needed and he would see that we got it. Tom and I walked back to the meeting point and found the other fourteen waiting for us.

"Sam, where did you find to store the materials we brought with us?"

"We are in the hay loft over the livery stables. I figured it would be warm and out of the weather for one or two nights."

"Excellent, Corporal Peters, we are going to need your blacksmith skills. The mounts for Tom's guns are on the freight coach which will not arrive for two days. Can you make us two mounts that can be bolted onto a heavy wagon?"

"Yes, Sir. I will need timbers."

"Any volunteers to help the Corporal?"

Two men went with the Corporal to the blacksmith shop and two volunteered to go and buy timbers at the saw mill. I told them where Colonel Johnson's headquarters were and sent them to get two wagons and have them pick up the timber and have it pulled to the blacksmiths shop tomorrow. Tom and I rode with the Colonel to Camp Floyd and met his executive officer, Major Allen. The Major said he knew where to find the Mormon militia, they were camped just inside the Utah Territory border. In fact, he said he thought that the militia had the road blocked at the border with overturned wagons.

"That will be our demonstration of will," I said. "Tomorrow we will arrive at the blockade and remove it with some Navy gunfire."

"Major, I want you and a detail of cavalry to escort Captain Caldwell and his men. Let the Navy do all the work, we are just there to watch and learn." said the Colonel.

"You are coming, Colonel?"

"Yes, I will ride as one of the cavalry escorts. I want to see what these Marines are up to."

By midmorning of the following day we had our two battle wagons ready. Tom was riding in one and Corporal Peters was riding in the other. Each wagon had extra rounds and a loader for each gun. We brushed the hay dust from our winter uniforms and made ourselves presentable. The Colonel showed up as we drove the wagons out the front gate of Fort Bridger. We drove to Camp Floyd and picked up our cavalry escort. Fifty men rode towards the border to face the militia. Two white flags were flying from short poles mounted on each wagon. We reached the overturned wagons blocking the road and swept the area with the Major's field glass.

"I see only two men on horseback at the moment." he said.

"Good, Sergeant Schneider, Corporal Peters, do your work."

Both battle wagons opened up with the deck guns and poured hundreds of rounds of heavy caliber shells into the overturned wagons in the next minute. Pieces of wood flew through the air and into the woods on both sides of the road. In the distance a bugle sounded, it was probably from the militia camp.

"Move out, troops!"

The wagons went first flying the white parlay flags. They were followed by the cavalry and then a troop wagon carrying the rest of the Marine Detachment. We had not gotten half- a- mile when militia cavalry met us on the road.

"We have a message for your supreme leader, Brigham Young, from the President of the United States, James Buchanan."

"What is the message?"

"It is a written packet of materials, letters of pardon and conditions for ending the hostilities," I said.

"Follow us."

The militia riders turned and led us into their camp. I noticed that there were not 5000 troops in camp, probably a couple hundred at most. The look of surprise on the Colonel's face was informative. He had withdrawn from the Utah Territory because he was facing a much larger force. Now he could come across the border and remove the threat.

At that moment, two riders came at a gallop into the camp. They dismounted and ran into a rather large tent. A few minutes later, the flap flew back and Brigham Young strode out of his command post and walked up to the first wagon and said, "What is the meaning of this?" I knew then that we had his attention. I dismounted, walked to the front of the wagon and removed a packet which was marked, *Commander Utah Militia, Blacks Ford, Utah Territory.*

I walked to him and said, "From the President of the United States, for you, Sir."

"What is it?"

"It is a series of documents, Sir. The first is a letter from the White House introducing me, Captain Caldwell, from the Army Navy Building, Washington City. The second is a series of Presidential pardons for anyone who has killed someone during the month of October, 1857. The third is an appointment for you to meet with the State Department to discuss Statehood for the Utah Territory. A Mr. Thomas Kane, from the State Department is on his way here to meet with you at your convenience."

"I hope he is diplomatic in nature, Captain Caldwell. My men just told me of your calling card at the border crossing."

"Time is critical for your response to the President and my instructions were to remove any obstacles towards producing a peaceful settlement. I viewed the blocked roadway as an obstacle. Would you care to sign for receipt of the packet, Sir? We need to return to Washington tomorrow."

I handed him a pen, kneeled down on one knee and bent my back so that Brigham Young, leader of the Church of Latter Day Saints, could use me as a desk. He signed the receipt with a flourish, turned on his heel and returned to his tent. I stood up, bowed to the militia captain who had brought us to camp and mounted my horse.

"United States Marine Detachment about face," I shouted at the top of my lungs.

We wheeled smartly around and left the camp riding towards Camp Floyd. We dropped the Major there and continued on into Fort Bridger. Colonel Johnson had not said a word until we arrived inside the fort and had dismounted.

"Remind me never to play poker with you, Captain Caldwell!"

"Colonel, you never know, we could all be laying dead in Utah!"

"Do you think Young will accept the President's proposals?"

"He is a fool if he does not, it will all be handled by the State Department."

"My job will be done as soon as the third packet is delivered. I have, in fact, two identical packets for Thomas Kane. One I will leave with you, addressed to him. The other I will mail with the Buttefield Service to Sacramento as we leave on the morning stage."

"Gone already, you just got here!"

"I know, remember what my Sergeant said about US Marines and their speed of travel?"

"Yes, I thought that was hilarious!"

"Well, this detachment of Marines is lead by a Navy Captain. And the Navy travels faster than the Marines." I said with a straight face.

"Aye, aye, Captain." He snapped a perfect salute and walked into his office.

I stood there in the mud and said, "Besides, the First Lady does like me to take long, out of town, trips."

38
Return to Washington
October 26, 1857

Fort Bridger awoke the morning of October 26, 1857, to a termination dusting by Mother Nature. The mountain people called a heavy frost of about a quarter of an inch, a termination dust. This meant the termination of summer. Tom was already up, dressed, down out of the hay loft and out of the livery stable. I had sent him to check on the two passenger coaches that we had kept aside when we arrived on the twenty-third. He was to see if someone would get the horses harnessed and return. He returned with a smile on his face.

"Captain, you are not going to believe this. The Colonel has Major Allen's cavalry escort outside as an honor guard for us."

"Marines, listen up. The Army is going to send us off in style. Everyone get the dust off your uniforms and look ship shape. You all know how I feel about you. Privates in the detachment, come to order! You now are Corporals, field grade. Corporals in the detachment, come to order! You are now First Sergeants, field grade!" I turned to Tom and said, "Sergeant, form the men in columns of two, we are marching out of Fort Bridger and getting on the Overland Express!"

"Columns of two, look sharp! F'ward arch. One, two – three, four."

"Sergeant, I think the men could use a little encouragement, how about a cadence call?"

> **"When we die, our mother's will cry;**
> **One, two – three, four,**
> **When Army boys bite the dust,**
> **One, two – three, four,**
> **They will go to heaven on their knees,**
> **One, two – three, four**
> **And when they get there, they will find,**
> **One, two – three, four,**
> **The streets are guarded by, United States Marines!**

When we reached the Colonel's horse, I shouted, "Detachment halt, about face, present arms!"

In unison the marines snapped their Henry rifles from their shoulders and brought them front and center. "Care to inspect the detachment, Colonel?"

Colonel Johnson dismounted and walked along the formation with me following him. "What is your name, Private?" the Colonel asked.

"Corporal D. D. Wilson, Sir."

"And what is your name, Private?"

"Corporal James, Sir."

The Colonel smiled, turned to me and said, "I like your style, Captain." He extended his hand and said, "Have a safe journey."

The sky looked a dark gray, yellowish color as the two coaches pulled out of Fort Bridger on the road to Big Pond. The freight coach had arrived last night and was loaded with our gear. Keets and Franks looked mended and not the worse for wear as they had additional amounts of sleep compared to the rest of the detachment. That meant that we were back to eighteen members and we were happy to be on our way to Julesburg station. If we could reach there before heavy snows, we would be back in Washington in mid or late November.

We had fresh horses and drivers at each station. We kept moving day and night until we reached Julesburg. Once there, we slept the night. From Julesburg to St. Joseph we slept every night in stations that provided overnights. We stopped at Hebron Station to send telegrams to; The White House, Army Navy Building, General Dodge and St. Joseph, Naval Depot. The President was given the mission completed statement in code. The Secretary was given the mission successful statement, again in code. General Dodge's message was a thank you for assistance. St. Joe depot was given a warning that we were about to need river boat transport for an eighteen man detachment. The origin point is St. Joseph depot and the termination point is Pittsburgh. We would be making a stop at St. Louis depot (confluence of Missouri and Mississippi rivers). The Cairo depot is located at the confluence of the Mississippi and Ohio rivers. The Cincinnati depot is on the Ohio. We would end our river transport at Pittsburgh. Transport request was not urgent. Layovers were preferred with two day leaves requested for St. Louis, Cincinnati, and Pittsburgh.

I decided that the rest of my money belt would be divided equally among the men so they could enjoy their leaves. The Navy would not miss it and the men would have memories that they could share with their children some day and I said to myself, "*I wish I had met someone earlier in my life and not at the end of my career.*" I made a mental note to write Louise.

We left Hebron Station and headed for the St. Joseph, Naval Depot. Upon reaching this point, the heavy equipment was packed into wooden crates and marked **_RR tools_**. The rest of our gear was carried aboard, stowed below and we headed for St. Louis. In St. Louis, I found a nice hotel and rented nine rooms for two nights. Once in my room, I located pen and paper began a series of letters. The first was to my family in South Carolina.

BELMONT HOTEL
St. Louis, Missouri
November 12, 1857

Dear Mother and Father,

I am spending a couple of days in St. Louis. My detachment is in route back to Washington City. This assignment into the West has given me an opportunity to think about my future. I have decided that I will finish my Navy Career at the end of the Buchanan Administration in 1865. I have been away from South Carolina for far too long and I miss it.

I have met someone in Washington City. If she will have me, I will bring her home to meet y'all. We will come home as soon as she can arrange to be away from her duties in The White House. More information when I can find time.

Your Son,

Jason

The next was harder to write. I started and stopped several times but when I finished I was happy with the results.

BELMONT HOTEL
St. Louis, Missouri
November 12, 1857

Dear Louise,

I am spending a couple of days in St. Louis. My detachment is in route back to Washington City. This assignment into the West has given me an opportunity to think about my future. I have decided that I will finish my Navy Career at the end of your brother's administration in 1865. I have been away from South

Carolina for far too long and I miss it. I wrote to my parents in Beaufort and told them how I feel about you. Actually, I wrote that I had finally met someone with whom I could share the rest of my life . I just needed to find out if she felt the same way.

If you will have me, as your life's partner, I will bring you to our future home in Beaufort. It is 353 Bay Street, overlooking the intercoastal waterway. At high tide it is beautiful, at low tide it smells like shell fish - but I love it and I hope you will too. I do not need the Navy to make my life complete now that I have found you. I am the owner of the Caldwell Shipping and Trading Company of Port Royal, South Carolina. I co-own with my father and brother, a sea island plantation. You and I will be kept very busy with the business and social activities of Beaufort. It is a long time until '65 — but I wanted you to know how I feel.

Lovingly,

Jason

When we docked in Cairo, Illinois, the following messages were waiting for me at Naval Depot.

THE WHITE HOUSE
Washington City

November 8, 1857

Jason E. Caldwell, Captain USN
Cairo Naval Depot
Cairo, Illinois

Dear Captain Caldwell:

I received your telegram and have read your after action report filed with Secretary Toucey. I share your belief that the situation in Utah is now defused. I agree with Secretary Toucey that it will be a matter of months before the State Department will make contact with Brigham Young.

When contact is made, the groundwork has already been done by your service to the Commander-in-Chief. Your willingness to be my special envoy on missions of this type is appreciated and will not be forgotten. Upon your return to Washington, set an appointment to meet with me about your future services and position of importance to this administration.

James Buchanan
James Buchanan
President of the United States
1st endorsement Department of the Navy

DEPARTMENT OF THE NAVY
Washington City

November 8, 1857

Jason Caldwell, Captain USN
Cairo Naval Depot
Cairo, Illinois

Dear Captain Caldwell:

I have received your after action report and forwarded a copy to the President along with my thoughts on how matters stand at this time He will, undoubtedly, want to visit with you upon your return to Washington. Your request for leave is hereby granted. Your recommendations for official promotions, making your field promotions permanent, have also been granted.

Isaac Toucey
Isaac Toucey
Secretary of the Navy

But there were no personals for me. I asked when we were scheduled to leave for Cincinnati. I walked the river front and was deep in thought when Corporal Peters approached and said, "Captain, they are about to push off."

"Thank you, Sergeant, tell the others that their promotions are now permanent."

We spent the next few days traveling on the Ohio River, stopped at Cincinnati for two days and finally docked in Pittsburgh. I was leaving the docks to get the men hotel rooms, when a Navy Chief said, "There are personals and messages for you, Captain." I took them and tore open the one marked personal from The White House.

THE WHITE HOUSE
WASHINGTON CITY
November 18, 1857

Dearest Jason,

Your heartfelt letter arrived to day and I am answering you immediately. My answer is, I will wait for you until you ask me to marry you. I do not think that you will have to wait until 1865 to retire, however. I am telling you this in confidence, my brother will not seek the nomination from the Democratic Party in 1860. He too, says he misses spending time with his life's partner and he plans to retire from public life after the election of '60.

My brother has accepted your invitation to visit you in South Carolina. He will bring us on the USS Charter Oak via Charleston. He will drop Secretary Toucey in Charleston and continue on to Beaufort. He has also told me that you are a man of honor and I would be fortunate to have you as a husband. I can not wait to embrace you again and to make our future plans together!

With all my love,

Louise

We were committed to the two day leave before heading back to Washington by train and I spent my time writing letters again. I hurriedly wrote to my brother, and parents.

Pioneer Hotel
Pittsburgh, Pennsylvania
November 24, 1857

Dear Mother and Father,

Today, I am in Pittsburgh. I will leave with my detachment for Washington on the 26 of November. I have heard from my friend in the White House. The news could not be better, she has agreed to marry me in the near future. We have not discussed where the marriage will take place, I assume it will be the Buchanan's home church in Pennsylvania. I will take her to see our church in Sheldon when we are home.

Her brother, the President of the United States, has agreed to bring them both to Beaufort to meet you both. I have no dates for their arrival at this writing but I will send the date of arrival with plenty of advance warning. A Presidential visit to Beaufort is rare indeed and we will want to prepare properly. Please open my house on Bay Street, have it cleaned and hire the necessary household staff to welcome the President.

There are probably many other things that I am forgetting. Please share in my joy and happiness. I will be home on leave for 30 days as soon as I can arrange for my temporary replacement at the Army Navy Building. Waiting to see you again, I remain

Your loving Son,

Jason

We arrived back in Washington City with no fan fare and no one meeting us at the train station. It had taken us nearly two months to accomplish a simple mission. The reason was the physical size of the nation. The nation needed a transcontinental railroad, telegraph and road system. Instead, the nation had a financial panic when the President tried to push the railroads westward. It was easier to send a telegram to England via transatlantic cable than it was to communicate with our own western territories. The territories of Minnesota, Utah, Oregon and others had applied for Statehood. I could not see my job getting any easier.

Two days after I was back in the Army Navy Building, the President sent for me. I walked over and sat outside his office. He will see you now, Captain. I rose and entered the Oval Office.

"Jason, I am glad to see you back at work."

"Thank you, Mister President. It was a long trip with so little to show for it."

"Nonsense. You have no idea how much I am beginning to rely on your creative solutions to the problems of this country."

"Thank you again, Mister President."

"Jason, I have had quite a few conversations with my sister these last two months. She has missed you greatly. I think it surprised her how much. She never thought she would meet a man that would make her life complete. She loves you completely."

"I feel the same way, Mister President."

"Please, Jason, if we are going to be brother-in-laws, I think you need to start calling me, James, when we are alone."

"I will try to remember that, Mister President."

"After we are finished here, find Louise and set a date for our visit to South Carolina. We both need to get away from Washington. This place will grind you up and spit you out. It is not at all what I expected when I was elected. When we return from South Carolina, I would like you to consider moving over to the White House on a permanent basis."

"What would you like me to do?"

"I need someone here at the White House to oversee the missions that you have been undertaking from the office of Naval Intelligence. You are too valuable to me to be gone two months at a time on a single mission. I would like you to run several missions from the White House at the same time. Do you think you could do that?"

"Yes, Mister President. I would like to keep my rank in the Navy, however, it would be helpful in getting things done."

"I am sorry, Jason, I can not do that. I have sent your name to the US Senate for conformation as our first Admiral from South Carolina and my new National Affairs Advisor. This will be a cabinet level position but without Secretary status."

"I, I am overwhelmed, Mr. President. Thank you, my father will be so proud to hear this."

"Jason, Jason. He already is proud of you. Now, go find my sister and give her the good news."

39
Home to South Carolina
February 1858

I was granted thirty days home leave and fifteen days travel leave. I asked Louise Buchanan if she would travel with me provided that the ship's captain could marry us. She did not blink an eye when she said, "Jason Caldwell, I thought you would never ask."

"We have waited long enough, I do not want to spend another day without you at my side."

"Oh, you southern gentlemen have a way with words. My brother will want to be at my wedding, Jason, how can I tell him we are going to do this without him?"

"We will tell him that a formal wedding is planned for the Episcopal Church in Sheldon, South Carolina. He will attend that, as my best man, on his Presidential Visit in March."

"I wonder how he will react? James and I have no brothers or sisters, only each other since our parents died. Did I ever tell you why there is such an age difference between us?"

"No, tell me."

"Our father was married three times, James is the oldest, from the first wife and I am the youngest from the third wife. James is nearly 60 years of age!"

"Yes, I know, that makes you almost 50, yes?" I got a sharp elbow in the ribs.

"I am not 50 years old, I am 20 years younger than James! He has always been there for his little sister. We have traveled the world together. He was foreign minister to both England and Russia, did you know that?"

"Yes, Louise. I am aware of your brother's career, ambassadorships, and Secretary of State service. He is ideally suited to be President of the United States."

"When do you want to leave, Jason? Do you think your family will like me? Oh, Jason, I am so scared!"

"My brother, Robert, will love you. His wife, Mariann, will be so impressed with meeting you that she will be worried that you will not like her. In fact, the whole family will be that way, you do not have to worry about a thing. My family probably thinks I am marrying way, way above my social status, but I do not think about things like that when I am around you."

"What do you think about?"

"Do you remember how we met? It was at a State function for some King, or other. Dinner was over and the ballroom was open for guests. Your brother does not dance and you were standing beside him, being the First Lady. I walked by you and you reached out and pinched my arm and asked if I danced."

"Yes, you looked so startled you could not even respond."

"When I found my voice, I said, "Of course, ma'am!" We had several dances that night and every time I looked into your eyes I was drawn in deeper and deeper."

"Jason, you are a romantic at heart."

"I guess, I am around you."

"That did not happen for me until you kissed me the first time."

"I never wanted to kiss a girl so much in my life!"

"What is the weather like, this time of year, in South Carolina?"

"Who cares? We will we spend all our time in the bedroom."

"Jason, really, control yourself!" She was giggling so I knew I was alright.

"Louise, you still have to function within the White House. When we get back, I will be in the office section of the White House all day and you will be occupied running the place. The only time we will have to ourselves is when we are alone in one of the upstairs bedrooms. Let us spend the next month practicing what people do best there."

She blushed and said, "I am ready when you are."

"Good, get packed for the trip and let us get started with the rest of our lives."

The ship taking us to Beaufort was a small steamer with comfortable cabins and a nice walking area all around the deck. The captain married us just outside the Chesapeake Bay. We floated down the east coast to Port Royal, South Carolina, on our honeymoon. My brother, Robert, had a carriage and driver waiting at the docks.

"How did you know when we would be arriving?" I asked the driver.

"Your brother told me to meet every ship docking during last three days. He wanted to impress you."

"Tell him, I am. May I introduce you to Mrs. Caldwell? I am sorry, I do not know your name."

"It is Kevin, Sir."

"Louise this is, Kevin, he works for my brother."

"Actually, I work for you. I am employed by Caldwell Trading and Shipping."

"Well, Kevin, get us to 353 Bay Street, so my bride can see her house."

"Admiral, you do know that the whole family; mother, father, brother, sister, cousins, nieces, nephews, etc.,etc. are waiting there."

"Better to get the introductions over all at once, Kevin."

I squeezed Louise's arm and she pinched me somewhere other than the arm. The carriage ride was bumpy as we left Port Royal and started for Beaufort. As we passed houses, inns, stores and what not, I talked nonstop.

"Jason, are you nervous?"

"Yes, I wonder why?"

"Take a deep breath and be a good boy, until everyone leaves!"

"Oh, Louise, I love you so much!"

Before I was ready, the carriage pulled into 353 Bay Street and stopped under a white painted portico attached to the side of the house.

"Oh, Jason, you said you owned a house. This is a mansion. How many rooms are there?"

I could not answer before the side porch filled with shouting, joyous people.

"Jason, Jason. Uncle Jason, over here. Hey, brother. Jason, Son, how are you?" The sounds came crashing down around us.

"Folks, line up so I can introduce y'all."

"Y'all? Jason, you are home, I can tell!" Louise was smiling as she took my hand and stepped down from the carriage.

"Mother, Father, this is Louise Buchanan Caldwell. Robert, Mariann, this is your sister-in-law. Carol and Carl, this is your sister-in-law. Dennis and Jacob, this is your cousin. Mary and Samuel, this is your cousin." This went on and on until my hand was tired of shaking and Louise was totally confused.

"Come inside and have something to eat. Kevin, get the luggage for them." My father said.

"Yes, Sir, Mister Caldwell."

People moved in mass across the porch and into the house. The mass broke up and flowed into the first floor rooms. Louise's eyes were wide as she tried to take in everything at once. A house keeper, I had never met, came forward and welcomed Louise to her home. Tears were rolling down her cheeks when Louise turned and said, "Thank you, thank you everyone for this."

My father, Robert Hays Caldwell the second, made a toast to the bride and groom. My brother, Robert Hays Caldwell the third, welcomed both of us to Beaufort. My cousin, Mary, welcomed us to South Carolina. And so it went on and on. Finally, Trey, my brother said, "Time to leave these newlyweds alone for awhile. Those of you who want to join us further down Bay Street, I am buying."

Everyone laughed, but they finally left one by one. We were exhausted as we walked up the center stairway to the second floor and were greeted by Louise's maid. She took Louise into the master suite and showed her where she had laid out her things, where she had hung some clothes and mentioned that she had taken some clothes down to the laundry. They would be returned tomorrow, unless she needed them for tonight.

"Jason, what time is it?"

"I do not know, I am going to take a short nap." I took off my shoes and fell on top of the bed. I awoke the next morning as the sun rose across the bay front. I had no clothes on! Louise was smiling at me. She was as bare as a new born also.

"Jason, are we always going to have the same bedroom?"

"You like one of the other bedrooms better?"

"No, I mean are we always going to sleep in the same bed? Some people have separate bedrooms after they are married awhile."

"I can not imagine not sharing every minute with you awake or asleep. Let us think about it and we can talk about it again in 50 years."

A knock on the door interrupted our conversation. "Mrs. Caldwell, Admiral, are you awake and ready for breakfast?"

"Yes, we will be down shortly."

"I have it on a tray, Sir, I will sit in the hall for you."

"Louise, what do you want to do today?"

"I need to go shopping, but before I do, I will need to rearrange this bedroom."

"Rearrange?"

"Maybe remodel would be a better word. Do you have a carpenter working for you?"

"Over in Port Royal, why?"

"We need to add shelves and places for women's things, Jason. It is obvious you were never married or lived with a woman before."

"What do you mean, what is wrong?"

"Nothing is wrong, except there is no room for women's clothes and other things. Trust me, let me give directions to your carpenter and you will be pleased with the results."

"You are the lady of this house, just like at 1600 Pennsylvania Ave. You can add, subtract or do anything inside that you want."

"We are only a few blocks from town and I would like to shop there for a few things today." Louise left the house after breakfast and walked down Bay street with her maid and scouted out every shop and dry goods store along Bay Street. They returned in a few hours empty handed.

"You were unable to find anything you liked?" I asked.

"No, I found a few things." Her maid rolled her eyes to tell me, not a few. "When I tried to pay for them the clerks would not take my money. They said you had an account there and they would send you a bill at the end of the month."

"So, are you upset?"

"Yes, I have money, Jason. We are married and I want to feel like I am contributing to our home and family here in Beaufort."

"Louise, you must understand, you are in South Carolina now, right or wrong, men control everything here. Do you feel like walking back to those shops? If you do, I will go with you and have my name taken off the accounts. Your name will replace mine. The bill will be sent to you instead of me. How would that suit you?"

"Great, we need to go back right now!"

The next day we walked back to town again, but this time we boarded the ferry to cross the river to the next barrier island called Lady's Island. My brother had a carriage and driver waiting for us and we drove along a dirt road until we came to another smaller stream called Cowen Creek. The horses and carriage forded the stream because it was low tide. We were on our way to the family plantation. It took two hours of fording at low tide or ferry to reach Datha Island. We left the carriage on Datha and stepped into a flat bottom boat to get to Pollawana Island. This entire island was a working plantation, owned by the Caldwell's since 1797. We got into a second carriage and started for the house. Field hands were working and I asked the driver to stop. I walked over to my childhood companion, Tobias, and asked him how his wife and children were.

" Mr. Robert said y'all were coming today, Mr. Jason. It sure is good to see you again. How many years have you been up there in Washington?"

"Too many, Tobias, it is good to be home in Beaufort again!"

"All us folks is coming to the feast that Mr. Robert has got laid out for you and your bride."

"See you then, Tobias." I walked back to the carriage.

"Jason?"

"Yes, Louise."

"Do you approve of slavery?"

"Certainly not. The Caldwell's do not own any slaves!"

"Who was that man you were talking to?"

"That was Tobias, my childhood friend. My father granted him his freedom when he became of age, he is the overseer here. I could have slaves on the docks at Port Royal, but I would rather hire workers already trained to do the work. The decision to bring slaves to work on the large farms in Maryland and the plantations of the southern states was made when we were colonies of Britain. Slavery was legal in Britain at that time and they sold them to us. All of the slaves that were held here on this plantation are now free or are indentured servants. Your brother has stopped slave ships from bringing Africans to this country. The slave market in Charleston deals only with American born slaves."

"But slavery is wrong, correct?"

"In my opinion, as it exists today, in South Carolina, it is no longer necessary. Your brother has talked about freeing all the indentured servants in this country because there is enough money in the treasury to do that. There is not enough money in the US Treasury after the Panic of '57 to purchase all the slaves in the United States."

"If there was enough, would that end slavery?" She asked.

"Yes, I believe that if plantation owners were compensated for property taken from them today, slavery would end today. It is much cheaper to hire workers during planting and harvesting times than it is to keep them year around. Louise, slavery will end in this country in just a short time, probably less than five years."

"Do you think my brother would end slavery if he could?"

"Without a doubt, he is the most honorable man I have met."

"That is what he says about you, Jason, no wonder you get along so well!" Louise was at ease the rest of the day as she met Tobias, his wife and children and the rest of the field workers.

"Why do they stay, if they are free, Jason?"

"I suppose it is a number of things. Freemen with black faces are assumed to be run away slaves in this State. It is hard for them to travel anywhere. Your brother is going to change that, I think. Another, it is a matter of income, they have wages here, I know it is not much. They do not pay rent for housing or food. Maybe it is the best they can expect when the country is divided like it is."

"Jason, when are we going to Sheldon? Why is it so important to you that we have a formal wedding there?"

"Sheldon was a small village during the American Revolution. About halfway through the war, a company of British Dragoons rounded up all the people of Sheldon. They placed them inside the church and burned it to the ground."

"Jason, that is terrible! Why would they do such a thing?"

"They were giving aid to Francis Marion's Militia. When my Great Grandfather heard this, he rode from Beaufort and wept at the burned remains. He returned to Beaufort and began raising money to rebuild the church in brick, not wood. After it was completed, he brought his family from Beaufort as regular members. Most of the family now attends St. Helena's in Beaufort, but my farther is a man of honor, every Easter he takes us all out to Sheldon to sit inside the church that his Grandfather helped build. We look out through the stained glass windows and are comforted that a brick church is fire proof.

40
Presidential Visit
March 1858

A Presidential visit anywhere is controlled chaos. The trip to South Carolina was planned and announced to the newspapers. Because he would travel by ship, Navy personnel were put in charge of the transportation. They would be responsible for the safety and well being of the Commander-in-Chief, his sister traveling with him, the Secretary of the Navy and an Admiral Caldwell. The USS *Charter Oak* was used by the President whenever he traveled on the East Coast of the United States. Naturally the President's suite was suitable for a head of state and was usually occupied by the Secretary of the Navy whenever the President was not on board. When the Secretary of the Navy was not on board, then the senior most Admiral would occupy the suite. I was the most junior in the Navy and would never see it.

Plans were progressing when the President's life was threatened by a South Carolina House of Representatives member during a heated debate in Columbia, the Capital of the State. The representative was detained by local law enforcement, the speech was reported in the State Newspapers and, therefore, had to be taken seriously. When news of this reached Washington City, I advised the President to take it seriously and to take the following precautions before his visit to Beaufort, South Carolina.

1. Provide a security force within the White House. This force would consist of at least four agents on duty around the clock. The agents would be trained military or police members dressed in plain clothes. Each would carry a pistol on his person and protect the President. The protection should begin immediately so they could become proficient before the trip began.
2. A chief of Presidential protection protocol be identified and hired before March 1.
3. A search should be made to hire a Presidential double.

James Buchanan always wore a black suit with vest, a white shirt with standup collar and a white cravat tried around his neck. If a man dressed identical to the President could be used during public travel then the threat might be reduced somewhat.

The President looked at my suggestions 1 through 3 and said, "Do you think this is necessary, Jason?"

"I do, Mister President."

"It seems to me that the best way to react to threats of bodily harm is to confront the threat, look it in the eye and say, here I am."

"Much easier to do if you have overpowering strength right by your side, Mr. President. As a personal envoy for you, I was always at ease. I never felt threatened, because I knew that the US Marines that traveled with me would give their lives for my protection."

"You may be right, and that may work. But what I want to do is face the threat. Can you get me an invitation to speak to the State House of Representatives while I am in South Carolina?"

"Yes, I think the best way to handle that is to announce in the newspapers here that you will be giving an address to the Nation while you are visiting South Carolina. The location is yet to be determined, you will meet with Governor Pickens in Columbia and if invited you will give the address to the Nation from the floor of the State House. Otherwise, city officials were planning for the address to be given in Beaufort."

"The State House will get the message, either way, is that your idea, Jason?"

"Exactly, Mr. President!"

"Go ahead with all three items, then."

It was during the preparations for item three, that things began to unravel. One of the actors to be interviewed for a double, appeared for his interview dressed like the President. He grayed his hair almost white and had shaved his forehead to match the receding hairline of the President. He was an unknown stage actor. Louise and I had seen a play at Ford's Theater where he was quite convincing as King Lear. He indicated that he had come for the interview on a dare from a fellow actor. He was hesitant about giving up his stage career and coming to work at the White House. I convinced him to come with me for a walk around the White House. We were walking down the stairway, when an upcoming clerk saw him with me and said, "Good morning, Mr. President. Good morning, Admiral."

I was very pleased with myself until we walked around a corner and there stood the President. "What is the meaning of this?"

"We are trying to see if anyone noticed the likeness, Mr. President." I replied.

206

"Jason." The President said smiling, "Scratch the third item. Nice to see you again, Mr. Booth, I enjoyed your King Lear performance the other night."

The look of shock on John Booth's face was immediate and I had to laugh. " Thank you for coming in, we will not be needing your services." I said. I walked him back to the interview room and he left the White House as I walked to the Oval Office.

"How are the plans getting along for the protection detail, Jason?"

"We are on schedule, Sir. I think I will have a commitment from Lieutenant Commander Lewis to move over to the White House. He will let me know, tomorrow. If he says yes, then we have commitments from two shore patrol officers, one city policeman, and five rapid response unit members. I know all five marines and they are very good."

"See you and Louise on the *Charter Oak* later today then. I have a pile of papers to sign before I leave."

The voyage south this time was consumed with the activities of the floating White House. We stopped at several seaports along the way. The President wanted maximum exposure so we stopped in Virginia and North Carolina before getting to Charleston. These were arranged ports of call with the White House. Telegrams were waiting at all three ports and replies were sent by the President. Secretary Toucey was given a warm reception at Fort Sumter as we raised anchor and moved slowly into the inter-coastal waterway towards Beaufort.

The town of Beaufort had never had a President of the United States visit since it was founded in 1712. Beaufort was built on a bay formed by the mouth of the Beaufort River. Bay Front is a street, a marina, and a place for people to gather in a large park. The founding fathers wanted the Bay of Beaufort to remain pristine for future generations. No building was permitted on the water edge, except for the marina where vessels could dock and a ferry which operated to the barrier islands along the coast. We tied up along side the park at high tide, across from the marina. Thousands of people filled the park to over flowing. The President came down the gang plank because of the tide, followed closely by his protection detail. The sight of armed body guards were not lost on some who pushed forward to greet him.

It took the President, Louise and the rest of the visiting party nearly two hours to move slowly through the crowd and into waiting carriages for the short drive to 353 Bay Street. We arrived and found the porches full of family members, not unlike a month earlier. The luggage was being unloaded from the ship and would be brought over later in the day. The President met my family with Louise at his elbow, trying to remember all those she had met. I was amazed at her ability to place faces with names and smile at the same time. She turned to her brother and said, "James, Jason and I want to welcome you to our home here in Beaufort."

My family beamed their happiness at hearing these simple words. They had accepted her as their daughter. James Buchanan smiled at the group of family assembled and said, "Louise has found the love of her life while working in the White House. After her visit here a month ago, she has found the large, caring family that she has always wanted." He turned to me, surprised me by

pulling me close to him in a huge embrace and whispered in my ear, "Thank you, little brother."

As fast as the emotion appeared, it was gone and the President asked, "Where can my speech writer work, Jason?"

"In my study, Sir. Come this way and I will show you."

Two days later we had arrived in Columbia by train. The President seemed distracted and distant. He entered the South Carolina House of Representatives after the bailiff shouted, "Mr. Speaker: The President of the United States." James Buchanan entered the great hall and walked to the podium. He opened his set of notes and began the Buchanan Proclamation of 1858.

I have chosen this place and this time to announce to the people of the United States, the following executive orders from the fifteenth President of the Union.

First. I have signed, today, executive order 178, which states that as long as I am President, every man, woman or child who presently are known as indentured servants shall be released from their service. I have instructed the Secretary of the Treasury to render payment to all those who presently hold contracts of service. The contract balances will be paid from any federal paymaster throughout the United States of America.

Second. I have signed executive order 179 ,which states that an attempt against the life of any federal employee, officer of a court or member of the United States Government shall be arrested by local law enforcement and remanded to the closest federal detention center. As of today, it is now a federal offense to make an attempt on the life of any federal official.

Third. I have signed executive order 180, which states that no state law enforcement official may cross other state lines in pursuit of fugitives. Once the fugitive has crossed into another state, that fugitive becomes a federal fugitive and when arrested, the fugitive will be returned to the individual state for federal prosecution.

Fourth. I have signed executive order 181, which states that individuals and their properties are to be protected under the laws of that state in which they are held, unless state law is in direct conflict with the federal bill of rights and the constitution of these United States of America. No state, within our union, can dictate how its people practice their religion, feed their families, protect themselves through the right to bear arms or enjoy their God given rights.

Fifth. I have signed executive order 182, which states federal territories who wish to join the union have 180 days to make application. The present rules for admittance to the union are waved until 1860. We have experienced civil war in Kansas and Utah. From this day forward, civil insurrection within states or territories will be met with the full weight of the Army and Navy of the United States.

After this proclamation, he continued with the rest of his speech. It had a homespun flavor. He mentioned how he was born on a farm in Franklin, Pennsylvania, in April, 1799, how he struggled to become a lawyer and he understood how hard working people in South Carolina lived. After all, his sister was married to a man born in Beaufort, South Carolina. He did not mention that his brother-in-law lived and worked in Washington City.

He then added some off the cuff remarks. "You know, this is a great country of ours, it was forged from the great American War of Independence. Men like Francis Marion, of your great State of South Carolina, kept the British from advancing out of Charleston and into the northern colonies. South Carolina has always taken the lead in the concept of 'death before dishonor'. As your President, I ask you today to dedicate, reaffirm and set forth your sense of honor. Honor your families, the state in which you live and the country you helped create less than a hundred years ago. We would still be British colonies today if not for the people of South Carolina. This country is your creation, your hope for the future and your destiny."

41
Proclamation Reactions
May 1858

The immediate reaction by my father to President Buchanan's address on the floor of the State House was to start the paperwork necessary for all the indentured servants working for him. This amounted to a windfall profit for the family. The executive order 178 did not apply to property held as slaves. Some of the larger plantation owners were angry, and some of them said, "Why should the Caldwells profit and not them?"

"You could have made your slaves indentured servants several years ago, as I did." My father replied. But they did not want to hear this and some stopped talking to him and took their business elsewhere.

Proclamation 180 caused another immediate reaction. Angry slave holders said the President was trying to make the return of run away slaves more difficult or impossible. Of course, that was exactly what the President had in mind when he wrote it!

The biggest reaction came from Proclamation 182, however. Minnesota applied for statehood and it was granted on May 11, 1858. Oregon applied and was granted statehood on February of 1859. Utah applied and was given provisional status until federal troops could be removed from the territory. This produced more free states than slave holding states. This caused the people of South Carolina to feel the need to strengthen their position on slavery. The supreme court ruling, known as the Dred Scott decision, put them squarely in the right to own slaves as property and further to move them from state to state.

So now it was up to those serving in Washington City to protect the property rights of those living in the South. Southern senators and representatives introduced bills of protection. Secretary Howell Cobb issued payment to slave holders after-the-fact in the State of Georgia. His agents were told not to check the dates that former slaves were made indentured servants. Secretary Floyd told his agents to ignore federal prosecution of run away bounty hunters.

"The amount of cases that this will produce are beyond our ability to prosecute on a case by case basis," Secretary Floyd said.

Secretary Thompson said federal funds would be made available to assist those property owners who wished to relocate their property from a slave holding state to a free state. When this reached the President, he sent for me.

"Jason, we need to sit hard on some of my cabinet members. You are my National Affairs Advisor, how can we get harmony and cooperation from Secretaries Cobb, Floyd and Thompson?"

"Cobb is from Georgia, Floyd is from Virginia and Thompson is from Mississippi. It is under-standable why they reacted the way they did. They are thinking about their futures back in their home states. If we can get them to listen to the moderates from their home states, then they may pull back somewhat."

The President nodded and said, "Continue."

"Suppose we can flood Secretary Cobb's office with requests for payment of freed slaves. What do you think would happen if the Atlanta Journal ran an article that quoted you as saying that the property owners in Georgia have the right idea? Free the slaves in seven years by making them indentured servants. You applaud Mr. Cobb in his attempts to free all the slaves in the State of Georgia using this means."

"Jason, if I do that, Howell Cobb will be in here in a matter of days telling me why he cannot make payment for this underhanded way of freeing every slave in Georgia." He was smiling.

"Now, for Mr. Floyd, what if you give the task of enforcement of the bounty hunters to a well known Virginian, say our Colonel Robert Lee? He is more popular in Virginia than Floyd and an order from the Commander-in-Chief is not questioned by a Secretary of War."

"Get me an appointment with Colonel Lee. What about Thompson?"

"What about him? Moving slaves from state to state is legal until the supreme court says it isn't. The funding of this may not be, however. The Department of the Interior has federal land management responsibilities only. That would mean the property owners would be moving slaves onto federal land, and I do not think that is legal. Your Attorney General could have a little talk with Secretary Thompson about violation of federal laws, misappropriation of federal funds, etc. etc."

"Thank you, Jason. See you at dinner."

I left the Oval Office and walked over to the Army Navy building. I asked at Secretary Toucey's office if they knew the whereabouts of Captain Benjamin Hagood, skipper of the USS *Intrepid*. I was told they were docked in Baltimore and would be there a few more days. I thanked them and said that the President would like to send a telegram through me. I wrote the following to be sent over the public telegraph.

Captain Benjamin Hagood
USS Intrepid
Baltimore Harbor

BEN – JASON HERE – NEED NAME OF YOUR FAVORITE EDITORIAL WRITER ATLANTA JOURNAL – PRESIDENT NEEDS TO SEND INFORMATION – RESPOND DIRECTLY TO ME.

JASON CALDWELL, ADMIRAL
OFFICE OF NATIONAL AFFAIRS
1600 PENN. AVE.
WASHINGTON CITY

The next day a response came to the White House.

Admiral Jason Caldwell
1600 Penn. Ave.
Washington City

JASON – BEN HERE – NAME YOU ARE LOOKING FOR – WILLIAM JAMES – CABLE DEPOT – ATLANTA JOURNAL – 1290 PEACH TREE PLAZA – ATLANTA. GRANTED 30 DAY LEAVE – WILL COME TO WASHINGTON IF INVITED. MUST MEET WOMAN CRAZY ENOUGH TO MARRY YOU.

BENJAMIN HAGOOD
USS INTREPID
BALTIMORE HARBOR

I smiled as I read the cable and walked out of my office in search of Louise. The following day an invitation was mailed to Baltimore. The First Lady had outdone herself.

THE WHITE HOUSE
OFFICE OF PROTOCOL

June 11, 1858

Captain Benjamin Hagood
US Navy Yards
Baltimore, Maryland

The President of the United States requests the honor of your presence on the evening of June 20, 1858. This date is the anniversary of the United States Rapid Response Detachment formation.

Dinner will be served in the State Dining Room at seven post meridian. Dress uniform will be required. RSVP to Mrs. Louise Buchanan Caldwell, Office of Protocol, 1600 Pennsylvania Ave, Washington City.

James Buchanan
James Buchanan
President of the United States

I wrote the following letter and sent it to Ben.

THE WHITE HOUSE
OFFICE OF NATIONAL AFFAIRS
June 11, 1858

Dear Ben,

You will get your invitation to the White House as promised, be looking for it. The President, my brother-in-law, likes to have people around him. He will have the detachment for a party on June 20. But, you come a week earlier if you can, train connections are good. You should not have any problems getting here. You know many of the detachment members from our time spent in Nantucket. Tom Schneider you will remember, I am sure. Sam Mason and his wife have a new baby. Life goes on. A Lieutenant Commander Lewis, you may not know from his time in the detachment, but he is the head of the Presidential Protection detail here in the White House and is an interesting character to say the least.

Louise and I have been home to South Carolina twice since we were married. She is getting used to Beaufort and southern hospitality. Hope your parents are

213

*in good health and looking forward to your visit home to Savannah. Waiting to
see you again, I remain*

Sincerely yours,

Jason Caldwell, Class of '37

Ben arrived four days early and I introduced him to the President.

"Captain, this is an honor for me. Jason has told me how the two of you
were responsible for the return of HMS *Resolute* in '56."

"It is an honor to meet you, Mr. President."

"I have a request I would like to make of you. It is not an order from the
Commander-in-Chief, it is something I want you to think about."

"Yes, Mr. President?"

"How would you like to form a rapid naval attack force? To begin with,
I think the Secretary of the Navy could spare two more ships besides the
Intrepid to cover the Atlantic coast. I would also like to have another three
ships in San Francisco to cover the Pacific Coast."

"Sounds like something the Intrepid would be ideally suited to perform,
Mr. President."

"It would mean you would have to give up being the Captain of the
Intrepid. Jason here, tells me you are a sailor and want to spend your time on
the ocean. I respect that. My question to you is, can you take command of
a small attack fleet as a Commodore?"

"Aboard one of the ships? Yes! Thank you, Mr. President, I will not let
you down."

"I know you will do everything in your power to serve the Secretary of
the Navy and your Commander-in-Chief. Tomorrow, I will have Secretary
Toucey complete the paper work for promotion and I will sign it."

The look on Ben's face must have been similar to mine when I was
nominated. I shook his hand and said, "Congratulations, Commodore
Hagood."

When we were alone, I said to Ben, "You do not know how happy I am,
Ben. I am no longer the newest one star in the Navy!"

He grinned and said, "Ah, shucks. This old boy from Savannah, Georgia,
will make you proud, brother!"

Ben and I spent as much time together as we could before the White
House affair to honor the detachment that I had commanded for three years.
We visited a tailor's shop in Washington City, measured him for size and
returned two days later for a fitting.

"Louise and I want to buy this gift for you, Ben. Every time you wear your dress mess, you can think of us."

The reception line at the White House consisted of President Buchanan, Louise, Secretary and Mrs. Toucey, Secretary and Mrs. Floyd, Secretary and Mrs. Cass, Secretary and Mrs. Cobb, Secretary and Mrs. Thompson, Attorney-General and Mrs. Black, Postmaster General and Mrs. Brown, National Affairs Advisor Caldwell and Commodore Hagood.

I had never seen my old detachment in dress uniform. Commander Lewis looked like a Commodore in his dress uniform with bright red sash and silver sword. Even the marines showed out with dark green jackets and pink pants. Every one of my marines and wives came over to our table to sit and talk for a minute. Louise was amazed at the informality of the conversation with first names used all around. Children's names were bounced around as well. It was still a tight little group, with the children growing up together in Washington City.

"You know, Louise, we knew about you and our Captain before anyone else." One of the wives said. "We used to call you, the Captain's Lady Friend."

"From the First Lady of the White House, to the Captain's Lady. You must all have thought I was a scarlet lady, indeed." There was laughter all around.

42
THE WHITE HOUSE
Christmas 1858

Our first Christmas together was spent in the White House with the extended Caldwell family from Beaufort, South Carolina. Louise had invited my parents, brother and sister, wives, husbands and cousins. Anyone else with the last name of Caldwell was welcome to purchase train tickets. A mob showed up on the train platform at Union Station, Washington City. Unfortunately, a great aunt, aged 92, sent me a note saying she was unable to stand the cold of a northern winter. Her bones just would not take it. I laughed when I read it and handed it around for all the family to read. I had hired as many cabs as I could find standing idle at the station. I told them to make round trips to the White House until everyone was delivered. My parents and my brother's family crowded into the first cab and were whisked away. Several trips later everyone managed to arrive at 1600 Pennsylvania Avenue.

We all ate our meals in the formal state dining room because that was the only place to seat everyone. Louise announced that the number of family in attendance had set a new record for the White House. The old record had been 57, and everyone laughed because there could not have been more than 40 now sitting and eating in the dining room.

The White House is a special place at Christmas. The first floor has a decorated tree in every room. Louise had instructed her staff to make ornamental signs for each of the trees. She hung the first sign which was carefully lettered. `Grandpa and Grandma Caldwell's Tree`. She instructed everyone who had brought gifts for my parents to place them under this tree. The next sign read `Trey's Family`. Her instructions were the same for gifts. The third read `Carol's Family`. The final sign read `Caldwell Cousins`. This, of course, caused a shopping fever to break out among the Caldwell women and shops within walking distance of the White House emptied their shelves.

Louise was in her element. James Buchanan, however, was not from a large family and he watched in horror as little children tore up and down the halls of the White House. When he complained to his sister, she replied, "Better get used to it, brother, Jason and I plan to have a large family."

"Louise, you are beyond child bearing age!"

"Yes, I am too old to bear children, but not to raise them. Jason and I have talked about adopting orphan children from the Epworth Foundation in Columbia, South Carolina."

"When will this be?" He asked in wonderment.

"When we return home in a year and a half."

"Louise, do you know what you are doing?"

"For the first time in my life, I do. Jason has more money than he can ever spend, he needs sons and daughters to leave it to." she said with a smile on her face.

"Louise, I never thought ... I mean I just assumed .....I never..."

"Yes, I know, brother. Things change. Lives change. And as soon as the Epworth home has a healthy baby boy ready, we plan on naming him James Jason Caldwell in your honor."

The President smiled and started to walk away until his sister said, "And the first girl baby ready will be named Ruth Louise Caldwell in honor of your mother. The second girl will be named after my mother."

"Wait, wait. Try your hand with two to start with to see if you like being parents."

And so that was how Louise and I arranged to start our family. We did not wait to go home. James came to live with us from an orphanage outside Alexandra, Virginia, and Ruth came to us from the Epworth home in South Carolina.

The rest of the Christmas holiday was a series of White House parties and trips out into the capital city of our nation. We attended concerts, a play at Ford's theater, walks through Lafayette square and on across for drinks at the Hay-Adams.

On Christmas eve, Santa Claus came to the White House and delivered gifts to everyone staying that week. Louise laughed when she saw me dressed as Santa. I handed her a bright red envelope and whispered in her ear, "Louise, you have been such a good little girl this year, open this now!" Inside was the deed for 353 Bay Street, Beaufort, South Carolina, in her name only. The family was indeed impressed until my father said, "Louise, welcome to the property owners association of Bay Street. You owe us 100 dollars for 1859 dues."

"Jason, write your father a check!" And the laughter began as a ripple and ended with everyone's sides hurting.

The week ended before we knew it. The Caldwells were driven back to Union Station and the White House became quiet again. The President smiled as he walked to work and Louise began writing her letters of inquiry.

43
Alexandra, Virginia
January 1859

After Christmas and the return home of the Caldwell family, Louise starting contacting children's homes in the Washington area. She wrote to church sponsored and state run facilities in the states of Maryland, Virginia and Delaware. She heard from each one, not surprising when they received letters of inquiry on White House letterhead. We started with the closest. It was located in Alexandra, Virginia, and was called the New Rochelle Home for Children. After the exchange of several letters, Louise informed me that January 21, 1859, was to be reserved for a visit to the home. We drove over the Potomac and into Virginia. Our driver from the White House had been instructed that this might take all day.

"Jason, are we doing the right thing?"

"Louise, do we want to be parents? Of course, we do. We have talked about this for a long time. We have been married a year with no success in that department. We are both over 40 now, healthy and eager for this, correct?"

"Oh, Jason, that is exactly how I feel. Do you think they can help us?"

We had arrived at the home. It was a large brick building placed back on a large green lawn that was several acres in size. It had a large portico for carriages in rainy weather and as we rolled under the portico a man and a woman were standing at the double doors, waiting. The man stepped forward and opened the carriage door.

"Good morning. You must be from the White House. My name is Damien Wilson and I am the administrator here at New Rochelle. Please, let me help you down, Mrs. Caldwell."

"Let me introduce, Nurse Schmitz, she will be taking you through the home for your inspection."

"We want you to see everything in the entire facility and how we care for the children here," He continued. "How long do you have this morning to spend with us?"

"We have the entire day, if necessary," Louise said.

"Fine, will you follow Nurse Schmitz, then? She will bring you both to my office after your visit and we can start the paperwork on the adoption."

I looked at Louise and she looked at me with raised eyebrows. *Can it be this easy*, we both thought.

"Mrs. Caldwell, we are so happy that you contacted us here at New Rochelle. I think you will find this to be a fine facility, run by caring people," nurse Schmitz said.

Near noon, we were shown into a large dining room where the older children came from their classrooms to eat as a group. The children seemed happy and well fed. They had been warned that visitors from the White House would be here today, so to behave themselves. One small boy came up to me and asked, "Are you the President, Sir?"

"No, I just work at the White House, but this is the First Lady of the United States."

"Whew, you must be really important. How many ladies are there in the White House?"

Louise laughed, told him there was just one and gave him a big hug. He ran back to his friends and said, "The President could not come today, so he sent his only lady and the man with her."

We both laughed and started to relax. Mr. Wilson found us after we had eaten a bite and said, "How did you like the nursery?"

"We are going to be new, first time parents, Mr. Wilson. When we walked in here we were looking for a male infant, but I would like to Mother them all."

"That is what we like to hear, Mrs. Caldwell. You and the Admiral have the right attitude about this. Did you find any children or babies that you were drawn to?"

"Yes, in the nursery there is an older infant boy, why is he there? Is he sick?"

"Yes, he is recovering from the chicken pox. We put him in there because the infants still have natural protection from their birth mothers."

"How old is he?"

"We have no idea, Mrs. Caldwell. He was a foundling. The baby was literally left on our door- step one night last month. I am sorry, we do not a birth date. We judge him to be between 8 and 10 months now."

"But he so tiny. He looks frightened."

"You folks have to understand what the conditions might have been like for a mother or a father to abandon their child. Oddly enough, mothers rarely abandon, single fathers are the most likely. They feel overwhelmed trying to raise an infant."

"Is it alright if we use today's date for his birth date?" Louise asked.

I knew then that we had found baby, James, and would bring him home with us as soon as the home would allow us to do so.

"Why not spend the rest of the afternoon with him today? What do you want his Christian name to be?"

"James." We both said at once.

"Start calling him by his name today, then. See me before you leave and we can set up a visiting schedule so that you can come and go as you please."

"I am not sure I can do that, Mr. Wilson. Can I stay the night with him?" Louise asked.

"Of course, Mrs. Caldwell, we have a room for 'parents to be'. You can stay there tonight."

"Mr. Wilson, can you and I talk about the paperwork while Louise spends this afternoon with James?"

"Of course, Admiral. Follow me to my office."

We walked to his office and Louise went to the nursery. After we sat down on a couch in his office, Mr. Wilson said he understood my wife's feeling about not wanting to leave James.

"That is a very positive sign. We look for that in each future parent that we screen here at New Rochelle. How do feel about James?"

"I would take him home today if it was permitted."

"Well, these are unusual circumstances, Admiral. We have never been contacted by the White House before. I think this time we can stretch our rules a tiny bit and release James to your care and custody so that the three of you can spend the night at home. You will still have the waiting period required by Virginia State Law. There is still paperwork to be completed and signed by you and your wife. But I do not see why we can not take care of that by courier, do you?"

"Here is a White House pass, when you or Nurse Schmitz come, just show it at the gate to the East Wing and you can deliver papers or inspect the nursery that Louise has waiting for James."

"Very good, Sir. I will inform the staff that you will be taking James with you later today. If James rejects either of you, then we will have to set up the schedule for visitations until he warms to the idea of parents. Does that seem reasonable, Admiral?"

"Very reasonable, Mr. Wilson."

I was walking to the Nursery, lost my way twice in the mass of hallways and finally found Louise in a chair holding James in her arms. He looked up at me and smiled, scratched a pox mark and squirmed to get down off Louise's lap so he could crawl around the floor.

"When do babies crawl?" I asked Louise.

"Depends, usually between six or eight months, why?"

"And when do they walk?"

"Depends, again on the age. Sometimes as early as a year, sometimes as late as two, why?"

"Just trying to figure out how old our son is."

"It does not matter, he was born today!"

"We have a couple more hours to spend here and then we have to go."

"I am staying the night, Jason!"

"Change of plans. If the three of us bond this afternoon, Mr. Wilson has bent the rules, probably broken some, so that we can all stay together at the White House."

"Thank you, Jason."

"Thank Mr. Wilson when we leave today, it was his idea."

"I know you, Jason, you bent the rules!"

"I did not!"

44
Sheldon Church
Easter 1859

Our first Easter season in the White House, as a family, was spent on home leave. We took baby James home to Beaufort. All three of us boarded the train at Union Station and rode to Yemassee, South Carolina. Trey had a carriage waiting for us. We took the road south to Sheldon, South Carolina. I asked the driver to stop at Sheldon Church and we walked around the graveyard showing James his relatives. James had not starting talking in sentences yet. He was big on one word commands; go, more and no!

"Look, Louise, here is the marble marker for the Bulls. They were ancestors of mine. Stephen Bull came from England to Charleston on the frigate, *Carolina*, arriving soon after the settling of the colony. As Lord Ashley's deputy, he was able to obtain large grants of land on St. Helena Island and on the Ashley River up in Charleston."

"Was he an important founder of the area, Jason?"

"Yes, it is said that he selected the site of Charles Town, and his son, William, did the same for Savannah. William built a magnificent home and named it Sheldon Hall for their ancestral home in Warwick, England."

"Is it still standing?"

"Yes, but it is in ruins. Years ago, Sheldon Hall became noted for its elegant hospitality. Later, when this church was built, the Bulls were large contributors. My grandfather used to tell the story that on Sundays the entire congregation, sometimes numbering over a hundred, would be invited to Sheldon Hall for midday dinner. Look at the top of the marker that is Governor Bull's coat of arms."

"How are the Caldwell and the Bulls related?"

"A Bull married a Caldwell in 1797. That is the date of our plantation on Pollawana across from Datha. It came into the Caldwell family as a wedding gift from John Bull's grandson. He owned two plantations on Bull's Island, which you remember we came by on our trip to St. Helena, last year. Though now it is called Chisolm's. It is across a small creek from Lady's Island. He also owned a small plantation across the creek from Datha. This is the plantation that you visited with me. Because land, in this state, is inherited from father to son, he passed the Chisolm Plantations, at his death, to his two sons. His daughter received the third small, 1200 acres, on her wedding day."

"Jason?"

"Yes, Louise."

"Why is it called Lady's Island?"

"Legend says, it was named in compliment to the women of the Bull family. Another version is that the island was called, 'Lady Blake Island', in honor of the wife of Joseph Blake, named Governor of South Carolina by the Lords Proprietors. Over the years it was shortened to Lady's Island."

"When did John Bull live on his plantation?"

"John was married to his first wife in 1714. She only lived a year or so, she was killed by Indians in 1715."

"Killed! What happened?"

"1715 is still referred to in Beaufort as the, 'Year of Tragedy'. It was the year of the uprising of the Yemassee Indians. They attacked Port Royal first, this allowed many people in Beaufort to flee their homes and avoid their murders. The small barrier islands, of course, were not warned and the people there were murdered."

"How was the husband saved?"

"Captain John Bull was in Charles Town with the militia who were being formed to put down the uprising. Returning days later to Bull Island, he found the island deserted, his home burned and the area strewn with bodies, all scalped. Consumed by grief, and later anger, he became one of the most relentless members of the militia that hunted down and exterminated the Indians."

"Oh, Jason, that is also very sad. Was an entire tribe exterminated?"

"Few survived, they disappeared from South Carolina westward into Georgia."

"What happened to John Bull? He must have had a family in order to have a grandson?"

"Yes, he remarried, but the memory of his first wife still occupied a place in his heart. Nineteen years after her death, in 1734, he gave St. Helena Episcopal Church, a silver communion service in her memory. We still use it today."

"Are the Caldwell founders buried here, Jason?"

"No, when we go to church in Beaufort, I will show you some markers. The family tree is interesting. John Caldwell was born in Ireland, in 1701. He came to South Carolina in 1731, much later than the Bulls. He is also known as an Indian fighter. The Tuscarora tribe in North Carolina ranged southward after the defeat of the Yemassee. Captain John Caldwell led a successful campaign against them and drove them back to North Carolina."

"What about your branch of the tree?"

"I am coming to that. In 1779, Robert Caldwell distinguished himself at Port Royal. This was during the American Revolution, of course. Anyway, he was under the command of General Moultrie and assigned to defend Port Royal. A large number of British landed and quickly surrounded the Carolinians. The company under his command was ordered to surrender. My relative called out to know what quarter they would have. 'No quarter to rebels' was the reply.

'Then men,' Captain Caldwell yelled, 'defend yourself to the last man. Charge!' In an instant the click of every gun was heard as it was cocked and presented to the face of the enemy, who immediately fell back."

"Oh, Jason, you are a story teller! You should write a book."

"This same Robert Caldwell was later Speaker of the House of Representatives in Columbia. He later became a representative in Washington. At one time there were seventeen branches of the Caldwell family in South Carolina. Most were in Beaufort, but they stretched from here into the Piedmont and one finally settled in Pickens. My great grandfather, Robert Gibbs Caldwell, built the four-story house overlooking the bay. It is the one we call, 'The Castle.' We were in that house last year for a party in your honor."

"I do not remember the house, we were in so many different places."

"You will remember this. You overheard two ladies talking about you. One said to the other, 'What is the President's sister like? I have not met her.' The response was, 'She is exquisitely beautiful, cold, quiet, calm, lady-like and fair as a lily, but with the blackest and longest eyelashes. Her eyes are so light in color, like the hue of cologne and water."

"Oh, yes, I was flattered, except for that 'cold' comment. You do not think I am cold, do you, Jason?"

"Oh, yes. About as cold as a bonfire! To finish my family tree, before I was so rudely interrupted. There were a lot of Robert Caldwells. Robert Woodward Caldwell was president of South Carolina College. His son, known as Junior, became an Episcopal Priest. And his son, known as Bubba, was the biggest horse thief in the county,"

As we left the church, Louise asked me how it felt to have a family and for that family to join in the Caldwell Easter Tradition.

"It is like a dream, Louise."

"How so, Jason?"

"Until I met you, I did not think in terms of being a father or having a family of my own. I always thought I would only be my father's son."

"Do you like it?"

"Like, no. Love, no. Whatever the emotion is, it is greater than love. Being a father is like looking far into the future, you will not make it there, but your children and your children's, children will."

"Children, Jason?"

"Yes, children, Louise. If you are ready, we need to start the paperwork at the Epworth home for another baby, Ruth."

45

The San Juan Dispute
June 1859

Another dispute with England arose in the summer of 1859. It involved the ownership of San Juan Island, which sat in a narrow channel between British Columbia, Canada and the United States. It came to the attention of President Buchanan in a cabinet meeting. Secretary Floyd asked for permission to have General Harney send troops to San Juan.

"Mr. President, the situation on San Juan has become desperate. As you know, the San Juan Treaty of 1846, provided for joint ownership of the island by both our countries. Both have protection forces stationed there. The Governor of British Columbia has doubled the number of soldiers in the last month. He is now trying to build a large fort to control the channel between our two countries. He has even requested the assistance of the Royal Navy. The Royal Navy may try to build a navy repair yard there, also."

"Who is our contact on San Juan?" asked the President.

"We can not make contact with the island at this time, Mr. President."

"Who is the closest military contact?"

"That would be General Harney, commanding the Washington Territory, Sir."

"Can we send and receive telegrams?"

"Yes, but it takes about ten days to send or receive, Mr. President."

"Send a message to General Harney to reinforce troops on San Juan and await further orders."

"Very good, Mr. President."

"This is a temporary measure, gentlemen, what are your suggestions for a permanent solution?"

The President had a habit of asking for ideas from the most junior member of his cabinet first. In that way junior members would not be influenced by the ideas of more senior members. Because this was a military matter the rankings in the cabinet were: 1) Secretary of War - Mr. Floyd, 2) Secretary of the Navy - Mr. Toucey, 3) Secretary of State - Mr. Cass, 4) Secretary of the Treasury - Mr. Cobb, 5)Secretary of the Interior Mr. Thompson, 6) the Attorney- General - Mr. Black, 7) the Postmaster General - Mr. Brown and 8) me - the National Affairs Advisor.

The President fixed his gaze upon me. "Admiral Caldwell, you may begin."

"Mr. President, I have contacts with the commander at the Royal Naval Dockyards in Bermuda. If plans are underway to build a Royal Navy Repair yards on San Juan he should know. In addition we have diplomatic contacts with Lord Napier of the Royal Navy. Secretary Toucey can find out if the Royal Navy plans to increase their presence in the San Juan Channel. Secretary Cass can start talks with the Prime Minister and Mr. Black can reread the San Juan Treaty."

"Thank you, Admiral. Mr. Brown, your ideas, please."

"Mr. President, I can find out exactly how to communicate with Washington Territory. You will remember that the postal service provided assistance to the Rapid Response team from the capital here in Washington City all the way into Utah Territory two years ago. I think we can go right on into Sacramento and up to San Juan. The telegraph system is nearly completed, it has open breaks. But the postal service can provide temporary riders between telegraph stations until the matter is settled."

"Thank you, Mr. Brown. Your comments, Mr. Black?"

"The justice department will review the treaty. But we can also provide federal agents because Washington is a territory not a state."

"Thank you, Mr. Black. Mr. Thompson, you are next."

"The department of the Interior will provide maps of the area for land or sea operations, Mr. President. We also have agents that have been throughout the upper northwest mapping and taking road placement studies, I will make them available to whomever may need them."

"That will be most helpful, Mr. Thompson. Mr. Cobb, what can the Treasury do?"

"The Treasury can pay for it, Mr. President." Everyone burst out laughing.

"That is probably the most important part of whatever we decide to do, Mr. Cobb."

Secretary Cass, and Toucey said they would begin with England and work back to officials in Canada. Secretary Floyd, who brought the matter to the President said, "I still need an answer about reinforcing our presence on San Juan."

"If we send troops from General Harney, what will the Canadian and British response be?" asked the President. "Are we ready to have an armed conflict on that island?"

"That is not the right question, Mr. President, we need to make both Canada and Britain think we are ready to protect our right to be on the island. If they build forts and repair yards, they will be in a position to close the channel if they so choose."

I had listened to each member express his ideas, but I could not let Secretary Floyd correct his Commander-in-Chief. "I disagree." I blurted out.

"Admiral?"

"Mr. President, YOU may decide to reinforce the island, but without information from San Juan about the situation we will not know which options may work. The idea is to settle the current problem, correct? Rattling our sabers and threatening to go to war is the last option, not the first!"

"I agree, Admiral. Mr. Floyd, you may respond to General Harney to send only a matching number of troops to be equal in force to what the Canadians have on the island. Leave the British out of it for the time being."

"That is not the right response, Mr. President!" John W. Floyd was getting angry.

"Well, when you are President and Commander-in-Chief, you may make a different response, Mr. Floyd. You are excused from this meeting."

I had never seen the President that angry. I liked it! Secretary Floyd just sat there deflated.

"Mr. Floyd, if you are going to forward those orders to General Harney, I suggest you start now. The rest of us will continue to work on the solving the problem as a team."

My God, I thought, "The President is going to ask for his resignation if Floyd does not start to move. James Buchanan, you do have a solid backbone! Floyd hung his head and said, "I am truly sorry for my outburst, Mr. President. I will issue the orders as you requested at this time." He arose from the cabinet meeting and left the room.

"Secretary Toucey, do you know where Commodore Hagood is right now?"

"Yes, Mr. President. He is aboard USS *Hornet* headed to San Juan Island. He will stop in Bermuda on a courtesy call."

"How can we contact him?"

"We have mail ships between Potomac Dockyards and Bermuda. One English the other US."

"Damn, the communication takes forever!"

"Yes, but our relations with the Royal Navy have never been better. I would bet that they are unaware of things on San Juan." replied Toucey.

"We need to get the Commodore from Bermuda to San Francisco as fast as possible with his reinforcement vessels, Mr. Toucey."

"Yes, Sir. We have sent his ships around the tip of South America, that will mean a long ocean cruise. That will take time, Mr. President."

"He has three fast attack vessels waiting in San Francisco. We need a commander, not necessarily the ships from Bermuda." The President looked directly at me and said, "Jason, this is really a wild thing I am thinking. Why not send you and the marines across land if things go to hell on San Juan and we need a naval response? You can be in Sacramento in a short period of time. A train ride to San Francisco and you can pick up three fast attack ships and be on your way. Have you commanded a group before?"

"Yes, Sir. USS *Black Warrior* affair in Cuba, Sir. It is in my service records." I could feel my pulse increasing. Oh, what was I thinking? I can not run off to a shooting conflict thousands of miles away. I am a married man, with a child.

"We need to make contingency plans, we will assume that Commodore Hagood will arrive with his ships from Bermuda before we need him. If not, Admiral Caldwell will take command until Hagood can get there."

"Let me know what happens with our orders to General Harney, will you Jason?"

"Yes, Mr. President, I will walk back to the Army Navy Building with Secretary Toucey and see what has been done for you."

"Thank you, Gentlemen, that will be all."

We left the cabinet room and started off towards Isaac Toucey's office.

"Jason, do you think the President will forgive and forget Floyd's little outburst?"

"I doubt it, they are like two dogs with a bone. What John B. Floyd does not understand is, that the President is a much larger dog. His bite will be painful and terminal. I know Floyd wants a free hand with the Army, but that is unreasonable."

"I think he will resign as soon as the election is over next year. He will not want to serve another term under the President. If I were the President, I would be looking for his replacement now." Said Isaac Toucey.

"You may be right, Isaac."

"And what was that about sending you out in command of a naval force from San Francisco?"

"Isaac, you do not know his sister. She will never allow me to go to war. The President is having a pipe dream with that one."

"But, you would go if ordered. I saw you sit up straighter and square your shoulders. Remember, Jason, I have seen that look in your eye. Once a warrior, always a warrior."

"War is for young men, not men of our age, Isaac."

"I predict that if you handle the situation on San Juan, it will be settled without firing a shot. I know your record for getting things done peacefully."

"I hope I am not put into the San Juan solution, Isaac."

We continued our conversation until we arrived at the door of the Secretary of War. "I bid you farewell, Mr. Toucey. I am about to enter the lion's den." Isaac laughed and continued on down the hall. I entered the outer office and asked to see the secretary. I was admitted and I sat before John's desk until he stopped shuffling papers and looked up.

"Jason, I am glad you stopped by. Can you talk some sense into him? He is your brother-in-law."

"Mr. Secretary, when we are in the cabinet room or the Oval Office he is my direct superior and Commander-in-Chief of the Armed Forces. I can not and will not question his judgement."

"But, Jason, you are his most trusted advisor. You are from the South. He is giving away the store here!"

"Are you referring to the Buchanan Proclamation?"

"Damn, right. He has put us in a box."

"Us, being the South?"

"Yes. He is driving the South to war."

"You are a federal employee sitting here, John. You are not an employee of the State of Virginia, are you?"

"I envy you, Jason, there is something about you, a calmness that seems to distance you from other people. You have a self-assurance that is obvious, and yet no arrogance at all."

"Thank you, John. When do you think you will resign and offer you services to the South?"

"I am considering a run for the White House or at least a running mate's slot in the next election. I am not ready to give up on a southern sensible White House, Senate or House."

"Good, glad to hear it. Either way you will be leaving in '60, right?"

"Absolutely, I can not function under the present conditions."

"Have you sent troop movement orders to Washington Territory, yet?"

"Yes, I have copied the President to cover myself, but I think it is a weak approach, what do you think?"

"Proportional, I would say. Navy tactics are different from Army tactics, John. I always use a proportional response in the middle of an ocean. I try to get the other Admiral to back away and fight another day. If I were an Army General, I would think and act like you."

"Jason, I really have tried to understand this President. What does he want to accomplish in the next year, besides putting out fires? I have no idea anymore."

"I think he is exhausted. The job was more than he was ready to handle. He is a President set upon saving the Union of these States. To him the federal government is the key to most of our well being, while you think the State of Virginia is the key."

"Well put. That is exactly how I feel."

"Then, how can you be the President of the UNITED States of America?"

I returned to the White House, sought out my wife, kissed baby James and headed to my office. The President was waiting for me.

"Well, Jason. What do you think about our Secretary of War?"

"He is just going through the motions, Sir."

"I feel that also, he needs to be replaced."

"I would agree, Sir, if you are nominated for another term and are elected then he should be replaced at that time."

"Jason, you know I will not seek the nomination."

"Yes, Sir. But I doubt Mr. Floyd knows that. You can keep him in his place for a few more months, if you want to."

"I will think about it, I would hate to go to war with him in the cabinet."

46
Titusville, Pennsylvania
August, 1859

The nation needed some good news. It came in the form of important mineral and oil discoveries. Besides the oil wells now in Pennsylvania, new coal deposits were found in the western United States. In 1859, it was estimated that the coal reserves in the United States were now equal to all the rest of the world. Gold was found at Pike's Peak, Colorado, and several other locations throughout the west. The Comstock Lode of silver was brought to light in western Utah Territory. The Rocky Mountain region discoveries were abundant in minerals of all types.

The panic of 1857, was soon forgotten with the new wealth of the nation. Oil amounted to millions of dollars added to the national economy. The Comstock Lode alone was estimated at a quarter billion dollars. Secretary Thompson of the Interior and Secretary Cobb of the Treasury kept the cabinet meetings filled with good news upon good news.

"What does the discovery of oil in large amounts mean for the US Navy, Mr. Toucey?" asked the President.

"We will be able to fire our boilers with oil and not coal. Oil is more compact and lighter than coal. It means, Mr. President, that we can steam farther without having to stop and refuel."

"How will the change over to oil affect industries like the whalers in Nantucket?" to no one in particular.

"Whale oil is used to light our homes because it is so clean burning," someone said.

"The oil in Pennsylvania is a light crude, almost brown in color when it comes out of the ground. It should not take much to refine it into lamp oil," another said.

I looked around at the faces in the cabinet room and thought, maybe national wealth derived from minerals will replace wealth derived from plants like cotton. I made a mental note to write to my father in Beaufort and other business letters.

THE WHITE HOUSE
Office of National Affairs

August 21, 1859

Dear Father,

 Today I have learned a rather startling fact. It is cheaper to make kerosine from the vast oil deposits in Pennsylvania, than it is to make turpentine from pine trees. You are always ahead of others where future trends are concerned. I advise you to stop making turpentine from the pine forests that we hold. The price will plunge when kerosine is produced in large quantities. When will this happen? I do not know. But as you always say, "Advanced knowledge is like gold."

 I have the information that you requested in your last letter.

   Mr. Edwin Drake
   Pennsylvania Rock Oil Company
   Titusville, Pennsylvania

 I would imagine that he would be most welcome to hear that he has another investor from South Carolina. My vision for Caldwell Trading and Shipping is to expand as rapidly as possible into mineral based assets instead of depending entirely upon agriculture based commodities. I have sent a letter to my Port Royal office and requested that our ships investigate ways of transporting oil from Pennsylvania to South Carolina.

      Louise sends her best.

      Jason

THE WHITE HOUSE
Office of National Affairs

August 21, 1859

Mr. Kyle Johnston
Director Port Facilities
Port Royal, South Carolina

Dear Mr. Johnston:

Thank you for your recent letter informing me that the sale of the Port Royal properties owned by Caldwell Trading and Shipping has been completed. Please send payment to:
Bank of Bermuda
Caldwell Trading and Shipping Account
St. George, Bermuda
Please send the lease forms to rent the same facilities from the new owners.

Sincerely yours,

Jason Caldwell

THE WHITE HOUSE
Office of National Affairs
August 21, 1859

Robert Whitehall
Caldwell Trading and Shipping
110 Boundary Street
Beaufort, South Carolina

Dear Robert,

The sale of the office, warehouses and other properties in Port Royal is now complete. I will forward a copy of the lease of same back to you. You will rent available warehousing as our needs dictate . A secure facility must be found in Port Royal for the shipment of Oil to South Carolina. Write to my partners at Pennsylvania Rock Oil Co. and find out how the oil shipments will be handled.

Also, you may want to contact the Comstock Mining Offices in Utah and get quarterly reports sent directly to you. I have directed the banks used in Utah and California to report deposits directly to you. Income from Utah should stay there for the time being. Income from Pennsylvania should stay there also. As you manage the company for me, be on the alert for mineral based assets outside of South Carolina.

What is the progress on the California water equipment purchases? Awaiting your response, I remain

Sincerely yours,

Jason Caldwell

Trying to run a business from the White House was not something that I would have to do much longer. The election next year would end my service in Washington City. Then Louise, the children and I would be free to live wherever we chose. I was putting away my stationary when Louise stuck her head inside my office and said, "I am glad I caught you."

"Louise, just the person I need to talk to. What does your schedule look like next week?"

"Nothing serious, why?"

"I need to travel to Titusville again and I was wondering if you would like to go with me."

"Do you want to stop by Franklin, it is only 19 miles away? I can show you the houses where James and I were born. We were not there together, but the houses are. I know all about your family history, Jason. You really have not seen where I am from, have you?"

"No, Louise. And it is time that I did. Do you trust the children with their nanny for that long?"

"Yes, they are safe here. The protection detail will not let harm come to them."

"You make fun of me for being the long term planner. I would like to find a house in Franklin that you like so the company can purchase it before we leave office."

"Do we really need a third house, Jason? The place you bought last year in St. George is beautiful, I could live there full time."

"I know you could. You love it and so do I.. Running a business will not be easy from there. Unless...."

"Unless, what?"

"Unless we have the State Department contact the British Embassy here and ask about dual citizenship so we can obtain British Passports."

"I do not understand, Jason."

"A British Passport allows us to conduct business in Bermuda as citizens. Foreigners in Bermuda pay additional taxes on everything. The house they live in, the items that they buy and most importantly the export/imports are taxed at an extreme rate. We could not afford to live in Bermuda unless we were citizens."

"You mean when we are in South Carolina or Pennsylvania, we are US citizens with US passports and when we are in Bermuda we are British citizens with their passport?"

"Exactly, we can travel anywhere in the United Kingdom as citizens also."

"I would like that, Jason."

"Alright, this is why I want to buy property in Pennsylvania. We become state residents. The children would be accepted by the people who live there and in South Carolina. It is important to me that our children have roots in both the north and south. They need to know about their mother's heritage also and not just about their father's."

"Jason, are you worried about what is happening in South Carolina?"

"Not just there, but everywhere throughout the south. They act like they want to be another country."

"Then we may be talking about trying to juggle three citizenships. Is that it, Jason?"

"Yes, in order to live our lives without fear, it will take some careful financial planning on our part. I have moved assets from South Carolina to Utah, Pennsylvania, California and Bermuda. We will be able to live a comfortable life in any or all of these locations."

"I will clear my schedule so we can go to Titusville."

"Before you go, I will need the name of a land broker in Franklin, Pennsylvania."

"You can ask James, but I think he used Beith Associates to search for him."

"Is that name spelled b- e- I- t- h?"

"Yes, James has just bought a home there and he was very happy with what they were able to find for him and his friend."

"Thank you, see you at dinner."

I walked over to the President's private secretary's office and asked for the telegraph information to contact Beith Associates in Franklin. I wrote out the request that needed to be sent and left it with him. In a few days, we would be stepping off a train in Franklin, Pennsylvania. I needed them to meet us at the train station and for them to arrange to show us property for sale.

Within the week, Louise and I were, in fact, standing on the train platform. "August is hot in Pennsylvania, Jason."

"Not as hot as Beaufort."

"Louise Buchanan, as I live and breathe, is that you?"

Louise turned to see who had called her name. "Cynthia?"

It turned out to a school friend, they had not seen each other in years.

"Your brother is moving back here. Are you?"

"Yes, this is my husband, Jason Caldwell."

"Oh, Louise, it will be like old times. Where did you buy?"

"We are here to look, we have not bought anything. An agent from Beith Associates is supposed to meet us."

"I have to buy my ticket to Erie. I hope to see you soon." And she was gone.

"Was she always like that, in a hurry?"

"That is Cynthia Majors."

The land agent found us and drove us to Winfield Township and showed us the farmsteads where James Buchanan and Louise were born. One was 183 acres and the other 172 acres. One was now a working dairy farm and the other was now a pig farm which Louise did not appreciate because of the smell of the place.

"You said you were looking for a working farm which has two houses. One will be used by you and Mr. Caldwell and the other for the farm manager. We do not have many farms like that around here."

"We are looking for an investment," Louise said. "You will need to find us something that will produce enough income to pay the taxes, insurance and operating costs." She continued. "I have lived my early years in Franklin and I want my children to live on a small farm, not in a small town or city like Franklin or Titusville. We will wait until you find us something."

The land agent looked at me and probably thought, *you poor, hen picked, man.*

"Mr. Townsend, my company, Pennsylvania Rock Oil will be the owner of this farm, not us. It should make a small income, but that is not the primary purpose of our purchase. You may have gotten the wrong idea from my wife's telegram. Louise and I are expecting to invest a considerable amount. We are not looking for something rundown, or less than 640 acres."

His attitude changed completely. "When will you be coming back from Titusville?"

"In two days, Mr. Townsend."

"Cable me when you will arrive and I will meet you again and show you something that I think you will like. It is very pricey, probably over a hundred thousand dollars, Sir."

"That would be fine with us."

Louise just stared at me with her mouth open. Later, when we were alone, she said, "Jason, were you serious back there with Mr. Townsend or were you trying to impress him?"

"Louise, we will have to pay that for the type of place we want. Speculators are trying to buy property between here and Titusville because of the discovery of oil. If they can not buy the land outright then they try to buy the mineral rights. Mr. Townsend will be calling people who are not even listed with him."

"Yes, but we cannot afford a 100 thousand dollars for al farm!"

"Louise, do you have any idea what the mineral rights to a 1000 acres of oil are?"

"No."

"It is a little over a 100 thousand dollars!"

"A hundred dollars an acre! That is more than the land costs."

"Yes, we could sell the mineral rights and pay for the farm. Or we could speculate and buy a large track of land up the road towards Titusville and form our own oil company."

"We have to find safe investments for as long as the oil income lasts." She mused. "Why not buy a bank, then?" She was giggling.

"We already own parts of banks in Utah, California and Bermuda." I said rather sternly.

"Then we need one in Pennsylvania!"

"Yes, that is why we are going to Titusville to buy a portion of Penn State Trust."

"I never did ask you why we were coming to Titusville. Why are you going to buy a bank in Pennsylvania, Jason?"

"Our company is called, Caldwell Trading and Shipping. Everyone can see the shipping portion of the company, it is hard to hide merchant marine ships and the men to sail on them. That is the smaller of the two parts. The larger portion of the company is trading in stocks, bonds, options and lines of credits."

"Oh, and in order to grant a line of credit, you have to own a bank. I understand stocks and bonds but what is an option, Jason?"

"Do you see the farm land we have been passing today outside the carriage window?"

"Yes."

"Every square foot may have minerals under it, in this case, oil. The property owner is free to sell his mineral rights or option them. If he options them, then he is in partnership with the drilling company which will come onto his land and drill a well. If oil is found, then the income is split between the land owner and the company holding the option."

"Do you have any options on land here?"

"Yes, about 5,000 acres so far."

"5,000 acres! Oh, Jason, we will be in the poor house."

"There is no money paid out for options, Louise. It costs only to drill a well." If I am successful in my offer to Penn State Trust Bank in Titusville, then we will form our own oil company. I would like to call it Seneca Oil. The Seneca Indian tribe used to range all along the South Carolina side of the Savannah River. There is even a town called, Seneca, up in the northwest corner of the State, Oconee County, I think."

"Oconee, another Indian name?"

"Yes, ma'am!"

"Jason?"

"Yes, Louise."

"I love you."

I could see that she would never change. Her world was one where she was a mother of her children, sister of the President, first lady of the White House and wife of a crazy sailor named, Jason Caldwell.

47

Ossawatomie, Kansas
September, 1859

The abolitionist, John Brown, began his impassioned speech to a group of about 130 people on the steps of the county court house.

"Good people of Kansas, hear my words. Slavery is the most evil arrangement that God fearing men of this, or any nation, have ever devised. I know, some people call me a fanatic, a religious zealot, or a crazy frontier preacher. If I am crazy, why has my brother traveled all the way from California to join our cause? Why are two of my brothers-in-law, standing behind me on these steps? Why then have my own sons; Owen, Oliver and Watson, joined the army of God that will leave tomorrow for Virginia? Why are over twenty runaway slaves risking their very lives to return to the cradle of slavery with us today?"

The excited crowd moved forward and John Brown thought, 'Today I will sign up the few who will slay the many'. "I will tell you why these brave men are going to travel across the country," he continued. "They are going to attack the federal government on its very door steps, to secure the means to arm every slave in the State of Virginia!"

A huge roar went up from the crowd, a few yells of, "Amen, Brother Brown," floated through the air. He continued, "When my brother and I planned this great uprising in 1855, we hoped that this day would come. We collected funds from every source known to us. Many of you standing here today have given us the money, courage and your blessing to enter the great land of Satan, known as, Virginia. We will prevail. We will provide the means for the slaves to free themselves from their master's grip of bondage!"

Unknown to Brown, a federal agent was standing among the "Good People". He had been sent to Ossawatomie to investigate some wild claims that had been sent to Washington. He had joined the Army of God as a member of Brown's trusted advisors. He had said he had just come from Iowa. His parents had died and left him a farm. He traveled from his home in Maryland to sell his father's farm and bring the proceeds to Brother Brown. He had placed a small pouch of gold upon the table and said he wished it was more. He asked only to be accepted as a foot soldier in the Army of God. Brown accepted this at face value.

Brown then began to question him about his home in Maryland. Where was it? Was it close to any Federal Arsenal? When he learned that it was directly across the Potomac River from the Federal Arsenal at Harpers Ferry he became very attentive. He and his brother had already decided they would attack either the national armory in Springfield, Massachusetts, or the depot at Harpers Virginia. When the Right Reverend O'Malley showed up from Iowa, God had answered his prayers.

That was a month ago. Now they would begin their great march east. When everyone was gathered at the train station in Topeka, they would travel in small groups by different routes and meet again at the train station in Frederick, Maryland. Brown had one hundred and eighty men to divide into small traveling groups. He asked Reverend O'Malley for advice on how to get his soldiers from the Baltimore and Ohio Rail Station in Frederick to the O'Malley farm in Brunswick, Maryland. O'Malley assured him that he could arrange wagons to carry twelve men at a time. All he had to do was telegram his brother and let him know the arrival times of each of the groups. Brown obliged and divided his "army" into fifteen units of twelve men each. He called each group his disciples. The reverend sent his telegram the next day. It read:

REVEREND TO HOME BASE – FIRST GROUP ARRIVES FREDERICK STATION 9-19 AM – PLEASE PICKUP AND DELIVER – SECOND GROUP ARRIVES 9-19 PM   FIFTEEN GROUPS IN ALL – TWO GROUPS EACH DAY. I WILL BE IN NINTH GROUP.

REV. JAMES O'MALLEY

When Brown's brother read the message he said, "Send it, Reverend, and may God be with us, a hundred and eighty unarmed men into the jaws of death."

A futuristic statement to say the least, because when the telegram was sent, the plan was to arrest each group of the 'disciples' as they stopped along the route. Because the groups were spread out, it should not be a problem for his "brother," special agent Thomas Kinsey of the US department of Justice, to arrest or detain the disciples. A federal arrest warrant was issued for John Brown and his three sons for the May 24th murders of five men at Pottawatamie Creek, Kansas. Agent Kinsey and his men boarded the train in Topeka a day before the first group of disciples was due to leave and rode to the first stop. They waited until the next day and boarded the train at the Lawrence, Kansas, station. Kinsey and his men did not have pictures of the Army of God and had no idea who the individuals were. They were looking for twelve armed men traveling as a group. There was no group. They began searching for armed men. There were no armed men. The disciples, however, were shaken that law enforcement was aware of their plans.

Each member decided it was every man for himself and they scattered. They had been seated in pairs traveling to Maryland. So, two got off in Lawrence to wait for the afternoon train. Two more entered the station and cashed in their tickets to Frederick and bought two for Topeka. The rest got off at stops along the way and faded into the communities and were never heard from again. The pair waiting on the platform boarded the train with the federal agents and tried to warn the next group of disciples. They were recognized by the agents as passengers from the morning train and they were arrested and held for questioning. During the arrest the second group of twelve left the train in panic and began to disappear within Topeka. These men were never found for questioning. When two men arrived from Lawrence at the Topeka Station, John Brown was shocked. How had the federal agents known where they would be?

The answer had to be that the Reverend O'Malley was not who he claimed to be. He and his brother left the station and returned to where the rest of the army, now 156, waited for their times to board the train to Maryland. Brown called them together and made the following speech to the waiting men.

"We have a problem. Federal agents are waiting for us on the train line to Maryland. Therefore, we shall change our plans slightly. We will not travel in groups of twelve. Instead of buying tickets to Maryland, we will purchase tickets only as far as Kansas City. This many soldiers would cause an alarm trying to board a train at the same time. Some of you may want to return to your homes and wait until I summon you. Those of you who want to leave, please do so."

The men were so shaken that more than one-half left for their homes in Kansas. So the army had now only 81 soldiers and it had not left Kansas. John Brown smiled and shook the hand of each man who left. One of those was the Reverend O'Malley. "Reverend, your gold was most appreciated and it will enable us to do God's work. Without it, we would still be talking about taking action. We have decided to attack the Springfield Arsenal instead. Pray for us brother."

He then took his remaining men to the Topeka Station and bought 40 tickets for St. Louis, and 41 tickets to Springfield. He had divided his force but a smaller force would be enough to do what he had planned. After all, when the slaves were armed, they would be his army. Before anyone boarded the train, Brown pulled his brother aside and said, "Follow the reverend, kill him if you can, if you cannot, board a train for California."

During the rail segment from Topeka to Kansas City, federal agents identified and held for questioning 18 of his soldiers which included a man who wore a full beard. This man carried papers that identified him as John Brown and was promptly arrested for murder. Agent Kinsey indicated to his superiors in Washington City that the plot to free the slaves of Virginia had been foiled. He suggested that agents wait in Frederick to pick up any who may have slipped through the net.

Brown and twenty-two of his followers stepped off the Baltimore and Ohio in Harpers Ferry, Virginia. When asked to identify himself, Brown produced papers showing him as Isaac Smith. They were free to go and they left for the farm Brown had leased nearly a year before near Brownsville, Maryland.

When the Attorney-General Black received and read the after action report from Thomas Kinsey, he was saddened at the death of agent Woodall. His body was found in Topeka, Kansas. Woodall was the best undercover agent in the Department of Justice. He closed the file, placed it under his arm and walked down the hall and into the office of the National Affairs Advisor. He laid it down and said, "Read this when you get a chance, Jason. I will not report this to the President until I get your assessment."

"I can read it now, if you like." Black lit a cigar and sat while Jason read the short, concise report.

"That should do it, if you have John Brown in custody, then it is over. I listened to one of his speeches while I was in Kansas for President Pierce. More like a rant and a rave, but people hung on every word out of the man's mouth. How many made it through to Frederick Station?"

"Not a one, Jason."

"I think something is wrong, a few should have been picked up there. Let us alert Harpers Ferry to expect trouble. What do you think?"

"Good idea, I will send the orders today."

"We should also bring the army in on this."

"I will check with John Floyd. I think that he has troops stationed nearby under Colonel Lee."

"Two weeks ought to be enough time to keep the army on alert."

"Yes, if they left Kansas on the nineteenth of September, we should be clear by the first week in October."

48
Harpers Ferry
October 1859

It was late in September when John Brown's party reached the farm where he planned to equip and train his men for the attack. He and one of his sons, Owen, had purchased rifles and hand guns the summer before, a few at a time. He had enough arms at this point for nineteen or twenty raiders, as he now called them. Each day, he brought them together so he could outline his plan of attack.

"Remember this, Raiders, there are two keys to the success of our endeavors. First, capture the weapons and escape south before word reaches Washington City. Second, we must go from plantation to plantation so that local slaves can rise up against their owners. We must find and cut the telegraph wires both north and south. John Kagi will climb and cut one set and Jeremiah Anderson will climb and cut another set. Trains running through Harpers Ferry should be stopped in both directions. William and Dauphin Thompson will stop trains coming into the station from the south. Oliver and Watson Brown will stop trains coming from the north. As soon as we are inside, Owen will load the wagons so that he, the two drivers and the two men riding shotgun can leave for the plantations. Tibbs, Coppeci, Merrien, and Anderson, you are going with Owen as drivers and guards. Oliver, you back up Owen. Barclay, Cook, Leary and Newby, you are also backups."

Some days, he interrupted the physical training to stress the importance of surprise. They would only proceed when the armory was closed on Sunday, probably at night. That meant that the raid would happen on the first Sunday in October or on the ninth or as late as the sixteenth of the month. It would depend on the progress of the men. He said, "If we are careful all should be well. If we are discovered before we reach the armory doors, protect each other, remember your assignments. If your comrade falls, then take his place. You know who you are paired with. If one cannot do a task, your replacement will."

He was preoccupied with which of the plantations should be given arms and which should not. Brown poured over his list of land owners in northern Virginia, while his men took target practice. The first Sunday in October came and went.

"We are almost ready, another week and we go."

On the ninth of October, it was pouring rain and Brown said, "God must be guiding our hands, wagons loaded with heavy weapons will not travel far on these country roads." And they waited and prayed for better weather. It came on the sixteenth.

In 1794, President George Washington had selected Harpers Ferry, Virginia, and the site at Springfield, Massachusetts, for the new national armories. In choosing Harpers Ferry, he was quoted as saying, "The benefit of waterpower provided by the Potomac and Shenandoah rivers will make this an ideal site." The truth of the matter was that Harpers Ferry was in his home state and since 1795, one or more of Washington's family had found employment there. Lewis Washington, the great-grand nephew of President Washington, was one of the family. He was just hired and was assigned as a night guard. On the evening of October sixteenth he was one of six night watchmen captured outside the arsenal.

"What do we do with these six?"

"Hog tie them, gag them and let us move forward." Brown ordered.

Suddenly, a voice called out, "Halt, show yourself!" Owen Brown raised his rifle and shot the unarmed man. There was no need for silence any longer. When Brown's men found the body they remarked, "He has a black face, we have just killed a slave who we have come to save." Hayward Shepard was actually a freed man working as a railroad baggage handler, but Brown's men could not have known this.

The killing and the capture continued until the small group now 19 members reached the doors of the arsenal.

"Who is down?" Brown asked.

"Kagi and Anderson." Owen answered.

"Have the telegraph lines been cut?"

"Yes, four men are now removing sections of Baltimore and Ohio rail north and south of the arsenal. That should keep the railroad from knowing what is going on."

"We need to start loading the wagons. Owen, get your men ready to leave for the locations that I gave you. Move, move, let God's work begin."

An hour later, 160 model 1817 Hall rifles were loaded along with twenty-two boxes of ammunition. Owen Brown, Charles Tibbs, Dale Coppeci, Francis Merrien and Osborne Andersen left the arsenal in two wagons heading to the plantations. They disappeared into the night and were never heard from again.

Brown's men had loaded two more wagons. His men had pulled the wagons out of the arsenal when shots rang out and two of his men were wounded on the wagons.

"Find out where those shots came from!" Yelled Watson Brown.

"Looks like the corner of High and Shenandoah Streets."

"Oliver, take two men and see if you can get him."

They found a local town policeman by the name of Thomas Boorly firing from a prone position. They circled him and killed him before returning to the arsenal. This awoke more townspeople and by sunrise of Monday morning, reporting Armory workers joined the townspeople in shooting at any movement that they could see inside the arsenal. The local Virginia Militia was informed and joined the mob surrounding the arsenal. During the first few hours, two more townspeople were killed, Jake Turner and the mayor of Harpers Ferry.

It was a standoff until a Baltimore and Ohio passenger train, north bound, stopped because of the missing rails. They re-spiked them and continued into Harpers Ferry. When the train reached the station, the engineer did not stop and tried to continue through town. He was stopped again on the north side of the station because of missing rails. Again, they worked to connect and spike them into place. They continued on to Frederick, Maryland. Here they telegraphed the news to Union Station, Washington City.

UNKNOWN NUMBER – INSIDE FEDERAL ARMORY – HARPERS FERRY – LOCAL MILITIA ON SITE – PLACE SURROUNDED – SEND TROOPS.

This message was received at 3:30 PM, Monday, October 17, 1859. It was forwarded to the War Department and Colonel Robert Lee, commander of the rapid response unit, was ordered to Harpers Ferry by Secretary of the Navy, Toucey. While Lee's unit organized and boarded a train, Brown realized that escape was not possible and he ordered, "Take the prisoners and move to the fire engine house, it is like a fort. We will be safer there."

"I am not going to be trapped in there," one man yelled back to Brown.

"Lehman, is that you?"

But before Brown could react, Samuel Lehman ran from the arsenal and jumped into the Potomac River. He began to swim across toward the Maryland shore. The townspeople, many of whom had been drinking corn liquor all day, began firing at him. He was hit, turned belly up and began floating down the river with the current.

On Tuesday morning, Colonel Lee and his marines arrived in Harpers Ferry. Lee's first order was to close the taverns in town.

"Lieutenant Stuart, get those saloons closed down! Arrest anyone with a firearm who appears to be drunk or disorderly."

"Yes, Sir."

"Oh, and Jeb, can you find me the commander of the militia? Have him report to me."

"Aye, aye. Sir."

While Lee awaited the commander of the militia, the commander, a Colonel Greene, was breaking down the doors of the fire engine house. Luke Quinn was the first militia member through the door and was shot and killed by Watson Brown. As more militia poured into the fire engine house, hand to hand fighting broke out and John Brown was wounded by a sword. When everyone inside the fire engine house was arrested, ten of Brown's men had been killed including his sons, Watson and Oliver. All of Brown's prisoners, including Lewis Washington, were dead. Colonel Lee was not pleased when he located Colonel Greene, commander of the militia.

"Colonel Greene, my Lieutenant will take charge of the prisoners."

"Hold on, Colonel. These are my prisoners captured by state militia forces inside state boundaries and will stand trial in Charles Town, Virginia. I will not allow them to be taken into federal custody, I have already placed them on a train for Charles Town."

Lee looked around and did not see any live prisoners. John Brown bleeding from his wound awoke in a box car headed for Charles Town. He called out, "Is anyone in here? Call out your names."

"Hazlat, Sir."

"Stevens and Shields, Sir. Shields is hurt bad."

"Copeland and Cook, Sir. Cook is dead."

"Copper, Smith and Ragland, Sir."

Five days later John Brown, still recovering from his sword wound, stood trial in Jefferson County Courthouse. The trial lasted four days and the jury found him guilty. Judge Robert Parker asked Brown if he had anything to say before he passed sentence.

"I am now quite certain that the crimes of Virginia and other slave holding states will never be purged away, but by blood. Let me be the first to die in a national civil war."

On December 2, he was taken from his cell in Charles Town and hung. Two more trials were held for four of the men who followed John Brown. On December 16, four more of his followers were hung. On March 16, 1859, the last two prisoners died while awaiting trial.

Lee stated in his after action report to the Secretary of the Navy, "The mob was out of control when we arrived in Harpers Ferry. The marines under my command controlled the mob by disarming the townspeople. The militia gained confidence from federal forces on station and so attacked the armory grounds on their own. No order was ever given by a federal officer for any arrests at the scene of the surrender by Mr. Brown. The survivors were arrested by local authority and my command returned to Washington."

When the report reached the Office of National Affairs in the White House, I sat down to read it. I thought, this will be the beginning of the end for states rights in this country. I began a series of letters home. The first was to Robert Whitehall, managing director of Caldwell Trading and Shipping. It directed him, at his earliest convenience, to board one of our ships in Port Royal and sail to St. George, Bermuda. He was to take the enclosed letter of introduction to a Mr. David Nelson, Bank of Bermuda, 224 Water Street, St. George. It was only a two block walk from the docks in St. George. He was to inform Mr. Nelson that the time was now right to begin the transfer of Caldwell Shipping to the docks in St. George. Dock space would be needed. A lease would be preferred. If leases are not available, then a purchase would be made from the Caldwell Shipping Account. If a dock purchase cannot be made in the next thirty days, then purchase land upon which additional docks can be constructed. Please remind him that I am now a dual citizen.

The second enclosed letter is to be taken to the commander of the Royal Naval Dock Yards. You will have to catch the Bermuda Railroad in St. George and get off at the termination point, which is the Royal dock yard. Stop at the gatehouse to the yards and ask for the letter to be delivered to the Admiral. Ask for a receipt. The third letter enclosed in a separate addressed envelope is for Lord Napier in London. Take it to the Perot Post Office in Hamilton as you pass through there. You may, of course, stay as many days as you and your wife like in the company house there. Take a carriage to Caldwell Place in St. George. If you like to walk, it is a short walk from the docks on Duke of York Street, past St. Peter's Church and continue until you come to Rose Hill Street. Turn right on Rose Hill and climb to the stone columns and gate with Caldwell Place worked into the iron work. Our house keeper is called Sally Trott and I will send her a letter to expect you. If by chance, you should like Bermuda, you might think about living there during the next year. I signed the letter, enclosed the others which I had written and walked to the mail room.

I thought, the die has been cast. Once the commander of the Royal Dock Yards gets my letter offering to sell coal and oil to his fleet, there will be no turning back. The cost of shipping coal or oil from the United States will be much cheaper than trying to bring it from Wales. My letter to Lord Napier was one of many over the last year. It outlined the advantages to the Crown for entering into contracts with Caldwell Trading and Shipping. We could deliver all types of goods and materials to St. George and the Royal Naval Dock Yards, Bermuda. I hoped he would find the time appropriate for the final contract to be drawn and signed by the Crown.

49

St. George, Bermuda
November, 1859

Robert Whitehall and his wife, Laura, stepped onto the Caldwell merchant mariner, *Cold Harbor,* on November 9, 1859. They were met by Captain Jacob, and shown to the owner's suite.

"Captain Caldwell uses this suite whenever he travels with us. I know you will be comfortable here. If you need anything, Mrs. Whitehall, I have instructions from Captain Caldwell to provide it. We are crossing at a nice time of year. Storm season is over for the middle Atlantic and we should have smooth sailing."

He left them to unpack their bags and settle in.

"Robert?"

"Yes, Laura."

"Why did Jason Caldwell want me to come along with you on this trip? You have been here before and I did not accompany you."

"This time is different. I think Jason is going to promote me. That promotion will be to Bermuda or England for at least one year. He is a very understanding company owner, he would never even ask me to consider Bermuda if you did not approve. He is married now. You have met his wife and have spent time with her. What do you think of her?"

"I think Jason Caldwell has met his match in her. She is beautiful and intelligent. Together, they are going to build a financial empire. She has the political connections from all those years with her brother and he has made some outstanding investments."

"How do you know that, Laura?"

"Women's gossip going around Beaufort. Did you know, she spent a small fortune remodeling their house on Bay Street?"

"What do you mean?"

"Well, I heard that she has installed running water and an eight foot marble bathing tub!"

"Laura, how would you know that?"

"Marge Shield's husband is a plumber and he installed the pipes inside the walls of the house."

"Gossip will tell us everything that we do not need to know, Laura."

"Yes, I know the Caldwell's own half of Beaufort and everyone is jealous of them, but they have been good to us, Robert. Did you ever think that you would be put in charge of Caldwell Trading and Shipping in Beaufort? Let us keep an open mind about becoming more than an office manager in Beaufort, South Carolina, shall we?"

"Laura, would you consider moving to Bermuda for a year?"

"It would depend upon what Bermuda is like."

Several days later the captain of the *Cold Harbor* announced, "We are several leagues away from the eastern end of Bermuda, Mrs. Whitehall. Notice the color of the sea has changed to a bright blue and aqua. We are sailing over the sidewalls of an ancient volcano. Bermuda is what is left of the volcano rim. Over the centuries the side of the rim facing America has dropped below the sea. This side, that faces east, remains above the sea."

"How did the island gets its name, Captain?"

"It was discovered by a Spanish vessel in the year 1515, they were looking for fresh drinking water. When water was not discovered, the island was added to the Spanish maps and named for the ship's captain, Juan de Bermudez"

"How did the English come to settle here?"

"An Atlantic storm caused a ship traveling to Jamestown Colony to crash on the coral outcropping in 1609. The captain of that ship, Sir George Somers, salvaged what he could and brought survivors to the beach just beyond this point that we are sailing around today. Look up on that bluff, that is Fort St. Catherine that guards the entrance to St. George Harbor."

"How did they survive without fresh water?"

"They had barrels of water with them. And more importantly, they discovered that it rained nearly very day during the winter months here. They built catch systems for storing rain water. They had to boil the drinking water, of course, but most water used in buildings and houses is not potable, anyway. Every building that you see today in Bermuda has a cistern, in fact, the roofs are now the collectors for the cisterns."

"What a remarkable people," Laura said.

The *Cold Harbor* entered St. George Harbor, dropped anchor, and prepared to lower a tender for us along side the dock at Somer's Wharf. "This is closer to Water Street, Mr. Whitehall, I will have to re-dock at Ship's Wharf across the harbor. If you need us before we sail, come there via St. David's Road and you will find us."

"When will you sail back to Port Royal?"

"We will remove cargo here and return in three days."

"We will let you know if Laura and I will be on the return voyage, Captain."

And with that conversation ended, Laura and I got into the tender carrying our two small bags off the ship without assistance and found a carriage for hire on Water Street. I told the driver to take us to Caldwell Place, and we were off on our adventure. We drove from Water's Street through Barber's alley and turned left into Duke of York, went one long block and turned right into Rose Hill Street.

"It is at the top of the hill," we said.

"Yes, Governor, I have been here before!" The driver said this with a perfect English accent.

"Welcome to Caldwell Place," I said to Laura.

The driver handed our bags to us and wanted twenty-five pence. We handed him a US dollar and said, "We are sorry, we do not have any Bermuda Pounds."

"Thank you, Sir. That is about right with the conversion."

We were standing under a carriage portico in front of a large, rambling, one story building with Caldwell Shipping Company lettered across the double doors. We went inside into a large entrance hall which must have been a lobby at one time. A woman's voice called out, "Be with you in a minute."

Sally Trott stuck her head around a corner, smiled and said, "You must be the Whitehall's I got a letter from Admiral Caldwell saying to expect you. Have either of you been here with us before?"

"No, I stayed at the White Horse Inn, down on Water Street when I was here last time. This is my wife's first visit to Bermuda."

"Well, then, let me show you to your living quarters and I will tell you a little bit about this place."

"Living quarters?" Laura asked.

"Yes, Ma'am. The Admiral said when you and his friend Robert move here you will be in charge of this converted golf course."

"Converted golf course?" I asked.

"I will be charge?" Laura asked.

"Yes, to both questions. You, Laura, are to be put on salary to manage the comings and goings of Caldwell employees while they are here at Caldwell Place. The Admiral purchased the whole club, golf course and all, as a company headquarters. The Admiral hopes that you, Robert, will be the new President of Caldwell Shipping Company."

"I need to sit down." We both said at once.

"Here is the Admiral's letter to me, maybe you ought to read it. Oh, and there are letters waiting for you in your office, Robert."

"My office?"

"Yes, it is over there to the left, see it?"

"We walked across and stopped before a heavy cedar door and read the gold leaf lettering:

Mr. Robert Whitehall, President

"Laura, your office is down that hall and off to your right."

"My office?"

"Yes, ma'am. It says, Laura Whitehall, Director Caldwell Place."

We both must have looked shell shocked because Sally looked at us and said, "I know what you must be feeling. The Admiral has a way with people especially his friends. You are looking at the new facility manager. My office is in a cottage behind that Bermuda stonewall over there. I have been busy interviewing cooks, chamber maids, grounds keepers, a golf shop manager, and others. When this place gets fully in operation, it will really be something to see."

The remainder of the day was spent reading our letters of one year appointments from Louise and Jason. We found our "living quarters", which were larger than our house in Beaufort. We followed Sally around the "Place" to get our orientation. Two other sets of living quarters were in different wings of the club. Individual rooms were provided for overnight guests which looked out through french doors onto a large swimming pool. A large conference room was adjacent to a large community eating area and kitchen area where food was prepared and then served.

"What do you think?" I asked Laura.

"Could be larger, I doubt that you could get more than a hundred in here." She said, with a smile on her face. "Thank you, Robert, this is too good to be true. Me, with a job." Tears were running down her cheeks.

"Thank Jason, this is his doing. He has not stopped helping my family since he bought the Bank of Beaufort in '37 when is was almost worthless. It saved my father from suicide, I know."

"I see Louise Buchanan, everywhere I look. Let us each write a letter of acceptance today."

"Should we at least see the country, first?"

"Yes, of course, we need to work hard to deserve this kind of treatment, Robert. I know he has been your friend forever, but this is different."

"We have letters to deliver and a train ride to take tomorrow. We will begin to see the whole country, from east to west end by train coach. Then we can make a final decision."

"Robert, I am staying. I want to start my employment tomorrow."

"What about clothes and other things that we will need from home?"

"Robert, I will only say this once. Everything we will ever need for one year is right here. Did you see those dress shops along Water Street? We have an expense account, you did read that part in your letter!"

"Yes, Laura."

The next morning we walked down to 224 Water Street and found the Bank of Bermuda. We went inside and found the office of David Nelson. We introduced ourselves and he said, "I am truly glad to meet you, Mr. and Mrs. Whitehall. I have several documents for you to sign. Robert, you can read and sign this bunch. Laura, you can read and sign this stack."

"It says here that Caldwell Place is a public inn. Is that true?"

"Why, yes. Mrs. Whitehall, that is true. You do not advertise the fact in Bermuda. Most of your guests are from the United States. Mr. Samuel Clemmons is a frequent visitor."

"Mark Twain?"

"Yes, ma'am. He loves Bermuda. Says he no longer believes in Heaven. He can not imagine a nicer place than Bermuda."

We picked up our account books, ledgers and copies of the signed documents and stood to leave.

"Just a moment, Mr. Whitehall. The Admiral wanted you to have this." He handed me a brown leather brief case with gold embossing on the cover, Mr. Robert Whitehall, President. I put both Laura's and my papers inside along with the letters I was carrying in my breast pocket. We walked to the train depot and waited for the next train to the west end.

"Robert, everything is within walking distance in St. George. I like that."

The train left on time according to the posted schedule in St. George. Our first glimpses of the country were while were we on St. George Island. The train was really a trolley that stopped every few minutes. We rode along with the Atlantic Ocean on our right hand and Castle Harbor on our left. We went across small stone bridges from island to island. Coney Island Park, then Bailey's Bay came into view. We had already passed Wilkinson Park and Abbot's Cliff Park before we stopped in Hamilton Parish. We passed Shelly Bay and Harrington Sound and crossed another bridge into Flatt's Village. We hugged the north shore until we came to a place called Pembroke Marsh where we bent south and into the town of Hamilton.

"We need to stop here, Laura. I need to find the Perot Post Office."

We walked past Victoria Park on Victoria Street, found Wesley Street until it took us across Church Street and onto Queen Street. Perot Post Office was in the middle of the next block.

"Robert, there was a post office in St. George, we walked right by it."

"I know, Laura, think of this as a treasure hunt. Jason is having his fun and he is showing us Bermuda and how easy it is to get places."

We spent the next hour exploring Front Street stores and shops. We found a truly amazing store called Trimingham's. It was called a department store. It

253

was having its Grand Opening. Laura spent her Bermuda pounds that she had exchanged in St. George and we trudged back up the hills above Front Street, back to the train depot. We found an open seat and placed her packages in it and stood as we pulled away from Hamilton and rounded Albuoy's Point and proceeded into Paget Parish. We were now inland and could not see the Ocean or the Great Sound. In less than an hour we were passing the modern Gibbs Hill light house built in 1846 and made of cast iron. At Seymour's Pond we caught sight of the Great Sound and kept it on our right side as we made stops for passengers in Jennings, Evans, Somerset, Scaur Hill and Mangrove Bay. The island grew very narrow with the Great Sound on our right and the Atlantic on our left. We went across bridges at Waterford, Boaz island, Grey's and at the Royal Naval Cemetery, the burial sight for the British Navy. The termination was at the Royal Naval Dockyards.

We left the train, with Laura's packages and found the main gate. I followed the Admiral's instructions and while we were waiting for a receipt, the guard asked if we had used any of the water taxis.

"No, can we take a water taxi to St. George?"

"Of course, walk down to the north basin and you can catch one there." We did. It was a bright beautiful day for a ferry ride. It took a fraction of the time to ride back to Ordnance Island terminal in St. George. We walked off the ferry and passed Sir George Somers Statue and into King's Square. We needed to sit and rest awhile. We found a little park called Somers' Garden, one block from the square. It was warm for November. The park was full of trees and flowers that we had never seen. When we had rested, we started walking down Duke of York looking for Rose Hill. We found it, turned right and started up the hill to Caldwell Place. My legs burned, the hill was so steep.

When we dropped our packages inside the main entrance, Sally smiled at us and said, "Are you hungry, have you eaten?" We both looked at each other and realized that we had not had anything since breakfast. We sat down in the dining room and we asked for anything that was ready to eat. Bermuda food was English basic fare with a dash of special island flavor. We ate until we could not take another bite.

The next day we signed our contracts, wrote letters to the Caldwells and took them down to the Captain of the *Cold Harbor* at Ship's Wharf. We handed him the mail packets and a list of items that we would like him to bring from our house in Beaufort on his next trip across. He smiled and said, "This is a nice place. I do not blame you folks for staying. See you next month."

50
The White House
Christmas 1859

Our second Christmas together was spent in the White House with a larger family than the prior year. Little James was a typical two year old, riding his tricycle up and down the halls, yelling at startled staffers to, "get out the way!" Baby, Ruth, was adorable. All she wanted to do was cuddle in your arms or sit quietly on your lap, while her brother James was known as the "little terror" of 1600 Pennsylvania Avenue. The "big terror" was an adoring Uncle James.

James Buchanan had settled into the affairs of state with renewed vigor. He shook off the Harpers Ferry affair, as he called it, and promoted Robert Lee instead of expressing any concern whatever. As a Brigadier, however, Lee's rank was too high to keep command of my old marine detachment. His command was passed to Colonel Jeb Stuart, another southerner, and a very able commander. So now, the annual Christmas RR celebration would include the original marines under my command, those of Lee's and the new men under Stuart. That should be an interesting party. Lots of "war" stories to tell around the tables, I thought.

The White House Protection detail had served with distinction and would celebrate their anniversary in March, and they had a very large Christmas party. Louise and I sat with Lieutenant Commander Lewis and his executive officer, Tom Schneider and their wives. Tom was promoted from Master Sergeant to Warrant Officer and he was running an efficient operation. Louise liked her protection detail and did not mind the shadowing outside the White House, she told them. They said they tried to stay in the background and be helpful. "Sam Mason goes with me everywhere I need to go." I said.

The Christmas trees on the first floor of the White House gave the home of the President, "a lived in feeling." Most of the time, the first floor was open to the public for tours. Every President to date, had said that the White House belonged to the people. The President's staff worked in the west wing and rarely went into the first floor unless it was decorated for a holiday season and there were parties to attend.

Louise's office was called the Office of Protocol. She had a staff that followed White House "rules and regulations" to the letter. When Christmas rolled around every year, her office flew into action. Live trees were purchased, usually from New England. They were brought to the White House and the First Lady was in charge of their placement throughout the White House. There were 135 rooms furnished and occupied in December 1859. The decorations were stored in the "basement" of the White House. After Thanksgiving holiday, the process of decoration began. All 135 rooms had at least one Christmas decoration. My office had a fat little Santa seated behind a large globe of the earth. A huge roll of paper was spread out over his lap and onto the rug of the centerpiece. I remember having to remove items from an end table in order to have Santa and his world view decorate my office.

People working in the White House, like most places of business became very territorial. Louise would laugh when a person would tell her. "What happened to my Christmas Santa and his elves? I always have them in my office at Christmas time!"

She would look up the master list of items stored in the basement, locate the missing Santa and have it taken to its proper place.

"I just can not believe how touchy some of these people are, Jason. That is not their property, it belongs to the White House."

"I know. By the way, your people have not found my Ten Days of Christmas decoration that I always have on my bookcase."

When the decorating was completed, then the parties began. Not just the White House parties, of course, but the Washington parties began. The ambassadors of all the embassies had to return the single party that Louise gave each year at the White House. That one party for foreign embassies spawned nearly a hundred invitations. Louise would answer each one, yes the President would be pleased to attend. No, we can not attend on that date, could we come another? Sometimes, she and her brother would leave the White House, go to one embassy for an hour, excuse themselves and go to as many as half a dozen in one night.

I usually found an excuse not to attend Christmas parties away from the White House. It became too much. It was worse than attending a cabinet meeting!

After Christmas, I made monthly train trips to Titusville to check on the construction of our new company head quarters for Caldwell Trading, called "Seneca Hill." The 640 acres upon which it sat were undergoing a dramatic change. A permanent residence for Louise, the children and me was to be located in a grove of trees atop a small hill. A stable and other out buildings were framed but not completed. A machine shop for Seneca Oil was down the hill in back of the house and out of sight from the country road which passed our place. The top of an oil rig could be seen from the road, however, and we called it our little money maker. The oil rig was not planned. When the water well people came to drill our well for the house, they hit oil. When the septic tank installers came, I warned them about oil tar deposits.

Septic systems were a modern replacement for cesspools. They were completely underground, whereby a cesspool was an open pond. We thought that with little children, an open pool would invite disaster. I questioned the installers about how it worked.

"Well, it is like your stomach, Sir. We put a shovel of horse manure in the bottom of the concrete tank and that starts the digestion of waste that you put in there."

"What happens when the tank gets full?"

"Water is flushed every time you add to the tank, Sir. That water rises to the top of the tank and is carried away through these clay tiles that we have placed in these here trenches. The water is taken away from the tank into a drain field. See the pattern of the trenches and the area that we have allowed for that?"

"Does the tank ever get completely full of solids?"

"Not if we do our job correctly. If it does we come out and pump it out for you, free of charge!"

"Well, that is good to know. Thank you."

The foundations were in for all of the buildings and the first story walls were beginning to rise. Louise left the outside appearance to my selection, while she busied herself with making sure that water pipes were installed within inside walls. I selected gray granite stone from New Hampshire for exterior walls. It was shipped by rail and stacked on site for the masons. I decided to have a slate roof, I picked a gray, green color and it was shipped from Erie. Copper flashing and copper sheeting would be used to cover roof valleys and porch roofs.

I made several side trips to Erie to order porch columns, windows and doors. Hardware of all types had to be selected. Whenever I asked Louise what she thought, she always asked. "Is that outside or inside? If it is outside, you have to decide, I am busy with inside stuff."

Sam never complained about traveling on weekends. He and Rachael had two children, also. And as new fathers, we compared notes and talked about what we would do after the election next year. Sam could go back to the Navy, but I doubted the Navy would need or want me. I had been a man sailing a desk for too many years. I had moved the international shipping part of the company to Bermuda. The State Department had been successful in obtaining dual citizenship for Louise and I. When we spent leave in Bermuda the protection staff all wanted to go along!

The reports from Western Utah Territory were getting better, we would soon be in the black ink within another quarter. So Christmas 1859, was a time of peace for the Caldwell family and the nation

51
Seneca Hill, Pennsylvania
Easter 1860

The announcement was given to the local newspapers that the President of the United States, Admiral and Mrs. Jason Caldwell and families would be spending the Easter Holidays in Franklin, Pennsylvania. No details were given about times of arrival. The Franklin Reporter contacted the White House and wanted minute by minute schedules. The Presidential Protection Detail sent a telegram which stated:

PRESIDENT TO ARRIVE MARCH 21, 1860, ON BALTIMORE AND OHIO. PLEASE CONTACT COMMANDER LEWIS ON TRAIN PLATFORM. MORE INFORMATION TO FOLLOW.

Of course, no additional information was ever sent. A Presidential Protection team was sent one week before the arrival and cleared the route that the President would take from the train station to the house that he had purchased in August. The housekeeping staff was assembled and questioned.

Do you live in the house? Do you travel to and from the house to work? Are you married? Are you single? Do you ever have guests inside the house with you? Who delivers items to the house? Do you buy things for the President in Franklin? Have you ever been arrested? Has anyone in your family ever been arrested? Do you have dependent children? Are there any firearms in the house? Do you carry a firearm for protection? Where do you keep this firearm? How far is the fire station? How far is the police station?

Jerome Lewis was determined that the Presidential visit to his planned retirement home would be without a single blemish. No advanced warning was given to the Baltimore and Ohio Personnel. They, therefore, had to have "special handling" personnel on stand by for each of the trains leaving Union Station on March 21,1860. The Presidential Protection Detail arrived at the station in advance of the time to board the train to Franklin, Pennsylvania.

They cleared each car in the train. When the President and his family got to the station, the detail members had already been in place three hours.

When the train finally pulled into the Franklin station, the children were asleep. So I carried one and James Buchanan, President of the United States, carried the other. We all walked onto the train platform and through the crowd of people trying to get a glimpse of the President.

"I wonder when he will come off?"

"He probably waits until all these other people are off."

"How long has it been since he was home?"

We continued to walk through the people and not a one noticed us. James Buchanan was a happy man. He kept his head down, talking gently to baby, Ruth. We were well away from the platform and into our carriages provided by the Protection Detail assigned in Franklin. The train detail reboarded for their trip back to Washington and handed us over. We were out of the station yard and on our way to a much needed vacation away from the White House.

We arrived at the "Pennsylvania White House", a large square, two story wood frame house on Willow Street in Franklin, Pennsylvania. James Buchanan was back in his element as he said, "I feel like a prisoner in Washington, here I can breathe!"

"The last four years have aged you considerably, brother."

"All three of us have. Look at Jason, Louise. He has crow feet around his eyes. He did not have those when I met him in President Pierce's office."

"Those crow feet are from squinting at all those small numbers on his accounts sheets." Louise said with a grin.

"I have mixed business with pleasure, these past two years. Not everything that we have tried has worked. And sometimes, what has worked so well, can never be told." I said.

"What do you mean, Jason?" Louise asked.

"When I was in Naval Intelligence, things were not always as they seemed. Your brother, here, talked me into accepting a Presidential Warrant from Franklin Pierce."

"What is a Presidential Warrant?"

"That is when I send your husband on an assignment that is likely to get him arrested by local authority. A warrant is like a Presidential Pardon in advance. The assignment is of such critical importance to the nation, that sometimes a state law is broken. A warrant allows, Jason, or whoever holds it, to continue without interference."

"Oh, I get it! It is like diplomatic immunity!" His sister beamed.

"Exactly right. My sister is intelligent, Jason."

"Jason, tell me about the assignment for Franklin Pierce."

"That really is ancient history. It seems so long ago, now. It was in December of '56, I think. Our relations with the British were strained to the breaking point over the dismissal of the British Ambassador to Washington."

"Why was he dismissed?"

"He had set up a scheme to enlist American seamen to serve on English ships. They were told they would be stationed in Bermuda. In truth, they were used wherever the Royal Navy needed sailors. They needed them in the Black Sea."

"The Black Sea, that is half way around the world!"

"I know. When the Ambassador's agent, Milton Black, could not meet the quota set by the Royal Naval Dockyards in Bermuda, Black started pressing seamen,"

"Pressing? What does that mean?"

"Forcing them into service - kidnaping."

"Americans taken by the British, that is incredible!"

"That is what Franklin thought!" Her brother said.

"So, what did you talk my husband into doing about it?"

"Franklin and I were sitting in the Oval Office and in walks this Navy Captain, your husband over there, and gives off this sense of confidence that I had never seen before. In those years, your husband ran the Naval Intelligence division for the Secretary Dobbin of the Navy. He spoke very softly and slowly with a hint of seriousness that made people pay attention. I remember thinking, this man is a warrior!"

"Jason, a warrior?"

"Yes, Louise. Your husband has been successful because once his mind is set upon the objective, he is determined to get results. It is surprising how many men and women lack this characteristic."

"Yes. But what did you and Franklin Pierce want him to do?"

"We wanted him to stop the pressing of American seamen."

"And did he?"

"Yes, he did. He and a special detachment of US Marines found where the British were holding the kidnap victims. One of his men set a trap for this Milton Black character and Jason forced him to take him and his marines to a waiting ship in Chesapeake Bay. They captured the ship, rescued the American seamen and everyone lived happily ever after."

All three of us had a good laugh at a funny, relaxed, James Buchanan. He then said, "Jason, can you at least call me, James, on this vacation?"

"I will think about it, Mister President." And we laughed again.

52

Western Utah Territory
Spring 1860

When silver was discovered in western Utah Territory in 1857, it was not met with the same "Gold Rush Fever" of ten years earlier at Sutter's Mill, California. It took almost a year for the news to reach prospectors and large scale mine operators. It was known within the White House, however, and in 1858 Jason Caldwell had sent his representatives to explore this business prospect. They were guided by two of his RR marines, corporals D.D. Wilson and Matthew James, now private citizens and employees of Caldwell Trading Company. When the Caldwell representatives, a mining engineer, surveyor and construction foreman, reached Carson Canyon they found 200 gold miners at work along the gravel banks of the canyon river with rockers, Long Toms and sluices. Most of the men complained about a heavy blue-black material which kept clogging their rockers. The Caldwell engineer thought this might be silver and when he had it assayed, it was determined to be almost pure sulphuret of silver. Traveling on up the river, they came to the town of Johnstone. Here they paused long enough to purchase a few lots upon which to build later. Jason Caldwell had insisted that they not pan for gold. Or they should not stake claims for silver, instead they should build a saw mill and obtain timber for the mill. He reasoned that mining required timbers cut from trees and water. They were to purchase any water rights that they could find. Then and only then, should they begin to buy up played out gold strikes, turning these into silver mining operations.

By the Spring of 1859, those who discovered the Comstock Lode had extracted all the gold and discounted the "blue-stuff". Patrick McLaughlin sold his interest in the Ophir Mine to Caldwell Trading for $3,500.00. Emanual Penrod sold his share for $8,500.00. Peter O'Riley held on to his share for a few months and sold to Caldwell Trading for $40,000.00 in order to build a hotel. One year later the Ophir Mine produced one and one half million dollars in silver dividends for stock holders. D. D. Wilson, manager of the saw mill, sold over a half a million dollars in cut timbers for the prevention of cave ins to other mine owners. Matthew James, director of Caldwell Water Company was selling sump pumps to keep the mines free of flooding from vast quantities of underground streams of hot water. The hot water was collected and sent to the town of Johnstone through pipes and sold there to businesses and townspeople. The proceeds from these enterprises were placed in the Bank of California until a bank could be built in Johnstone and later Carson City.

There were no railroads into Utah Territory, Caldwell Trading noticed this and began a shipping operation. Freight and passengers were transported by mule teams of from 10 to 16. Ore was hauled from the mines to the mills for refining by Caldwell Shipping. They brought to the mines all the timbers, mining machinery and supplies. No wagon made an unloaded run anywhere. Goods and merchandise needed by small mining towns was hauled over the Sierras from California on the return trips from deposits of pure silver and gold from the refining mills. Caldwell investments would have flourished by shipping contracts only, but it was the Caldwell Water Company that became the real "Gold Mine."

In 1859, the flow of water from natural springs was adequate to supply the needs of the miners and small towns of Johnstone, Virginia City and Gold Hill. As population increased, wells were dug for domestic needs, and the water within several mine tunnels was added to the available supplies. As the refining, smelting mills and hoisting operations multiplied, the demand for water for use in steam boilers became so great that it was impossible to supply it without creating a water shortage. To fill this need, the Caldwell Water Company began hauling water to whomever needed it. Water tank wagons became common sights as they traveled from the Sierra Nevada mountains to the Virginia ranges that lay in the Washoe Valley. The Caldwell engineer, Herman Schussler, began working on a plan to replace the wagon trains by a cast iron pipe line. The 7 mile distance between water source and water demand could be met with a 12 inch diameter pipe which would produce 92,000 gallons of water per hour. Caldwell Water Systems Construction Company, CWSCC, now became the leading manufacturer of water systems for towns in Western Utah Territory.

In the spring of 1860, D. D. Wilson sent his first report back to the home office in Pennsylvania. He had the accountants provide an annual statement of saw mill production, sales and expenses. His salary was $10.00 per day, he itemized his expense account, and indicated that his profit sharing of 2% of timber production for that year was $10,000.00. Employees were paid at $1.00 per day plus expenses and ½% profit sharing or $2500.00. The cost of timber purchased that year was $40,000.00. Equipment and supply costs were $28,000.00. Transportation costs were $11,250.00. This left roughly $240,000.00 on deposit in the Bank of California for payment of outstanding debts. The mill had been constructed at a cost of $80,000. The interest on the loans for operating expenses, equipment and transportation showed a balance of zero. Not apparent to a casual reader was that the interest was paid to a Caldwell bank, trans- portation costs were paid to a Caldwell firm and timber purchases were to a Caldwell firm.

Matthew James sent a similar annual report for the water company. It had a balance of $650,000 on deposit in the bank of California to pay outstanding debts; interest, transportation, machinery purchases, pipe and supply purchases. His annual salary was also $10.00 per day, plus 2% of net operating profits or $13,000.00 His expense account was not itemized, but it was modest, it included one trip to Indiana.

When the copies from the lumber company, water company and Caldwell Mining and Shipping were forwarded to Jason and Louise Caldwell in the White House that year, they were pleased. The western assets were now worth well above 14 million dollars and that year's income to them was a little over 1 million dollars. When Louise reviewed the statements, she said, "Jason, D.D. and Matthew have done an outstanding amount of work for us in the last two years."

"I agree, they signed contracts with us for five years. If this income level keeps up, they will want a bigger piece of the pie."

"How long do you think the silver will last?"

"Herman says it looks like a fifteen to twenty year run until the veins of the Comstock are completely gone."

"And what about the oil in Titusville, Jason?"

"That should last longer, it will not disappear in our life times, and not in the children's."

"But, if both the silver and oil are gone?"

"Then you will have to settle for the "poor boy" you married from South Carolina, who owns an international shipping conglomerate in Bermuda."

"Are you going to be sad to leave the Navy and your time here in the White House, Jason?"

"Louise, your brother is keeping this country held together as best he can, but the future for a United States does not look good. We will have to see where we can best survive if there is a national war between the states."

"Does a war bring profits for a company like ours?"

"I would think that we will loose everything in either South Carolina or Pennsylvania depending upon which is occupied territory. We will need to write off holdings in one state or the other. The western assets look secure for the moment. Utah has applied for statehood and Nevada will follow as soon as Utah is admitted. They will be free states."

"Jason, what will happen to your parents and the rest of your family if a war breaks out?"

"I have talked with my father about coming to Pennsylvania or Bermuda, but I doubt he will want to leave his home and business. I will make the offer to move them if they want. It is really up to them. My sister and Carl might consider it, but Robert is too tied down as manager of the plantations and all."

"Could they manage their business's from a remote location, like you do, Jason?"

"Louise, I have excellent people I have met in the military service that manage for me."

"They need to find people they can trust. You trust people, Jason."

"Evaluate first, then trust. Then I never have to say, what in the hell is this?"

"What?"

"Master Chief Gunnerman, my DI in Annapolis, taught me a lot about how to handle people. He always assumed that I would not do things correctly, and therefore, I did not try very hard to please him."

"What are you getting at, Jason."

"I assume that people will do the right thing, because they want to please me. The fear of letting someone down is much greater than the actual fact. You try harder, you correct things on the fly, when things go awry."

"Jason, that is exactly how you are with my brother."

"Of course, practice what you preach!"

53
The White House
July 1860

The meeting with Senator Douglas had gone well, I thought. I waited until the President had signed the warrant and handed it to me. I read it, signed it and returned it to him.

"Jason, you will notice that the warrant becomes active if Lincoln is elected in November. I want you in Beaufort well before the election this fall. You hand pick from the RR detachment the men you need. I do not want Lee or Stuart to know anything about this."

"But, Sir, Stuart will know as soon as the detachment leaves Washington without him."

"Maybe, maybe not. I am sending his detachment on a special mission to San Juan Island in September. He is to meet with Commodore Hagood in San Francisco. By the time he gets back, you should have things under control. I am sending you because I do not want any blood shed down there, Jason."

"This is intelligence gathering in nature, so I will need only the men I can trust with me. Sam Mason, of course, and I will need Tom Schneider from the White House. I will need to talk to

Commander Lewis to find out if any others are from the southern United States. I can not take anyone with a Yankee accent. We are supposed to 'blend in' not call attention to ourselves. We will sail from Potomac Dock yards to Port Royal and await the election. If the Democrats win, we will be back in the middle of November. When would you like us back if the Republicans win, Mr. President?"

"The reactions are going to be immediate, Jason. I would like you back for the Inauguration, February at the latest. It will be someone else's headache after March 4 th. I have reserved a coach on the Baltimore and Ohio to take us home to Pennsylvania on the afternoon of the 4 th, I want you, Louise and the children with me."

"I will tell Louise, Mr. President."

"Jason, it pains me to say this, but do not send any information to the War Department. Use the Navy or the White House for communication with me. Do not allow Secretary Cobb, Floyd or Thompson to know where you are going or what your mission entails. I meant it when I said, I have only three cabinet members that I can trust to help me keep the Union together."

"You have my letter of conditions for Governor Pickens, right?"

"Yes, Sir. I do not know when I will get to Columbia, but it should prove helpful if someone questions our authority to be in South Carolina."

"Do you have my orders for the commanders of federal forces, Fort Sumter, Castle Pinckney, Fort Moultrie and Fort Johnson?"

"Yes, Sir."

"What am I forgetting, Jason?"

"Do I have your authorization to abandon Castle Pinckney if it is under attack, I would like to save everyone by moving to Fort Moultrie. In fact, it might buy us time to design a collapsing bubble, whereby troops are moved from the smallest to the largest, Fort Sumter. Fort Sumter can hold until March 4, 1861."

"Jason, my desire is not to start a shooting war with the State of South Carolina. I am convinced that if I turned Secretary Toucey loose with the Navy, every port in South Carolina would be in his hands within a week. Unfortunately, a war would result. I am trying with all my effort to protect the citizens of South Carolina from hot heads like David Jamieson and Governor Pickens, for that matter."

"I understand that, Mr. President. A holding action until the President-elect can take the oath is what you are after. You can depend upon my best judgement in how to do that."

"I know I can, brother, I am counting on that!"

"Mr. President, there is no way that the State of South Carolina can capture Fort Sumter. It is not like the other three fortifications. Even if Moultrie is captured, her guns can do little damage to Sumter. It is simple, if Fort Sumter is re-supplied, she can hold her own."

"I hope that will not be necessary, Jason. Start picking your men. Take only those you can trust."

I left the Oval Office and wondered what the next few months would be like. I was to begin training for a mission that might not be called upon. I stopped by Jerome Lewis's office and sat down in front of his desk. He looked up and said, "There are 135 rooms in this building and you have to rest here?"

"The President has given me another warrant, this time for Governor Pickens in South Carolina."

"You are going to South Carolina to arrest the Governor, when?"

"Before the election on the first Tuesday of November, probably in the middle of October."

"Why are you telling me this? Is the President accompanying you?"

"No, but you are involved. The President wants you to counsel me."

"Counsel?"

"More like the old days, Jerome. He wants a small force of men, like the RR group that you and I put together, to accompany me."

"I know you are not going to like this, but I need Tom Schneider and my personal body guard Sam Mason from your staff."

"Why not just take the RR unit?"

"The President has taken Stuart, Lee and Floyd out of the loop. Please do not mention this conversation with any of them."

"Jason, are you serious? Is this a black operation, off the books!"

"Absolutely. We travel on civilian transport, wearing civilian clothes with documentation from the White House. We will look like your protection detail, armed and ready to take action."

"That is why you need Schneider!"

"In the next two months, I need for *Warrant Officer Schneider* of the White House to become *Gunny Schneider* of the United States Marines. I need the same thing from Mason and anyone else you assign to this mission."

"How many do you need? We have applications a plenty here for you to go through. We should not take anymore from the White House, it will be noticed. Instead, look at these files, pick who you want and I will hire them."

"I can always count on you Commander Lewis! Your ideas are always better than mine, that is why I do what you suggest, but tell everyone that it was my idea."

I walked to my office with a bundle of files under my arm so that I could begin the selection process. I looked for prior or current military service, place of birth, backgrounds that may cause a security clearance problem and any interesting special talents. In the next couple of days, I found ten men I thought might have the makings of an insertion team and sent them to Lewis. He interviewed them, over a three day period, for employment in the White House and sent each to my office. As I met each one, I followed the same format:

Good morning, thank you for coming to see me. You have been hired by Commander Lewis as an employee of the White House. You will not be serving in the White House, you work for me. You have passed your security clearance for TOP SECRET. Do you know what that means? (Pause) You have been selected to serve federal arrest warrants outside the United States. You will travel with me to where every the President sends us. Think of yourself as Marshall Wyatt Earp sent to get the bad guys, if you like. Only you are a United States Federal Marshall and not some gun slinger in Dodge City. (Pause) You have been highly recommended to accept this position. Do you accept? (Pause) Raise your right hand and repeat after me.

I _____, do hereby pledge myself to serve as a United States Federal Marshall under the direct command of the President of the United States. I will faithfully and to the best of my ability, fulfill all the orders given to me. So help me, God.

After the last of the ten men had taken the oath, I now had a team of men to be lea by two capable commanders called Schneider and Mason. I felt better, not good, but better. We packed our bags and left Washington on October 12, 1860. We were aboard the *Cold Harbor* bound for Port Royal, South Carolina. Schneider and Mason found their sea legs and marine manners within a few hours of departure. They talked quietly to the men in two separate groups, never raising their voices. Showing them how to break down and clean the weapons that we brought with us.

"A Navy Model 1850 deck gun is meant to shock and awe the enemy." I heard Tom say to a wide eyed group of five.

"A killing knife is quiet and best used when close to our enemy. Keep it in your boot." I heard Sam say as I walked by.

"A Henry repeating rifle is compact and highly accurate. It is not like the Springfield or the Hall rifle that you may have used. Always use lethal force. Never try to overpower an opponent. We are not equipped to take prisoners. We serve warrants, if they resist, we kill them. We are not nice. We are survivors. We enter dangerous ground where others would not. The people we serve with warrants are better dead than alive. If they survive, we hold them in the nearest federal detention center and move on to the next on our list." This was my speech to the men every day aboard *Cold Harbor*.

"We will dock in Port Royal, South Carolina. There will be wagons waiting for us. Tom, a gun mount has been added on the last wagon for you. We will be traveling with our gear to an island called Pollawana. We will train there until November, when we will either serve our warrants or return home to Washington," I said on our last day of the voyage.

54

The Election of 1860
November

The Washington Post had the following headline after the presidential election of 1860.

Democrats Split Vote: Lincoln Wins

	States	Popular Vote	Electoral Vote
Lincoln	17	1,866,352	180
Breckinridge	11	845,703	72
Bell	3	389,581	39
Douglas	2	1,375,157	12

The election of Lincoln put our Presidential Warrant in force. We packed up our camp on Pollawana and returned to Port Royal. We boarded the *Cold Harbor* as newspaper men and sailed to Charleston. Phase one, was to wait and listen. Report to Washington if the reaction was violent. Phase two, was to take counter measures. Phase three, execute arrest warrants. Phase four, get the marshals out of Dodge.

Phase one was in affect as we walked the streets of Charleston asking folks how they felt about the election.

"The people of South Carolina will never surrender our rights as Americans. As President Buchanan, himself, said inside our legislature, 'Defend your rights.'"

"You can quote me on this, Lincoln is not my President."

"Them damnyankees better not stick their noses in our business."

"The South will rise up, as one and make this right, you wait and see."

And wait to see, we did. I sent telegrams to the Washington Post where Jerome Lewis's man picked them up and returned them to the White House.

NOVEMBER 23, 1860, CHARLESTON, SOUTH CAROLINA

FOR IMMEDIATE RELEASE – PEOPLE ON STREET HERE – NOT FAMILIAR WITH MR. LINCOLN – WHAT HE PLANS TO DO WHEN HE TAKES OFFICE – COMPLETE ARTICLE TO FOLLOW.

NOVEMBER 30, 1860, CHARLESTON, SOUTH CAROLINA

FOR IMMEDIATE RELEASE – TEMPERS COOL – A WAIT AND SEE ATTITUDE PREVAILS. WILL VISIT FOUR MORE SITES ALONG THE COAST – COMPLETE ARTICLE TO FOLLOW.

We began phase two in December. We proceeded to Folly Island to locate the US facility known as Castle Pinckney. We were still using the disguise of newspaper men on assignment whenever out on the streets. But approaching the island in a tender from the *Cold Harbor*, I decided to change our cover story somewhat. We tied up on the castle quay and told the guard that we had a message for the commanding office.

"May I see some identification, Sir." I handed him the following:

THE WHITE HOUSE
WASHINGTON, CITY
October 12, 1860

TO WHOM IT MAY CONCERN: ADMIRAL JASON CALDWELL, USN, IN CONNECTION WITH HIS MISSION FOR ME, WILL TRAVEL TO SUCH PLACES AT SUCH TIMES AS HE FEELS APPROPRIATE, ACCOMPANIED BY SUCH STAFF AS HE DESIRES.

ADMIRAL CALDWELL IS GRANTED A TOP SECRET/WHITE HOUSE CLEARANCE, AND MAY, AT HIS OPTION, GRANT SUCH CLEARANCE TO THOSE HE MEETS ON MY BEHALF.

US MILITARY AND GOVERNMENTAL AGENCIES ARE DIRECTED TO PROVIDE ADMIRAL CALDWELL WITH WHATEVER SUPPORT HE MAY REQUIRE.

James Buchanan

JAMES BUCHANAN
PRESIDENT OF THE UNITED STATES

"Jesus Christ!" The guard blurted. "You and your men had better come with me, Sir"

We went down the quay, over a stone revetment and into the castle. He took us to the officer of day and said, "These men are from the White House." I handed him the same set of orders that I had shown to the guard. I got a similar reaction. He recovered and said, "You can get back on guard duty now private."

"We are looking for a Colonel Gardner, Lieutenant."

"Colonel Gardner is no longer in command, he has been recalled by Secretary Floyd."

"Has this been recently, Lieutenant?"

"Yes, Sir."

"Who is in command at the moment?"

"I am, Sir. But I report to Major Anderson."

"Where is Major Anderson?"

"Fort Moultrie, Sir."

"Not Fort Sumter?"

"No, Sir. The Fort was just completed last summer and the War Department has not sent a full compliment. Head quarters are still in Moultrie"

"Lieutenant, how can I make immediate contact with Major Anderson?"

"I can send a rider, Sir."

"You do that. Tell him you have a representative from the War Department."

"Do you have enough men to escort my detachment to Fort Moultrie?"

"Yes, Sir."

"Good, get the rider off now. We will follow as soon as you can get us horses."

The detachment and escort left Folly Island, crossed the bridge into Charleston and rode for Sullivan's Island and Fort Moultrie. Major Anderson asked for our orders from the War Department and I handed him the same set of orders.

"These are not from the War Department, Admiral."

"No, they are from the Commander-in-Chief, the War Department takes orders from him."

"Yes, I know. Secretary Floyd has said he is doing everything he can to send us troops."

"Secretary Floyd will be replaced, as soon as I report to the President." I lied. I was angry, but that was no excuse. Officers do not lie to a subordinate.

"Do you have secure telegraph here, Major?"

"Yes, Sir."

"Good, I want the following telegram sent to the President. Code Alpha, repeat, code Alpha. Place John Floyd, Secretary of War, under restraint. Suspicion of treason. Sign that, Admiral Caldwell and get that off immediately. Send it, eyes only, James Buchanan."

"Yes, Sir."

"We should hear back from the White House within the hour. Can my men billet in Fort Sumter?"

"Yes, Sir. We can ferry men and supplies."

"Excellent, Major, here is what we have to do in just the next few days." I handed him my plan for the defense of Fort Sumter and Charleston Harbor. He began reading it and a sergeant entered his office and said, "Major Anderson, we have a reply from the White House."

"Give it to the Admiral."

UNABLE TO COMPLY WITH CODE ALPHA MESSAGE. JOHN FLOYD NO LONGER SECRETARY OF WAR. JOSEPH HOLT NOW ACTING SECRETARY.

CONTINUE PHASE TWO AND REPORT.

JAMES BUCHANAN, PRESIDENT USA

I read it and passed it to Major Anderson. He read it and said, "God help us, we do not have enough personnel to hold Fort Sumter."

"You might if you close down Pinckney and transfer everything moveable to Sumter. You have fourteen 24- pound cannon, four 42-pound, four 8-inch howitzers, two mortars and four light field pieces. Destroy anything that cannot be moved, Major."

"Sounds like the RESOLUTE plan, right Admiral?" Tom Schneider said.

"Major, my detachment has done this thing before. We would like to assist you if you agree with the plan of action you have just read."

"What triggers the plan, Admiral?"

"If the State of South Carolina tries to take any federal installation. We are here to protect federal property. The best way to do that is put every able bodied man in defense of Fort Sumter."

"Oh, I agree, Admiral. We also have military dependents here in Charleston. Where will they be safe?"

"Why not use Fort Johnson, for that?" I replied.

So a plan of action, or reaction, was formed. And we waited.

55

The State Convention
December 1860

The State Convention of South Carolina met in Charleston on the 17 th, with David Jamieson as presiding officer. On the 20 th, the following resolution was unanimously adopted by the one hundred and sixty-nine delegates.

> *We the people of South Carolina, in convention assembled, do declare and ordain, and it is hereby declared and ordained, that the ordinance adopted by us in convention on May 20, 1788, whereby the Constitution of the United States was ratified, and also all acts and parts of the General Assembly of the State, ratifying amendments of the said Constitution, are hereby repealed, and the Union now subsisting between South Carolina and other States, under the name of the United States of America, is hereby dissolved.*

The excitement generated in Charleston reached the dependents of federal military members before it was known at any of the federal installations. Business in Charleston was shut down to celebrate. People filled the streets. Posters of the articles of secession appeared in public places for all to read. Church bells rang and everyone in Charleston was delirious with joy, while 12 men sent from Washington and Major Anderson's troops began spiking the heavy cannon at Castle Pinckney. Everything of value was quickly moved to Fort Sumter. Dependents were moved to Fort Johnson. All dependents were settled into their temporary quarters and told that they would be taken to Washington when the federal marshals returned or they were free to arrange their own travel away from Charleston. None would be taken to Fort Sumter. The political events were going to happen at a rapid rate. Governor Pickens appointed special representatives to board the train in Columbia and travel to Washington. Here they would present the "papers of transfer" from the federal government to the state government of all federal property within the State of South Carolina. President Buchanan sent me the following:

REPRESENTATIVES SENT HOME WITHOUT CONTACT. SEND LETTER CONDITIONS TO GOVERNOR PICKENS. EXECUTE PHASE THREE AND REPORT.

JAMES BUCHANAN, PRESIDENT USA

I called the marshals together and showed them the President's telegram. "Gentlemen, this is the hour that we begin to earn our pay. Tom, take your five men to the home of General Butler here in Charleston. Have him read the detention warrant. Tell anyone else in the house that he is wanted for questioning and will be held at Fort Moultrie. Sam, take your five to the home of the Charleston Harbor Master. Have him read the warrant. Tell anyone else in the house where you are taking him. We have practiced these arrests at Pollawana. Tom, after you deliver the Charleston Militia General, go to the next person on your list. Sam, do the same thing."

"Admiral, are we to kill anyone for resistance?"

"The President has told me that these arrests are to show the people of Charleston and Governor Pickens that the federal government will react. He does not want anyone killed, render them unconscious if they physically resist arrest. They will be released unharmed by Major Anderson on March 4 th. Please make sure that this is made clear to each of the persons arrested. They are to be questioned by federal authorities and released."

"Do you want us to start tonight or today?"

"We need to start at sundown and be finished by sunrise. Gentlemen, you may proceed."

I was waiting at Fort Moultrie for the first arrival. It was General Butler.

"Admiral, we found the good general trying to burn letters from the Treasury Department, you had better read some of these."

"Take General Butler to an interview room and I will be there shortly."

I sat and read some of the letters. I found one from Secretary Cobb confirming the transfer of funds from the US Treasury to the Charleston Militia. I found another from Secretary Floyd authorizing the transfer of arms from the federal arsenal to the Charleston Militia. I could not believe my eyes. I stopped and read every letter carefully that Tom had found before sending the following telegram to the White House.

CODE ALPHA, REPEAT, CODE ALPHA. PLACE SECRETARY HOWELL COBB UNDER RESTRAINT. WRITTEN PROOF OF MALFEASANTS.

ADMIRAL CALDWELL

The reply from the White House confirmed my worst fears.

UNABLE TO COMPLY WITH CODE ALPHA MESSAGE, HOWELL COBB RESIGNED POSITION AND HAS RETURNED TO GEORGIA. PHILIP THOMAS NOW ACTING SECRETARY. CONTINUE PHASE THREE AND REPORT.

JAMES BUCHANAN, PRESIDENT USA

I was stunned. What had the other southern secretaries done? Could I find evidence to forward to the President? The next arrest might give me some clues. Tom and Sam returned with men in handcuffs. Each was placed in a separate room and interviewed with armed guards present.

Near sunrise, I was convinced that we had all the captured documents and intelligence that we were apt to obtain, so I sent the following telegram to the White House.

FOLLOWING PERSONS IN FEDERAL PROTECTIVE CUSTODY, HEAD CHARLESTON MILITIA, HARBOR MASTER, PRESIDING OFFICER STATE CONVENTION, GOVERNOR'S COMMISSIONER, AND MAYOR OF CHARLESTON. AWAITING FURTHER INSTRUCTIONS.

ADMIRAL CALDWELL

When the news of our activities reached the authorities of Charleston they were enraged. They declared that our actions as federal agents was a virtual declaration of war. Hundreds of militia demanded that they should be allowed to attack the four federal fortifications. This was immediately stopped by Governor Pickens. In the letter that I had sent to the Governor for the President, it stated the conditions for the US Army and Navy to land troops in South Carolina. The militia overran the Castle first and then Fort Johnson but found nothing. In frustration they seized the US Customs House, post office and federal arsenal. A patrol vessel, *William Aiken,* was asking questions of the *Cold Harbor* captain.

When this information was passed to Washington, the following message was received:

TO FEDERAL MARSHALS IN FORT SUMTER – EXECUTE PHASE FOUR.

JAMES BUCHANAN, PRESIDENT USA

It was Christmas Eve, when we informed Major Anderson that we had recall orders from the President and we would like to withdraw by December 27, 1860.

"Admiral, I would like your men to help in the transfer of the women and children to the *Cold Harbor*. We can remove the last of the food and materials and the 85 men from Fort Moultrie."

"Major, you have been sending secure telegrams from Fort Moultrie. Do you have secure telegraph from Fort Sumter?"

"Yes, until the Charleston officials find the underwater cable and cut it. Why?"

"I would like you to request food and other non-military supplies from Caldwell Shipping in Beaufort. If for some reason you can not contact Beaufort, try contacting a Mr. Robert Whitehall in Bermuda. He can get things done that people here may not be able to do."

"Thank you, Admiral. It will help to know that I am not isolated in Fort Sumter. My requests to the War Department have not been answered."

"Major, you can contact me anytime via the White House Office of National Affairs, or better yet, send your requests directly to the Department of the Navy, Army Navy Building, Washington City."

"That would be out of channels, Sir." He was smiling.

"I will leave a copy of my orders from President Buchanan for you. If anyone asks if you are out of channels, you can refer them to paragraph two, which I will endorse by my signature. This tells them you are granted Top Secret/White House clearance from the President. This places you directly under the Commander-in-Chief as far as decisions concerning Fort Sumter. Your orders regarding the Fort are not to be questioned by anyone other than the President. This endorsement lasts until March 4, 1861. After that date, I will be Mister Caldwell, not Admiral and President Buchanan will be Mister Buchanan."

I located one of several copies that I carried, signed the second paragraph and handed it to him. He saluted and said. "Tell the Commander-in-Chief that the Commander of Fort Sumter will hold this location until March 4 th and well beyond."

"Before we leave Fort Moultrie, Major, I have several telegrams to send. I will be down in the telegraph dispatch station if you need me."

"Yes, Sir."

The first telegram went to the Office of Protocol, The White House.

MISSION HERE ENDS IN TWO DAYS. HAVE LOCATED TRANSPORT TO YOUR LOCATION. WILL ARRIVE AFTER CHRISTMAS. SORRY TO MISS LAST HOLIDAY. HUG CHILDREN. SEE YOU SOON.

JASON

The second went to the Commander-in-Chief.

ACKNOWLEDGE LAST TRANSMISSION. ARRIVAL BACK BEFORE THE 1 ST.

ADMIRAL CALDWELL

We spent the last couple of days helping Major Anderson is his effort to close Fort Moultrie and occupy Fort Sumter. It was difficult to abandon the federal installations in and around Charleston Harbor, but it was the best military option. The Castle was a small masonry fortification constructed in 1810. It was used in the War of 1812, but saw no action until the Nullification Crisis of 1832. It was now used primarily for the storage of gunpowder and other supplies.

Fort Johnson was a much older fortification, built in 1704 and did not see action until the Revolutionary War and the War of 1812. It, too, fell into disrepair and was unoccupied until Major Anderson opened it for storage. Fort Moultrie was under construction during the Revolutionary War and could not be used. It was destroyed by a hurricane in 1804. It was rebuilt in 1809-10 and saw action in the War of 1812. It was the main defense for Charleston Harbor until Fort Sumter was built. Fort Sumter was a new modern facility in 1860 and here Major Anderson began his defense of the federal facility.

56
The Cabinet Changes
January 1861

President Buchanan was in a trying situation. His secretary of war, John Floyd ,was indignant that a force of men, some kind of federal marshals, were sent to Charleston without his knowledge and approval. At the last cabinet meeting that he attended, Floyd angrily insisted that he be allowed to withdraw all federal troops from South Carolina. The President had not gotten my telegram indicating Floyd's interference with the opening of Fort Sumter and the replacement of commanding officers. He asked for Floyd's resignation and sent him home to Virginia.

Howell Cobb, his Secretary of the Treasury, was a violent secessionist. Having done his upmost to finance the cause, resigned on the 8th of December before my telegram arrived in the White House. Four days later, Secretary of State Cass, resigned. This was odd, I thought. Cass was from Michigan. Cass stated in his letter of resignation that he was unable to convince the President to follow his proclamation of 1858 and send federal troops to reinforce the federal properties in South Carolina. The revolt in South Carolina should be met with the Army and Navy in full force before the revolt spread to other southern states. Jeremiah Black was now acting Secretary of State and Attorney- General. Philip Thomas was from Maryland and was acting Secretary of the Treasury, until John Dix of New York was appointed.

The President at this juncture issued another proclamation recommending the fourth of January as a day of fasting, humiliation and prayer. There was observance throughout the North. I could not fail to see the peril gathering over the nation. I felt that South Carolina knew that, if war came, she would be the first to receive the blow. When the Charleston militia began to search for General Butler, they came first to the Castle and found it deserted and devoid of anything of a military value. This immediately was reported to the Governor in Columbia and he had an unusual response.

"No shots have been fired, in this, our hour of peril, and none will be fired by the State of South Carolina." This had been one of the conditions stated in the President's letter that I had mailed to the Governor. And, so far, the Governor was following the conditions.

The President, who had been accused of weakness by the northern US Senators, gained confidence that his plan would work with the cooperation of both sides in the conflict. The next step that he took was to make Edwin Stanton, Attorney-General. Stanton possessed great ability and tireless energy. At his urging, the unarmed supply ship, *Star of the West,* was sent to Fort Sumter. This action so offended Secretary of the Interior, Thompson, that he resigned and proceeded to return to Mississippi. So far, President Buchanan had lost his Secretary of War, State, Treasury and Interior.

All three southern gentlemen appeared at the general convention of the seceding States held in Montgomery, Alabama. Howell Cobb was chosen chairman. In his address he asserted that the secession of the states was "fixed, irrevocable and perpetual." John Floyd submitted a series of resolutions, declaring that it was expedient to form a confederacy of the seceded states. At the suggestion of Jacob Thompson, it was agreed that the assemblage should be known as a congress. At the urging of these three men, it was decided that the Constitution of the United States, with a few changes, should be used by the Confederacy. The provisional President of the Confederacy was to hold office for one year, and Jefferson Davis accepted this appointment.

Each state within the Confederacy was to be a distinct judicial district. The several districts together composed the supreme court of the Confederacy. Wherever the word "Union" occurred in the United States Constitution, the word "Confederacy" was substituted. The African slave-trade was prohibited and the Congress of the Confederacy was empowered to forbid the introduction of any slaves from any state not a member of the confederacy. In order to fill the treasury of the Confederacy, appropriations were to be upon the property owners within the Confederacy at the demand of the President. When Louisiana seceded, the United States mint in New Orleans was seized. The treasury of the Confederacy was richer by $254,820.00 in gold double eagles and $1,101,316.00 in silver half-dollars. The gold and silver bullion not already struck has held in reserve.

Members of the Congress of the Confederacy were not to be prohibited from holding honorary appointment under the administration of the Confederacy. Here, the three from Buchanan's administration took full advantage of the situation. Howell Cobb became the advisor to the President for financial affairs. John Floyd became special advisor to the President for War. Jacob Thompson became chairman for the design of the CSA flag. Many designs were submitted to him and he selected a design that consisted of two broad bands of red, separated by a white band of the same width. In the upper lefthand corner was a blue field with seven stars forming a circle in its center.

While President Buchanan's former cabinet members were meeting in Montgomery, the newly appointed Washington cabinet was meeting. My absence from cabinet meetings was obvious when I missed the November and December regular sessions. The President covered this by saying, "Admiral Caldwell is in Charleston, South Carolina, as my envoy since the election." When I returned for the January meeting, Secretary of War, Holt asked to be briefed on my mission. I looked at the President. He nodded his head and I began.

"Gentlemen, I can report success in my meetings. Governor Pickens has agreed to the conditions set forth in the President's letter of October 12, 1860. He will abide by these conditions until fired upon by federal authorities. The commander of Fort Sumter has informed me that he has an adequate number of troops at this time. He has decided to evacuate Pinkney, Johnson and Moultrie and they have been occupied by South Carolina Militia. The dependents of married men serving in Charleston have been transported to Washington. The following have been detained for questioning; Mayor of Charleston, Commandant of Charleston Militia, Harbor Master of Charleston, presiding officer of South Carolina State Convention, and the Governor's Commissioner sent to Washington City."

"What do you mean, detained?"

"They are to be released to Governor Pickens on March 4, 1861 as outlined in the letter of conditions sent to him by the President." James Buchanan was smiling.

"We have no hope, at this time, of recovering the other seized federal property." I added.

"Besides the three land fortifications, what other properties were seized?"Secretary Holt asked.

"US customs house, the federal arsenal, post office and a harbor patrol boat."

"I have reviewed your finding, Admiral." The new Attorney-General said. "There is more than enough information to charge former Secretary Floyd with dereliction of duty, this is a death sentence in time of war. I have reviewed the facts in the case of funds sent to South Carolina by Secretary Cobb. This is a prison sentence offence. I have issued federal warrants for their arrest and they will be served by the Department of Justice, should they ever set foot in Washington.

"What has happened to Fort Sumter?" Asked Secretary Toucey.

"Major Anderson is a very capable commander, he will be requesting aid from both you and Secretary Holt, I am sure. Food will be the critical element. If is alright with you gentlemen, Caldwell Shipping Company will attempt to deliver non-military items from Beaufort, South Carolina. This offer does not have to be submitted for approval. It is a non-governmental offer of assistance. It will continue on a regular basis until the Confederacy stops it by force of arms."

"Do you think they will use force against humanitarian aid?"

"If they do, they will be in violation of the letter of conditions sent by the President and agreed to by Governor Pickens. The Governor can control state forces. Confederacy forces under Davis, I doubt Pickens can do anything about. My offer of assistance is until March 4, 1861."

Now, I was smiling as I heard my brother-in-law say, "Admiral, on behalf of the nation, I thank you for serving in my administration."

57
Recall to Washington
January 1861

The Presidential Warrant was now complete. Everything was in place for a "lame duck" session to begin as soon as we were back in the Potomac Dockyards. We had assisted Major Anderson with the civilians wanting transport back to Washington with us. We put them on board the *Cold Harbor* Christmas night. The next night, December 26, 1860, Major Anderson evacuated Fort Moultrie. There was a full moon and it shined brightly but did not give away the series of small boats that were used to ferry 85 men out to Fort Sumter. The guns on Moultrie were spiked, wagons and carriages were burnt and the flag staff was cut down. Major Anderson folded the flag in the proper manner and carried it under his arm standing in the bow of one of the ferry boats.

"He looks like George Washington!" Sam Mason said to me as we pulled in the opposite direction to find the *Cold Harbor* at anchor. We left the small boat we had used, adrift and climbed aboard.

" Sneak us out of Charleston Harbor will you, Captain Jacob?"

"Aye, aye, Admiral."

The *Cold Harbor* was one of my merchant mariners from Port Royal and had made many stops in Charleston over the years. A night sailing was not unusual and besides there was some confusion within the Harbor Master's Office, because he was missing. Captain Jacob raised the anchor and we slowly began a turn towards Fort Sumter, then pulled sharply eastward and out to sea.

Tom and I stood at the rail and watched as Fort Sumter disappeared on the horizon.

"What did you think of Major Anderson, Admiral?"

"He has guts, Tom, I hope he has some luck to go along with that."

"How long can they last with the food that they have in stores, Admiral?"

"If they are not supplied by late March or early April it will get critical. I will make sure that the Major gets everything that I can provide between now and March 4 th. Caldwell Shipping may be able to enter Charleston Harbor again, who knows? I would venture to say that *Cold Harbor* is not welcome here again after they figure out what happened."

"What about other ships from Caldwell Shipping in Beaufort?"

"Time will tell. They should be free to come and go. You have not seen the letter that was sent to Governor Pickens and I did not read it after the contents were discussed with the President. If what was discussed, wound up in the letter, then we will be alright."

"What do you think the letter said, Sir?"

"I think the President reminded the Governor of the Buchanan executive order 182 which stated, 'We have experienced civil war in Kansas and Utah. From this day forward, civil insurrection within states and territories will be met with the full weight of the Army and Navy of the United States.' I also think he dared the Governor to start an insurrection."

"Every one says Buchanan is weak. That does not sound weak to me, Admiral."

"You know, Tom, I find he is very patient with people. People may mistake this for weakness. I know for a fact that our Secretary of War did that, and now he is a fugitive from justice. I understand that our new Attorney-General may file charges for dereliction of duty."

"What about Cobb? What he did in Charleston is not forgivable. When I found those papers in General Butler's house, I wanted to kill the bastard."

"I feel the same way, Tom. When I was younger, you will remember that I ordered you to make certain people disappear."

"Yes, I remember, Sir. People like Milton Black deserved what they got. Never mess with the United States Marines."

"Tom, you have been one hell of a Marine, Presidential body guard and now a US Marshal. I am going to miss not seeing you every day in the White House."

"Admiral, I can not imagine you out of the Navy."

"I left the Navy when I agreed to move over to the White House, Tom."

"Why did you do that, Sir?"

"I felt that being away for months at a time was not a good thing for a new husband and father. We have been away from Washington since October 12 th. It will be nearly three months this time. It seems more like three years to me. A baby changes so much in a month."

"I know, Sir."

"You can call me, Sir, until March 4 th, Tom. After that, I am just a simple, Mister, just like you and Sam over there."

"I am going to stay on with Commander Lewis, wherever the Navy sends him."

"I doubt that the Navy will send him anywhere. Did you know that there has been a threat to kill the President-elect?"

"No, when did that happen?"

"He is still in Illinois and it was made there."

"Good, God. What is this country coming to?"

"I heard that the President-elect is considering doubling the White House protection. It is to be funded and operated out of the Department of the Treasury. The detail is to be called the, "Secret Service.""

"Sounds to me, they probably want to operate a bunch of spies out of that department. I wonder what will happen to Naval Intelligence or even the shore patrol. I would hate to see Commander Lewis's work just set aside."

"I know Jerome will appreciate that, Tom. But if you ever need or want a job outside the Navy, you look me up in Pennsylvania. I will give all ten of you men a letter of employment with Caldwell Trading and Shipping. All you have to do is date and sign and a job will be waiting for you."

"I appreciate that, Admiral. If things go to hell in a hand basket, I will show up with the wife and kids on your door step in Pennsylvania."

"You know, Tom, things can get pretty hairy in the world of business. Things in Utah are not often civilized, like they are back here on the east coast. My shipments of refined ore have been stolen off wagons when I try to ship it from Utah to California. Men have been killed working for me."

"Does not sound like business, Admiral."

"No, it is still the wild west. If you ever get lonesome for a Naval deck gun mounted on a heavy wagon, you can work for me in Utah."

"Well, I am a US Marshal!"

58
Inauguration Day
March 4, 1861

On march 4, 1861, an immense crowd was present in Washington City. Early in the forenoon the President-elect went from the White House to the Capitol. Between one and two o'clock, accompanied by President Buchanan, they entered the Senate Chamber. The two men were arm in arm. The President-elect was pale and disturbed, while the President was cool, though his face was slightly flushed. The inaugural address was delivered in the presence of the Supreme Court, both Houses of Congress, foreign ministers and members of his cabinet.

The address was in good taste, as Buchanan had suggested. The new President declared that there was no ground for the fears that had been expressed in South Carolina. Southern States were not in danger from the Republican Party. He had no purpose of interfering in any way with slavery in those States where it existed. He would follow the Buchanan Doctrine of 1858. In this, he was so explicit that there was no room for mistake. He had sworn to support the Constitution and the laws, and nothing could swerve him from that purpose.

He so liked the changing of the cabinet members between the Pierce and Buchanan administrations, that he asked his cabinet to meet with their counterparts. There is an old tradition where the outgoing administration leaves something for the incoming. Laying on the President's desk in the Oval Office was an envelope marked from #15 to #16. In the office of National Affairs Advisor, was an envelope marked from #1 to #2. In the office of the Presidential Protection Detail was an envelop marked from #1 to #2. In the US Marshal's office was the same. It occurred to those of us who left the service of the fifteenth President of the United States that a number of offices had been created under his administration. The nation had been held together for four years and now great danger faced us all. For me, the possibility of returning to South Carolina any time soon was out of the question. South Carolina had issued an address to the other slave holding states, inviting them to join her in the formation of a Confederacy of Southern States. The following States called conventions and passed ordinances of secession in January, 1861: Mississippi, 9 th;

Florida, 10 th; Alabama,11 th; Georgia, 19 th; Louisiana, 26 th and Texas, February 1, 1861.

On March 4, 1861, President Buchanan, his sister and his brother-in-law along with his niece and nephew left Washington on the 3:15 pm Baltimore and Ohio train bound for northwestern Pennsylvania.

59
Washington City
July, 1861

President Lincoln had sent me a letter which arrived at my home in Pennsylvania shortly after my retirement from public life and my service to President James Buchanan as his National Affairs Advisor. He had invited me to spend a day with him in the Oval Office of the White House. I answered his letter and indicated that I was not sure what I could do for him. I was no longer the advisor to the president for National Affairs. I was a private citizen and a business man. A second letter arrived and it was more revealing, he felt he now needed a National Advisor from the business community. On July 2, President Lincoln had authorized the suspension of the right of habeas corpus and requested my time for only one day. I boarded a train and headed for Washington.

On board the train, I still did not know what information I had that would matter to the Republican Administration of Abraham Lincoln. President Buchanan was elected in 1857, and served until March 4, 1861. It was now clear that the Union that President Buchanan and I had fought to preserve had failed. On April 15, following the attack on Fort Sumter, President Lincoln proclaimed a state of insurrection. He had issued a draft for 75,000 volunteers. On April 17, Virginia seceded from the Union, the eighth and closest to Washington City. April 19, found Union troops marching to Washington City attacked in Baltimore. During the ensuing riot, fourteen people died. Lincoln then ordered the blockade of all Confederate ports. On May 6, Arkansas and Tennessee seceded from the Union. One week later, Queen Victoria recognized the Confederate States of America. One week after that North Carolina seceded.

From the White House, Abraham Lincoln could see Confederate flags flying in Alexandria and the Army of Virginia campfires at night. Baltimore was ready to explode because fewer Union Army volunteers had arrived in Washington City than the 75,000 called for. When Union troops began moving into Alexandria on May 20, a close friend of Lincoln's was shot and killed becoming the first combat death. June 10, saw Confederates forces beat back a Union attack at Big Bethel. The battle of Rich Mountain in western Virginia was a minor Union victory by George McClellan. This gave encouragement to General McDowell and he moved towards Richmond in a effort to capture the Confederate Capitol. General Beauregard, General Butler's replacement at Fort Sumter, was deployed along Bull Run River near Manassas, Virginia. Here in July, Union forces were routed by Confederate forces in a battle watched by Washington residents, who had come to view the grand battle. The next day a congressional resolution was passed that the war was being fought to preserve the Union, not to abolish slavery. One week later, Lincoln replaced McDowell with McClellan as commander of the Army of the Potomac.

All of these events of the last four months were in my mind as I rounded a corner in the hallway of the White House and there was the Oval Office that was so familiar to me. I knocked on the door and it was opened by the President's private body guard, Pinkerton. I entered and was greeted by the President. "Please sit down so that we can tell you why we have asked you here."

"Thank you, Mister President."

"Admiral, you are a graduate of the United States Military Academy, class of '37, correct?"

"Yes, Mister President."

"You are a resident of the State of Pennsylvania, the State of South Carolina and Bermuda, is that correct?"

"Yes, it is, Mister President." *I wondered where he was going with this.*

"That makes you one of a kind and qualified to be my National Affairs Advisor. I would like you to consider the same position in my cabinet, Admiral."

"I was an advisor to the last president on how to preserve the Union. The Union is now in two pieces, both having the same constitution."

"Yes, and if I accept that, then I would be trying to locate someone that Jefferson Davis could trust as my minister to his government and someone who is still loyal to the Union, even though his background and family resides in the Southern Confederacy. That makes you unique for that position as well. But I will not accept the concept of two separate but equal nations sharing the same constitution. I am trying to readmit the seceded states back into the Union."

"I understand that, Mister President. I am not sure I am the right person for that position in your administration, however. I have a major business to run. Caldwell International has several companies that will be vital to the well being of the north in this upcoming struggle to put the nation back together. I could not move back to the White House and be able to do both things for you."

"I understand that now, Admiral. Jefferson Davis has sent a representative to meet with Mr. Pinkerton, here in Washington City. We have no idea what the topic of concern will be. Would you be willing to assist Mr. Pinkerton by attending that meeting today?"

"How can I help?"

"You can listen and give me your ideas. You can represent the position of the past administration. Whatever Jefferson Davis has in mind, I would like you to hear it and give me your reaction to it. If Jefferson Davis requires a meeting with me, I would like you to represent me. You know him from when he was the Secretary of War under Franklin Pierce. You may be able to become a roving ambassador so that you can travel on diplomatic missions between us, using your British Passport. You would be given a safe conduct through enemy lines by both Presidents."

"I do not understand, Mister President. Can I travel by ship and enter a harbor that is blockaded by the US Navy?"

"Yes, you can. You can board trains in both territories and travel between the two as you wish."

"I cannot be away from my business for any length of time and travel is a time consuming process. I wish I could help you in your choice of this special envoy or roving ambassador. If I think of someone, I will give that person's name to you."

"Have you considered the lives that may be saved by an immediate cease to the hostilities?" Said Pinkerton.

"Yes, an end now would mean two separate nations. Is that your goal?"

"No, I will accept nothing but the readmittance of the seceded states back into the Union."

"Well, I hope you have a private army, because you are going to need them when the Armies of Virginia, South Carolina and North Carolina sweep across the Potomac, capture Washington and arrest the President" I turned to President Lincoln and said, "Mr. President, I do not know where you are getting your military advice, but I would fire them if I were you." I stood to leave because I thought my welcome was probably worn out.

"Admiral, do you always say what you think to your superiors?" Pinkerton said.

"Not when I was in uniform, I waited to be asked and gave them the honest truth, as best I could. It would seem, Mr. President, that your advisors are telling you what they think you want to hear, not what the plain truth is. You are not prepared to fight and win a civil war. You can fight and lose in less than two years unless you make some basic changes, now."

"I am listening."

"Item (1), we need to begin a war tax system to finance the war effort. The present $189 million, that Mr. Pinkerton mentioned before, will not finance a large scale civil war over the four to five years that it will require. Any advisor who tells you that a war can be won in less time, is either a liar or is out of touch with reality.

"Oh, I do not think we will spend $189 million on this conflict." Pinkerton interrupted.

"Mr. President, can you ask Mr. Pinkerton to leave us alone or keep his opinions to himself?"

"Are you angry, Admiral?"

"Yes, Sir. I am. You asked for advice and I am trying to give you my best estimates. Mr. Pinkerton may be your bodyguard, but he is not a military, political or governmental expert. He seems impressed that the US Treasury has $189 million dollars, so do most major companies in the US, including mine. I would not even consider going to war with the Confederacy with the worth of my company. You must begin thinking in terms of billions, not millions."

"Mr. Pinkerton, will you leave us for a few minutes?"

"Oh, Mr. President, I would not advise that!"

"That was not a request, Mr. Pinkerton. Please continue, Admiral."

I watched a very angry Chief of Detectives leave the Oval Office, and said, "I am sorry, Mr. President, I can not abide fools."

"Admiral, let us start over. Just you and me. Sitting down to chat about what to get done before the roof falls in on our heads."

"Good idea, Sir. Now, where was I?"

"Item (1), we need a federal income tax. Consider it proposed to the congress sometime this week. Item (2)?"

"Item (2), General Fremonte is unbalanced, in my opinion, and needs to be replaced."

"Consider him replaced." Lincoln picked up a pad of paper and a pencil.

"Item (3), consider a Confiscation Act which will authorize the appropriation of all properties from any seceding state. I am amazed that Maryland is still with us, Mr. President."

"I have arrested and detained several Maryland citizens since July 2 nd, Admiral."

"Item (4), authorize the Secretary of the Navy to draft US citizens, former slaves and anyone else to serve, we are going to need many more sailors than you think."

"Where are we going to get the ships for them to serve on?"

"Item (5), purchase as many civilian merchant marine ships as you can find. My company has several available. Purchase war ships from any European Nation, but not England."

"Consider that in the works." He said as he wrote on the pad.

"Item (6), this is critical, replace or promote General Scott."

"Why? He is my General-in-Chief, the best brain in the military."

"He was during the last war with Mexico, he was a genius. But he is of advanced age now, he is not up to the task required of him. It will break his heart. But it has to be done."

"In for a penny, in for a pound." And he continued to write.

"Item (7), prepare for war with England, the Queen will not tolerate being cut off from the products she buys from the southern United States."

"How can we possibly fight two wars, Jason?"

It was the first time that he called me, Jason, and I thought our new President might start to make the sacrifices needed to put the Union back together again.

"Prepare for war, not fight one. You can announce to the newspapers that you are considering a civilian advisor board for national affairs. The chairman of this board will report directly to you, not to a cabinet member. I would like to be a member of that board, Mr. President. My contribution to the board will come from my contacts in Bermuda. My staff, in Bermuda, can monitor the Royal Navy Dockyards and the Admiralty in London. England fights most wars on the sea. She will fight through our blockades in order to trade with South Carolina."

"Jason, this has been one of the most productive meetings that I have had since I have been in the White House. Thank you for coming. I will prepare the announcement of the advisory board for the newspapers and I will indicate the chairman, Admiral Caldwell, now recalled to active duty for the duration of the war, has already accepted this position and has started work. How does that sound?"

"Have a copy sent to my home office, Caldwell Place, St. George, Bermuda, will you, Sir?"

"I will. Where will you get your staff?"

"You will appoint them, Mr. President. They will be: Commander Jerome Lewis, US Navy. Warrant Officer Thomas Schneider, USMC Master Sergeant Samuel Mason, USMC."

"You better slow down, I am writing those names down."

"You will be getting a list of ten other names from Officer Schneider, Mr. President, these men are all serving in the United States Marine Corps. Can I ask you something, Mr. President?"

"Of course, Admiral."

"Do you trust, Pinkerton?"

"With my life."

"Good, can you ask him when I am to meet with this mysterious messenger from Jefferson Davis?"

"Yes, why do you want to do that, now that you will be in Bermuda?"

"If the contact is genuine, there should not be a problem for the Confederate States of America to send a minister to either England or Bermuda. If they are serious in having contact, then we could do that in Bermuda, in either, Hamilton or St. George. The Government Houses have been moved from St. George to Hamilton, Sir."

"Then we should establish a US Conciliate Office in Hamilton as soon as we request permission from the Queen. You can present your credentials from me to the Lord Governor of Bermuda when you get there. That way you will have diplomatic protection, should you ever need it. I will call Mr. Pinkerton back in and tell him to set a meeting for later today, in your hotel, before you leave Washington. I do not want to attend this meeting."

"That is wise, Mr. President, if the contact is an assassin, he will be unable to find you outside the White House."

"Admiral Caldwell, it is an honor to have you serve your country again."

"Thank you, Mr. President. Written communication will be sent twice a week on the steamer between the Potomac Dockyards and the Royal Naval Dockyards, Bermuda. Diplomatic pouches are sealed and can be delivered directly to your office, if necessary. I must admit, I will enjoy being back in St. George again. Let us hope that I am wrong and the war will end in a short time. I will resign my commission at the end of the war."

"Jason, you are a man of honor, indeed."

"Mister President, we both know that I am a warrior, not a diplomat. My reason for being in Bermuda is to keep watch on the British, report their naval movements through Bermuda and may act as a line of communication to Jefferson Davis. I will, of course, sail to South Hampton whenever you need an envoy to the Admiralty. Lord Napier is a personal friend, as well as a fellow Admiral."

"I will send a White House messenger over to the Hay-Adams when we get things together on our end, Admiral. Thank you for coming to Washington and agreeing to do this for me. I will not forget what you are about to do for your country, or what you have done for the past two administrations."

60
Washington City
Hay-Adams Hotel

I left the White House and walked across Lafayette Square and into the Hay-Adams Hotel. I stopped at the desk and asked for the key to my room and a telegraph pad and pencil. I had just gotten my message to Louise, James and Ruth written out when a knock on my room door interrupted my thoughts. I walked to the door, opened it and there stood Pinkerton and Ben Hagood. I must have looked confused because Pinkerton smiled and said. "This is not the messenger from Davis, Admiral. Admiral Hagood was asked by the President to brief you on the blockade of southern ports and to sit in on the conversation with Davis's envoy. The meeting will begin when he gets here. He is staying in the hotel."

Now, I was really confused.

"How long has he been checked in?" I asked.

"A week."

"A week?"

"Yes, he checked in right after the battle along Bull Run."

A loud knock sounded. We opened it and in walked General Butler who I had detained in Charleston last winter.

"Hello, Admiral. It is good to see you again. Mr. Pinkerton, Admiral, is it?"

"Yes, Ben Hagood, General. How do you know Admiral Caldwell?"

"He arrested me in Charleston, held me in Fort Sumter until I was released with the others on March 4 th. Now I am the personal representative of President Davis. He has sent me to Washington to meet with Mr. Lincoln, but so far, all I have managed to do is spend time with Mr. Pinkerton, here. Can we get started?"

"Of course," we all said at the same time.

"I am here unofficially and President Davis will not make any of these contacts public."

"Neither will President Lincoln." said Pinkerton. "He will speak only through Admiral Caldwell."

"As long as a dialog begins, my President is not concerned how it is arranged."

"I will be Minister to Bermuda from the United States. Does the Confederacy have a Minister to Great Britain?" I asked.

"We do. You know him, Admiral. He was the US senator from Virginia and a close personal friend of Mr. Davis."

"James Murray? Does he have an undersecretary for Bermuda?"

"Yes, you are looking at him." General Butler said with a smile.

"How can that be? I did not know that I was going to Bermuda until today? Do you have a spy in the White House?" I said smiling.

"No, Murray has not left Charleston and will not arrive in London until October. He will drop me off in Bermuda, after a stop at the Royal Naval Dockyards."

"The Confederacy has permission to use the docks in Bermuda?"

"Yes, Admiral. It was granted when Queen Victoria announced Great Britain's neutrality and granted us the right of 'belligerent nation status.'" I looked at Pinkerton and then Ben Hagood, raised my eyebrows in a signal to remember to tell that to the president. "Well, General, what is your new title?"

"Minister to Bermuda and Undersecretary to Ambassador Murray, London."

"Will you be sailing back and forth, you know, to London and Bermuda? Minister Butler."

"Of course, I thought maybe we could use British vessels and travel together, Admiral Caldwell."

No one, besides the president, had called me, Admiral since I had retired until now. I liked the sound of it. "We could get many things discussed during the voyage, I hate wasting my time." I said.

"I think we have accomplished everything here, I need to get back to report to my president and then to Charleston."

"You are in the middle of Washington City, how are you going to do that?" I blurted out.

"It is surprisingly easy, when the federal troops retreated into Washington City, I just walked in with them. No one seemed to notice another newspaper reporter. I will use the newspaper credentials to take a carriage across the Potomac and then show my safe conduct from Davis and get on a train all the way into Richmond. You can travel anywhere, the situation is very fluid."

"Yes, it is. I have to ask you this. What happened after Manassas? Why not take Washington City? It was left unprotected by General McDowell."

"Too many Generals on the Confederate side of the lines; General Longstreet , my replacement Beauregard, and General Johnson. Longstreet was still wearing his Union uniform and was nearly shot during the battle of the first day. Johnson was not even at Manassas when the battle began, he was moving his troops from the Shenandoah Valley by train. The Army of the Virginia was split between two locations and Beauregard's Army from South Carolina did most of the fighting in the center of the line the first day. When Beauregard troops were in danger of collapsing from the center on the second day, he sent a rider to the Shenandoah Valley troops newly arrived under Colonel Thomas Jackson. He asked for an immediate advancement to his center. Either Jackson did not understand or was slow in responding, because a second message was sent to him stating, 'You are standing like a stone wall. Advance. Damn it! Or I will replace you.' I am afraid that he has been nicknamed, 'Stonewall Jackson'. So you see, there was confusion and failure on both sides. We had no idea that General McDowell would leave Washington City unprotected. We considered ourselves fortunate to completely defeat the federal volunteers. Our newspapers are reporting our great victory and volunteers are reporting faster than we can process them."

I again looked at Pinkerton and Hagood before I spoke. "What is your message for President Lincoln from President Davis?"

"The Confederacy has no desire to replace or become the United States of America, we are content to be the Confederate States of America. If a USA army crosses the Potomac again into the CSA,

it will be defeated as before. My President proposes that the two nations be divided along the Potomac River, North and South. The capitol of the north being Washington City while the capitol of the south already is Richmond, Virginia. Mr. Davis is moving his cabinet to Richmond as we speak. Let there be peace between our two nations. If President Lincoln agrees to this proposal, he will withdraw the naval blockades of our ports and peace will be insured. If he refuses this peace offer then we will protect the C SA with the eleven armies at our command."

"That is crystal clear, Minister Butler. Of course, we have only a verbal commitment from your government. Will there be a written version sent to the White House?"

"No, Sir."

"Alright, there will be no written document of this meeting either. I will depend upon Admiral Hagood and Mr. Pinkerton to report the offer to my president. I am leaving on the afternoon train, unless summoned to the White House. From one South Carolinian to another, can you report back to your president that he has my word, upon my honor, that if President Lincoln asks my advice, I will recommend that he accept your offer of peace."

"Thank you, Admiral, I can ask for nothing more. Good day to y'all." The room was strangely quiet after Butler left. The three of us sat and pondered the conversation. Ben was the first to speak. "Jason, we are in a fine mess, the President is not going to like this."

"Report it just as you heard it, Ben. Take Mr. Pinkerton with you and see the president as soon as you can. The longer we wait, the more we will forget. Why are you here, anyway? I already know about the blockade."

"The president sent a messenger with a hand written note to the Army Navy Building for me. Here, do you want to read it?"

I read it. "I must have made an impression on him. This says you are to provide my transport to and from Bermuda, London and Washington City. He must feel that Washington is safe. I have my own transport, Ben. You will need every ship you have and more for the blockage"

"Thank you, Jason. I will report that to the president."

"I will need you to take the sloops and briggs that you and I bought from the Navy in '37 and have them rearmed so that they can protect themselves. Can you do that?"

"Consider it done. Send them from St. George to the Potomac Dockyards for refitting."

I turned to Pinkerton who had said very little during the entire meeting and said, "I do not know your first name. If we are going to be working closely together, I can not keep calling you, Mister."

"It is Allen, Sir."

"Call me, Jason, Allen. I think we got off on the wrong foot in the Oval Office."

"We sure did, I am sorry about that. I had no idea that President Lincoln thought so highly of you."

"Do you think, he knows I am a Democrat?" I said smiling.

"Jason, at this point, it would not matter if you had two heads and came directly from the Devil!" Pinkerton blurted out.

Ben had sat long enough and had kept his opinions to himself until he could not control himself any longer. "The President already has a two-headed Devil in the White House, he is chief of his protection service!" All three of us broke into laughter.

61
Washington Post
September 1861

The mail steamer from Potomac Dockyards came twice a week to deliver the diplomatic pouch to the US Conciliate's Office in Hamilton. It passed by the Royal Naval Dockyards on the west end of the island chain and steamed into the Great Sound and on to the capital, Hamilton. The pouches and other mail from the US were left in Hamilton and the steamer entered back into the Great Sound and steamed on eastward to St. Georges, the site of the first people to set foot on Bermuda. The staff at both locations, eagerly awaited the three or four day old copies of the Washington Post. The events of this past August, as reported therein, began with the news of the congressional passage of the first income tax for the United States. Every person who earns an income will report this income to the new federal internal revenue service, so that the tax to support the war can be determined and levied. "This new income tax law, along with The Confiscation Act of 1861, will help finance the effort to readmit those states in rebellion, back into the Union." This was the direct quote from the secretary of the Treasury to this reporter.

These new laws require that property owners in areas occupied by Union Forces appear in person to pay their taxes. The first property seized under The Confiscation Act has been the estate of the Curtis family overlooking the Potomac. General McDowell took the residence, known as Arlington House, as his headquarters until he was replaced by General McClellan this month. In other news of Union Generals taking command, General Fremonte has been transferred to Missouri where he was quoted as saying, " My first order shall be to declare martial law. I then will proclaim that all slaves are to be set free."

The President's cabinet has been active this past month, also. Secretary of the Navy, G. H. Welles authorized the enlistment of run away slaves and recent freemen. Secretary Seward announced that Queen Victoria has accepted his undersecretary, Jason Caldwell, as minister to Bermuda. Lord Napier, of the Royal Admiralty, was quoted as saying, "Great Britain is very aware of Admiral Caldwell's capabilities and is strongly supportive of this appointment and we look forward to his visits here in the United Kingdom."

A smile walked its way across Louise Caldwell's face as she sat at the breakfast table at Caldwell Place. "Look, Jason, the paper reports that items 1 through 4 of our national affairs advisory committee have been implemented. It does not even mention you or the committee as having suggested them in the first place. It does say that you work for Secretary Seward."

"What? That can not be right. Oh, wait, that is a newspaper article, right? They rarely get anything correct."

"It says that Winfield Scott is still the General-in-chief of the army. And look what General Fremonte is quoted as saying! You said he was unbalanced, but this is something. He thinks he can free the slaves living in Missouri."

"Well, he is partly correct, because the Secretary of War sent him to Minnesota to put down an Indian uprising. Missouri is only two states away. Milton Fremonte has never gotten over the fall off his horse years ago. He was unconscious for over a week and when he awoke he was in a fog. Some mean spirited folks say he is still asleep, he should be retired, not sent anywhere in command."

"Are you going into Hamilton today, Jason?"

"No need. If there is anything important in the pouch, Jerome will send someone over here. I think I will take James down to the beach so he can build a sand castle."

"Do you feel guilty about sitting out the war over here in Bermuda, Jason?"

"Hell, no, you and I have served our country to the best of our abilities for over twenty years. Besides the war is just underway, there is going to be plenty of action regarding Bermuda and England before it is done. I will be gone for a month at a time when things heat up. You and I should enjoy these days with the children for as long as they last."

"Oh, we have a letter from Beaufort here. It is postmarked in Havana, Cuba, but I recognize your father's handwriting. Why did it go to Havana?"

"This came on the British mail steamer HMS *Trent*. Blockade runners take the mail from Charleston to Havana and transfer it to a mail steamer. The steamer stops here in Bermuda before it reaches England."

"Open it and read it to me, Jason."

"Oh, thank God."

"What is it, Jason?"

CALDWELL HOUSE
874 Bay Street, Beaufort, South Carolina

September 1, 1861

Dear Jason,

Trey has managed to lease the remaining family property for four years here in Beaufort. Our plans are to accept your kind offer to visit you, Louise and the grandchildren. So far, only your sister Carol remains steadfast in remaining here. Everyone else, and I mean everyone, has purchased tickets on a "runner" to Havana. We will leave Charleston sometime next month when there is a slight storm brewing in order to make a clear escape.

Seeing not a one of us speaks Spanish, I have a letter written in Spanish which requests passage on a mail steamer bound for Bermuda. You can go ahead and find your mother and I a little cottage in St. Davids.

More later, RHC

Your loving father

"Give this letter to Laura or Sally to start looking for a lease on St. Davids, will you Louise? I need to get James ready for the morning on the beach."

Before I could get James packed up for the beach, Robert and Laura came into the dining room for breakfast. Louise handed the letter to Laura and explained what needed to be done in the next month or so. Robert and I got caught up in the status of the requests from the War Department for the lease of some of our older merchant ships.

"What is the Navy going to do with these ships, Jason?"

"They are going to refit them with modern deck guns, rocket launchers and mortars so I can use them here in Bermuda. You need to make sure that they are stripped of anything that belongs to the company. No sense letting our fittings sit in Potomac Dockyards when we can use them in our store of supplies."

"Jason, I have no record of when these ships were purchased by Caldwell Shipping. Do you remember when or how you came by them?"

"Louise, Laura, come over here with Robert and me. You may enjoy hearing how Ben Hagood and I began Caldwell International Shipping. I graduated from the US Military Academy in '37 when I was not yet 21 years of age. The Naval Academy was not split away until '44 or '45 and the Army

301

had little or no use for the training vessels used down in Annapolis. These were ships that were used in the War of '12, but built in the later 1790's or early 1800's. Most of these were solid oak, no iron plating of any kind. The Point saw no use in keeping them around so they offered to sell them as scrap to whoever would place a bid. Ben Hagood was twenty-one years of age, so I had him write out a bid for $400.00 for a Brig named USS *Providence*, never thinking that we would get it. The *Providence* had first seen action in 1797. No one else even entered a bid.   So, Ben says, 'Your family is filthy rich. Why not write to your father and ask for a business loan?' Well, I did. He sent me a thousand dollars and said not to bid over a hundred on anything. Ben and I thought we at least could pay the four hundred that we owed and return the balance to my father. As a lark, Ben bid one hundred dollars on six more ships: two Brigs, called the USS *Spitfire* and USS *Jersey*; two Ketches, called the USS *New Haven* and USS *Trumbull* and two Snows called the USS *Congress* and USS *Philadelphia*. We got all six. So now, we have seven ships and no way to get them to Port Royal where I wanted to repair and work on them in order to start a shipping business."

"How did you get them to Port Royal?" Laura asked.

"A Brig needs a crew of eight seamen and two officers. Ben and I were the officers, so we ran an advertisement in the newspapers asking for able bodied seamen who wanted to relocate in South Carolina. As soon as we had 8 sailors, ready to trade work for transport, we requested leave from the Navy and started sailing them to Port Royal. Ben and I left the seamen in South Carolina and caught a ride on my father's schooner, *Westwind*, back to our stations. Every few weeks we had eight more sailors and we again requested leave to transport another ship to Port Royal. A Brig and a Snow are the same basic ship except for how the sails are set on the forward and aft masts. A Ketch or a Sloop is a much smaller ship and has only a single midship mast."

"Jason, my records show none of those ship names."

"I know, all of them were renamed by the Caldwell men who loved them. My father named one of the Snows *Cold Harbor*, sounds like my father and his puns! My brother, Robert, liked historical names, so he picked names of English Admirals like Somerset and Nelson."

"Jason?"

"Yes, Louise."

"How much are you renting those ships to the government for?"

"Robert, you have the figures right in front of you, tell them."

"The company leased four at $14,000.00, two at $22,000.00 and one is not for lease." replied Robert.

"Which one is that, Jason?" Asked Laura Whitehall.

"The *Cold Harbor*. I will never sell or lease that ship. Too many memories for everyone around this table. Too many trips to far away places, trips to Bermuda for both Louise and me. And for you and Laura also. Just too many good times on that old bucket to ever sell her."

"That reminds me, have you heard from your brother and father?"

"Yes, we got a letter today, Laura has it, she will let you read it. My father would like to 'let', as the English call it, a small cottage near you and Laura over on St. Davids. Do you still like it over there? No trouble getting to work over here every day?"

"No, Sir. We love our place. We made an offer to buy it. We should hear soon from the owner. When the war is over, we would like to keep it as retirement home."

"We have done the same thing here and I think we will enjoy having a place away from Pennsylvania when it comes winter time." Louise said.

"Laura, have you found places for Tom Schneider's and Sam Mason's families yet?" I asked.

"Yes, I found two places in St. Davids and two places in St. George for them to look at when they get here."

"The ten single marines are going to use the cottages here at Caldwell Place. The cottages are not modern, but they will do until they find something better."

"How did Jerome Lewis and his family like the house in Hamilton that Laura found for them?"

"They have not complained about being away from St. George. When the entire detachment is located here in Bermuda, they will be scattered all over the islands. Thank you, Robert and Laura, for taking on the extra work load. Louise and I really appreciate your work."

"Hey, there is a war going on!"

62

Bermuda Station
Caldwell Place

Everyone finished breakfast and I located James playing on the lawn outside one of the cottages which dotted the grounds of Caldwell Place. "James," I yelled. "Want to go down to the beach this morning?"

"Yes, Sir. Can I ask Sally to pack us a lunch?"

"Sally is busy this morning, why not ask Mommy to pack us a lunch and bring Ruth along?"

In an hour we were packed and ready to get on a carriage for the short ride down to Tobacco Bay Beach. The driver looked at the two adults, two children and related gear and said, "I will need 50 pence instead of the usual 25, Admiral."

I paid him and we were on the beach in a few minutes. "Pick us up in two hours, there is an extra 50 pence in it, if you can."

He smiled and said he would be right here in two hours. We walked to a smooth, sandy spot and put up a small umbrella for sun, sat the picnic basket down and got both children covered with skin cream of some sort that Louise had brought with her. James built his sand castle and Ruth ran in and out of the water, too many times to count. James then said, "Daddy, can we play our drawing game in the wet sand?"

"Sure, find me a stick and I will test your memory of old fashioned sailing vessels of the Revolutionary War."

"Which one is this?" I asked after I drew a three masted, three decked outline which had sixteen sails set off the masts.

"That is a Ship of the Line, it had 60 to100 cannon and a crew of 3 to 5 hundred."

I wiped out the sketch and started another. I had only gotten to the double masts and James cried, "Two masts, that is a Snow, Brig or Schooner, Daddy."

"The placement of the masts will tell you which one, Son."

"Let me see, how many decks are there?"

"Oh, that would make it too easy! Let me draw you some sails."

"It is a Schooner! See that large single sail off the aft mast, Mommy."

"Yes, I do. How do you know that is not a Brigantine. It had a single large sail on the aft mast, also."

"Cause Daddy never draws a Brigantine, he says the forward sails are a mess!"

We all enjoyed a laugh together. I pulled out my pocket watch and said, "It is time we started back if we want to catch the carriage up Rose Hill and back to Caldwell Place. The kitchen will have the lunch crowd finished and they can fix something for us."

The carriage was waiting for us and we loaded our beach gear and headed up the Duke of York Street until we reached Rose Hill, turned right and rode up the steep hill to Caldwell Place. As we pulled into the portico, Sally stuck her head out of the front doors and said, "You have guests from the United States." We met the detachment sitting in the dining room finishing their noon meal. When Tom Schneider saw me, he jumped up and out of habit yelled, "Officer on deck."

I laughed and told him and the rest of the detachment to sit down, I was not assigned to the Navy, I was a trusted member of the State Department. I shook each of the men's hands starting with Sam Mason and ending with Tom Schneider. They all looked seasoned, fresh from a short ocean voyage.

"How did Admiral Hagood arrange to have you Marines sent here so fast?"

"We got our orders from the White House, Sir. Admiral Hagood says to give you his best, the *USS Providence* has been recommissioned and ready for action. It is in St. George Harbor. He saw us off from the Potomac Dockyards in the *Providence*."

"Did he indicate when your families would arrive?" Louise asked.

"No, he said that the paperwork was in the mill and that they would follow in a few days, Ma'am."

"I will go and tell Laura to expect the families in a few days, then."

"The cottages that you and your families will be staying in are spread around the grounds of this old golf course. You are standing in the former club house. You and your wives have kitchens in the cottages, but you are welcome to eat meals here in the dining room whenever you like. I have never been a foreign diplomat before and I am sure that you may have a new experience as well. You all know Commander Lewis, he and his family are located in the US Conciliate quarters in Hamilton. It is a short train, a trolley actually, ride from here. You will all have to catch it this afternoon to report in there. Commander Lewis will have your work schedules for you sometime today. There is quite a bit of responsibility with being a Marine assigned to a foreign office, especially this one. I know each one of you. I requested the President to assign you here. We have to not only protect the people serving inside the Hamilton Office, but our families here at Caldwell Place. Our primary mission is to monitor the goings and comings of the Royal Naval Dockyards on the west end. If England tries to enter the war on the side of the Confederacy, they will go through here in great numbers on ships of the line and troop carriers."

"Admiral?"

"Yes, Tom."

"Does someone have our cottage numbers for us so we can dump our gear and get into civilian clothes?"

"The only Marines in civilian clothes will be those close to the dockyards, watching and reporting. Always wear a dress uniform when on duty in Hamilton. You can leave your dress uniforms in Hamilton, if you like. The natives will come to respect the US Conciliate as US property if we make a show of protecting it. Always travel to and from Hamilton in uniform and when on duty. Off duty, is civilian all the way, be comfortable."

"Can we dump our gear?"

"Yes, Sally Trott is the manager here at Caldwell Place. She has the cottage closest to the club house. Her office is there and she will have your cottage assignments. Sam and Tom will you stay behind and let the detachment find Sally?"

"What is it, Sir?" Sam asked after everyone had left the dining room.

"I am not sure we have enough Marines to do everything the President wants done here. I did not want to mention this in front of the men, but we are going to be stretched really thin to do this. We have to find a contact inside the Royal Naval Dockyards to get current information. I will leave that up to you two. You have done this before, remember the Resolute Matter?"

"Aye, aye, Sir!" They both said with a smile.

"Tell the men not to call me, Admiral. The natives here in Bermuda do not need to know that we were once a smooth running military unit. Sir, is alright and Minister, is fine. But try to keep the military courtesy to a minimum."

"Got you, Sir."

"Good, now think about how you want to make contact with someone who can help us inside the Dockyards of the Royal Navy. It should be someone who is not happy with his or her level of responsibility and will trade information for US gold coin. You both will carry a money belt full of coin, so let us see what the greed of an Englishman can get for us. You two are the only ones of the guard detachment that will have this task. Go slow, do not take chances with the British system of justice. Report only to me or Commander Lewis, no one else."

"Will we have to stand guard duty in Hamilton, Sir?"

"No, your assignment is information gathering only. Are either one of you familiar with a simple substitution code for sending messages to Washington?"

"No, Sir."

"Let me explain, then. Every day diplomatic pouches are sent to Washington from Hamilton. They contain letters, orders, and coded information. A coded message has a key. I will write something on this piece of paper so you can watch." I lettered the following name.

G E O R G E   J E F F E R S O N   W A S H I N G T O N 1 2 3 4 5 6 7

This is the key. Under each of the letters in this name I will write the alphabet.

G E O R G E   J E F F E R S O N   W A S H I N G T O N 1   2 3 4 5 6 7
a b c d   e f   g h I j   kL   m   n o p q r s t

Notice that UVWXYZ do not have a substitute code, so our messages will not contain those letters when we send them, just leave blank spaces. So in the diplomatic pouch when we have really something of military value to send to Washington, such as "British troops arrived Bermuda." We would send that as:

E5WMW6K   M52236   G55W9JR   EJ5T8RG

"You both will be sending coded messages from Hamilton to Washington on a regular basis as things heat up here in the middle Atlantic."

"And we thought this was going to be a babysitting operation," Tom said.

"No, the success of the US Naval Blockade depends on us keeping the British off the Navy's back. And to make things worse, General Butler will arrive to set up a foreign office for the Confederates which will try and get the British to come into the war on the C.S.A. side."

"The General Butler we arrested in Charleston?"

"The same, he is now Minister to Bermuda for the C.S.A. We need to monitor his activities while he will try to monitor ours."

"Sounds like a cat and mouse game, Sir."

"That is what life in Hamilton will be for the twelve of you men that have just arrived. Commander Lewis has been running the entire operation until today, he will be very happy to see you men report to him."

Tom and Sam left the dining room to find their cottages. They stored their gear and got into clean uniforms. Shortly, we were all walking to the St. George train station. We waited for the next train and caught some interesting glances from the townspeople. We got off the train in Hamilton and walked to the US Conciliate Office. Jerome Lewis was ready to have his Marines report for duty.

"Gentlemen, welcome to Bermuda and the US Conciliate's Office. It is good to see everyone again. I have work details for each of you. The front gate should be guarded at all hours of the day. If we use 8 hour shifts, then the day is divided into three parts. We will need two uniformed personnel on each shift so that means 6 of you men will have front gate duty. That leaves only four to roam the grounds and inside the building for security. I know it will be extra work because we are short handed here, but I have worked out the following schedule. You will work 8 hours, sleep 8 hours inside the building here and have 8 hours of free time every day. The schedules are rotational so that you can have days off. In that way we will try to fool the public into believing that we have a full company of Marines here."

"Commander Lewis is the assistant undersecretary here in Bermuda and you report directly to him." I said. "Warrant Officer Schneider will be available most of the second eight hour shift to answer any questions you might have. Master Sergeant Mason will be available most of the third shift to do the same thing."

"Minister Caldwell has an office here in this building and in St. George. If I am unavailable for any reason, you can contact him in an emergency." Said Jerome.

"Yes, remember, we function as a protection detail with things handled at the lowest level possible. We are here to protect the war secrets of the United States as well as the personnel and families of everyone assigned to this State Department Outpost. We need for everyone to get some rest, I know you traveled several days to get here. Your assignments can wait twenty-fours, is that correct, Commander Lewis?"

"It is Minister. I would like to visit with each of you as you leave the building today. Let us begin with Corporals Wilson and Clemens please. As they leave, Simmons and Farley are next. Then Smith and Wallace, Norwich and Olsen, Saunders and Marlin. That is the rotation that I have set up and I want to make sure that it runs smoothly."

Tom Schneider and Sam Mason looked at me and nodded their heads. We walked into my office and Tom said, "I wish we had some of the patrolmen who joined the US Marshal's Office here on this. These young Marines are going to be fine on guard duty, but they will not work on undercover assignments."

"I was just thinking the same thing, Tom. Let me get a request off to the White House and see if Allen Pinkerton can find us some policemen."

"Sam and I will start finding out where the British Marines and officers go for rest and recreation. If we find anything out in the next few days, we will let you know, Admiral. I mean, Sir."

In less than a week, Tom returned with the following information. "It seems that the pressed seamen are not ever released from the dockyards. We found out from talking to an officer at the 'Country Squire Pub', that the makeup of an average crew of a royal naval vessel is 75 men. Fifty percent of these are pressed seamen, twenty-three percent are volunteers, fifteen percent are from jails and twelve percent are foreigners. That means for every ship in the dockyards, thirty-seven are held and not available to us for gathering information."

"Where is this Country Squire Pub?"

"It is close to the dockyards, in a place called 'Mango Grove', that is in Somerset, Sir".

"Who was this officer?"

"There were two officers that we talked to; both Lieutenants, A. J. Schmidts and Horatio Farnsworth. We learned that Farnsworth was demoted from an Admiral's Aide, a major, I think."

"He sounds like he might have some useful information if you go slow and let him tell you what he knows. He might try to impress you with his experience as an Admiral's Aide."

"I think so, too, Sir. The other one feels he is not being used to his fullest capacity. He is a marine but he never gets on a ship. He can use one of the those new Underwood typewriters so he types letters and communications all day long."

"He could be a gold mine of information, Tom. I wonder if he remembers anything that he types and would like to impress you or Sam with what he knows? What is your cover when you see these officers?"

"We are both are AWOL seamen from a Confederate ship that stopped at the Royal Dockyards last month."

"Be careful with that cover, you could wind up as pressed seamen on an outbound vessel."

"We are careful, always together and armed to the teeth. The Brits are looking for easy pickings, Sir. We will be fine for a few more visits anyway. By that time, the additions from Pinkerton can take over that part of the operation."

"What do you think of having them sail directly into the Royal Naval Dockyard as survivors of a running gun battle with a US Naval vessel. This Confederate vessel could be a blockade runner whose captain and most of the crew have been killed, say, only five or six survivors. These members would not know anything about passwords or agreements with the Royal Navy. They would just be requesting aid. How much information could we get about British plans to run through or destroy the blockade of ports?"

"I can code up a message and send it through the State Department to Admiral Hagood for his reaction after I talk to Commander Lewis. The Commander always adds things to my plans to make them better, Sir."

"Commander Lewis and you are two of the best idea men I have, Tom. Do not tell him it was my idea, let him develop it for us. He will put on the necessary touches here and there that will make it viable. How do like Bermuda so far, Tom?"

"Better now that Beth and the kids are here. We really like the house that Laura Whitehall found for us in St. Davids. But I can not get an answer from her on how much rent we owe her."

"The house is part of the per diem expenses forwarded from Washington, Tom. All you need to buy is food for the family. All other expenses should be paid through the Conciliate in Hamilton."

"Thank you, Sir."

"Because you are on duty for eight hours a day and sometimes have to sleep inside the building, you will be given an increase in your normal Navy pay, also. Commander Lewis went through all that with you and Sam, right?"

"Yes, Sir."

"Anything else that we need to talk about?"

"No. Sir."

"Good, then get out of here and get back to your families on St. Davids."

"Aye, aye. Sir.

63
The Trent Affair
October 1861

The night of October 11, 1861, was dark and the sea was boiling. Rain came down in sheets as a Confederate blockade runner slipped out of Charleston, South Carolina, carrying Robert Hays Caldwell the second and his son "Trey" along with their families. They had purchased the last available spaces on the run to Havana, Cuba. The cabin spaces had been reserved for Confederate foreign ministers, James Murray and John Butler. Robert knew John Butler. He was a general in the State of South Carolina Militia. He had no idea that James Murray was a Virginia lawyer who had served in both houses of congress before he was appointed as Ambassador to England by Jefferson Davis. Before the cruise was over, however, he knew that James Murray was a tobacco-chewing, swearing, staunch states' rights Democrat who had drafted the Fugitive Slave Act of 1850. He also knew that Murray was a close personal friend of President Davis and had served on the US Senate Foreign Relations Committee with him, because the man never stopped talking about himself. There was another foreign minister, David Slidell, bound for Paris after Havana, but he kept to himself. Trey had talked with him some and found out he was a US Senator from Louisiana before the war, but he had a New York accent and Trey doubted he was telling the truth.

Robert Hays Caldwell II was 64 years old when he decided to leave his home in South Carolina and board the runner to Havana. If the war lasted the four or five years as his son, Jason, had suggested, he hoped he would live long enough to return home. He and his wife, Mary Elizabeth, had five children, two had died in infancy and three had grown to be his pride and joy. He had not talked to any of his children about how or where he was to be laid to rest, but he hoped that he would be laid beside his babies in the Beaufort, St. Helena Church yard whenever the time came. His daughter, Carol, and her husband had stated flatly that they would not leave Beaufort no matter what her brother, Jason, said. It was typical of a brother and sister.

He hated to have his family separated but he also trusted Jason's judgement. Ever since '37 and his purchase of surplus ships to start an international shipping business in Port Royal, Jason had made one good judgement after another. Jason and Louise had said to leave Beaufort with no luggage. Do not give any indication that it was anything other than a weekend trip to Charleston. Each of us carried a small overnight bag, even the grandchildren. We arrived in Charleston and stayed at the Planters Inn. Trey had gone down to the harbor to find the cutter to Havana. He found it and asked what date the runner would try to get out of the harbor. The first mate said as soon as the weather gets stormy, we would leave at night and have the best chance of getting through. If we were stopped, then we would be fined and returned to the harbor to try again later. It seemed rather ordinary and not at all unusual. He had already sold the three private cabin spaces, but there was room below decks among the cargo for bedrolls for all the Caldwells. So, Trey paid a retainer and started checking every afternoon until the eleventh, when the first mate indicated that we would try to go tonight.

We boarded the boat in the driving rain, flashes of lightening frightened the grandchildren while the smells coming from below decks did not seem inviting. We had not gotten the beds rolled out before the boat began moving. The captain had a full head of steam and he was not waiting around for a patrol boat to spot us leaving the docks. Blockade runners were primitive vessels in '61. We relied on the darkness of night, with all ship lights extinguished, a rain storm to block the moonlight and the cloud of steam produced by the ships boilers. It was several hours before a crew member came below and said we were in international waters. We were to try and get some sleep. He would return at sunrise.

Passengers were not usually allowed on deck when making the short run to Havana, but the captain relented and let the men only come up on deck to stretch their legs. After they had some exercise, they could return and the women could do the same. No children would be allowed on deck. We spent the time in shifts and said we would never try this again. It was a beautiful day when we entered Havana. James Murray announced that he and the other two ministers, Slidell and Butler, would board HMS *Trent,* the mail steamer, bound for London and Paris. The rest of us could wait for the next ship to Bermuda. Mary Elizabeth announced that she thought that was an excellent idea.

"Robert, he is an awful person and I do not want to spend another minute with him. Use your Spanish language letter and see what cabin space is available to Bermuda. Otherwise, I would enjoy staying in Cuba for a few more days." Robert had lived with Mary Elizabeth for 45 years and knew that when she said something, she meant it!

"Trey and I will look today. But before we do that, we need to find the nicest hotel in Havana. Then you, Mariann and the children can have baths. We need to buy new clothes and become civilized again."

"Thank you, Robert. You need a bath, also!"

We found two carriages and managed to communicate that we needed a hotel, "Casa del Resort, Amigo." The driver nodded his head and instructed the other carriage driver to follow and we headed for our place of reorganization as Mariann called it. We gave the drivers a US gold five dollar coin. By their reactions we knew that we had overpaid them. They carried our hand luggage inside the hotel lobby. One of the drivers could speak a little English and asked if we had "Del Casa Reservacion?" We shook our heads, no, trying to indicate we had just come from the United States. He walked to the desk and spoke to the desk clerk, showed him his five dollar gold coin and returned to us. He says that for another gold coin you can stay two days at this hotel. "Gratias, Amigo."

The next day Robert Caldwell showed his letter of introduction to the Harbor Master and found cabin space on the next ship to Bermuda. At about that time, the HMS *Trent* was approached by the USS *San Jacinto*. The *San Jacinto* was a first class steam powered sloop. It had 13 guns and weighed 1446 tons when it was built in 1850 at the Brooklyn Ship Yards. When the Trent did not stop, the *San Jacinto* captain ordered two shots fired across the Trent's bow. The US and England were not at war and this was a flagrant violation of international maritime law. Captain Charles Wilkes demanded that a Mr. Murray and Slidell be placed on his ship for transport to Boston. They were being arrested for treason. There was no arrest warrant and the captain of the Trent was outraged.

"This will be reported as soon as we land in the United Kingdom."

Murray and Slidell were taken to Boston and jailed while the Trent sailed on to Bermuda.. The US newspapers rejoiced over the capture of Confederate diplomats, but none indicated how Captain Wilkes knew that the diplomats would be on that ship in that location. Congress passed a resolution thanking Captain Wilkes for his actions while Queen Victoria had a different reaction. She sent a message to Abraham Lincoln via transatlantic cable.

YOUR GOVERNMENT HAS DETAINED A MINISTER TO GREAT BRITAIN. UNDER INTERNATIONAL LAW, YOU WILL RELEASE HIM IMMEDIATELY. WE SHALL DETAIN YOUR AMBASSADOR IN LONDON UNTIL MR. MURRAY ARRIVES HERE IN ENGLAND.

LORD PALMERSTON FOR HER MAJESTY

When HMS *Trent* stopped at the Royal Naval Dockyards in Bermuda, The captain of the Trent reported the arrest of Ministers Murray and Slidell. Minister Butler reported his credentials to the Lord Governor at Government House, Hamilton, and walked to the US Conciliate Office. He was angry and shaken at the removal of Murray and Slidell. He would lodge his own complaint with the US Minister to Bermuda, Jason Caldwell. How had the Captain of the *San Jacinto* known to stop the mail steamer and why had he escaped arrest? It had to be Slidell, he must be an informant. He was stopped at the front gate to the US Conciliate by two armed US Marines in dress uniform.

"Can I see your credentials, Sir?"

He handed a copy to one of the guards and said, "I must see Minister Caldwell on a very important matter."

"You may see his deputy, assistant Minister Lewis."

"Fine, let me in and I will see him."

A few minutes later John Butler, former General of the South Carolina Militia was cooling his heels in an outer office waiting to see Jerome Lewis. He was not used to treatment like this, the longer he waited the angrier he got. When a secretary admitted him to see Mr. Lewis he was livid. "Where is Jason Caldwell?"

"Admiral Caldwell, Under Secretary of State and Minister to Bermuda is not in at the moment. I am his assistant and have his full authority to act in his absence. Can I be of help, Minister Butler?"

"Yes, I would like to give an eye witness account of an abduction of two foreign ministers upon the high seas."

"Who were these foreign ministers?" Jerome Lewis asked as he reached for paper and pen.

"James Murray, Ambassador to Great Britain and David Slidell, Ambassador to France."

Jerome was taking names and information and as he wrote, he asked. "These two Ambassadors were in transit, from where to where?"

"Havana to London and Paris."

"And how were they taken?"

"The USS *San Jacinto* was captained by a Charles Wilkes and he fired upon the HMS *Trent*."

"The same Captain Wilkes who was the first American to sail around the world? This is incredible. He must be nearly 70 years of age. I doubt that this is accurate, Minister Butler. Perhaps a privateer posing as Wilkes boarded the Trent. Did you see this man who said he was Captain Wilkes?"

"Yes, I did."

"Did he look 70 years old to you?"

"No, he did not."

"Alright, I will report this to our State Department after Minister Caldwell gives me his permission. I would suggest that you accompany me when I report to him. Do you have the time?"

"I would be delighted to see Jason, again."

"You know him?"

"Yes, the first time was in Charleston when he arrested me and held me unlawfully for three months. The second time was in Washington City, where I met with Admiral Hagood and a Mr. Allen Pinkerton."

"The President's bodyguard?"

"Yes, and I believe that Admiral Hagood is the Atlantic Fleet Commander in charge of the Union Blockade of Charleston Harbor among others."

"You are well informed, Minister Butler. Have you just now docked at the Royal Naval Dockyards?"

"Yes, why?"

"You must be exhausted from your ordeal. Why not meet at the C. S. A. Embassy here in Hamilton? Do you know where that is, Minister?"

"I have a street address, I can find it."

"Do you want to meet later today, or would tomorrow be better for you?"

"I would like some action on this matter today, if possible."

"We can meet you at your embassy in three hours. The train schedules are accurate here in Bermuda. I will leave immediately and contact the undersecretary, that will take an hour, the return trip another hour, three hours would be about right."

"Tell the Admiral that I was traveling with his family and I would like his attention to this matter at his earliest convenience. People traveling from the Confederacy on neutral nation's ships should not be attacked in international waters. We must put a stop to this at once."

"I understand, and agree completely, Minister Butler. I have notes on the matter and we will find a solution as soon as possible."

"Thank you, Mr. Lewis, you have been most courteous and helpful. You are not a southern gentleman by any chance, are you?"

"Louisville, Kentucky, Sir."

"Close enough, see you and the Admiral in three hours."

64

CSA Embassy
Hamilton, Bermuda

In three hours, Jerome Lewis had sent a message with one of the roving marines to alert me that a meeting was going to be held in the C. S. A. Embassy at 4 pm. The St. George train had delivered me promptly to Hamilton and I had walked to my office, picked up Jerome and we were walking to the C.S.A. Embassy while we talked. "Did he say why my family did not come with him on the HMS *Trent*?"

"No, Sir. He is too shaken to be diplomatic, maybe the three hours will help him get his poise."

"He thought he was absolutely safe on a British ship. I would assume the same thing. I wonder what really happened?"

We were on the steps of the Confederate Embassy next to the Government House, Hamilton. There were no formal gates to enter, no guards of any kind to stop our progress. We tried to open the doors, but they were locked and a small sign said to ring the bell. We did. John Butler opened the door in his shirt sleeves and said, "Good to see you again, Admiral. Come inside please. I assume your assistant here has told you what happened?"

"Yes, what a deplorable act."

"Almost as bad as kidnaping a sleeping General from his bed in Charleston." He said with a smile.

"I had an arrest warrant, General. And you were a citizen of the United States then." I said smiling.

"Yes, I do not understand how the *San Jacinto* found us, Admiral. Can you tell me what you know?"

"Of course, Mr. Lewis gets a weekly briefing on all USS ships and their stations. One week ago the *San Jacinto* was on patrol off the coast of Africa. I doubt it was the *San Jacinto* that stopped you."

"Mr. Lewis has indicated the same thing earlier today. The man who claimed to be her captain was not the right age, we know that."

"What about the ship itself? I play a game with my son where I draw an outline of the ship and he tells me the class of ship. Do you think you could draw an outline of what the ship looked like?"

He reached over on his desk and got a pad of paper and a pen. "I am an army general, not an admiral, so excuse the crudeness of my artwork." He handed it over to me.

"That is a steam powered sloop alright." I said as I studied his sketch. "Did you see any markings or was this at night?"

"No, it was in broad daylight. There was lettering along each side which said USS *San Jacinto*."

"Give us enough time to contact Washington and find out what they know. Mail ships are back and forth, both British and US, so it should not take very long. Have you notified Richmond?"

"Yes, I told the British captain of the Trent to have the Royal Admiralty send a transatlantic cable to Canada and have them forward it to Richmond."

"So, Richmond is unaware of what happened because the Trent has not reached England." I said.

"Yes, I suppose so."

"The first thing I think we should do is figure out a way to send messages directly to Richmond. Does the telegraph still work between South Carolina and Richmond?"

"Of course, we can send and receive telegrams anywhere inside the Confederacy. Richmond and Washington City are very close and we cannot communicate between them, but we can send a telegram to Texas and get a reply in an hour. What a situation!"

"What if we figure out a way to communicate with someone close to the Confederacy? Say Havana or Mexico City?" I offered.

"The British mail steamers make frequent runs between Bermuda, Canada and Cuba. I can send a message to Havana and have a runner try to take it into Norfolk" He said.

"Do that. You can indicate that you have talked to me and I am cooperating fully. We will have additional information in a few days, but I would not wait, Richmond needs to be notified."

"Good suggestion, I will do that, Admiral."

"Commander Lewis said you were traveling with my family?"

"Yes, we shared the same runner out of Charleston. When we got to Havana, the Trent cabin space was sold out and your father checked into a hotel."

"It was probably a good thing, seeing what happened to you. Do you have any idea why they took Slidell and Murray and left you aboard the Trent?"

"I have thinking about that. Maybe they wanted the kidnaping reported as soon as the Trent docked in Bermuda."

"Of course, how stupid of me, the captain of the Trent would report to the British and you would report to Richmond. The only people in the dark are in Washington. They have created an international incident so that England will give the Confederacy more than just recognition of nation status. I wonder who, they are? I doubt very much if the US would do this, they can only be losers in this affair. I will refer to this as the Trent Affair in my communication." Said Jerome Lewis.

"Welcome to Bermuda, Minister Butler. This is going to be a very interesting time to be in the middle of the Atlantic Ocean, I think. Well, Commander Lewis and I have some messages to send. I will, of course, let you know what I find out about the Trent Affair. We should know some of the answers within a few days. Do you know where the *San Jacinto* was headed?"

"The man posing as the captain said he was taking them to Boston. That is all I know."

"Thank you, we will start there. And, feel free to visit me here in Hamilton whenever we can be of assistance to you, Minister Butler."

65

USA Conciliates Office
Hamilton, Bermuda

We left Butler's office and headed down the street to the US Conciliates Office. "Do you think he has told us everything, Admiral?"

"Yes, it is just as big a mystery to him as it is to us. If this 'Captain Wilkes' or whoever, was stupid enough to land in Boston then we will find out something immediately. When we get back to the office, I will let you send what we know to the President of the United States, through Secretary Seward, of the State Department. That way if Seward or someone tries to bury the information, we will have a copy in our files. We need to send a blind copy of the information to General Butler. At this point we are seeking information and clarification only. There is no need to send secret coded messages in the dark of night."

"I agree, Jason. This will blowup for whoever ordered this action. I can not imagine a ship's captain doing this on his own. How did he know that there were Confederate Diplomats on that particular ship at that particular location? I doubt we ever find out what started this or why, the coverup has already started."

"It will take several days for a response from Washington. Why not try through the US Department of the Navy, also? I will send a personal to Ben Hagood and see if he knows or can tell me if he knows."

I left Jerome to get to work and I walked to the train station in Hamilton to catch the last train to St. George. Five days later we got our response from the State Department in the sealed diplomatic pouch.

TO: Jason Caldwell, National Affairs Committee
ROM: Secretary Seward
SUBJECT: Receipt of eyes only President

The White House has no information to share with you on this matter at this time. Inquires are being made to location and recent actions of USS San Jacinto. White House not aware that Confederacy was planing to send diplomats to England until transatlantic cable from Lord Palmerston arrived. Copy attached.

In the regular mail pouch we received the following personal from Admiral Hagood.

Jason,

Got your inquiry about our Spanish friend not being at home. That is true. He had to return to Cuba to see his sick Aunt Maurry. I understand that the doctors in Cuba could not help her and she was sent to Boston General Hospital for observation and isolation until the sickness is identified.

Glad I could help.

Ben.
PS I have enclosed some newspaper articles on another unrelated topic

When Jerome showed me the items in the two pouches, I said. "Contact General Butler and let him read this first response and the attached cablegram. The fact that Lord Palmerston has placed our ambassador under house arrest, may give him cause to pause and communicate this to Richmond. Do not show him Ben's personal. What that tells us is that the Navy was instructed to take Murray and Slidell but leave Butler so he could get to Bermuda to open the lines of communication. Someone did not think this through very carefully. The President can suspend the right of habeas corpus on US soil, but not on the high seas or anywhere in the Confederacy. He still thinks the southern states are states within the Union."

"Look at these London Times press clippings, Jason. 'If Captain Wilkes is typical of USN officers then the entire breed from the Northern United States can be judged. They are an uncivilized nation built on a foundation of vulgarity and cowardice.'"

"Here is another from The London Daily. 'Perhaps Secretary of State Seward thinks that war with Great Britain will bring the seceded states back to the Union'."

"Here is a quote from the Washington Post. President Lincoln has said, 'One war at a time.'"

"There must be twenty clippings here, Jason."

"Yes, the British business world is upset. They are frustrated by the Union blockade. Lord Palmerston is playing to the fear and frustration. In this article, he says that the Admiralty is sending 8000 troops and 40 ships to rescue the diplomats. Read that as an attempt to smash the blockage of southern ports."

"Do you think they will come through Bermuda?"

"Yes, I do. We need to start to squeeze the two officers that Tom and Sam have found and try to get information to Washington as soon as we can."

Tom Schneider and Sam Mason began their vigil at the Country Squire. They met with the two contacts separately on several occasions buying drinks and making small loans of gold coins.

"It is about time that England comes to our aid. The blockade is a joke, it needs to be removed by force. From what we have seen, the Royal Navy can sweep the blockades away from our Confederate ports any time they choose." Tom said.

"The Admiralty has warned us to expect heavy ship traffic through the dockyards starting November 1. We cannot process that many ships at a time so they will come through in groups of twenty. It will take us a month to pass through 40 ships and 8000 marines. Of course, most of the ships are fast cutters to run through the blockades at Charleston, South Carolina. If they are successful there they will open Norfolk and a pathway to Richmond with the 8000 marines." Lieutenant Farnsworth proudly announced. Tom made mental notes and stopped off to see Commander Lewis on his way home to St. Davids.

"Commander Lewis, Sam and I have nearly the same stories from the Lieutenants Farnsworth and Schmidts. They have been put on alert to receive a small fleet for refueling and provisioning. The fleet consists of 38 vessels. Two ships of the line will serve as escort, each have 150 guns. Our largest ship of the line was the Pennsylvania with 120, it was captured on station in Norfolk harbor. The rest of our ships all carry 84 guns. So we will need four vessels to match that number of guns. There are no Frigates in the English fleet, so that is helpful. They are to receive eight first class steam sloops, all screw operated, no side wheelers. They are to expect eight screw, and eight side wheelers of second class sloops, ten third class steamers and four steam tenders."

"Excellent work. We need to send a coded message for the outgoing diplomatic pouch. Make it simple. Say, confirmed from multiple sources; a number of blockade running vessels in route to Bermuda; escort consists of two men-of-war. Number of marines on board ships unknown. Will report ships as they arrive. Will report number of troops as they pass through. Early indication is Charleston Harbor, not Boston. Repeat, not Boston. Can you do that for me, Tom?"

"That is a long coded message, Sir. Will you review it before I type it up?"

"I will, but I doubt you will have any trouble with it. I will put it on tomorrow's mail steamer so the Admiral can make last minute changes if he likes. Has his family arrived in Bermuda?"

"Yes, they are all at Caldwell Place. You should see the dining room over there, it is a three ring circus. These cousins have not seen each other for two years! His father looks ten years younger. The blockade running must have stirred up a few juices."

"Good, the Admiral is a strong family man. I am glad that he got his family out of South Carolina."

"The Admiral takes care of all us, Commander. Did you know that he tried to hire us as company men after we finished the operation last winter in Charleston?"

"What did you tell him?"

"I told him that I would go wherever the Navy sent my unit as long as you were the unit commander. If the Navy did something stupid and split up the unit, then I would see him in Pennsylvania."

"I think we all think along the same lines, Tom. Since the Republicans have taken over the White House and therefore the military, it has been like a basket upset. The newspapers report how many army officers went with the Confederacy, but no mention is given about Navy transfers. Last year when we were in the White House, there were ten ships of line in the entire Navy, four of those were in Norfolk harbor and were taken when Virginia seceded. There were ten Frigates, three were in Norfolk. There were twenty Sloops of War, we lost four of those. There were three Brigs, we lost one. And the list goes on, 30 to 40 per cent are now Confederate Navy vessels. The shipyards of the Confederacy are building full speed, especially Jacksonville."

"I had no idea, I knew we lost some to Florida and Virginia. How does this affect the blockade of southern ports?"

"We are making progress in the Gulf and up the Mississippi, but it is slow going. The blockade is along the east coast, nothing in the Pacific. No ground troops have taken harbors or ports away as of yet. If that happens, then we have a chance to win."

"What if this British fleet descends on Charleston?"

"If they can run off the blockade vessels and land 8000 marines, then the Confederacy will hold the city and harbor for the entire war. More importantly, the British might try to do this again in Norfolk."

In the last week of October, we received several reports in Hamilton via the mail steamer from Washington. The first was the after action report of the Battle of Ball's Bluff near Leesburg, Virginia. President Lincoln could not get his newly appointed General of the Army of the Potomac to leave Washington City and cross the river into Virginia. The Union Army was close to 200,000 by late October, but General McClellan was unwilling to cross and engage the Confederacy. Lincoln's close personal friend was senator Edward Baker from Oregon. He also was a colonel in the army reserve, having served in the war with Mexico. Lincoln had confided in him that he was disappointed in the lack of progress towards the prosecution of the war across the Potomac. He offered Baker an appointment as a brigadier and command of a small brigade, 1700 member reconnaissance force. Lincoln was convinced that the Confederate line was porous and could be penetrated. He encouraged Baker to find this opening and report it to McClellan. On October 21, Baker lead his brigade from Maryland to Virginia. At the river's edge, they found a swollen river from fall rains and a hundred foot high bank on the Virginia side of the river called Ball's Bluff. Baker sent his men up and down the Maryland side looking for any available boats to ferry his men across. They found three boats. In dozens of trips back and forth, good fortune seemed to smile on them as all 1,700 were ferried across safely. The way up the bluff was a narrow pathway with Virginia sharp shooters killing every fifth man who plodded up the bluff side. When eighty percent of the force reached the top, they found themselves on open ground and confronted by four Confederate regiments. Baker was killed in the first volley. In a frenzied panic, the force raced backward and fell to their deaths at the bottom of the bluff.

The second report was even more incredulous. Lincoln replaces Winfield Scott with the General who refuses to fight across the Potomac and prefers to "protect" Washington, General McClellan. "Jerome, have you read this?" I asked.

"Yes, it is what you recommended, Admiral."

"I know, but Scott at least has a brain. I am not sure about McClellan. He lacks the will to lead his army against the enemy."

"Then you do not want to read this last report, Admiral."

"What is in it?"

"An assessment of our undercover work regarding English intentions in either Norfolk or Charleston."

"Go on."

"The War Department, in particular the Secretary of War, has informed us that we are in error. The war department has just ordered 2,300 tons of gun powder from Great Britain. Why would they sell us gun powder to kill their troops if they were planning an attack?"

"I cannot abide fools, Jerome. The man has 'ordered' not received gun powder. Now England knows that we need gun powder for the ships on blockade! What an idiot!"

"What do we do now, Admiral?"

"Report how many Royal Navy ships are re-supplied in November, where they are headed and the number of troops aboard. What else can we do?"

"We could send a blind copy to Admiral Hagood, after all, it is his men that will die on the blockade ships because of the lack of gun powder."

"Thank you, Jerome. You are always one step ahead of me."

66

Royal Naval Dockyards
Bermuda, November, 1861

November 1861 found the Royal Naval Dockyards crowded with British shipping. From captured French luggers used as troop transports and supply ships to sloops, frigates and two ship of the line came the shrilling of whistles and stamp of feet as the crews of more than 40 vessels settled down to the day's routine. In the cabin of HMS *Revenge,* Admiral Lord Willingsworth studied the charts of the waters off Norfolk Harbor. For "Black Billy," as his seamen called him, had been given the task of smashing the North American blockades, first at Charleston and then Norfolk. This was to be punishment for the kidnaping of an ambassador to Great Britain that was held in Boston. Why he was not attacking Boston was unclear to him. Lord Palmerston had been very clear that his orders were to be followed unless the diplomats were released and Black Billy considered his role as the one to rattle the saber and show the Union Jack. He was positive that a war with America was not about to happen. His task force was too small for such action, but it was the right size to send a serious message to both the North and South. To the North, it would indicate that England would not tolerate the interference with free trade and to the South it would indicate that they were a separate nation, an equal trading partner. The violation of international maritime law had been the excuse necessary to begin the operations he was sent to complete.

Suddenly a tremendous explosion jarred the dockyards out of its morning routine activities. Those nearest the explosion saw a tall column of water collapsing into a large cloud of gun powder smoke. No sooner had this occurred before several smaller bangs were heard off the stern of HMS *Revenge* and HMS *Rapier.* In an instant the dockyards was in an uproar. Drums beat to general quarters as the Queen's ships prepared for action. Men were heard yelling, "Search for mines, get the divers under the hulls, move, move." Officers shouted orders to fire the boilers, prepare to get under way. Other ship captains that were aboard, cut mooring lines and started to drift into quays and wooden pilings. With that many ships in such a small space, more damage was done in one hour by ship collisions than the United States Navy could hope to accomplish on the high seas.

The chaos in the dockyards was seen from a hillside less than a quarter mile away. Tom Schneider and Jerome Lewis had been in the Royal Navy Graveyards since before sunrise. They had brought a picnic basket filled with sandwiches and other snacks. It also contained two spy glasses, a map, a train schedule, pen and paper. As they sat with their backs to grave markers, glasses to their eyes, they were enjoying what was unfolding below them.

"The stupid bastards brought the entire fleet into the dockyards. Just like Admiral Caldwell said they might. This will teach them a lesson." Tom said.

"There was absolutely no need for all that destruction. Look, Tom, that tender was literally torn apart by that steam powered sloop screws."

"The damage done to the dockyards is as great as anything done to the ships. Look at all the secondary explosions and small fires that are everywhere. Smoke will soon block us from seeing much of anything. We had better start writing down which ships are damaged and those that have left the dockyards under their own steam."

Notes from observation team 11-17-61

2 *Man-of-war hit by small mines, blown steerage - still in docks.*
6 *steam sloops left docks - now in Great Sound anchored.*
2 *sloops afire, minor explosions below decks, assume boilers out.*
4 *steam tenders destroyed by collisions with sloop screws - sunk.*
8 *second class sloops took out several docks and themselves in panic to get out of dockyards.*
8 *side wheelers left dockyards and are headed east for St. George.*
10 *French luggers are still tied up, not damaged in the melee.*

The raid on the dockyards had been planned after Admiral Caldwell said something should be done to give Admiral Hagood some time to respond to the threat. He said he could not know how the delay was caused but offered any equipment we might need, including a Bushnell Turtle, from his dockyard in St. George. Jerome Lewis had heard of the submersible repair device, but he had never seen one until he and Sam Mason had seen it in St. George.

"We will need to construct small charges that will destroy the two escort vessels steerage. No deaths, just confusion and fear. Do we have everything for that?" Jerome Lewis, master planner of chaos, and assistant minister to Bermuda was making a list of needed materials.

"Yes, Sir. Good swimmers can place these charges, why do we need the Bushnell Turtle?"

"For the main event, Sam. There is an empty prison hulk right in the middle of 40 ships. If we can either set it afire or blow it up, the resulting chaos might be interesting!"

"So, how do we blow it up?"

"We use the Admiral's turtle. A bushnell turtle was last used to blow up a man-of-war in New York Bay."

"When was that? I never heard about it."

"It was a little before your time, Sam, it was September 7, 1776."

"Oh. No wonder I never heard about. Who is going to operate the turtle?"

"You have two weeks to learn how to master the craft. You can start by studying these diagrams the Admiral gave me. See here is a cutaway view of the turtle. The two clam shell sides are seven feet long and it looks about six feet in diameter when it is closed. Tom will not fit inside the turtle, but you are just the right size. You have to master the hand cranks for horizontal and vertical propellers."

"When do I master the controls?"

"You will be here in the Caldwell Shipping docks until you do. Do not report for duty in Hamilton until you can prove to me that you can navigate the turtle as well as use the attachment auger, foot operated rudder and ballast pumps. I do not want to let you into the Royal Dockyards so you can drown in this oaken bucket."

"Aye, aye, Sir."

Every day of the first week, Sam practiced on the water's surface around the wooden docks of Caldwell Shipping Company. He sat on the pilot's seat and looked through the tiny portholes of the conning tower. The tower was about as tall as his head. Snorkel tubes extended above the tower about six inches, so there was fresh air until you had to submerge. It was fun trying to learn how the propellers and rudder worked. He bounced off of and bumped into every wooden piling in the dockyard. Finally he tried to submerge by cranking the intake valve by his right foot. Water came into a holding tank and the turtle sank below the surface. The snorkel tubes closed and he could stay under about thirty minutes before the air became fouled. His depth was shown by a vertical glass tube, closed at the top and leading to the water outside through a brass, water tight fitting. Any increase in water pressure forced the column of water upward, any decrease dropped the level of the water in the tube. As a safety precaution a 200 pound lead keel could be released from inside the turtle, counteracting any tendency to sink. This was also the anchor, since it was fastened to a rope.

The second week, Sam practiced attaching the mine. He would navigate to a wooden platform in the water, submerge one foot and propel himself under the platform. He then practiced the use of the metal auger. This was very tricky since the turtle tended to settle down when the auger tried to fasten itself to the wood. But with practice and patience he mastered the attachment of the egg shaped wooden cask containing the powder charge of 250 pounds and a clockwork timing device. When the mine was released from just above the rudder on the turtle, it floated to the bottom of the practice platform and became inverted. This set the timing device for one hour. Sam needed to get way to a safe distance in that hour. After that, a flint gunlock set off the charge.

In the early hours of November 17, 1861, the turtle was dropped from a Caldwell Sloop that was passing into the Great Sound, adjacent to the Royal Naval Dockyards. The sloop continued on into Hamilton and tied up at the wharfs. Sam was like a floating child's top until he managed to get some water into the ballast tank and the turtle settled to the depth of the conning tower. It was past sunrise, but just barely. His heart was pounding while he turned the hand crank of the horizontal propeller. The turtle edged into the middle of the vessels tied up inside the dockyards. He spotted the old deserted prison hulk and propelled himself towards it. When he was along side, he again turned the intake valve and slipped below the surface of the water. He watched his depth gage and maneuvered under the hull. He released the auger and placed it for attachment. Slowly he turned and the metal bit caught and the attachment bolt was firmly in place. He pulled the release level for the mine and prayed that his fellow marines had built an accurate timer. He did not wait for the mine to float up and invert. Instead he placed both hands on the horizontal propeller and turned as fast as he could. He would need to blow some water out of the ballast tank so he could rise to the surface and get his bearings. As he pumped the ballast tank, he slowly rose and broke the surface. He wondered if the two marines assigned to place the charges on the escorts had been successful. If they were unable to place the charges then all his work would be for nothing. He followed the sea walls out of the Royal Navy Dockyards and entered the Great Sound. He kept as near to the shore as he could. There was a waiting fishing boat to pick him and the turtle up a quarter mile away. He kept turning the horizontal propeller and praying.

"Please, God, get me safely out of this machine so that I can see Rachael and the children once more before I die."

He found the fishing boat waiting and had cracked the hatch to crawl out when he heard the first giant explosion followed by two, then two more bangs.

"We had better get that turtle secured and towed back to Hamilton before the British figure out what happened here." Said Timothy Saunders.

An hour later, they were tied up beside the Caldwell sloop and began the loading process for the return to St. George. Sam left them to continue and walked to the US Conciliate Office across from the Government House in Hamilton.

"Reporting back, Sir." Sam said.

"You mean reporting in. I have no idea where you have been Sergeant Mason or what you may have done on your two week leave." I said with a smile.

"Are Tom and the Commander back?"

"No, they will ride the train back and it will take longer than your boat ride."

"I heard the explosion go off, Sir. I have no idea if blowing that deserted hulk did any good or not."

"We will be getting a report from our observers soon, Sam. Be patient and hope that the escorts are held up for repairs four to six weeks."

The next day we prepared and sent our messages on the outbound mail steamer to Washington.

TO: EYES ONLY PRESIDENT OF UNITED STATES
THROUGH: SECRETARY OF STATE SEWARD
FROM: JASON CALDWELL, NATIONAL AFFAIRS COMMITTEE
SUBJECT: DELAY OF ENGLISH NAVAL FLEET

IT HAS COME TO OUR ATTENTION THAT AN ACCIDENT HAS OCCURRED IN THE ROYAL NAVAL DOCKYARDS, NOVEMBER 17. A BRITISH PRISON HULK APPARENTLY EXPLODED FROM THE IGNITION OF METHANE GAS. NEARBY VESSELS WERE DAMAGED AND ARE NOW UNDER REPAIR. OF THE FORTY SHIPS IN THE INVASION FLEET, 4 TENDERS WERE DESTROYED BEYOND REPAIR, 8 SLOOPS ARE NOW IN ST. GEORGE HARBOR UNDER GOING REPAIRS BY THE CALDWELL SHIPPING COMPANY. THE CALDWELL COMPANY ASSURES ME THAT THE REPAIRS CANNOT BE MADE BEFORE SIX OR EIGHT WEEKS.

TWO ESCORT VESSELS ARE CURRENTLY UNDER REPAIR IN THE ROYAL NAVAL DOCKYARDS. BUT THIS WILL ALSO TAKE SOME TIME, SINCE THE DOCKYARDS ARE ALSO UNDER REPAIR. NUMEROUS FIRES WERE CAUSED BY FLYING DEBRIS FROM THE HULK. MOST WERE EXTINGUISHED IN A MATTER OF A FEW MINUTES BUT ONE COULD NOT BE BROUGHT UNDER CONTROL UNTIL IT HAD DESTROYED A REPAIR BAY AND SHIP'S HOIST. THE REPAIRS TO THE STEERAGE OF THE ESCORT VESSELS WILL NOW HAVE TO BE MADE BY "CAREENING" INSTEAD OF HOISTING THE VESSELS, THIS WILL CAUSE A DELAY IN THE REPAIR PROCESS.

It is the advice of this committee, that the actions that caused the formation of this fleet, be removed by the prompt release and return of the diplomats held in Boston. I would be available for the assignment of personal envoy to return the English diplomat in question. A letter, from the President, recognizing that he had been taken illegally would make my mission somewhat more palatable to the British. Awaiting your response

We also sent the following to the Confederate Embassy, Hamilton:

TO: Minister Butler
FROM: Minister Caldwell
SUBJECT: Disaster at Royal Naval Dockyards

Please be advised that repairs on eight of the vessels damaged on November 17, last, are currently underway at Caldwell Shipping Co., St. George Island, Bermuda. Docking space is also available for Confederate ships that would normally be repaired at the West End. I have informed my government that all repairs to the English vessels shall be made in a timely manner and that the holding of the Confederate diplomats would only bring further reprisals from Great Britain.

I proposed the diplomats being held in Boston be released to you and me. If it is agreed upon in principle, could you get permission to travel with me from Bermuda to Boston and then on to London via the port of South Hampton? Awaiting your response

It was now time to send a personal to Ben Hagood.

Ben,

Jason here, just wanted to let you know that the foreign group of travelers will be delayed. The two guard dogs are unable to proceed at this time. Estimates are a month to six weeks, if this time estimate changes, I will update you.

Jason.

The incoming mail had some interesting after action reports. They began with another account of a defeat for Union forces. The morning of the 7 th a group of 3000 Illinois volunteers under Colonel Grant floated down the Mississippi River in barges from their camp in Cairo. Here, Grant's forces met a smaller group of Confederates and they pushed them back down the river and into Belmont, Missouri. Here, they over ran the camp and started looting the Confederate supplies when they came under heavy artillery fire from a hill across the river. These troops were commanded by General Polk, a West Pointer. Now Grant was faced by twenty-seven hundred troops who began crossing the river toward him. The troops who he had temporarily pushed down the Mississippi turned and advanced. This caught Grant's outnumbered troops in a pincher movement. Grant ordered his troops to retreat to the barges for a quick return to Cairo. He was forced to leave his wounded and the captured Confederate supplies. Grant was fortunate to escape with his troops and his life. General Polk could see Grant and offered his sharp shooters $100.00 if they could bring him down. Grant dived into the bottom of the barge and hid from sight. Unconfirmed reports are that Colonel Grant was drunk at the time of the engagement.

"Well, at least Grant is willing to engage the enemy." Said Jerome Lewis as he read the report.

"Too bad he has to find courage in the bottom of a bottle." I replied.

"Maybe we should find out what he drinks and send a bottle to General McClellan." Jerome was smiling.

"Lincoln has said, 'One war at a time', maybe he is letting McClellan hide in Washington until all the east coast seaports are either captured or contained by blockades." I offered.

"The press likes to cover land battles, they do not like sea engagements. It is hard to send a telegram from a location at sea. The war will be won by which side has the most effective Navy. So far, we control the sea lanes everywhere. The rivers are another matter. Lincoln should let Grant clear the Mississippi and Ohio rivers of all Confederate forts and gun boats. I like Grant, he goes to battle in barges or gun boats, he is really a marine in disguise!" Jerome was laughing now.

"You may have something there, Jerome, Firm it up and I will let you send it off as an official suggestion from the committee, which reminds me I must send out some missives for the rest of the committee to read, agree with or vote no. I am heading to my office to construct the first set of letters to be sent on the next mail steamer. If you need me, you know where to find me."

The committee members were all captains of industry or financial firms in the northern United States. President Lincoln had written to each and asked for their service for one year. Those that accepted became my committee list. Because they were located across the country, I wrote whenever I needed to bring matters to their attention. I took out the list and began to write the letters to the following:

Asa Parker Mansion
122 Penn ave.
Scranton, Pennsylvania

John Nesbitt
1311 Redwood Way
Sacramento, California

Henry Huttleson Rogers
One Wildon Lane
Titusville, Pennsylvania

John Peirpoint Morgan
550 Park Ave.
New York, New York

Henry Brooks Adams
1100 Commonwealth Ave.
Boston, Massachuttes

Amos J. Stillwell
22 Post Fort Road
Des Moines, Iowa

George Hiles   Wisconsin
349 Elm Street
Madison, Wisconsin

Simeon Brock
1101 High Street
Camden, Maine

Isaac Norris
11 Cardinal Gannon Street
Erie, Pennsylvania

J. Caldwell, Chairman
Seneca Hill
Titusville, Pennsylvania

The letters would all be the same and I began to put my thoughts into writing:

November 18, 1861

Committee member name
Street Address
City and State

Dear _____,

It is time again to convene our committee by mail. In the near future, I am hoping that the President will find the time to sit down with us in the White House. The committee can reach Washington by train with the exception of John Nesbitt and myself. We will need some advanced notice in order to plan an ocean voyage. If an emergency meeting is ever called, I will send my proxy via Admiral Hagood of the Army Navy Building. John, if you could select a proxy also, that might be helpful.

The matter to report today is the progress towards the solution of the Trent Affair. The British fleet to remove the blockades of Charleston and Norfolk has been held in Bermuda for the next six to eight weeks. I have requested that Minister Murray be released to me for transport to London. This half baked idea of detaining Confederate Diplomats has caused a great deal of strain on US Navy resources. We have only 42 ships at the present time to maintain the blockade of the southeastern coast line. The gulf effort is progressing, but the number of Confederate ships outnumber us in this region. We should recommend to the President the following:

1. Promote US Grant to Brigadier.
2. Order him to engage all Confederate forts along the Ohio, Tennessee and Mississippi Rivers.
3. Recruit US Marines to serve on Grant's barges and gun boats.

I was about to finish the form letter when Jerome stuck his head through my office door and said, "Your family is here to see you, Minister."

"Tell them I am on my way out!"

Louise, James and Ruth had brought everyone to Hamilton shopping. My father was insistent that he needed a suit of clothes. Mother had shopped in St. George with Laura and Louise and had found most of the things that she needed or wanted. We all walked down to front street so that father could either buy off the rack at Trimminghams or get measured at a tailors shop. Trey and Marriann and the three children tried to buy Trimminghams out of stock. I was happy to see everyone enjoying their time together. Louise said, "What is the matter, Jason?"

"Trey, Louise and I are going upstairs to the tea room here at Trimminghams. Can you or Mariann watch James and Ruth?"

"Mariann will take them with the girls to try on dresses."

"None for James, please!"

When we reached the third floor, we slipped behind chairs and ordered a pot of tea. "I may have to go to London, Louise. I would like you to go with me."

"Can the children go, too?" She asked.

"Let me tell you what it is about, then you can decide. I think that President Lincoln is going to release the Confederate Diplomats held in Boston."

"He is going to release them to you, if you agree to take them to London, is that it?"

"Exactly, he has written a letter of apology to Queen Victoria and he wants it hand delivered by someone she has met and trusts. I can answer any questions she might have."

"How are you going to get them?"

"I think Ben will send a steam powered sloop or larger vessel if he can find one not doing blockade duty. He will pick us up in Bermuda, return to Boston, pickup the diplomats and then head for South Hampton."

"Could you change his mind?"

"About what?"

"I would like for the whole family to leave Bermuda in the Cold Harbor and sail to Boston. Your family needs to feel like they are not trapped on this island. Your Mother and Father can really shop in style. James and Ruth can stay in Boston with Trey's family or with Grandma and Grandpa. I will write to my brother at Wheatland and see if he can come to Boston by train and meet us. I think he would like to go to London again. He could even smooth over some of the rough spots created by that Republican in the White House."

"No wonder I married you, Louise. This can be our December Christmas presents to each other. I missed last Christmas by being away for your brother. If we can work out the details, I would enjoy this very much." I bent over and kissed her on the lips.

"Jason, control yourself, we are in public!" But she was giggling again like she always did.

We returned to the Caldwell family shoppers and my father announced, "We have way too many packages to get on a train. Let me hire a carriage and a wagon to get us back home."

"Home, father?"

"Yes, Jason, this is home now. My family around me and a wonderful climate to live in. What more could a man ask for?"

"How about a shopping spree to Boston?" I asked.

"Jason Caldwell, do not tease about something like that!" My mother said.

"I am not kidding, I may be sent to Boston on business and there is plenty of room in the Cold Harbor for any Caldwell who would like to tag along."

"Would we spend December in Boston?" My father asked. "No thanks, on that one."

"Oh, Robert Caldwell, you are such an old fuddy duddy. Think, snow for Christmas!" Mother said. Everyone began to talk at once. "Wait, wait. I do not even know that I am going. I will find out as soon as the mail steamer gets back from Washington."

"When will that be?" Mariann said. "I have lots more things to buy before I get on another ship!" Everyone laughed as my father returned with a carriage and drivers in tow. "Children do you want to ride in the wagon with the old 'fuddy duddy'?" They piled in around the packages and Grandpa sat next to the driver. The adults climbed into the carriage and we headed for home.

67

Solution of Trent Affair
Bermuda Station

The next day in Hamilton the mail pouch came into the office and we opened and read the following:

> TO: JASON CALDWELL, NATIONAL AFFAIRS COMMITTEE
> FROM: SECRETARY SEWARD
> SUBJECT: RECEIPT OF EYES ONLY PRESIDENT

THE WHITE HOUSE APPROVES YOUR PLAN TO RETURN MINISTERS MURRAY AND SLIDELL. YOU WILL PROCEED TO BOSTON TO MEET ADMIRAL HAGOOD AT YOUR EARLIEST CONVENIENCE. ADMIRAL HAGOOD WILL PASS TO YOU A LETTER FROM THE PRESIDENT TO THE QUEEN. USS INTREPID RELEASED FROM BLOCKADE DUTY TO TRANSPORT DIPLOMATS TO LONDON AND PARIS.

A TRANSATLANTIC CABLE SENT THIS DATE TO THE QUEEN INFORMING HER OF YOUR ARRIVAL AT SOUTH HAMPTON. COPY ATTACHED.

In the regular mail pouch we received the following personal from Ben Hagood.

Jason,

Ben here, got your inquiry about meeting in Boston. Sounds good to me. I will be traveling with you so I can eat humble pie for the one who approved the snatch of the diplomats. I am to personally apologize to Lord Naiper for the Trent Affair. See you in a few days. Oh, I have been asked to request that you bring your formal naval uniform in as much as the President has been granted permission from the US Senate to give you a third star.

> *Ben*

I stood looking at the personal and laughing. "Ben is up to his old tricks again, Jerome. He thinks I will fall for that old trick?"

"I do not think so Admiral, here is a message from the Army Navy Building with a copy of the resolution from the Senate. It says for meritorious service to the Navy on November 17, 1861, you are hereby promoted to Vice

Admiral, in the United States Naval Reserve on Presidential assignment in Bermuda. It does not say you are retired. This means you are now back in the Navy! Congratulations, Sir."

"Congratulations, my ass. Lincoln did an end run on me. I will write and process my retirement papers again if necessary."

"I think the President is trying to protect you on the trip to England, Sir. If you traveled as a diplomat the Queen might hold you like Lincoln held her diplomat. But holding a Vice Admiral and a Fleet Admiral, like Ben Hagood, would be next to impossible."

"I will think about that, Jerome. But returning to active service is out of the question. I will not raise a hand against my native state."

The next day, I sent the following information to the Army Navy Building.

> TO: FLEET ADMIRAL HAGOOD, ARMY NAVY BUILDING
> FROM: CHAIRMAN NATIONAL AFFAIRS COMMITTEE
> SUBJECT: COMMISSION IN UNITED STATES NAVY
>
> AS A VOLUNTARY MEMBER OF THE STATE DEPARTMENT, I THANK THE SENATE FOR THE VICE ADMIRAL TITLE. WOULD YOU PLEASE PASS MY APPRECIATION TO THE SECRETARY OF THE NAVY AND HAVE HIM BRING TO THE ATTENTION OF THE PRESIDENT THAT I AM A RETIRED ADMIRAL. I AM NOT A MEMBER OF THE RESERVE. IF A MISTAKE HAS BEEN MADE, THEN I HEREBY RETIRE AGAIN FROM THE NAVY.
>
> MY CHAIRMANSHIP DUTIES FOR THE PRESIDENT ENDS AT THE END OF THE WAR, AND I LOOK FORWARD TO RETURNING TO PRIVATE LIFE AND TO BEING THE FULL TIME CHAIRMAN OF THE BOARD FOR CALDWELL INTERNATIONAL.
>
> JASON EDWIN CALDWELL, ADMIRAL, USN RETIRED

I left the office early to return to St. George. Had I done the right thing? I thought. What role was I playing in the civil war that was tearing families apart? I had used my best judgement on not violating my oath as an officer in the United States Navy when I was on active duty. Now that I was retired, how did I feel? The train stopped in St. George and I was still pondering the thoughts as I walked up Rose Hill and into the front doors of Caldwell Place. There was not a sound of any kind in the office wing, everything was closed and locked, that was strange. I headed to the main dining room to find the entire extended family sitting around a large table, tears streaming down their faces.

"What happened?" I asked.

"Oh, Jason, your father just got a letter from Beaufort. Your sister, Carl and the children have been killed."

"Killed? What happened?"

"Carl was assigned to Fort Beauregard. It was bombarded by the Navy Warships when they invaded Port Royal. All the Fort's Officers and families were killed when their living quarters were hit by heavy mortar fire."

I held Louise for a long time and wept. I looked over at my father and brother and said, "Thank God, you came to us." They both could not speak, they just nodded their heads in agreement.

68

Christmas in Boston
December, 1861

Christmas is a special time of year, a time for family gathering and celebration. This year the death of my sister and her family hung like a cloud over the rest of us. My father and mother said they would like to stay in St. Davids for Christmas. Trey and Mariann said they did not feel like going anywhere either. They would like James and Ruth to celebrate with them while Louise and I were gone to Boston for a few days. I suggested that the Whitehalls and Caldwells move into the Inn so they could all be together and they agreed. My father pulled me aside and said, "Please do not go to Europe, come back to Bermuda when your business is finished in Boston."

"I will make the necessary arrangements with the White House, do not tell anyone this yet, but Louise and I will try to be here for Christmas, if we can."

"Thank you, son!" He held me close and it reminded me of James Buchanan's embrace in the parlor at 353 Bay Street. Another time and another place, ages ago, it seemed now. Louise had not written to her brother, she would instead take a train from Boston to Wheatland if things took more than a few days to accomplish. I contacted Captain Jacob of the *Cold Harbor* to see what day he could leave St. George. He indicated that it was now December and anytime would be fine with him. I told him to prepare to leave in two days and returned to Caldwell Place and told Louise to pack. I needed to get on into Hamilton and send off the mail for the White House and Army Navy Building.

"Jason, are you all right, you look pale?"

"Yes, I have been fighting with myself about a decision that I must make." I left her to pack and I boarded the train for Hamilton. It arrived an hour later and I walked to my Office to visit with Jerome Lewis.

"Jerome, I have made a decision. You were right. It does not matter if I am a member of the US Navy Reserve or not. The task that I have undertaken requires me to function as a three star Vice Admiral on active duty. I cannot continue to walk a fine line between serving the country that I love and not harming the State where I was born. All that changed with the invasion of Port Royal and the deaths of my family members. I advised the President to invade each seaport and harbor along the southeastern coast. Her death was caused by my advice and recommendations."

"Admiral, on November 7, 1861, Captain Samuel Dupont caused the deaths of your family by ordering the attacks on Fort Walker and Beauregard. You are not to blame for the deaths of anyone. I cannot remember a time that you ordered anyone killed, it is not in your nature to do so. You, cannot take the responsibility of your sister's death, Sir. It will destroy you."

"Maybe you are right, Jerome, but the way I feel now, I cannot ever set foot in Beaufort again."

"Admiral, you need some time off, go to Boston. Let me write the communications for the mail pouch and you can read and sign them. Do you still want me to be acting minister to Bermuda in your absence?"

"I have thought about this some, Jerome, you are ready for a promotion. How would you like to be an Admiral's Aide, Captain Lewis?"

"Captain? Admiral's Aide? Are you out of your mind, Sir? I am a policeman!"

"That was a long time ago, Jerome, you have been my aide for a year now. Let us get the paperwork off to Washington." I signed and we sent the following:

TO: SECRETARY OF STATE SEWARD, WHITE HOUSE
FROM: ADMIRAL JASON CALDWELL, BERMUDA
SUBJECT: CHANGE FOR MINISTERS MURRAY AND SLIDELL

DUE TO DEATHS IN MY FAMILY, I WILL BE UNABLE TO ACCOMPANY ADMIRAL HAGOOD IN HIS DELIVERY OF MINISTERS MURRAY AND SLIDELL TO THEIR POSTS. I WOULD LIKE YOUR PERMISSION TO RETURN THEM TO BERMUDA WITH ME. MINISTER BUTLER, HERE IN BERMUDA, IS UNDERSECRETARY FOR GREAT BRITAIN AND WILL ACCEPT THEIR RELEASE. HE WILL THEN INFORM LONDON AND PARIS OF THE TRANSPORTATION ARRANGEMENTS TO THEIR POSTS. THIS IS CONSIDERABLY EASIER THAN TAKING NEEDED SHIPS FROM THE BLOCKADE EFFORT IN ORDER TO TAKE TWO PEOPLE TO EUROPE. AWAITING YOUR RESPONSE

TO: SECRETARY WELLES, ARMY NAVY BUILDING
FROM: ADMIRAL JASON CALDWELL, BERMUDA
SUBJECT: PROMOTION OF COMMANDER JEROME LEWIS

PLEASE DISREGARD ANY COMMUNICATION THAT YOU MAY HAVE HAD WITH FLEET ADMIRAL HAGOOD. I AM DELIGHTED TO RECEIVE MY THIRD STAR. IN THAT REGARD, I WOULD LIKE TO NAME COMMANDER JEROME LEWIS AS

MY AIDE. THE PROBLEM IS THE RANK OF LEWIS. HE IS A COMMANDER AND MOST ADMIRALS HAVE A CAPTAIN AS THEIR AIDE. HE HAS SERVED IN THAT CAPACITY FOR OVER A YEAR AND DESERVES PROMOTION. I HAVE NAMED CAPTAIN JEROME LEWIS AS MY AIDE EFFECTIVE TODAY.

> TO: ABRAHAM LINCOLN, PRESIDENT, UNITED STATES
> FROM: ADMIRAL JASON CALDWELL
> SUBJECT: CHANGE ON THE NATIONAL AFFAIRS COMMITTEE

I REGRET TO INFORM YOU OF THE DEATH OF JOHN NESBITT IN CALIFORNIA. YOU SHOULD CONSIDER A REPLACEMENT BEFORE WE MEET IN WASHINGTON. BY THIS TIME, I AM SURE THAT YOU HAVE BEEN NOTIFIED OF MY ACCEPTANCE BACK INTO THE USN RESERVES BY SECRETARY WELLES. I HOPE THAT THIS PROMOTION WILL NOT AFFECT MY SERVICE TO SECRETARY SEWARD IN THE STATE DEPARTMENT. IN TIMES OF WAR, AN OVERLAP IN SERVICE CAN SOMETIMES BE HELPFUL.

IN ANY REGARD, I LOOK FORWARD TO YOUR ASSIGNMENT AND I SERVE AT YOUR PLEASURE. YOU HAVE MY FULL AND UNDIVIDED SUPPORT OF THE WAR EFFORTS MADE TO THIS DATE.

I left Jerome with the mail and walked to the C. S. A. Embassy. I rang the bell and a woman answered the door. "Is Minister Butler in?" I asked.

"Yes, who shall I say is calling?"

"Admiral Caldwell."

"Jason, I am so sorry to hear about your sister and her family." John Butler greeted me with a genuine sadness in his eyes.

"Thank you, John. Do you have news of what has happened in Beaufort? We have had only the one letter informing us of the deaths."

"Yes, come in and I will tell you what I know." He handed me a letter from his aunt in Beaufort.

November 12, 1861

Dear JB,

I have some terrible news from Beaufort. It was overrun and captured by Yankees. General Dunavent's regiment was camped between Port Royal and town. They could hear the heavy mortar rounds explode in the water. Every man under sixty was asked to go to the two forts, Walker and Beauregard. Some of the officers took their wives and families with them thinking they would be safer there than at home in Port Royal. A terrible tragedy occurred at Beauregard when the one of the war ships hit an officer's quarters and destroyed the building and everyone inside.

Most of Dunavent's men survived but the folks in Beauregard were never found. A few body parts were buried in the Port Royal cemetery yesterday. The marker just says defenders of Fort Beauregard. The next day, the war ships came on high tide and are now tied up in Beaufort opposite Bay Street. Several of the Caldwell Mansions have been seized under the Confiscation Act. A general is living in one and rest are hospitals for Union wounded.

I did not read any more of the letter, I thanked him and said, "I will be leaving in two days to bring Minister Murray and Slidell to your embassy. Will you accept their unconditional release?"

"Of course, Jason. How are you getting to Boston?"

"I will use a Caldwell ship, probably the Cold Harbor. There are no USS ships available, they are all active on the blockade of C S A harbors, as you well know. They have not stopped the faster C S A ships that you have been building in Florida. I hope that you can continue to carry mail pouches to Norfolk and then to Richmond, John. I am so sorry that this war will be one of blockades, fort seizures and starvation. No one should have to suffer for politician stupidity."

"I could not agree more, Jason. I no longer think the war will be won in a year or two by the C S A. There will be no winners, only those that lose, less."

"Well put, John. You are becoming a diplomat instead of an army general."

"Not a diplomat, Jason, only a realist."

"Do not let Murray hear you say that, John. He is bound to be angry over his illegal detention in Boston and he will want revenge."

"Yes, I do not envy the trip back to Bermuda with him bending your ear. Could I be of any assistance to you on the voyage up or back?"

"I think that would be a very good idea, John. That way the newspapers will report that they were released to a C S A representative in Boston. I can stay in the background."

"What is the date and time of sailing, I will be on the docks in St. George, an hour before."

"I will have my aide drop off a note to you, John."

I left John Butler with a better feeling than I had felt for several days and I realized that it was talking to someone from home that made me feel that way. The war would rage on, but people you knew would remain the same or disappear from your life forever. I realized that my function for the US Government would be one of trying to shorten the war wherever possible.

We left St. George Harbor on December 12, 1861, and headed north by northwest until the windy weather drove us below decks and into our cabins. Louise and I were in the captains quarters below the poop deck. The captain had moved to the first mates cabin off the quarter deck, the first mate bumped the tiller's mate and so on. John Butler was given the guest cabin under the forecastle deck. It was a two day trip by steamer, but the Cold Harbor was built in 1797 and it was a sailing vessel from times past. It was quiet on deck, only the sound of wind in the sails. Louise and I bundled up in coats and sat in deck chairs and just enjoyed the time alone.

We entered Boston Harbor on December seventeenth. We were met by a representative of the Navy, a Commander Whitsill. He saluted sharply and then handed me a garment bag that he had carried down to the docks. "A present from Admiral Hagood with his compliments, Sir. He would like you to wear this during the handing over ceremony."

"There is going to be a ceremony?"

"You know the Navy, Sir. I will wait for you to change before I escort you and General Butler off your ship, Sir."

I returned to our cabin and said, "A present from Ben Hagood."

"What is it, Jason?"

"Probably a joke, knowing Ben." I pulled the garment bag open and there was a brand new dress uniform for a Vice Admiral. "So much for staying in the background."

"Put it on, I want to see how you look, Admiral. Can I see your 'rear', admiral?"

"Not anymore, my 'rear' has been promoted to 'vice'".

Twenty minutes later, I was top side and found the Commander and John Butler. Butler smiled and said, "You look splendid with three stars on your shoulder, Jason. I would have worn my one star if I had known this was a masquerade party." He was smiling from ear to ear.

"This is not my idea, General. A friend of mine is returning a favor, when he got his first star, Louise took him to a tailor and had a dress uniform made for him. He has waited a long time for this."

"You deserve to be recognized for your service to your country, Jason."

"Thank you, John. So do you!"

"Where are you taking us, Commander Whitsill?" John Butler asked.

"To Boston General Hospital, Sir."

"To a hospital?"

"Yes, Sir. Both men are ready to be released, all you have to do is sign them out."

"Good, I want to be home for Christmas not stuck in Boston, God Damn, Massachusetts." He said.

The Commander led the way and we left the ship and got into a carriage headed for Boston General Hospital. The newspaper reporters were everywhere when we arrived and stepped out of the carriage. They all asked questions at the same time. I said nothing while John Butler was in his element, he answered questions in a direct way. He said he was the representative sent by President Davis. Yes, they would be released today. No, the foreign ministers were not spies, they were on their way to London and Paris. Yes, it had been nearly two months since they were detained.. No, he did not know when the ministers would arrive in London.

We broke away from the reporters and headed into patient receiving. Here we met a doctor who took us to the mental ward. We passed through locked doors and into a hallway marked 'patient holding'. There sat David Slidell and James Murray. Murray jumped to his feet and ran to Butler and hugged him.

"John, you have finally come to rescue me from this hell hole of a place!"

"Actually, Admiral Caldwell here rescued you. I am here to accept your release and to certify that you have been well cared for." Murray was about to moan and complain again when David Slidell rose to his feet and said, "Admiral Caldwell, on behalf of the Confederate States of America's, Paris Embassy, I thank you."

"You are most welcome, Minister Slidell. On behalf of my government, I apologize for any mistreatment that may have befallen you. Commander, the ambassadors have luggage, you will fetch it for them."

"But, Sir. The handing over ceremony is to be ....."

"There will be no 'handing over ceremony', Commander. These two men are foreign diplomats, not criminals."

"I do not know, Sir. I have my orders."

"Were they given to you by a three star Admiral commissioned before 1837?"

"No, Sir."

"Then my orders stand, ya hear?" I realized that the madder I got the more pronounced my southern accent became. John Butler had a grin on his face.

"But, Sir, the reporters."

"General Butler here is an expert on handling reporters. Doctor, do have anything for the General to sign before we leave?"

"No, Sir."

"Good, then we are on our way back south. Commander, find the bags and meet us on the docks."

The four of us walked out of the mental ward, through the hospital patient receiving and out the front doors. I did not look back, the carriage was still waiting, we got in and started for the docks.

"I was kidding about getting home for Christmas, Jason."

"I think that is a very good idea, John. I cannot abide fools or the messes that they create."

Neither Murray or Slidell had said a thing until James Murray said, "Admiral, were you a captain in the Army Navy building when David and I were in the Senate?"

"Yes, Sir. I was. Navy Intelligence."

"Do you have any idea why we were detained, Admiral?"

"Not a clue, Ambassador. All I know is that I was given the job of cleaning up the mess."

"Sometimes you have to create a mess in order to cleanup another. Right Admiral?"

I glanced over at John and said, "I did not give any orders to destroy any British property anywhere in the last year, General."

"Well, orders or no, it worked and I thank you on behalf of President Davis."

"As one South Carolinian to another, John, you can report to your President that Jason Caldwell will never raise a hand against his native state. That is more than I can say for the United States Navy."

We were now on the docks and in a few minutes, Commander Whitsill appeared with two very large suitcases. We walked up the gangway and I shouted to Captain Jacob, "Permission to come aboard captain?"

"Permission granted captain."

"He called you 'captain', Admiral." Murray said.

"That is correct, I own this vessel. It is part of my commercial fleet. I was a ship's captain long before I was a captain in the Navy. Captain Jacob there trained under me when I was his captain and he still thinks of me as his captain."

"Oh, that, Caldwell." I could hear the items falling into place for Murray.

"Gentlemen, we will be getting underway shortly. I will have your bags taken to your cabins, they are next to General Butler's. You might want to refresh yourselves before dinner, it will be at six

bells." I walked away towards the captain's cabin to find Louise.

"What happened? Why are you back so soon?"

"Every thing was in order and we came right back here to avoid newspaper reporters and so that I could get out of this monkey suit."

"Oh, Jason. You look so good in that uniform."

"I bet you say that to all the sailors you meet!"

"Just the ones I find in the White House."

"We have had quite a marriage, my love, I was lucky to find you!"

"I feel the same way, Jason."

"What would you like for dinner? I told the three gentlemen to expect a light supper at six bells. I am on my way to Hop Sing and give him the dinner order."

"Tell him no onions!"

"Very good. When I return, we can go topside and see the lights of Boston, it is getting dark."

"The lights of Boston?"

"Yes, I have been told that they have gas lamps throughout the city, just like London. Did you find the gas lamps in London interesting when you were there with your brother? You had better bundle up, it is getting cold."

I left the cabin and headed for the galley where I would find our Chinese cook, Hop Sing. The captain's cabin is at the aft and the galley on the *Cold Harbor* was down one deck and behind the fore mast. I found Hop Sing and asked him if he had found anything in Boston Harbor that was fresh.

"Yes, Captain, I found plenty of sea food for sale right on the docks."

"Did you find any shrimp or lobster?"

"Yes, captain, I got plenty of both."

"We have two additional guests for dinner at six bells, can you prepare one of your famous shrimp and lobster dishes?"

"In the main salon, Captain? At six bells. It will be done, Sir."

"Thank you, Hop Sing. You are a wonder, I can always count on you to impress my guests."

He was beaming as I left the galley and looked for Louise on the topside. I found her talking with James Murray and David Slidell. They had been viewing the street lamps glowing throughout the city of Boston. "Can anyone join the viewing?"

"Hello, darling, I was just telling the Ambassadors that I spent several years in both London and Paris and the lights of Boston can surely compare. Did you know Ambassador Slidell can speak French?"

"No, I did not. Louise can speak excellent English, not like mine, Russian and French. I feel like my military education was lacking when they did not give us at least Spanish. I needed that during the last war."

"You were in the Mexican War, Admiral. I did not know that." James Murray said.

"Yes, I was a Fleet Admiral's aide in the Gulf of Mexico. That seems a life time ago, now. What did you do in the last war, Ambassador?"

"I was elected to the House of Representatives and that way I missed the war altogether. I wished I had served, I heard Winfield Scott was something of a genius."

"He still is, Lincoln should keep him as an advisor. He is so angry at being forced to retire, he will not be of any help to the President."

"Scott's been replaced?"

"Yes, that happened when you were detained, Ambassadors. That is news to you, I forgot."

"Gentlemen, if you will escort me to the main salon, I would be most grateful, it is getting cold up here. Jason has refurbished the *Cold Harbor* after it was built in 1797. He had the Stern Galleries converted to large dining room. The deck to overhead windows provide a magnificent view from astern. We can continue to enjoy the light of the city and have warm drinks if you like."

"Mrs. Caldwell, allow me." David Slidell offered his arm and they walked ahead of us. We went down one deck and knocked on John Butler's cabin door. He joined us and we found our way aft. The main salon was warm, out of the slight breeze, and the window wall was aglow from the city lights. The ships bell began to toll, it stopped at six. Hop Sing threw open a side door and stepped into the salon and said, "Captain, the seafood surprise is ready to be served."

"Thank you, Hop Sing, we may proceed. Would you ask one of the cabin stewards to come in and take the drink orders?"

"As you wish, Captain." He disappeared and a young man in a starched white uniform appeared with a pad and a pen.

"Ma'am, what you like before dinner?"

"A white wine with dinner, please, for now bring me a hot chocolate!"

"Ambassador Slidell?"

"The same, thank you."

"Ambassador Murray?"

"That would be wonderful!"

"Ambassador Butler?"

"I hate to be different but could I have some southern comfort?" The cabin steward looked at me for guidance.

"That would be some my finest sipping bourbon. I will have the same, Won Sing."

"Jason, I am beginning to like you more and more. When you arrested me, I thought you were the devil himself."

"Well, John, I was supposed to put the fear of God into you so that you would not fire on Fort Sumter 'till I was out of the White House." We both laughed as the drinks were rolled in on a cart and handed to us. "Louise, will you show us the seating for dinner? We do not want Hop Sing's special to get cold."

The *Cold Harbor* was still tied to the Boston Docks as we feasted on a culinary delight known as the 'Hop Sing Special'. It was a five course affair, equal to anything I had ever eaten in the White House. After dinner I asked John Butler if he had arranged for the London and Paris trips. He replied, "Yes, Jason, I have and I want to warn these two gentlemen on my right that the food on a British mail steamer is nothing like this!" Everyone laughed and I said, "Yes, my family found Hop Sing and his family stranded in Charleston a number of years ago. Now they are part of the crew of the *Cold Harbor*, my father likes his creature comforts, so we remodeled the entire ship for family business use only. It really should be replaced with a steamer, but the romance of travel will be lost. I will use a steamer if speed is essential, otherwise, I like the quiet of a sailboat and the safety of the last century Snow Architecture."

"You lost me there, Jason, I am a general, a real land lubber, what is a Snow?"

"I wish our son, James, were here General Butler, he and Jason play a game of Revolutionary War ship identification." Louise said.

"Yes, I know, Jason and I have already played that game, that is how we identified the *San Jacinto*."

"Now all the rest of us are lost." Louise countered.

"Right after the Trent Affair began, I drew an outline of the Sloop that stopped us."

"The Trent Affair?" Both Slidell and Murray said.

"Yes, that is what the newspapers called your detentions, you are both famous." John Butler reached into his breast coat pocket and took out a folded newspaper article from The Boston Globe, he began to read:

Captain C. Wilkes commander of the scientific expedition around the world in 1842 to 1843, and now captain of the USS San Jacinto recalls the arrest and detention of commissioners James M. Murray and J. David Slidell. My orders were to intercept the Theodora on route to Cuba from Charleston. I waited for the intercept, but by the 26 th of October, I realized that I had missed them. I then went into Cuba for a re-supply of coal and learned that Messrs. Slidell and Murray, with their secretaries and families, would depart on the 7 th of November in the English steamer Trent for Bermuda on their way to England.

"I made up my mind to leave Havana and find a suitable position. On the morning of the 8 th, her smoke was first seen; at 12 our position was to the westward. We beat to quarters and orders were given to Lieutenant Fairfax to have two boats manned and ready to board her. He was to take Messrs. Slidell, Murray, and Butler prisoners and send them immediately aboard."

"The steamer approached and hoisted English colors. Our emblem was hoisted and a warning shot fired across her bow. She maintained her speed and showed no disposition to heave to. Then I fired another shot and this brought her to. I hailed that I intended to send a boat to board and Lieutenant Fairfax, with his armed men in two boats left to do so. The captain of the steamer declined to show his papers and passenger-list, force became necessary. Messrs. Slidell and Murray were located, but Butler was not found. Their wives were offered my cabin on the San Jacinto, but they refused and remained on the Trent. They and their luggage were then taken aboard. The Trent was suffered to proceed on her way to Bermuda.

It was my intension to take possession of the Trent and tow her to Key West as a prize for resisting the search and carrying these passengers, who had no federal identification, no passports. But the large number of passengers on board bound for Europe, who would be put to great inconvenience, decided me to allow them to proceed to Bermuda. We then proceeded to Hampton Roads and after taking on more coal and reporting to the Navy Department, I continued on to Boston. I handed over the prisoners to the commandant of Fort Warren."

"We really have been out of touch What else has happened?" Slidell said.

"I can fill you in on the Union side, if John will give you the Confederate."

"Everything that I have is either classified, or of no great importance. But I would love to know what the Union side thinks is important the last two months."

I laughed and began a run down of all the defeats for the Army of the Potomac. I did not mention the actions of the United States Navy and Marines in South Carolina because John Butler had the same sadness in his eyes and a pained look on his face. I finished with, "And that is all I know about current events in the last two months." As the last word came out of my mouth, I could feel the ship start to pull away from the docks.

"Gentlemen, we have a begun our trip south. Everyone and everything on the *Cold Harbor* is at your call. If you need anything during the night, there is a steward on duty, just pull your bell cord and he will answer. Until then, you are free to move about the ship. She is 175 feet long and 40 feet in beam so you will not get very far if you like to walk and explore. The lower holds are for cargo we have unloaded some in Boston and some remains. Above that are two passage ways in which you can barely stand. It is a working space for ropes, metal cables, capstans, tiers, winches and what not. It is definitely not a place for dress clothes. There are two main decks above that and you are welcome to explore anywhere you like. Meals can be brought to your cabin or you can eat with Louise and me here in the main salon. The meals are plain, not fancy like tonight, there is also a crew salon, where you will find coffee and snacks nearly any time of the day or night."

"Louise, have I missed anything that they should know?"

"Only that Captain Jacob is really in charge, not my husband. If he gives you an order, it is for your safety and well being, follow it explicitly. That was really hard for me to understand when I first sailed on the *Cold Harbor*." She said with a smile. "The *Cold Harbor* is the safest ship I have ever traveled on and it will get us home even through a hurricane."

"Louise, we need to give these Confederates some time alone to get caught up with what they have missed in last two months. Good night, gentlemen."

We retired to our cabin and Louise said, "What did you think of David Slidell, he is an interesting man."

"Stay away from him, he probably pinches!"

"His French is better than mine and I do not think he is from New Orleans as he claimed. Can you find out more about him, Jason. He may be a Yankee spy."

"Oh, Louise, you are as bad as John Butler, that is what he thinks."

"He does? What do you think James Murray thinks?"

"James Murray only thinks about James Murray." I said with a smile.

The next morning we did not see our three guests in the main salon. Noon came and went and still no sign of them. "Do you think we should go to their cabins and check to see if they are alright?"Louise asked.

"I will have one of the stewards knock and say he wants to change the bed linen, he will report back if anything is a miss."

In a few minutes the steward returned and said all three were sound a sleep. " They look healthy, they rolled over when I opened the cabin door but did not awake."

"Thank you, Won Sing."

"Jason?"

"Yes, Louise?"

"Why not go back to our bed and change our linens?"

Sea air always had this affect on Louise and I made a mental note to sail with her more often. We awoke in the middle of the afternoon, got dressed and took a walk on the open decks. We stood by the Hammock Rail and gazed out to sea. "Jason, do you think we will always be in love?"

"It took us thirty-eight years to meet, and a year to get to know each other. We got married at sea. We had our honeymoon aboard ship. I think if I can keep you at sea we will last fifty years. What do you think?"

"I think fifty-five!" She stood close and I wrapped my great coat around both of us. "Jason, do you want to have another child?"

"We can see if we can find a children's home in Bermuda, if you like."

"We will not need a children's home, Jason."

"Why not? Do you want to get a child from Pennsylvania?"

"No, we will get it from me! I want to call her Carol."

"And if it is a boy, we will call him Carl."

69
Lincoln's Council of War
January, 1862

On January 11, 1862, President Lincoln contacted his National Affairs Committee and requested that they meet with him in the White House. Jason thought that the President had finally decided to meet the committee in person, instead of dealing with only him through the State Department. He was wrong. Three days earlier a group of Republican Senators had met with him in the White House. They were critical of Lincoln's conciliatory manner toward the seceded states of the South. In particular, they doubted that General McClellan was the correct choice for General-in-chief. He was a democrat, he had a slow pace in moving across the Potomac, and he was unconcerned about the defeats at Bull Run and Ball's Bluff. They indicated that Lincoln's assumption of dictatorial powers and the arrest of Maryland citizens was un-American. They told him that they saw no choice but to provide a Congressional Joint Committee on the Conduct of the War, to oversee the president to root out corruption and inefficiency in the Union Army and Navy.

Lincoln indicated that such a committee already existed, would they like to join the National Affairs Committee? They indicated that they would like to appoint three nonvoting members for coordination with their committee. Lincoln said that would be alright if he could appoint nonvoting members from the National Affairs Committee for coordination, also. It was agreed that Franklin Wade would serve as Chairman, Joint Committee and nonvoting member of Jason Caldwell's Committee. Zachariah Chandler and George Julian would also serve. Lincoln appointed Jason Caldwell, JP Morgan and John Nesbitt, who he had forgotten was deceased and he had not yet been replaced.

When Jason Caldwell received this information in the diplomatic pouch, he wrote to the Secretary of State, Seward. He explained that he would not accept the three members of the Joint Congressional Committee, as oversight to his committee. His committee reported directly to the President and he would resign before he accepted them. He also indicated that he would poll his committee, but he doubted anyone would want to serve with or on a Congressional Oversight Committee. He also suggested that the President ignore the committee and get on with the prosecution of the war. He further

351

stated that the so called corruption of the war department could be solved by the removal of the Secretary of War, Simon Cameron. "He would make an excellent Ambassador to Moscow!" wrote Admiral Caldwell on January 17, 1862. "It is also time for the President to decide how he wants to divide and conquer the Confederacy. The fastest way to end the war is to split the Confederacy into two parts. The western commander should seize the Mississippi River and all the forts along it. New Orleans should be taken by the Navy. The Navy should supply gun boats and marines for the western commander. The most capable General for this, is US Grant."

"My committee has suggested that the eastern commander should cross the Potomac and march toward Richmond. If Richmond is taken, then the Confederacy will have to move its capital and the government will be thrown into confusion. The committee, also suggests, that the General-in-chief should not be the eastern commander. If General McClellan is unable or unwilling to accept direction from the Commander-in-chief of the Armed Forces he should be replaced with someone who understands who is in command."

The following message arrived from the State Department:

TO: ADMIRAL JASON CALDWELL, BERMUDA
FROM: DEPARTMENT OF STATE, THE WHITE HOUSE
SUBJECT: RECEIPT EYES ONLY PRESIDENT, JANUARY 21

THE WHITE HOUSE HAS INDICATED TO SENATOR WADE THAT NO MEMBERS OF THE NATIONAL AFFAIRS COMMITTEE HAVE AGREED TO SERVE AS NONVOTING MEMBERS OF HIS COMMITTEE. AND FURTHER THAT NO CONGRESSIONAL MEMBERS WILL BE ACCEPTED ON THE NATIONAL AFFAIRS COMMITTEE. THE PRESIDENT HAS THEREFORE STATED THAT HE WILL NOT ACCEPT ANY OVER SIGHT FROM CONGRESS. THE SEPARATION OF POWERS STATED IN THE US CONSTITUTION CLEARLY SET THE MILITARY GUIDANCE WITH THE ADMINISTRATIVE BRANCH OF GOVERNMENT.

HE, THEREFORE, HAS MADE THE FOLLOWING APPOINTMENTS WITHOUT CONGRESSIONAL APPROVAL:

1) SIMON WADE APPOINTED AMBASSADOR TO RUSSIA,
2) EDWIN STANTON APPOINTED SECRETARY OF WAR,
3) GENERAL HALLECK WESTERN COMMANDER OF THE ARMY,
4) VICE ADMIRAL CALDWELL WESTERN NAVY COMMANDER,
5) GENERAL-IN-CHIEF HAS BEEN ABSOLVED,
6) GEORGE MCCLELLAN APPOINTED EASTERN COMMANDER,
7) BENJAMIN HAGOOD APPOINTED EASTERN COMMANDER, NAVY.

YOU WILL REPORT TO THE GULF OF MEXICO TO ASSUME YOUR COMMAND WITHIN THIRTY DAYS. ASSISTANT MINISTER JEROME LEWIS WILL MAINTAIN HIS STATION ON BERMUDA AND REPORT TO YOU. YOU ARE TO RETURN TO BERMUDA AS SOON AS THE WESTERN NAVAL OPERATIONS ARE COMPLETE.

I sat and read the message again. "Well, Jerome, my big mouth just got me in trouble again."

I handed him the message. He read it and said.

"Your newly pregnant wife is not going to like this depending upon how long the capture of the Mississippi takes."

"The sooner I get started, the sooner I can get back to Bermuda." And we sent the following:

TO: GIDEON WELLES, SECRETARY OF THE NAVY
FROM: VICE ADMIRAL JASON EDWIN CALDWELL
SUBJECT: ASSUMING WESTERN COMMAND, JANUARY 27, '62

I WILL NEED SEA TRANSPORT FROM HAVANA, CUBA TO NEW ORLEANS. REQUEST THE USS *SAN JACINTO* IF IT IS ON STATION THE ABOVE DATE. I WOULD LIKE ORDERS FOR FLAG OFFICER, ANDREW H. FOOTE, TO CONTACT GENERAL US GRANT ON THE UPPER MISSISSIPPI TO COORDINATE HIS FLOTILLA CONSISTING OF THE USS *CINCINNATI, ESSEX, CARONDELET,* AND *DE KALB* PLUS THE WOODEN GUN BOATS *CONESTOGA, LEXINGTON* AND *TYLER.* FOOTE IS TO PLACE HIS MARINES UNDER GRANT FOR LAND ACTION AGAINST FORT HENRY ON THE TENNESSEE RIVER. THIS ACTION SHOULD COMMENCE ON OR BEFORE FEBRUARY 10, 1862. IF ACTION IS DELAYED FOR ANY REASON, APPOINT FLAG OFFICER JOHN C. HALSTON AS HIS REPLACEMENT.

FOLLOWING THE FALL OF FORT HENRY, WHICH IS LITTLE MORE THAN A PILE OF DIRT, THE NAVY UNITS ARE COMMANDED TO PROCEED TO FORT DONELSON. THIS FORT IS COMMANDED BY THE FORMER SECRETARY OF WAR, JOHN FLOYD. PLEASE RELAY TO GENERAL GRANT THAT FLOYD IS A WANTED MAN, DEMAND HIS UNCONDITIONAL SURRENDER. HE IS TO BE ARRESTED ON A FEDERAL WARRANT AND TAKEN TO WASHINGTON CITY TO STAND TRIAL FOR TREASON UNDER THE BUCHANAN ADMINISTRATION.

FOLLOWING THE FALL OF FORT DONELSON, THE NAVY WILL PROCEED TO NASHVILLE AND CAPTURE THE STORE OF SUPPLIES CONTAINED IN THAT CITY. THIS ACTION SHOULD BE COMPLETED BY APRIL 1, 1862. IF GENERAL GRANT IS IN DISAGREEMENT WITH ANY OF THESE OBJECTIVES, THEN THE NAVY SUPPORT IS TO BE WITHDRAWN. THE NAVY IN THE WESTERN THEATER WILL SUPPORT ONLY THOSE ARMY GENERALS WHO WILL ADVANCE AND CAPTURE.

New Orleans will be attacked after the Tennessee campaign so that Commodore Foote can proceed down the Mississippi towards New Orleans. I would like orders for Flag Officer David Farragut to proceed into the Gulf of Mexico to meet me at or near the Mississippi Delta. While David is over sixty years of age, I have served with him in the Gulf in the last war, he knows how to break through the Confederate Naval lines and sail up and into New Orleans. If action is delayed for any reason, appoint Commodore David Porter as his replacement.

I leave Bermuda for Cuba aboard the *Cold Harbor*. When in Havana, I will be able to send and receive mail by steamer. I will report success or failure of missions as soon as possible, after actions will be sent by ships pouch. This means that you will probably read about the success or failure of these actions in the newspapers before you receive my reports. It is important to note that the success of these actions will be the efforts of Admirals Foote and Farragut, only the failure will be my fault for not planning and executing the mission in a timely manner. The ship yards in New Orleans are constructing modern steel plated battleships that will destroy the Union Navy if this is not captured or destroyed.

"Jerome, please copy the Secretary of War, Edwin Stanton and Secretary Seward, eyes only the President."

"Admiral?"

"Yes."

"Good to see the warrior again, Sir."

"Let us hope that my wife feels the same way, Jerome. I need to be back by late May or early June or I will miss the birth."

"Sir, you are a three star Admiral and the Western Theater Commander, you can come and go wherever and whenever you like. No one can question your actions, unless he is the Secretary of War."

"Good point, Jerome, see you in May then."

Captain Jacob had me in Havana a day before the *San Jacinto* pulled into port. It was February 10, 1862, and I needed to get to New Orleans before the action started on the Tennessee River. The new captain of the USS *San Jacinto* said he needed to stay a week in Havana. I replied, "We leave in two hours. If you are unable to comply with my orders than your executive officer just became the captain of this ship." His eyes grew wide and he said, "Aye, aye, Sir."

"Tom, you and Sam get your gear aboard. I will handle getting the 'ten little Indians' on board. We had become accustomed to calling the marine guard detachment in Bermuda the ten little Indians. They had served with distinction until Allen Pinkerton had sent us ten policemen to replace them last year. Now they did odd jobs for Jerome or me, as we needed them. I figured I would need all the help I could get to start fires under Navy butts from here to the upper Mississippi.

The cruise from Havana up into the Gulf was uneventful and we linked with Admiral Farragut in three days. I transferred my flag from the *San Jacinto* onto Farragut's Ship of the Line.

"Permission to come aboard?"

"Permission granted, Admiral Caldwell", David Farragut returned my salute.

"What is the status of Commodore Foote's forces on the Mississippi, Admiral?"

"They have linked with Grant. The iron sided Cincinnati, Essex, Carondelet and De Kalb should be fine but there are a pitifully small group of gunboats with too many marines crammed on board. If any of the boats are hit, there will be a great loss of life."

"I feared as much, in my orders to Commodore Foote, I suggested taking any small boats that he could find along the Tennessee under the Confiscation Act."

"Well, he must have done that, because Fort Henry has fallen and so have several newly constructed ones between Henry and Donelson. As you indicated they were poorly defended and Foote has a large number of captured and wounded enemy that are slowing him down."

"How often do you send and receive the mail pouches?"

"Every day since the campaign began, Admiral."

"Excellent, how soon can a message reach Foote?"

"I would guess more than a month while the fighting is current, after that a message should find him in a couple of weeks."

"The Navy needs to do something about communications, the time required is ridiculous." I looked at David Farragut and he was smiling. "What?" I said.

"I remember an Admiral's Aide in the last war saying the same thing right here in the Gulf. It has not improved a whit, has it!"

"No, Sir. It has not. I still need to get a message off to Foote to congratulate his taking of the forts before Donelson."

As I sat down to write, Foote was advancing on Fort Donelson with his iron clads, gun boats and towed boats full of marines. Fort Donelson was not a quickly constructed pile of dirt and the stone walls stayed intact while the iron clads could not make any penetration. The cannon fire from the fort put the Essex out of the fight with 42 killed. In sharp fighting, Foote's marine force was driven backward as General Grant watched through his field glasses. He ordered a counterattack by his army forces. This caught the Confederate defenders out in the open and sent them reeling back into the fort. These Confederate forces were led by General Gideon Pillow and when he reported what had happened to the fort commander, John Floyd, he was shaken. Grant knew Pillow was a political appointee and Foote knew that an arrest warrant waited for Floyd. As Grant and Foote discussed how to take the fort with their combined forces, two things happened. Nathan Forrest, a Confederate cavalry officer, ordered his men to mount and break through the lines to protect the supply depot at Nashville. During this action, both Floyd and Pillow deserted, in the face of the enemy, to save themselves. Command now rested with Simon Buckner. He decided to request the terms of surrender from the combined Union forces.

General Grant replied with the following which was to make him famous: "Sir: Yours of February 16, 1862, proposing armistice and appointment of commissioners to settle terms of the capitulation, is received. No terms other than Unconditional Surrender can be accepted. I propose to move immediately upon your works." The fall of Fort Donselson was front page news and the reporters decided that Grant's initials stood for Unconditional Surrender. General Buckner was quoted as saying the initials stood for 'Unchivalrous and Sanctimonious'.

Foote and Grant now had thousands of prisoners, some able bodied and some wounded. The wounded were loaded onto the boats that the marines had towed to battle in and the marines joined the army of Grant for the march to Nashville, the last objective in the northern Mississippi campaign of 1862. The able bodied prisoners were told to march between an armed federal troop. Grant ordered his men to cut willow branches from the Tennessee river banks and the Confederates carried these like rifles. From a distance the army looked twice its size. On February 25, 1862, Grant's army approached the city of Nashville. When scouts saw the size of the army, they surrendered without firing a shot. The campaign of the northern Mississippi was over for Grant. He took the supplies stored there and locked the Confederate prisoners in the empty warehouses. Foote continued down the Mississippi towards New Orleans.

On board the USS *Hartford*, flag ship of Farragut's fleet of seventeen ships, I watched as Farragut, veteran of the War of 1812, the Mediterranean and Mexican Wars led his fleet into one of the greatest naval battles of the Civil War. Before the engagement of the Confederate defenders they faced numerous obstructions, including fire ships. These were barges that were piled with wood and set ablaze. A large iron chain was strung across the river from Fort Philip to Fort Jackson on the other side. For six days and nights these forts were pounded by mortars from flat bottom barges by Commodore David Potter. They were reduced to rubble. As Farragut's fleet advanced, he commanded six sloops of war, sixteen gun boats, twenty mortar barges and five other vessels. He continued to pour cannon fire into the fifteen Confederate ships which lie in wait. When it was over, Farragut had run the gauntlet of the forts and opposing fleet with the loss of only one ship, 37 men killed and another 147 wounded. This was less than the losses of Foote on the upper Mississippi.

On the morning of April 25, 1862, Farragut's ships steamed into a defenseless New Orleans. Jason stood on board to see and later write, "desolation, ships and steamers destroyed all in a common blaze, along with 20,000 bales of cotton, coal and cord wood. The *CS S Mississippi*, stood in the ship yards uncomplete, its iron ribs like a decayed animal dead upon the prairie." General Benjamin Butler stood beside Jason and said, "I will be in the unfortunate situation of having my forces try to occupy New Orleans."

"Yes, your job will be to seize the US Mint and the rest of the land objectives outlined from the War Department. Yours is the real job of the capture of New Orleans. I will leave my detachment of marines and you will decide when it is safe for them to advance up the river to meet Foote."

I handed him a letter from the White House similar to the one President Buchanan had made for me to use in Charleston. He read it and said, "I think Officer Schneider will be telling me when he is ready to leave for the meeting with Commodore Foote!"

THE WHITE HOUSE
WASHINGTON CITY
January 15, 1862

To whom it may concern:

Vice Admiral Jason Edwin Caldwell and Warrant Officer Thomas Q. Schneider, USN, in connection with their mission for me, will travel to such places at such times as they feel appropriate, accompanied by such staff as they desire.

Warrant Officer Schneider is granted a Top Secret/White House clearance, and may, at his option, grant such clearance to those he meets on my behalf.

US Military and governmental agencies are directed to provide Officer Schneider with whatever support he may require.

A. Lincoln
Abraham Lincoln
President of the United States

"Officer Schneider is unique, I trust him with my messages and orders for Commodore Foote. I have left my orders for Admiral Farragut to split his fleet, the sloops of war will stay here in New Orleans for your protection, the gun boats and other vessels are to proceed up the Mississippi to join with Commodore Foote."

70
Return to Bermuda
May, 1862

On May 10, 1862, Sam and I boarded the USS *San Jacinto* for passage to St. George, Bermuda. I had sent my after action reports, but the newspapers were full of the accounts of the western campaign. I doubted that my reports would cause much of a stir. When the USS *San Jacinto* docked in Bermuda, Sam and I stepped onto the pier. The *San Jacinto* pulled quickly away, knowing its reputation among the British. We were greeted by our families, even Louise who looked like she was going to have twins. I put my arms around her and held her close, not wanting to hurt the baby.

"Give me and her a hug!"

"I do not want to start labor."

"I am fine, the doctor at the hospital in Hamilton says I am healthy as a horse, he says we should have more children."

"No, Louise, three is enough, just as your brother said it was!" We both laughed at this shared memory.

Louise could not walk very far before she had to sit on a bench and rest, but we made it to the square in St. George and caught a carriage to Caldwell Place. We kissed for a long time. "Oh, Jason, we are going to be so happy with our family here in Bermuda." She put her head on my shoulder and fell asleep. We stopped under the portico at the Inn and another crowd of people were there. I thanked them all for coming and put Louise in her bed for a nap. I returned to the dining room to find Jerome Lewis waiting for me.

"Hello, Jerome, there are 42 rooms in this place and you decided to rest here?" It was a running joke from our White House days and Jerome smiled and said, "I brought some after actions for you to read. I think you will find them interesting."

"Did you summarize them for me, Jerome, I am too tired to read them all."

"I did, the page on top is all you need to read for now."

AFTER ACTION REPORTS: January - May, 1862

1-11 Lincoln calls for Union offensive, General War Order No. 1. At the request of the President, General McClellan made a plan of operations. It was his belief that the decisive struggle would be fought in Eastern Virginia. He drew up a plan of support for his efforts to take Confederate forces away from Virginia to defend the western area along the Mississippi. He urged that western Virginia be allowed to break from Virginia and form their own free state, which would support the Union. Likewise he urged eastern Tennessee to break from western to form another support area for the Union. He urged a military campaign along the Tennessee and Mississippi rivers. He suggested that all Confederate strongholds along these rivers be seized and held. Troops should be sent to West Virginia, Baltimore and Fort Monroe should be occupied with a sufficient force kept within call of Washington to hold it secure. By capturing the cities of Richmond, Charleston, Savannah, New Orleans, Montgomery, Pensacola and Mobile, the Confederacy would be driven to the wall and would see the hopelessness for further resistance.

2-13 West Virginia Constitutional Convention is formed. By this action, federal troops have taken command of West Virginia and have driven all Confederate troops from the state. The Confederacy responded by sending General John B. Floyd to reinforce General Wise at Lewisburg, on the Greenville River. When General Floyd faced federal forces in the field, a ten hour battle killed seventy-five per cent of the troops he commanded. During the night he fled the field. The remnants of the forces driven from West Virginia had been gathered at Monterey and were placed under the command of General Robert Lee.

2-16 Fort Donselson surrenders (report to Washington).

2-25 Nashville surrenders (your report to Washington).

3-9 Battle of Hampton Roads considered a moral victory by Admiral Hagood. While you were commanding in the wester theater, a battle between the Monitor and the Merrimac occurred near Norfolk Harbor. The Merrimac sunk one Union vessel and nearly destroyed several others before being badly damaged itself. It was rechristened the Virginia and then sunk to prevent capture.

3-11 General McClellan is demoted in rank. The reshuffling of command results in a demotion/promotion for McClellan. He is no longer general-in-command, because he refuses to see the big picture coming from the White House, he is given command of the eastern theater- Army Operations.

4-4 McClellan begins Peninsular Campaign, advances between James and York rivers. In its first major offensive, the Army of the Potomac advances toward Yorktown on the peninsula between the James and York rivers. Little or no resistance encountered.

4-7 Grant wins at Pittsburgh Landing, Tennessee (Shiloh).
Two days of furious fighting and tremendous casualties (Federal: 1,735 dead, 7,882 wounded and out of action for rest of war, 4,044 missing and assumed dead; Confederate: 1,728 dead, 8,012 wounded, 959 missing) end when Grant forces General Beauregard to withdraw after the death of the commanding Confederate General Albert Sidney Johnston.

    I read this with tears in my eyes, Sid Johnston, my friend from Utah was gone.

4-7 Island Number Ten, falls to Foote on Mississippi, Union controls Upper Mississippi. Before meeting Grant at Shiloh, General Johnston left a force to defend Island No. 10 (an earthworks fort). A combined land and naval attack was made by Commodore Foote. Commander Walke, of the *Carondelet* volunteered to lead the attack. The *Pittsburg* pounded the batteries of the fort taking out two ten inch columbiads, four eight inch guns, five thirty-two pounders and five sixty-four pounders, 5000 men surrender to Foote.

4-10 Fort Pulaski outside Savannah falls to General Gilmore of eastern army command. In less than two days, the imposing masonry structure near the mouth of the Savannah river is reduced to rubble, there were no Confederate survivors.

4-10 Lincoln signs a congressional resolution to free slaves in Washington City.

4-25 New Orleans falls to Farragut, he proceeds up to Natchez (this is your report).

5-4 McClellan occupies Yorktown, Virginia.

5-12 Natchez falls to Farragut (this is your report).

5-14 McClellan stops five miles from Richmond, says he faces overwhelming forces.

"It appears that there is a war on more than one front, that will shorten the war, the south is not equipped to fight on two fronts."

"Do you think Washington will realize how close they came to having the CSS *Mississippi* and her sister ships destroy the blockade, Admiral?"

"No, they probably think they can fight them to a standstill like at Hampton Roads. We will never see wooden ships built for the Navy again, an era has passed. Just like steam engines replaced the sail, steel has replaced the wood building, except for pleasure craft."

"What do you think your next assignment will be, Admiral?"

"The Mississippi River is in Union hands except for Vicksburg. It may take General Grant some time to completely split the Confederacy into two parts. I am sure that the Secretary of the Navy will want a plan other than a 'siege and starve them out' plan. Foote should be able to patrol the river north to south if we can find him enough gun boats. I assigned Tom and his detachment to a tour of duty with Foote. I will send a letter through Secretary Welles asking if he needs extra officers and plans for the seizure of docks on either side of the river within the Confederacy."

"What if something happens involving England again?"

"That would be Ben Hagood's decision, it is in the eastern theater of naval operations."

"Do not tell Louise this Jerome, but I am home only for the birth of our baby. I may have to return to Washington to command the western theater of naval operations soon."

"Your secret is safe with me, Sir."

"When the baby is born and the war is under control, we might move back to Pennsylvania and I can take long weekends by train. I have to wait and see what the Secretary of War has in mind."

I sent the following to the Secretary of war:

TO: Edwin Stanton, Secretary of war
FROM: J. Caldwell, Commander Western Theater
SUBJECT: End of naval campaign Mississippi and Tennessee

At this time both rivers are in control of USN surface craft. This does not mean that there is no Confederate boat traffic. My standing orders are to capture or destroy any Confederate vessels that our patrols contact. All shore batteries have been silenced except Vicksburg, Mississippi. As of this writing the city

IS SURROUNDED BY THE ARMY UNDER GENERAL GRANT. THE RIVER IS BLOCKED SO NO SUPPLIES CAN REACH THE DOCKS. OFFICE SCHNEIDER AND HIS DETACHMENT HAVE PENETRATED THE CITY AND REPORT THAT THEY CAN LAST ONLY A MATTER OF WEEKS. HIS LAST REPORT IS ATTACHED FOR YOUR REFERENCE.

I WISH TO RECOMMEND THE FOLLOWING OFFICERS FOR MERITORIOUS SERVICE TO THEIR COUNTRY:

ADMIRAL DAVID FARRAGUT: I CONTINUE TO BE AMAZED BY WHAT THIS FLAG OFFICER HAS DONE IN THE LAST FEW MONTHS: THE ABSOLUTE DESTRUCTION OF THE CONFEDERATE FLEET IN THE GULF, THE CAPTURE OF THE CITIES OF NEW ORLEANS, NATCHEZ, MEMPHIS AND FINALLY VICKSBURG.

COMMODORE ANDREW FOOTE : THE CAPTURE OF FORT HENRY, FORT DONELSON, THE CITY OF NASHVILLE AND THE SIEGE OF VICKSBURG. I RECOMMEND THAT HIS SECOND STAR BE AWARDED.

BRIGADIER GENERAL US GRANT: I AM DIRECTLY OPPOSED TO THE RECOMMENDATION FROM GENERAL HALLECK. GRANT IS FUNCTIONING AT THE LEVEL OF A THREE STAR, NOT A ONE STAR. I RECOMMEND THAT HE BE PROMOTED TO THE RANK OF MAJOR GENERAL AND TRANSFERRED TO THE EASTERN THEATER OF OPERATIONS FOR THE ARMY. HE WINS BATTLES! HE DOES NOT CODDLE THE ENEMY, EITHER THEY SURRENDER OR HE KILLS THEM - THAT IS WHAT WAR IS IN ITS SIMPLEST TERMS.

WARRANT OFFICER THOMAS SCHNEIDER: THE UNITED STATES MARINE CORPS HAS NO FINER OFFICER THAN THIS MAN. I DESIRE THAT THIS OFFICER BE PROMOTED SO THAT HE CAN BECOME AN ADMIRAL'S AIDE, HE HAS FUNCTIONED IN THIS CAPACITY SINCE MY ASSIGNMENT AS WESTERN NAVAL COMMANDER.

CAPTAIN JEROME LEWIS: THIS OFFICER IS PRESENTLY THE ACTING FOREIGN MINISTER TO BERMUDA, IT IS TIME TO PROMOTE HIM FOR HIS SERVICE IN THIS CAPACITY. THE ACTING SHOULD BE REMOVED SO THAT HE CAN BECOME THE FOREIGN MINISTER. A JOINT RECOMMENDATION FROM YOU AND SECRETARY SEWARD TO THE PRESIDENT SHOULD ACCOMPLISH THIS SO THAT I MAY FOCUS MY FULL ATTENTION UPON THE WAR EFFORT.

Three weeks later the following was received from Secretary Stanton:

TO: Vice Admiral Jason Caldwell, USN
FROM: Edwin Stanton, Secretary of War
SUBJECT: Recommendations, President to Congress

At this writing the following are awaiting Congressional Approval:

1) Promotion of US Grant to Major General United States Army, commander western army
2) Promotion of David Farragut to four star flag officer, commander western naval theater
3) Promotion of Andrew Foote to two star flag officer, assistant commander western naval theater
4) Promotion of Jason Edwin Caldwell to four star flag officer, assignment Army Navy Building Undersecretary of the Navy
5) Promotion of Thomas Schneider to Captain USMC and Admirals Aide, Washington City

Under separate cover from the State Department, you should receive notification of the appointment of Jerome Lewis as foreign minister to Bermuda. You are hereby ordered to report for duty three months after the birth of your third child in Bermuda.

PS
Jason, you have performed your duties and have succeeded beyond our hopes and dreams here in Washington. Congratulations on your appointment and I will see you when you report here.

Ed Stanton

71
Davis's Council of War
June, 1862

In Richmond, President Davis was frustrated. The Confederate armies were successful in many of the battles fought to date. The Confederate navy was another matter. When the war began, there were only ninety vessels in the United States navy, and of these, twenty-seven were out of commission. Twenty-one vessels were unfit for service, leaving only forty-two in commission. Of these forty-two only eleven carried one hundred and thirty-four guns, were in northern harbors. The rest had been scattered around the globe or were in southern harbors. The total number of officers of all grades in the navy, August 1, 1861, was fourteen hundred and fifty-seven. Three hundred and twenty-two officers resigned and entered the service of the Confederate Navy.

By July, 1862, President Davis now understood that the war would be won or lost by his navy. He ordered his government to begin at once to replace its naval power lost at New Orleans and Hampton Roads. Merchant vessels were bought from England and converted into war vessels. Construction was begun on eight additional sloops-of-war at the Jacksonville, Florida ship yards. Numerous contracts were let in Mississippi and Alabama for heavily armed gun boats. These were known as the "ninety-day boats", because they were begun and completed in that period. The same vigor was shown in the building of "double-end" side wheelers for river and ocean service.

As he addressed his council of war he said, "We have all learned of the glorious record of 'Old Ironsides' from our history lessons. Let us build the same kind of war vessels and place men of honor to serve upon them. Nearly all of the ports within the Confederacy were taken by us in 1861. Let us now pledge to retake those taken from us. Let us begin the process with Fort Pickens in Florida. I am today ordering General Anderson to capture the town of Santa Rosa, a mile distant. He will approach from land while the remaining Gulf fleet will attack from the sea.

If that is successful we shall take Fort Hatteras and Fort Clark with our surviving Atlantic Fleet. I have given the mission of the recapture of

Charleston via Beaufort to Admiral Josiah Tattnall. What I need from each of you here today is the following:

1. Vice President Stephens, I would like to raise the capital for a new navy via foreign contacts, begin with England, France and Russia. 2. Secretary Toombs, I want you to visit the countries that agree to loan us funding for the rebuilding of our navy, thank them and get their advice on how to improve our foreign trade. 3. Secretary Memminger, I want you to replace the assets lost at New Orleans, see if we can interest anyone in the western states to help us. 4. Secretary Walker, continue with the ground campaign by allowing our Generals to cross the Potomac and fight the Union armies in Pennsylvania, Maryland, West Virginia or anywhere we have the advantage. It is no longer a defensive struggle on our part, we must crush the Union and replace it with our own. 5. Secretary Mallory, it will be your job to oversee the rebuilding of the Confederate navy and the undermining of the Union navy. Send your naval combat troops to destroy Union shipping in northern ports. Ask for volunteers to move into northern harbor cities so that they can report the activities of the Union navy. 6. Secretary Reagen, try to improve our ability to send timely commands from the battlefields to the government and return. 7. Attorney-General Benjamin, appoint a committee to increase the borrow limit authorized by our congress from $15,000,000 to $30,000,000 and to accept another 100,000 volunteers. We need to conscript another 100,000 before the end of the year."

The room was deadly quiet, usually a cabinet gathering was loud and opinionated during its several hour duration. "Mister President?"

"Yes, Secretary Walker, you have a question?"

"Why should we fight so far from home? The Army of the Potomac is led by an idiot! Why not let him come up into Virginia as far as he wants and then crush him? He left Washington by ship to land at Jamestown with a modest size infantry and no naval support. He could have come straight down through Alexandria, Virginia, and captured Richmond months ago. We should hope that the Union forces are led by party Generals who would rather be in a Washington parade. We have seasoned Generals who have graduated from West Point who lead our armies. Lincoln is not a military man, he is a lawyer and a do-gooder. People who have been around him for any time will tell you he is an idealist, but has no practical knowledge on how to get things done. I would consider your idea of invading the north, ill-conceived and if you continue with this, I will resign my office. Let them come to us. We can kill them in familiar surroundings easier than we can travel hundreds of miles. The death rate at Shiloh proves that the leadership of the north cares nothing for the lives of their soldiers."

"Does anyone agree with Secretary Walker?" Jefferson Davis asked.

A chorus of seven voices said, "I do Mister President."

"Mr. President, as your Secretary of the Navy, I would advise along similar lines for the time being. We need to construct more vessels and then attack, but not to retake ports that we have already lost. We need to be thinking about how we can protect our rivers and trading ports. Why would we want to sail up the Chesapeake and fire upon the White House as the British did in 1812? Let us concentrate on building blockade runners to get our products to market in England and France."

"I agree, as your Vice President, I should be trying to encourage the Europeans to assist us through a lend or lease of war materials, ships, armaments of all types. We can buy ships faster than we can build them."

"Wait, wait, I see your positions and you can do all that besides what I have suggested. The biggest mistake in my life was not letting Stonewall Jackson take his army from Manassas into Washington City to arrest Lincoln and end this mess a year ago. Look what Jackson did this March in the Shenandoah Valley. As a result, the Union army fled across the Potomac to protect Washington. The Union army is still unled and disorganized. It will crumble if attacked and pursued across the Potomac."

"We understand you are upset about the failure in the Mississippi and Tennessee river campaigns, Mister President. Our Generals there were political appointments, Floyd has turned tail and run in the last two engagements, he should be arrested and court marshaled along with that Pillow fellow."

"We have no need to panic, at this point the war has progressed according to our schedule, we do not need to upset that schedule by trying to recapture what the Union forces have done. Why not meet again in a few months and evaluate what we have accomplished?"

"You have given me new confidence. I shall not attempt to undertake the winning of the war single handed!" Laughter followed the President's comment and peace was restored to the council. "I would like to consider our contact in Bermuda. One year ago, I sent General John Butler through the lines at Manasses to contact the White House and offer our hand in friendship and peace to Mr. Lincoln. He never spoke to Mr. Lincoln, he could not get anyone other than his body guard to respond. I think Lincoln wanted to deny the offer from us. John Butler did meet with his National Affairs Advisor, an Admiral Caldwell, who was born in Beaufort, South Carolina, and graduated from West Point. Caldwell is now the foreign minister to Bermuda where John Butler is now our representative to Bermuda. As you may remember, from the Trent Affair, that it was settled by the intervention of Caldwell and Butler. They have maintained a friendly and cordial working relationship ever since. With your permission, I would like to use that relationship to our advantage. Minister Butler can inquire if Caldwell has any contact with Lincoln through the department of state. If we draft an offer of an armistice between our two nations, maybe Lincoln will consider it this time."

"An armistice would give us time to rebuild our navy and recruit infantry for our armies, Mr. President. That is an excellent idea. Even if Lincoln rejects our offer again, it still slows down their efforts to create new free states, like West Virginia. It concerns me that we may be two nations which have divided states like; North & South Missouri, East & West Tennessee. We still have slave holding states which have not joined the Confederacy. We should approach Maryland and the others to see if they would consider joining us if an armistice is signed." Secretary Toombs said.

"I agree, we should send representatives to the western territories to see if they would like to consider statehood in the Confederacy. Utah is still not accepting federal troops on their soil. That might be an area that we can tap for funding." Secretary Memminger said.

"Yes, I like all those ideas, begin at once to explore them, gentlemen. I will contact Minister Butler through the normal channels and have him meet with Caldwell in Bermuda." President Davis was smiling for the first time in several months.

He left the council of war meeting and sent the following instructions to Bermuda through the blockade at Norfolk:

CONFEDERATE STATES OF AMERICA

Office of the President, Richmond, Virginia

June 14, 1862

Dear General Butler:

Begin the discussions with your contact in Bermuda for an armistice with the Union. The war council has approved the following guidelines:

1) immediate cease fire to go into affect July 4 th, 1862 (seems an appropriate date),

2) withdrawal of all troops from western Virginia and return of property to State,

3) removal of all enemy forces from each nation (includes harbors and rivers within state boundaries),

4) failure to accept this offer, changes our position from defensive only to an offensive position whereby we will march on Washington City.

Jefferson Davis

When this missive arrived in Hamilton, John Butler was overjoyed. He needed to meet with Jason Caldwell as soon as possible. He called his secretary into his office and said, "Did I hear that Louise and Jason Caldwell had a baby girl?"

"Yes, Sir. She delivered a baby at the Hamilton hospital last week, I think it was the seventh of June. I sent a note of congratulations for you. I know how much they both mean to you, Sir."

"Thank you, Petterson, you take good care of me. I need to walk down to front street and get a baby gift at Trimminghams for them. After that I will catch the train to St. George and walk on up to Caldwell Place and deliver it."

"Very good, Sir."

"I will gather up a few papers and be off, see you tomorrow, Petterson."

He closed and locked his office, bought a small baby thing that the clerk in Trimmingham's said was in fashion and he caught the train for Caldwell Place.

"Hello, Mrs. Whitehall, I hope I am not interrupting your business day. I have a small gift for Mrs. Caldwell and the baby. Is she at home by any chance?"

"Yes, Mr. Butler, baby Carol and the Admiral are with her in the nursery. Let me go and tell them you are here." She disappeared down a hallway and was gone for a few minutes and returned with a smiling Jason Caldwell.

"John, how good of you to call. Louise is nursing the baby, but she will meet us along side the swimming pool when she is finished and the baby is asleep." He motioned for them to exit through a set of french doors onto the pool deck.

"Have a seat John. What really brings you to see us? You are a bachelor and not really into babies are you?"

"I must confess that you read me like a book, Jason. Of course, your joy in fatherhood can not be appreciated by a bachelor, but just seeing your face just now leads me to believe that you have never been happier."

"You are absolutely correct, my friend."

"We are friends, are we not, Jason?"

"We are."

"Then as a friend, I would like you to send this letter directly to the President of the United States."

I took the letter and read it. "Do you think this is a genuine offer of peace? Or is it a ploy to buy more time to rebuild the Confederate losses?"

"I am sure it is both. The south is exhausted with the effort required to defend itself from attack. If an armistice is put in place, both sides will rebuild and the conflict will continue again at a much larger and frightening scale. The battlefield at Shiloh had 19,357 men from both sides laying dead or in the process of dying when we took the body of General A.S. Johnston and withdrew. The reports that were given to me is that the ground was covered body to body, the results of hand to hand combat. When and how will all this end, Jason?"

I shook my head that I did not know and said, "I first met Albert Johnston in Utah, he was a gentle soul and the best natured man I have ever met. I was moved when I learned how he died." I cleared my thoughts and said, "I have been replaced here in Bermuda, John. Jerome Lewis is now your contact for peace talks. Do you want to show this offer to him?"

"No, Jason. We need to decide how to get this directly to your president."

"You are afraid that it will be buried in the State Department?"

"Yes."

"Is time critical? Can I hand carry this to my president?"

"Oh, Jason, that would be wonderful!"

"Did you make a hand written copy of this for your files? Can I carry this original?"

"Yes."

"Well, then can I offer you some southern comfort?"

"Yes, you can."

I got up to go into the dining hall and find two glasses when Louise walked over and gave me a kiss. "Thank you, Daddy."

"For what?"

"You know what for, she is asleep in her crib. The nanny is with her. I wanted to see what John brought for her."

"He is pool side, I am trying to find a bottle of bourbon to fix him a drink."

"I will be thanking him for his thoughtfulness, bring your drinks out when you finish."

I did and we had an enjoyable afternoon catching up on the changes in our lives. We told him that we were not looking forward to life in Washington

City again. We would be opening the house at Seneca Hill for the household staff, Louise and the children. I would have to ride the train back and forth to Washington. I had no idea what an undersecretary did. We hoped that he would continue to write to us, mail still passed from Bermuda to the Union. We told him that we had lost our homes in Beaufort, they were now government property, they might be returned as I had already petitioned the war department that they had seized property of a serving United States Admiral. I was told that the house at 353 Bay Street did not belong to me. It belonged to someone named Louise Buchanan. He laughed and said she did not need another house at the moment.

72
Caldwell Place
September 1862

We were scheduled to leave for my service at the Army Navy building in Washington on September 7, 1862. I planned on meeting with the president as soon as I arrived. My extended family decided to stay in Bermuda. My mother and father were looking for a larger house on one of the islands that dotted the Great Sound. Their house, that they had purchased in St. Davids was for sale. I did not know if they would ever return to South Carolina. Their fortune was safe in the Bank of Bermuda and they had applied for British citizenship. My brother, Robert, was another matter, he was restless and wanted to see the war damage in Port Royal, Beaufort and on Pollawanna plantation. He did not want to be a British citizen and I understood that. I could work out my frustrations with the war by trying to do something to stop or shorten it. He could only sit and wait for it to end. I decided to talk to him and I walked to his living quarters in Caldwell Place.

"Robert, I need your help."

"Sure, your departure date is coming, need help with the sea trunks?"

"Not that kind of help. I want to start a new venture here on Bermuda."

"A business, you know I am not good with that, you and father always did the business at home."

"No, it is not a business with a lot of paper to shuffle. Robert Whitehall is my paper shuffler here in Bermuda. I want to start to raise crops here in the islands."

"What kind of crops?"

"They have to import almost everything they eat here, Robert. What would you think of renting or buying as many small plots of land as we can find to raise produce (fruits and vegetables) for sale here?"

"That makes good sense to me, Jason. We can always import those that will not grow here. First I will have to make test beds here on Caldwell Place. I need to take soil samples and have them tested for contents. I can check with the southern chain of Carribean Islands to see what grows well there, maybe we can grow bananas, that would really be something! I need to walk down to St. George and talk to the green grocer there and see what he orders and from where. Then I can ask him if he ever considered buying from someone local, like me. Jason, can I use Caldwell shipping to start bringing in some produce before we start to plant? I am going to need field hands here. Boy, this is really going to take a lot of my time."

He was talking to himself by this time, I had gone looking for Louise, with a smile on my face. I was going to tell her how the Caldwell Produce Company of Bermuda was formed and to look for the Caldwell label when purchasing her fruits and vegetables.

The last communication from Washington informed me that between June 26 and July 2, Union and Confederate forces fought a series of battles: Mechanicsville, Gaines Mill, Savage's Station, Frayer's Farm and Malvern Hill. On July 2, 1862, the Peninsular Campaign was finished and so was McClellan. On July 11, 1862, he was demoted and replaced by General Halleck for the Union forces. In August, Union General Pope was defeated at the second battle of Manasses. On August 29th, Union General Fitz-John Porter was defeated and General McDowell began the defense of Washington. Jefferson Davis's fears were calmed and a replacement Confederate Navy was never formed.

73
Army Navy Building
September, 1862

It was strange returning to the building where I started my career with Navy Intelligence so many years ago. Gideon Welles was there to greet me and we sat in his office and talked about what he expected the Navy's role to be for the remainder of the war. I did not say much until he finally said, "Admiral, what is wrong? You seem to be somewhere else."

"Yes, Sir. I would like you to read this and tell me what you think." I handed him the letter that John Butler had given me to hand deliver to the president.

He read it and said, "This is dated three months ago, why have you not forwarded it to the president through the state department?"

"It is written to John Butler, the minister to Bermuda. He gave it to me to hand deliver to the president. He was afraid that it would be ignored inside the state department."

"I do not follow you, Jason."

"The one and only time I have met the president he asked me to go over to the Hay-Adams and meet with John Butler, Allen Pinkerton and Ben Hagood. The president said that an envoy from Davis was waiting to talk to an envoy representing the Union. Mr. Lincoln chose me as his envoy."

"When was this?"

"July 1861, right after the first Battle of Bull Run."

"How did a Confederate get through our lines and into Washington?"

"There were no lines of defense, anyone could have entered the city without any security check what-so-ever. I believe that the south sent a number of people into Washington and they are still here sending information to Richmond."

"Incredible! You know this for a fact?"

"Yes, John Butler was one of them."

"We need to get this information to the president as soon as we can, it would appear that a general invasion of the north may be upon us. Are you aware that Lincoln has replaced General Pope who was defeated at Bull Run, with McClellan?"

"No, I had not heard that." We stood to walk to the White House and contact the president's scheduling secretary.

"Jason, this does not change why you were brought to the Army Navy Building to work for me. Even if the president will not see us, we have important work to be done. The Secretary of War was very impressed with your battle plan for the Mississippi and Tennessee river basins. It was the best use of land and sea assets I have ever seen. You have a knack for this, mind telling me how you came to use the Navy marines off the ships?"

"President Buchanan felt that the marines were under used, they should consist of a ground force controlled by the Navy. In the eight years that I served under Presidents Pierce and Buchanan, I used a detachment of marines wherever I went. I cannot remember of any action that I have been involved in that has not included marines used as group forces. In fact, my service record shows that most of my combat experience has been on the ground, not the sea. I believe that ground forces should be moved from place to place by water, not marching for days or even weeks to get to the battlefield."

We had cleared the guard stations and were admitted to the White House. "I suppose that Allen Pinkerton will want to sit in on this?" I said.

"Allen is not at the White House, he has been assigned other duties." Gideon Welles was smiling.

"Two to see the president, Mr. Ambrose."

"What day, Mr. Welles?"

"Today, Admiral Caldwell has a letter from Jefferson Davis."

"The President of the Confederacy, Davis?"

"That is the one."

"Can I take the letter into the oval office and let President Lincoln read it and decide when he wants to see you?"

"Of course." I said. I handed the letter to him and we sat on some very small chairs that were not comfortable.

"It seems that these chairs do not encourage people to come and 'camp out here'."

I smiled remembering that Franklin Pierce had selected these chairs for the very reason stated. Mr. Ambrose returned with the letter and handed it to me.

"The President has told me to tell you that this was a very interesting letter and if Jefferson Davis would compose another up-to-date letter and send it to him here at the White House, he would read it."

"Read it?" Gideon Welles said.

"Those were his exact words, Mr. Secretary."

"Can you tell him a former member of his National Affairs Committee has recommended that he try to begin a conversation with Jefferson Davis." I said.

"The president knows that you are with Secretary Welles, Admiral. He will deal directly with Mr. Davis, not through anyone else. His decision is final, gentlemen. Good day to you both."

We looked at each, shrugged our shoulders and began walking back to our offices. "Has he always been this unavailable to his cabinet members?" I asked.

"Since the death of his friend, Senator Edward Baker at Ball's Bluff, he has been depressed. He has shut most of us out of his inner circle. The only time I see him is in cabinet meetings."

"I had no idea that things were that bad here in the White House, Gideon."

"That is another reason that I asked you to resign from his advisory committee and get away from the Department of State. A hand full of men will save the Union and right now Abraham Lincoln is not one of them. Unless he can get control again, he will just react to things, not cause them to happen. I worry for sake of the Union. The armies of the Confederacy can sweep across us on land whenever they please, unless a few army officers and the Navy stop them."

"My God, I had no idea!"

"You are a welcome sight here for those of us who work in the Army Navy Building, Jason. Secretary Stanton wants to greet the man who planned the Mississippi campaign, he wants to pick your brain on how to stop the Confederate invasion that is sure to come, now that Mr. Lincoln has closed the door on Jefferson Davis."

By this time we were back at his office and he said, "I will take you to Edwin Stanton's office, Jason. I think you will find him like a breath of fresh air. He has changed since he was in the President Buchanan lame duck cabinet"

"Good morning, Ed. I have Jason Caldwell with me, can we have a minute of your time?" He said as he stuck his head into Stanton's office without bothering to stop at the secretary's desk or even knock on his door.

"Yes, come right in. I want to see this four star Admiral of ours! It is good to see you again, Jason."

He held out his hand across his desk and grabbed mine with a very firm grip. "Sit down, sit down both of you. You do not look like you breathe fire and spit death, Admiral."

"Sir?"

"When I asked Admiral Farragut to command a strike force into Norfolk Harbor, he refused, saying he would not raise a hand against his home state. He did say, 'I would be happy to serve under Jason Caldwell who was my aide in the Mexican War. He breathes fire and spits death! Once his mind is made up, the enemy is either dead or captured. He is the Ulysses Grant of the Navy.' "

"So that is how my request for David was answered in such a short time frame. You both should have been with me at New Orleans and seen how David Farragut is still the best Admiral in the Navy."

"A mutual admiration society, he says the same thing about you!"

"So, can I use him again, if it is not in Virginia?"

"Sure, what did you have in mind?"

"I have not discussed this with Gideon, so maybe we should talk first."

"You can tell Ed, anything that you would tell me, Jason. We actually like each other. Not like the last two Secretaries of the Navy and War under the last administration. Speaking of that, did you know that John Floyd was finally arrested?"

"Yes, I heard that Jefferson Davis had ordered a court marshal."

"Now, tell us how you would use David Farragut if he was not the commander in the west."

"I think the next several battles of the civil war will be fought in the north. The information that I have says that Davis must act quickly to end the war before we get midyear, 1863."

"Where did you get this information?"

"General Order: 191, from his minister to Bermuda."

"We have a copy of that from Pinkerton. Go on."

"That means he will rely on his army, not his navy. They will have long marches to get to the battlefield. I suggest that we put a smaller land force near the water as bait and maybe a Confederate General will try to attack them. We can bring both our naval fire power and marine corps to trap them and destroy the invading armies from the south."

"Interesting. How can we do this?"

"Station the armies of the north near a river or the ocean. If the south wants to dance, they will have to find us. We choose the location of all future battles. Under no conditions should we ever have another engagement without Navy involvement. Our only victories to date have been with navy coordination or command. We will be defeated whenever we have to fight single handed (army alone or navy alone). Look at what happened to Ben Hagood at Hampton Roads when the navy went alone into battle, look what has happened when the army is left on its own. Fight with both hands."

"My God, Gideon, no wonder you wanted this man! From this day forward the standing orders from the White House should be, Army, where is the Navy? Navy, where is the Army? Simple, yet effective, both branches fight together." Ed Stanton was smiling.

"Well, planning is the key to any military operation, that is why I want David Farragut or Andrew Foote to plan the battles that we fight in the west. I think they will see action in Kentucy next, maybe while Ben Hagood sees a campaign in Maryland."

"Kentucy, first. Why, Kentucy?"

"I think that Davis will send the remainder of his Tennessee forces under General Bragg, into Kentucky, then swing east to invade western Virginia. I graduated with Braxton in '37 and I know how he thinks. We can wait until he reaches Virginia or set up an ambush along his route of march. Navy intelligence should find out for us the probable dates and locations. I would guess, late September or early October."

"Now Maryland. When and where?" Stanton asked.

"Again, it is my guess, that the remainders of several armies will be joined under the command of General Lee to cross into Maryland along the upper Potomac anywhere from Sharpsburg to Brunswick. Again, armies do not move in a vacuum, as soon as there is movement naval intelligence can send word to us to set the trap. We will need many more gun boats to patrol the upper Potomac and transport the marines into fighting position."

"You mean, set our spy network run by Pinkerton to watch Generals Bragg and Lee?" Stanton quipped.

"Exactly. Whenever they move, we will know, dates and directions of march." I replied.

The discussion went on for two hours, Edwin Stanton's focus and concentration was amazing. "Admiral, you have given us your thoughts for the remainder of 1862. Any guesses on '63?" Asked Gideon Welles.

"God willing, the war will be over after the invasion of the north is crushed." I answered.

"Then I will inform the White house that the three of us expect a Confederate attack north and east from Tennessee and across the upper Potomac River into Maryland. This will be supported by our reports from intelligence agents in the field." Said Stanton.

"Why the three of us? Why not include General Halleck. He is the only four star, at the present time, in the Army." I said.

"And at the present time, he is the only one who is inside the inner circle of the president. I would not be surprised if he was meeting with the president and that is why he would not let us in the oval office today." Gideon Welles said.

"We need to tell you who we think the president trusts and who is in the circle. It does not leave this office, Jason, understand?" I shook my head, yes, and sat forward in my seat.

"We think he is taking his advice from a small group of generals headed by Halleck. Pinkerton is the spy master and he listens to him. Whenever the two sources confirm current or future events, the president reacts with general orders from the White House."

"There is no cabinet level input?"

"If the cabinet was uniformly opposed to something, in a cabinet meeting, then the President might change his mind. But none of us sitting in this office will see him on a day-to-day basis, he will not consult with or send for us on an individual basis for consultation. General Halleck sits in on every cabinet meeting as my undersecretary, even though he is not. He is an automatic consensus vote for Lincoln's positions on agenda items. You will attend the next cabinet meeting as Gideon's undersecretary to see what the reaction is from the president. We hope that he will see you as another consensus vote. What the two of us would like, is for you to speak your mind, just like you have done in this meeting. Can you do that?"

"Be honest, tell the truth, try to bring the President out of his depression, yes, I can do that."

"Thank you, Jason, that is the reaction that we hoped for."

"We should let Admiral Caldwell get back to his office, Ed, he has not even unpacked his things and found a billet for his aide. What is your aide's name, Jason?"

"Captain Thomas Q. Schneider of the United States Marines, Sir."

"I should have guessed that one!" replied the Secretary of the Navy.

As we walked back to Gideon's office he said, "What else do you need to begin work, Jason?"

"Several items, we must improve the speed of communication within the military. We can no longer rely on paper messages that take days or weeks to deliver. I will pay for and have installed private telegraph monitors in my office, your office, Ed's office. I already have one in my office at Seneca Hill. I will hire morse key operators for a 'basement' station here in the Army Navy Building. Right now we send and receive telegraph messages through the White House 'basement.'"

"Telegraph monitors?"

"Yes, I first saw them five years ago in Council Bluffs, Iowa. General Dodge, who I think is inside the circle with the president by the way, had one installed from the railhead to his home office. It looks like a stock market ticker and translates morse code to a small strip of paper."

"Do it. We do not need permission from the White House if the monitors are property of Caldwell International. Thank you, Jason, you have no idea how this will help me. I can send messages via the key operator from our building to whomever can receive them."

"Yes, you can send back and forth to London, if you like. I visit with Lord Napier at the Admiralty on a regular basis."

"You do?"

"Yes, that is why I know that the 8000 British Marines have not returned home. They have left Bermuda, I know that. The British ships of the line are still in Bermuda. They are waiting to get an order from Jefferson Davis to enter the Chesapeake and sail up the Potomac to burn the White House again, I am sure of it."

"You mentioned several things, what else do you need?"

"I will need the freedom to move around. I can not be effective locked inside an office here at the Army Navy Building. After the telegraph station is installed here, I will monitor things on a hourly basis. I will of course be available for cabinet meetings and other functions, but I plan to work from my office at Seneca Hill, not the office here.

My aide will be sitting behind my desk here and he will keep me informed. I trust his judgement. And as you become familiar with him you will find that he functions exactly as I do."

"What if that is not satisfactory?"

"Then my career as an undersecretary has been one day long!"

"I am not sure about this, Jason."

"Why not think about it? I will return to my office and have a letter of resignation written for you, I will not date it. You keep it in your office and when my service is not satisfactory you can date it."

"That would be satisfactory, very satisfactory indeed. I am going to do the same thing and give it to the President, I am tired of sitting outside the circle. I either want to be part of the future of this country or I want to leave the future to someone that the President trusts."

"You can always come to work for Caldwell International, I know the boss!"

In two days the telegraph station for the Army Navy Building was up and running. I sent a test message to myself before boarding a train for Seneca Hill. I welcomed Tom to his new office and asked him if his family had arrived from Bermuda. He indicated that they were in transit on a Caldwell ship. On September 17, I received the following message from Tom:

ADMIRAL, UNION FORCES UNDER McCLELLAN MET LEE'S ARMY IN MARYLAND AT A PLACE CALLED ANTIETAM, NOT FAR FROM WHERE YOU

PREDICTED. ADMIRAL HAGOOD'S GUNBOATS PRODUCED ONE OF THE BLOODIEST SINGLE DAYS OF THE WAR SO FAR. HE ESTIMATES 23,000 DEAD OR DISABLED FROM GRAPE SHOT AND MORTAR SHELLS. LEE HAS RETREATED BACK INTO VIRGINIA. WE DOUBT HE WILL BE BACK. WE FOLLOWED YOUR PLAN AND THE ADVANCED INFORMATION CONTAINED IN THE CONFEDERATE GENERAL ORDER 191 TO PINPOINT ENEMY STRENGTH AND WEAKNESSES.

THOMAS Q. SCHNEIDER, CAPTAIN USMC

Being at home with Louise, James, Ruthie, and baby Carol was a Godsend. I found that I loved family life, especially Ruthie. She was talking a blue streak. She would run to my side and scream, "Up, daddy, up". Then she would whisper in my ear that James had hit her on the arm.

"Does it hurt? Show daddy where he hit you. I cannot see anything. Do you want me to kiss it and make it better?" I would and then sit her down to run and tell her brother, James, "Daddy fixed it for me and he says if you ever hit me again, you are in BIG trouble."

Louise would then look at me and say, "I have an ouchy, daddy, can you kiss it for me and make it better?"

"Sure, where is it? No, I cannot kiss that in front of the children." And we would both burst out laughing. I found I liked being a husband and a family man.

On September 23, I received the following:

ADMIRAL, UNDER SEPARATE COVER I AM SENDING THE PRELIMINARY TEXT OF THE Emancipation Proclamation. It will take affect on January 1, 1863.

THOMAS Q. SCHNEIDER, CAPTAIN USMC

On September 27, I received the following:

ADMIRAL, THOUGHT YOU MIGHT LIKE TO KNOW THAT YOUR GENERAL BUTLER, THE ONE IN NEW ORLEANS, NOT THE ONE IN BERMUDA, HAS JUST FORMED THE FIRST OFFICIALLY RECOGNIZED NEGRO REGIMENT. BLACKS HAVE VOLUNTEERED AT A RATE NOT SEEN PRIOR TO THIS DATE.

THOMAS Q. SCHNEIDER, CAPTAIN USMC

These three telegrams proved that the system I had set up for communication was working. I replied to all three and sent separate congratulations to Admiral Hagood and General McClellan. There were no more messages until October 8.

Admiral, a second Confederate invasion of the North under General Braxton Bragg has been checked by Union General Don Carlos Buell at a place called Perrysville, Kentucky. Same battle plans were used. River gun boats caused second most casualties in the civil war. Bragg retreated.

Thomas Q. Schneider, Captain USMC

When the Army Navy Command suggested that General McClellan not pursue Lee back into Virginia and be caught away from naval gun fire support, he was dismissed from military service by the president. He was replaced by Ambrose E. Burnside, an inside the circle, General. George McClellan sent me the following letter:

November 15, 1862

My Dear Admiral:

Working with you these past two years have given me an insight to what our military needs are going to be in the next few years and beyond the civil war. Lincoln has a small group of advisors, as you well know, we were not part of the inner circle and, therefore, unable to reach him with what would work on the battlefields of our nation.

I have thought about this since leaving the military and I will form a committee to seek the nomination from the Democratic Party to run for the White House. I would be honored if you would run with me. Lincoln cannot be allowed to remain in the White House and prosecute the war in the way that he has. The confederacy should not be allowed to exist another day. The reconstruction of the war torn south must begin immediately.

I await your decision before I form the committee.

Faithfully yours,

George McClellan

I responded with a personal letter and a letter of credit for $100,000.00.

In December I received two messages:

Admiral, December 13, 1862, General Burnside, without naval support, crossed the Potomac and attacked the Confederate

FORTIFICATIONS AT FREDERICKSBURG, VIRGINIA. HE WAS ROUTED WITH LARGE UNION CASUALTIES.

THOMAS Q. SCHNEIDER, CAPTAIN USMC

I responded to both Stanton and Welles asking if the inside circle was really that INANE!

ADMIRAL, ADMIRAL FOOTE REPORTED ON DECEMBER 31, 1862, THE BATTLE OF STONE RIVER, TENNESSEE, IS OVER. COMBINED NAVAL GUN BOAT AND ARMY ARTILLERY FIRE HAS CAUSED 25,000 CONFEDERATE DEAD OR DISABLED FOR THE REMAINDER OF THE WAR.

THOMAS Q. SCHNEIDER, CAPTAIN USMC

I responded to both Stanton and Welles asking when will they understand, it is a matter of numbers!

A one line response came back from the Army Navy Building.

NOT THIS YEAR!

74
State of the Union
Washington City, 1863

It must be admitted that the state of the Union had seen substantial progress during 1862. The important victories were Mill Spring, Forts Henry and Donelson, Pea Ridge, Shiloh, Fort Pulaski, Corinth, Roanoke Island, New Orleans, opening of the Mississippi River, Seven Pines, Antietam, Perrysville and Stone River. The Union lines had been extended across the entire State of Tennessee and it was out of the fight. Ben Hagood's blockade of the southern ports was becoming more rigid with the sinking of the following ships trying to run out of Charleston; Osiris 10/61, Peerless 11/61, Governor 11/61, Rattlesnake 3/62, Experiment 4/62, Samuel Adams 4/62, Edwin 5/62, Nellie 5/62, and Minho 10/62. There had been a vicious outbreak of the Sioux Indians in Minnesota, but troops were sent and quiet was maintained.

But the truth was, that the suppression of the rebellion was no easy matter. In January, 1,300,000 volunteers had been called for, the number of vessels in the US Navy was now 600 and the war expenses now reached the total of $3,000,000 a day. Just as I had predicted to President Lincoln in July of 1861, a year's cost was now one billion, ninety-five million dollars. After both invasions of the north had been turned back, President Lincoln issued the Emancipation Proclamation.

In 1863, the government issued paper money in bills, which became known as "greenbacks", because of the color of the ink with which the bills were printed. These bills became legal tender. But because of the need for vast sums to pay war debts, the price of gold rose quickly to 285 dollars a troy ounce. This made the paper dollar worth about 35 cents in gold. Caldwell International had a huge inventory of paper bills because the gold coming out of Nevada was exchanged for paper money. A large portion of the war debt was paid by war bonds, a form of loan with interest to be repaid by the government. To aid in the sale of bonds, the National Banking system was established and Caldwell International now owned; two national banks, seven state banks, one territorial bank and one foreign bank. I figured with my net worth, I could finance about a week of the war.

I struggled with the duties of the undersecretary of the Navy. There were four Union Army Navy forces in the western theater of operations. Rosecrans/

Foote near Murfreesboro, Tennessee, Grant/Farragut near Vicksburg, Mississippi, Banks, who had succeeded Butler in New Orleans and a fourth was in Arkansas, where the Confederates were comparatively weak.

So far this year, the Union armies in the western theater alone had taken over 80,000 prisoners, including three major generals, nine brigadiers and about a hundred thousand pieces of military hardware. Grant summed it up best by stating: "The engagement of the enemy in five separate campaigns; (Chancellorsville, Vicksburg, Gettysburg, Chickamauga and Chattanooga), the occupation of the entire states of Mississippi and Tennessee, and the elimination of troops and materials to equip two Confederate armies have fallen into our hands."

Of all the records kept in 1863, the battle of Chickamauga was the most costly to the Union. The percentages of losses was greater than those incurred by the British army in a hundred years, including those of Waterloo and the entire Crimea War. Thirty regiments, composed of western soldiers, lost fifty percent. This percentage was more than fell in the "Charge of the Light Brigade" from British failed efforts.

Of all the records kept by the confederacy in 1863, the battle of Chancellorsville was the most costly to the south. The percentages of losses were greater than those of the Union at Chickamauga. Lee was unable to replace these losses suffered in May, before he met General Meade at Gettysburg on July 1, 1863. On November 19, 1863, Lincoln visited the battlefield and delivered his memorable "Gettysburg Address." The outcome of the war was no longer in doubt. But a strange thing happened in Washington City. General Halleck suddenly resigned and George Meade replaced him as commander of the Army of the Potomac. The inner circle was drawing ever smaller.

The President seemed less depressed and he ventured out of the White House as far as Gettysburg in Pennsylvania and around Washington City he was seen on a regular basis. He would often walk over to the Army Navy Building and talk to either his Secretary of War or his Secretary of the Navy depending upon which could answer his question at that moment. He walked into the undersecretary of the Navy in late November and asked to speak to whomever was in charge.

"The Admiral is not here, Mr. President, he is at sea with Admiral Hagood." Answered his aide, a captain in the marine corps.

"Well, tell him to stop over and see me tomorrow, will you?"

"Sir, I have no way of reaching him, he is at sea, on a ship somewhere between here and Cape Hatteras, North Carolina."

"What are they doing there? Who gave that order?"

"You did, Sir. War order no. 157. I have a copy of it right here, Sir."

"Never mind, if I gave an order, then I gave an order. Tell the Admiral that I would like to see him as soon as he returns to his office."

"Aye, aye, Sir."

"What did you say?"

"That was, Yes, Sir. In the navy, Sir."

"Well, you are not in the Navy, you are in the Army Headquarters Building, Washington City, USA."

"Yes, Mister President."

"Thank you, that was better. What did you say your name was soldier?"

"I am in the navy, Sir."

"Then what are you doing in the Army?"

"Just visiting, Sir."

"No wonder we are losing......" And the President collapsed onto the floor of Tom Schneider's office.

Tom rushed out of his office, crying, "Someone get the White House doctor." A clerk heard the cry and ran into the hallway and found a messenger to send to the White House to find the President's doctor. By the time that the doctor arrived, the President was sitting up and shaking his head.

"Did you faint again, Mister President?" The word 'again' was not lost on Tom Schneider.

"Yes, I must have. Where am I?"

"In the Army Navy Building, Mr. President."

"Oh, yes. I came to see Secretary Stanton, but he was not in. So I was looking for Welles."

"This is not Secretary Welles' office, Mr. President. It is down the hall. Do you feel dizzy?"

"No, I am fine. Help me up and I can find Welles' office."

He was helped by his doctor and they left for Welles' office, Tom grabbed a pad of paper and began writing down what was said so he could tell the Admiral what had happened. He finished his notes and walked down the hall to see if Secretary Stanton was in his office. He was there.

"Excuse me, Sir."

"Yes, Captain, what can I do for you?"

"Have you been in all morning?"

"Yes, why?"

"Did the President find you? He was looking for you or Mr. Welles."

"No, I will go down to Welles' office with you, Captain."

They walked down to Welles' office and asked, "Did the President find you a few minutes ago, Gideon?"

"No, I have not seen him, what happened, Tom?"

"He fainted in my office, Sir." Tom related the conversation as best he could remember it without his notes.

"He gets confused right before he faints. They are really small seizures, his doctor says they come on when he is under a great deal of stress. Something must have happened or someone has resigned that was part of the inner circle."

"Ed, it must be either Burnside or Meade who has called it quits, either one could trigger a seizure."

"For the sake of President Lincoln, let us hope it was both and we can convince him to appoint General Grant!" Said Tom Schneider without thinking. Both of the Secretaries glared at him.

"I am sorry, Sirs. I should not have said that."

"It is alright, Tom, we were thinking the same thing."

Tom retreated to his office and checked his calendar to see when the Admiral indicated he would return with Admiral Hagood. It would be just before Thanksgiving, a new holiday that he and his family would be celebrating this year in Seneca Hill, Pennsylvania. He would try to remember to tell the Admiral how the President had acted and what was the last thing that he had said just before he fainted. Was it *losing* or was it *choosing* something? He could not remember. He went home that night still bothered by what had happened, even though the cabinet members seemed to think that this was a common occurrence whenever the President was under extreme stress.

The train ride from Washington City to Pennsylvania was enjoyable for his wife Beth and the two children; Tom Jr., called JR and Emily Schneider. They had not seen the northwestern part of Pennsylvania before and the train ride was exciting for the children. Tom was met at the train station by a carriage from Seneca Hill and in a short while they were traveling on country roads that twisted through that part of Pennsylvania. They came over a rise and spotted the house on a hill. It looked like a mansion to Tom. It had giant white columns in front and a huge wrap around porch that had several french doors that led into different rooms on the ground floor. A side carriage portico was towards the right hand side of the first floor and the carriage stopped here to unload passengers and baggage. Louise Caldwell and her son James were waiting on the porch to welcome them.

"Tom, Beth, it is good to see you again." She hugged them both and smiled at the children. "James do you remember Emily and JR from Bermuda?" She asked.

"Yes, ma'am. Hello, JR, want to see my pony?" And they were off running towards a stable at the rear of the house.

"Emily, you are not going to believe how much Ruthie is talking now. If she bothers you, just tell her to leave you alone." This was said just as Ruthie came bounding out of one of the french doors and ran into Beth Schneider and fell to her knees.

"Sorry, Mrs. Schneider, I was trying to hurry and beat daddy and baby Carol out to see you." Jason Caldwell came through the open doors carrying a beautiful seventeen month old baby girl who looked exactly like her mother.

"Oh, my. She is the image of her mother!" Said Beth.

"Thank God." Said Tom and everyone laughed.

"Admiral, we sure wish we were going with you and your family to Bermuda this Christmas. We miss your brother and especially your father."

"I will tell him you said hello, Tom."

"When you get to be an Admiral, Tom, maybe you will take us somewhere special for Christmas." Beth said teasing.

"Marines do not have admirals, we have generals just like in the real army." Everyone laughed. "Besides I need to make major before we dream of anything more."

"You will, Tom. I think your performance in the Army Navy Building will get you that promotion."

Tom looked pained and said, "Admiral, can I talk to you in private?"

When he had finished telling Jason everything that was written on his notes, Jason said, "That explains several things, Tom. The President seemed as normal as you and me when I met with him in July of '61. I have not seen him since. He is avoiding all kinds of stressful situations and being around me would be extremely stressful because I tell him that his military advisors are addle minded."

"Admiral?"

"Tom, when we are alone, you can call me, Jason."

"I will think about it, Admiral." I began to laugh. "What is wrong, Sir?"

"That is always what I used to tell Louise's brother when I was in the White House."

"I remember, Sir. I made a small error in etiquette also." And he told him how the remark slipped out about hoping that both Burnside and Meade had resigned.

"Tom, that will do more to get you promoted than anything I can think of."

"Thank you, Jason."

"You are welcome, Tom, let us get back to the others before they think we resigned."

Before the long weekend was over I had my telegraph operator send the following message to the Secretary of the Navy:

MY AIDE, CAPTAIN SCHNEIDER, HAS BRIEFED ME ON PRESIDENT LINCOLN'S BEHAVIOR IN HIS OFFICE THIS PAST FORTNIGHT. I MUST APOLOGIZE FOR MY CONSTANT CRITICISM OF HIS CONDUCT OF THE WAR. I REALIZE THAT HE AVOIDED ME BECAUSE I ALWAYS WANTED HIM TO DO MORE THAN HE WAS CAPABLE OF AT THAT MOMENT. HIS WAS A CONSTANT BALANCING ACT BETWEEN WHAT WAS RIGHT FOR THE COUNTRY AND WHAT WAS POSSIBLE WITH THE RESOURCES AT HAND. IN MY OPINION, HE ALWAYS CHOSE 'GOD BEFORE COUNTRY' NOT MY 'COUNTRY ABOVE ALL ELSE.' FEW MEN WOULD HAVE DONE THAT. I CANNOT BELIEVE THAT I WAS ONE OF THE LATER. MY EYES ARE NOW OPEN AND I WILL NOT TRY TO 'SHORTEN THE WAR'. THE COUNTRY MUST GO THROUGH THIS 'CLEANSING PROCESS', I REGRET THAT SO MANY YOUNG MEN AND WOMEN HAVE DIED TO DATE. THE DEATH OF MY SISTER, IN COMBAT, STILL HAUNTS ME.

CAPTAIN SCHNEIDER REGRETS HIS REMARKS MADE TO YOU AND SECRETARY STANTON. HE IS THE FINEST OFFICER I HAVE EVER MET. HE FUNCTIONS WELL ABOVE HIS PRESENT RANK AND HE IS NOW READY TO ASSUME NEW DUTIES WITHIN THE MARINE CORPS. IT IS MY RECOMMENDATION THAT HE BE ASSIGNED TO THE MARINE COMMANDANT.

After Tom and his family had returned to Washington and Tom returned to the Army Navy Building, I got the following response from Secretary Welles:

ADMIRAL CALDWELL.

I SHARED YOUR TELEGRAM ABOUT THE PRESIDENT TO ALL THE CABINET MEMBERS AND THEY AGREE 100 PERCENT WITH YOUR DESCRIPTION OF THE LAST SEVERAL MONTHS IN THE WHITE HOUSE. WE ARE ALL IN AGREEMENT THAT THE PRESIDENT HAS TAKEN ON WAY TOO MUCH OF THE WAR EFFORT. SECRETARY STANTON HAS REORGANIZED THE MILITARY TO FUNCTION AS CORPS DIVISIONS INSTEAD OF THE WESTERN OR EASTERN THEATERS OF OPERATION. THE FIVE STAR ARMY AND FIVE STAR NAVY FLAG OFFICER WILL BRIEF THE PRESIDENT AT APPROPRIATE INTERVALS. THE PRESIDENT IS NO LONGER RESPONSIBLE FOR EVERY DECISION AT EVERY LEVEL OF THE MILITARY. YOU EXPRESSED REGRET THAT CAPTAIN SCHNEIDER WAS GROWING TO THE POINT THAT YOU WERE HOLDING HIM BACK. I AGREE AND HAVE RECOMMENDED THE FOLLOWING TO THE MARINE CORPS:

PROMOTION TO MAJOR AFFECTIVE JANUARY 1, 1864 ASSIGNMENT TO SECRETARY OF THE NAVY, ARMY NAVY BUILDING. AREA OF RESPONSIBILITY: RECRUITMENT AND TRAINING USMC. I NEED YOUR SELECTION FOR YOUR NEW AIDE, IN YOUR NEXT MESSAGE.

Without hesitation, I sent the following reply:

Promotion of Warrant Officer Samuel Mason, present assignment Bermuda, to Captain USMC. Transfer to Army Navy Building affective January 1, 1864.

75
Winter Campaign
Washington City

Winter activity during the war was a time to slow or stop major campaigns. This time was used to train new recruits, both volunteers and the draftees. Both the north and south could no longer depend upon volunteers to fill the ranks and both sides resorted to conscription of men to serve between the ages of 25 to 45. Leaves were granted from the Army Navy Building during these times and I had gotten a 30 day leave to return to Bermuda. Granted, it was a working leave in that we needed to bring Jerome Lewis and his office into the new communication loop that we had devised for the Army Navy Building. Secretary Seward had his own 'basement' operation in the White House but he saw the advantages of our network. The problem was no cable from the United States east coast to Bermuda existed. Tom Schneider reminded me of what we did in Navel Intelligence during the Utah missions.

"Remember, Sir. We used the telegraph where the lines were strung and in between we had the pony express deliver the message to the next line operator."

"So, what we need is pony boat express!"

"Yes, Sir. How do we do that?"

"I will talk to the Postmaster General and see what is available. We use mail steamers now. I wonder if there is anything faster?"

I walked to the White House in search of the Postmaster General. I found him in his office and said, "Montgomery Blair, just the man I need to see!"

He appeared to be startled, as few cabinet members ever addressed him in the cabinet meetings, he was just there, the chief mailman of the United States. "Yes, Admiral, what can I do for you?"

"Well, I have a question."

"I hope I can answer it. What is it?"

"I need to get messages back and forth between Washington City and Bermuda Station faster than the once a week mail steamers."

"You need a telegraph cable."

"Thanks, when can you have it installed?" He really looked startled now, his glasses nearly slid off the end of his nose.

"I mean the American Telegraph Company, not the post office!"

I laughed and said, "I did not mean that you should lay a cable, Monty."

"Seriously, Jason, you need to talk to the people over there. They are expanding in every direction. All you have to do is pay for the rent on the line and allow them to send public messages as well."

"Really! What do you suppose the monthly rent on a cable is?"

"Thousands of dollars, I would imagine, I do not know."

"Monty, I hate to ask this, but could you come down there with me to talk to them? I am a nobody in the message world, but you are a real somebody. They might listen to you."

He puffed out his chest and said, "Finally, somebody appreciates what I try to do around here." He stood and strode out of his office and told his secretary, "If anyone is looking for me, I will be on a secret mission with the Admiral here!" He kept on walking and I had to hurry to keep up with him. He hailed a White House carriage and we were off to downtown Washington and the American Telegraph office. He was well known there and he breezed past the hired help and we were sitting in the company president's office, a Mr. Dewitt, and were visiting like old friends.

"So, the Postmaster General here, says that you install and then rent underground telegraph cable. Is that correct?"

"Yes, Admiral. But we do not do anything for the federal government, it is a matter of payment, you see. The fact is, the feds are always late or unpaid in their bills since the war started."

"This would not be for the federal government. I am president of Caldwell International, you know the holding company for American Telegraph?"

"Oh, my God. I did not put two and two together Mr. Caldwell, I am sorry!"

"It is, Admiral Caldwell, until the war is over, Mr. Dewitt. It is 600 miles to Bermuda, correct?"

"That is correct, Admiral."

"So what is it going to cost Caldwell International to lay 600 miles of cable?"

"Well, it will not cost Caldwell International anything since you own us. I mean, the cost will be our costs, I mean, our cost will be paid by others that use the cable." Montgomery Blair was really enjoying this.

"Good, so we have established that it can be done. What is the time frame; weeks, months or years?"

"Certainly not years or weeks, General, but months should do it."

"It is, Admiral, and can you start tomorrow?"

"Yes, Sir. All we need is a signed authorization from you to begin."

"Have your secretary type it up, Mr. Dewitt. Monty and I are going to lunch and then we will be back and we will sign it."

"We, Admiral?"

"Yes, we, Monty. The United States Post office just became our first public customer!"

He laughed and said, "Agreed, Admiral, it will be the best buy of my administration." We had that lunch. And every Wednesday we had lunch, until Louise and I left for Bermuda and our Christmas break.

76

State of the Confederacy
Richmond, 1863

In Richmond, President Davis was considering the progress made by the army and navy in the last six months of action. Galveston, like all the other seaports of the South, was blockaded by the Union fleet. General Magruder, after collecting artillery at Houston, occupied the works erected opposite the island on which Galveston stands. Two steam packets were converted to gunboats and strong bulwarks of cotton bales made them 'small arms proof'. These were manned by Texas cavalry men. They steamed up and engaged the Union gunboat *Harriet Lane*, while Confederate troops were marching over the long railway bridge that connects Galveston Island to the mainland. The *Harriet Lane* drove off one of the gunboats, but the other ran alongside and under brisk rifle fire, the Texans leaped aboard the *Harriet Lane* and killed Captain Wainwright and the crew. The *Westfield* tried to go to the aid of the *Harriet Lane* and it too was destroyed with all hands. Meanwhile, the land troops had captured the city and the blockade was lifted and it looked like it would now stay in the hands of the Confederacy.

President Davis also had limited success in obtaining Great Britain's assistance in the launching of privateers upon the high seas. Privateers were licensed by a government to capture merchant ships upon the sea and sell them in European ports of call. So long as the Confederacy was not recognized as a distinct nation by other governments, its privateers could not take their prizes into any port to sell them. So far, the privateers for the Confederacy were stopping and robbing US Merchantmen of everything worth taking and then burning the ships.

Confederate privateers would have had a difficult time in fitting out and getting to sea without the help of England. In April, Davis bought the HMS *Oreto* and renamed it the CSS *Florida*. When ready, the Florida was sailed to Nassau, Bahamas. She then appeared off Mobile harbor flying the British Union Jack. Commander Preble, of the Union blocking fleet, had been warned about giving England another Trent Affair. He did fire upon her and she entered the harbor safely. The *Florida* received her armament and came out again, under the command of Captain Maffit. She inflicted immense damage on the blocking fleet and sailed off into the middle Atlantic towards

Bermuda. The second ship built in England was named the CSS *Sumter*, it was captained by A. J. Semmes. The *Sumter* was not as fortunate as the *Florida* and it was sunk by the USS *Tuscarora*. Captain Semmes escaped and returned to England for another ship. The one built for him was the CSS *Alabama*, the most successful privateer to date for the Confederacy. The CSS *Nashville* was sunk by the USS *Montauk*.

Davis ordered that all blockades be destroyed by the Confederate Navy and privateers, starting with Charleston Harbor. A Union fleet of ironclads blocked the harbor. Captain Ingraham of the CSS *Rampage* ran out accompanied by two gun boats and scattered the ironclads and captured a Union gunboat. He then sent word to President Davis that the blockade was broken. And it was until the next day, when Admiral Du Pont, was ordered to attack and occupy the city of Charleston by Admiral Benjamin Hagood. The ironclads now formed a line of battle with the USS *Weehawken* under the command of Captain J. K. Rogers. A cumbrous "mine sweeper," in the shape of a raft, was fastened to the front of the *Weekawken* and it slowed the advance of the line. The *Weekawken* now came under fire from Fort Moultrie and then exploded a mine under the bow and put her out of action until repairs could be made. The second in line was the USS *Keokuk* and it too came under heavy fire from both Fort Sumter and Moultrie. She was struck ninety times in the course of half an hour and sank to the bottom of Charleston Harbor. The third in line was the new USS *Ironsides* and it had a remarkable escape from sinking. Her rudder was shot away and she became entangled with three other ironclads, the four of them lay in deadlock for quarter of an hour trying to free the mine that lay under them. A hundred cannon from Fort Sumter pounded the entanglement until Admiral Du Pont signaled by flags that the fleet should withdraw. The blockade fleet retired to Port Royal Harbor and for another day the blockade was lifted.

The failure of this attack was a great disappointment to Admiral Hagood. He ordered Admiral Du Pont to return and establish the blockade. He was instructed not to allow the enemy to put up new defenses on Morris Island. Admiral Du Pont's reply dwelt so much on the risks involved, he was replaced by Admiral Jab Dahlgren, who made plans for a coordinated land and sea attack on Charleston. General Gilmore, the hero of Savannah, was to lead the land attack and capture the three land forts of Charleston while Admiral Dahlgren would silence Sumter and occupy it.

The conventional plan of attack used at Fort Pulaski in Savannah did not work in Charleston. General Gilmore ordered General Strong to take the first land fort while Union gun boats pounded it from off shore. General Strong was wounded and seventy-five percent of this troops were killed in the first day of action. Gilmore was enraged and ordered the gun boats to level the fort. After 14 hours of shelling the fort grew silent and the rest of Gilmore's troop cheered. The summer temperatures were reaching 100 degrees and Gilmore said his troops could wait until the cool of the evening to occupy the fort. At dusk his troops advanced and met murderous cannon fire from the fort. While Gilmore rested, the Confederates reinforced the fort from Charleston. Gilmore was now livid and ordered the city of Charleston to be shelled at random. It threw the general population of the city into panic. General Beauregard, defender of Charleston, sent an impassioned message to Gilmore, "Never before, among civilized nations, has a commander ordered the murder of non- combatants without prior notice so that those might leave and save their lives." The battle for Charleston lasted another forty-two hours. The southern wall of Fort Sumter was in ruins. The loss of life was minimal, however. The other forts held and the inner line of defenses extending across James Island towards Sullivan's Island were impregnable. The combined attacks by Union forces had failed and the victory was reported to Richmond.

Upon hearing the news from Charleston, Davis said, "It is time to start the great naval uprising of the South." He was referring to his preparation for battle order no. 211 which had been issued after the fall of New Orleans. It stated that next to New Orleans, Mobile was the most important seaport on the Gulf of Mexico. Accordingly, the fullest preparations shall be made for its defense. A naval force was formed under Admiral Franklin Buchanan, the hero at Hampton Roads. He ordered the construction of five heavy gun boats at Selma, one hundred and fifty miles up the Alabama River. The Confederate ironclad the CSS *Tennessee* was built in this shipyard. It was on station with eighteen officers and one hundred men.

Buchanan believed that he could destroy the blockade of Mobile with surprise and the darkness of night to aid his efforts. On the night of May 18, 1863, he planned to destroy the blockade, then destroy the entire Union Gulf Fleet under Farragut, capture Fort Pickens at Pensacola, then on to New Orleans and finally sail around the tip of Florida and free the entire east coast. Quite a grandiose plan for one ironclad and five heavy gun boats! But then, Franklin Buchanan was a dreamer like his cousin James. Like all grand schemes, they come to an end. The *Tennessee* ran aground in the dark and remained immovable until after daylight. With the chance of taking the blockade fleet by surprise gone, he waited for the tide to change and refloat the *Tennessee*. He anchored, under the guns of Fort Morgan, at the mouth of the Alabama.

No place in the South was more powerfully fortified than Mobile. Fort Gaines was a brick fort on Dauphin Island and had a garrison of 864 men. Fort Powell commanded the principal pass to Mississippi Sound. Fort

Morgan was the main fortification and mounted its guns in three tiers. The ship channel was spanned by a double row of surface mines called 'torpedoes'. Buchanan's delay of the Tennessee and his obvious intention of defending the Port of Mobile gave enough time for one of the blockade vessels to steam to the Union Gulf Fleet and warn them. The Fleet promptly sailed for Mobile with Admiral Ben Hagood on board the USS *Hartford*.

The Union Gulf Fleet consisted of twenty-one wooden vessels and four ironclads. Admiral Farragut's plan of attack was to pass up the channel close under the guns of Fort Morgan, where a free channel had been left for the blockade runners. The vessels were to sail in pairs, with the larger ship on the left to give fire support. Farragut's intention was to lead with his flag ship the *Hartford*, but at the urgent request of Admiral Hagood, he gave that perilous post to the Captain James Alden of the *Brooklyn*. They were to attack in the morning of the next day and David Farragut could not sleep that night so he sat up and wrote to his wife.

"We are going into Mobile in the morning, if God is with us, as I hope He is, and in Him I place my trust. If am to die tomorrow, I am ready to submit to His will. God bless and keep you if anything

should happen to me."

Before seven the next morning the fleet crossed the bar and moved up the channel in a battle line. Farragut climbed up and took position in the port main shrouds on the upper sheer ratline, twenty-five feet high. He could see the USS *Tecumseh* open the battle by firing at Fort Morgan. His monitors like the *Tecumseh* and *Brooklyn* were expected to draw the fire from Fort Morgan. The CSS *Tennessee* and her five escorts came out from Fort Morgan and opened fired on Farragut's fleet. The enveloping smoke screened the ships from his view and he climbed higher on the ship's rigging. Ben Hagood was closely watching Farragut, fearful that some accident might befall him, he ordered a seaman to climb the rigging with a rope to secure him to the shrouds. The thickening smoke made Farragut go still higher. He could signal, by flags, to other ships in his fleet from here and he did so. He called for the ships to close up ranks. The larger ships obeyed and they poured broadsides into the fort.

Captain Carvin, of the *Tecumseh*, was eager to meet the *Tennessee*. He paid no attention to fire from the fort, making straight for the *Tennessee*. A change of direction by the *Tennessee* caused him to run directly over the line of torpedoes. Suddenly there was a muffled explosion and a massive column of water leaped into the air. The *Tecumseh* lurched to port, her bow dropped, her stern tilted up, the screw turning in the air and she slipped below the water carrying all hands to their deaths. Farragut was watching the disaster and signaled to look for survivors. He watched as he saw his line of battle become entangled with the line of torpedoes. He shouted below to the *Hartford* crew, "Damn the torpedoes, full speed ahead." Ben Hagood could not believe his ears, he was about to die at the battle of Mobile. What he did not know was that David Farragut, high up in the riggings had seen a clear line directly through the network of torpedoes and had signaled the other ships to follow in single line after the *Hartford*. Ben held his breath, expecting to see the noble old flagship and her heroic admiral blown to bits.

"No more decisive test of bravery is conceivable," He would later tell his friend Jason, "than that of the men below decks on the *Hartford*. Standing in awed silence, they heard a strange, grating noise along the entire hull of the *Hartford*. They knew it was the cables attached to the torpedoes. That hideous scraping sound slid off into silence. They had missed the *Hartford*."

The Confederate commander of Fort Morgan was watching and would later declare, "The admiral clinging to the mizzenmast was as calm as he could be and his quick perception saved the Union fleet that day."

Farragut's action now placed the *Hartford* in the lead of the line of battle, Ben Hagood was shaking with fear as the huge CSS *Tennessee* bore down on them and hit them with a percussion shell. For the second time in two minutes, Ben Hagood feared for his life in Mobile. A jagged hole was torn in the Hartford's hull, but it was above the water line, she had escaped the second peril. Then Buchanan drove the CSS *Tennessee* towards the *Hartford*, intending to sink her, as she had the USS *Cumberland* at Hampton Roads. Farragut signaled to evade the charge and to sweep up the channel. The CSS *Tennessee*, having missed the *Hartford* continued down the line of battle. She raked broadsides into the rest of the entire line, but all Union vessels continued up the channel after the *Hartford*.

Fort Morgan had been passed with the CSS *Tennessee* and her gun boats retreating and holding under the fort. Mobile harbor was now in full possession of the Union fleet, who anchored some four miles above the fort. But so long as the *Tennessee* waited to attack again, the victory was not complete and Farragut was determined to destroy the monster as soon as he had given his men a few hours rest. But Buchanan did not wait to be attacked, he slowly started creeping towards the Union fleet. The parapets of the three forts were crammed with soldiers to watch the destruction of the fleet.

Slowly swinging around, the *Tennessee* steamed out to engage the fleet. Farragut had his signalman transmit the following:

"Raise anchors - attack with bow guns - ram at full speed."

Farragut reasoned that his ships guns would do little to slow the *Tennessee*, he would have to sink her by ramming. Farragut had iron plating on the bows of his wooden ships, not fully iron construction. When the USS *Monogahela* rammed the *Tennessee* , the iron prow was torn off. The *Tennessee* developed a small leak. When the USS *Lackawanna* rammed the *Tennessee*, she rolled fifteen degrees to starboard. Now the *Tennessee* was hurt. Not out of fight, she turned towards the *Hartford* and they engaged. Ben Hagood knew this time he was dead. A wooden ship cannot stand against a larger, all iron, vessel. He said his prayers and waited to die.

At a critical moment, the captain of the USS *Manhattan* cut across the bow of the *Tennessee* and fired the largest guns of the US fleet, fifteen inch. The *Tennessee* turned like a wounded animal to face its new threat. She turned directly into the USS *Chickasaw* and received a ram under her stern, locking the two vessels together. Ben Hagood had to smile, the *Chickasaw* looked like a bulldog biting a horse in the ass. The *Chickasaw* had eleven inch guns and she fired point blank into the stern of the *Tennessee*. Meanwhile the USS *Winnebago* rammed the helpless *Tennessee* amid ships and she rolled again. The *Manhattan* was now in position to fire the fifteen inch guns and the *Tennessee* was in trouble. Admiral Buchanan had his leg blown off below the knee and before he died, he turned command over to Captain Johnston to try to make an escape. Escape was impossible and he surrendered.

The Union fleet now turned its attention to the three forts. They shelled Fort Powell and a white flag was raised over the fort. Fort Gaines was now addressed with similar results. Only the monster, Fort Morgan, remained. It was shelled for two days and it surrendered. Mobile was now a Union seaport. Admiral Farragut was transferred from the *Hartford* to accompany Ben Hagood to Washington and a hero's welcome. In this furious battle, the Union lost all hands on the *Tecumseh*, 52 killed on other ships, 170 wounded and 4 missing, assumed lost at sea.

1863 was a year of bitter disappointment for President Davis and his war cabinet. Stonewall Jackson was killed after the victory at Chancellorsville by friendly fire. When Vicksburg fell to Grant and Sherman, the entire State of Mississippi was now in Union control. The disaster at Gettysburg further reduced the size of the standing army in the east. In the fall, a victory cheered Richmond, it was the battle of Chickamauga. The defeat at Chattanooga released General Sherman from Grant's Command to begin his Atlanta Campaign. The only bright spot was in December when General Bragg released General Longstreet to drive a Union force into Knoxville and trap them there.

77

CSA Embassy
Bermuda

From Bermuda, General Butler reported that the English invasion fleet that was supposed to enter the Chesapeake in support of the Confederate States of America, had sailed for home. The 8000 Marines had landed in Brunswick, Canada. The US Consulate Office was closed for thirty days and John Butler wished he could jump on a trolley and visit the Caldwells in St. George. His attention from his paper work was interrupted by the ringing of the door bell at his front office door. He walked to the door and peered through the side lights. It was Jerome Lewis, his friend from the US Consulate Office. He threw open the door and said, "I was just thinking about you."

"You were? Can you spare a few days? Louise and Jason are spending the holidays at Caldwell Place. Does the embassy have a petty cash jar?"

"Of course."

"The Inn has a reservation for you. Jason says you can come and visit for a few days if the Confederacy is not bankrupt!"

"Are you headed there now?"

"Yes, my family is already there. I was sent to fetch you."

"Come in and I will pack an overnight bag and we can leave." They rode the train from Hamilton, passed through the Flatts section of Bermuda, across stone work bridges and blue sparkling waters. The temperature was 72 degrees in the middle of December and John Butler thought the winters in Charleston are not that bad, but they could not compare with the beauty of Bermuda, he would be sad to leave this place. Then he had a strange thought, "I am a bachelor, I can live anywhere I want, why not here? Jerome, what are you going to do after the war?"

"I have to decide if I want to stay with the State Department or return to the Navy as my full time career. I was a policeman in Louisville, Kentucky before I joined the Navy. So, I have some options."

"Would you ever consider staying here in Bermuda?"

"As long as I was the minister here, yes. It is a beautiful place to live and work."

"I have decided not to go back to South Carolina."

"You have! I am surprised, General."

"That is just the point, Jerome. At home I would be the defeated General from the Civil War. I want to start over with a clean slate."

"Well, you could not pick a better place. Have you ever been interested in a business, John?"

"Yes, I ran a small business in Charleston before the war. I was also a General in the State Militia. It was an honorary title. I have never commanded troops in battle."

"Talk to Jason this week, John, I think he might have something for you."

"Here in Bermuda? That would be great."

"And even better if you could start before the war ended. What he has in mind would be in no way a conflict of interest for you, John."

"What is it? You have gotten my curiosity going."

"Caldwell International is bringing a telegraph office to Hamilton and St. George."

"The country is so small, why connect Hamilton and St. George."

"Not if you connect Hamilton, St. George, America, Canada and England. Think about it, John. The cable is in place between Canada and England. The US is already connected to Canada to have transatlantic cable service. What if a cable was laid from Bermuda to America?"

"This is Jason's doing. He has found a make work job for me?"

"Not at all, John. He would never even ask you if you wanted to work in Bermuda. He is from South Carolina and he knows how you Carolinians think. He asked me to broach the question with you so you could turn him down gracefully. He wants you to run the Bermuda Telegraph System. The offer is genuine and it will be open for you to think about. The cable is being laid from St. George to Maryland as we speak in both directions at the same time. Jason never does things half way, John."

"My God, my prayers have been answered!"

"I take that is a, yes?"

"Damn right it is a, yes. Where do I sign on?"

"Caldwell Place in about ten minutes, looks like we are almost there."

The train pulled into St. George station and we walked down Duke of York Street to Rose Hill and up the steep incline to Caldwell Place. We were both out of breath when we hit the front doors.

"John Butler, it is good to see you again." Louise Caldwell gave him a hug and held on to his arm. "Let me introduce you to everyone. Everyone, this is General John Butler from Charleston. That man over there is Jason's Father, Robert and next to him is his brother, Robert and next to him is another Robert, Robert Whitehall." People began to giggle and Louise said, "What?"

"Too many Roberts." Said Mariann.

"Oh, that is right. If you forget someone's name just call them Robert!"

Louise never did get the rest of the introductions finished, but John Butler did not care. He was among his fellow South Carolinians and he loved it. Jason and James came into the room with a large tablet of paper and James said, "Hey, Uncle John, want to play identify that ship?"

"Hulls and masts, or do I have to identify sails? I am lousy at sails."

"So, is Dad. He cheats, so watch him."

They laid the large paper tablet on one of the serving tables in the dining hall and James began his first lesson. He drew three masts. " The first mast is called the foremast, it has three sections. The section closest to the deck is called the lower foremast, the middle is called the fore-top mast."

"Wait, why not call it the middle foremast?"

"Cause that would make it too easy for you land lubbers!" The room erupted in laughter.

"James Jason Caldwell, you will apologize to your Uncle John or go to your room!" Louise was red in the face.

"I am sorry, Uncle John, my mouth ran away with itself."

"Let me get this straight, all three masts have lower masts, right?"

"Right."

"And all of the masts have top masts, right?"

"Right."

"Then why not call the middle, the middle?"

"Cause the middle sections are named after their masts, like mizzen, main and fore."

"I get it, cried John Butler!" And everyone laughed again.

"Now, on to the hard part. The sails are called yards."

"Can someone get me a drink?" John Butler was having the time of this life. Or maybe he was introduced to family life for the first time, as an adult. Jason left, fixed him his favorite, returned and handed it to him.

"You can tell where the yards are by which mast they are on. For example, main yards are on the mainmast, fore yards are on the foremast and mizzen yards are on the mizzenmast."

"Wait a minute, are you making this up as you go, James?" The laughter got louder.

"No, honest the mizzenmast is the most important because the jiggermast can be raised or lowered."

"Good God, I need another drink!" The main dining hall erupted again.

"Really, Uncle John, it is simple, just look at my sketch!"

"Where is this jiggermast?"

"I have not drawn it, yet!"

"Because you just made it up, right?" And the dining room was in stitches from laughter.

I glanced over at Jerome, he smiled and nodded his head, yes. I said, "That is enough, James, go find your sister and tell her your mother wants to talk to her." I gave a shrug of my shoulders and said, "When you have time, Uncle John, I would like to talk to you about a business venture that I am starting in Bermuda'.

78
Virginia City, Nevada
Spring 1864

When silver was discovered in Nevada five years ago, it was not met with the same "Gold Rush Fever" at Sutter's Mill, California. It took almost a year for the news to reach prospectors and large scale mine operators. It was known within the White House, however, and Jason Caldwell had sent his representatives to explore this business prospect. They were guided by two of his RR marines, corporals D.D. Wilson and Matthew James, now private citizens and employees of Caldwell International, now just known by its initials (CI). When the CI representatives; a mining engineer, surveyor and construction foreman, reached Carson Canyon they found 200 gold miners at work along the gravel banks of the canyon river with rockers, Long Toms and sluices. Most of the men complained about a heavy blue-black material which kept clogging their rockers. The CI engineer thought this might be silver and when he had it assayed, it was determined to be almost pure sulphuret of silver. Traveling on up the river, they came to the town of Johnstone. Here they paused long enough to purchase a few lots upon which to build later. Jason Caldwell had insisted that they not pan for gold. He also indicated that they should not stake claims for silver, instead they should build a saw mill and obtain timber for the mill. He reasoned that mining required timbers cut from trees and water. They were to purchase any water rights that they could find. Then and only then, should they begin to buy up played out gold strikes, turning these into silver mining operations.

By the Spring of 1860, those who discovered the Comstock Lode had extracted all the gold and discounted the "blue-stuff". Patrick McLaughlin sold his interest in the Ophir Mine to CI for $3,500.00. Emanual Penrod sold his share for $8,500.00. Peter O'Riley held on to his share for a few months and sold to CI for $40,000.00 in order to build a hotel. One year later the Ophir Mine produced one and one half million dollars in silver dividends for stock holders. D. D. Wilson, manager of the saw mill, sold over a half a million dollars in cut timbers for the prevention of cave ins to other mine owners. Matthew James, director of CI Water Company was selling sump pumps to keep the mines free of flooding from vast quantities of underground streams of hot water. The hot water was collected and sent to

Johnstone through pipes and sold there to businesses and townspeople. The proceeds from these enterprises were placed in the Bank of California until the CI bank was built in Johnstone in 1861 and 1862 in Carson City.

There were no railroads into Nevada, CI noticed this and began a shipping operation. Freight and passengers were transported by mule teams of from 10 to 16. Ore was hauled from the mines to the mills for refining by CI, Shipping. They brought to the mines all the timbers, mining machinery and supplies. No wagon made an unloaded run anywhere. Goods and merchandise needed by small mining towns was hauled over the Sierras from California on the return trips from deposits of pure silver and gold from the refining mills. CI investments would have flourished by shipping contracts only, but it was the CI Water Company that became the real "Gold Mine."

In 1860, the flow of water from natural springs was adequate to supply the needs of the miners and small towns of Johnstone, Virginia City and Gold Hill. As population increased, wells were dug for domestic needs, and the water within several mine tunnels was added to the available supplies. As the refining, smelting mills and hoisting operations multiplied, the demand for water for use in steam boilers became so great that it was impossible to supply it without creating a water shortage. To fill this need the water company began hauling water to whomever needed it. Water tank wagons became common sights as they traveled from the Sierra Nevada mountains to the Virginia ranges that lay in the Washoe Valley. The CI engineer, Herman Schussler, began working on a plan to replace the wagon trains by a cast iron pipe line. The 7 mile distance between water source and water demand could be met with a 12 inch diameter pipe which would produce 92,000 gallons of water per hour. CI Water Systems Construction division now became the leading manufacturer of water systems for towns in Nevada.

In the spring of 1861, D. D. Wilson had sent his second report back to the home office in Pennsylvania. He had the accountants provide an annual statement of saw mill production, sales and expenses. His salary was $10.00 per day, he itemized his expense account, and indicated that his profit sharing of 2% of timber production for that year was $10,000.00. Employees were paid at $1.00 per day plus expenses and ½% profit sharing or $2500.00. The cost of timber purchased that year was $40,000.00. Equipment and supply costs were $28,000.00. Transportation costs were $11,250.00. This left roughly $440,000.00 on deposit in the CI Bank of Johnstone for payment of outstanding debts. The mill had been constructed at a cost of $80,000. The interest on the loans for operating expenses, equipment and transportation showed a balance of zero. Not apparent to a casual reader was that the interest was paid to a CI bank, transportation costs were paid to a CI firm and timber purchases were from a CI firm.

Matthew James sent a similar annual report for the water company. It had a balance of $850,000 on deposit in the bank of Johnstone to pay outstanding debts; interest, transportation, machinery purchases, pipe and supply purchases. His annual salary was also $10.00 per day, plus 2% of net operating profits or $13,000.00 His expense account was not itemized, but it was modest, it included one trip to Indiana to ask his school sweetheart to marry him, now that he was a rich man.

In 1864, when the copies from the lumber company, water company, mining and shipping were forwarded to Jason and Louise Caldwell at Seneca Hill, Pennsylvania, they were pleased. The western assets had increased from the 14 million dollars in 1860 to 44 million for 1864. When Louise reviewed the statements, she said, "Jason, D.D. and Matthew have done another outstanding amount of work for us in the last three years. We have increased their profit sharing by 2% each of the last three years. That means they make $30,000.00 and $36,000.00 a year in profit sharing plus their annual salaries. I am pleased that you took them off hourly and gave them salaries so they stay content and with us."

"I agree, they signed contracts with us for five years. The contracts are due to be signed again. I should travel to Nevada as soon as I can find time."

"Oh, Jason, I do not know about you going all that way, just to sign contracts! The length of time that you will be away from the Army Navy Building, will they give you leave?"

"In 1862, General Dodge started building from Council Bluffs westward along the trail that I took to Nevada in October of '57. In five years he is past the point where you turn south off the overland stage route and head into Fort Bridger. I will book passage from Washington City on the train and ride it to the end of the line, somewhere in Utah. D.D. Wilson, Matthew James, Herman and the other managers can meet me there. It will take some coordination, sure. But you must keep face to face contact with your managers, wherever they may be. I will suggest that we meet in California when the Central Pacific meets the Union Pacific coming from Council Bluffs. They estimate that it will be somewhere around Ogden, Utah. As soon as that is completed, you and I can get on a train in Pittsburgh and get off in Sacramento, California."

"Why is it necessary to go before the railroad is finished then?"

"I wrote to DD telling him about Congress authorizing a United States Mint for Carson City."

"What did you ask him to do?"

"To check with Herman, our mining engineer to get a new estimate on how many more years the silver will last. Last time I asked him, he said it looks like a fifteen to twenty year run. After that, the veins of the Comstock will be completely gone. I want to stop taking our silver to California, I want to start selling it to the mint right there in Carson City. They will strike silver and gold coins."

"And what about the supply of gold in Nevada, Jason?"

"That should be gone soon, we will still haul refined gold from California to Carson City, Nevada."

"But, if both the silver and gold are gone?"

"Some day that will happen, but not in our life times."

"Are you going to be sad to leave the Department of the Navy and your work there for Gideon Welles, Jason?"

"Louise, this country has held together better than I thought it would, the future for a Union with the south still does not look good. We have survived and even prospered during the national war between the states."

"Has the war brought additional profits for a company like ours?"

"Yes, I told you earlier that we would loose everything in either South Carolina or Pennsylvania depending upon which is occupied territory. At this point, neither side is going to occupy the other. They will fight until one side or the other is completely ruined and unable to continue the war effort. We have temporarily lost our holdings in South Carolina. The western assets are secure and will remain so. Nevada has applied for statehood it should be granted later this year.

"Jason, what will happen to your parents property and the rest of your family when the war ends?"

"I have talked with my father about coming back to South Carolina with me and Robert, but I doubt he will want to leave Bermuda, he can run Robert's business for him. I will make the offer to move them if they want. It is really up to them."

"Could they manage their business's from a remote location, like you do, Jason? We have excellent people that manage for us. They need to find people they can trust. You trust people, Jason."

"As we have said before, evaluate first, then trust. Then we never have to say, *what in the hell is this*?"

"What?"

"Remember me telling you about Master Chief Gunnerman, my DI in Annapolis?"

"Yes, you said he taught you a lot about how to handle people. He always assumed that you would not do things correctly, and therefore, you did not try very hard to please him."

"Yes, Louise, we assume that people will do the right thing, because they want to please us. The fear of letting someone down is much greater than the actual fact. You try harder, you correct things on the fly, when things go awry."

"Jason, that is exactly how you are with your brother and father."

"Of course, practice what you preach!"

"So, when will you leave for Nevada?"

"I need to calculate how many days of train travel, both ways. Then add a few days for interruptions and at least one day for the meeting. Then I can inform Gideon how many days I will be gone."

"You inform him?"

"Yes, we have an agreement. I work for him for one dollar a year and I have as much time off as I need. If I am gone too much, he will simply date my letter of resignation and I will be retired again."

"Sounds sensible."

"Louise?"

"Yes, Jason."

"Do you always have to have the last word in our conversations?"

"No, it just works out that way!"

Sam and I were on our way west the next week. It took us three days to get to Independence, Missouri, on a nonstop sleeper. We had boarded the train at Union Station and stepped off the train whenever it stopped for mail or water to stretch our legs. Nonstop meant you could sleep on board. From Independence westward the new railroad was built along side the old Butterfield overland stage route. It still operated but now it ran shorter routes from the train stations to outlying areas and back again. We had an overnight at Chimney Rock and then proceeded on into Fort Laramie in Wyoming Territory. My managers were waiting at the end of the line. They had a much shorter distance to travel but it took the same number of days.

The train came to a chugging stop. Six men on horseback greeted us. D. D. Wilson was no longer the boy who was excited upon being promoted from private to corporal in '57. Beside him sat Matthew James, his side kick in the marine detachment that I commanded in western Utah Territory a few years ago. Peters and Keets sat next to them, grown men no longer shave tail marines. Peters wore a star on his vest, indicating that he was the Johnstone town Marshall as well as a CI employee. William Burns and Herman, "the German," Schussler, my mining engineer, looked older but they were older when I hired them to open the Caldwell venture.

"Hello, Cap'n, welcome to the wild west." D. D. Wilson said.

"Hello, gentlemen. Have you got horses for us?"

"Yes, Sir. Have you got bags and bedrolls?"

"Bedrolls, you have got to be kidding, D. D."

"Yes, Sir. I just wanted to scc the expression on Sam's face, Sir."

"Stop calling me sir and help me get up on this beast. Do you have any idea how long it has been since I have ridden a horse?"

"Let me do some calculations? You were last on a horse in Nebraska in 1857 or 8, correct?"

"Yes, but I was only 39 years old then. I am as stiff as a sixty year old now."

"You have had a lot of miles on the old body since then, Cap'n. I read you were in the battle of New Orleans with Admiral Farragut. How was that?"

"I was never so frightened in my life!"

"And what about Captain Hagood, he was in Mobile with Farragut, correct?"

"Ben and I see each other regularly, but he admits that sailing with Farragut is a death wish experience for sure. How about you marines? Do you ever miss being at sea?"

"The last three years have been a continuation of the mission that we took out here with you, Cap'n. We have all worked hard, fought Indians and highway men at one time or another. But I like it, I think that D. D. and the others all love it here, Sir." Matthew said.

"How is your wife you brought out here from Indiana, Matt?"

"Connie is fine sir, expecting our first any day now."

"What is Tom Schneider doing, Sam?"

"He is in the Marine Commandant's office in the Army Navy Building." Sam replied.

"Jerome Lewis is still in Bermuda. Sam and Rachel were assigned in Bermuda when I was there. When I got promoted, we moved back to Washington."

"I bet Rachel's folks liked that, Sam."

"Yes, D. D., she and the kids see them everyday."

"Kids? How many do you have?"

"Three, just like Louise and the Admiral here, they can be a handful."

The conversation kept our minds off the pain in our butts and it was no time at all until we rode into a small mountain town called "Paradise." It was a typical Rocky Mountain town with dirt streets that were more mud than dirt whenever it rained. We stopped at a livery stable and handed our horses off for the night. We grabbed our single bag and headed for the only hotel on the three block main street. Eight men walked into the lobby and rented the entire hotel's upper floor. It was not a large hotel. And it was not a large town, but it had a telegraph office, a saloon, a restaurant on the first floor of the hotel. A livery stable with black smith kept the town connected with others. A doctor's office which doubled as an undertaker kept three churches and four graveyards busy. A one room school house taught the children of the town through the eighth grade. A boarding house rented women by the hour to provide all the creature comforts of an American town in 1864.

I walked to the telegraph office and sent a message to Seneca Hill. It was the tenth since we had left Washington. I gave Louise the station number and asked her to telegraph me back. The office would deliver it to the hotel. That evening we all met downstairs for a western T- bone steak that covered the entire plate, I could not eat it all. We adjourned to the saloon for a night cap and a few stayed to play some cards. I left to read my telegram, it should be at the hotel by now. I picked up my key and asked if I had any messages. "None, Sir," was the reply, so I thought Louise must really not have approved of this trip west. I slept, off and on, all night and arose at daybreak. I needed to read the contracts one more time before I talked to each of the men I had come to see.

My individual meetings began to take place near six o'clock because Matthew James was an earlier riser, also. We began with a verbal rundown of what had happened at the CI water companies since I had last seen him. I asked him, " Would you like to sign another contract with CI., Matthew?"

"Yes, I enjoy company management and the freedom that you have given me to operate it as I see fit. I would like to hire additional employees that would not involve the one half of one per cent profit sharing, however. Once the company gets to 200 employees there will be no corporate profit for CI."

"I will think about that, Matthew. I can not foresee a time when we have 200 management employees reporting to you, but you never know. We already have hourly paid employees, the profit sharing is only for yearly salaried employees. And remember, Matthew, the one half of one per cent is for net profits only. CI already has a corporate profit built into it with the holding company concept set by our lawyers. Our intent is to show no profit after the employee profit sharing, that way the individual company income taxes are reduced to almost nothing. The corporate taxes are the only income taxes that will be paid to the Nevada Territory and the United States Government."

"I realize that the lion's share of my income comes from my profit shares. How can I reduce my personal income tax, Sir."

"You should talk to the company lawyer in Carson City, Matthew. He will probably recommend that you invest some of your profits to purchase stocks or bonds in other companies. You are a trusted member of CI management, but that does not mean you should not invest in other companies. I have started a new company called American Telegraph and Telephone, you should look for opportunities like that."

"What is a telephone?"

"It sends a voice over the telegraph lines. The concept was demonstrated at the 1854, World's Fair in New York by an Italian inventor Antonio Meucci. It took me until 1860 to interest him in selling his Italian patent rights. We are not interested in building the devices, we are interested in providing compatible lines over which they will operate. We have just finished laying a cable from Maryland to Bermuda for telephone and telegraph messages. All new lines installed by us in the future will be compatible for voice or telegram."

"Could I try to do that in California and Nevada?"

"Yes, either on your own or with help from CI. You could begin by stringing poles and wires to connect the capitol in Carson City with other towns and cities in Nevada. In a small area, voice communication could be possible within a year. I believe that men and women must have something that excites them in some way. Life should be a growth process, whereby a good idea takes care of itself. I can talk with my family in Bermuda via this new process whenever I like because I can afford to pay the line rental. Right now, voice communication is too expensive for the common household. In your lifetime, Matthew, I would judge that most households in California will have telephones." I could tell by the look on his face that he doubted that!

D. D. Wilson, manager of the first profit making venture in Nevada for CI, was waiting when Matthew left my room. He sat down and said, "Where is the new contract, Cap'n, I would like to read it and make some changes."

"Changes?"

"Just pulling your leg, Cap'n. I would like to read it, but you have made me a rich man beyond my dreams and I trust you. I see nothing but opportunity here in Nevada. Next year we will expand the lumber mill so that we can produce other products besides mine timbers and ship lap products. We will see a huge increase in building of towns throughout that area of Nevada."

"I agree D.D., you can get together with William Burns and build banks in each of the new towns once they reach 2000 people or so. I also want you and William to use the blueprints from the bank that was built in Carson City to build a second bank there. We will call it Nevada State Bank. Statehood has been granted by congress but no one in Nevada knows, yet. I want to be the first to use the name Nevada State. My lawyers are drawing up the papers."

"When do we start, Cap'n?"

"Yesterday! D. D. Wilson, you were one of the men in my detachment that I always knew would have a bright future. Here is your new contract, read it and sign it before tomorrow. Send in the next one waiting outside, will you?"

We shook hands and he left the room and sent in the company engineer, Herman Schussler. Herman had immigrated to the United States from Germany. He had trained in Switzerland and was the finest mining engineer I had met.

"Jason, I read the papers you sent me on Meucci's paired electro-magnetic transmitter and receiver. Can you send me a pair for testing? Have you tried these?"

"Yes, they are of good fidelity but the signal is weak. We had to increase the inductive loading of the telegraph wires to increase the long distances between Maryland and Bermuda. This, unfortunately, causes a great deal of heat. The heat is fine underwater. But serious burns result when the telegraph line is strung overhead on poles, the wires burn through and break the connection. We will continue to work on the heating of the wires. We also experienced what my English engineers in Bermuda called sidetones, I call them feedback or echoes. We had several pairs of wires in the cable between Maryland and Bermuda so we just used two pairs, one to send and the other to receive. Unless this problem is solved we will need to string two pairs of telegraph wires for a telephone circuit."

"Well, it is damned exciting. Just think sending your voice over wires. It would make this meeting unnecessary in the future."

"Except, I want to look at the people I talk to. When we send pictures along with the voice, then I will telecommunicate with the western CI companies. How are things progressing on your efforts on secondary recovery of metal ores and oil deposits?"

"Here are my plans for the oil recovery in Pennsylvania. We should have a method to process silver and then gold from waste water and the slag produced by the smelting mills here in Nevada. How are you going to get the mills to give us their waste, Jason."

"We are going to use some business pressure, Herman, we are going to inform them that they can no longer discharge waste water back into the streams or on to the ground. We fear the future contamination of our water sources. We will, however, provide for the removal of this harmful, unwanted water. Matthew assures me that he can build a pipe system that will return the water from the mills directly to us. We, also, will begin to offer free dump sights where they can bring their solid waste. When each mill begins to shut down for lack of raw ore, we will buy it and begin the recovery process of the solids. We will, by then, have our own water recovery system, something that we have not attempted to build in the past. If you are certain that your process will work, you will be a very rich man by signing your new contract."

He read it, signed it, thanked me and sent in the construction company manager, William Burns.

"William, have you read Matthews plan for building a return waste water system for polluted mill water?"

"Yes, but I do not understand why we want this water."

"Because it is full of silver that the mill did not get in their processing of the ore."

"Is the amount significant?"

"Herman, says he will recover about a million dollars a year!"

"Wow, that will pay for the pipeline in two years!"

"Make that paid out in three to five, will you, William?"

William smiled and said, "Something about taxes, Captain?"

"Exactly, we do not want the federal government to think we are getting filthy rich, just filthy from processing all that dirty water. We will tell them that we are trying to be a good neighbor and stop the dumping of contaminated mill water into fresh water streams and rivers."

"Understood, Captain. Do you want me to sign a new contract?"

And it continued through the waiting CI managers outside my room until everyone had signed or taken his contract to consider it until tomorrow. I was hungry and I walked over to the Saloon and had a late lunch and beer recommended by Herman. It was made by some German brothers he knew who had moved from Colorado and began their own style of brewing using clean mountain water.

I walked over to the telegraph office and sent another telegram to Seneca Hill and wished that we had perfected a way to talk to Louise and the children without burning up the wires. I returned to the hotel and made ready for my return trip the next day. Sam found me and handed me three telegrams from Louise.

"These have just now caught up with you, Admiral. We moved too fast coming out here. When you sent a telegram from a location when we stopped, she must have sent a reply to you along our path, but we were already past that point. Anyway, I am glad these finally got to you."

"I thanked him and tore them open to read all about what was happening in Pennsylvania. Our communication system in the United States still had a long way to go to catch up with our transportation. I had a very good night's sleep and in the morning, I had all the signed contracts in my bag. We had decided to meet next time in California. They would ride directly west instead of coming north to meet us. Louise and I would take the train directly to Sacramento and then south to meet them. Sam and I, along with a livery stable hand, mounted our horses and set off for the railroad end point. When we reached it, we thanked the livery hand while he tied the two horses to the back of his saddle for the return to Paradise.

"What did you think of Paradise, Sam?"

"Every thing being equal, I like Pittsburgh better." We both laughed and found our seats on the train.

79
Presidential Nominating Conventions
May - July 1864

The Republicans had two conventions because they split into two rival groups. The first was a group of radicals who nominated General John Fremonte for the Presidency on May 31, 1864. With the outcome of the war still in doubt, some political leaders, including Simon Chase, Benjamin Wade and Horace Greeley, opposed Lincoln's renomination on the grounds that he could not win. And if the Republicans lost the White House, the graft and corruption, that is common in war time, would pass to the Democrats. Besides the monetary issues, this group was also upset with Lincoln's position on the issues of slavery and post-war reconciliation with the southern states. When it was apparent that the Republican party would not give Lincoln another nomination, the Lincoln delegates left the convention and formed a new political party called the National Union Party. The Democrats were overjoyed, until they found that the pro-war faction of their party promptly joined the new party.

The National Union Party held their convention in Baltimore, Maryland, from June 7 to June 8, 1864. They nominated Abraham Lincoln. Lincoln, dissatisfied with the radical Vice President, Hannebal Hamilen, chose a war Democrat, Governor Andrew Johnson of Tennessee. Johnson was ideally suited to run as a vice presidential candidate with Lincoln. He had strongly supported the Union, he was a southerner and he was a leading member of the war Democrats. It took two ballots:

Presidential Nomination Ballot Voting 1864

	First Ballot	Second ballot
Abraham Lincoln	494	516
Ulysses S. Grant	22	0
Not voting	3	3

In the balloting for Vice President nomination:

Andrew Johnson	200	492
Hannebal Hamilen	159	9

| Jason Caldwell | 149 | 0 |
| Daniel Dickinson | 11 | 27 |

Jason Caldwell received a telegram on the evening of June 8, 1864, from the convention chairman, informing him that his name had been placed in nomination for Vice President by Montgomery Blair, to run with Abraham Lincoln on the National Union Party ticket. In the first balloting he had received 149 votes just behind the current Vice President. He did not tell him that Lincoln had chosen Andrew Johnson, and on the second ballot Johnson was given overwhelming support by the convention. Jason finished reading the teletypewriter message, tore it off the machine and walked with it to find Louise.

"Louise, where are you?"

"In here, honey."

"What do you suppose Monty did at the convention?"

"He placed your name in nomination for President?"

"No, Vice President."

"You are not even a Republican, Jason. Why would he nominate you for a Republican ticket?"

He nominated me for something called the National Union Party, it is half moderate Republicans and half war Democrats."

"But it was at the Republican convention?"

"No, the Republicans nominated John Fremonte."

"Jason, quite kidding. Tell me the truth."

"The Republicans are split into two parties. We will definitely have a Democratic President in November. That is the only reason Lincoln was elected in '60, because the Democrats split into two parties."

"My brother will be happy to hear that. George McClellan will get the nomination and he has the money, thanks to you, to reach newspaper readers across the Union states. The south will not vote in this election, will they?"

"No, this will be the first time in our country's history that some Americans will not be allowed to vote in a Presidential Election."

"Jason, I have never voted in a Presidential or any other kind of election!"

"And that is not right, Louise. Why not start the movement for women's vote in the next election? Caldwell International will fund the movement at the same level that it is funding George McClellan."

"You mean it, Jason?"

"Yes, you and I will hire some editorial writers to place ads right along side McClellan's. That way the wives can urge their husbands to vote Democratic.

It will appear that George is supporting the women's movement, even if he is unaware that he is!"

"I love the idea, Jason. I will start contacting people tomorrow, I will start with Cynthia Majors.

The Democrats held their convention the weekend of July 4, 1864, and again, as they did in 1860 split along two different party lines. There was a distinct group of "peace at all costs" and the remainder of the war Democrats that did not join the National Union Party with Lincoln. John C. Breckinridge was again nominated by the war Democrats and he selected Daniel Dickinson who was unsuccessful in his bid to become Lincoln's running mate. The peace Democrats suggested that the party postpone the convention and move it to Chicago. The war Democrats said they had a candidate and would not attend a "second" convention.

In Chicago, tens of thousands of Democrats from political activists to con men showed up at the convention. The Amphitheater at Michigan Avenue and Eleventh Street was restricted to convention delegates only, but they were subjected to the crowds of special interests none the less. Four years into the Civil War, most Democrats were tired. Many thought President Lincoln had gone too far, especially concerning the Emancipation Proclamation. Chicago was pro-union, but many Chicagoans had ties to the South. These pro-south representatives wanted to play on Republican corruption. They wanted to bring the nation to peace. And they selected George McClellan as their candidate on the first ballot. The real fight was for the Vice President slot. McClellan indicated his choice was Admiral Jason Caldwell and on the first ballot the voting was:

Jason Caldwell	65.5
George Pendleton	55.5
L .W. Powell	32.5
George Cass	26
John Caton	16
Daniel Voorhess	13
General A. C. Dodge	9
Joseph Phelps	8
Abstaining	.5

Before the second balloting began, Powell, Cass, Caton and Voorhess met with George Pendleton and asked for several future favors. They then announced that they were withdrawing from consideration and releasing there delegates to support George Pendleton. When George McClellan heard this he sent for Jason Caldwell.

"Jason, I want to offer you a cabinet position. I will name you as my Secretary of the Navy."

"You have a much bigger problem than who should be your Vice President, Sir."

"I do? And what is that?"

"You should be offering the Vice president position to John Breckinridge. He was Vice President four years ago and he would make a much better candidate than either myself or Pendleton."

"He will not see me, Jason. I have tried. He thinks he wants to be a Presidential candidate again."

"And the same thing will happen again. You and he will spit the Democratic vote. Remember, in the last election Lincoln had two million votes, but Douglas and Breckinridge together had over three million. If you can not come to some agreement with Breckinridge, I will have to withdraw my letter of credit for your campaign."

"Why would you do that? I am going to win this thing. The Republicans are split too."

"No, you and John Breckinridge will insure that Lincoln will win. Fremonte will have little or no effect on this election. I am sorry, George, I can no longer support you." I left his hotel room and made arrangements to leave for Seneca Hill. As I was checking out, I was paged for a telegram:

JASON

DO NOT ACCEPT VP OFFER FROM MC CLELLAN. JUST LEARNED FREMONTE HAS MET WITH LINCOLN. HE HAS OFFERED TO DROP HIS CAMPAIGN IF THE PRESIDENT WILL DISMISS SOME OF HIS CABINET APPOINTMENTS. IT DOES NOT LOOK GOOD FOR YOU. LINCOLN HAS ASKED WELLES TO SIGN YOUR LETTER OF RESIGNATION. LINCOLN FEARS YOU WILL BE RUNNING AGAINST HIM IN NOVEMBER.

MONTY

As I rode the train home to Pennsylvania, I tried to put my thoughts together. "I will be getting a telegram from Welles, telling me what he has decided to do and when. I have little personal items in my Army Navy office. Sam Mason can bring everything I need, including the morse code writers, to Seneca Hill. I will offer a job to Sam. If Monty gets caught in the political squeeze, there should be room for him at American Telegraph and Telephone in Washington City."

The train pulled into the Titusville Station and I thought what the nation needs is some good news. I had been to meet with the Caldwell employees of Nevada and had seen first hand the excitement that these Americans felt. It had come in the form of important mineral discoveries. Besides the oil wells now in Pennsylvania, new silver deposits were found in the western United States. When the Comstock Lode of silver was brought to light in Nevada, it was estimated that the silver reserves in the United States was now equal to all the rest of the world. Gold and silver was still being mined in California, Colorado, and several other locations throughout the west. The Rocky Mountain region discoveries were abundant in minerals of all types.

The last four years of war in the east should be balanced with the new wealth and welfare of the nation. Oil amounted to millions of dollars added to the national economy. The Comstock Lode alone was estimated at a quarter billion dollars. I should use this "good news" and financial windfall to assist in the rebuilding of South Carolina. I made a mental note to write a series of letters when I got home to Seneca Hill.

SENECA HILL
Office of Caldwell International

August 1, 1864

Dear Father,

I have returned from the Democratic National Convention in Chicago. You or I have represented the Caldwells of South Carolina in the last ten conventions. We are always ahead of others when predicting the future. I can now predict that Mr. Lincoln will be re-elected. General McClellan refuses to make peace with John Breckenridge and put him on the ticket as Vice President.

I may be asked to resign from the department of the Navy. When will this happen? I do not know. But as you always say, "Advanced knowledge is like gold." And I have asked Sam Mason to pack up my things when the time comes.

I also have the information that you requested in your last letter. I will send you that in a telegram directly to Caldwell Place. Letter writing always helps me clear my head and you are a good listener. I have been giving some thought as to what we might do to help rebuild South Carolina. My vision for Caldwell International is to expand as rapidly as possible into banking, development of our mineral based assets and ignoring our agriculture based commodities. As soon as we are allowed back into the state, we should return with all the resources necessary to assist the City of Beaufort and the State of South Carolina.

Louise sends her best.

Jason

CALDWELL INTERNATIONAL
St. George, Bermuda

August 1, 1864

Mr. Kyle Johnston
Director Port Facilities
Port Royal, South Carolina

Dear Mr. Johnston:

Please be advised that within a few months, at the end of the war, I will be sending you an offer for the purchase of the Port Royal properties formerly owned by Caldwell Trading and Shipping. Please send notice of amount due to:
Bank of Bermuda
Caldwell Trading and Shipping Account
St. George, Bermuda
If a purchase is not possible, please send the next year's lease forms to rent the same facilities from the owners.

Sincerely yours,

Jason Caldwell

T H E ARMY NAVY BUILDING
Department of the Navy

August 1, 1864

Robert Whitehall, President
Caldwell Trading and Shipping
St. George, Bermuda

Dear Robert,

The offer to purchase the office, warehouses and other properties in Port Royal is enclosed for your information. Please mail it to them for me. If a purchase is not possible, I will forward a copy of the lease of same back to you. We can always rent available warehousing as our needs dictate . A secure facility must be found in Port Royal after the war for the shipment of Oil to South Carolina. I will arrange for Seneca Oil to begin shipments as soon as I get clearance.

Also, you may want to contact the C I Offices in Nevada and get quarterly reports sent directly to you again. I have directed the banks used in Nevada to report deposits directly to you. Income from Nevada will now be used to rebuild our holdings in South Carolina. Income from Pennsylvania can be used also. As President of the company, decide where you would like to live, inside or outside of South Carolina.

For the time being, there is an advantage to the Bermuda location. Awaiting your response, I remain

Sincerely yours,

Jason Caldwell

Trying to run a business while serving part time in the Army Navy building was not something that I would have to do much longer if the telegram from Monty proved correct. The election this year would end my service in Washington City. Then Louise, the children and I would be free to live wherever we chose. I was putting away my stationary when Louise stuck her head inside my office and said, "Have you read your morse code incomings yet."

"No, there is a stack of them here, I was about to go through them."

"I have read most of them as I took them off the writer. Louis Napoleon has landed troops in Mexico."

"What?"

"Maximilian, Archduke of Austria, has been appointed by Napoleon III as the Emperor of Mexico."

"I had better start with the earliest date and read all of these."

JASON

AS DISCUSSED IN OUR CABINET MEETINGS THIS SPRING AND SUMMER, THE LOSSES IN BATTLES AND BY DISEASE HAVE BEEN APPALLING. WHEN IS THIS BLOODSHED TO END? IS THE UNION WORTH SO MANY LIVES? ARE WE NOT PAYING TOO HIGH A PRICE FOR ITS PRESERVATION? INDIFFERENCE IS NOW COMMON PLACE AMONG THE CABINET MEMBERS WITH THE EXCEPTION OF WELLES AND SEWARD. THE REST, INCLUDING MYSELF, HAVE SUGGESTED A WAY OUT. VICE PRESIDENT HAMILEN, HAS SUGGESTED THAT HE BE AN ENVOY TO RICHMOND TO LEARN UPON WHAT MUTUAL TERMS PEACE COULD BE HAD BETWEEN THE TWO PARTIES.

THE PRESIDENT WAS ANGRY, BUT INDICATED THAT HE WOULD TAKE OUR SUGGESTIONS UNDER ADVISEMENT. MY FEELING IS THAT THE PRESIDENT WILL NOT RELINQUISH EFFORTS TO RESTORE THE UNION. HE WILL INSTEAD REPLACE ALL WHO DISAGREE. HE ALREADY HAS REPLACED THE VICE PRESIDENT BY CHOOSING JOHNSON AS HIS RUNNING MATE.

MONTY.

I placed that message in a new pile and picked up the next.

JASON

WE KNOW YOU ARE AWAY FROM SENECA HILL ATTENDING THE DEMOCRATIC CONVENTION. BUT YOU SHOULD BE AWARE THAT LOUIS NAPOLEON HAS JUST FORMALLY RECOGNIZED THE CONFEDERATE STATES OF AMERICA AS A SEPARATE NATION; WITH THE ASSISTANCE OF ENGLAND AND SPAIN HE HAS LANDED TROOPS IN MEXICO. HE ALSO HAS CREATED THE EMPEROR OF MEXICO TO REPLACE THE REPUBLIC OF MEXICO, PRESIDENT JUAREZ. THIS IS FLAGRANT VIOLATION OF THE

MONROE DOCTRINE AND THE PRESIDENT HAS RESPONDED.
CONTACT US AS SOON AS YOU READ THIS.
    EDWIN STANTON, SECRETARY OF WAR
    GIDEON WELLES, SECRETARY OF THE NAVY

I did not place that message in the new pile. I ran to find my key operator,
Peter. I had him send the following response:

SECRETARIES STANTON AND WELLES
    WHAT WAS PRESIDENT LINCOLN'S RESPONSE?
            JASON CALDWELL, UNDERSECRETARY

We waited. Four minutes later the morse code writer began to chatter.

ADMIRAL:

MESSAGE RECEIVED AND A COPY EACH WAS HAND DELIVERED
TO BOTH SECRETARIES. STAY ALERT FOR MESSAGES TO
FOLLOW.
            SAMUEL MASON, CAPTAIN USMC

Again, I sat and gazed at the morse code writer willing it to come to life with
a message response. An hour later it did.

JASON

THE PRESIDENT HAS PREPARED A SERIES OF RESPONSES.
    FIRST, HE HAS HAD THE AMERICAN AMBASSADOR IN PARIS
FILE A FORMAL COMPLAINT WITH NAPOLEON. IT INFORMS
HIM THAT WE ARE SENDING TROOPS TO ASSIST PRESIDENT
JUAREZ. GENERAL SHERMAN WILL BE ORDERED TO BREAK
OFF HIS ATTACK THROUGH THE SOUTH AND BOARD TROOP
TRAINS FOR THE MEXICAN BORDER AND ADMIRAL HAGOOD
IS DIRECTED TO LAND MARINES VIA THE GULF.
    SECOND, HE HAS SENT ORDERS TO GENERAL GRANT TO
BREAK OFF HIS SIEGE OF PETERSBURG, VIRGINIA AND BOARD
TROOP TRAINS FOR CANADA. GENERAL GRANTS ORDERS
ARE SUBJECT TO GREAT BRITAINS FORMAL RECOGNITION
OF CSA AND HER CONTINUED SUPPORT OF MAXIMILIAN IN
MEXICO.
    THIRD, HE WILL BE SENDING YOU ORDERS TO COMMAND
THE SIXTH FLEET TO INVADE CUBA WITH THE FOURTH

MARINE DIVISION IF SPAIN FORMALLY RECOGNIZES CSA AND CONTINUES THEIR SUPPORT OF MAXIMILIAN.

FOURTH, AND I THINK A BRILLIANT STEP, HE HAS SENT COPIES OF THE MONROE DOCTRINE TO THE KING OF SPAIN, QUEEN OF ENGLAND, AND NAPOLEON III. ALONG WITH DOCTRINE IS A PERSONAL LETTER TO EACH STATING THAT A STATE OF WAR NOW EXISTS BETWEEN THE UNITED STATES AND FRANCE FOR VIOLATION OF THE MONROE DOCTRINE AND IT WILL EXIST WITH ANY OTHER EUROPEAN COUNTRY WHO VIOLATE IT.

My God, I thought, we are going to be at war with Europe! I reread Sam's message. It stated to be alert for the messages to follow. I carefully read the last message again. It jumped off the sheet at me, there is no sixth fleet, where did that come from? There is no fourth marine division. I smell a rat! I had Peter key another message to Sam, this time partly in code.

HAVE READ FIRST MESSAGE. I AM PREPARING TO TAKE COMMAND OF THE SIXTH FLEET. NOTIFY GENERAL SCHNEIDER OF THE FOURTH MARINES THAT HE IS TO BE READY TO SAIL UPON MY ARRIVAL IN POTOMAC DOCKYARDS. USE FOLLOWING SUBSTITUTION CODE FOR REMAINDER MESSAGE.

474J48474HTYGDMMVKKFJGU998E77E6E6FGCBBSMMDJJSSMSMSSM3
M4M4M5M JASON CALDWELL, ADMIRAL USN

I received the following in code.

ADMIRAL, THE SECRETARIES WERE WORRIED THAT YOU MIGHT NOT GET THEIR LITTLE PLOY. OUR OUTGOING AND INCOMING ARE BEING READ BY THE ORION SPY GROUP THAT WAS SENT NORTH WITH GENERAL BUTLER AFTER BULL RUN ONE. I ASSURED THEM YOU WOULD CATCH ON, THANKS FOR THE PROMOTION TO GENERAL. PINKERTON HAS IDENTIFIED FIFTEEN MEMBERS STILL ACTIVE INSIDE ORION. THEY REPORT EVERYTHING THEY CAN TO RICHMOND. IT IS OUR HOPE THAT THE PRESIDENT'S OUTGOING TO GENERALS SHERMAN AND GRANT WILL BE REPORTED TO RICHMOND. WE NEED TO MAKE SURE THIS IS REPORTED TO LONDON, PARIS AND MADRID. CAN YOU LET THIS SLIP OUT IN BERMUDA SO THAT LONDON WILL GET IT? THE STATE DEPARTMENT IS ALREADY LODGING FORMAL COMPLAINTS IN THE THREE CAPITALS, YOUR INFORMATION WILL CONFIRM IT.

SAM

Peter and I were going to have a busy night. We sent telegrams to Jerome Lewis in Bermuda assuming they would be read by ORION. I wrote a rather carefully crafted telegram, again for ORION's benefit, to our embassy in Paris informing them of the plans to land a force of marines on the eastern shore of Mexico. I also sent a message to the Madrid Embassy saying that the fourth marines would invade and capture Cuba unless Spain formally announced that they were no longer were in support of Maximilian in Mexico. I sent a telegram to the Washington Post for them to run in the next available edition.

ATTENTION SAILORS ON LEAVE FROM SIXTH FLEET
REPORT TO YOUR STATIONS BEFORE O800 AUGUST 6, 1864,
FOR IMMEDIATE DEPLOYMENT.

ADMIRAL CALDWELL, USN

In between Peter's key tapping of various messages, I read the rest of the incomings and placed them into two piles. We sent brief returns on the second pile and then fell into our beds for the night.

Early the next morning I was on the train for Washington. I picked up a copy of the Washington Post from the train platform and the headline read.

US Gears up for War in Mexico

The reporters never got anything right. Others from the Army Navy Building were already at work leaking information to the newspapers on the cover story. The reporter for the article that I read said he had, from confirmed sources, that Mr. Lincoln would not tolerate a dictatorship in Mexico. Lincoln had already alerted the 4th Division of the Marines to return from leaves so that an invasion force could land on the east coast of Mexico. I smiled and said to myself, "No, the 4th is going with me to Cuba — try to get the lies straight, will you?"

I stepped off the train in Union Station and was met by a group of reporters. I was in uniform, so I was an easy target. If you want to get a bull's attention you wave a red flag, right! The uniform of an admiral is like a red flag to reporters. I tried pushing through them to meet Sam Mason, but I stopped just in time, looked exhausted and said, "What is it? I have got to get to Potomac Dockyards."

"Are you the fleet commander for the sixth, Admiral?"

"The President has just issued orders to that affect."

"Can you tell us if you are going to Cuba?"

"The fleet is scheduled to perform a sweep of the Gulf of Mexico to hunt down any remaining CSS ships of the line and destroy them even if we have to chase them to Cuba."

"Will you land the 4th Marine Division in Mexico, Admiral."

"I think you have the wrong admiral, Fleet Admiral Benjamin Hagood is the supreme commander and he decides where and when the Marines will land on foreign soil. He could decide to take them to Canada, Cuba or Charleston, South Carolina for all I know." You are a liar Jason Caldwell, I thought.

The next day all of the papers, had from confirmed sources, the fact that Admiral Hagood was going to land a marine division on the east coast of Mexico while Admiral Caldwell would begin a blockade of all Canadian east coast ports until England withdrew their support of the French Army in Mexico. Sam and I sat in my office in the Army Navy Building sending messages by telegraph to nonexisting marine detachments, to please hurry to the Potomac Dockyards. Gideon Welles had ordered everything that could float to begin to build steam in their boilers and make ready to sail away from the dockyards. He even had gun boats that were in for refits ready for towing so late the night of August 6, 1864, the dockyards could be emptied of all vessels. Most of these were towed around the Chesapeake for a few days and then gradually they were brought back one at a time.

The gamble worked. On August 21, 1864, the State Department reported that Madrid had contacted the American Ambassador to explain that a formal letter of Spain's neutrality in the American Civil War was in route to both Richmond and Washington. The State Department then informed Madrid that the sixth fleet would be redirected to the Gulf of Mexico. Secretary Seward walked into my office on the 22nd and said, "Jason, your sixth fleet is not going to invade Cuba."

"Good, they are needed in Mexico or Canada, I have not decided which one." I smiled and thought, "My last acts as an Admiral in the USN are deceptions and misinformation for the enemy."

No word was forthcoming from either London or Paris, so the War Department decided that Richmond had taken the bait that Sherman was in the process of moving his army to Texas and Grant was in the process of moving to Canada. Word was sent to Pinkerton to determine the actions of Confederate General Hood, the defender of Atlanta. He sent reports to Washington that indicated that Richmond believed that only a small portion of Sherman's Army remained near Atlanta. General Hood was free to leave his intrenchments and capture the Union Army that remained.

On the night of August 25th, two corps on the extreme left abandoned their intrenchments and marched to the southwest. Then other corps followed the next day to destroy the Union Army. The people of Atlanta were delighted to learn that the Union Army had withdrawn which meant the lifting of the siege of Atlanta. General Hood did not learn of the deception until it was too late. His army was caught in the open by a superior Union force. The terrifying news spread thorough Atlanta. Hood saw the fatal trap into which he had been led and knew that his only hope was in getting out of the city at once. A portion of his military stores were loaded on wagons and the rest were set on fire. The skies were lit up by the glare of the fire and the exploding munitions. This set the entire city ablaze. Sherman sat upon his mount outside the city and viewed the lighting up of the heavens. " In years to come, my army will get the blame for the burning of Atlanta."

80
The ORION Network
Richmond, Virginia

President Davis was alarmed so much when he learned of the capture of Atlanta from the ORION network, that he and his Secretary of War, L. "Pope" Walker, hurried from Richmond to Hood's army to learn first hand the actual situation. They found most of Hood's army intact and Hood planning to attack Sherman who had moved his headquarters into the State Capitol of Georgia. Hood, Walker and Davis sat together in Hood's tent.

"Mr. President, the tables are turned. I have him bottled up in Atlanta. I have sent for addition reinforcements, in fact General Hardee has left Lovejoy Station and should arrive within the hour. When they arrive, we will surround Atlanta and starve him into submission."

"Can you keep Sherman here for at least a month, General?" Asked Pope Walker.

"Of course, why?"

"I am ordering the ORION Network to commence operation Archangel!"

General Hood had no idea what the hell, "Archangel," was. But he did not want to let the Secretary of War and head of the ORION spy network know of his ignorance. It sounded like an act of desperation to him, however. He changed the subject by telling his President, his version of what had happened in Atlanta the night of September 1, 1864.

"I have been told that Union General Slocum rode into Atlanta at daybreak on September 2nd and was met by the Mayor of Atlanta who presented him with a folded US flag. The general had the state flag of Georgia removed from the top of the capitol and the US flag raised."

"First, Mobile by Farragut and now this by Slocum. We must cut off the head of the dragon before the entire Confederacy is eaten alive."

"Yes, Mr. President, Sherman has ordered all civilians out of Atlanta, he intends to defend the city to the last person. He can not escape me, I will destroy him. His advance from Chattanooga has cost him over 5,000 dead, 22,000 walking wounded and over 4,000 missing. CSA lost 3,000 during the advance. Neither Sherman or Grant seem to understand that the Conscription Act is not a bottomless pit of humans ready to fight for their country. ORION reports that thousands are sick of the fighting and are now avoiding the draft by going to Canada."

"Yes, yes, General; but what do you think of operation Archangel?" Pope Walker asked.

"Do you think it will work, Mr. President?"

"Archangel is a bold move, not an act of desperation. If Lincoln is re-elected in November, we will put it into action."

"I have until November then to starve Sherman out of Atlanta. I can meet Sherman's support coming from Chattanooga and defeat the general commanding them, correct?"

"If an opportunity presents itself to defeat a whole Union army coming to the rescue of Sherman, that would be an added bonus. The main item of battle is to keep Sherman in Atlanta and prevent his escape. If he escapes, his army will destroy every major city in his path, look what he did to Atlanta."

Major General Hood did not tell his president that he was the one who burned Atlanta. He rode with his president to board his train for Macon, Georgia. At Macon, Davis had the train stop and he gave a speech to the awaiting crowds. "My fellow citizens of the Confederacy, General Hood has managed to trap the animal, Sherman, inside Atlanta. The entire city is surrounded and he can not escape. General Hardee's army from southern Georgia has joined him in this great effort to starve the Union army inside Atlanta and to advance north toward Chattanooga to meet the Union General Thomas who will try to free Sherman. Before November, the war in Georgia will be over with a great victory for us."

In a nut shell, Jefferson Davis revealed the entire southern strategy for the battle of Atlanta. A Pinkerton agent was standing in the crowd at Macon listening and he remembered nearly every word, which was promptly forwarded to Sherman headquarters in Atlanta. Hood's plan was to completely surround Atlanta when Hardee's army arrived and then set off for Chattanooga to defeat General Thomas in battle. Hardee was late. Sherman's Cavalry rode from Atlanta to meet Thomas and warn him of the upcoming battle. Sherman's orders were; he should not engage Hood, but fall back with his forces until he could be supported by the Army of the Cumberland. Sherman gave orders for Thomas to "look after Hood." The advance party from Chattanooga was commanded by General Schofield. He fell back before the advancing Hood fighting a delaying action until the Army of the Cumberland could reach him. Schofield met Thomas outside of Nashville, a Union stronghold. The month of September passed with light fighting around Nashville, while Sherman broke out of the containment around Atlanta and defeated General Hardee's army in another month's time. The end of November came with a slight victory for Hood's forces outside of Nashville. But that was the last that he would see of victory. General Thomas attacked out of Nashville with a superior force, capturing 54 cannon, 4,460 prisoners and 2000 missing Confederate loses. In two days the Confederate Army under Hood fled in confusion for a second time. Thomas pursued with relentless energy and Hood and his demoralized troops forded the Duck River then the Tennessee River and then disappeared into the country side. More importantly, Sherman was allowed to take Macon. Macon was defended by Howell Cobb, former Secretary of the Treasury under President Buchanan. Cobb's 10,000 volunteers were no match for Sherman's 60,000 and they were swept aside like dry leaves before the wind. No one stood between Sherman and Savannah.

Sherman arrived in Savannah on the 10th of December. The famous "march to the sea," was over. The three hundred miles were straight through the heart of the Confederacy, and for most of the men leaving Atlanta, it was no more than a pleasure excursion. The remainder of Hardee's forces in Atlanta had withdrawn into South Carolina.

In Richmond, ORION ordered the commencement of operation Archangel. Pope Walker was not amused by the total disappearance of General Hood and his army. This coupled with the retreat of General Hardee into South Carolina reduced his options for delaying the war. Winning the war was no longer an option. The most he could hope for was a draw and Archangel would give him this much needed delay and the opportunity to council with the new administration in Washington. Walker sent his one line, coded message, to the Grand Dragon, Army Navy Building. *Commence Operation Archangel.*

81

The Election of 1864
November

The Washington Post had the following headline after the presidential election of 1864.

Democrats Split Vote Again: Lincoln Wins

	States	Popular Vote	Electoral Vote
Lincoln	22	2,218,388	212
Breckinridge	1	1,225,110	13
McClellan	4	1,812,807	24

The election 1864 was the first time since 1812 that a presidential election took place during a war. For much of 1864, Lincoln believed he had little chance of being reelected. Confederate forces had won at the battles of Mansfield, Crater and *Cold Harbor*. In addition, the war was continuing to take a high toll. The prospect of a long and drawn out war started to make the idea of "peace at any cost" offered by the "copperheads" look more desirable. Because of this, McClellan was thought to be a heavy favorite to win the election.

However, several political and military events made Lincoln's re-election possible. First the Democrats nominated two candidates and split their party at the convention. And they remained split, unlike the Republicans who joined forces in September to run an effective campaign. The political compromises made at the Democratic convention were contradicting and made McClellan's campaign inconsistent and difficult. McClellan was also mystified by the number of newspapers who ran his announcements beside the announcement of the Women's Right To Vote!

At first McClellan laughed at the newspaper's coincidence, then when it happened again outside of Pennsylvania his campaign workers contacted the newspapers involved. They reported that a Mrs. Louise Buchanan Caldwell, had a standing order to place her announcement whenever the General placed his and she had paid for 100 in advance.

The final straw for McClellan was Union Generals Sherman and Grant. Sherman was advancing on Atlanta and Grant was pushing Confederate General Lee into the outer defenses of Richmond. It became increasing obvious that a Union military victory was inevitable and close at hand. McClellan hopes faded when John C. Fremonte announced that he was encouraging his followers to vote for President Lincoln. Fremonte announced, "Mr. Lincoln has agreed to stop the corruption within his cabinet by dismissing Postmaster Montgomery Blair and his stooge Undersecretary of the Navy, Jason Caldwell."

The Lincoln and Johnson ticket also ran their newspaper announcements also and Louise Caldwell was there to answer with her own. Only 24 states participated, because 11 had seceded from the Union. Three new states voted for the first time, Nevada, West Virginia and Kansas. Tennessee and Louisiana were completely under federal control and voting took place, however, their electoral votes were not counted.

On November 24, 1864, Abraham Lincoln dismissed Montgomery Blair and appointed William Dennison as the new Postmaster General of the United States. No one was calling for the dismissal of Jason Caldwell and Gideon Welles never dated his letter of resignation. More importantly, Mr. Lincoln did not date Gideon Welles' letter of resignation. On December 11, 1864, Lincoln did ask for and receive resignations from the Secretary of the Treasury, William Fessenden, he was replaced by Hugh McCulloch. He than dismissed Attorney General Bates and replaced him with James Speed. Gideon Welles, William Seward and Edwin Stanton were now the only remaining members of the cabinet that had not been replaced.

The Grand Dragon left his office in the Army Navy building and was walking to Lafayette park to clear his head. He stopped at the third bench from the Jackson Memorial and reached under the left side to find a sheet of paper folded several times and wedged between the bench and the front leg. He pulled it out, unfolded it and read.

Commence Operation Archangel

It has come to this then, he thought. He refolded the sheet of paper and placed in the pocket of this great coat. He stood, stretched and then walked to the Hay-Adams to send a telegram. He sent a telegram to his family saying he was called away from the Army Navy Building to deliver a message and he would not be home for two days. That way his disappearance from work and his survival would not be questioned during the investigation of the horrible tragedy that befell Washington City.

He walked back to his office and withdrew a small bottle marked, MEDICINE, and walked to the basement of the Army Navy Building. He found the water supply tank for the boiler and poured the contents in. He immediately left the building and waited in Lafayette Park for the Archangel Squad to meet. Before long he was met by a young page from the House of Representatives, and then from the Senate. They both nodded their heads that the medicine had been administered. They waited nearly an hour before the janitor from the White House arrived. He was calm but could not stop talking about what he had done.

"Shut your mouth. We must never speak of this again. We have just killed hundreds of people." The Grand Dragon and commander of the Archangel Squad said.

They did not leave the park and go their separate ways as was planned. Each had a cover story for being out of their buildings. One was delivering a message, one was sick, another had a sick mother at home and the forth had cut his hand and was at the doctor's. They stared at the buildings wondering how long it would take for the poison gas to work. It did not take long. A muffled sound came first from the Army Navy Building and then smoke from the basement windows could be seen. The boiler had exploded. Workers came streaming out of the building to stand on the sidewalks facing Lafayette Park. Then the same sound came from the White House with the following results. The Archangel Squad left for their prearranged destinations. Similar boiler explosions in both the houses of Congress forced federal workers into the December cold of Washington City.

The next day the Washington Post carried the following headline and article.

BOILER BREAKS GIVE FEDERAL EMPLOYEES EARLY CHRISTMAS VACATIONS

IT WAS REVEALED TODAY THAT THE STEAM BOILERS IN THE WHITE HOUSE, ARMY NAVY BUILDING AND HOUSES OF CONGRESS WERE SLIGHTLY DAMAGED BY MINOR EXPLOSIONS WHEN CLEANING FLUID WAS ACCIDENTALLY ADDED TO THE WATER TANKS BY WORKMEN THIS WEEK. THE PRESIDENT AND HIS STAFF HAVE MOVED TO BLAIR HOUSE WITH AN EXTRA ADDED MARINE DETAIL FOR SECURITY. BOILER REPAIRS IN THE WHITE HOUSE ARE EXPECTED TO TAKE A WEEK OR SO. THE AFTER ELECTION WORK OF THE WHITE HOUSE CONTINUES. IT WAS REPORTED THAT THE NEW POSTMASTER GENERAL,

ATTORNEY GENERAL AND SECRETARIES OF THE INTERIOR AND TREASURY HAD NOT MOVED INTO THEIR OFFICES WHEN THE BOILER BREAKS OCCURRED.

The Senators and the House of Representatives will begin their Christmas breaks early this week and the repairs to their buildings will be completed after the first of THE YEAR. MANY HAD ALREADY HEADED HOME FOR THE HOLIDAYS. THE ARMY NAVY PERSONNEL NOT VITAL TO THE WAR EFFORT, WERE ALSO GIVEN AN EARLY VACATION.

SECRETARY OF WAR, EDWIN STANTON. WAS QUOTED AS SAYING, "WE NEEDED A BREAK FROM THE WAR, BUT THIS WAS NOT WHAT I HAD IN MIND. GENERAL SHERMAN, UPON HEARING OF OUR 'OUT IN THE COLD', HERE IN WASHINGTON, HAS NOTIFIED ME FROM SAVANNAH THAT THE WEATHER THERE IS WARM, WHY NOT COME TO INSPECT THE TROOPS!"

THE SECRETARY OF THE NAVY HAD THE FOLLOWING COMMENT. "THE TEMPERATURE IN THE ARMY NAVY BUILDING WILL REMAIN PLEASANT AS LONG AS THE ARMY AND THE NAVY CONTINUE TO REPORT VICTORIES FROM THE FIELD AND SEA LANES THROUGHOUT THE SOUTHERN UNITED STATES."

MEANWHILE, THE OFFICERS INSIDE THE ARMY NAVY BUILDING ARE WEARING THEIR GREAT COATS AND STAMPING THEIR FEET WHILE CONTINUING TO MANAGE THE WAR EFFORT. UNDERSECRETARY OF THE NAVY, ADMIRAL CALDWELL HAD ALREADY TAKEN HIS CHRISTMAS BREAK WITH HIS FAMILY IN SUNNY BERMUDA. HE WILL BE UNAWARE OF THE COLD WORKING CONDITIONS UNTIL HIS RETURN.

The Grand Dragon sat at his kitchen table in Washington City reading the Washington Post and wondered why ORION had given them cleaning fluid to dump in the water tanks of the building in which they worked. He would have to walk over to the Hay-Adams and send another telegram to his control agent.

War Secretary Walker sat at his breakfast table in Richmond, reading the overnights and learned of the disaster of Archangel. Now they would have to do it the old fashioned way and a list for assassination was hand written on a piece of paper. It began:

1. *Abraham Lincoln (send free theater tickets to the White House)*
2. *Andrew Johnson (explore security at Blair House)*
3. *Seward's home is not secure, attack same date as Ford*
4. *Stanton's home is not secure, attack same date as Ford*
5. *Fressenden is in the hospital (ORION find out condition)*
6. *Dennison is unmarried address unknown (find location)*

7. *Speed has not moved to Washington (find location)*
8. *Welles lives in Maryland (easiest hit of the cabinet)*
9. *Usher? (ORION report current information)*

On or before April 1, 1865, plan a concurrent attack on the homes of Seward, Stanton, Welles, Caldwell and the newly appointed members of the cabinet. These are to be attempted only after the Dragon has been found outside the White House and eliminated.

82
Christmas in Bermuda
December, 1864

Christmas has always been a special time of year for the Caldwell family, a time for gathering and celebration and we were all in attendance at Caldwell Place, St. George, Bermuda. This year Louise and I had closed Seneca Hill and given the household staff a month's paid vacation. They had agreed to return January15, 1865, and reopen the estate. My father and mother said they would like to stay in Caldwell Inn for Christmas. They had locked up their new estate on the island they had purchased in the Great Sound and had come to St. George by water taxi. Trey and Mariann had purchased our parent's house in St. David and the cottage next to it. They hired work men and had constructed a connection between the two cottages. They now had a place large enough for their children and a small household staff. James; age 7, Ruth; age 5 and Carol, age 2 had not seen their cousins for two Christmases and it was a loud and cheerful Christmas vacation. I suggested that the Whitehalls and John Butler move into the inn so they could all be together and they agreed. My father pulled me aside and said, "You do know that John and Sally have been seeing each other, Jason. He already lives with her in her cottage here at Caldwell Place."

"John and Sally?"

"Yes, son! What do think of that?"

"John, has found someone? I did not know that."

"Few people did until he told Sally he wanted to live with her, it seems he is proud of it."

"Well, if Sally loves him, he should be. You know, Dad, Sally is a fine person and one of the finest managers we have ever had anywhere in Caldwell International."

"Oh, Jason, I did not mean it that way. I am happy for John, just like I was happy for you and Louise. I figured you were a confirmed bachelor, what with all the ladies that came and went in your life."

"Dad, Louise knows nothing about when I was young and stupid. We need to keep it that way. I never asked her about other men in her life. It has never mattered to me."

He held me close and it reminded me of the Christmas of '62 when Louise and I went to Boston. He whispered in my ear, "Louise and Sally are both fine women, Jason, you and John are lucky to have them in your life. I love you, son."

"What are you two up to?" Mother said.

"He told me what he wanted to get for you for Christmas, Mom. I told him that I doubted you could get into one of those new body corsets."

"Robert Hays Caldwell, you had better not even try to get me one of those foul things!"

"Well, then Jason and I are leaving for Hamilton to do some more shopping. Are you coming?"

"No, I am not!"

My father knew that I needed to get on into Hamilton and get the mail from the Army Navy Building. So we walked together, down Rose Hill and into the Duke of York turned left and ended at the Bermuda Railroad Station.

"Jason, are you all right, you look pensive?"

"I have been trying to decide if I need to stay with the US Navy until the end of the war. Or another option might be to stay until the end of Lincoln's second term. I am a confirmed Democrat, Dad, I can not go along with many of the things that the Republicans stand for."

"Stanton is a Democrat, right? How does he do it, Son?"

"Stanton is a politician, Dad, he thinks that he can be useful to the Republicans that seem to be lost most of the time."

We were pulling into Hamilton and I left him to walk to Trimminghams on Front Street and I headed for the US Ambassador's Office to visit with Jerome Lewis. "You go ahead on home when you have finished your shopping, Dad, I have no idea how long I will be with Jerome."

"Jerome, I have to make a decision. You have been my counsel for many years now. I always feel better talking to you. I am not getting anything accomplished as the undersecretary of the Navy. For the last several months, all I have done is send off fake messages to non-existing units under my fake command."

"Welcome to my life as an Ambassador, Admiral. That is exactly all I have done here and I am sick of it. When you figure out how to get us back in the war, count me in."

"Jerome, I had no idea."

"Before you decide anything, Admiral, read these incomings from the State Department. It seems that someone tried to poison the people working in the White House, Senate, House and Army Navy Building."

"What?"

"Just go through those, it is all there. Those stupid bastards nearly killed five hundred non- combatants."

I began reading and when I finished I said, "Jerome, this may be what we are looking for. Who ordered this? Are they active in Washington or were they sent to do this thing on a one time basis? We can find out. Together, we can do something about this. We are not without resources."

"What do mean?"

"Jerome, someone who would not be noticed added the poison to the water tanks, right?"

"Right."

"Then they are employees! We have Confederate sympathizers or Confederate agents working in these buildings, probably a group known as ORION."

"My God, you are right, Admiral. I have other messages here that mention the ORION network."

"Thank you, Captain. How would you like to help me identify the members of ORION?"

"Can you do that?"

"Of course, I am an Admiral. See the big red A on my undershirt!"

"How can I get one of those? Only, make mine a big blue C."

"Either I will transfer you within 30 days or I will resign my assignment and return to Bermuda and we can work from here."

"From here?"

"Yes, I think we will find the answer to the puzzle from the Ambassador to Bermuda."

"John Butler, he is harmless."

"He is a member of ORION did you know that?"

"God, no. How did you find out?"

"He told me in a hotel room at the Hay-Adams, only I was not listening."

"I do not understand."

"You will, do you want to help me in this? You will have to come to Washington. You can use your diplomatic cover to get a lot of things done that you could not get done as a Captain in the USN working for me."

"If you return to Washington as a member of the State Department, it would be better, agreed."

"Agreed, oh, my wife is going to kill me, she loves it here."

"She and the children should stay here, Jerome, tell her you are assigned to Washington on a short temporary assignment. I will try to get you a 90 day leave of absence from Seward to work for me. In the meantime, come out to St. George and spend a few days with us, the inn is nearly empty. Let me get busy on the communications that should be sent."

I wrote, so Jerome could send the following in diplomatic pouch:

TO: SECRETARY OF STATE SEWARD, WHITE HOUSE
FROM: ADMIRAL JASON CALDWELL, HAMILTON, BERMUDA
SUBJECT: CHANGE IN ASSIGNMENT FOR JEROME LEWIS

I WOULD LIKE YOUR PERMISSION TO HAVE JEROME LEWIS RETURN TO WASHINGTON WITH ME. I WILL NEED HIS EXPERTISE FOR 90 DAYS, AFTER THAT TIME HE COULD RETURN TO HIS DUTIES AT HIS STATION IN BERMUDA. FURTHER INFORMATION ON THIS MATTER IS AVAILABLE FROM SECRETARY WELLES. AWAITING YOUR RESPONSE.

TO: SECRETARY WELLES, ARMY NAVY BUILDING
FROM: ADMIRAL CALDWELL, BERMUDA
SUBJECT: NINETY DAY LEAVE OF ABSENCE FROM MY DUTIES

CERTAIN INFORMATION HAS COME TO MY ATTENTION REGARDING THE BOILER BREAKDOWNS IN WASHINGTON. IT HAS COME FROM SOME UNUSUAL SOURCES IN BERMUDA AND SOUTH CAROLINA. IF TRUE, THE NETWORK, I REFER TO SHOULD BE "ROLLED UP" BEFORE ANOTHER ATTEMPT IS MADE UPON THE PRESIDENT'S LIFE AND THE MEMBERS OF HIS CABINET, INCLUDING MYSELF. I HAVE MANAGED TO IDENTIFY THE MEMBERS OF THIS NETWORK, THOSE WORKING OUT OF RICHMOND AND THOSE PRESENTLY ASSIGNED IN WASHINGTON. ADDITIONAL INFORMATION IS AVAILABLE FROM SECRETARY SEWARD AND I WILL FORWARD CODED MESSAGES AS INFORMATION BECOMES AVAILABLE.

AWAITING YOUR RESPONSE.

TO: ABRAHAM LINCOLN, PRESIDENT, UNITED STATES
FROM: ADMIRAL JASON CALDWELL, HAMILTON, BERMUDA
SUBJECT: SPECIAL ASSIGNMENT DUTIES

I HAVE REQUESTED A SPECIAL 90 DAY ASSIGNMENT FROM SECRETARY WELLES. THIS ASSIGNMENT IS CRITICAL TO THE OUTCOME OF THE WAR AND IT DEALS WITH THREATS TO YOUR LIFE. I ONCE ASKED YOU IF YOU TRUSTED ALLEN PINKERTON. PINKERTON HAS WITHHELD ACTION ON ORION BECAUSE HE LACKS INFORMATION ON HOW TO IDENTIFY ITS MEMBERS. I NOW HAVE THAT INFORMATION. IF SECRETARY WELLES CAN NOT GRANT THIS ASSIGNMENT, THEN I MUST, IN ALL GOOD CONSCIENCE, RESIGN MY POSITION

AS UNDERSECRETARY. I WILL THEN RETIRE FROM MILITARY SERVICE, AND PROCEED ON THE ASSIGNMENT AS A PRIVATE CITIZEN. IN ANY REGARD, I AM PRESENTLY GATHERING DATA ON THIS ASSIGNMENT. YOU HAVE MY FULL AND UNDIVIDED SUPPORT OF THE WAR EFFORTS MADE TO THIS DATE.

I left Jerome with the mail and walked to the C S A Embassy with one of Jerome's incoming messages. I rang the bell and a woman answered the door. "Is Minister Butler in?" I asked.

"Yes, who shall I say is calling?"

"Admiral Caldwell."

"Jason, I am so glad to see you." John Butler greeted me with a genuine warmness.

"Thank you, John. Do you have news of what has happened in Washington regarding the attempt at a mass murder?"

"Yes, come in and I will tell you what I know."

"John, I do not want you to say anything until I show you something." I removed my great coat, jacket and vest. I rolled up my left sleeve to just below my elbow and said, "Do you have one of these?"

"Yes, Jason, I do."

"It is a tattoo of the constellation O' rion. You are required by South Carolina fraternal tradition to consider me a fellow warrior."

"I always have, Jason. You are my brother in arms."

"This damn Civil War has placed brother against brother. Did you know that a group of crazy people have been trying to kill Mr. Lincoln?"

"Yes, I walked into Washington City with thirty-five of them, I told you that at the Hay-Adams four years ago."

"I was too stupid to put it together, John. I know you cannot tell me anything, honor requires that you keep your word. I have figured out a few things, can you shake your head, yes, if I tell you some things that I fear might be true?"

He shook his head yes, sat down at this desk, smiled and waited for me to begin.

"You and I were given these tattoos when we were very young, probably after our second birthdays." He shook his head, yes.

"It consists of a very large group of men in the south?" He looked straight ahead and said nothing. "It consists of a group of men only from South Carolina?" He shook his head, yes.

"These men are presently divided between Richmond and Washington, except for you and I." He shook his head, yes.

"John, you should know that I am going to arrest those in Washington. Pinkerton will probably keep an eye on those now in Richmond." He shook his head again. "John, the war is almost over, why is Richmond trying to keep this bloodbath alive?"

"That can not be answered by shaking my head, Jason. It is madness. Only those in Richmond can answer you. I quit being of any use to Richmond a long time ago. Sally and I are going to get married and have a family here in Bermuda, the Confederacy is dead to me. You must believe me."

"I do, John. I knew your heart was not in this when we met at the Hay-Adams."

"I wish I had a list of names to give you, Jason. I do know that the assassination squad you are looking for is called, Archangel."

"Thank you, John. You have just saved many innocent lives."

I left John's office and walked back to Jerome's office. "We need to send some additional information, Jerome."

> TO: Secretary Stanton, Army Navy Building
> FROM: Admiral Caldwell, Bermuda
> SUBJECT: Special coded message

The information that I have obtained and forwarded to Secretary Welles should not wait until my return after the first of the year. A subgroup within the ORION network has been activated by Richmond. This is an assassination squad that calls itself *Archangel*. They are the ones responsible for the attacks on the buildings there. I have confirmed this from two different sources. They will try again before the end of the year.

You can identify an ORION member by a small tattoo of the constellation just below the left elbow. If the tattoo has been removed, a scar will appear where the tattoo was. The O'rion tattoo consists of two bright stars, Betelgeuse and Rigel, surrounded by smaller stars to represent the "great hunter." The O'rion organization is similar to the Masonic Order and dates from similar times. It was carried to the United States in 1701 by Stephen Bull when he settled in South Carolina. The tattoo is common in South Carolina, both my brother and I were members as children. It is not common outside of South Carolina and anyone found with one in Washington should be held for questioning until I can return.

You will find at least one member working in the White House, Senate and House, and in the Army Navy Building. They would not be questioned when entering or coming from a basement, so they are probably posing as workmen, repair men or labors. Look at the

EMPLOYMENT DATES FOR ALL EMPLOYEES, MY SOURCES SAY THEY WALKED INTO WASHINGTON AFTER THE FIRST BATTLE OF BULL RUN. THEY WOULD NOT HAVE WORKED IN WASHINGTON PRIOR TO THAT TIME. LET ME KNOW WHAT YOU FIND. CAN YOU SPARE MAJOR SCHNEIDER TO ASSIST ME IN THIS ASSIGNMENT FOR 90 DAYS?

"Did John Butler confirm this, Admiral?"

"Yes, he did. Thanks to him we have the name of the assassination squad and who their targets are."

"Who is the second source?"

"My father."

"Your father?"

"He is very proud of his family history and he has told both Robert and me stories of the O'rion Fraternity in Ireland and what it was used for in South Carolina. I have no doubt that these members are working for the Confederacy in Richmond. It will be a race to see if we can round them up before they have completed their assignments."

"Do you think the targets have any idea that they are being hunted?"

"Lincoln should, there was an attempt on his life just after the election of '60, remember?"

"Yes, we were involved in the stopping of that too."

The day after Christmas the diplomatic mail pouch was delivered to Jerome's office. It contained the following:

TO: ADMIRAL CALDWELL, ON LEAVE, BERMUDA
FROM: SECRETARY SEWARD
SUBJECT: RECEIPT OF EYES ONLY PRESIDENT

THE WHITE HOUSE HAS GRANTED YOUR REQUEST FOR REASSIGNMENT. YOU WILL LEAVE YOUR PRESENT LOCATION ON OR BEFORE JANUARY 2, 1865, AND REPORT TO THE AMBASSADOR'S OFFICE, HAVANA, CUBA. HERE YOU WILL MEET MAJOR THOMAS SCHNEIDER AND HIS INVASION FORCE OF US MARINES. YOU WILL PROCEED AT THE BEST POSSIBLE SPEED AVAILABLE TO THE GULF OF MEXICO AND LAND MAJOR SCHNEIDER'S MARINE FORCES JUST SOUTH OF BROWNSVILLE, TEXAS. MAJOR SCHNEIDER HAS A LETTER FROM PRESIDENT LINCOLN TO PRESIDENT JUAREZ. HE WILL BE RESPONSIBLE FOR ALL LAND OPERATIONS AND THE LINK UP WITH PRESIDENT JUAREZ'S ARMY. YOU ARE NOT PERMITTED TO SET FOOT ON MEXICAN SOIL. UPON THE SAFE LANDING OF THE MARINES, YOU ARE TO REMAIN ON STATION FOR EVACUATION OF MAJOR SCHNEIDER AFTER HIS MISSION IS COMPLETE.

Your request for retirement from the USN is hereby denied. All officers presently serving will continue until the war ends, plus six months.

If you ignore these orders and return to the United States, you will be arrested along with all other members of the ORION network and detained at St. Elizabeth's Hospital. No further communication is desired from you on this matter or any other until your assignment in Mexico is complete.

"Jerome, did you get any mail?" I said weakly as I handed the communique to him to read.

"No, I did not. This is sent in the open, Admiral, it was sent so ORION could read it."

"We sent everything in code, right?"

"Then there will be no Archangel members to arrest in Washington. They have failed to detain anyone for questioning. What do you make of that?"

"Not sure, Jerome. I am not permitted to send anything to the State Department. I will send orders for Sam Mason to box everything in my office and send it to Seneca Hill by January 15, 1865. He then should make his way to Pennsylvania and meet with my staff there to send and receive messages in code."

"What have I forgotten, Jerome."

"Protection to Havana. We have more 'palace guards' than I need. Take six of the most experienced marines that I have. You may be arrested when you step off the ship."

"Not if I go on the *Cold Harbor*. I do not think Tom will arrest me, Jerome. He trusts me completely, even if the White House does not."

"The War Department does not even have enough army replacements for Grant or Sherman. If Tom shows up with marines, they will be raw recruits that he has just trained through his office in Washington. Maybe a hundred. He will need squad leaders like the six you will take from here. It may be just smoke again for France and England to absorb through ORION. Just for the record, Jason, I will do everything I can to assist you in the next few months, this stinks!"

"Whatever it is, Jerome, they have gotten my attention. Sam will be sending telegrams to you, I will be sending ship's mail to you and you can send mail to me, I will let you know the ship's name etc. as soon as I can. It will be a slow process, I am sure."

"A suggestion, Sir."

"Go ahead."

"How many recommisioned ships do you have in St. George?"

"You mean former USS ships of the line, vintage 1799?"

"Yes, it might be a good idea to show up in Havana with everything that floats if you want to sell the concept of an invasion force instead of a mail delivery to the President of Mexico in exile."

"You mean if ORION is watching they will see a large number of ships. Oh, that is a good idea, Jerome. We have a few days before I have to leave. I can get as many vessels as I can locate, even if I have to rent some. This is going to be fun."

"Can I come, Admiral?"

"Do you have orders to the contrary? Do you have earned leave that you can request?"

"No and yes."

"Do it!"

83

Flotilla to Havana
January, 1865

On new years day 1865, seven ships left St. George's Harbor, Bermuda and set sail for Havana, Cuba. Our orders were clear, "leave on or before January 2, 1865. The following ships left one day early. The *Cold Harbor*, a Snow, had its crew and passengers; Admiral Caldwell, Mrs. Caldwell, Captain Lewis, Mrs. Lewis, General Butler, Mrs. Butler (on their honeymoon), Mr. Robert Whitehall and Mrs. Whitehall. The *USS Somerset*, a Brigg, had its crew and six marine guards from the US Council's Office, Hamilton. The *USS Nelson*, a Brigg, had its crew. The *USS Providence*, a Snow, had its crew. The *USS New Haven*, a Ketch, had its crew. The *USS Trumbull*, a Ketch, had its crew. And finally, the Brigg *USS Spitfire* with its crew left for Havana. These were all sailing vessels, none were steam powered. They made quite a sight when all yards were put to the wind. A fast steam powered Sloop of War could make the trip from Bermuda to Havana in two and one half days. We would take a week.

"Admiral, what if the Navy had taken you up on the offer to sell these ships to block Charleston Harbor, we would not be in one of the last wind driven fleets to enter the Civil War."

"You are right, Robert. The Navy got a better offer from the whalers in Nantucket. No one will ever suspect that we are the means for the invasion of Mexico. I like it!"

"Jason?"

"Yes, Louise?"

"You are sure all of us are safe doing this?"

"Unless we meet something unexpected in Havana, say a steam powered fleet of seven vessels, we will be fine. If the Navy has provided us with ships, then you and the others will have had a nice winter vacation. You can stay as long as you like in Havana and take the 'fleet' back to Bermuda. I am not the most popular person in Washington right now. I doubt Tom and his recruits even find a ship to meet us there."

"Then what, Admiral?"

"Then, Captain Lewis, we wait in Havana until the end of the war waiting for the USMC to get there. Those were our orders and by God we will obey them to the letter."

"Do not curse God, Jason, it is bad luck."

"Let us all get down to the main salon for some of Hop Sing's food and enjoy the rest of this week. We can not send or receive messages until we arrive in Havana."

We did just that, and the week flew by with everyone enjoying themselves, especially John and Sally Butler. John had sailed on the *Cold Harbor* with us to Boston and he was getting his sea legs. He enjoyed telling Sally all about the names of the masts, how they were divided, how the yard arms carried different types of sails. This was all courtesy of James Jason Caldwell's lessons of course. We hated to see Havana Harbor and a single ship, the new USS *Philadelphia,* anchored there. That meant that the US Marines were already in Havana. I reported to the harbor master that one Snow, the *Cold Harbor,* would like to dock, the other six would anchor just inside the harbor. Captain Jacob lowered a long boat for Jerome and I. Two crew members helped us row out to the *Philadelphia.* A Sloop of War looks huge from a long boat. Jerome hailed the *Philadelphia,* "Admiral Caldwell to come aboard."

"Permission granted."

A gangway was lowered but it would not reach the long boat. It was about three feet above the gunwales of the long boat. "Can I give you a boost, Admiral?" After two tries, I was boosted onto the gangway and Jerome followed. We scrambled up and onto the deck of the *Philadelphia.* The ship's captain saluted us and said, "Welcome Admiral Caldwell, we have been expecting you." He was smiling a wide handsome grin.

"If you will follow me, I will take you to the briefing room."

"The briefing room?" I thought. I wonder who is on this ship?

We entered a long narrow room just port side of captain's quarters and there sat Secretary Welles and Major Thomas Schneider. Without thinking, Tom bellowed, "Flag Officer on deck!" He and everyone else, except Gideon Wells, leaped to their feet.

"As you were, everyone." Welles said without looking at me. "The *Philadelphia* is scheduled to leave in two hours, we need to get this over with. Admiral Caldwell, here are your written orders from the President of the United States. Major Schneider, you were given your orders by the President when you met with him in the Oval Office, correct?"

"Aye, aye, sir."

I was speechless. I had met President Lincoln in July, 1861, and had not seen him since, now Tom has a meeting with him? Maybe I was all wrong about what this mission is supposed to entail. I must have had a blank look on my face because Gideon Welles said, "Relax Jason, you are among friends, no one here believes that you are a member of a Confederate spy ring." That broke the tension and everyone burst out laughing. He continued, "You gave an excuse for the President to slap you down, Admiral, he does like you very much. Probably because you say and do whatever you think is best. If I had as many millions as you, I would probably do the same thing." Smiles instead of laughter met his last remark.

"The point is, this is a real mission, not something to fool the Confederate listeners. That is why the President sent me to see you, Jason. He wants France to withdraw their troops from Mexico and the only way that will happen is if we land troops of our own to assist the Mexican Army in the overthrow of Emperor Maximilian."

"How many Marines have you brought with you Mr. Secretary?" I asked.

"I have 875 well trained and eager to show what they have learned to the Mexican Army. Can you fit that many in your flotilla, Admiral?"

"Of course, I have had no communication on how many billets I would need, so Captain Lewis and I planned for a 1000."

"Captain Lewis, it is good to see you again. I remember what an excellent job you did with President Lincoln's protection detail after he was elected. We need someone just like you in the White House now."

"Thank you, Mr. Secretary."

"Gentlemen, I must cut this short. You have to get your marines onto their transport. You are dismissed. Jason, can you stay a moment?"

"Of course, sir." When the others had left, he said, "Jason, I think the President is wrong. ORION will not stop until he is dead. I think he knows that he will not live out his second term and he is taking unnecessary risks with his own life. The rest of us have hired extra security in our offices and our homes. You should, also."

"I will, sir. And thank you for this chance to get out of the President's dog house. Tom Schneider will do an excellent job for you, sir."

"I know he will, look who trained him!" And with that said Gideon Welles shook my hand and said, "Be careful with your wife and the guests that you brought with you, Jason. A war zone is no place for women and Confederate spies."

I must have had a shocked look on my face because he said, "You are not the only one with spies working for them, Jason. Have Robert Whitehall send me the lease agreement for the flotilla so that I can process payment. I was just kidding about you not needing payment because you were a millionaire, Jason."

I thanked him and told him the guests would be staying in Havana for a few days before sailing back to Bermuda. I left the briefing room to find Jerome and Tom. Jerome, Tom and the six marines from Bermuda had their heads together getting caught up on the time apart from each other. I heard Jerome telling Tom that he had brought the six sergeants from the US Council's Office in Bermuda, could he use them? Tom just smiled and said, "The 875 raw recruits are like babies, now they have six more fathers!" He had a big smile on his face.

"All master sergeants take one step forward, you are now first lieutenants!"

A smile was crossing my face, " I said that very thing in Utah Territory a few years back to encourage my men, I thought."

"All staff sergeants take one step forward, you are now second lieutenants! Now you six lieutenants can go and meet the 875 marines and get them transferred to the Admirals Flotilla."

"Aye, aye, sir." They all said in unison.

We met the two hour deadline for the transfer of the marines to the three Snows, three Briggs and one Ketch. We would leave one Ketch, the *New Haven*, for the return of guests to Bermuda when they had finished their vacation in Havana. Tom Schneider, Jerome Lewis and I returned to the *Cold Harbor*. We enjoyed another great meal, put the families on the docks with their suitcases to say goodbye before the fleet sailed for the Gulf of Mexico. I waved from the bridge of the *Cold Harbor* as we pulled away from the docks and headed for the five anchored troop transports. We pulled along side the Brigg, Somerset and Tom transferred for the sail out of the harbor.

Jerome and I were standing at the starboard rail and we could see Key West off the starboard side. "Secretary Welles was not kidding about you returning as chief of protection for the White House, Jerome. He is worried that Allen Pinkerton's men will not keep up the same level of protection now that the war is about over. If you do not take his offer, would you consider chief of protection for Caldwell International? Gideon thinks there will be attempts on the lives of the cabinet members, including mine."

Jerome said, "I already have a new job. Secretary Welles hired me and the six sergeants as your protection detail two weeks ago. I do not have the heart to tell Tom that he will have his six new lieutenants for only the trip to Mexico and the unloading of war materials, after that they will return with me as part of your detail. We go wherever you go. That includes Washington, Pennsylvania or the moon. It is an honor to serve you again, Admiral."

"Jerome, is this what you want?"

"Yes, sir. I have sat on my butt the entire war. Now I feel like I am doing something important."

"What about the wife and kids?"

"The kids are old enough to return to the US after the war. The wife will stay in Bermuda with the others at Caldwell Inn."

It would be another five more days until we were close enough to land the marines south of Brownsville, Texas. According to Captain Jacob's charts, it was 1050 nautical miles from Key West to Carboneras, Mexico. We had already come nearly 1400 miles from St. George to Havana. We posted lookouts on the main masts, we should not meet any CSS vessels, they were completely bottled up now that Fort Fisher had fallen. We had heard in Havana that Admiral David Porter's squadron of warships had subjected the fort to terrific bombardment while General Terry's land troops took it by storm. Wilmington, North Carolina, was the last resort of the blockade-runners and it was sealed off. This trapped the only remaining Confederate war vessels.

A few hours off the Mexican coast, a marine who was top side, spotted the Laguna Madre a long narrow barrier island that protected the fishing village of Carboneras located at the mouth of the Conchos River. Captain Jacob found the break in the barrier island and slowly led the six ships into the intra-coastal waterway. A flag man signaled the other ships in line and we anchored just off shore. A boat was lowered and the three Spanish speaking marines joined Tom to row to the village docks. They tied up the boat and walked to the nearest canteen. President Juarez had his army hidden in the Nuevo Leon Mountains but had sent watchers to the coastal villages of La Pesca, Ciudad Madero and Carboneras. Tom met them and asked for assistance in unloading the boxes of muskets and other surplus materials that were offloaded from the *Philadelphia* into the holds of the three Briggs. He explained, through his interpreters, that President Lincoln had sent nearly a thousand men to support the Army of Mexico and its fight against the French. These troops would remain in Mexico until the French were driven out. He explained that this was just the first of many shipments to be made by the fleet now anchored at Carboneras. He also told them that General Sherman and his army would be sent to McAllen, Texas, ready to invade Mexico, should President Juarez request them. They indicated that the French were not in this part of Mexico and the marines could march to their camp in the mountains, or they could ride to the closest encampment and get soldiers to offload the needed supplies. Tom indicated that he would need a hundred workers if they could find that many. He would wait until they returned and he waved goodbye as they rode out of Caboneras.

Tom returned to the *Cold Harbor* and visited with Captain Jacob and me. "It is going to be difficult to unload heavy materials into long boats and row to the docks, but I do not see any way around that. There are no French troops near here so we should be able to take our time and unload as soon as the Mexican Army sends us a hundred men."

"A hundred men? What are you going to do with that many hands that may not be familiar with ships and long boats?" I asked.

"I am going to begin training my men, Admiral. There must be some common words between the two languages that my men can learn and use in conversational work, right?"

"I suppose so." I said doubtfully.

Before the month was out, Tom had his men learning simple Spanish commands mixed with sign language. Every time an American marine used a signal for lift up, the Mexican soldiers would cry out the Spanish for, lift up, and then they would laugh until the marine could repeat it correctly.

"You know, Tom, this is going to work. We will return to Havana to meet the *Philadelphia* and transfer another shipment. Will you be alright when we leave?"

"At some point, Admiral, it is a leap of faith. If we march into a French ambush, so be it. There will be a lot of dead Frenchmen buried in Mexico."

"Be smart, Tom, if you cannot find this President Juarez, leave and return for a pickup here at this location. Always have someone you trust watching for our return."

"Aye, aye, sir." He snapped to attention and gave me a salute.

84

Advisors in Mexico
February, 1865

Tom Schneider and his marines had moved inland from their landing points at Carboneras, La Pesca and Ciudad Madero. They were led by their guides sent from President Juarez's encampment in the Nuevo Leon Mountains. President Juarez had also sent 100 Mexican soldiers to help with the unloading of the armaments and supplies sent by President Lincoln. The soldiers were unarmed except for rather long knives or short swords that they carried in their belts. During the unloading process, 875 English speaking US Marines began to learn simple Spanish commands. The tons of supplies were stacked in a storehouse in the fishing village of Carboneras and Tom sent one of the guides and ten soldiers back to President Juarez to request horses, wagons and pack mules. Until they returned, all Tom could think of to do was train the 90 remaining Mexican soldiers. Tom had three Spanish speaking privates within his 875 marines and he found a dozen Mexican soldiers who indicated that they spoke English.

For the next week, several crates were opened and surplus muskets from 1845 were cleaned and test fired. Each Mexican soldier was asked if he could fire a musket. Every one nodded his head, yes, even if he could not. Tom formed two lines with loaded guns in each row. After the first row fired, they knelt so that the second row could fire. The exercise did not go well. The first row fell flat upon the ground at the sound of muskets firing behind them. When they realized that they were unhurt, they leaped to their feet and cheered. When the second row managed to fire each of their weapons and a celebration began.

"No, no. You must reload and fire again!" This command was translated into Spanish, but most of the soldiers looked at their US counterparts to see what to do. The demonstration was simple. Place the musket butt on the ground. Reach into your kit and drop a musket ball down the muzzle. Place a paper wadding in the muzzle. Remove the tamping rod from the muzzle and ram the wadding so that the musket ball would not roll back down the barrel. Replace the tamping rod in its holder along the barrel. Raise the musket across your arm, cock the hammer. Reach again in your kit and get a twist of gun powder, bite the end off and pour into the powder chamber.

"Be careful at this point," Tom said, " the hammer is still cocked." But he was too late, as several of the muskets fired some into the air and some into fellow Mexican soldiers. The first casualties of the Mexican War with Maximilian were self inflicted.

"Everyone place your muskets on the ground." Tom shouted. "Sergeant Daniels, you and rest of the marines form two lines and we will demonstrate how to fire, load and fire again."

The marines had not fired muskets in their basic training and they were no better than the Mexicans watching. "Cease firing! Get me a musket and I will show you how it is done." Thomas Q. Schneider was like a machine. He loaded, fired, loaded, fired and loaded again in less than forty-five seconds. He turned to the startled Americans watching and said, "This is what a French Infantry Soldier can do against us. We will all have to do this against them or we are dead."

When this was translated to the Mexicans, there was no more cheering and hugging of their compadres. Grim looks began to appear on the faces, mixed with fear for the French Infantry Soldier. The next day when the ninety volunteers were supposed to report for training, there were two hundred and eighty men, women and older children present.

"What is the meaning of this, Jose?" Tom asked his senior Mexican officer.

"Mia, Major, we are determined to learn how to fight. Yesterday, only a few of us had ever fired a weapon. If you are to train us properly, everyone in the village of Caboneras must learn. The French are beginning to build forts into this part of Mexico. They must be driven out!"

"Jose, anyone who wishes to learn will begin today. Translate that for me." Jose turned with tears in his eyes and said, "Mia, Americono Major, will teach us!" The cheering began again.

"Jose, I need to talk to you, come into my tent."

They walked off the dusty patch of ground and across a grassy area on the outside of the village where the marines had their encampment. "Jose, I will show you a map. Show me where the French have established outposts." Tom unrolled a map of northeastern Mexico.

"Here is my capitol, Mexico City. It is 400 miles from here. The French puppet, Maximilian, stays here. He has sent the French troops north to occupy the our forts at Pachucal, Tampico and Tamaulipas. From Tamaulipas they sent out small groups to locate suitable places for the French to steal what they need from the villages."

"Have they come to Carboneras, Jose?"

"No, Mia, Major. They keep further to the south, in villages like Hidalgo and Santa Jimenez."

"Santa Jimenez is only 48 miles from here! They will be here next, Jose. We must act before they find the storehouse with the supplies. We must make them think that we did not land at Carboneras. We must attack and draw them away from here. Go see if Admiral Caldwell's ships have returned to the harbor."

A breathless, Jose, returned in an hour and he reported sails on the horizon. The Caldwell Flotilla was returning from Havana with another shipment of equipment and supplies. Tom and his aide were waiting on the docks as the first long boat tied up.

"Take us out to the flag ship, we must talk to Admiral Caldwell." Tom ordered.

"Can we unload first, Major?"

"Just set everything on the docks as fast as you can, my men will take it to the storehouses."

On board the recommissioned USS *Providence*, Tom explained what the French were attempting to do in northeast Mexico. "I would like you to take my marines from here back down the coast to La Pesca and up the river to Soto La Marina. This is south of the French at Tamaulipas. We only need one vessel, the shallowest draft. We will attack French patrols and seize the horses and wagons for transport of the supplies in Carboneras to President Juarez. I do not feel comfortable with 30,000 muskets sitting in a storehouse, we need to get them to the Mexican Army."

"I agree, Tom. I would like to mention something that might be helpful. I would not bury any dead French in this part of Mexico. I would load them on wagons and return the bodies to the *New Haven*, it has the shallowest draft. The *New Haven* can bury them in the Gulf of Mexico. Any prisoners should also be held in our larger vessels for transport to Havana."

"The idea is to make them disappear! I like that, Admiral. Put some fear into the French."

"And one other thing, take Jerome with you and he can report back to me after the operation is over."

"Done, when can we get started?"

"As soon as the *New Haven* is unloaded, we will unload her first. Have your marines here before sundown so we can land you at night."

Before sunset a thousand men showed up for transport. "Where did all these come from? I thought you were taking 800 marines?" Jerome Lewis asked.

"I am, Jerome. I have 800 marines on this operation and 75 left to guard the storehouses in Carboneras. The extra 200 are Mexicans eager to kill as many French as they can find."

"Do they realize, that we will be on foot until we captures horses?"

"I will try to buy horses as we move inland from Soto La Marina. I have gold in my money belt."

"I better signal for the other ketch, USS *Trumbull* to accompany us, Tom."

A thousand men on two small ketches was a sight to be seen as they left the fishing village of Carboneras for a short run down the coast of Mexico. They stood shoulder to shoulder, some in United States Marine Uniforms and some dressed like Mexican farmers, because that was what they were until they had some training in how to fire a musket. The USS *Trumbull* and *New Haven* entered the river and stopped at Soto La Marina. It was a dark winter night and the village was asleep as the 1000 made their way towards Ciudad Victoria, the first French outpost past the Fort of Tamulipas. About ten miles into the march, they came upon a French encampment consisting of tents full of sleeping French cavalry, their horses and wagons. A single sentry was posted but was fast asleep. Two marines crept up on him, covered his mouth and placed a knife between his ribs and into his heart. The first French death was recorded by Jerome Lewis for report back to Washington. The sleeping camp was awakened by a 1000 screaming marines, some American, some Mexican. The draft horses were hitched to the wagons. The single dead French soldier was placed in it and the prisoners were marched back towards the waiting ketches at Soto La Marina. Tom gave orders to take the rest of the wagons and horses directly to Carboneras and begin the loading of supplies. He ordered the supplies to be taken to President Juarez immediately.

The company was now down to 900, 800 marines and 100 Mexican nationals. As the sun rose they came upon a small village and Tom used some of his gold to buy every wagon and horse that he could find and these were sent to Carboneras to help move the supplies to President Juarez. At around noon, a dust cloud was visible on the horizon. This meant that a large number of horsemen were probably on the road towards the Fort. Tom drew his sergeants around him and told them what he wanted them to do.

The French Cavalry officer signaled for his column to halt. Six Mexican bodies lay in the roadway, apparently dead or dying. One of the farmers raised his hand and motioned for the French to help him. The troops dismounted to rest the horses and that is when the marines raised from their cover along side the road. They rushed the column with fixed bayonets screaming, "Ferma La Fenettra." A Mexican who said he spoke French had told them it was "Surrender the fight." It turned out that it meant, "Close the window." But the result was the same, the entire column surrendered without a fight. This was more than Tom had hoped for. There was only one dead, the sentry and many prisoners. The horses were tired together in groups of three and a single rider was assigned to each group. The groups were told to ride for

Caboneras and use the horses as pack animals to move the remainder of the supplies. Tom ordered the remainder of the company to begin the march back to the waiting ketches at Soto La Marina. French cavalry were used to riding, not walking and they began to complain. Some sat by the side of the road and refused to move. Tom drew his revolver walked to the first French man and shot him in the head. He walked to the second French man and started to shoot him, but he jumped to his feet and said in perfect English, "We need to rest."

"You can rest on your trip across the Gulf of Mexico. I will shoot any man who refuses to march." The French man turned to his officer and translated. French orders were shouted down the line of prisoners and we began to march again towards the waiting ships. We reached them before sundown and loaded the prisoners on one ketch and the remaining marines on the other. By sunrise, the following day, Caldwell Flotilla was prepared to sail back to Havana.

85

Return to Havana
March 1865

We sailed on the morning tide. We had had no communication with what was happening in the States until five days later when we docked in Havana. The USS *Philadelphia* was not there. We anchored just inside the harbor again and docked the *Cold Harbor*. The lone seaman who could understand Spanish went with me to the US Ambassador's Office in Havana. There we learned that General Sherman had driven across North and South Carolina with only token resistance. The Confederacy was finished. Lee was now faced by two Union armies. Lee had attacked Grant at Petersburg and was defeated. Richmond was under siege. Jefferson Davis moved his headquarters west by train. February had been a very good month for the Union and March promised to be even better. The *Philadelphia* made Havana two days later and we began the transfer of French prisoners onto and the war materials off of the *Philadelphia* by lashing the Briggs to the Philadelphia and transferring boxes by sheer force. In four days we were ready to make the return trip to Carboneras.

"With this trip we will have provided over 50,000 muskets with bayonets, 60,000 side arms, 10,000 crates of muskets balls, wadding and gun powder, Admiral. Sherman's army could not have done what the USN has done in as short a time." Jerome was looking out to sea trying to spot Key West.

"It will not be long until we can stop at Key West and resupply, Jerome, the Confederacy is falling apart. It is only a matter of months, probably weeks."

"Thank you for getting me into Mexico with Tom on his mission, Admiral, I thought maybe I would not see any action during the great war to save the Union."

"Yes, and when our grandchildren ask us where we fought in the Civil War, we will have to say, 'Mexico'". We both laughed and then remembered that nearly 900 US Marines depended upon the bimonthly runs from Havana to Carboneras, Mexico.

We brought food stuffs and most importantly mail. The mail pouch was stuffed with letters for the marines now in Mexico. They will appreciate getting these, I thought. There was mail from Bermuda for the crews of the flotilla and there were letters for me. The one written in Ruthie's hand was the best letter I have ever read. I folded it and placed it inside my tunic. During the next two months, whenever I was lonely, I reached inside and unfolded it and cried again.

On your last return trip to Havana, we anchored the flotilla and docked the *Cold Harbor* as usually but this time the US Ambassador was there to meet us. We lowered a gang way and he boarded the *Cold Harbor*. He was not a navy man, because he did not ask for permission.

"Admiral Caldwell."

"Yes, Mister Ambassador?"

"You have been recalled to Potomac Dockyards, here are your orders."

"Captain Lewis. Here are your orders to return to duty in the White House as soon as the *Cold Harbor* can untie. I am sorry, I know you look forward to shore leave and mail. The mail is here in this pouch. You and the crew of your ship are to be in Washington, immediately."

"What has happened, Mister Ambassador?" I asked.

"The President and Secretary Seward have been assassinated!"

"Oh, my God, Jerome, we should get the *Cold Harbor* turned around as fast as we can. How is the fresh water and food supply? Do we have enough for a week or more?" A hundred things ran through my mind. Then I remembered the most important thing.

"Mr. Ambassador, what do I do with the rest of my ships, they need provisions if they are to accompany me to Washington. It will take days to resupply all of us."

"We have no orders that involve your ships, Admiral."

"Fine, they can sail twenty-four hours after we set sail. Send the following message to Secretary Welles:

" Today's date, today's time, message received and understood. Have split flotilla into two parts. Flag ship and one escort to enter Potomac no less than three days. Rest to follow for needed repairs."

Jerome and I realized that we were still holding the sealed orders from the Ambassador. We tore them open and learned. During our last trip to Mexico, Richmond fell. General Lee surrendered at Appomattox Courthouse. General Johnston was in conference to surrender to General Sherman and on the evening of April 14th Archangel struck.

86

Washington City
April, 1865

On April 14, 1865, the President received the news of Lee's surrender to Grant two days earlier. Johnston had not surrendered to Sherman, as yet, but his surrender was certain within a few days. He asked his secretary if the White House had received any free tickets to Ford Theater that week.

"Yes, sir. We have had several tickets sent everyday this week. Should I notify the secret service that you and Mrs. Lincoln will be attending tonight?"

"Yes, Jamison, Mary has been wanting to see 'Our American Cousin' for a month. Send in a messenger and I will see if Mr. Welles and Mr. Stanton over in the Army Navy Building would like to go. Find Secretary Seward and see if he and his wife would like to join us."

"Mr. Seward is home in bed trying to get over that bad fall he took yesterday, sir."

"I had forgotten that, Jamison, forget about the Sewards, then. Do we have six tickets? Mrs. Lincoln wants to meet the star, can you send a White House card to Mr. Booth at the theater asking him to come to the President's box during intermission?"

"Yes, Mr. President."

"Good. Send in the messenger, will you? Oh, here you are. Will you run over to the Army Navy and see if you can get a response from Secretary Welles or Stanton on a night out at Ford's?"

"On my way, sir." Mr. Lincoln did not notice that the messenger had a small tattoo just above the left elbow. The messenger had been employed at the White House for four years and was trusted with messages of a verbal nature. He walked at a normal pace until he was out of the White House and then he ran across the street and into Lafayette park. He carried a small piece of paper and wedged it where he usually did. He then walked over to the Army Navy Building and went to the office of the ORION commander, who also had a small tattoo just above the left elbow.

"It is tonight, sir."

"Are you sure? I do not want to disturb the Grand Dragon with another false alarm."

"Yes, sir. I heard them talking. I was sent to ask Stanton and Welles if they would like to attend with the President."

"We have to attack Welles and Stanton at home. Go to both Welles and Stanton and indicate that the invitation is for them alone, not their wives. If anyone asks you later, indicate that you got confused about the invitation for the wives."

"There was no mention of the wives, sir. I assumed that the invitation was for them alone."

"Very good, that reduces our chances that both will accept. After you find out who has accepted, return here to me."

"I will be back soon, sir."

The Grand Dragon was sitting in Lafayette Park reading the drop message from the White House messenger and wondered if he had all the pieces in place. He had assigned the most dangerous task of cutting off the dragon's head to himself along with the assistance of a Maryland Confederate, John Booth. Four members of his group would be assigned the homes of each of the cabinet members for elimination tonight. He looked up at a particular window of the Army Navy Building and wondered if his second in command would perform his tasks correctly.

The second in command waited for the messenger to return. "Sir, both Mr. Welles and Stanton indicated that they could not accept tonight, maybe another time."

"Excellent, go back to the White House and indicate exactly what was said by each. Then add that a Major Rathman, one of the aides and his fiancee, a Miss Clara Harrison would be happy to accompany the President and Mrs. Lincoln. If he asks who this Major Rathman is, you tell him, he is the stepson of Senator Williams from New York. There will not be time to check that out by one of the secret service's men."

"Very good, sir. Do you want me to come back here?"

"No, take your place in the line of messengers and act as everything is normal. And remember to report to work tomorrow. We must remain in place for another assignment if necessary."

"Yes, sir."

It was intermission as the actor, John Booth, entered the hallway to the President's Box in Ford's Theater. He was immediately stopped by a secret service man and asked for identification. Booth handed him his invitation from the White House.

"Very good, sir. You may enter. You will have to give me that stage prop dagger, though."

"It is only rubber, sir. See", he bent it nearly double.

"I guess no one can get hurt by that, you can go in."

Booth entered the box and saw four people seated looking forward. The two men sat together with the wives at each end of the row of four seats. Just as he was about to introduce himself to the President and Mrs. Lincoln, the man seated next to him raised his arm and shot the President behind the left ear. Booth was dumb struck but he still carried the stage prop dagger. The plan was for the Grand Dragon to shout "assassin" and then shoot Booth before he could protest. He would then place the pistol in Booth's hand. Plans do not always work smoothly, because Booth recovered and grabbed Rathman's arm to wrestle the pistol from his hand. The pistol fell to the floor changing the plan. Rathman placed his free arm under Booth and pitched him over the box rail and onto the stage floor. He hoped that the fall would kill Booth by breaking his neck. But a sprained ankle was all that happened. Booth was in a panic, he was a known southern supporter and everyone would believe that he had shot the President, he must get away and he fled the stage and the theater. He was closely followed by two ORION members.

It was several minutes before the audience returned from intermission and realized what had happened. The President still sat beside a weeping Mary Lincoln and a shocked young couple. An Army major opened the box door and shouted for the secret service agent.

"Mr. Lincoln has been shot by the actor, Booth! Get a doctor! Hurry Please!"

"What happened, Mr. Rathman?"

"The actor, Booth, shot the President. You certainly saw that?"

"No, I heard a shot and saw you trying to get the gun out of his hand. Oh, this is terrible, look Mrs. Lincoln has fainted." A doctor entered the box and declared that the President was injured but not dead. He stopped the flow of blood and gave Mrs. Lincoln a stimulant.

"We can move the President whenever you would like." The doctor said to the secret service agent.

"Can you help us, Major? More agents are on the way, he should be moved to a bed. See if you can find a house next to the theater that will accept the President."

"I will be right back as soon as I find someone."

The Grand Dragon ran next door, to the house of a Mr. Peterson and explained what had happened. He ran back and helped move the President to a bed where he lingered until seven the next morning before he died. Major Rathman and Miss Harrison disappeared in the confusion and when White House personnel were questioned the next day by the secret service's men, no one knew a Major Rathman or a Miss Harrison.

Intermission was scheduled at Ford's for 9:45 PM. At ten o'clock four men approached the homes of Secretaries Seward, Stanton, Welles, and Blair

House. The four men assigned to Seward's home had individual assignments. One man approached the front door and knocked. A house servant opened the door and inquired who he was and what he wanted at this hour. The man replied, "I have been sent with medicine by the doctor for Secretary Seward."

He then tried to push by the servant. The slight disturbance alerted the house security. The Secretary's son was awake and confronted the man at the door and was knocked unconscious by a blow to the head from a pistol butt. By this time a security guard rushed in to help and was shot by a second man who appeared in the doorway.

"The bedrooms are on the third floor, get up there."

Two ORION agents rushed up the stairs looking for the Seward's bedroom. They threw open each door until they found Mr. Seward along with his daughter and her sailor boy friend. The boy friend immediately tried to stop them but one of the attackers held him at gun point while the other shot the secretary in the face and neck. ORION members were always told to shoot the head of the victims, never to shoot the body. Seward fell to the floor wounded but not yet dead.

At the home of Secretary Stanton, four men were assigned the same mission. One held the get away horses, another acted as a lookout and two tried to gain entrance. This time the security was better and the two trying to gain entrance were shot and killed at the front door. The remaining two escaped into the night. At the home of Secretary Welles, entrance was gained and a man sleeping in a bedroom was mistaken for Welles and killed with all four men escaping. At Blair House, the security was the best and Vice President Johnson slept through the night without incident, four riders passed on the street but did not even slow beyond a trot.

The belief that a new ORION attempt was afoot for the assassination of the leading officers of the government, caused Secretary Stanton to take immediate steps to protect Washington City against further attacks. Additional guards were placed around Blair House, and St. Elizabeth Hospital where Secretary Seward was now located and clung to life. Stanton ordered the secret service to learn the truth of the plot and to bring the criminals to justice.

87

Washington City
April 15, 1865

The next day, April 15, 1865, as provided by the Constitution, Andrew Johnson was sworn in as the seventeenth President of the United States by the Supreme Court Chief Justice. He took the oath in the cabinet meeting room before a small group of cabinet members and his invited guests. Johnson was an ardent Democrat, but when the storm of secession swept over Tennessee, no man was more intensely Union than he. He was the US Senator elected from Tennessee in 1857. When Tennessee seceded he stayed in Washington and Lincoln appointed him Military Governor after the fall of Tennessee. His violent expressions against the secessionists, who he declared ought to be hanged, led to an attempt to lynch him in May, 1861. He met the mob, revolver in hand and drove them off, killing three. It was this man who assumed the office on April 15, 1865.

His first order of business was to gather his cabinet together. Secretary of State, Seward, was still in the hospital but the others met with him for his advice. The meeting began by the President saying the following to his cabinet.

"I am not Abraham Lincoln. I am Andrew Johnson. I have been your Vice President for a little over six weeks and now I am your President. Will you all give me a few days to adjust to this sudden change of events? I will, of course, accept resignations from those of you present that do not want to continue in my administration. Make no mistake, it is now my administration. I will make the final decisions after considering your areas of expertise. I will not listen to anyone who tries to speak outside of his area of expertise, however. Let me begin by going around the table and telling you each what I already know about you. Some of you, I have never met. Others, I have met before, but know little about you."

He stopped and gazed around the cabinet meeting table waiting for questions. When none came he began. "Secretary Seward will be recovering for sometime and I will appoint an acting member to replace him until he can return to work in the White House." Heads bowed in agreement.

"Secretary Stanton, your area of expertise is the War Department and as a fellow Democrat, I expect the same level of service that you gave Mr.

Lincoln. I trust you completely and probably know you the best from my time as Military Governor of Tennessee. You will not direct the secret service to do anything for you. The secret service does not work in the Army Navy Building, they work for the White House, in fact they will all be fired today for gross incompetence in regard to the ORION network. I have asked, and he has accepted, Captain Jerome Lewis, the former head of Presidential Security to begin work as soon as he can get here from Cuba." Heads again bowed up and down with exception of Stanton.

"Who will serve as security until he can get here?" asked Secretary Stanton.

"I have asked Secretary Welles to provide United States Marines as armed guards to be placed throughout the White House and the Army Navy Building. You better remember the passwords that will be given to you at the end of this meeting, because if you forget it and can not repeat it you will be shot and killed." Stanton swallowed hard and looked at the rest of the cabinet members who were all frowning. Security was no longer a joking matter.

"Secretary Welles, that brings me to you. Can you get Admiral Caldwell back from Cuba with Jerome Lewis?"

"I can send another telegram, Mr. President, Lewis is presently in charge of the protection detail for the Admiral and I think it would be a good idea for them to travel together."

"If Admiral Caldwell will accept my apology for the stupidity shown by the White House in regard to the threat from the ORION network, he may agree to accept my offer of a cabinet level position that I will request. But I doubt that a man of his caliber and great ability will want to serve in the White House, again."

"Sir, I do not understand why you think so highly of Caldwell, he is a member of ORION for God sake!" Said William Dennison.

"You will refer to me as, Mister President, in the future, Mr. Dennison, or I will replace you with Montgomery Blair so fast it will take your breath away. You are unqualified to be Postmaster General in my opinion and I hope you decide to resign before the end of the day. Your appointment was a political mistake by Mr. Lincoln and frankly you will be an embrassment to this administration if you do not learn what the Postmaster General is supposed to be doing. I have asked Montgomery Blair to be your immediate supervisor. He will take a 90 day leave from his position as CEO of American Telegraph. If you do not meet with his approval after 90 days, you Mr. Dennison, are history. And as far as Admiral Caldwell being a member of ORION, that is ridiculous, he identified the entire network working in the White House and the Army Navy Building and your precious secret service did nothing, damn them, I think Pinkerton was a member, not Caldwell –

you fool." Andrew Johnson had lost his temper, but like Jason Caldwell, he could not abide fools.

"Now, where was I? Oh, yes. We are up to you, Mr. Mc Culloch. You are the third Secretary of the Treasury in four years. The two before you were thieves. If I ever hear of improper conduct from your department, I will have you arrested. Is that clear?"

"Yes, Mister President."

"Good. Now on to you, Mr. Speed, as Attorney General, I expect you to keep me out of jail." The tension was broken around the table and everyone laughed except Dennison, he was still smarting from the dressing down from the President.

"That leaves you, Mr. Usher, I have no knowledge of you or the Department of the Interior. I have no first hand knowledge of anything that you have done in the last four years. That is my fault, not yours. Could I get a one page summary of what your department has done?"

"Yes, Mister President."

"In fact, I would like a one page summary from all of you by the end of today." He stood signaling that the meeting was over. "Gentlemen, see the lady at the doorway for your passwords."

The President walked from the cabinet room to his working office with two secretaries in tow, one male and one female. The woman had been hired at the beginning of the day. He had told her, "You will be replacing Mr. Lincoln's secretary, a man, can you do that?"

She smiled and said, "Yes, Mister President."

"I want you to transcribe everything that is said in the cabinet meetings, we are going to make some enemies before this is over and I want a record of what was said and by whom."

When the two secretaries entered the President's working office, he said, "Please, sit down, I have some dictation for both of you."

"But, Mister President, I do not take short hand." George Jamison said.

"Then you are excused ,Mr. Jamison, I am sure that you have plenty of typing back at your desk."

"Yes, Mr. President."

"Shall we begin, Mrs. Wainwright?"

"Whenever you would like, Mr. President.

"Personal to Secretary Stanton.

Item One. Jefferson Davis and his cabinet are now fugitives upon the evacuation of Richmond. It is my fear that he will try to reach Kirby Smith in the southwest, and with his help, he will attempt to prolong the life of the Confederacy. I, therefore, as commander and chief of the armed forces order General J. H. Wilson to use every effort with his cavalry to capture the fleeing

President. I do not wish to discuss this order with you or have you issue it through General Grant. This is a direct order from me to General Wilson. I want you to make it clear to the General that I expect Davis to be in custody before May 1ˢᵗ, or his letter of resignation on my desk by May 2ⁿᵈ.

Item Two. Issue an order for General Grant to move south until he engages General Johnston of the remaining Confederate Army trying to protect Davis' escape. You are to direct General Grant that I want Johnston's unconditional surrender, identical in terms that were granted General Lee. I am tired of General Sherman's pussyfooting around Johnston. Tell Grant that either Johnston surrenders or he has orders from President Johnson to attack and take no prisoners. I desire no input from you or General Grant on this matter. I want the war ended by May 1, 1865.

Item Three. Issue an order for General Sherman to pull out of the fight against Johnston and march towards McAllen, Texas. If he meets any Confederate resistance he is to take no prisoners. If the Confederate mentality is to die on the battlefield, tell Sherman to do his best to kill every damn one of them from as far away as possible with artillery fire. Barring that, use the new long range rifles to drop the enemy where he stands. General Sherman is not to stop and bury the enemy dead, he is to let them lay where they fall. The message must be introduced that the war is over, only death remains for those foolish enough to resist.

Item Four. General Sherman is to remain within the US boarders, but he is to send scouts into the mountains to locate Major, (make that Colonel), Schneider's marine force. President Juarez will be offered Sherman and his troops to hunt down and kill every God Damn French troop they can find. The French have been told by President Lincoln to withdraw. I will not ask them again. I will find and kill as many as I can until they get the same message as delivered to the Confederacy. The longer we wait, the more Union deaths we will encounter.

End of personal."

"Do you want me to read that back to you, Mister President?"

"Yes, please."

When she had finished he said, "A good start. Let us try another. Send a blind copy of the Stanton personal to Admiral Caldwell, acting Secretary of State, will you?"

"How do I do that, Mister President?"

"After you have typed the personal for Stanton, take it to the basement and it will be keyed to our Havana Embassy. You will only have to type it once. After the message is sent to Havana, hand carry it to Stanton and place it in his hands only. Let no one else see it. Take a receipt slip and have him sign for it. Never use a messenger for paper work inside the White House or the Army Navy Building."

"Yes, Mister President."

"When that is done come back in here and we will twist another cabinet member's tail."

She was smiling as she said, "Aye, aye, sir."

"Your husband must be a marine, Mrs. Wainwright. I like Marines."

"He would like your take charge attitude Mister President."

"Send in the messengers waiting outside with Mr. Jamison, one at a time."

"Yes, Mister President."

The first member of the messenger squad entered the President's Office.

"Roll up your left shirt sleeve."

"Yes, sir. May I ask what this is about Mister President?"

"Of course, I am promoting all messengers today. The ones with large biceps will be given a raise in pay."

"Really!"

"Yes, you qualify for the pay increase. Please roll down your sleeve and stand along the wall over there, I might need your help."

In this fashion, Andrew Johnston, seventeenth President of the United States, personally arrested three members of the ORION network not listed on the White House known list. He had to use a revolver that he had placed in his top desk drawer only on one of the three. When news of this spread throughout the White House, a panic started within the remaining members of ORION network working in other parts of the White House and they were arrested by Marine guards as they were trying to flee the grounds. At the same time, Gideon Welles, was doing the same thing with all members of the Department of the Navy. Two were arrested and when this happened a panic started in the Department of War and fleeing members were arrested as they tried to exit the Army Navy Building. The Grand Dragon was in Lafayette Park watching the events unfold and told himself, "I think I will like Canada this time of year and he headed for the train station."

Captain Jerome Lewis arrested John Stuart for the attempted assassination of Secretary Seward. His sister lived in Washington City and her house was known to be the meeting place for ORION members. When she was questioned, she was not recognized as Miss Harrison. A man who claimed to be a Simon Payne was found to have dyed his hair and shaved off his beard, but was identified as John Stuart. For the next ten days, Jerome Lewis' men searched for the actor, Booth. Booth had returned to Maryland with Daniel Harrold and William Bilts in close pursuit. When Booth stopped for sleep one night in a Virginia barn, the two ORION agents set fire to it. Booth awoke with a start and yelled "Who is out there?"

"Federal Marshals, come out, Mr. Booth, the real assassin has been caught."

Booth's last words were, "Thank God you found me."

He was shot in the head and left for dead. His body was found by Lewis' men and taken to Washington where a post-mortem examination was made. The remains were taken to St. Elizabeth's for processing. Lewis' men continued to arrest ORION members that were known to them from the secret service's list that was four years old. Twelve were arrested in all. Only Miss Mary Stuart and the Grand Dragon survived the search for and the arrest of the assassins.

Acting Secretary of State Caldwell sat behind his former boss's desk and said to himself, "Here I go again, a fish out of water. I wonder what Ben Hagood is doing?" He had several meetings with President Johnson and he was given the job of dealing with Jefferson Davis after his capture. On May 1, 1865, he received the following telegram from General Wilson:

HAVE LOCATED SUBJECT IN QUESTION SLEEPING IN A TENT OUTSIDE IRWINSVILLE, GEORGIA. NO SHOTS WERE FIRED. ALSO HAVE DETAINED; MRS. DAVIS, DAVIS CHILDREN, AND VARIOUS AIDE-DE-CAMPS. THEY WILL BE ESCORTED BY COLONEL PRITCHARD OF THE FOURTH MICHIGAN CAVALRY TO MACON, GEORGIA. AWAITING FURTHER INSTRUCTIONS.

GENERAL J. H. WILSON

I carried the telegram to Mrs. Wainwright and let her read it.

"When he has time, show him this and ask what we should do about the others arrested with President Davis.

"Let me see what he is doing, Mister Secretary." She opened the Oval Office door and stuck her head inside. She softly closed the door and said, "He has his head down on this desk and is sound asleep, poor dear."

I smiled and said, "Come and get me when he is wide awake and wants to see me."

She nodded her head and I went back to my office.

An hour later, a refreshed Andrew Johnson stuck his head around my open door and said, "Guess what? It seems that no one can find the Undersecretary of War. Stanton is making all kinds of excuses for him. What do you make of this?"

"Mister President, either he was an ORION member or he was killed by an ORION member, what other conclusion can we make?"

"Exactly what I thought! That dumb, sumbitch Stanton had a spy working for him and did not even know it. Or worse, Stanton is a secret, southern sympathizer."

"Mister President, I do not think Edwin Stanton is either of those things. I think he was using his assistant to feed misinformation to Richmond. He thought he could control him and the reverse was probably true."

"Where do you think he is now?"

"The Undersecretary?"

"Yes."

"Canada, Mister President."

"Exactly, I judge a man's intelligence by how much he thinks like me. You, Admiral, are one smart, sumbitch!" He turned on his heel and was gone.

"Tomorrow, Andrew Johnson will be twisting Stanton's tail again and asking Gideon Welles to do many of the things that should be sent to the War Department." I thought to myself.

88
General Amnesty
Summer 1865

President Johnson issued a proclamation of general amnesty for all former Confederate combatants. Certain classes of people were not included in this amnesty. Any West Point Graduate above the rank of Colonel, those persons that had voluntarily taken part in the rebellion whose property values were in excess of $20,000.00, a former US Senator, a former US Representative and twelve other cases which totaled sixteen classes of persons were excluded from the amnesty. The amnesty proclamation did provide for a special written application for Presidential pardon. Because of this, General Lee wrote the following:

Richmond, Virginia
June 13, 1865

"His Excellence, Andrew Johnson, President of the United States"
    "Sir: Being excluded form the provisions of amnesty contained in the proclamation of May 29, 1865, I hereby apply for the benefits and full restoration of all rights and privileges, extended to those included in its terms."
    "I graduated from the Military Academy at West Point in June, 1829; resigned from the US army, April, 1861; was a General in the Confederate Army and included in the surrender of the Army of Northern Virginia, April 9, 1865."
    "I have the honor to be, very respectfully, your obedient servant,

R. E. Lee

There was no letter requesting pardon from Jefferson Davis, who was a former US Senator, he was unaware of the proclamation. He and his male companions were taken to Fort Monroe to stand trial for treason. The date of this his trial was fixed several times, but postponed. The legal question of whether or not the Constitution forbade the withdrawal of a state from the Union could not be answered, the Constitution dealt with how to add states, not remove them. The acting Secretary of State said, "If Mr. Davis should make an honest effort to escape from Fort Monroe and flee to Canada as so many have done, I think he would succeed."

No one saw more clearly than President Johnson, the difficulty in fixing upon the wisest course to be pursued with the prisoner and he sent for his acting Secretary. "Jason, come sit down. What have you decided to do with Mr. Davis?"

"I would like to send him to another country to remain in exile for the remainder of his life, Mr. President."

"Sort of like Napoleon I, hope he does not escape and return like that French bastard!"

"Well, there is a problem with finding a country that will accept him. England has closed all of her ports, harbors and waters against any vessel bearing the Confederate flag or Confederate officers. I thought we had a chance with France, but now they have done the same thing. So far, eight countries have refused to grant him entrance. I do not think exile is an option, Mr. President."

"What is his health at this moment, Jason? Can he live much longer in a cell at Fort Monroe?"

"The doctors in Richmond say he is very weak and depressed, he is not eating normally and he has lost a lot of weight."

"What if we arrange for someone famous, like Horace Greeley, to announce that the New York Tribune will post a bond for his release from Fort Monroe while he waits for his trial? We then delay the trial month after month until there is no need to prosecute a dead man!"

"I will have my editor friend at the Washington Post leak that very idea, Mr. President. It will be an accomplished fact in few weeks."

"Jason, how is Secretary Seward coming along? I saw he was in his office yesterday with you."

"He is healing nicely, Mr. President, I will be leaving in a few weeks."

"What are your plans, Jason?"

"I graduated from the Military Academy, Anapolis in '37, so I have eighteen more months until my retirement from the Navy. I will report to Secretary Welles for my assignment."

"I have suggested to Secretary Welles that he consider you for the position of Marine Commandant, assignment Army Navy Building. It would mean that you would have to become a four star Marine General instead of your four star Admiral status. What do you think?"

"My son would never forgive me, Mr. President. He is a future Anapolis man through and through, he loves the Navy and everything it stands for, just like me. However, I am a loyal American and I will follow my orders wherever they send me and whatever they may entail. President Lincoln taught me that."

"President Lincoln was a fool for not listening to you and your advisory board, Jason. The war would have lasted about two years if he had invaded the South through their seaports with Marines. The army should have been used to hold what the Navy captured for them. You can reach Richmond by gunboat for God's sake!"

"Yes, we butted heads the entire war."

"Jason, you will be happy to know that on July 1, 1865, we passed the eight hundred thousand mark for mustered out of service, soldiers, sailors and marines. These men have reentered private life, returning to what they were doing before conscription. Only the volunteers remain on active duty, mostly in Mexico and on the Texas/Mexico border. Over a million men are now on inactive reserve in case there is a national emergency. I have you to thank for the ideas that made this possible."

"It is nice to be useful and appreciated, Mr. President."

"Do you ever think you can call me Andrew?"

"The day you leave office, Mr. President."

"I would be honored to have you as a friend, Jason. You may have heard that I have forwarded a list of names for Vice President to the Senate, I am tired of butting heads with them. They can pick the one they would like. I plan to ignore whoever they choose, that is why your name was not on the list."

You never got the last word with Andrew Johnson and I left his working office to find Monty Blair and to twist the tail of his apprentice, Postmaster General Dennison.

"Monty, what are you doing for lunch?"

"Jason, I was wondering if you would show up, it is Wednesday, you know. I understand the Hay-Adams has a wonderful New York strip steak and a fine red wine today."

"How many days before you have to go back to American Telegraph, Monty?" I said this loud enough for Dennison to overhear.

"It depends on how fast my understudy can grasp the simplest tasks, I have permission from the holding company that owns American Telegraph to remain another 90 days if need be." I saw Dennison sag in his chair.

We left Monty's office and headed for Jerome Lewis' office to pick him up for lunch. "You know, Monty, we should really stop with Dennison. Is he ready to do the job?"

"Sure, he was ready a week ago."

"Monty, I need you back at American Telegraph as CEO. The profit margin is down and it should be way up with the war over and all these troops returning home."

"I will tell the President, Jason. I was just having some fun with the political appointee!"

"I am a few weeks away from a new assignment with the Navy, myself. I have no idea where they will send me. I have a meeting with Gideon this afternoon."

Jerome Lewis heard me say that as we found him in his office and he said, "They should let you be an advisor from either Pennsylvania or Bermuda, if there is any justice left in the world."

"Or better yet, Military Governor of South Carolina." Monty said.

"Now that would really be a disaster!" Jerome said. We all laughed and left the White House in route to the Hay-Adams for a Wednesday lunch.

After our lunch we walked slowly across Lafayette Square, we said goodbye and the two of them headed for the White House and I walked towards the Army Navy Building. I found Gideon Welles at his desk behind a huge pile of papers. He peered over them and said, "Jason, good to see you again. Are you getting tired of the White House and need a real assignment with the Navy?"

"Yes, that about sizes it up from where I stand."

"Jason, did you know that Andrew tried to get you confirmed as his Vice President before he offered you the position of acting Secretary of State?"

"I had no idea, he did say he was tired of butting heads and he sent a list from which they could choose a name."

"The Senate will never confirm anyone for any position that he chooses. They have a two-thirds majority, just like the house and they will over ride any veto that he makes. It is a standoff. Too bad for the country. He could get many things done for the country if they would leave him alone and let him do his job. I am ashamed to be a Republican. The house is considering impeachment, did you know that?"

"There are no grounds for impeachment! My God, Gideon, what has this country come to?"

"I think that is why Lincoln chose a 'War Democrat' as a running mate. He knew his days were limited and he did not want someone else to get the credit for saving the country. If Andrew would just take the reconstruction plans that Lincoln had in his office and publish them, then they would be adopted without question."

"Do you think someone like me should suggest this to him?"

"No, you have been assigned to me for the next eighteen months and you are going to be too busy to make helpful trips to the White House. Starting today, you are granted 30 days home leave and 30 days travel leave. After all, you have a home in South Carolina that you have not seen in four years." He handed me my leave papers, signed and ready for my signature.

"You will need to stop off at Seneca Hill so that Sam Mason can bring you up to date on the ORION network now active in Canada. He will travel with you to South Carolina, as your aide, as will a protection detail of marines (I have called them the RR unit)". He was smiling as he handed me those orders. He continued, "The President wants to send a message about mustering out soldiers and sailors. He has decided to do something special in your case. He thinks it would be symbolic if you personally handed the orders to the CO in Beaufort and placed him and his troops onboard the Caldwell flotilla for return to Washington."

"When you have completed that, I want a report from you on how Bermuda has managed to have a working telephone system installed. That will require you to travel to Bermuda to discuss with the chairman of Bermuda Telegraph and Telephone company how this was done. You should not take more than 90 days on this mission, however. You will file your report from the Bermuda Conciliate's office, a Captain Milroy now has Jerome Lewis' duties there." He handed me a third set of orders.

"Your report from Bermuda should indicate how the telephone cable from Bermuda to the Maryland Eastern Shore can be extended into the Chesapeake and up the Potomac. It is time that we have secure voice communication throughout Washington City. I also have orders for you to report to the American Ambassador in Havana as soon as your report is sent, the time table of course is to be determined by you." He handed me another set of orders. My head was swimming.

"Sir, is that stack of paper in front of you all for me?"

"Yes, it is. Jason, I guarantee that these orders will take at least 18 months to accomplish, maybe longer. Some are more important than others, you can sort them out and even have some of them done by others as you see fit. From Havana you will take the Caldwell Flotilla back to Mexico and get Colonel Schneider and four of his marines and deliver them to Potomac Dockyards. After the Colonel's report, he will be assigned to you to complete the expulsion of Maximilian from Mexico by force." He handed another set of mission orders from his stack in front of him and then he said, "Jason, it is up to you. You can leave the Navy at the end of the next 18 months or you can complete the missions I have outlined for you." He pushed the entire stack of papers across his desk, they rested in front of me like Mount Everest.

"If you will give me a free hand on procedure, I will complete the missions in the order that you have suggested. I will need time with my family, at my discretion. I also need the normal letters of introduction from you and the

White House to carry along to convince doubters that the mission has been authorized and a Canadian visa for my passport."

"It is all in your stack, Jason, and some other things that you might find useful, like a US Treasury voucher for purchase of needed materials while on a mission."

"I hope to survive the next three and one half years in this office, if I do not, I hope my replacement has the good sense to find men like you to command men in the service of their country." He stood and extended his hand across his desk and said, "Do you remember the day I took this job from Secretary Touche?"

I shook his hand and said, "Yes, I do, sir."

"I thought then that the wrong man had been selected for the job, it should have been you, Jason. If you complete these missions for me, I will be the most successful Secretary of the Navy since John Paul Jones was a USN Captain."

I reached out and gathered the pile of papers and said, "I will have Montgomery Blair come over and talk to you about American Telegraph installing a telephone compatible underwater cable. You do realize, that there are no above water lines in Bermuda, sir. John Butler has installed underwater cable from the connection point that American Telegraph left him to connect the tiny chain of islands that make up Bermuda. Bermuda is an ideal place for such an installation because the cable must be kept from overheating and burning through the wire carrying the signals. From my house in St. George, I can talk to my father and mother who live on a tiny island inside the Great Sound, my brother who lives on St. David's island or the City of Hamilton, Government House. We ran a cable from Government House to the Royal Naval Dockyards. They think it is a private line, but we can listen to anything being said."

"Why did you have American Telegraph run a cable from Maryland to Bermuda?"

"So we could talk to anyone connected to the transatlantic cable. There are now three lines across the Atlantic Ocean, sir. You can send a telegram to London, or you can talk to them if you like."

"How do you talk to Bermuda from Seneca Hill?"

"We installed an underground cable from Seneca Hill to Erie. Once we connected to Erie, we used Lake Erie and just dropped the wire in the water until we got to the canal connecting Lake Erie and Lake Ontario. From Ontario we used the St. Lawrence to connect to the transatlantic cable to Europe. I was able to talk to the Lord Admiralty before I was able to talk to Bermuda, however. As more and more telegraph cable was installed we kept bridging the open spaces until we had a Bermuda crossing from Salisbury, Maryland."

"So what I asked you to do from Salisbury to Washington is a minor thing compared to what you have already done?"

"I would think so, but I have no knowledge of how this system works, it is really the brain child of Monty Blair. The best thing that ever happened to American Telegraph was when Monty was fired as Postmaster General by President Lincoln. I had a chance to hire him and he has made over fifty million dollars for the company at ten times his salary here in Washington."

"Then why did he come back at Andrew Johnson's request?"

"His salary continues at American Telegraph and it was only for 90 days. This is his last week at the White House, so it is important that you talk to him today or tomorrow. Shall I send him over?"

"Are you going back to your office in the White House, Jason?"

"Yes, I need a larger brief case to carry all these papers home to Seneca Hill."

"I will walk with you and see Montgomery. Why do you call him Monty, everyone else calls him Montgomery?"

"I am the only one he allows to call him that. It started as a joke. We were sitting in the Washington office of American Telegraph trying to convince them to lay a double bonded telegraph connection from Salisbury to St. George, Bermuda. The office manager had no idea that Caldwell International was the holding company for American Telegraph. Monty turns to me and says, 'Jase, this man does not know who he is talking to, he knows me from the White House.' He turns to the office manager and says, 'Let me introduce the Chairman of Caldwell International.' The man's eyes bugged out and said, I had no idea, Mr. Caldwell, please forgive me."

"That does not sound like Montgomery Blair."

"I know, he was putting on an act". I turned to him and said, "Well, Monty, let's go to lunch so he can sort it out for us and we will return in a couple of hours to sign the contracts. This was on a Wednesday."

"So that is how the Wednesday lunches began between you two. That drove everyone in the White House crazy trying to figure out what you two were doing."

"We were having lunch!"

We walked into the White House and Gideon Welles said, "That reminds me of a joke. A factory worker left work one night pushing a wheelbarrow full of straw. The night watchman looked through the straw but found nothing. This happened night after night until finally the night watchman said to the worker, 'I know you are stealing something. If you tell me what it is I will not report you to the management.' The worker replied, 'wheelbarrows'".

We were both laughing as we found Monty's office and I said, "You will be getting telegrams as updates until your telephone is installed in the Army Navy Building. Thank you for allowing me to serve the last eighteen months in the Navy with dignity, I will not forget this, Gideon." We shook hands again and he entered the Postmaster General's office. I heard him say, "Montgomery Blair, just the man I was looking for."

"Call me Monty."

Well, that is off to a good start, I thought as I continued on to the Secretary of State's office. I found out later from Monty that Gideon Welles was amazed by what American Telegraph could do with a pair of copper wires. Monty gave him the cost of laying a private, government line verus a public line which was free of installation costs but carried a monthly fee, paid every month or the line went dead. Monty estimated that as soon as everyone else heard of his plan, especially the White House, that additional lines would be required. He warned him that dropping the cable in the Chesapeake and Potomac was a rapid process, once you came on land, the costs skyrocketed because ditches needed to be dug and water pipes for cooling were then installed. He indicated that the trench from Seneca Hill to Erie cost over 650 thousand dollars to construct.

"You have to understand Mr. Secretary, the telephone system that we use is very costly because of the over heating of the cable. Soon, say ten years or less, it will be possible to send telephone transmissions through wires in the air and the cost will be cheaper than a telegram. I predict telegrams will decrease in popularity as the telephone becomes common place in America."

Monty explained that the Federal Government was heavily in debt because of the war. After the Revolutionary War the debt was 75 million, the War of 1812 drove it to 127 million and this war drove it to over12 billion, the yearly interest being 140 million dollars. Monty doubted that Gideon or even the President could get an appropriation through Congress for the amount necessary to construct a private line. The cost would be in the neighborhood of ten million dollars.

"How can American Telegraph afford to make such a large investment?" Secretary Welles finally asked.

"It is a cost of doing business, the monthly rent on the use of the telephone line will be 50,000 dollars."

"That is six hundred thousand dollars a year!"

"Correct, a lot cheaper than the ten million to construct a private line. You have to understand, Caldwell International is one of the largest holding companies in the world. Jason Caldwell has no idea how much he is worth, it varies daily. I would say he could buy Morgan and Chase and have money left over. A million dollars to him is pocket change."

"No wonder he wants out of the Navy!"

"If he worked really hard at business he could remove the national debt in a year, Mr. Welles. Jason Caldwell is my hero. There will never be another like him for a century."

"I am beginning to understand why people either love or hate him. The jealousy factor alone must be a constant thorn in his side."

"Think of it this way, Mr. Welles, how many Admirals do you know that take their own private fleet with them on assignments for the Navy. The lease agreement you have with him is causing him to lose thousands of dollars a day in lost revenue. He thinks nothing of it, just a loyal American serving his country."

"Thank you, Monty, I will talk to the President about what we have proposed, but I think we will be sending telegrams well into the future!"

"You can reach me at my office in town if you change your mind or need a written, formal proposal from American Telegraph."

I was still packing things from my few months as the acting Secretary of State, when Gideon Welles stopped and entered the office.

"That was an interesting conversation, Monty is a remarkable man. No one bothered to spend much time with him during his first four years here. That was our loss, I see now."

"He is a very quiet man. Very confident with who he is and what he is capable of accomplishing. If I had twenty more like him, I could run a hundred companies with ease. Right now Caldwell International is trying to find college graduates that speak at least one foreign language and understand how to make a profit from a business enterprise. Do you know that Spanish or French is not required for graduation from college anymore?"

"Mon Dieu, Comonques quelltelle que sollerie!"

"Very funny, you know that neither French or Spanish is required for graduation from the US Military Academy. What did you just say?"

"I have no idea, but it sounded really good. You would be surprised how many people respond with Oui, Oui and nod their heads like they speak fluent French."

"Gideon, I am going to miss not seeing you every day. But my boss has given me this impossible list of tasks and only eighteen months to complete them."

"Jason, the telephone thing will have to wait. After talking to Monty, you can cross that off the list as something to look forward to in the future. You should sort the list and complete the most important, first. And go home to South Carolina, that is an order!"

"Aye, aye, sir."

89

Home Leave
Fall 1865

I was sitting on the train out of Washington bound for Seneca Hill, Pennsylvania. I had boxed what few items I could not carry and mailed them to my home. I had a long train ride ahead of me so I managed to get a private compartment with a small writing table that dropped drown from the wall. I opened one of the two brief cases and began reading and making notes with my new fountain pen that Louise had given me from her shopping spree in Havana. I started by reading the orders for the Naval commander, occupation forces, Beaufort, South Carolina. Gideon Welles reasoned the best way to remove these forces was to place them on the ships of the flotilla and bring them back to Potomac Dockyards for mustering out of the service. Gideon had forwarded the original orders to a Commander Davis (no relation to Jefferson Davis, I mused) and had placed a copy in my stack of 'to make' notes. That was good, it would not be a complete surprise when a four star Admiral shows up on his door step with orders from Washington. I placed everything related to the trip to South Carolina in one pile and made the following notes:

1) Pay taxes on 353 Bay Street, check condition of house, hire household staff, reopen;
2) Check rental properties and homes of Father and Brother;
3) Check conditions of Caldwell Properties in Port Royal;
4) Find Carol's grave in Port Royal and have remains removed to St. Helena's Churchyard for internment in family plots with markers for her husband and children. Even if the remains can not be found, they should each have a separate marker and place of honor.....

I realized that I could no longer see through my tears. "Is the war really over?" I asked no one.

I worked the entire time the train traveled the 220 miles to Pittsburgh. I realized I was hungry, locked my compartment and found the dining car. After a meal, I felt like pouring through my papers again and I returned to work while the train continued on to Erie. I would get off before Erie at a little stop called, Clarks Mill, here I changed to a coach seat for Franklin and on into Oil City. Oil City was the closest train station to Seneca Hill, here Sam Mason would be waiting with a carriage to take me the rest of the way. As I stepped off the train and onto the platform I heard, "Oh, it is Daddy, right over there, Ruthie, can you see him?" That was all it took for Ruth to run headlong into my knees and hold on tight, she would not let loose. James, as old as he was, jumped up on my back and held on for dear life. Louise was smiling and holding on to Carol's hand so she could make her way across the platform and place a giant kiss directly on my mouth.

"Really, Louise, control yourself, we are in public!" I said this with a giant smile, because she always said this to me when we showed any affection in public.

"I do not care. You are my husband and you never have to go back to Washington again in our life times. I will kiss you whenever and wherever I please until the day you die." She was crying.

"Why are you crying, Mommy?"

"Because your Daddy is home to stay, Carol."

Sam and Rachael came forward with their children and we had a giant, group hug. Sam grabbed my two brief cases and said, "Welcome home, Admiral. I have two large carriages waiting just outside, we should get the children out of the cool air and into Seneca Hill."

"I am completely in agreement, is it a 'fires in every fireplace', time yet?"

"The household staff has planned something special for you, Admiral, try to act surprised. They really have been working to provide a proper homecoming for you."

We rode a few miles and the house on the hill called, Seneca Hill, came into view. Every gas lamp in the place was ablaze, even the outside carriage portico was well lit. And there, standing with his arms crossed waiting for us, was Louise Buchanan Caldwell's brother, the fifteenth President of the United States. "How long has he been here?" I asked Louise.

"He came over from 'Wheatland' last week. He is so excited about going to Beaufort with us, Jason."

"He is going to South Carolina? You are going to South Carolina?" This was not in any of the papers that I studied.

"Yes, he got a letter from President Johnson informing him that he could be of great assistance to you in the normalization of South Carolina and her return back into the Union. He loves Beaufort, Jason."

I felt a lump in my throat as James Buchanan threw his arms around me and gave me a warm embrace. "Jason, Jason. The war we tried to avoid is finally over!"

"Yes, it is." Was all I could think of to say.

"Daddy, Uncle James has a present for you. It is inside all wrapped up in a tiny box can we go inside and see what it is?"

"Yes, James. Help Sam with my brief cases and we will see what it is."

We all trooped in through the front entrance and greeted the household staff who were all lined up like a White House reception line. I spent some time with each one and thanked them for the years of faithful service to my family. James could not stand it another minute. "Daddy, have Uncle James tell you about his present to you."

"Jason, past presidents are not without some influence." He cleared his throat and continued. "When I heard that President Johnson was at war with his own Senate, I wrote to the Republican majority in an open letter asking for them to consider something I thought was important."

He flipped open the box James thought was wrapped and inside was the Presidential Medal of Freedom. I could not speak.

"It took two Presidents to get this done, Jason, but it is long overdue! Please accept this with my congratulations. Here is a letter from President Johnson that he would like you to read to your family."

"You will have to do that, James, I am afraid I could not make it through without embarrassing myself." I said while wiping my nose with my handkerchief.

He opened and began reading:

THE WHITE HOUSE
September 25, 1865

My Dear Friend Jason,

Your brother-in-law has managed to do something that I have been unable to do for two months. He, and he alone, convinced the United States Senate to approve my granting of the Presidential Medal of Freedom to you on this day.

In all of my years of public service, I have never met anyone more deserving of this recognition. You are the loyalist American alive today. May your retirement from government service be blessed with good health, (you already have the wealth), happiness and continued success in the things you find important to your family.

Andrew Johnson

Everyone was quiet until Ruthie said, "That was a nice letter Daddy, was it as nice as mine?"

"No, it was not." I reached into my tunic and found the letter that I had over my heart. I unfolded it and began to read:

SENECA HIL

DEAR DADDY,

MOMMY SAYS MY PRINTING IS VERY GOOD. I TRY HARD TO DO WHAT MY TUTOR SAY TO ME. DO YOU KNOW SHE HAS ONLY ONE EAR RING. JAMES STILL HITS ME. I TOLD HIM YOU TELL HIM NO NO. I ASKED MOMMY WHY YOU ARE AWAY. SHE TOLD ME THAT SOME PEOPLE DO NOT LIKE TO FOLLOW RULES. THE RULES ARE FOR SO WE CAN ALL LIVE TOGETHER. SHE SAID YOU WERE TELLING SOME PEOPLE NO NO. DO YOU MISS ME. I MISS YOU ALL THE TIME. I GIVE YOU A BIG HUG WHEN YOU ARE BACK TO ME.

RUTH LOUISE CALDWELL

I folded the letter and placed it back inside my tunic. I had read it so many times that I could read it without tears filling my eyes but most of the people in the room had never heard it and they were affected the same way I was when I first opened it months ago. I looked around the room and found many of the listeners shaking their heads, yes.

The welcoming home party continued on into the night until the children fell asleep in chairs and I carried them to their rooms and tucked them in for the rest of the night. Louise looked on and said, " They do not need night shirts tonight, Jason. They can sleep in their underwear."

"Mrs. Caldwell, is everyone else assigned to their sleeping quarters?"

"They are, Admiral, the rest of the night is ours."

90
Mission to South Carolina
Winter 1865

The next morning found us planning our trip to South Carolina. James Buchanan, Sam, Rachael, Louise and I sat around the breakfast table drinking our last cup of coffee and visiting.

"You know, Jason, a past presidential visit anywhere is a nonevent. The last trip that I took to South Carolina was March, 1858. It was planned and announced to the newspapers, no announcement need be given in the fall of 1865. We can travel by train from Seneca Hill to the Potomac Dockyards to board the Caldwell Flotilla. The President has offered us the use of Charter Oak."

The USS Charter Oak was added to the flotilla by President Johnson. He had indicated in his letter to James Buchanan that he should use the Presidential Ship. He had also offered six members from his protection detail. We would meet the members from Jerome Lewis' office at the dockyards. They would be responsible for the safety and well being of the past president, his sister traveling with him, Admiral Caldwell, the three Caldwell Children and Captain Sam Mason. Sam's wife, Rachael and their children would remain in Washington with Rachael's parents. Naturally the President's suite was suitable for a former head of state. I remembered the last time I was aboard. I was the most junior Admiral in the Navy.

"How are the plans getting along for the protection detail, Sam?"

"We are on schedule, Sir. I think I will have a commitment from Captain Lewis for a detail of six from the White House. He will let me know, tomorrow. If he says, yes, then we have commitments from two former shore patrol officers, two former city policemen, and two former rapid response unit members. I know all six and they are very good."

"We will be on the Charter Oak later this week then. I have a pile of papers to sign and a few telegrams for you to send before we leave."

The voyage south this time was consumed with the political awareness of the flotilla. We stopped at several seaports along the way. President Johnson wanted maximum newspaper exposure so we stopped in Virginia and North Carolina before getting to Port Royal. These were arranged ports of call with the White House. Telegrams were waiting at all three ports and replies were sent to the President. The final telegram telling of our arrival in Port Royal was made by Sam as the flotilla moored next to the piers in Port Royal, the Charter Oak continued on into Beaufort.

The town of Beaufort had never had a President of the United States visit until James Buchanan in March of '58. Beaufort was founded in 1712 and was built on a bay formed by the mouth of the Beaufort River. Bay Front is a street, a marina, and a place for people to gather in a large park. The founding fathers wanted the Bay of Beaufort to remain pristine for future generations. No building was permitted on the water's edge, except for the marina where vessels could dock and a ferry which operated to the barrier islands along the coast. The Charter Oak tied up along side the park at high tide, across from the marina. Thousands of people filled the park to over flowing in '58, no one seemed to care in '65. The Past President, Louise and I came down the gang plank because of the tide, followed closely by our protection detail.

In 1858, it took James Buchanan, Louise and I nearly two hours to move slowly through the crowd and into waiting carriages for the short drive to 353 Bay Street. Today, no one greeted us and we could not take a carriage to 353 Bay Street because it was occupied by Union Naval Officers assigned to Beaufort. We did find a carriage for hire and asked to be taken to the Commanding Officer's headquarters. His headquarters turned out to be my Uncle's house on Boundary Street. I wore my naval fatigues with four stars on the collar points. A dress uniform would send the wrong message, I thought. It would be better to be one of the sailors on this trip. We paid our driver and the three of us walked up the front steps of the CO headquarters. We entered the house used as an office and found the duty officer.

"Can we see Commander Davis?"

"Do you have an appointment?"

"On your feet, sailor!" I shouted. Louise jumped and James Buchanan was smiling. "Are you in the habit of addressing an Admiral in such a casual tone?"

"No, Sir. I mean, I did not see your rank, Admiral."

"Get Commander Davis out here right now. Tell him the President of the United States would like to see him!" Now James Buchanan was chuckling, he had seen this act before. Louise had a terrified look on her face and when the ensign ran from the outer office. I bent down and gave her a kiss on the cheek.

"Try to keep a straight face while I try to get your house back for you, honey."

Both the ensign and a commander came running into the outer office. "Admiral, Sir. No one told me you were coming. Where is the President?"

"Right here, son." And James Buchanan held out his hand for Commander Davis to shake it.

"It is so good to meet you, Mister President. What can we do for you?"

"You could offer us a chair to sit down."

"Of course, how stupid of me, come into my office. Ensign Jensen, bring another chair for the lady."

We marched into his office and waited for Louise to be seated. James Buchanan was enjoying this.

"Commander Davis, you did get orders saying that you would be transported to Potomac Dockyards some time this week, correct?"

"Yes, Mister President, we can be ready to depart in twenty-four hours."

"Good the fleet is moored at Port Royal. We will see you in Port Royal tomorrow at this time."

"Tomorrow?"

"Yes, that is twenty-fours from now."

"I meant twenty-fours from official notification to disembark."

"How official can we make it, Commander?" I said smiling. "You and everyone under your command will sail tomorrow from Port Royal. It may take us more than one day to complete our business. It seems that you have commandeered this lady's house for the past four years. May I introduce Louise Caldwell, the owner of 353 Bay Street."

The commander said, "How do you do, Miss Caldwell."

"That is, Mrs. Caldwell, commander, and this Admiral is my husband."

"Oh, dear me, we had no idea that it was your house, Admiral, or we never would have ....."

"It is not my house, commander, it belongs to the lady."

"I do not understand."

"How soon can Mrs. Caldwell move in to 353 Bay Street so she can list any damages for payment by the US Navy?"

"We cannot pay any damages to Confederate property during the last four years, Admiral."

"The house at 353 Bay Street belongs to a loyal 'Yankee' from Pennsylvania, you did check the property deed before you commandeered her house?"

"No."

"Then you may have made a career ending decision, Commander Davis. However, I think this can be fixed in short order. I want you to walk over to that address and tell all the officers that they have twelve hours to pack their things and get themselves to Port Royal for the voyage to Washington. The troop ships there are comfortable, ask the marines where they are to put their gear. Oh, and tell them if they have taken souvenirs from the house they will not make it all the way back to the Potomac Dock Yards. Do I make myself clear?"

"Yes, Admiral, I am on my way right now."

He left in a hurry. "Jason, that was a terrible thing to do." Louise was not amused, her brother was.

"Louise, Jason handled that just right. The fear of God will be in every sailor, not to steal the home owners blind when they leave tomorrow."

"We are leaving tomorrow?"

"No, the flotilla full of US Navy personnel will leave Port Royal exactly twenty-four hours from now." Her brother said. "The Charter Oak is under my command, sorry, Jason, but it leaves when I say so."

"Aye, aye. Mister President, what are you going to do when the commander finds out you are not, Andrew Johnson?"

"We never said I was Andrew Johnson, besides, I have a letter from Andrew that I can show him."

The look on Ensign Jensen's face was incredulous.

"Ensign Jensen, that is kind of a tongue twister. Do you type ensign?"

"Yes Sir."

"Good. Type up a promotion form for me to sign. I like, Lieutenant Jensen much better than Ensign Jensen."

"Thank you, Sir."

"You are welcome, Lieutenant."

He rushed off to find the proper form and we walked out on the front porch. A boy, older than James, was riding a bicycle down the sidewalk of Boundary Street. I waved and called, "Son, you want to earn a dollar?"

He skidded the bike to a stop and said, "Yes Sir!" He jumped off his bike and walked over to us.

"Here is a dollar. I would like you to ride down to Bay Street and tell every shop keeper that the Navy is leaving Beaufort tomorrow and that Admiral Caldwell is home and will make sure any outstanding bills will be paid. Tell them to bring the bills to this house. Oh, and if you see a carriage for hire, will you bring it back here and I will pay you another dollar?"

"Thank you, General, Sir."

"It is Admiral, but you are close. See you in a few minutes."

We waited on the porch with our protection detail, sitting in white rocking chairs. "What do you think of the southern past time of 'sitin and rockin', Sergeant Major?"

"I could get used to this, Admiral." He said with a smile.

Ensign Jensen found us and I signed his promotion papers. "Make sure those get in today's mail pouch, Lieutenant."

"Aye, aye. Sir."

We were waiting for a carriage so that James Buchanan could complete his list of items that had to done the first day. Louise was about to say something when Commander Davis came walking up the street with a Navy Captain.

"Jason, I thought that Commander Davis was the ranking officer here in Beaufort?"

"So did I, James, I wonder where Davis found him?"

"Admiral Caldwell, may I introduce, Doctor Belks, from the Navy Hospitals here in Beaufort."

I stood and said, "And may I introduce my wife and President James Buchanan."

The look of confusion on the Commander's face was evident.

"Good morning, Mister President, Mrs. Caldwell. I have come over here with the Commander to inform you that I am not under his command, I have a command of my own and therefore I cannot leave my billet at 353 Bay Street until the hospital is evacuated."

I looked at him and did not say anything, just stared at him. The seconds turned into a minute and then James Buchanan said, "Doctor, it is good to met you. I have a letter here from President Johnson, I think you should read. You will find that we are here to evacuate the hospitals. In fact we are waiting for a carriage to tour the several houses that you have turned into hospitals here in Beaufort. Perhaps you would like to give us a tour?"

"I am too busy for that, I decide when my patients can be moved, not you, Mr. Buchanan. It will be weeks before some of them can be evacuated."

I had seen James Buchanan perturbed, upset and even angry at times. Usually the quieter he got, the more upset he was. He rose from his rocking chair and walked directly up to the doctor until their noses were less than an inch apart. "You are saying, that you refuse an order from the President of the United States?" He was whispering.

"No, Mr. Buchanan, I am saying I refuse an order from you."

"And if Admiral Caldwell gives you the same order, you will refuse him?"

"Yes, Sir. The Navy Medical Staff does not take orders from the military command."

"I have read your records, Doctor Belks, you have been here the whole four years of the war. That is a little unusual."

"No, Sir. I was responsible for taking the largest Confederate Houses here in Beaufort and turning them into top notch military hospitals. That is why I have been here four years."

"Were you the one responsible for removing all the household contents from these magnificent homes, piling it on their front lawns, soaking it with kerosene and burning it?"

"Yes, it was the most efficient way to dispose of the contents."

"Did it ever occur to you that some of these homes are not Confederate?" You could barely hear his words.

"They were all Confederate, Mr. Buchanan."

"Sergeant!"

"Yes, Mister President?" He was at attention and standing beside James in one giant step.

"Arrest this ass hole. Put him in handcuffs. Take him back to 353 Bay Street and have any other officers present find every personal item that the doctor has including underwear and pile it on the front lawn, pour kerosene over it and burn it. He will leave tomorrow with only the clothes on his back. Personally, take him to Port Royal and have the marines lock him in the brigg of the USS *Providence* to await court martial."

"Aye, aye. Sir." Sergeant Major Clyde Hawks stood a good six inches taller than the doctor and he was not gentle putting the handcuffs on him and dragging him off the porch towards Bay Street.

"Commander, you better go with them. There are other Navy doctors here?"

"Yes, Sir." He said with a smile on his face.

Louise stood up and said, "James, I have never seen you like this."

"Your husband was too angry to deal with him. Jason cannot abide fools and I can not abide flaming ass holes."

"What is the difference?" She managed to ask.

"A fool does not know he is an ass hole. A flaming ass hole knows he is."

I burst out laughing and it was contagious, first the other sergeants from the protection detail, then Louise and finally James Buchanan could hardly stand up. Our young man came riding his bicycle followed by a carriage. "You owe him another dollar, Jason."

The three of us sat in the carriage and the two sergeants stepped on the foot rails and we were off to visit the hospitals. The first place we stopped was "The Castle", a large four story Caldwell family town house. It was constructed of tabby, covered with stucco and it looked like a small manor house in England. The stucco had not been cleaned in four years, it needed paint on all the wood trim and shutters. The grass was not clipped and the flower garden, I remembered as a child, was over grown and neglected. It did not look like a hospital. I gave the driver a dollar and told him to wait, we would be going to all the hospitals. He nodded and we walked inside the castle. It was damp and musty smelling. A nurse sat behind a desk and asked, "Are you here to visit, folks?"

"Yes, we are." Louise said.

"Are you relatives?" She asked doubtfully.

"We have come from Washington with a letter of evacuation from President Johnson." She replied.

"Oh, thank God. I have prayed for this day. These men need to get home to their families. I must warn you that most of the war survivors are amputees. They may be on crutches or in wheel chairs but they are still men, or some just boys, that need the support of those they love."

"Can we visit the wards?"

"Of course, follow me."

We walked up one flight of stairs and entered a large room. You could still see where the walls had been removed from several smaller rooms to make the ward. The walls were lined with cots.

"You do not have hospital beds?" Louise asked shocked.

"No, ma'am. Doctor Belks says that canvas cots can be washed after the patients die and can be used over and over again."

"That flaming ass hole." I heard Louise say under her breath.

"What was that, dear?"

"That claim is old. I have heard it before, but I do not believe it."

"You are absolutely right, my dear. A bed is much better."

We stopped at the foot of cot where a young boy was recovering from his wounds. "Is he a local boy that was injured and treated here?" Louise asked.

"No, he is a Private that was brought here from Columbia when Sherman came through."

"What is your name, Private?" Louise asked.

"Peter Loresmith."

"How old are you, Peter?"

"I will be seventeen my next birthday."

"What are you doing here if you are only sixteen, Peter?"

"I was a private with the Rhode Island 4th, Ma'am."

"No, I mean why are you in the army?"

"They took me, Ma'am."

"Who took you?"

"The army recruiters in Rhode Island. Two men came to my Mother's cottage and said that she would have to pay 300 dollars or sign me up. She said my Pa was already in the army. It did not matter, either pay the 300 dollars or I would be drafted."

Louise began her silent crying that I had seen only once before. Large beads of tears slowly rolled down her cheeks. She bent over and kissed the boy on the forehead and said, "We are here to take you home to your mother, Peter." She straightened to her full height and said to the nurse, "Admiral

Caldwell has transport ships in Port Royal, can any of these patients be moved by carriage tomorrow?"

"They all can be, Ma'am."

"That ass hole, and to think, I felt sorry for him."

"Ma'am?"

"You are a Navy nurse?"

"Yes, Ma'am."

"Then you will be leaving tomorrow, also. Where is home?"

"Pennsylvania, Ma'am."

"We are from Pennsylvania! Where are my manners? Let me introduce my brother, James Buchanan and my husband, Admiral Caldwell."

"I thought I recognized both of you, Franklin County, right?"

"Are you the only one on duty here?"

"Oh, no. There are several others on different floors."

"Good, go and tell them what has happened. They have a full day ahead of them, packing supplies that they will need. We will have a wagon here in an hour for them to start putting everything together. You nurses will be in charge, not Dr. Belks, he has been arrested and jailed, awaiting court marshal."

"Praise the Lord, it is about time that sadist has been put behind bars. I would like to testify at his trial!"

"You shall. After you talk to your nurses come back outside and you can show us what we need to know at the other hospitals." Louise Buchanan Caldwell was now in charge of the evacuation of the hospitals in Beaufort. She stomped down the stairs and out on to the porch of the castle and found one of the protection detail. "Walk over two blocks and towards the bay and you will find a livery stable, hire a wagon and have it brought here. You can catch up with us, we will be visiting each of the hospitals."

"Yes, Ma'am." He was off on a trot.

"Louise, slow down, you have a week here in Beaufort, more if you need it."

"Oh, Jason, a week will not begin to be enough. I am here until the people of this town have their dignities returned to them."

"What do you mean?"

"Jason, it is going to get worse. We are going to find things that will be beyond our understanding. Please, let me do what only a woman can do. You and James deal with the criminal actions, let me try to pick up the pieces of these people's lives."

"Yes, Ma'am." I saluted and turned to find her brother.

James came walking out of the hospital with the nurse. "This is nurse Bellamy. Jane Bellamy, I know her family."

"Nice to meet you, Jane. James, your sister is now in charge. She finally understands what you and I tried to avoid four years ago."

"Admiral, before we go to the next hospital there is something I think you should see." We now had two carriages hired for the day and the first carriage stopped at the St. Helena's Episcopal Church, my church. Nurse Bellamy stepped down and said, "Follow me." We walked through the outer walled section of the church graveyard and stopped in our tracks.

"Where are the grave markers?" I said in horror.

"They have been stacked at the rear of the church after it was abandoned as a hospital."

"My church was a hospital?" I was numb.

"It was a surgery during the war. Hospital ships brought the wounded here. In good weather, amputations were done about here." She pointed to the bare ground where not a blade of grass grew.

"Why has the grass been removed?" I asked.

"It was not removed. Three head stones at a time from the graveyard were used as surgery tables. Two as legs and the large flat ones as table tops. The surgery was done, several patients at a time. The table surfaces were washed down with water to remove the blood. Human blood has caused the grass to die."

"Oh, my God." Was all I could manage to say. I felt weak.

"What about in winter?" I asked softly.

"In winter they moved them inside."

We entered the church and my childhood memories were destroyed. "How could they do this to a place of worship?" Stone surgery tables still stood where some of the pews had been removed. I walked over to them and read the inscriptions on the surfaces, they still held dark black remains of human blood. I turned and faced my wife. "You are right. We are not leaving Beaufort until this has been made right! I do not care how long it takes."

James Buchanan was silently weeping as we left the church and returned to the graveyard. "There must be a master plot plan I can get from the church sextant, Jason. I am in charge of returning all the markers to their proper places. What an outrage to the families. Where were your family buried, Jason?"

"Over there by that giant live oak, a few of the smaller markers are still there."

"You are not going to like hearing the rest, Admiral."

"The rest, there is more?" I almost shouted.

"Yes, the Union soldiers that died on the operating tables were buried on top of the grave sites you see here. This was when action was slow. When the bodies were piling up from so many, the dead were piled, soaked with kerosene for a funeral phyre."

"The bodies were burned, not buried?"

"Yes, Sir. Right over there in that shallow pit, where the ground is still charred black."

"I will have it filled, Jason." James said with a hollow voice.

"Certain organs and bones will not be completely burned only charred, they were gathered each day and buried in a hole on top of an existing grave."

"Were records kept of the dead? Do we have those?"

"Yes we do, Admiral. I know where Doctor Belks kept them. I will be responsible for all the records that I can find for you."

The four of us stood looking at the aftermath of the horror that must have occurred here from 1861 to 1865. James Buchanan turned to his sister and said, "Now you understand what Jason and I tried to avoid my four years in office and what we both endured watching this last four years. I will dedicate the next four years to the people who suffered both North and South."

James Buchanan was a prophet. He died four years later, 1869, in Wheatland surrounded by his family and friends. He had written to Andrew Johnson and said he wished a closed casket be placed under the Rotunda of the Capitol and the usual State Funeral with burial of the casket in Pennsylvania. His remains, however, were cremated in honor of the soldiers in St. Helena's Churchyard and his ashes were spread, by his sister, on the surface of beautiful Beaufort Bay.

91

Requiem Mass
Saint Helena's Church

The Episcopal Church in Beaufort, South Carolina, had a service on Wednesday, December 21, 1865, to honor those who fell during the last four years. It was a musical tribute to those who died and a solemn celebration of the restoration of the Church and adjoining graveyard. All of the markers had been replaced according to the plot plan that James Buchanan had found. He faithfully went every day from 353 Bay street to the church. He supervised and paid for the restoration of the graveyard. He directed that three tablets be erected in the manner that they were used by surgeons during the war and had a bronze plaque attached. The plaque described what happened on this spot, 1861 - 1865.

The missing pews were found in a warehouse on Boundary Street and lovingly restored and placed where they belonged. The silver communion service that was donated by John Bull in 1734 was never found. Louise Buchanan Caldwell had an identical set made by a silversmith in Sheldon and donated it during the mass. Father Timothy Brightwell gave the following sermon:

"Enclosed in a high brick wall, she sits like an ecclesiastical poem among its grayed lichened gravestones; its slender spire piercing the green masts of the trees like a clear bugle call. Ancient live oaks, with their swaying banners of gray moss, weave myriad leafy designs of light and shadow to fling against its mellowed, pinkish walls of brick and tabby.

When the wind blows, the palmettoes chant a requiem for those who sleep beneath the stones. The tall sycamores, green in summer, gold in autumn, silver green in spring, march two by two like loving sentinels from the east gate. In early spring, a purple flame of wisteria creeps along the walls, creating a scene of such breathtaking beauty that artists' easels set up along the path seem almost a natural part of the scene.

We now sit in one of the oldest ,as well as the most beautiful, of the early churches in America. Built to fill the need of a struggling young colony, it is simple in design, almost to austerity, rising four square and solid to withstand storms, wars and time.

This old church has witnessed prosperity and adversity. She is filled with memories of joy and sorrow. She has witnessed the heartbreak of death and parting. For many generations tiny infants have been christened at her font. Young girls in gossamer white and solemn little boys, have knelt at her altar for first communion. As I look out upon you, her congregation, I see a people who will not tolerate the death of a church or its people. Within these walls is Beaufort's unwritten story of birth, faith, life, war and death. It can not be erased by an invading army. It can not be wrought asunder by those who plundered its valuables. The valuables that we hold dear are each other and the families that have toiled so many hours to restore this Church.

A former President of the United States sits with us today and has transferred his membership from Pennsylvania. He and his nephew have donated countless hours to our building and replacement efforts here at Saint Helena Episcopal Church. His sister married a man from this congregation and she has returned with him to help heal those of us in need. She has paid all of the outstanding taxes on all of the homes of this congregation because she knew the need of some of us and she understood our refusal to pay a union tax collector's call for payment. She has encouraged all of us to have faith in God and in each other.

It is the pride that God gives all of us to enjoy his blessings, that we rededicate this church today and every day that we enter and kneel in prayer."

I was holding Louise's hand siting with her and her brother. Next to James Buchanan sat his nephew who had become his shadow these last three months in Beaufort. Everywhere that James the elder went, his nephew was there watching and learning. Next to James sat his sister, Ruth. She no longer complained of James' torments. James had changed. He had grown into a sensitive older boy and I wondered if we might have a future Episcopal Priest or even a statesman in our family. It would be his choice, not mine. Even our baby, Carol, had changed these past three months, or maybe we saw her differently. The entire family knew that our mission to Beaufort was about over. Beaufort would always be my birth place, a special place in all our hearts. Our lives were in other parts of the world, however. James Buchanan would return to his home at Wheatland, his nephew was old enough to visit him often, it was a short train ride from Oil City to Wheatland.

I had sent and received reports of what we had accomplished on our trip to South Carolina. In twenty-four hours, the main body of the Caldwell Flotilla had left from Port Royal. All of the Navy personnel were on board as well as the hospital staff and their patients. The Captain of the USS *Providence* had thought that a mistake had made by locking Doctor Jonathan Belks in the brigg and he released him to care for his patients. He was seen about the ship the first day and then he vanished. He was reported as lost at sea. Three of his patients died of natural causes before reaching the Potomac Docks and were buried at sea.

A week later the USS *Charter Oak* sailed for Washington with Sam Mason and the protection detail. Sam carried a number of reports and letters important to Secretary Welles who had sent me on this mission. One of the reports I had written, I decided not to send. It was heart wrenching to me personally, but it would result in no action whatsoever. I would read and reread it over the next few years of my life.

REPORT OF GENERAL SHERMAN'S TROOP BEHAVIOR
FILED NOVEMBER 23, 1865
ADMIRAL JASON EDWIN CALDWELL REPORTING

THE PREVIOUS REPORTS HAVE DEALT WITH THE EVACUATION OF FEDERAL TROOPS FROM BEAUFORT COUNTY, SOUTH CAROLINA. I HAVE DISCOVERED SEVERAL DISTURBING FACTS ABOUT GENERAL SHERMAN'S TROOP BEHAVIOR ON THEIR TAKING OF THE CITY OF SAVANNAH, GEORGIA. THEY PASSED THROUGH BEAUFORT COUNTY DESTROYING EVERYTHING IN THEIR PATH. NONMILITARY, CIVILIAN HOMES, CHURCHES AND PUBLIC BUILDINGS OF EVERY DESCRIPTION WERE SET AFLAME. THE HATE CAUSED BY THIS WILL NEVER DISSIPATE FROM THIS AND FUTURE GENERATIONS OF THIS LOCALE. A TYPICAL EXAMPLE FOLLOWS:

THE PEOPLE OF SHELDON, SOUTH CAROLINA, HAD A HISTORICALLY SIGNIFICANT CHURCH THAT HAD AN INTERESTING HISTORY. IN 1780, WHEN THE BRITISH UNDER GENERAL PREVOST PASSED IT ON THEIR MARCH FROM SAVANNAH TO THE SIEGE OF CHARLES TOWN, DECIDED TO LEAVE A MESSAGE FOR THE REBELS. THEY GATHERED AS MANY OF THE TOWN'S PEOPLE AS THEY COULD FIND AND LOCKED THEM IN THE WOOD FRAMED CHURCH AND BURNED IT TO THE GROUND WITH EVERYONE INSIDE. THE METHODIST-EPISCOPAL CHURCH OF AMERICA DECLARED IT A HOLY SHRINE OF MARTYRDOM. THE PEOPLE OF BEAUFORT COUNTY, INCLUDING MY GREAT GRANDFATHER, REBUILT THE CHURCH OF BRICK SO THIS TRAGEDY WOULD NEVER OCCUR AGAIN. AND IT SURVIVED NEARLY A HUNDRED YEARS UNTIL SHERMAN'S CAVALRY DECIDED TO USE THE CHURCH AS A STABLE. THEY IGNORED THE BRONZE PLAQUE DESCRIBING IT AS A HOLY SHRINE. THEY GUTTED THE INSIDE SO THAT STRAW COULD BE PLACED ON THE FLOOR IN ORDER TO STABLE THE HORSES OF HIS CAVALRY. HORSES DEFECATING ON A HOLY SHRINE SHOULD HAVE BEEN ENOUGH. WHEN THE CAVALRY MOVED ON, THEY WERE ORDERED TO BURN THE CHURCH. ANYTHING WOODEN PERISHED, EVERY THING BRICK SURVIVED. IT STANDS TODAY, A GHOSTLY REMINDER OF MAN'S INHUMANITY TO HIS FELLOW MAN, A CRUEL ACT BY ONE GROUP OF AMERICANS UPON ANOTHER.

The people of Sheldon have decided never to rebuild. Each Easter they will gather and celebrate a sunrise service for generations to come. As a small boy I remember my Grandfather taking me from Beaufort to Sheldon to celebrate Easter mass within the beautiful brick walls of the church. Every Easter, that I am alive, I will take my Grandchildren to sit upon the grassy mounds and celebrate the sunrise and the renewal of the hate generated by General Sherman.

One of the reports that Sam carried had to do with Sam's present assignment as my aide decamp, it read.

Plan for Sam Mason's Mission to Canada
Filed November 23, 1865
Admiral Jason Edwin Caldwell Reporting

One of the hardest things for a fleet commander to do is the promotion of an aide back into active duty. Sam Mason has been an exceptional aide and I will hate to have him assigned back to the Army Navy Building in Washington. But, it is time for his promotion and advancement within the service. I would suggest that he be given the Canada mission of trying to establish the whereabouts of former ORION members. He is returning with six members of the protection detail and he works well with them. I suggest that you assign some additional marines to make up the RR Unit and send them off on the Canadian Mission, post haste.

I have ordered the return of the Caldwell Flotilla to Port Royal and will proceed with the evacuation of Colonel Schneider from Mexico in a timely manner. They should arrive in the Potomac Dockyards sometime in early December.

Another report dealt with housekeeping matters.

Report of the use of US Treasury Vouchers
Filed November 23, 1865
Admiral Jason Edwin Caldwell Reporting

The banks in Beaufort, South Carolina, finally accepted my use of Treasury Vouchers for the resupply of the vessels used to transport the Navy occupation forces and the Navy hospitals here. They should start arriving in a few days for payment.

THE FEDERAL RECONSTRUCTION REPRESENTATIVES ASSIGNED HERE ARE A BUNCH OF "SCALAWAGS AND CARPET BAGGERS" AS ONE LOCAL HAS LABELED THEM. THEY STEP OFF THE TRAIN WITH ONLY A SINGLE PIECE OF LUGGAGE MADE OUT OF WHAT LOOKS LIKE A PIECE OF CARPET. AND THEY HAVE A NEW SET OF ORDERS AND PROCEDURES FROM WASHINGTON, OFTEN COUNTERMANDING PREVIOUS ORDERS. I AM CONSIDERED ANOTHER ONE OF THE "DAMNYANKEES" (ONE WORD) FROM WASHINGTON. AN EXAMPLE FOLLOWS:

I AND MY DAUGHTER RUTH ENTERED THE BEAUFORT COUNTY COURTHOUSE TO PAY THE NEW FEDERALLY IMPOSED TAXES ON MY HOUSE AND FAMILY PLANTATION. I WAS IN CIVILIAN CLOTHES, MINDING MY OWN BUSINESS WHEN ONE OF THE "CARPET BAGGERS" NOTICED ME AND ASKED ME TO GET IN THE FRONT OF THE LINE OF PEOPLE WAITING TO PAY. I REFUSED. I WAITED MY TURN. WHEN I FINALLY GOT TO THE HEAD OF THE LINE, I WAS MISSING ONE OF THE FORMS THAT I NEEDED FROM THE AUDITORS/ APPRAISERS OFFICE. IN A LOUD VOICE, THE "SCALAWAG" SAID, "ADMIRAL, THESE NEW TAXES ARE FOR CONFEDERATES ONLY, YOU ARE A MEMBER OF THE UNITED STATES NAVY AND ARE EXEMPT FROM SUCH TAXES." I HEARD A MUTTERING FROM THE LINE BEHIND ME, "DAMNYANKEE". RUTH AND I SAT DOWN ON THE FLOOR AND I SAID, "I WAS BORN HERE, YOU FOOL, I AM HERE TO PAY MY TAXES. WE WILL NOT MOVE UNTIL YOU RECEIVE OUR PAYMENT."

HE FINALLY AGREED TO TAKE MY PAYMENT. THE NEW TAXES APPEAR TO BE A FORM OF PUNISHMENT, AS A SOUTH CAROLINIAN I THINK THEY ARE A BAD IDEA AND WILL ONLY CAUSE FURTHER DELAY IN THE ACCEPTANCE OF THIS STATE BACK INTO THE UNION.

Ruth and I spent a great deal of time together. James and James worked at Saint Helena's Church. Louise and Carol were busy with the restoration of the Church and the house at 353 Bay Street. So, father and daughter went first to Port Royal to check on the location of the grave described by John Butler's aunt. We checked with the sexton's at the Port Royal Churches and various graveyards to find where the "defenders of Fort Beauregard" were buried. We were told that no such grave existed. I asked if they remembered the firing on Beauregard during the US Navy invasion of Port Royal. Sure, they remembered it alright, "The cowards defending the fort ran at the sound of the first shot fired, no one was killed because the fort was empty!"

"Where did they go?" I asked dumb founded.

"In all directions, some went back to Beaufort, others made their way to the uninhabited islands like Fripp and Pritchard."

I must have looked upset because Ruth asked, "What is wrong, daddy?"

"Your Aunt, Uncle and cousins may be alive, if I can find them."

"If WE can find them." She corrected me.

"If we can find them." I said with a smile.

The next day, Ruth and I were on the ferry to Lady's Island. We hired a "two-wheeler" and searched the little villages like "Frogmore"until we reached the ford crossing to Datha Island. We stopped and talked to people asking them if they knew of anyone who had escaped from Beaufort or Port Royal in 1861. We explained that we were looking for Robert Caldwell's daughter and her family. They all knew of the Caldwell plantation on Pollawana, but they had not heard of anyone escaping to locate there. We crossed over to Pollawana and found Tobias Caldwell and his family still on the plantation. I asked him if he knew anything about my sister, Carol.

"She was blowed up over in Port Royal, Mr. Jason. She is buried in a mass grave somewheres over there."

"Thank you, Tobias. Can I show my daughter the old deserted house where I was born? Is it still standing over in the grove of live oaks?"

"Yes, Sir. Mr. Jason. It is still there. Folks 'round here says it is haunted, it has lights at night."

My heart jumped. Maybe that is where she is, I thought. We hurried over the sandy road until the horse was winded and we stopped before the old plantation house. No one could live here, it was deserted and beyond repair. We got out of the carriage, tied the horse to the hitching post and walked up to the front steps.

"Be careful, now honey, these steps look rotten, we do not want to fall through them."

"Lift me up on the porch, daddy." I did and hoisted myself up after her and we stayed away from the steps. The front door stood ajar and we pushed it open and birds flew in all directions. They frightened us and we jumped. We were standing in the great foyer that my mother was so proud of when she greeted her guests forty years ago.

"Over here is the parlor, Ruth. And upstairs are bedrooms where my brother, your Uncle Robert and my sister, your Aunt Carol, used to sleep and play with our toys."

"You had toys, daddy?"

"Of course, I was little just like you when I lived here."

"I am not little. I am small for my age!"

"Yes, I keep forgetting that you are really six going on twenty-one."

"What does that mean, daddy?"

"You are six years old, but think like an adult."

"Oh, is that good?"

"Sometimes."

We finished our tour of the house, untied the horse and started back to Tobias' house on the other side of the island. We ate lunch with them and then continued on to the Fripp Island ferry. This ferry was a privately owned means of getting from Hunting Island to Fripp. We talked to the man in charge and asked about visitors that might have come and gone.

"This is a working plantation, Admiral. You remember Captain John Fripp's kids inherited it from him. There is only one main house, close to the beach. They have servants, but they are former slaves that have been with them for years. There are no white people, other than the owners. I do not think your sister and her family are here. I know you want to find them, Admiral. The truth is there were only a handful of casualties at Fort Beauregard, the survivors ran for their lives. They did not find any remains to bury, Admiral. Your sister died inside Fort Beauregard, let her rest in peace. The folks in Port Royal made up a nice story about the 'defenders of Fort Beauregard' for future generations. The truth is the Fort was not defended, it was destroyed by US Naval cannon fire."

"I think you are right, besides it is getting past time to get back to Beaufort."

"You and your daughter should hurry so you catch the ferries between Hunting, Saint Helena and Lady's Islands."

"Will do, thank you for what you said. It helped me clear my head."

As we rode from ferry to ferry, Ruthie asked, "What was Aunt Carol like, daddy?"

"Well, let me remember. Her hair was about the color of yours. She liked to talk nonstop, like you. We had left the plantation and moved to Beaufort so that Robert and I could go to elementary school. She was too young and she was upset that she was left at home. Your Grandpa hired a private tutor to come to the house in Beaufort so she could begin her lessons early."

"Just like me, I have a tutor."

"Yes, you do. You learn everything as quickly as she did. When it was time to go to first grade in Beaufort, she lasted only about three days and Grandma was called to school for a visit with her teacher. It was decided that she should be moved to the second grade because she already knew how to read her letters and make her numbers."

"Just like me. When will I go to second grade, daddy?"

"You have a private tutor that lives with us. I am sorry to tell you that you will be stuck with her until you pass your exams into second level."

"What is second level, daddy?"

"The first level is beginning, or elementary. Second level is for really smart children, like you. You will get a new tutor and your tutor will become your little sister's tutor."

"Oh, goodie. I would hate not seeing Miss Templeton every day."

"But you can not bother her, she will be busy with Carol."

"Carol, same name as Aunt Carol."

"You figured it out, your sister is named in honor of Aunt Carol."

"Why do James and I have tutors? Why are we at home and not in school?"

"If we lived in one house, in one location, then you would be in a school. Your daddy's job takes him all over the world. And because I love you so much, I take you with me."

We had by this time found our way to the livery stable where we had rented the carriage for the day. I paid the livery hand and we walked to the Beaufort Ferry.

"Daddy?"

"Yes, Ruthie."

"I love you."

"Me, too, 'Ruthie Two Shoes.'"

"Why do you call me that?"

"When you were a little girl, not like the big girl you are now, you kept losing one shoe under your bed or wherever and I had to help you find it. So I started called you, 'Ruthie Two Shoes'."

"Daddy, will it make you mad if I tell you that I used to hide one shoe so that you would help me find it?"

"I think I figured that out after the umpteenth time, Ruthie. And no, I will never get mad at you for wanting to spend time with me. There will be a time, many years from now, when you will meet a nice young man and fall in love with him, like I did with your mother."

"Then what happens?"

"Then, I hope the nice young man holds on for dear life, because life with you will be one hell of a ride."

"You swore, daddy!"

"I know. Do not tell your mother!"

"Where are we going for Christmas, daddy?"

"To your home in Bermuda, the flotilla is back in Port Royal and it is time that the crew members get back to Bermuda to be with their families for Christmas."

"Why do you call the ships a flotilla?"

"Because there are not enough of them to be a fleet, and they are unarmed merchant ships."

"Then why is one of them called USS *Providence*, it has cannons."

"Yes, it does. It was built for the US Navy about 70 years ago. I bought it and changed it into a merchant ship and used it for many years. When the war broke out, I loaned it back to the Navy."

"Do they pay you rent?"

"Yes, they do. You know, it seems I have had this same conversation with your mother!"

"Are we rich, daddy?"

"In more ways than you can imagine, honey. This family is truly blessed."

"Will we ever run out of money?"

"Never!"

"Promise, daddy."

"Promise, Ruthie"

92

Bermuda Mission
Year 1866

Part of my mission package from Secretary Welles was a fact gathering trip to St. George, Bermuda. He had devised a set of assignments that would allow me to return to civilian life with the ghosts removed. I realized that he had ordered me to South Carolina so that I could confront the guilt caused by the death of my sister. And more importantly, the fact that I had not resigned my commission with the U.S. Navy and joined the C.S.A. Navy as nearly 320 other officers had done in 1861. Gideon Welles had become my protector, he understood me better than anyone else now serving in Washington. He allowed whatever time I needed in each of the locations where ghosts waited for me. We were all returning to St. George on the *Cold Harbor*. The flotilla from Port Royal now numbered ten ships and it was time to return some of them to the Caldwell Shipping and Trading Company so that Robert Whitehall could began using them.

"A penny for your thoughts?" Louise said as she slipped her arm through mine.

"Oh, you startled me!" I said. "It is cold out here in the wind. Are you warm enough?"

"Yes. How long do you think we will be in Bermuda, Jason?"

"Until all the ghosts are gone, probably all winter and spring."

"Ghosts? I do not understand, Jason."

"A ghost is created whenever you think you have caused the death or demise of another."

"Are you talking about Carol?"

"She was a ghost, but she is gone now. Ruthie and I put her to rest the last three months."

"So that is what she was talking about."

"Did she tell you about our search for her Aunt and Uncle?"

"Yes, I guess you had to do that. What was all the talk about money?"

"She worries about family finances, Louise. She is just like you."

"What did you tell her?"

"Well, we had quite a conversation between ferries coming back from Fripp Island. She asked if we had enough to live on if I quit my job as Admiral in the Navy."

"She was worried about income?"

"Both of you have no concept of what Caldwell International is worth. I explained it this way. Suppose that ten golden eagles, were placed one on the top of another?"

"Oh, I see. A hundred dollars would be about an inch thick."

"She got that part just like you did. But not when I told her that the number of gold eagles that Caldwell International has would be several miles high."

"Now I am lost."

"So was she. I tried it this way. If an inch is 100 dollars, how much is a foot high?"

"1200 dollars."

"Correct, how much is a 1000 feet?"

"1,200,000.00, oh my God, Jason, a mile is over six million dollars! How high was the stack you told her?"

"Several miles."

"Several times 6 equals more than billion. Oh, Jason, that cannot be right, can it?"

"That is what the company was worth last quarter, it varies from day-to-day, up and down. It will drive you and Ruth crazy if you try to keep track of it. Think of it this way. God has truly blessed this family. He made it all possible and he can take it all away in the blink of an eye."

"Then, we should do something worthwhile with some of it before God decides to blink. Jason, set up a foundation to help others less blessed than we are."

"Good idea. What should we call this foundation and who should run it?"

"The director should be James Buchanan, can you think of anyone you trust more?"

"Agreed. Now, the name." I said.

"United States Development Foundation, USDF for short. If my brother does not want to be part of this, tell him he has to until President Johnson leaves office. You trust him?"

"How can you not trust someone who thinks you deserve the Presidential Medal of Freedom?"

"Who would be funded from the foundation and why?" I asked.

"All western territories or former states seeking admission to the Union! The federal government has indicated that they will not pay for reconstruction of what Sherman did to the south. USDF will. The first hurdle, or rule for assistance, will be that the government has refused to help. The second will be that no northern state need apply, only western territories or CSA states. The third rule will be that once a state is admitted ,or readmitted , it is no longer eligible."

"Louise, you should be the director. You have it all figured out."

"I cannot. I am the executive secretary and treasurer so I can keep an eye on our money."

"That is not how it works, Louise. Once the foundation is funded, the money is no longer ours to do with as we see fit. We will create the funding each year that we pay federal income taxes at the limit allowed by the tax codes. That way we pay the foundation instead of the federal treasury."

"I like the sound of that!"

"You become more southern every year you live, you know that, Louise?"

"And you become more northern, Mr. Business Tycoon."

We laughed and noticed that the colors of the offshore waters were beginning to turn a bright blue and coral. St. George would appear in about an hour. We went below and finished our packing.

USDF was formed and James Buchanan became its first director. He sent letters to each of the provisional governors in the former CSA appointed by President Johnson. The confusion was soon apparent. Many governors thought USDF was a department in Washington and following the USDF guidelines to the letter, they called state conventions to do three things:

First they repealed the ordinances of secession, second they repudiated the state debts incurred in the aid of the Confederacy and, third they ratified the Thirteenth Amendment to the Constitution, which abolished slavery. Once this was done the funding arrived in Virginia, Tennessee, Louisiana and Arkansas. Tennessee was readmitted to the union in early 1866 and was shocked to learn that they no longer qualified for USDF funding. And further shocked when the governor's letters of protest, addressed to USDF, Washington City, were returned with the letter marked, "No such agency". The "Civil Rights" bill passed by congress in 1866 gave the right to veto to all Negro men. This caused considerable concern in the northern states. The US House of Representatives was based upon the voting population. Therefore, the fourteen southern states with freed slaves, suddenly increased their representation from 52 to 76 members of congress. The majority of congress was Republican, but the majority would change once the rest of the states followed Tennessee into the Union. The Republican majority decided that they needed to slow down, or stop, the readmission of southern states into the Union until they could modify the right to vote sections of the new civil rights bill. They proposed that every person who desired to vote should be able to read and write his name before voting. A poll tax would be required. A voter was required to own property. This applied to every state in the Union. And the right to vote was to be an adoption to every state constitution. They reasoned that no southern state would grant the right to vote to former slaves. This would keep them from readmission to the Union. This backfired when all fourteen states of the former CSA added this requirement to their state constitutions. Massachusetts, Colorado, Connecticut, Rhode Island, Wisconsin and Minnesota all refused to change their state constitutions and if you were a black man living in these states, you could not vote. Black men who had fought for the north in the war could not vote when they returned home if they lived in these states.

The "Radical Republicans" became alarmed when the USDF taught black men to sign their names and read them. The annual poll tax was paid by the USDF. Deeds to one square foot of land were made out for black voters and paid for by the USDF. The USDF funding applied only to those states and territories seeking admission or readmission to the Union. So southern states began to seek readmission and were fully qualified to do so with USDF assistance. The quarrel in the thirty-ninth congress was bitter. When the southern members of the house of representatives were elected in the midterm elections of 1866 and came to Washington to serve their terms, they were refused upon the grounds that they had not taken their loyalty oaths to the United States. When each presented a copy of their sworn oaths, provided by USDF, a new requirement was passed by congress. No member of congress should have been connected in any way with the former Confederacy. This reduced the number by half. The remaining half were told to return home while the other half would be investigated by the reconstruction committee of Congress. The committee recommended to the congress that southern representation be limited to the 1860 membership levels until the census of 1870 could be made to determine the correct number of representatives from each of the southern states. This recommendation was passed by both houses of congress and vetoed by President Johnson. The veto was overridden by a two-thirds majority.

Thaddious Stephens, a Republican member of the House from Pennsylvania, was the leader of the drastic measures regarding reconstruction. He was implacable and intolerant of opposition carrying his views into effect by the imperious force of his iron will. His real object was to preserve the Republican two-thirds majority by keeping the southern Democrats from being seated as voting members of the US House of Representatives. The midyear elections of 1866 had eliminated the two-thirds Republican majority. Representative Stephens was seventy one years old and rapidly failing in health, but this did not stop his savage vigor, showing no mercy to the other members of his party who might disagree with him. When a fellow Republican protested to him on the floor of the House, that his conscience would not permit him to support some of his radical measures, Stephens replied, "To hell with your conscience man, this is your country!"

The reply to that comment was, "Your position is a concept foreign to me. I do not believe in, my country right or wrong. I believe in, God before country. Right is always on the side of God. It would appear to me that your radical point of view is wrong for the country and wrong for the Republican Party."

He received a standing ovation from the members present and the Republicans lost several votes to the minority on each of his proposals from that date forward. President Johnson had vetoed each of the measures that the radicals put forward but he was overridden in each case. This so angered him that he decided to take his case for "God before Country" directly to the people. He decided to make a train tour, extending from Washington City to Chicago which he described as "swinging around the circle." He invited James Buchanan to accompany him. The director of USDF agreed and met him in Washington City. James Buchanan was never popular with the people after his Proclamation of 1858, and this further injured Johnson's popularity. They were viewed as two failed Democratic

Presidents complaining directly to the people. After one train stop the two Presidents reviewed their progress to date.

"James, why is it so difficult for some of these people to see a fairly simple concept of right over wrong?"

"It is more complex than that, my friend. The Republicans have convinced the populace that several thousand uneducated former slaves do not have the ability to vote properly (translated, they will not vote for them). As soon as they can convince the black men of voting age that the Republican party is the only party for them, things will change in a hurry."

"Why are the Republicans fearful that the black vote is a Democratic vote?"

"The Democrats welcomed them into the party. Republicans are uncomfortable around people of color. 'White men only' is the defacto motto of the Republican party. They failed to see that after the war with Mexico, there were more men of color within the new territories and states in the west than white voters. Therefore, that is a Democratic strong hold. The south is not the only Democratic area of the country, look at both of us. If Louisiana is readmitted, for example, the black voters will out number the whites by forty percent."

"And these are all Democratic votes!"

"Correct. The struggle between you and the congress is one of political might and keeping control."

"There is supposed to be a separation of powers between the branches of government, James. I have been unable to get anything done, I might as well resign."

"Thanks to the Republicans there is no sitting Vice President, they will never confirm a Democrat and you will never appoint a Republican. If you resign, then the White House goes to the Republicans."

"I have only the next two years then, I will not get re-elected."

"Andrew, you have to face what I had to face. You will not be nominated."

"Then whoever is nominated at the Republican convention is our next president?"

"Unless the black men of this country are allowed to vote, yes. Even if the southern states are readmitted in time for the election, the congress will find a way to keep Democrats from taking their seats. It is all about keeping control."

"I had such high hopes for this country, James."

"So did I. The only thing that kept me sane the four years I was in the White House was a young man by the name of Jason Caldwell, my brother-in-law."

"I wish he was part of my administration."

"He is too smart for that, Andrew. He will get more accomplished through USDF than you or the next Republican president."

"You have convinced me, James. How can I get some of the things that I feel are important to USDF?"

"You are talking to its director. Give me a list."

"I want to change my cabinet members."

"You will have to convince them to resign on their own, Andrew. A dismissal requires Senate approval for just cause."

"Just 'cause I want to, is not enough?" He asked with a smile on his face.

"Who are we talking about, surely not Gideon Welles?"

"Hell, no. Gideon Welles is the only Republican I know that his head screwed on straight. He is best of the cabinet."

"I agree. Who then?"

"Edwin Stanton."

"Edwin? My God he is a Democrat! He was a member of my cabinet."

"I know, he opposes everything I try to do inside the cabinet. Did you know he had a Confederate spy working for him in the Army Navy Building?"

"Yes, Gideon Welles thinks the spy is in Canada, of all places."

"Not anymore. Captain Mason reports from Canada that the 'Grand Dragon' passed through there on his way to England. Those English bastards supported the Confederacy for four years by building ships of the line for them, all the while declaring that they were neutral. Those sumbitches!"

James Buchanan was smiling. Jason had told him of Andrew's colorful language when he was mad.

"The first thing that you have to do is hold your temper in public and in private meetings. Use it only to drive a point home and only rarely. That way it is tool, not a character trait."

"You are right, Mr. President, I, Andrew Johnson, am properly reprimanded for my barnyard approach. I will try to do better."

"Trying is not good enough, Andrew. Doing, is what is important to you the next two years. Do what you can get done, forget trying things that do not work. Quit trying to bump heads with the congress, ignore them and get what you want through USDF. And do not give them any grounds for impeachment, Andrew. If you do, they will use it."

"Thank you, James."

James Buchanan was smiling again, he remembered Jason saying, "You will never get the last word in a conversation with Andrew Johnson!"

"No, thank you for inviting me on this trip around the circle."

"I really needed your support, James. You will not see another veto from the White House."

James Buchanan was smiling again. "Did I ever tell you about the time
....

93
Wheatland
1867

James Buchanan found the state of the country alarming at the beginning of 1867. Anarchy prevailed in many quarters and was rapidly spreading. When the armies of volunteers were disbanded at the close of the war, fifty thousand troops were retained for service in the south. They were insufficient to preserve peace and enforce the laws. Stanton resigned his office and was succeeded by General Schofield. Congress thanked General Sheridan for his service as military governor of Louisiana after Louisiana was readmitted. The House of Representatives impeached President Johnson because he ignored them and he was acquitted in the Senate by a single vote.

And yet the blessed work of USDF went on by itself, independent of these revolutionary proceedings. Those that now worked for USDF were mostly veterans of the war. Some had worn blue uniforms and some gray. They were coworkers, not enemies. USDF left the wrangling to the politicians and began to get things done. USDF capital began to build up the war torn places in the south. Not one dollar was ever assigned for war damages in the north. Southern states, in the next two years would all be readmitted, one by one, until all became ineligible for USDF aid. Nebraska was admitted as a state this year and USDF aid stopped flowing to Lincoln, the state capital.

James Buchanan had an interesting visitor from Washington City that year. It was Secretary of State, William Seward, looking fully recovered from his brush with death and full of energy. He had been having discussions with Russia for the purchase of Alaska. Congress had called the proposal, 'Seward's Folly" and refused to even consider it.

"James, think about what this purchase will mean to the United States. Russia is the only country with territories on three continents. Russia's treasury is nearly empty because of her wars with England. USDF can purchase 577,390 square miles for twelve dollars a square mile or .02 cents an acre!"

"William, I think you made a trip to Pennsylvania for nothing. You are aware that USDF owns nothing and is forbidden to keep property of its own. That is why I work out of my house. We are even forbidden to pay office rent.

One of the founding precepts is that funds will never be given to the federal government for any reason."

"I understand that, Mr. President, but Alaska will become a US territory and territories are eligible for funding, correct?"

"Correct. And once Alaska is a territory we can certainly help. We are not in the business of doing things as large as the Louisiana Purchase. You are asking for a purchase nearly two and one half times what it cost the federal government in 1803. As long as I am director of USDF, I would veto such an action. You are free to speak to the incoming director, however."

"Who is that?"

"The honorable, Andrew Johnson."

"When will that be?"

"Well, we thought it would be this year but the impeachment failed and his appointment date will be March, 1869."

"Would it do any good to talk to Jason?"

"You can speak with him if you like, but you and I will have to catch a train to Oil City and get a carriage to Seneca Hill."

"Is Jason home, I thought he was still in Bermuda?"

"He is, you talk to him over the telegraph line."

"Several telegrams will not do anything, I need to have a conversation with him."

"You will, voice communication over the telegraph is called a telephone. Surely you have telephones in the White House by this time. Jason offered to install them free. Oh, I forgot, President Lincoln did not think much of Jason, did he? He would not listen to most of his suggestions. And he fired Montgomery Blair, who is now chairman of American Telegraph and Telephone. Different management style, I guess. I found Jason to be invaluable to my administration."

"Jason worked for me, James. I know what he is capable of when he puts his mind to the task. Why was I not told about this telephone thing?"

"I think there were several things that were never forwarded to the cabinet, or credit was given to someone else for the concept. Do you want to go on to Seneca Hill? We can talk on the train. I think you should know some things about Jason Caldwell and Andrew Johnson that you might find useful." James Buchanan was smiling a devilish grin.

Both men stood and James asked his butler for his carriage driver to pick them up under the portico. He walked to his desk and wrote a short note. He handed the note to the butler and said, "This is what we will need when we get to Oil City. Send a message to Seneca Hill through our private telegraph line will you?" A short time later they were on their way to the train station.

"Jason Caldwell has decided that the well being of the country is too important to be left to those who are presently in the White House, that includes you, William, and those up on Capital Hill. This next election he will fund any honorable candidate that will run against an incumbent Republican. He will spend whatever it takes to defeat the incumbents of the two-thirds majority. He is tired of the good old boy network presently at work in the White House. I pity whoever the next president chooses for his running mate and cabinet members. Jason has given orders to dig all the dirt on these individual's past and publish it in all the major newspapers from New York to San Francisco. He is tired of the scandals that rocked the Lincoln White House. He will crucify any wrong doing. I predict that cabinet members of the next White House will come and go like a revolving door. A Democrat or a Republican, it will not matter, Jason is no longer a Democrat he calls himself an Independent."

"That is a strong statement, James. He will not be able to do a thing to change things, however."

"William, are you blind? The federal government is four billion dollars in debt! The truth is, there is nothing in the federal treasury to do a damn thing. You, who serve in the White House better understand that Caldwell International has no debt and a war chest of billions that it can spend on the defeat of anyone they target. It is a new age in politics in this country and unlimited funding is the new power behind the throne."

"Maybe I am wasting my time by asking USDF for aid?"

"If you think it will go into the federal treasury, you are."

"How should I approach Jason?"

"He might consider buying Alaska as a private estate, that way Russia would not have a territory holding in North America. Other than that, I cannot think of an approach."

"Be serious, we are talking about seven million dollars here."

"Jason has more than that invested in Bermuda, California, Nevada, Pennsylvania, New Mexico, Old Mexico, South Carolina and probably a few other places abroad. Seven million is pocket change to this man. He might consider a personal loan to the State Department!" James Buchanan was enjoying himself.

"I do not understand?"

"I am sure you do not. Jason Caldwell is the last of the great American patriots. He does not have a greedy bone in his body, he works hard and expects others to do the same. When they do not work as hard as he, he comes down on them like a ton of brick. I warn you, when you talk to Jason, be totally honest with him. If he finds out you lied to him, look out for falling brick."

They pulled into the train station and brought two round trip tickets for Oil City, Pennsylvania. They continued to talk, but William Seward could not get his mind around the fact that a single individual had twice as much net worth as the federal debt. Then he realized that anyone with a positive bank account had more available funds than the federal government. Only red ink was used inside the federal treasury offices and the borrowing continued.

"The war has nearly ruined this country, financially. We are so far in debt that our grandchildren will have to pay it off."

"William, I think you are beginning to see the light. The south is in much better shape than any northern state, thanks to USDF and it will continue in that vein as long as Jason Caldwell is alive."

They boarded the train for the short ride to Oil City and Sam Mason started from Seneca Hill to meet the past president and his guest. Captain Sam Mason had lead a small party into Canada to find out what they could about Confederate spies, former troops or anyone entering Canada during the last two years from the southern US. The information was spotty at best. They learned that a band of former Confederate cavalry was living in Canada and raided across the Vermont State line to rob banks and then flee back into Canada. The Americans mounted a joint effort with the Royal Mounted Police and captured seven bank robbers over a three week period. The raiding across the boarder worked both ways. A volunteer detachment from Boston was composed of all Irish emigrants. They kept their arms when the war ended and used them against our northern neighbor as the best way to get back at the English, who they hated. They raided continuously until the US Marine detachment, under Sam Mason, had a heart to heart talk with them. They had never seen a naval deck gun in action and when seventeen of them were wounded in the first burst, they were eager to talk and surrender their arms. Sam did not arrest any of them. He just said that he would return with a full complement of US Marines if they did not behave themselves. Sam was still smiling when he pulled into the train station at Oil City. His passengers were standing on the platform waiting.

"Over here." James Buchanan called to Sam. "Sam, this is Secretary Seward, you probably met him when you served in the Army Navy Building."

"Mr. Secretary, nice to see you again. You look fully recovered, better than the last time I saw you."

"Thank you, Captain. Why are you at Seneca Hill?

"My military service was no longer required, so to speak. Now I am an employee of Caldwell International. I like it so far, it is close to my wife's family and we get to see them often. And the huge increase in salary has really helped my family. Admiral Caldwell offers ten times the military salary for any of his former Rapid Response Unit members that would like to come to work for him."

"How many have been employed?" William Seward asked.

"Almost all of them. They are spread out. Four are in Nevada, two in California, two in Mexico, four in South Carolina, four in Bermuda, I am here in Pennsylvania with three others. Did you bring any bags, Mr. President?"

"No Sam, we are just here to use the telephone."

"I have it all set up, the Bermuda end is waiting for your call, Sir."

They rode in silence as William Seward began to absorb what James Buchanan had told him on the way to Seneca Hill. He was amazed when they entered the house on Seneca Hill, he had never seen a private home larger than the White House. It sat on 640 acres in front of a working oil well. There were several out buildings and small cottages scattered throughout the property.

"Let me show you how the phone works." Sam said.

"You call Bermuda by turning this crank, it generates a ringing sound in Erie, Pennsylvania. A telephone operator asks which cable you wished to be attached to."

He went through the steps and spoke into a black shinny cone shaped mouth piece. "Operator, this is a call from Seneca Hill to St. George, Bermuda. Can you patch me through? Over." Sam then pressed a button and waited for the operators reply.

"Go ahead, Seneca Hill. Over." A voice said out of the second cone placed beside the first. William Seward was impressed.

"Bermuda, this is Seneca Hill calling for retired Admiral Jason Caldwell. Over."

"Sam, how is everything at the hill. I miss not being there, we are packing here to start our voyage. Over."

"Admiral. I have Secretary Seward here to speak with you. Over."

"Mr. Secretary? Over."

"Hello, Jason. Over."

"Hello, this must be important for you to come all the way to Seneca Hill to talk. Over."

"It is, Jason. I need your advice on a proposal I am making to Russia. Over."

"How can I help? Over."

"Alaska is for sale. The Russians need to raise capital. Over."

"What is the problem? Over."

"The congress thinks I am crazy. Over."

"Why would they think that? Alaska is close to the north pole and covered with snow most of the year. Over."

"Alaska is more than that, Jason. It is 577,000 square miles that stretch from the Sea of Japan into the Bearing Sea and down the Canadian western coast. It has an abundance of timber and other natural resources, including furs and fishing. Over."

"And the Russians want to sell it? Over."

"Yes, for 7.2 million. Over."

"You need to convince the congress that it is a good investment. Bonds will need to sold to raise the capital for the purchase. Put me down for a million shares, at one dollar a share, at twenty percent. I must run, nice to talk to you again, William, call anytime." No more noise came over the line and into the cones.

"What just happened?" William Seward said.

"You just raised 1 million of the 7.2 million you need, William, and Jason just doubled his money every five years that the bond is in force. Put me down for the .2 million." James Buchanan was smiling. "Jason never makes bad investments."

"Put me down for a thousand shares." Sam Mason said grinning. "Here is the list that Mr. Buchanan asked me to copy for you. It is the Admiral's advisory committee, they are some of the richest men in America you should have no trouble selling the remaining bonds, Mr. Secretary."

"So that was the note you were writing before we left. You had an idea that Jason would help on a personal level."

"Yes, I did. But I do not speak for the richest man I know. Would you like to send telegrams to the list from here?"

"Can we talk to them?" William Seward was like a little kid with a new toy.

"Only if they have a telephone or are visiting Jason in Bermuda." James Buchanan was smiling.

Just then, a loud bell rang and the three men jumped. "That is loud!" Said William Seward.

"Yes, we have to hear it all over the house. I have asked the Admiral's wife to install a bell in each of the rooms, but she says that it would cost to much." Sam was now smiling as he pressed the answer button and said. "Seneca Hill, answering. Over."

"Sam is that you? Over."

"Yes, Admiral. What can we do for you? Over."

"Is William Seward still at the hill? Over."

"Standing right here, Sir. Do you want me to put him on? Over."

Sam stood up and William Seward sat at the desk and said, "Jason? Over."

"No, this is JP. Put me down for 6.2 million shares at twenty, will you? Oh, and Mr. Seward do not contact anyone else on Jason's list until we have done some estimating here at Caldwell Place. You will be hearing from us in thirty minutes." .... Hi, Uncle James, you need to say Over when you are done speaking Mr. Morgan and then release the button."

"Mr. Morgan, I do not have 6.2 million shares left. Over."

"Damn, how many shares do you have left? .... you have to say over."

"James Buchanan has bought 200,000 shares and Captain Mason has bought a 1000 since we talked to Jason. If you want the rest at twenty percent, I guess that would be alright. Are you sure I should not contact the rest of the list? Over."

"The rest of the list will want all kinds of guarantees that you can not give them at the present. You better jump on this deal, Seward. It is now or never. .... you have to say over. Damn, Over."

"You have a deal JP. Over."

While William Seward was convincing congress to sell interest bearing bonds at twenty percent for the purchase of Alaska, Colonel Tom Schneider, his 875 marines and 50,000 Mexican troops were beginning to surround the French Army. Fifty thousand Mexican Nationals under the command of President Juarez of the Mexican republic had been trained and supplied over the last two years by the Caldwell Flotilla. The end came at Queretaro, Mexico, on May 15, 1867. Maximilian surrendered and was held for trail by a council of war and sentenced to be shot.

A general sympathy was felt for Maximilian in Europe, and many efforts were made to save him, but his execution was a military and political necessity, which he had forced upon the Mexican Government. The Mexico City newspapers reported: "If Maximilian should receive pardon and return to Europe, he would be a standing menace to the peace of Mexico. He would still call himself Emperor and have a court in exile. Some powers would recognize him in the event of a return to Mexico. A message must be sent to Europe that if you invade Mexico you will be caught and shot." Maximilian and his two top generals, Miramon and Mejia were executed on the 19th of June.

The 875 Americans serving in Mexico were evacuated by the Caldwell Flotilla under the command of Admiral Jason Caldwell. This was his last action as a flag officer of the United States Navy. He retired from the Navy on June 30th.

94

A Night With Dickens
Caldwell Place, Bermuda

Laura Whitehall came rushing into the main dining room at Caldwell Place with a piece of paper in her hand. She was of breath and Louise told her to sit down and tell her what was wrong.

"Nothing is wrong. I have a reservation for Mr. Charles Dickens from London, England. The, Charles Dickens. Can you imagine what this place is going to be like when word of this gets out to the public?"

"Are you sure it is, the world renowned novelist?"

"Yes, he is meeting Samuel Clemens here. They are going to write a new novel called, The Mystery of Edwin Drood."

"Wait, Laura, slow down. Samuel Clemens is living in Virginia City, Nevada, he writes for the Territorial Enterprise, the county newspaper. I have read several of his articles over the past years."

"He did live there, Louise. He moved to Virginia City with his brother, who had been appointed Territorial Secretary. When Nevada became a State, the brother moved back to Missouri. Mr. Clemens moved to San Francisco where he began writing humorous fictional accounts of the local citizens. His first book was called, The Jumping Frog of Calaveras County, published under the pen name 'Mark Twain'. Have you read it?"

"Of course, I had no idea that Mark Twain was our Samuel Clemens from Virginia City!"

"Yes, I think our young Mark Twain will become the American Charles Dickens. This novel could make Mark Twain a household name, as famous as Mr. Dickens."

"How long will they be here, Laura?"

"Mr. Dickens said at least a fortnight in his letter! Oh, Louise, this is going to be something to tell our grandchildren."

"Laura, we need to write to both Mr. Dickens and Clemens. If they are going to be here two weeks, maybe we can persuade them to meet with the citizens of Bermuda. Why not have a town meeting to answer questions and advertise their upcoming novel one evening? We will call it *a night with Charles Dickens and Mark Twain*. How many people can we seat here at Caldwell Place, Laura?"

"Well, that depends upon whether we sit outside or inside. There are over 50,000 people living in Bermuda, Louise. If they all show up we will need to seat them on the rolling hillside of the golf course. Hole number 4, closest to the Inn would be best."

"And now we need to find somewhere to seat a 1000. How times change, Laura."

"Yes, I think we can get this evening with the authors organized, Louise. We can start tomorrow."

The next morning we walked down to 421 Feather Bed Lane off York Street and found a print shop. We went inside and found the office clerk. We introduced ourselves and he said, "I am truly glad to meet you, Mrs. Caldwell. I have printed several things for Mrs. Whitehall at Caldwell Place. What can I print for you today?"

We handed him a piece of paper with the announcement of the town meeting to be held at Caldwell Place. "It says here that Caldwell Place is a public inn. Is that true?"

"Why, yes, that is true. We do not advertise the fact much in Bermuda. Most of our guests are from the United States. Mr. Samuel Clemens is a frequent visitor, while this will be the first visit for Mr. Dickens."

"Mark Twain and Charles Dickens hosting a town meeting. I will be there for sure!" We looked at each other and smiled, maybe this will be an event that people will attend, we thought. We left the print shop after placing our order and began walking back to the inn.

"Robert says everything is within walking distance in St. George. I like that."

"Yes, but the walk back is a real killer!" Louise was not looking forward to it.

Samuel Langhorne Clemens, a 32 year old American novelist, better known as Mark Twain checked in two days before Charles Dickens arrived from London. Mr. Twain usually stayed in Hamilton and he was fascinated by how old St. George was. Americans were always impressed by things older than the 1776 Declaration of Independence. Bermuda was discovered 261 years before 1776 and St. George was founded 167 years before 1776. He enjoyed walking and explored the town from one end to the other. He was very patient with the people who showed up unannounced to visit with him and ask him all sorts of questions.

1. "Yes, my pen name did come from what the river boat men on the Mississippi used in taking depth soundings."
2. "Yes, I was born in a little town called Florida, Missouri, on November 30, 1835."

3. "Yes, I worked in newspapers as a typesetter and composer in St. Louis, New York, and San Francisco."

4. "In 1851 I gave up printing and became a steamboat pilot on the Mississippi River. No, I do not miss it."

5. "I fought for the Confederacy and when the war was over I moved to Nevada with my brother who worked for the Territorial Governor. Yes, I miss Virginia City and the mountains there."

6. "The newspaper that I wrote for in Virginia City was called the Territorial Enterprise. Mostly my articles were about local folks, they did not appreciate my humorously, exaggerated descriptions of themselves, so I took a job on the Calaveras County Gazette. I tried mining for gold, I was a poor excuse for a miner."

7. "I am presently working on my second book entitled 'Innocents Abroad', it is about my travels to islands in the Pacific."

8. "No, I have no idea why Mr. Dickens has asked me to co-author a novel with him. His novels about America, Martin Chuzzlewit and American Notes for General Circulation are about the funniest things I have ever read. He does not need me to be humorous!"

9. "Yes, I will meet him for the first time in a few days."

10. "I came here on the American Steamer Good Hope, it docked right here in St. George at Terminal Island."

Laura had ordered a 100 copies of The Jumping Frog of Calaveras Country. They were sold within two days, all signed by the author. "I underestimated the demand for Mark's book, Louise, I should have ordered 500."

"How many Dickens' novels did you order, Laura?"

"I ordered a hundred copies each of: Posthumous Papers of the Pickwick Club, Oliver Twist, Nicholas Nickleby, Hard Times, The Old Curiosity Shop, Barnaby Rudge, Tale of Two Cities, Christmas Stories, Martin Chuzzlewit, David Copperfield, Great Expectations and his latest novel, Our Mutual Friend."

"Laura that is 1200 copies! Where did you put them? Are we going to be able to sell them?"

"In my office closet space, based on what happened with The Jumping Frog, I would say we will run out in the first few days Mr. Dickens is here."

Charles Dickens arrived from London aboard the HMS Trent on its mail run to Havana, Cuba. He was surprised at the number of British sailors and marines that were waiting for him as he docked at the Royal Naval Dockyards on the west end of Bermuda. He shook several hands extended to him and said, "My father was a Navy man stationed in Portsmouth. I was born in Landport, a suburb, on February 7, 1812, too young to join the fight against the bloody Americans." This drew peals of laughter from the crowd. "But I feel younger than my 55 years, and if war breaks out, I am ready to fight." Laughter again greeted him. "My father moved us from Portsmouth to London where I grew up, poor and improvident. I spent considerable time studying in the British Museum. I learned short hand and was a court reporter for many years. This is where I watched and learned how to create characters like Oliver Twist and the Artful Dodger. I was a reporter in the House of Commons and there I saw the real thieves of London." Considerable laughter followed this remark as most seamen did not trust politicians.

"My first success as a novelist, was Sketches by Boz, you probably know it as the series of articles I wrote for the Evening Chronicle. Most of my early works were newspaper articles and stories before they became books. You have book shops here, I am sure, and if you have purchased any of the books and would like them signed, I have brought my pen." He held his new fountain pen high in the air and looked for a place to sit and begin the signing. A long line formed and the process began. He had spent nearly an hour signing books when an American handed him a copy of *David Copperfield* and said, "This is my favorite, Mr. Dickens."

"Who would you like me to dedicate it to?"

"My name is Samuel, Sir. Samuel Clemens." Dickens did not look up and started writing. When he finished he handed the book back and said, "Nice to meet you, Mark. Can you get me out of this line of British sailors."

Mark Twain asked Charles Dickens to stand up from the shipping crate he had been using as a chair so he could stand upon it to address the remaining British seamen. "Gentlemen, I have been sent here from St. George to meet Mr. Dickens and take him to his lodging while he is in Bermuda. Those of you on leave are welcome to join us on the ferry to St. George where Mr. Dickens would be happy to talk to you and sign your books. For those who could not find copies of his work in the local shops, it is because 1200 copies were purchased for resale at the Caldwell Inn in St. George, you may purchase them there on your days off. I encourage all of you listening to attend a town meeting which is scheduled for next Wednesday evening at the Inn. There is no admission charge and the meeting will last until you get tired of us. I will be sharing the host's chair with Mr. Dickens, as I am his co-author for his next book. Thank you all for coming and join us as we move to the ferry terminal for our trip to St. George."

He stepped down off the crate and whispered, "Your bags are being picked up for you. We need to start walking towards the ferry, follow me, Sir." They pushed their way through the sailors not on leave and took those on leave with them as they walked towards a waiting ferry bound for St.

George. They found a bench seat and collapsed into it. " Is it always like this?" asked Mark.

"Yes, Mark. When they stop asking for your signature, then you know the book sales are down and you might go hungry. Is it true that Laura Whitehall purchased 1200 copies of my books?"

"Yes, Sir. She says that will not be enough, but it is all that she could find in the last month."

"Call me, CW or Charles, Mark. We are going to be working together here for a couple of weeks and by letters after that. You understand that the letters are the main vehicle for the chapters in the book. My idea was for two writers on separate continents to solve a missing person's case. The man missing is Edwin Drood, naturally an Englishman and assumed to be in America. I wrote all this to you, right?"

"Right, that is why I agreed to meet you here in Bermuda. Do you think the two writers will meet in the book at a midpoint like Bermuda?"

"They already have, Mark. You are like me in a sense that you soak up your surroundings and they appear in your stories. You write for newspapers just like I did when I started. I am old enough to be your father, but our life experiences are very similar. Neither one of us had any formal education, I think that is why we write the way we do, we listen and learn from those around us."

"From your body of work, I sensed your great humor. You possess immense creative power, the number of characters must be in the thousands. To me, the essence of your art is caricature and for comic relief you exaggerate the abuses you attack. In character building you hit upon some oddity and transform it into a delightful type never to be forgotten. Tiny Tim, for example."

"Mark, we are going to get along famously, you are young and full of energy and understand my style completely. I am more into a reflective stage in my life. I need someone to build a fire under me so that I can complete this last great effort. There will be no more Dickens novels after this. This is my swan song."

"Oh, CW. Fifty-five is not old, I plan to live to be a hundred."

"In that case, my young friend, I want you to deliver my ullage. The Queen has indicated that I am to be buried in Westminster Abbey."

"CW?"

"Yes."

"A ullage is a quantity of wine, brandy or other liquor, isn't it?"

"Yes, it is. Just seeing if you were paying attention. There will, of course, be drinking at my wake!"

The sailors sat and listened to the two authors until the ferry docked in St. George. Everyone of them walked down the Duke of York and turned on Rose Hill Street and headed for Caldwell Place. A small welcoming party was waiting inside the lobby. Sally Butler introduced her staff. Laura Whitehall said she was delighted to meet the two authors she had been corresponding with over the last couple of months. Louise and Jason Caldwell were introduced and they welcomed the men to their place of business and corporate retreat. Mr. Dickens said he was tired of traveling and would like to take a nap.

"Your bags will be held here in the lobby, let us know when you are awake and we will deliver them to your room, Sir." Sally said.

"Excuse us ma'am, but where are the Dickens' books for sale?" A sailor asked.

"Come right this way gentlemen, I have them on display in the next room." Said Laura Whitehall.

An hour later the dining room was clear of sailors, Charles Dickens was fast asleep and Mark Twain sat with a cup of coffee. He visited with John Butler, two former Confederates musing about what might have been. Jason Caldwell and Robert Whitehall joined them for a cup and the visiting continued. The next twelve days flew by and the grand night of the town meeting was a roaring success. Fourteen hundred people attended, purchased all the books available and asked questions for over four hours. Finally Mark Twain said, "I do not know what course others may take, but for me it is past my bedtime." He stood from the canvas deck chair and walked two steps to his co-author and extended his hand in friendship. Charles Dickens grasped it and pulled himself to his feet, placed both arms around Mark Twain and gave his friend a bear hug. The crowd roared its approval as the two writers walked slowly off the forth hole of the golf course and into the lobby of Caldwell Place.

95

The Election of 1868
November

The Washington Post had the following headline after the presidential election of 1868.

Third Party Hurts Democrats: Grant Wins

	States	Popular Vote	Electoral Vote
Grant	26	1,766,352	214
Seymour	8	945,703	80
Dickenson	0	699,581	0

The election of Grant was greatly assisted by the addition of a third party. Instead of taking away votes from the Republican Party it split the Democratic vote tally again, but this time the Republican candidate's vote total (1,766,352), was greater than the Democrats and Independents vote total of (1,645,284). This had not been the case in the last two elections where Lincoln's totals were less than his opposition. And the unlimited funding policy of the Independents made inroads into the senate and house of representatives where Independents were elected from Maine, New Hampshire, Vermont, California, Nevada, Nebraska and New York. This was the first time in our history that Independent party candidates were elected to a federal office. The two-thirds majority of the Republicans was gone as Democrats were elected from the newly admitted and readmitted states.

The celebration of the inroads made by the Independents and Democrats did not last long, however. President Johnson refused to sit in the same carriage with the President-Elect on inauguration day. When a compromise solution was found whereby two carriages would be used side by side down the Pennsylvania Avenue, President Johnson refused to appear in the parade at all. General Grant rode to the capitol in an open carriage, with his favorite staff officer, General Rawlins. General Grant was devotedly loyal to his military friends and he continued to do this his first year in office. He appointed military friends to his cabinet. When they were attacked in the newspapers as not having any practical experience in there present positions and that some of them had rather colorful backgrounds, President Grant was shocked. The criticism heaped upon his cabinet was taken personally and he tried to defend them. The newspapers had a field day and it appeared that Grant was either a fool or unqualified to be President. Grant was loath to believe wrong of his cabinet and he continued to protect them until a delegation from congress indicated that his cabinet would be impeached unless he replaced them. He slowly began the process. His selection process was, of course, flawed and he selected replacements as unqualified as the first round of selections. A complete list of the cabinet members during the Grant administration follows: **Secretary of State** – E. Washburne, of Illinois replaced by Hamilton Fish, of New York. **Secretary of the Treasury** – G. S. Boutwell, of Massachusetts replaced by W. A. Richardson, of Massachusetts replaced by B. H. Bristow, of Kentucky replaced by L. M. Morrill of Maine. **Secretary of War** – J. A. Rawlins, of Illinois replaced by W. T. Sherman, of Ohio replaced by W. W. Belknap, of Iowa replaced by A. Taft of Ohio replaced by J. D. Cameron, of Pennsylvania. **Secretary of the Interior** – J. D. Cos, of Ohio replaced by C. Delano, of Ohio replaced by Z. Chandler of Michigan. **Secretary of the Navy** – A. E. Borie, of Pennsylvania replaced by G. M. Robeson, of New Jersey. **Postmaster General** – J. A. Cresswell, of Maryland replaced by J. W. Marshall, of Connecticut replaced by J. N. Tyner, of Indiana. **Attorney General** – E. R. Hoar, of Massachusetts replaced by A. T. Ackerman, of Georgia replaced by G. H. Williams, of Oregon replaced by E. Pierrepont, of New York replaced by A. T. Taft, of Ohio.

The prophecy of James Buchanan had been correct, the cabinet offices became revolving doors whereby men entered, determined to work for the new president only to find their backgrounds reported in newspapers from New York to San Francisco. A member of the senate committee to approve cabinet selections was asked by the newspaper reporters, why the senate approved members without a background check. His reply was, "We will not in the future, we will read the newspapers, they are doing the background checks for us."

This caused a series of articles that attacked the senate and its members as being unqualified to even run a simple background check on its members, or future members, of the White House Staff. The senators ducked for cover and were careful of what they said in public.

"Where is all the money coming from to make these hundreds of backgrounds checks?" The President asked his newest Attorney General. "You are a lawyer, Mr. Williams. Is that correct?"

"I was when I awoke this morning, Mr. President. This will all blow over in a few weeks."

But the pressure did not blow over, it lasted the entire first four years of the Grant administration. After the senate, the house was given a through background venting and the embrassment continued. When the newspapers uncovered a price fixing scheme by two close business friends of President Grant, the spotlight was again upon the White House. A Wall Street firm of Smith, Gould and Martin convinced the president that the US Treasury should stop selling gold. This caused the price of gold to increase from 140 dollars a troy ounce on September 22, 1869, to 164 dollars on Friday, September 24, 1869. Jay Gould had planned to sell his gold at 200 dollars. His associate, Jim Fisk, sold at 164 and cleared eleven million dollars in profit. Near the middle of "Black Friday," a source in Nevada starting selling gold at 165, then 155 then, 145 and finally at 133, until the panic stopped. That same source notified the papers of the price fix and Jay Gould was arrested by New York Police. The White House took the blame for the scheme and a new Secretary of the Treasury was appointed.

Many businesses failed during the Grant administration and city fraud continued unabated. An example was the city of New York. The newspapers reported the "Tweed Ring" had defrauded the city of millions of dollars. William Tweed was superintendent of the street department and was known by the locals as "Boss Tweed". A political organization known as "Tammy Hall" ran the entire state of New York for their own financial gains through building contracts and the funneling of public funds into their own accounts. Tax payers were defrauded a total of 160 million dollars before the newspapers reported the scheme to the public and arrests were made.

Some of the failures were not due to graft, fraud or other criminal acts, but by acts of God. Sunday, October 8 th, the great fire of Chicago destroyed nearly a third of the city. Fifty-seven of the insurance companies involved were bankrupt. The country lost many of its leaders during the first four years of Grant's administration. Robert E. Lee, President of Washington and Lee College choked to dead on a piece of fried chicken at his home while eating dinner. Edwin Stanton, Secretary of War under Lincoln and appointed to the Supreme Court by Grant, died of natural causes. Admiral Farragut passed away suddenly, followed by Secretary Seward and Generals Thomas, Meade and Morse. Chief Justice Chase, Presidents Fillmore, Johnson and Buchanan died of strokes.

The Grant administration was unpopular with many newspapers. The New York Tribune, founded by Horace Greeley, was a leading critic. Greeley was a founding member of the Republican Party. He opposed Grant's programs and plans for reconstruction at every turn. He encouraged another Republican, Senator Sumner from Massachusetts, to introduce an amendment to the constitution, by which a President should be ineligible for a second term. Many of those known as, active Republicans, openly declared that if Grant were nominated for a second term, they would not support him.

Greeley became the embodiment of the opposition to the administration and at a convention held in Cincinnati, the "Liberal Republicans" nominated him and Gratz Brown, Governor of Missouri, as his running mate. They openly invited the Democrats to join them in the defeat of Grant for a second term. The Democrats met in Baltimore and adopted Greeley's platform. They made an honorary nomination of John Quincy Adams as a symbol of their disgust for anything Republican, but pledged to support the campaign of Horace Greeley for President.

96
West to California
Summer 1869

Jason Caldwell sat in the dining car of the Union Pacific West bound, having breakfast in Ogden, Utah. He was reading the Washington Post and shaking his head. "The Democrats have given up the race for the White House, Louise. They are supporting Greeley for President. The race will be between two Republicans, Greeley and Grant. Neither has a clue what the country needs." He was still shaking his head.

"When will we arrive in San Francisco, Jason?"

"In a few days. We are stopped here until the east bound Central Pacific can be turned around."

His complete answer was interrupted by a call for, "Telegram for Mr. and Mrs. J. E. Caldwell."

"Oh, Jason, that cannot be good!" She rose and waved for the telegram, tore it open and read it quickly. A look of relief spread across her face.

"Well, what is it?"

"It is from your son. I will read it to you. 'Mother and Father – I have been informed that I have passed my exams into second level. My tutor got a telegram from the Pennsylvania State Board of Education. Have a good time in Alaska. Your loving son, James.' Oh, Jason, my brother would have been so proud of him." She began to cry softly at the loss of her only sibling.

"Louise, they got to spend a lot of time together these last few years of his life. Back and forth from Oil City to Wheatland. He did not suffer, he was unconscious from the stroke and went peacefully into heaven."

"It is unusual for an entire family to be with you when you breathe your last, I guess." She said. "Do you think he knew we were all there and I was holding his hand when he passed?"

"Of course, my dear."

A porter came walking through the dining car announcing that all bags had been transferred to the Central Pacific and we would be leaving in twenty minutes. We would need to walk back into our coach compartment and tell Miss Templeton and Carol that we would be moving across the platform onto the train headed for San Francisco. As we walked across, we heard, "Captain

Caldwell, we are over here." There was D.D. Wilson and his wife who would be traveling to Alaska with us.

"Where are James and Ruth, Louise?" asked Corene Wilson.

"James stayed in Seneca Hill with his tutor to take second level examinations, we got a telegram from him a few minutes ago that said he passed and to have a good time in Alaska."

"Did Ruth stay with him? You said in your last letter that she has refused to leave his side since your brother died."

"Yes, it is the oddest thing. They used to torment each other all the time, but they changed the three months that we were assigned in South Carolina. We all did, even Carol here."

"Hi, Mrs. Wilson." Carol Caldwell had a soft, lightfull voice like her mother's.

D.D. Wilson had been a private and then a corporal in the rapid response unit under the command of Captain Caldwell. By the time his first tour of duty was complete, he was sure that he would like to return to Utah Territory and work for the Caldwell Shipping and Trading Company owned and operated by his Captain. He always called him, Cap'n Caldwell, even after the captain became a one star through four star, Admiral. D.D. had met Corene (no last name) when an Indian tribe was driven from western Utah by the United States Cavalry. Corene had been taken, as a child, from a family of settlers and adopted by the Indian Tribe until she was 15 years old. After she was abandoned by the Indians, she walked to the nearest settlement called, Paradise, Utah, and worked as a maid in the hotel. She worked to regain her English speaking skills and was progressing at a reasonable rate until she met a group of men staying at the hotel. The group of eight had rented the entire second floor of the hotel. One of the men could not take his eyes off of her and it bothered her. She had learned, living with the Indians, the warriors took what they wanted and if you smiled at an Indian Brave, he would claim you for his lodge. She tried to avoid the man, but everywhere she turned, there he was smiling at her.

"Why are you following me?"

"Hello, my name is Dewayne David Wilson. But everyone calls me D.D., what is your name?"

"You do not need my name, Sir."

"I do if we are going to get married, it is required on the license."

She burst into tears and the story of her abduction from a white family of settlers burst from her like a broken dam from too much flood water. She stood shaking in the hallway and D. D. placed his muscle bound arms around her and held her like a new born baby. "Tell me your first and last name and I will find out where your family is located."

"My name is, Corene something, I do not remember my family name, I was so young when I was carried off by my people."

"My people?"

"Yes, the tribe was called, 'My People,' that is all I ever heard them called."

"Well, Corene, it would seem fair to call you Corene Peoples. If I am to write to you, I have to know the name and address. Do you live at the hotel?"

"Yes, in the attic."

"In the attic?"

"Yes, all of us do."

"Who else lives there?"

"The maids and the footmen. We pull a curtain across the attic to make two sleeping spaces."

"Come with me, Corene."

"Where are we going? I cannot leave work. I will be fired."

"How much do you make here?"

"Twelve dollars a month, Sir."

"I think you need a new job, Corene Peoples. We are going to the bank."

They found the only bank in Paradise and walked into the manager's office. "Hello, we are here to open an account."

"Very good, Sir. Under what name is the account to be registered?"

"Miss Corene Peoples and Mr. Dewayne Wilson. It will be a joint account. Here is a hundred dollars to open it and we will be back tomorrow with another 500. Each month, we will make a twelve dollar deposit until the account is closed. Is that agreeable?"

"Very. Wait here until I return with the papers to sign."

"Dewayne, I cannot read or write English. I can only speak it." She was blushing.

"Do not worry about that, Corene, it is easy." He grabbed a blank sheet of paper from the manager's desk and a carbon lead pencil. He wrote C o r e n e. He handed her the sheet of paper and the pencil. You try to draw over what I just did. Follow it closely. She did and then he said, "Now, move to the side and repeat what you have just done, do it slowly." He watched her do it perfectly. Without thinking he gave her a hug and said, "Corene, you are a natural writer! Now your last name and they repeated the process until Corene Peoples could write her name with ease and confidence.

"Thank you, Dewayne, no one has ever shown me how to write before."

"It is really easy. And you are smart as a whip, Corene Peoples. Do not let anyone ever tell you otherwise."

The manager returned and the papers were signed with ease and Dewayne David Wilson was in love for the first time in his life. "Mr. Sellers, do you know of a nice little house for rent in town?"

"Why, yes the bank has a house by the Church. But I am afraid that it is very expensive."

"How much is it?"

"Ten dollars a month." D. D. tried to keep a straight face, he spent more than that on a Saturday night.

"Can you deduct the ten dollars from Miss Corene's new account every month?"

"Of course. Because we know we will be paid every month, the rest of this month is free."

"Is the house furnished?"

"No, it is completely empty, ready to move in."

"How much if you furnish it?"

"We could do that, but again, it would be very expensive, probably another 15 or 20 dollars."

"We have to decide on an amount, Mr. Sellers, why not make it an even 30 dollars a month with the first month free?"

"Mr. Wilson, you have a deal." Corene Peoples' head was spinning.

"We are going to walk down to the church and see your new house, Corene. Mr. Sellers, it was good doing business with you." D. D. handed him 10 gold eagles. "I will be back tomorrow with 25 double eagles, Mr. Sellers."

They left the bank, hand in hand and found the house by the church and D. D. Wilson carried Corene Peoples over the threshold and sat her down in an empty house he had just rented for her. "There is no lock on any of the doors, Corene. I will have the general store put locks on before I leave tomorrow."

"You are leaving me?"

"Only for a few days, Corene. I live close to Virginia City down in Nevada and I have to return and hire a manager to replace me for a few months. You do not like long engagements, do you, Corene. A few months should let you know if you could learn to love me. I will not marry someone who I do not love and who does not love me."

"You love me?"

"Yes, Corene, it happened like a thunderbolt. You are the most beautiful person I have ever met."

"Oh, Dewayne, you are a crazy man. We have not even kissed yet." He made a giant step toward her and swept her into his arms and kissed her on the mouth until she could not breathe. "Dewayne, I cannot breathe."

"Use your nose. That is why God gave you one and he kissed her again, longer this time."

The next morning he signed his next five year contract without reading it. Caldwell Shipping and Trading would just have to get along without him for a few months until he could convince Corene to quit her job at the hotel and move to Nevada with him. It took only five months for Corene Peoples and D.D. Wilson to decide to get married in the church next door. They had been living in sin for the entire time but Corene had no concept of white man's sin or even a God, until D. D. had mentioned that a God had given her a nose.

"So, what do you two think of the offers?"

"I am sorry ,Cap'n, I was a million miles away thinking of how Corene and I met."

"D. D. everyone in the hotel knew how you felt about Corene, with your mooning over her every minute." Cap'n Caldwell was smiling and Corene was blushing.

"Run the offer by us again, I will pay attention this time." The four adults sat in the dining car as the train pulled out for San Francisco.

"It is a straight forward deal, D. D.   I had the CI lawyers prepare a deed for the saw mill in your names see, Mr. and Mrs. Dewayne David Wilson. Matthew James and his wife, Connie, will get the water works in Johnstone."

"I do not understand, the mill belongs to CI."

"Not any more." Louise said.

"You are giving it to us?"

"Yes, you and Corene have worked very hard these past few years. We would still like you to stay with the company and take care of the lumber yard for us. The housing you have built around Virginia City has produced a windfall profit for CI. You will continue to get your annual salary and profit share in the lumber yard. But you and Corene own the mill outright, it is yours."

"I do not know what to say, Cap'n."

"Start by calling me, Jason."

"Yes, Sir, Cap'n Jason." Corene started to laugh first and then we all did.

"D. D., you know the best builders in Virginia City. Louise and I want to build on the tract of land that CI bought, near Johnstone, when you first came out west. It is now close enough to the town that the Indians have moved on west and they would not burn or plunder a ranch house and the barns."

"Ruth and James are avid horse riders. Louise and I are going to build a horse ranch and give it to them when they reach twenty-one years of age."

"I know just the man for the job, Cap'n. Do you have a set of plans?"

"No, we do not know what is required for life in Nevada. You wear a cowboy hat and a side arm, D. D. I could never get used to that."

"Sir, Corene is a drafting expert. Leave it to her. Corene get your note pad out of your purse and have Louise tell you what she wants."

"Cap'n, tell me what you would like the outside to look like."

"I would like the base of the house to be mountain stone about three feet high with the rest whole logs that we will buy in Alaska on this trip. How does that sound to you D. D.?

"If you do not find anything that you like on this trip, I know someone who owns a saw mill.

97
North to Alaska
Summer 1869

And so the days into San Francisco were spent designing the horse ranch in Nevada and watching D. D. and Corene, still mooning over each other. Miss Templeton had Carol do her lessons until we arrived at the station in San Francisco and transferred our bags to a hotel. We would buy tickets on a steamer, the Victoria, which left San Francisco and headed north to Vancover Island. In two days we were all berthed on the Victoria and entered the Straight of Juan de Fuca, leading to the inland passage to Alaska. Arriving at the Island of Victoria we turned and passed Port Townsend, the port of entry for Puget Sound. We continued along the inside passage. It was summer time but the nights were cool and we bundled up to go on deck. We passed Canadian Indian villages and white trading posts until we came to the city of Vancover. It looked like any city in the United States in the 1870's. We kept steaming up the straight of Georgia and into the Queen Charlotte Straight which led to Queen Charlotte Sound. Instead of re-entering the inland passage, the captain headed across the sound and stopped at Prince Rupert for fuel.

Alaska territory was less than eighty miles and we started our search for the purchase of timber in Ketchikan, Alaska. D. D. and I visited several saw mills and were not impressed by what we saw.

"These mills are primitive by our standards, Cap'n, we are interested in whole logs for your house, but we need them milled and keyed so that you do not have to clinch between the logs. They should fit together like a child's set of building blocks. I would not import any of the timber from here. The Nevada stands of timber are better."

"You gentlemen should stop at the old Russian capital, Sitka. Sitka pine and spruce are the finest logs in the world, prized for ship building." The foreman of the mill told us.

The four women, Corene, Louise, Miss Templeton and Carol, explored Ketchikan on their own. When they returned, they had found many interesting things to buy. Green jade and other gem stones were in many of the shops and Louise loaded down with everything she could find as gifts for the family and friends. We re-boarded and headed for Sitka. Sitka had some of the tallest and straightest trees I had ever seen.

"The foreman was right, Cap'n, Nevada has nothing to compare with this. How in the hell are we going to get them back to Nevada?"

"What a shame, D. D., Caldwell Shipping can tow float the logs as far as San Francisco but our building site is on the eastern side of the Sierra Nevada Mountains. There is no way we can haul such huge logs over the mountains. We will use plan B where Louise and I will come to Virginia City and hand pick the Ponderosa from the Caldwell stands of timber. It is the best we can hope for. What a trip this has been for us, D. D. Did you ever imagine that Alaska was so beautiful!"

"If it were summer all year long, Corene and I would move here, Sir."

"So would I, but Louise will never leave Pennsylvania for more than a few months a year. I will be lucky to get her west to Nevada and east to Bermuda to spend time in our other homes."

"Why not build a lodge on the property in Nevada?"

"You mean, an inn? Like we have in Bermuda?"

"No, a lodge. This is a western thing. Wealthy people go away for a month at a time and stay in a *resort lodge*. Lake Tahoe may someday be a popular place for tourists."

"You think so? Have Corene draw a dashed outline on the map of the tract in Johnstone and letter it 'future resort lodge'. That way we have our bases covered if James or Ruth want to build."

98
Building in the West
Fall 1869

In many ways the acceptance of Alaska as a United States Territory on July 27, 1868, and the completion of the transcontinental railway on May 10,1869, eliminated the intense rivalry between the northern and southern section of the United States east of the Mississippi River. The Union Pacific and Central Pacific rail lines met in Ogden, Utah. Begun in 1863, in the midst of the war between the states, little was accomplished during the first two years. The eastern division of the road was from Council Bluffs, Iowa, to Ogden under the command of General Dodge, a distance of 1,032 miles through the great plains. The western division was begun from San Francisco to Ogden, a distance of 882 miles through the Rocky Mountains. The west was defined as everything west of the Mississippi, an area twice as large as everything east. Alaska alone was as large as the United States before the Louisiana Purchase. Business organizations and construction firms now looked westward. They began to join Caldwell International, in its development of the natural resources found here.

The Southern Pacific Railroad built spur lines north to connect with the transcontinental at Reno, Nevada, and it was now possible for Jason and Louise to ride by horse drawn carriage to Oil City, buy a ticket to Pittsburgh and then transfer to the Union Pacific westward. At Reno, they could change trains and head south by spur lines into places like Carson City, Virginia City and even Johnstone. The only train gap was from Seneca Hill to Oil City and Jason considered building a short spur from Seneca Hill to Oil City until Louise heard about it and vetoed it as out of hand.

"We are not so spoiled that we need our own railroad, are we, Jason?"

"No, Louise, I just thought ...."

When the Wilsons and Caldwells returned from Alaska, they arrived at the port of San Francisco. They boarded a train headed east until it arrived in Reno. They transferred to the spur lines and took a short ride into Virginia City, Nevada. They stepped off the train fully refreshed after traveling thousands of miles. "What a great country this is!" remarked D. D. "No horse and buggy rides anymore."

"Except between Oil City and Seneca Hill."

"Get over that, Jason, there is no need for a railroad from our front door."

"Yes, Louise."

"Louise, Corene needs to show you all the building that Caldwell International has done here." He was trying to get Cap'n Caldwell out of hot water. "The guest house for CI visitors is really nice, it is a smaller version of what Corene has designed for you. I will get a carriage and you can rest up before we drive out to look at the tract of land where the new Nevada Horse Ranch will be built."

Louise, Jason, Carol and her tutor had decided to take a short nap before D. D. and Corene returned for the trip over to Johnstone. They were asleep when D. D. came back and he let them all sleep. He returned to the carriage and told Corene that he was not going to wake them. Louise, particularly, was exhausted, he had never heard her be short with the Cap'n before.

"What do you mean short? Louise is shorter than Jason."

"Short is a way of saying that she is not angry, but has run out of patience with him. No, that is not right either. Let me see. What does 'short' mean?"

"Does it mean that she is abrupt with him because she is tired, but she really loves him like I love you?"

"That is it, Corene. You are getting better and better at this English thing."

She answered in her native American Indian language. "Itsewa sandusai ectimasici loughe." She was smiling.

"Yah, yah. I love you, too." He leaned over and gave her a kiss.

The Caldwell party slept for ten hours without waking. It was four in the morning before Jason stirred from his slumber. It was pitch black outside and inside the CI guest house and Jason could not sleep. He pulled himself out of bed and lit a lamp. He rummaged around in a piece of luggage until he found Corene's sketches and began to study them. He walked throughout the house lighting lamps until the entire house was brightly lit. He realized that Corene had designed the guest house, her style was unmistakable. She had a natural talent and it included more than just the ability to sketch a picture. She was technically competent to design the houses that he had planned for the next subdivision of Virginia City. Confederate officers and soldiers, who could not afford their property in the southeast, were beginning to move west. Why not Nevada? He would have Corene design an advertising campaign for the southeastern United States and run advertisements in the newspapers.

"Jason, why are you still up? Come to bed."

"We have been asleep about ten hours. I woke up and could not get back to sleep so I was looking at the sketches that Corene made for you. She is really talented, Louise."

"Let me make some coffee and we can look at them together." Louise left for the bedroom and returned in a robe.

"It is freezing in here." She began to boil water on the kitchen stove while Jason spread the drawings over the kitchen table. He pulled a chair out for Louise and she handed him a cup. He felt of her head and said, "You have a slight temperature. Maybe you caught cold."

"Jason?"

"Yes Louise."

"I love you and I am sorry."

"For what? You are right, a railroad track to our front door would look a little silly!"

"I was not talking about the railroad track. I have been terrible to you and Carol for a week now. I do not know what is wrong with me? I am tired all the time. It is an effort to put one foot in front of the other."

"The doctors are better in Pittsburgh than they are out here in Virginia City. To be on the safe side, I will ask Corene who they use and we will have the doctor come here today as soon as it gets light."

"Oh, Jason, do you think that is necessary?"

"Yes, I do. You are my entire life when it comes to happiness."

Jason left at first light and walked the mile and a half into Virginia City. He got Corene and D. D. out of bed and told them Louise was sick. Corene dressed and went and got a doctor. We introduced ourselves and we rode out to the guest house.

The doctor listened to her heart beat and said, "It is strong and regular, no problem there." He listened to her lungs breathe air in and out and said, " You have 'walking pneumonia'. That is very rare for summer or fall time."

"We have just returned from Alaska, doctor." I said.

"Did you encounter any snow or wild changes in temperatures?"

"No, snow. But wild changes, yes."

"Mrs. Caldwell, you need bed rest and sleep. Do not stay in bed more than eight hours at a time, otherwise you will lose your strength and you will take twice as long to recover. This is not serious, I will give you some medicine from my bag. I will write out the directions for your husband. I will come out every other day to check on your progress. Drink lots of hot liquids and get some bed rest. You should be over this in a few weeks."

"In a few weeks? I have to get back to my children in Pennsylvania!"

"Listen to the doctor, Louise. I will telegraph Sam and Rachael Mason and have them bring the children to us. That will be seven tickets. I will ride back into town with you doctor, if that is alright?"

"I have no other stops to make this morning, Admiral."

We left the Caldwell Shipping and Trading guest house and rode the few minutes back into Virginia City. "I really appreciate your coming so early this morning, doctor. I did not want to wait until we got back east to see about treatment."

"Keep her out of cold drafts and wild shifts in room temperatures. We do not want her catching a cold or something else on top of what she has. If she starts to run a higher temperature, that means the infection is getting worse. Pneumonia is caused by a bacteria that settles in the lungs. Modern medicine has nothing that kills bacteria except alcohol and we cannot get that into the lungs. The Indians have a cure for this type of thing and we should have Corene Wilson look at her, also."

"Are you serious?"

"Corene has been a 'God Send' these last few years she has lived here. She helps me with all my difficult cases and I trust her."

We stopped at the telegraph office and I sent the telegram to Sam and Rachael Mason, explaining what had happened. I walked over to see if I could find D. D. Wilson at his office. He was there and I brought him up to date.

"Let me go get Corene and her medicine bag Cap'n. She can help, she is a wonder." He rushed out of the office and I sat with tears running down my cheeks. I had insisted that we make this Alaska trip and to build in Nevada. I wanted so much not ever to have come on this western trip.

"Are you ready to go?" D. D. was back with Corene and we jumped into the wagon and drove off for the guest house. Corene boiled a pot of water until it was steaming and added what looked like some bits of tree moss and other dried green stuff. She stirred the mixture and poured it into a wash basin.

"Come over here, Louise, I know you do not feel good, but this will help."

She lowered Louise's face over the bowl and covered her head with a towel. "Breathe deeply, Louise. Deeper I want to hear you pant."

"Good, God, this smells awful, Corene."

"Good, then I mixed it correctly."

She waited a few minutes and boiled another pot of water. This time she added some alcohol from a bottle she had and repeated the process.

"We need to do this every day until the doctor says her lungs are clear, Jason. Stop crying, she will be alright, I promise."

I did not realize that I was teary again and I blew my nose and said I must have caught a cold.

"Stick his head under here, Corene." We heard this from under the towel and we all laughed in spite of our concerned feelings for Louise.

A few days later the Mason's arrived along with James and Ruth. They got off the train in Virginia City and D. D. brought them out to the guest house. Louise was sitting in a large overstuffed chair with her feet up on an foot stool when her children ran into the house and threw their arms around her. She was too tired to stand and greet them. We were all teary except Carol, who announced that she and Miss Templeton were going to take a ride into Johnstone and see what the town was like. They called it a 'field trip' to gather information for a story that Carol was assigned to write about life in the wild west.

"I do not think it is very wild anymore, Carol. You should have been here with your father and me ten or twelve years ago." D. D. was beaming. "Miss Templeton, you and Carol will need an escort I will contact Marshall Peters over in Johnstone and he will meet us halfway and take you the rest of the way. Alright, Cap'n?"

"Alright, Corporal Wilson." And I saluted, the first I had given in years.

He snapped me a return and turned sharply on his heels and marched towards the door. "I guess we are going, Daddy."

"Good bye, Carol. Have a nice time and do not forget to write." I always said this when one of the children had threatened to run away from Seneca Hill.

D. D., Miss Templeton, and Carol left in the wagon that had brought the Mason's. They rode into Virginia City while we made Sam and Rachael comfortable. D. D. needed to send a telegram to the Marshall's office in Johnstone. Sam stored the luggage and came back into the kitchen where we all gathered and were talking.

"Alaska was sooo beautiful, Rachael. Maybe like what California looked like two hundred years ago when the Russians were driven out by the Spanish." Louise said. "But you know, Jason, up and back no time to play, work, work, work." She was smiling.

"I thought you did not like it there, Louise. The reason we made a business trip was to see what the territory was like and if we should sell our Alaska bonds for a profit or not."

"Sam and I are holding on to ours." Rachael said.

"The other thing was to see if we could buy some heavy timber, cheaper there than off the sides of the mountains here. We were disappointed to find out that we could not. But it does not matter now, I think the building plans are on hold."

"What do you mean?" Louise was staring hard to me, I had seen that look before.

"I mean, we may have the cart before the horse. Look at how beautiful this house is here. What do we need with a bigger place to live. This is perfect. Just add a horse barn behind us. Corene should be using her talents for commercial uses." I spread out the sketches and plans that Corene had drawn. "Look, my finger is on the dashed outline marked future resort lodge. This is where she and D. D. should start building."

99
The Light Shines Forth
Nevada, 1869

While we were planning our next financial mission, Miss Karen Templeton met Marshal Eugene Peters half way between Virginia City and Johnstone, Nevada. A man on a white horse rode towards them with the morning sun at his back. He had a large light gray Stetson cowboy hat that cast a shadow across his face. His shiny silver star twinkled in the sun light. He carried the largest revolver that Karen had ever seen, strapped to his waist and right thigh. He pulled his horse from a trot and said, "Mornin' D. D., this the Cap'n's kid and the school Mar'am?"

"I beg your pardon? I am Carol Caldwell's tutor. I am not a school Mar'am."

His manner changed completely, he dropped his western speech patterns and sounded like he was from Pittsburgh when he replied. "Too bad miss, we need a school teacher in Johnstone. We had three, but one took off for California, better pay, I suppose."

D. D. looked back and forth between the two of them. "Oh, oh. I see some 'mooning' going on here." He thought. The Johnstone Town Marshall, a former marine in the United States Navy, dismounted and gave his horse to D. D. He climbed up on the wagon seat and sat beside Karen Templeton. "Be careful with that horse, D. D. he has not been completely broken yet and he likes to pull to the right a little. He will throw you off, if he can. I will bring them back after the little one has seen her father's tract of land and we have seen the town of Johnstone."

"Thanks, Marshall, we really appreciate this."

"Anything for the Cap'n, D. D., you know that." He flicked the reins and they pulled away towards the town of Johnstone. The Marshall had not seen, or smelled, anyone as sweet as Karen Templeton since he left Pittsburgh to join the Marine Corps.

"I am sorry, if I offended you. I have not been back to Pittsburgh for fifteen years and I have lost my manners living way out here. Let me introduce myself, I am, Marshall Peters from Johnstone, but before that I was a sergeant in the rapid response unit for Captain Caldwell. I was the sharp shooter for the detachment. The Captain always called me, 'dead eye'. It was just a joke.

I was no better a shot than anyone else in the detachment. The Captain always made us feel good about ourselves. He would watch us and find something unique about each of us. He would build us up and give us something to be proud of. I would not have found this job as town marshall if everyone around here did not think that I was this special 'sharp shooter' from the USMC."

"What does the USMC stand for?" Carol asked.

"That is United States Marine Corps, little missy. What is your name, little honey?"

"It is, Carol Caldwell, and I guess it is okay for you to know my name since you used to work for my daddy."

"I still do. I am head of Caldwell International Security for the Nevada Region. And what is your name, big honey?" He was looking directly at Karen Templeton, boring into her eyes, but strangely she was not embarrassed or uncomfortable.

"My name is, Karen Templeton. Are you married?" She blurted out.

"No, never found the right woman, until this morning."

"What is the school house like in Johnstone, Marshall?"

"Maybe you better call me, Eugene. I am a town marshall and my first name happens to be Marshal spelled with one L. It got really confusing when people began calling me Marshal marshall. My middle name is, Eugene."

"Johnstone town marshall, Marshal Eugene Peters, sort of has a ring to it." Karen was smiling and she had a beautiful smile.

"The school house is closed for the summer. But I have a key. I have a key for every building in Johnstone just in case of fire or emergencies. I will let you in when we get there."

The three of them rode on in pleasant conversation until they came over a hill and there stood the pride of Nevada, the cleanest town west of the Mississippi. It had about 8000 people according the town marker as they drove by. It had several churches and one large red brick school house with a white bell tower. They pulled up in front and tied the horse to a hitching rail. Eugene pulled a large ring of keys from his pocket and searched for the right one.

"Here it is, Karen, right where it should be." As he began to place the key in the door, it opened and one of the teachers was startled to see the town Marshall standing on the front porch.

"Marshall, what are you doing here?"

"I had planned to show the school house, here, to Miss Templeton and her student, but since you are here ,I think you could do a better job, Mrs. Wentworth. I will be back in a few minutes."

"It is not much of a school, Miss Templeton. We have eight classrooms but only two teachers left after this spring. I have no idea where the Mayor, who is also the school board chairman are going to get six more teachers. I really do not." She was almost in tears.

"Now, now. Mrs. Wentworth, the Caldwells may be here when school starts in the fall and if they are, I will bring Carol and her sister Ruth and I will teach one of the grades. Do not worry, the Admiral will not desert his town in their hour of need."

"The Admiral, is here?"

"Yes, Ma'am. My daddy is an expert at hiring people for jobs, just tell him what you need." Carol was beaming. Ruth always got all his attention. Now she would be able to have a really good conversation with him about something important.

They were walking from room to room through the school house when Eugene found them. He was with a another man, a short balding man with eyeglasses perched on the end of his nose. "I am the Mayor of Johnstone, Miss Templeton, I understand that you are a teacher."

"Yes, she is. She was just telling me that Admiral Caldwell has arrived in Virginia City and plans to come here. She also said she would be able to substitute for us if she was here in the fall." Mary Wentworth blurted out.

"Is that right?" Both the mayor and Eugene said at the same time.

"I believe that we should talk with the Caldwells to find out what their plans are for this summer and fall before we make any decisions." Said Karen Templeton.

"I will speak to my father." This was from an eight year old girl who sounded like she was much older.

"Thank you, Carol. Your father would do anything that you ask of him."

"He would?" This sounded like an eight year old.

"Of course, you have him wrapped around your little finger. You are very special to him."

"I am?"

"Trust me, Carol. If you asked your father and your mother to remain in Nevada until fall, they would do so."

"And I could go to a real school with desks and everything?"

"Yes, Carol ,with real desks and everything."

Karen Templeton was on one knee looking directly into Carol Caldwell's eyes when she spoke to her. She glanced up and looked into the eyes of Eugene Peters and saw the man with whom she would spend the rest of her life. His eyes were full of tears but he was smiling and she could see that he was very happy.

The rest of the day passed in a blur and they were back at the guest house before the sun was down. Carol was the first one down off the wagon and ran for the front door. "Mommy, mommy, I got to see a real school house with separate rooms for every grade, with desks and chalk boards and a room with books, thousands and thousands in just one room along the walls. I have never seen so many books and we got to meet one of the teachers there, a Mrs. Wentworth and she asked if I would be coming to school there in August with Miss Templeton as my teacher and I said, yes, and then we ......"

"Carol, slow down. What happened, Miss Templeton?" Louise Caldwell did not look happy.

"Carol should tell you about her day, Mrs. Caldwell, after she calms down. She is very excited about what she has seen in Johnstone today. Frankly, I am amazed at what we saw. Johnstone looks like it belongs in northwestern Pennsylvania, not in Nevada. When you get stronger, you will see what I mean. It is what I have been looking for all my life. I have been offered a public school teaching job there and I am considering it. I have until August first, to make up my mind."

"Is this something that you would consider? I thought you were happy with us?" Louise had a panicked look on her face.

"I will know in the next month or so."

"You are staying here two more months? What about Carol's education?"

"It is summer, Mrs. Caldwell, children need some time to unwind and relax. I know, I do. I will be leaving in the morning to find a place in Johnstone. Eugene will be here to pick me up."

"Who in the hell is, Eugene?" I asked, after listening to the conversation.

"Eugene Peters, he is the most interesting man I have ever met, Admiral."

"Marshal Peters?"

"Yes."

"That must have been some field trip." I said.

"Probably the most important in my life, time will tell." She left the room to pack.

"Carol, take a breath, come sit down on your mom's lap and tell us what you saw today."

The story took nearly an hour to tell and when it was over the parents looked at each other and said, "We had no idea you wanted to go to a public school, honey, we will need to see this school and talk to the people in Johnstone. We live in both Pennsylvania and Bermuda during the school year and a private tutor seemed the best solution." Her mother said.

"Just go into Johnstone and talk, you will see what I mean." Carol had big clear, icy blue eyes like her mother and she could melt you with them, if she tried and she was trying.

I glanced at Louise and she looked exhausted. "Go and get Miss Templeton, will you Carol? I want to talk to your mother." I must have had that look, because she jumped down and ran to find her tutor.

"Louise, we are not moving to Nevada so that Carol can go to public school. I have an idea, let me see how far I get with it."

"Oh, Jason. I feel the same way."

"Admiral, you wanted to see me?"

"Yes, Karen, sit down will you?"

"I have made up my mind, Admiral."

"I know you are leaving us tomorrow and we will be glad to see you go."

"You will?"

"Of course, it sounds like you were really smitten today. I understand completely, it only took one look at Louise, here, for me to decide the same thing." Carol was still standing beside her mother's chair and she was wide eyed.

"We want to help you, Karen. You have been a loyal tutor through three of our children. We will continue to pay your salary until the school starts here in August. And we would like to come to some arrangement for you to tutor Carol every summer that we return to Nevada."

"I am not going to go to school with Miss Templeton in August?" Carol interrupted, she had tears in her eyes.

"Yes, you are. If that is what you choose. You can stay here with D. D. and Corene. They do not have any children and I would think that they would love to have you during the school year. Your brother's school in Pennsylvania does not begin until September and that is when the family will leave so that your brother James can enroll in his second level private school. Ruth will have to decide if she stays here in Nevada or returns with us to Pennsylvania. I want you girls to understand that public school is not good enough for most students to get into a college, you will need special tutoring from Miss Templeton here, but it is more important that you get what you want, is that right?"

"Oh, Admiral. Oh, Daddy." They both started at once.

"What is it, Carol?"

"I do not want to live here without my family."

"You next, Miss Templeton."

"Do not take Ruth out of private school, Sir, she is very bright. She will be able to get into any college that she chooses."

"But not if she goes to public school?"

"No, I am afraid not. Colleges take only the brightest and best prepared students."

"And what about Carol, here. Is she as bright as Ruth?"

"She is different, Sir. She can be anything she chooses to be."

"But not if she goes to public schools?"

"If you go to public school with me, Carol, you will be unable to get into any college."

"Oh, why not?" Carol had tears in her eyes.

"Your father is right, Carol. You will need private tutoring to get into a high quality second level school and into college beyond. You will waste your chance at a bright future if you stay in Nevada public schools."

"Can I spend some time with you and Eugene this summer?" Carol was accepting the hardship of life when a loved one moves on without them.

"Of course you can. Did you not hear your father say that I was employed all summer? Oh, and Admiral, I would like for Carol to spend the time this summer learning what a teacher does to prepare for the next school year. Would that be alright?"

"Perfect solution, Miss Templeton, I am glad you thought of that. Would you tell the chairman of the school board that I think I know where he can hire several teachers for next fall?"

"That would be wonderful, Admiral. These children in Johnstone deserve a quality education too."

"They will if you are a member of the staff, Karen. God bless you and take care of Marshal Peters, he is so lonely." Louise said.

Miss Templeton left our employment and a young woman came to live with us that Carol could not stop comparing with Karen Templeton. Not in a negative way, but in a very constructive, positive way. I heard her say, "Boy, Miss Carlton sure knows more about history than Miss Templeton did. She wrote comments all over my paper! I will have to rewrite the whole thing. Miss Templeton never found as many mistakes as Miss Carlton, she is really a good tutor!"

Louise took her 'treatments' from Corene everyday until she finally said, "Enough, I am completely cured!" We rode into town and visited Doc Williams and he agreed. We continued on into Johnstone and it was a nice little town that looked a little bit like western Pennsylvania, except for the huge ponderosa pines. We walked the tract of land we had purchased and relocated the site for the Johnstone Lodge. The views in every direction were wonderful, mountain lakes, streams full of trout, dense forest and peaceful quiet. "When I die, Jason, bury me here."

100
A Message from London
1870

Mr. Samuel Clemens
The Mark Twain Suite
Caldwell Inn
St. George, Bermuda

Queen Victoria is sadden to announce the news of the death of Charles Dickens at his home in Gadshill. His passing will leave a giant hole in the literary production of this country. The Queen considered Mr. Dickens to be the preeminent English author of our time. You are named in his last will and testament and as a personal friend you are invited to the memorial service before interment in Westminster Abbey on the tenth of the month.

RSVP   Lord Nevel A. Napier
Office of the Admiralty
London, England

101

Ready to Leave Nevada
Spring 1870

The summer and fall of 1869 had taken a lot of the strength out of Louise while she fought what the mountain people called 'consumption.' We delayed our trip back to Pennsylvania until the Spring. We had sent James back to begin his studies at a preparatory boarding school since the Masons were returning to Seneca Hill so their children could begin school that fall. James wrote to his mother often and he sounded like he enjoyed his classmates. He was a teenager, small for his age, but he was determined to study hard and get into Harvard or Yale, he said he would accept an appointment to the Naval Academy if the Secretary of the Navy would recommend him in four years. Ruth and Carol kept their tutor and attended the Johnstone Public School. I took them every day to meet Miss Templeton and the other five new teachers hired that fall. Four were men, all with bachelor's degrees in education from Iowa State Normal College in Cedar Falls, Iowa. General Dodge had run my ad in the Cedar Falls Gazette which offered any new graduate twice the starting salary offered in Iowa, plus transportation to Nevada, plus board and room. The school board had fifty-seven applications and chose the four best.

A building principal was hired from California. She had a master's degree in school administration. In August, when the school bell rang, each room had its own teacher and the school had its first principal. The town marshall of Johnstone came by the school once a day to "check on things", but everyone in town knew he was sweet on Miss Templeton. After school he would walk with her to the little house that she had rented at the edge of a park and they would sometimes just sit on a bench and hold hands. They had found each other, and that was enough for now. They talked about their marriage and decided not to go back to Pittsburgh, there were churches in Johnstone. The school board did not usually accept married teachers, Mrs. Wentworth was an exception because she had been single when she was hired. They would wait until the school board passed on Karen's letter of permission to get married before they did anything rash.

The US Census takers of 1870 came to our ranch house outside of Virginia City and interviewed us for the State of Nevada. Louise did most of the talking and I listened to her with a smile on my face.

"Are you residents of Nevada?"

"Yes, we live here. This is our home. We also have a home back in Pennsylvania."

"Are you a resident of the State of Pennsylvania?"

"Yes, we are residents of both states."

"For our census taking, you must declare which state you are full time residents and which state you are part time, Mrs. Caldwell."

"That is nonsense. We are dual nationals, United States and Bermuda. We have homes in South Carolina, Nevada, Pennsylvania and St. George, Bermuda.. We are part time in all of them."

"Are you counted in the population of Bermuda?"

"Yes, of course. Caldwell International is the largest employer in Bermuda."

"We do not have a place to mark that on our census form."

Louise was beginning to look at the US Census taker like he was either incompetent or a fool. She said, "Mr. Timmens, if it would be easier for you, you do not have to record that we are dual nationals. This is the US Census only, correct?"

"Correct."

"I own a house in South Carolina, mark that as my primary place of residence. My husband owns a house in Pennsylvania, mark that as his primary place of residence. My son owns the house you are sitting in, his name is James Caldwell, mark him as the primary resident of Nevada. My daughters own the Bermuda property, mark them as living with us until they are twenty-one at which time they will declare their places of residence." She sat and stared at him with her icy stare.

"Thank you, Mr. and Mrs. Caldwell, that would make my job a lot easier." He marked his census form and was gone.

"Louise, do you realize what you have done! You have just given James three shots at the US Naval Academy if he wants to use them."

"I did?"

"Of course, he is a resident of the State of Nevada. How many kids in Nevada want to join the navy? Until he is twenty years of age he can qualify from the State of Pennsylvania, and from the State of South Carolina."

"I do not understand."

"Cadets are chosen by the Secretary of the Navy from a list of candidates given to him by an admission board. The admission board, composed of United States Senators, usually reduces the list so that no more than two young men are selected from each state. The age for admission is from 15 years of age to twenty. Most 15 and 20 year olds are not selected, most are selected at age 16 and graduate at age 20, like I did."

"So why was Ben Hagood twenty-one when he graduated?"

"He entered just after his seventeenth birthday and he was barely twenty-one when we graduated in June."

"Well, it was a good thing for you that he was or you would never have had an opportunity to buy surplus ships and start a shipping business out of Port Royal."

"Yes, I wonder where the Navy sent Ben last year?"

102
Return to Seneca Hill
Summer 1870

We left Virginia City before Easter which was in mid April. Marshal Peters and Karen Templeton rode on the same train as far as Pittsburgh. Both were from the Pittsburgh area and they wanted to meet the opposite's parents and relatives before they were married in June. Karen was surprised to learn that when the barns and stables were built for us in Virginia City, Marshal had D. D. begin a house for them in Johnstone. Corene designed it and D. D. supervised the construction. It would be completed before June. Sam Mason and I had kept in touch through the telegraph. The Seneca Oil company was producing record profits and there was little concern for our holdings in Pennsylvania. Sam could telephone my office at Caldwell Place and talk to Robert Whitehall whenever things were needed for any of the holding companies for CI. Monty Blair and John Butler were busy running American and Bermuda Telegraph and Telephone. I walked around the house at Seneca Hill, looking for something to do. The postman rode up the lane to the house and I walked out to get the mail.

A letter arrived from Horace Greeley.

THE NEW YORK TRIBUNE

April 30, 1870

Admiral J. E. Caldwell
Seneca Hill
Oil City, Pennsylvania

Dear Admiral Caldwell:

It has come to my attention that the US Development Foundation, formerly directed by past president Buchanan, is now without leadership. The current state of affairs within the Republican Party makes this recommendation a little strange. Have you ever considered past Vice Presidents? Hannebal

Hamlin of Maine is honest and hard working and is really not a typical republican. He is a "come-outer" just like me. I am so opposed to the present Republican Administration that I can no longer call myself one. Your funding for investigative inquiries by this paper have opened my eyes to the fraud, graft and outright incompetency of both parties.

I am presently seeking support for a run for the White House in '72. I would be most interested in your reaction to this radical idea. I will, of course, seek the approval to the Democratic Party and their nomination, another third party race would give the Republican candidate a clear field to victory. I understand your commitment to honest and efficient government. Any thought you might have would be most appreciated.

> *Horace Greeley*
> Horace Greeley, Editor and founder
> New York Tribune

I sought out, Peter Clivestone, my butler, valet, key operator and anything else that I needed done and we sent the following telegram to the New York Tribune.

MR. GREELEY

THANK YOU FOR YOUR LETTER OF APRIL 30, 1870. THE DIRECTORSHIP OF THE USDF HAS BEEN FILLED - ANDREW JOHNSON. I HOPE TO SEE YOU AT THE DEMOCRATIC CONVENTION - YOU HAVE MY FULL SUPPORT.

JASON CALDWELL, RETIRED ADMIRAL USN

I reread the telegram and thought, "Retired four star admiral. Where had all the time gone since I graduated from the US Military Academy as a Lieutenant in '37? I had studied at the Naval War College in Rhode Island, earning a master's degree in Naval History. Instead of the second summer cruise, I was released to write my thesis on the *Ships and Seamen of the American Revolution*.

My thesis was read by Secretary Dickerson of the Navy, a close, personal friend of the former Vice President, John C. Calhoun, from South Carolina. The Secretary was following up on the candidates he had recommended for admission and who had graduated from the 'Point.' In his letter to me, he recommended that I seek another degree as soon as possible. He was a member of the board of visitors for Georgetown College in Washington City and would recommend me for the degree in Business Administration. I accepted and packed my bags for Georgetown.

When my second master's degree was completed, the US Navy had paid for three college degrees. It was late1839, and I was given my first Naval Training Depot assignment in Port Royal, South Carolina. The 'Panic of 1837', had caused several changes in Port Royal and throughout South Carolina. President Jackson was opposed to the United States Banking System and wanted to abolish it. The act which created it was due to expire in 1836, and Congress wrote a new bill which extended it for fifteen years. Jackson vetoed it and ordered his Secretary of the Treasury to remove all deposits of public money. The bank panic of 1837, resulted and the Bank of Port Royal closed its doors and paid out partial payments to its depositors. The Bank of Beaufort would have done the same thing, except Caldwell Shipping had its deposits in that bank. It also had lines of credits with other banks. The assets of the merchant fleet were used to buy shares in the Beaufort Bank until the bank withstood the rush of depositors for their withdrawals. Caldwell Shipping now became Caldwell Shipping and Trading Company.

I taught at the Naval Training Center in Port Royal until '43. I was then transferred to a teaching position at West Point until the Naval Academy was moved to Annapolis in '45. I helped fight the Mexican War 1846-48, as aide to Admiral Farragut (I still missed his passing). I was assigned to the Army Navy Building in '49. I became the head of Naval Intelligence, promoted to a one star under President Buchanan. I retired from the White House in '61, only to be brought back under President Lincoln where I earned my second and third star in the Gulf again. I was nominated for my fourth star by President Lincoln but the senate had not acted until after the 15th of April. My fourth star came by accident because the "Caldwell Flotilla" kept getting bigger as ships were added to it after the blockade was no longer needed. St. George harbor could not hold them all and the Royal Dockyards at the west end had to take the overflow."

I was tired and I went into my study where I dropped down into a heavy, over stuffed, leather covered chair. I continued to remember how my career had started.

"The graduation of the United States Military Academy in June 1837, was held at West Point for the Army cadets and Annapolis for the Navy cadets. A single military academy held both branches but the Army and Navy had separate missions and had separate ceremonies. The graduating Navy Cadets were taken by the Mohawk and Hudson Railroad to Annapolis for the ceremony. I was about to graduate from the US Military Academy and searched the spectators for my mother and father, Robert and Elizabeth Caldwell. They should be sitting next to my brother and sister. I could not find them among the crowd, but I knew they were there. I had welcomed them the day before. They had come all the way from Beaufort, South Carolina, on one of my father's packet ships out of Port Royal, South Carolina. It was not until I walked across the platform and received my bachelor's degree and commission as an OF - 2, officer second grade, that I heard a 'rebel yell' from my brother, Robert, and located where they were sitting."

"Jason, wake up you are snoring."

My eyes flew open, "I was dreaming, Louise, it was graduation day June, 1837, and my whole family was there!"

"Yes, I know. You were talking to Carol, something about eating Chesapeake crab."

"I have to find out where Ben Hagood is."

"Jason, Jason. It was only a dream."

"I know. Ben was not in it. I need to find out where Ben is, something is wrong, I can feel it."

"Jason, calm down and send a telegram to the Army Navy Building."

"Good idea!" I rousted Peter again and we keyed another telegram.

DEPARTMENT OF THE NAVY

I AM TRYING TO CONTACT FLEET ADMIRAL BENJAMIN HAGOOD. DO YOU HAVE HIS PRESENT LOCATION?

ADMIRAL J. E. CALDWELL, RETIRED USN

We sent it and I paced the room waiting for a response. "Why do the White House and other government buildings refuse to get a telephone?" I thought. The teleprinter was silent and I stomped out of the house and walked to the stables. I talked to the horses and groomsmen who were working on them, trying to clear my mind. Peter Clivestone came walking slowly towards the stable with a telegram in his hand.

ADMIRAL CALDWELL

ADMIRAL HAGOOD'S APPOINTMENT IS CURRENTLY SUPERINTENDENT, OF THE UNITED STATES NAVAL ACADEMY, ANNAPOLIS. WE HAVE BEEN TRYING TO REACH YOU, SIR. I AM RECOMMENDING YOU FOR SUPERINTENDENT OF THE NAVAL INSTITUTE. AS YOU KNOW THIS IS PRESENTLY HOUSED IN

THE ARMY NAVY BUILDING HERE IN WASHINGTON , PLANS
ARE TO MOVE IT TO ANNAPOLIS.

IF YOU WOULD BE INTERESTED IN A PART-TIME ACTIVITY OF
THIS NATURE, PLEASE CONTACT ME.

ADOLPH E. BORIE, SECRETARY OF THE NAVY

I handed it back to Peter and said, "Let us see what the Secretary of the
Navy has in mind for me."

"Mrs. Caldwell is looking for you, Sire. Shall I tell her you are in the
stables, or shall you be coming to the house?" Peter had an English accent,
but I doubted he had ever been in England.

"I am walking back with you, Peter. We had better see what the first lady
of Seneca Hill thinks about my going back and forth to Washington."

"Very good, Sire. You miss the action, Admiral?"

"You know me very well, Peter. I wonder if Louise has sensed the same
thing?"

We rounded the corner of the covered porch that ran the entire length of
the house and saw Louise sitting and talking with Rachel Mason. "Hello,
you two. Where is Sam?"

"He is in our bedroom packing an overnight bag for you." Louise was
smiling, but Rachel was not happy.

"Rachel, I will not need Sam to go with me to see Secretary Borie."

"Admiral, you know I love you and Louise like family, but I miss not
being close to my family in Washington."

"Why not make it four traveling? Sam can get us four tickets on the train
and you can see your folks."

"Thank you, Admiral, but that is not what I meant. Sam and I need
to move closer to my folks so that they can see their grandchildren more
often."

Louise was looking at me and glancing back to Rachel. "I think my
wife has the solution to this problem. Why not tell Rachel what you think,
Louise?"

"I think in a few weeks Jason Caldwell will accept an offer from the
Secretary of Navy to become Ben Hagood's right hand man. Ben is the
new Superintendent of the Naval Academy, Rachel. Jason will become the
new Superintendent of the Naval Institute, presently located in the Army
Navy Building, Washington. He will move it to Annapolis and he will be
part-time administrator and full time faculty at the Academy. Jason cannot
do what is needed unless we move, temporarily back to Washington. We

means; you, Sam, your children, my children, me and whoever is needed to get this job done. You and Sam can live in Arlington close to your folks if you like, Rachel."

Rachel rose from her chair, walked over to Louise and kissed her on the cheek. "Only a woman could have understood my feelings and frustrations these last few months. Thank you, both of you."

I looked at Louise and Rachel and said, "Sam and I are lucky men to have met you two."

103
Trip to Washington
Fall 1870

Four adults and a carriage driver left Seneca Hill for the train station at Oil City, Pennsylvania. It was the first day of fall, August 22, 1870, and the heat in Washington was going to be unbearable. Sam had booked us two suites in the Hay-Adams across Lafayette Square from the White House. Sam and I could walk to our meetings in the Army Navy Building and the wives could catch up on some serious shopping. Rachel had written to her parents in Arlington and asked them to take the train into "Town," as they called Washington.

On August 23rd we had a meeting with Secretary Borie. We dressed in business suits and walked across the square and into the Army Navy Building. "Some things never change, Admiral, it looks the same. It only needs a coat of paint."

"Sam, this is summer break for most of the federal employees, I wonder why Secretary Borie picked this date?"

"We should find out soon. Here we are, I will knock and see if his office secretary is in." He knocked and no one came to the door. He tried the knob and it was open. We walked into an empty office.

"We must be early, Admiral."

At the sound of Sam's voice, the inner office door swung open and there stood President Grant. "Come in gentlemen, Adolph and I have been expecting you."

The meeting began with an offer from Secretary Borie for me to become Superintendent of the Naval Institute. I accepted. He outlined what he and the President had decided to do with all the documents pertaining to the Navy. When he had finished, I asked the following questions.

"Mr. President, do I understand that you would like to move all the archives of historical documents to the Academy, but there is no suitable storage available?

"Yes, Admiral."

"Could we build a suitable storage facility?"

"We could if we had the funds, Admiral."

"I would like to make those funds available to an independent contractor, Mr. President, would you approve that?"

"That is why I wanted to attend this meeting, Admiral. If you provide the funds, I will approve the plans of construction that will be carried out under your supervision. I would, also, like you to accept an appointment to the Naval Academy as Professor of Naval History."

"I would be honored to accept such an offer, Mr. President. Who hires and fires at the Academy?"

"You would report to Admiral Hagood as far as teaching is concerned, but you would report directly to me as Superintendent of the Naval Institute. This appointment will be made by the President, with Senate approval, from this day forward. I would like to begin your service to this administration September 1, 1870. Can you do that?"

"Of course, Mr. President."

"Jason, I remember what you did for me during the war. Your recommendation got me out of the western theater and my third star. I feel a certain closeness to you and Admiral Foote for the military success that I have enjoyed. This is not a reward to an old comrade in arms, however. You will work your butt off."

I smiled and said, "I would not have it any other way, Mr. President."

The President turned to Sam and said, "Captain Mason, you were invited here because I would like to appoint you as Admiral Caldwell's Aide, either as a civilian employee or as a Major in the United States Marines. You decide."

"Mr. President, I am a civilian and so is "Professor Caldwell", I would very much like to be an assistant professor."

"I will make that suggestion to Admiral Hagood. I cannot promise what his answer will be. But a letter of recommendation from the White House should help your case. Well, gentlemen, I have to get back over to the White House. I will leave the three of you to talk over the rest of the agenda." He stood and the three of us stood and said goodbye.

"Captain Mason, you came up through the ranks and have not attended a college. Is that correct?" Secretary Borie had a skeptical look on his face.

"It is, Sir. I realize that I can not teach courses in algebra, geometry, trigonometry, French, Spanish or the like. I was thinking of the practical courses like; ordnance, artillery, infantry drill, seamanship, battery drill, gymnastics, signals, steam tactics, torpedo placement and marine training of all types."

"What do you think, Admiral?"

"I agree with Sam If I am to be a Professor of Naval History, I do not need to know how to speak French or Spanish, or any type of mathematics, these will be taught by others."

"Well, Professors, let me be the first to welcome you to the United States Naval Academy. Here are two letters of appointment from Admiral Hagood, he sent them to me last week in hopes that I could talk both of you into joining the faculty." He handed us the letters. We read and signed them, returning them to Secretary Borie.

He placed them in his out box to be mailed to Annapolis. "Now, for the other task. You both will be teaching in Maryland and the documents are spread over the following sites: Rhode Island, Washington, Annapolis and points unknown. I would suggest that you move your families into the housing provided for you on the Academy grounds. From there, you should be able to supervise the document collections from other points."

Sam's face fell as he realized that Annapolis was not Arlington, Virginia. I interrupted the Secretary, "We cannot be both places at once, Mr. Secretary. I suggest that Sam begin here in the Army navy building and start his teaching the second year at Annapolis and then only on a part the time basis until the Naval Institute is up and running."

Sam chimed in, "Yes, we must locate critical documents here in the Army Navy Building. I suggest that you assign that office marked 'record storage' in the basement to us for at least two years. After that the Naval Institute Building will be constructed at Annapolis and we can begin to teach more on a full time basis."

"Mr. Secretary, I think Sam has a very good idea. Why not let me move onto the campus at Annapolis as you suggest so it will be ready for us the second year. That would be very helpful. Sam should maintain the basement office here in Washington. I will have Monty Blair, from AT&T, run a telephone line from here to Annapolis, at no charge to the government. Is that satisfactory?"

"Very, gentlemen. Welcome to the Grant Administration. Oh, by the way, Jason, the White House has asked American Telegraph and Telephone to install telephones in every government building within the district."

"District?"

"Yes, government buildings are being built outside Washington City limits. These are referred to as district building. The combination of buildings will be called the, 'District of Columbia'".

"What a mouthful, that will never catch on, Mr. Secretary." Sam and I said almost together.

104

Hay-Adams Hotel
next day

We had said our goodbyes to the Secretary and promised to report in on September 1ˢᵗ. We had walked across Lafayette Square, stopped at the front desk to pick up any messages. I had sent a telegram to Monty Blair's office here in Washington City before we left Seneca Hill. We invited him to come to our suites for a short meeting at his convenience.

"Yes, Admiral, you have a message from American Telegraph. A, Mr. Blair, has sent a telegram saying he will meet you in the lobby, today."

"Hello, Jas!" Came from across the lobby. "I am over here."

We walked over and sat down beside him. "My God, Jason, you look pleased with yourself. What have you done, now?"

"Monty, you are looking at the newest Professors hired at the Naval Academy." I said.

"What a natural fit, you two will be excellent!"

"Monty, I sent you a telegram because I was unable to telephone you. When do you think we will have Washington City wired for telephone?"

"Interesting question, Jason, we have a contract for all the federal buildings in DC."

"DC?"

"Yes, the 'District of Columbia', you know the federal sprawl outside the city limits. We are digging trenches as we speak. It will be a very long, time consuming process."

"That is what Sam and I asked to see you about. We have learned from our meetings the last two days, that water cooled telephone lines may be a thing of the past. Do you know a Professor Alexander Melville Bell from Canada?"

"Never heard of him, should I know him?"

"He has immigrated from Scotland to Canada. He is the inventor of 'visible speech' an aid for the teaching of the deaf and dumb. His son, Alexander Graham Bell, is a professor at Boston University and he is interested in a speaking device for the hearing, what we have called 'the telephone'. I want you to go to Boston and meet with him. See if he is using water cooled lines or air cooled. If he is experimenting with air cooled, make an offer to sponsor his research through Boston University. Bell will own the patent on his new device. Boston University and he will both share royalties if American Telegraph is given permission to build and market the device to the public. Use the standard 'iron clad' contract and run it by the lawyers at CI, will you?"

"How soon do you think he will have a prototype?"

"I have no idea, I would bet that he has a device now. He probably will not show it to you. That does not matter. We need to offer assistance to anyone we hear of that is working on an air cooled system. Remember we have telegraph poles everywhere. I would say within five years we will have Bell's air cooled wiring hanging from every one of those poles. Until then we will continue to sell the water cooled system with the idea that when an air cooled system makes the water cooled system obsolete, we can use our underwater lines to offer a cheap form of a telegram. You need to be ready with an advertising campaign to begin selling 'air time' over the water cooled systems that we have installed."

"Do you think the telegram will become obsolete?" Sam asked.

"God, let us hope not!" Monty looked pale.

"Gentlemen, it will be forty, fifty or more years before telephones are common in households in America. Until then we need to make the telegram, the cheapest form of communication in America. The federal government will be sending telegrams to individual households well into the next century."

Rachel Mason and Louise found the three of us talking and offered to take us to lunch. Monty was overjoyed. His office was too far away from the Hay-Adams and he missed our "Wednesday Lunches". We followed the women into the restaurant and ordered Monty's favorite, a New York strip steak, salad and a glass of red wine. The table conversation ran the normal news of the day. "Did you hear the census figures are now final? The population of the country is 38 million plus. That is an increase of only 7 million in the last decade. The loss of life during the war has taken its toll."

"It was a terrible thing that happened to General Lee. He died at the supper table, surrounded by his family. No one in the family could free the food that was stuck in his throat! How very awful!" Louise said.

"Edwin Stanton, the new justice of the Supreme Court, died in his sleep. President Grant will have to nominate another to take his place. The Civil War figures are beginning to pass. The 'Rock of Chickamauga', General Thomas, died last week and Admiral Farragut's passing was difficult for me." I added.

105
Naval Academy
Annapolis, Maryland

The next day we began our train ride to Annapolis, Maryland. We took a cab to the train station, Louise bought the tickets while I sent a short telegram to Ben. I did not know if he was back from one of the summer cruises for new cadets or not. He would meet us at the train station and take us out to the Academy if he got the telegram.

From about the first of June until about the first of September, the Midshipmen are embarked on war vessels for the summer cruises. They are instructed on the various duties of their profession. For several years the practice vessels have been modern war vessels temporarily detached from the fleet, the fourth class spending half the summer on the sailing training ship *USS Severn* and half at the Academy. The fourth class is composed of incoming cadets, called Freshmen on most college campuses. But the Navy has its own way of doing things and Fourth Class (freshmen) is followed by Third Class (sophomore year), followed by Second Class (junior year) and ending with the First Class (seniors). After four years at the Academy the training continues for two more years at sea before the Midshipmen are commissioned as officers. This was a change from when Ben and I were at the US Military Academy at West Point, Naval Division.

Most of Sam's courses would be in the last two years of the six year commitment as a naval midshipman at the Academy. Mine would be in the first four years on campus and not at sea. We stepped off the train in Annapolis and found no one waiting for us. "Ben must still be on summer cruise, probably with the incoming cadets. He loves to tell them 'war stories'". I said.

"We can find our own way, Jason. Look there is cab waiting over there." She pointed out. We located a porter and had our suitcases taken to the cab I would hire.

"Take us to the Naval Academy, driver. My husband is a new Professor there."

"Are you Mrs. Caldwell and the Admiral?"

"Why, yes we are."

"The Superintendent told all of us cab drivers to be on the lookout for you two. I will take you on a short tour of the grounds and end with your billet. Is that alright with you?"

"Yes." Louise said.

"Good. The Naval Academy was begun by an act of Congress in 1845. That was after you and the Superintendent graduated, Admiral."

"Yes, we graduated from the US Military Academy, not the Naval Academy."

"Most of the buildings you will see on the grounds date from 1845, the oldest is twenty-five years old. The newest will be the Naval Institute building, you will see construction stakes already in place on the building site as we go by. We are turning off of John Paul Jones Way onto Blake Road, a street leading to the main gate. You will have to show some identification when we are stopped, Admiral."

"I was here last in 1836, for a summer cruise, the town has really changed."

"Yes, it has, Admiral. It will take a few weeks for you and the Mrs. to get your bearings. Do you own a boat? We are passing the marina on our left."

"His boat will not fit in that city marina, driver. It is a three masted Snow called the *Cold Harbor*." Louise was smiling.

"Oh, the *Cold Harbor* just arrived at the Academy, Admiral."

"It has?"

"Yes, I saw it yesterday. What a beautiful ship!"

"Ben has been up to his old tricks, Louise. I bet we do not have a place to sleep and he has contacted Captain Jacob and told him to bring the *Cold Harbor* from Bermuda."

The cab stopped at 121 Blake Road, the main gate to the Naval Academy. A midshipman walked to the cab and spoke to the driver. The midshipman stuck his head inside the carriage and asked, "Are you Admiral Caldwell?"

"Yes, I am."

"The Superintendent welcomes you to the Academy, Sir. I will open the gates for you to pass. I am signed up for your class this fall."

"This fall?" Louise looked at me with one of her looks.

"Louise, I am teaching only one course this fall. It is naval history. He must have been one of the unlucky ones to get me as the instructor."

"Oh, Jason. You will be fine. Just tell them what you have done since 1837, and you will be one of the favorite instructors of all time. Better yet, tell them what happened to you and Ben Hagood when you got off the train at Annapolis. That should hold their attention!"

The carriage jolted forward and we were on the grounds. Green lawns were spread out before us. Red brick buildings trimmed in bright white paint dotted the green spaces. The driver continued his monolog. "Notice that the original buildings that date from 1845, have been supplemented after the war. Congress has spent nearly ten million dollars here since 1865 and it shows. On your left are the original accommodations for the Midshipmen, they became inadequate and unsuitable until they were remodeled for Fourth Class. On your right, are the new accommodations for Upper Classes. Up ahead you will see some of the new academic buildings, science laboratories and lecture halls. In the next block on the left is what we call, Admiral's Row. Notice the Superintendent's house, it is the largest because he has to entertain a lot there. The next largest is for the new Superintendent of the Naval Institute." He pulled his horses to a stop in the driveway. "And that, folks, ends the short tour of the US Naval Academy, Annapolis, Maryland. I hope you will enjoy your stay here, Admiral, the Superintendent has been looking forward to seeing you".

He handed us our suitcases, tipped his hat and said, "I have already been paid, Admiral. Put your money away." He got back up in the driver's seat and backed the carriage down the driveway.

"Look, Jason, there is a sign in the front lawn. It has your name and position printed on it. Admiral J. E. Caldwell, Superintendent Naval Institute. I like the sound of that!"

"Are you sure about this, Louise. You and the children will be stuck here for the next two years, at least until we get everything organized. We will see very little of Seneca Hill or Caldwell Place while we are stationed here."

"Yes, but think of the opportunity for James. He will see up close what the Academy is like and if he wants to attend. The girl's tutors will be here in this house with us. We need to see how many bedrooms this place has." She walked up the front sidewalk and the door opened as she approached. Ben Hagood was standing just inside with a giant grin on his face.

"Did the driver take good care of you, Jason?"

"Yes, he did. Thank you."

"You can thank him yourself after he takes the horses to the stables. He is your academic aide for your first semester here at the Academy. We give all new professors this assistance for one semester only, after that you are on your own, brother!"

There was movement behind Ben, then a shoving match to see who could get out the door first. My brother Robert elbowed his way forward and said, "I brought the *Cold Harbor* so you would have a cook and household help." He was elbowed aside by his wife, Marriann, who said, "It was my idea!" Then came the Caldwell family in mass. My mother was followed by my father. Robert's three children; Robbie, older than James, our son, Karen and Sharon, the twins, came next. Then Hop Sing, his wife, Sui Lin, and their children; Won Sing, Rho Qui Sing, and Quo Lin Sing. The next persons out the door were John Butler and Sally Trott Butler followed by Robert and Laura Whitehall.

"Is their anyone left in Bermuda?" asked Louise.

"Oh, yes. Ambassador Lewis sends his regards and wishes he was here for the celebration, Jason." John Butler was beaming.

"We will sleep on the *Cold Harbor*, Louise, we can take care of ourselves." My mother said. And they did, for a week people were coming and going from the Admiral's house to the *Cold Harbor* docked at the water's edge at the Naval Academy in Annapolis, Maryland. It was a family reunion that would not soon be forgotten. Hop Sing organized the kitchen, cooked the meals and gave all the household staff orders, "Shape up or ship out!"

I asked him where he had heard that saying and he replied that it sounded like a Navy command and he had a lot of shaping up before the *Cold Harbor* could ship out for Bermuda.

When the organized chaos was at its height the Caldwell children, tutors and Peter Clivestone arrived from Seneca Hill. "Sire, the children would simply not stay at home any longer."

"That is fine, Peter, they should be part of the family reunion too, as should you."

"Oh, Sire. A gentleman's, gentleman is never part of the family. He allows the family to function as a smooth running entity."

"Well, good luck with that concept. I see you have never met Hop Sing. Let me find him and introduce you two." We found Hop Sing in the pantry moving things onto shelves.

"Hop Sing, you have heard me mention my butler, Mr. Peter Clivestone. Peter, this is the real commander of the *Cold Harbor*. He has been a part of this family for over 15 years."

Hop Sing did his "Chinese Peasant act" for Peter, bowing over and over again and saying in broken English, "I, Hop Sing. Wery glad to meet honorable butler. Captain Kaldwil talkie muchly bout you, Sir."

He then turned to me and said, "Admiral, this pantry needs a major overhaul. Do you think you could get your butler here to straighten it out for me?" He turned on his heel and left us standing alone in the pantry.

"See what I mean, Peter, as long as you two are together in the same house, you work for him."

"As you wish, Sire. But if that Chinese misfit ever sets foot at Seneca Hill, he better keep a civil tongue in his head. And he better be the best damn cook in the world!" He said with a smile.

"Welcome to the family, Peter. You understand Hop Sing perfectly."

I turned and left Peter to organize the pantry and found my father and brother sitting at the dining room table. They had a bundle of papers spread out before them.

"Jason, come sit down and look at these account sheets for the plantation on Pollawana." My brother called me over.

"How did we do last year?"

"Not as well as we should have, Jason. You boys are in your fifties now and that means I am in my seventies. I am too old to go back and make this a profitable venture. What do you think, Robert, of having Robbie move back on the property?"

Robbie was my brother's son and he was the fourth generation of Roberts. My grandfather was Robert Caldwell, my father was known as junior, my brother was known as Trey and his son was called ,Robbie. "Where is Robbie? Find him, Jason, and we will ask him what he thinks about being a gentleman farmer. Tobias does all the management anyway. Robbie would just be there to have a Caldwell on site, so to speak."

"Good idea, father. I will go and ask Peter to find him, he does not want to help Hop Sing, anyway." I said with a smile on my face.

"What?"

"You had to be there. Hop Sing did his dumb act on him."

"You tell Peter, to leave Hop Sing alone. He and his family are the best thing that ever happened to this family. Servants come and go, Hop Sing is forever."

I left the dining room in search of either Peter or Robbie and returned a few minutes later with Robbie in tow. "Sit down a minute with us, Robbie."

"Okay, Uncle Jason."

My father began his recital of the Caldwell Plantation Tale. The adults in the family have heard it before, but I doubted Robbie had ever heard it. "Robbie, you are Robert Hays Caldwell IV. You may claim your birthright today if you want it. Do you know what a birthright is, Robbie?"

"No, Grandpa, I do not."

"I will tell you a story about your family. It will take a few minutes and you can interrupt me with questions whenever you would like."

"Okay, Grandpa."

"What does this word, 'Okay' mean, Robbie?"

"It means, yes Sir."

"I prefer, yes Sir."

"Yes, Sir."

"Good, now where was I?"

"You were going to tell me about my birthright."

"Oh, yes. In South Carolina, property is passed from one generation to another through marriage or father to the first born son. You are the first born son of your father and you are entitled to his property upon his death or sooner if he 'quit claims' it to you."

"What is a quit claim, Sir?"

"A legal document that passes the deed to the property to you and your family."

"I am not married."

"But someday you might marry, Robbie. That is not part of my story."

"Sorry, Sir."

"The property known as Caldwell Plantation on Pollawana Island in Beaufort Country was quit claimed to your father when we all moved to Bermuda. I inherited it from my father, who became the owner by marriage to my mother."

"I do not follow, Grandpa."

"You will. One of your ancestors was Stephen Bull. Do you know about him?"

"Yes, he was famous. Stephen Bull came from England to Charleston on the frigate, *Carolina*, arriving soon after the settling of the colony. As Lord Ashley's deputy, he was able to obtain large grants of land on St. Helena Island and on the Ashley River up in Charleston. He was an important founder of that part of South Carolina."

"Yes, it is said that he selected the site of Charles Town, and his son, William, did the same for Savannah. William built a magnificent home and named it Sheldon Hall for their ancestral home in Warwick, England."

"Yes, I know about that, Grandpa. How are the Caldwells and the Bulls related?"

"Martha Bull married Robert Hays Caldwell in 1797, a year later I was born."

"That makes you seventy-two years old, Grandpa. You sure are a young acting 72!"

"Thank you, Robbie, but that is not the end of the story. The point is, that the date of our plantation on Pollawana across from Datha is, 1797. It came into the Caldwell family as a wedding gift from John Bull's grandson. He owned two plantations on Bull's Island which, you remember, we came by on our trip to St. Helena, last year. Though now, it is called Chisolm's. It is across a small creek from Lady's Island. He also owned a small plantation across the creek from Datha. This is the plantation that you visited with me and your father last year. Because land, in that state, is inherited from father to son, he passed the Chisolm Plantations, at his death, to his two sons. His daughter received the third small, 12,000 acres, on her wedding day."

"Grandpa?"

"Yes, Robbie."

"Are you trying to ask me if I liked the plantation that we visited last year?"

"Yes, I am."

"I would be honored to live on the plantation, watch over it and protect it from all who would bring harm to it. It is the living legend of our family. I have studied the plantations on Lady's island, Sir. Legend says, they were named in compliment to the women of the Bull family. Martha Bull would be my Great, great grandmother, correct?"

"You are correct, Robbie."

"When did John Bull live on his plantation?"

"John was married to his first wife in 1714. She only lived a year or so, she was killed by Indians in 1715."

"Killed! What happened?"

"1715 is still referred to in Beaufort as the, 'Year of Tragedy'. It was the year of the uprising of the Yemassee Indians. They attacked Port Royal first, this allowed many people in Beaufort to flee their homes and avoid their murders. The small barrier islands, of course, were not warned and the people there were murdered."

"How was the husband saved?"

"Captain John Bull was in Charles Town with the militia who were being formed to put down the uprising. Returning days later to Bull Island, he found the island deserted, his home burned and the area strewn with bodies, all scalped. Consumed by grief, and later anger, he became one of the most relentless members of the militia that hunted down and exterminated the Indians. Few survived, they disappeared from South Carolina westward into Georgia."

"What happened to John Bull? He must have had a family in order to have a grandson?"

"Yes, he remarried, but the memory of his first wife still occupied a place in his heart. Nineteen years after her death, in 1734, he gave St. Helena Episcopal Church, a silver communion service in her memory. It disappeared during the occupation of Beaufort by your Uncle Jason's navy. But your Aunt Louise had an exact copy made by a silversmith in Sheldon."

"I would like to know about our family tree, Grandpa."

"If you decide to accept your birthright, I will show you the grave markers when we go to church in Beaufort. I will also show you some markers in Sheldon Church Yard. The family tree is interesting. John Caldwell was born in Ireland, in 1701. He came to South Carolina in 1731, much later than the Bulls. He is also known as an Indian fighter. The Tuscarora tribe in North

Carolina ranged southward after the defeat of the Yemassee. Captain John Caldwell led a successful campaign against them and drove them back to North Carolina."

"What about your branch of the tree?"

"I am coming to that. In 1779, Robert Caldwell distinguished himself at Port Royal. This was during the American Revolution, of course. Anyway, he was under the command of General Moultrie and assigned to defend Port Royal. A large number of British landed and quickly surrounded the Carolinians. The company under his command was ordered to surrender. My relative called out to know what quarter they would have. 'No quarter to rebels' was the reply.

'Then men,' Captain Caldwell yelled, 'defend yourself to the last man. Charge!' In an instant the click of every gun was heard as it was cocked and presented to the face of the enemy, who immediately fell back."

"Oh, Grandpa, are you sure? That sounds like a story to me."

My father looked at my brother and me and said, "It is time. Roll up your sleeves boys and I will roll up mine. You see the three tattoos on me, your father and your uncle?"

"Yes, Sir."

"Do you have one of these?"

"Yes, Sir. It is the O'rion Constellation."

"Do you know it means?"

"No, Dad always said it was special to the men in the Caldwell family."

"Yes, it is. It comes from Ireland. It is the mark of the warrior. It means that if you are ever in trouble you can count on others who wear the same mark. You are brothers in arms."

"Wow, I had no idea."

"What is this word, wow?"

"It means without, other, words to express joy or surprise, Grandpa."

"Robbie, will you teach me some of the new language?"

"Sure thing, pops!"

"Robbie, your grandfather is not through telling his story, let him finish." My brother said.

"Okay, pops." Robert Hays Junior rolled his eyes and finished his story.

"This same Robert Caldwell was later Speaker of the House of Representatives in Columbia. He later became a representative in Washington. At one time there were seventeen branches of the Caldwell family in South Carolina. Most were in Beaufort, but they stretched from the coast into the Piedmont and one finally settled in Pickens. My great grandfather, Robert Gibbs Caldwell, built the four-story house overlooking the Beaufort Bay. It is the one we call, 'The Castle.' We were in that house last year when we were home."

"That finishes the family history lesson, Robbie." I added. "The living male members of the Robert Hays Caldwell family are sitting around this table today, Robbie. Your Grandfather, your father and your uncle are ready to pass the torch to you, if you are ready. All three of us will help in any way that we can to make your move to the plantation home."

Robbie turned to his father with tears in his eyes and said, "I can not do this alone, can you and Mom move with me and help me get started?"

"Of course."

"Uncle Jason, I have no money. Can you loan me some?"

"Of course."

"Grandpa, do you remember what the original plantation house looked like? I would like to restore it, not push it over and build new. Could you and Grandma come home and supervise the restoration?"

"Of course. Robbie, the cost of the restoration should not come from the operational loan from your Uncle Jason. Your Grandmother and I will pay for everything needed."

"Robbie, the loan that the Bank of Bermuda will grant for you is never to be paid back. You understand? You will pay one half of one per cent after the annual harvest in the fall of every year. The plantation is large enough to produce other things in addition to field crops. Let your father tell you about what he has done these past years in Bermuda."

My father and I rose from the table and left the dining room so the father and son could talk about their plans for the Caldwell Plantation in South Carolina.

106
Naval History 101
September 1870

After the family reunion, my academic aide and I began to review the course syllabus for fourth year, newly entered, cadets to the Naval Academy. It was dry and boring.

"What can be changed and what must remain intact so that cadets will be able to move on into History 201, Mr. Edwards?"

Merrill Edwards was about my age, had served in the Navy until 1865 when he was released with many other thousands of returning sailors to civilian life. He was wise beyond his years and I think that is why he was chosen to be an academic aide. He thought about my question and replied, "Admiral, the content is the same whether it is presented by a person truly interested in its content or by someone who reads his notes to the class. A reader is typical of European colleges and it is boring. If I were you, I would not write out everything that you say in a lecture. I would make a list of the important points or topics from the syllabus and make sure that you covered them in class. You decide how you want to make it interesting to them. These are just kids, first year from home, scared to death that they will make a mistake. You need to relate to them and you will be fine.

"Relate to them?"

"Yes, before I was drafted into the Navy, I was a public school teacher. I went to normal training sessions after my formal education was completed in Maryland. This qualified me to teach in the public schools of the state, but it did not teach me 'how to teach.' I learned that on my own. Every teacher is different, no two styles are the same. You can not copy another person's style. That will not work for you. Kids can sense when you are being yourself and when you are putting on an act. For example, the course syllabus has two topics and five points for a lecture that you will present to them. You may begin the lecture by walking to the chalk board and writing the two topics down for them. Then turn and face them and say 'we only have a little less than a hour each day this semester. It is impossible to cover both of these topics in an hour. I will cover the first for you and you will go to the library and find out as much as you can about the second topic.' It might be a good idea to use a little humor and explain to them where the library is and what it looks like on the outside."

"Good idea, Merrill! I need to make them want to learn what the syllabus has listed."

"That is it in a nutshell, Admiral. Your experience is so vast compared to theirs, remember you have a master's degree in Naval History. This is their first exposure to it. And another thing, the very best students, who love history, are the ones who will volunteer their time in the Naval Institute. Remember the Naval Institute is the warehouse for the history of the United States Navy."

We spent many hours together during my first semester at the Naval Academy, but Merrill Edwards put me on the right track straight out of the gate, before I ever walked into a classroom. The first day of classes came and I was confident that I would be the best teacher ever to set foot in a classroom. I came down to breakfast that morning and suddenly I could not eat a bite. My stomach was upset and my legs felt like they were made of rubber. I forced myself to walk from Admiral's row to the lecture hall just to fill my lungs with pure, fresh air. I found the classroom a minute or two before the class was to start and opened the door to hear, "Officer on deck!" The cadets leaped to their feet, waiting for me to say something. All I could think of was, "Please, sit down." They remained at attention. My brain clicked back into gear and I bellowed, "As you were, gentlemen." Everyone sat down.

I walked to the lectern and placed my briefcase on a small table beside it. And I began my first lecture, "This is Naval History 101. Anyone who thinks they are somewhere else should take this opportunity to get to their proper class." I walked to the chalk board and wrote;

Professor Jason Caldwell, BA
United States Military Academy '37
MA Naval History, Naval War College '41

"That gentlemen is who I am and why I am going to teach this course this semester. I was a member of the United States Navy for thirty years and I am proud of that, but I am not a member of that service today and you do not have to give me the military courtesy of saluting or standing in my presence. Is that clear?"

The entire class responded, "Sir. Yes, Sir."

I opened my brief case and took out my list of topics which I had penciled on a small piece of paper and my pocket watch so I would not go over the hour with them. I started with the first topic which was the outline for the course. "This first course is a history of the world's navies, how they were formed; what rivers, seas and oceans that they sailed and why. The course will end when we are still the 13 British Colonies. For those of you who thought you would learn all about the US Navy, you will. Because, the USN is based largely on what the British established for us as a pattern. The British stole from the Spanish, who stole from the Dutch, who stole from the countries inside the Mediterranean. So I guess you can say that navies are composed of a bunch of thieves."

Not a chuckle, not a smile anywhere on the faces of the fifty-five cadets. I am not reaching them, I thought. "Gentlemen, it is okay to smile at my corny jokes. Not only were there thieves serving in the British Navy, there were also convicted murderers, rapists, and men who were escaping debtor's prison and imprisonment by the Queen's courts. Many times the ranks could not be filled by volunteers and those escaping judgements. Some times the British had to kidnap their own citizens and citizens of other countries to fill the ranks. This is a true story that I was involved in when I was a Captain."

"President Pierce had met with James Buchanan shortly after the election and confided in him what must be done with Great Britain and Queen Victoria for allowing her embassy in Washington City to kidnap Americans. We must capture a British Man-of-war upon the high seas and tow it to the nearest US friendly port. We must also remove all of the seamen aboard and then claim that we found the ship afloat, abandoned. After resupply, a US Navy crew will sail the ship to South Hampton and return it to the Queen.

Britain still considered the United States a complaining little nation where the minister from England to Washington City had every right to contract American seamen. It did not matter that sometimes kidnaping and pressing them into service aboard HMS ships was a more common practice. The message to the Queen's Government was this - stop the unlawful pressing of seamen on our shores or we will make the entire British Navy disappear one ship at a time.

I took a breath and looked at my pocket watch. Where had all the time gone? I had only five minutes left. I cleared my throat and said, "Unfortunately we are out of time and I will have to finish this story tomorrow in class, if you are interested."

"But Sir, what happened with the pressed seamen?"

"Did you find the British Ship?"

"Tell us the rest of it after class, Sir."

I knew then that I had reached a few. I looked around the classroom and said, "I notice that some of you have not placed pencil to paper. Do that now. Letter the following, T A K E   N O T E S . Underline that please. For those of you who I notice take short hand, please share your notes with your classmates. I hate to repeat myself. I will see you all tomorrow."

The next day I ate a full breakfast and decided to get to class ten minutes early so as to avoid the military courtesy thing. I open the classroom door and heard again, "Officer on deck!" All fifty-five cadets had beaten me to the classroom.

"As you were, gentlemen! Who is the senior most cadet present?"

"I am, Sir, I missed this class last year, I am a third year midshipman not a cadet."

"What is your name?"

"Midshipman Casey Caldwell, Sir."

"Well, you certainly have a naval last name, Mr. Caldwell."

That brought about a few chuckles and we progressed from there. I went to the chalk board, wrote the topics to be discussed today and those that were to be studied in the library (the joke about how to find the library actually got a giggle.) I saved the last ten minutes of the hour to pick up the story about the pressing of American seamen and we finished a second day. On the third day I showed up 30 minutes early and found the classroom full with another course and fifty-four cadets and one midshipman sitting alongside the hallway walls. Before Midshipman Caldwell could bellow, 'Officer on deck', I said, "As you were, gentlemen. How many of you have a class after mine?" None raised his hand. "Good, I will use the time between classes to add another fifteen minutes to the story telling. I will also check to see if there is a class scheduled after ours."

"The room is empty, Sir. I checked." Said Mr. Caldwell.

"You will make a fine officer, Mr. Caldwell, some days I might need more than 25 minutes to finish a story." They actually laughed out loud.

107
The Naval Institute
Spring 1871

The United States Naval Academy was moved from Annapolis, Maryland to Newport, Rhode Island at the beginning of the Civil War. The fear of capture by the southern navy or over run by CSA armies was a real concern. This combined the Naval Academy with the US Naval War College, the Torpedo School and the US Naval Records and Archives held within The Naval Institute. At the close of the war, the Academy was returned to Annapolis, but the other branches stayed at Newport or were moved to the Army Navy Building in Washington City.

It would be the job of the new superintendent of the Naval Institute to locate missing records at Newport. He would then pack all existing records in the Army Navy Building, Washington City and move everything to Annapolis. It would take Jason Caldwell until January 2, 1873, to declare that the Institute was open for business. The entire process had been a labor of love by a team of volunteers, including the superintendent. The majority of the volunteers were faculty members, cadets and Midshipmen at the Academy.

In the spring of 1871, Admiral Jason Caldwell stood at the ground breaking ceremony for the new building on the Naval Academy grounds and said the following: "I welcome all of you here today to the official ground breaking for the United States Naval Institute. This building will house an organization founded by the officers who have taught at the Naval Academy since 1845. The institute has for its object the promulgation of knowledge concerning naval affairs among the officers of the United States Naval Service. During the first years of its existence it issued occasional copies of its proceedings, but now the publication will be made quarterly. In addition to papers submitted by officers, the review will contain the naval work of the world in the 'Professional Notes,' which aim to give all available information concerning new ships, guns, torpedoes and the latest research and naval advancements made in the preceding quarter.

The Institute will offer a gold medal, each year, a life membership and a prize of $200 for the best essay on any subject of interest to the USN, reserving the right to withhold the offer if no worthy essay is presented. All officers of the Navy and persons holding positions of administration under the Department of the Navy, Washington City, are eligible for membership. Students of the Naval Academy beyond the first year cadets are also eligible to join. This year's Medal goes to Midshipman Casey Caldwell (no relation). Will he please come forward and accept the medal and a check for $200?"

The best student in my fall course came forward and I placed the medal around his neck, handed him a check for $200 with my left hand and shook his hand with my right. "Do you want to say a few words, Casey?"

"Yes, Sir. I do."

He asked for a pen and walked to the lectern. He turned the check over and endorsed it. He then spoke in a clear voice and said, "Professor Caldwell has not checked with the Commandant of Midshipmen or he would know that I can not accept this check during my study here at the Naval Academy. I have, therefore, endorsed it and written below my signature, for deposit only United States Naval Academy Infirmary. The next time I am in sick bay, they better treat me nice!"

The crowd broke into laughter and then applause as they realized what the young man had done. Casey turned and winked at me as he took his seat. I stood there for a moment and thought what a great life teachers have. I walked to the lectern and continued by saying, "The present membership of the Institute includes about two-thirds of all the officers in the navy and is steadily growing."

I removed my reading glasses and glanced at the visitors assembled before me. I smiled at my wife and my son, James, who had been accepted into the Naval Academy for the fall of 1873. Next to James sat my oldest daughter, Ruth, who had scored the highest marks ever given at the Harvard preparatory school for girls. She would be making application at the Society for Collegiate Instruction for Women, Harvard University, Cambridge, Massachusetts. If accepted she would be one of only 1107 undergraduate students enrolled at the university. Next to Ruth sat Carol, a beautiful young girl, a miniature version of her mother. She still studied with her tutor, Miss Carlton, and spent her summers at the ranch in Virginia City. She did not ride horses, she helped Karen Peters prepare her classroom for the next fall. It was apparent that Carol would apply to the Teacher's College of Columbia University when her time came for a college education.

On the other side of Louise Caldwell sat Admiral Benjamin Hagood, the Superintendent of the Naval Academy and the best friend of Jason Caldwell. His hair was thinning where it was not gray. Crows feet were prominent when he smiled and he smiled a lot. He hated not having a swaying deck under his feet, but after all, a fifty-six year old sea captain was rare indeed. Admiral Farragut was older when he entered the battle of New Orleans but few would ever match this naval officer. Ben was happy in Annapolis, he had his own sail boat that he sailed often. He went on summer cruises with the new cadets and told them stories of the battles he had been in. But mostly he told them of his remarkable friend from Beaufort, South Carolina, who did not break his oath to defend the United States against all enemies both foreign and domestic.

108

Summer Vacation
Nevada

Classes ended on May 29, 1871, and the Caldwell family headed west to Virginia City, Nevada. We packed only personal items as we now had western clothes waiting for us at the ranch. We boarded a train in Annapolis, Maryland and changed trains in Washington. Then we retraced our train trip across the country in 1869. We arrived in Virginia City 12 days after we left Annapolis and we were all exhausted. It was June 10 th and we slept most of the following day. James and Ruth began to trail ride the next day with Corene Wilson. Carol, Louise and I rode into Johnstone and talked for a few minutes with Karen Templeton Peters, Marshal was not home. Karen told us the good news that they were expecting their first child sometime in the Spring.

"I am sorry, Carol, but I will not be working at the school this summer as I usually do, my doctor has said to take it easy and I plan to do just that. I will work here at home some and we can spend some time together going through my teaching things that you might want to keep. The school board will not let an expecting woman teach. I will be dismissed as soon as the chairman finds out Marshal and I are going to have our baby."

"That hardly seems fair, Karen." Louise said.

"I know, but Marshal and I knew this when we planned on having a family."

"Would you consider tutoring, again?"

"When the baby is born, that will be the only thing open to me as a teacher, Mrs. Caldwell."

"Would you consider coming back to us on a full time basis, if you did not have to leave Johnstone?"

"Yes, I would! What did you have in mind?"

"Jason and I have talked about a private school here in Johnstone for college preparatory students. At present these students have to travel into Virginia City to get second level schooling in the public schools. Why not arrange for a few to get their second level here in Johnstone? You can begin as the head mistress with teaching duties and if it takes off like we think it will, you can be the principal, full time."

"Oh, I would like that very much. Marshal was wondering what to do with me after the baby is born and school starts here in Johnstone."

"We are here to help in any way that we can. Jason and DD will begin construction of the Johnstone Lodge this summer and this should bring new people into town. What do you think, Jason. Can we find someplace for Karen to open a small private school?"

"I will let the town marshall and head of CI Western Security find us a place. After all he has keys to every building in town, right Karen?"

"He will know of something that we can rent. Carol and I will be busy getting the place in shape to teach students, I will supervise with my feet up and Carol can tell the workmen what to do."

"Oh, that will be fun!" Carol was beaming.

"Can Carol stay with you during the week, Karen? She would be a great help to you and Marshal this summer." Louise had that look in her eye.

"Oh, that would be wonderful. Would you like that, Carol?"

"Yes Ma'am!"

We left a happy Mrs. Peters and began looking for the town marshall. We found him in DD's office. "Carol is over with your wife, Eugene. They have something for you to do, if you can."

"What is that, Cap'n?"

Louise took over. "We heard about what the school board policy is about women having babies. I think that is way out of date and probably, illegal as well. Who do they think got them the teachers that they have! Jason did with his connections at Iowa State Normal School, that is, who!" She was working herself up.

"Eugene, we offered to employ your wife as head mistress of a new second level school that Louise is planning to build here in Johnstone. She has not checked with DD yet to see if a second school building is feasible, but we think it might be. The problem is we are already under construction with the Johnstone Lodge and DD will need to find another construction crew for the school. Can you find Karen a temporary storefront or other building that she could begin to use this fall?"

"This fall?"

"Yes, the baby is not due until spring, is it?" Louise asked.

"No, do you think it would be alright for Karen to work?"

"Of course, she is a strong, determined woman. She will rest and take care of herself and the unborn within her."

"I will ask around town. There are two possibilities that I know of now. The tanning shop has built a new place outside of town to get rid of the odors caused by curing leather. But the place may not ever be free from the stink, I am not sure about putting school kids in there. The other would be better.

It is above the dry goods and public bath house over on Orchard Street. It was supposed to be boarding rooms for rent but it never got off the ground with the new hotel built a few years ago."

"Good, let Karen know what you find and she will use Carol and some others to get it ready for fall." Louise was smiling.

I looked at DD and said, "What does the Lodge site look like?"

"It has been graded with scoops and horses as soon as the spring thaw let them on site. The trenches for footings have been dug and they have been filled with stone from up on the ridge. Herman, the German, says this is the best for the yearly freezing and thawing that occurs in this part of Nevada. We will begin to mortar the cut stone for the basement walls tomorrow. You and Louise might like to ride out there and watch them. These masons from China are something else."

"You hired masons from China?"

"No, they are from California. Some came off the railroads when that was finished and some have experience in city building in San Francisco. We are building the first project in Johnstone or Virginia City that is more than three stories high, the locals are scared to touch it. But if your ancestors built the Great Wall of China, a little building like a lodge does not phase you."

"Can they read blueprints? Can Herman communicate with them?"

"Yes, most understand English. A few are multilingual and they understand Herman in English or German. It is funny to watch them and Herman. When Herman gets mad or excited he reverts back to his German and they answer him in German. The first time that happened, Herman did not even notice that he had switched from English to German. His favorite comment now is, 'Mine Got, dis vorkers ish schmart!'"

"So where will we be at the end of the summer?"

"You should see all the exterior stone walls and the wooden floor framing in place. There will not be interior walls in place or stairwells, it will be a dangerous place for kids, so keep James and Ruth away form there unless one of us is with them."

"When will the roof be framed?"

"We will put down the sub-flooring on each story and then we are free to begin the roof members. As soon as the roof is framed we will put on the permanent roofing materials that you will chose and it will be what they call 'dried in'."

"Dried in?"

"Yes, we can work through the winter on some of the inside items like room and hallway framing."

"When do we have finished hotel?"

"Probably two years. This is a big project. The biggest undertaking in the western United States."

"In two years we can open for guests?"

"Probably, depends on how the grounds and support buildings are coming."

"Support buildings?"

"Yes, your master plan calls for hotel stables which will contain the carriages which will transport guests from the railhead onto the lodge property. Also, guests may rent riding horses or a private horse and buggy to explore on their own. Some guests will want to hunt or fish and a separate sportsman building is being provided where you can learn how to shoot or fly cast, for example. Gear of all types will be available for sale or rent. Several smaller buildings will be used for storage, material handling and the like. In all the complex will contain over a half a million square feet of commercial space. Your guests will live, play, eat and sleep all on the same complex, most will check in for a month at a time. Nothing else will exist like it in the United States."

"Oh, Jason, we will be in the poor house over this project!"

"Not at all, Louise." D.D. explained, "The windfall profits pouring in from your western holdings will all go to pay taxes unless they are reinvested and soon. This project came along at just the right time. Jason had a very good idea when he decided to build the lodge before anything else here in Nevada."

Louise and I left DD's office shaking our heads and wondering when God might blink his eye and all this would be just a wonderful pipe dream and be blown away in the wind. The summer raced by and we found the five of us back on the train headed east.

109
History of Naval Tactics
Fall 1871

Jason walked to his first class of the new school year and greeted a mixture of new and returning cadets and Midshipmen. "Welcome to another year at Annapolis. You have signed up for 302 History of Naval Tactics, make sure you are in the right section so I can give you an idea of what this course is about. The science of arranging combinations, groupings, movements and the methods for handling ships and other weapons is called naval tactics. The art of carrying these plans forward is no different than army infantry, field artillery or marine corps troop landings. Remember, first is the 'science' or how to do it by the textbook, and second is an art that is unique to every theater commander. Anyone can memorize how to do it, only the really few gifted commanders can offer unique sequences and often unexpected tactics that ensure victory. That is truly an art. I have watched this art performed by the best fleet commanders in the United States Navy during the Mexican War and the last war between the states. Whenever possible I will insert my direct observations of Naval Tactics and the results of battle."

"I want to set the stage for you today. Roughly speaking, tactics may be said to solve the question of 'how' a certain operation may be performed. It contains the strategy to furnish the reason 'why' it is likely to be desirable. The how and why are mutually dependent; tactics only provide for effecting conditions found desirable by strategy. And, cadets, strategy is confined to operations which are tactically practicable. In its broad sense naval tactics include the manipulation of all naval assets – the movement of a ship or a fleet, the methods of mounting guns and placing torpedo tubes, etc. In a narrower and more usual sense it is understood to mean the handling of the fleet.

With this in mind, the most important thing is to oppose the enemy fleet at the point of contact as a superior force. This may mean more powerful ships, numerical superiority, or a better arrangement for attack or receiving an attack. More powerful ships may be design, gun placement, or number of guns. Numerical superiority is obvious. You have more ships in your fleet than the enemy. And finally, the third item I just mentioned is ship arrangement. After a battle begins the ship arrangement changes and good maneuvering is the key to many battle outcomes. In your final year, you will take a course taught by Admiral Hagood and myself. We joking call it the 'battle of the Superintendents'. We are at sea with a fleet of ten sailing ships, not steam powered like today's Navy. Now Admiral Hagood has spent nearly all his years at sea, while I have sailed a desk at Naval Intelligence, Army Navy Building. So far, Admiral Hagood has never beaten me at sea. You know why? I spend most of my time as a tactician and strategist because I know I do not have the experience that he has and he is supposed to beat me. For instance, the better protected ships I will send in close action. In a mock battle, like we fight in this situation, we do not use lethal force. No grape shot is used, rock salt the same diameter is substituted. If you get hit with rock salt it will not kill you but it will take off some skin. Cannon rounds are replaced by shot sided bags filled with white wash and will leave a giant stain on whatever it hits, and so on. Battle damage is easy to see by the battle judge or referee. If I have a ship with a heavy bow or stern cannon and gun placement, I will make sure it is directed for maximum coverage and referee scores. Even when we change ships for the next battle the outcome is the same, my ships score more direct hits. You all will remember from your first course from me that we covered the battle tactics of the Galley Period where ships rowed to battle with hundreds of oarsmen. Then sails were used to drive the ships into battles. The battle tactics of today most resemble the Galley Period and not the Sail Period because steam, like manual power, enables any sort of combination of ships to be made and kept with reasonable precision. And, of course, the development of signaling has added to the facility of affecting these combinations, though the most experienced naval officers believe, that after a fleet action has begun, the changes in formation should be simple and few in number."

"Let me give you some blackboard examples. There are three principle formations; *line, column and echelon*. I will use a small fleet of twelve ships."

[12] [11] [10] [9] [8] [7] [6] [5] [4] [3] [2] [1]

"This gentlemen is called a line. You divide the fleet into **squadrons** like so:"

[12] [11] [10] [9] [8] [7]   and   [6] [5] [4] [3] [2] [1]
2 nd Squad.   1st Squad.

"In this manner you can send signals to either squadron. Each squadron is divided into **divisions** like this:"

[12][11][10]   [9][8][7]   [6][5][4]   [3][2][1]
4 th   3 rd   2 nd   1 st

"Or **sections** like this:"

[12,11] [10,9] [8,7] [6,5] [4,3] [2,1]
6th   5th   4th   3rd   2nd   1st

"A section can never be smaller than two ships. Ships fight in pairs, never alone. In the various navies of the world the subdivisions of a fleet are different. In some navies, ships fight in threes instead of pairs. In the US, a fleet consists of two or more squadrons, a division is usually half a squadron, which consists of five or more ships and sections which are two ships. The numbering of ships in a line is from right to left because John Paul Jones was left handed and that is the way he drew his battle plans."

"Now we will look at the column formation.

[1]
[2] sec. 1
                    } 1 st Division
[3]
[4] sec. 2
                                        } 1 st Squadron
[5]
[6] sec. 3
            } 2 nd Division   } Fleet
[7]
[8] sec. 4

[9]   } 2 nd Squadron
[10] sec. 5
            } 3 rd Division
[11]
[12]sec. 6

You will notice that John Paul was not dyslexic because he numbered from top to bottom."

"And finally, I think we have time for me to diagram the signals used to form each of these formations before our time is up, today. For tomorrow, I want each of you to bring to class the following variations of these three formations. They are: line indented, column indented - inverted order, double column, column squadron right - echelon squadron left, form column from line, squadron - counter form to line from double columns. It would be a good idea to find the signals for these also."

"Signals used in the Sail Period were for daytime use only and were flags raised from the signal mast. These flags were either square, shallow tail or pendent with special markings or colors. The use of flags for signals is wide spread and is of ancient origin. The Venetians used signal flags and there is good reason to believe that simple signals of this type were used on land in ancient times. In 1856, the British Government devised a system of signals which has been adopted by all maritime nations. The flags are hoisted singly or, in combinations of one, two, three or four. One-flag at a time signals are important, two-flags are urgent, three flags are normal communication and four flags at a time signify geographical positions such as seaports, islands, bays and a vessels distinguishing numbers. The numbering flags can be found in the American signal code book published by the Hydrographic Office of the Navy Department and is divided into three parts."

"And now my favorite time of class, the last ten to fifteen minutes are devoted to my experiences with today's lecture. I was a Farragut's Aide in the Mexican War. David Farragut was ......

110
Presidential Conventions
1872

There were three nominating conventions in 1872, plus one pre-conference for liberal Republicans. The pre-conference was called by Horace Greeley. Horace had been, for many people, the most famous editor in the United States. He founded the New York Tribune, and his forceful power of expression made that journal a strong factor in the politics of the country. He was a man of great simplicity, honest, a vigorous fighter with his pen, a theoretical farmer, as opposed to cutting down trees as did Prime Minister Gladstone of England. He was impetuous and quick tempered sometimes finding relief in profanity and with a hand- writing so execrable that few could read it without special instruction.

Greeley was one of the kindest hearted of men. He lost thousands of dollars through loans of money to friends. As soon as the war ended, his hatred of slavery and rebellion changed to charity for those that had been engaged in upholding the two. It has been reported how ready he was to become one of the bondsmen of Jefferson Davis. He opposed the severe measures, that the Grant Administration used in reconstruction, with so much earnestness that the two became foes. In January 1872, he and others who opposed the drastic measures in Missouri, issued a call for a national convention in Cincinnati. The Tribune ardently supported the movement, and was joined by several other influential journals. Those that were dissatisfied with the Grant policy, acted with them. Senator Summer proposed an amendment to the Constitution, by which a President should be ineligible for a second term, and many of those known as active Republicans openly declared that if Grant were nominated for a second term, they would not support him. The members of the pre-convention set the date of May 1, 1872, as the official convention date for the new party.

Greeley became the embodiment of the new party and called themselves the, "Come-outers". He was placed in nomination for the Presidency along with Gratz Brown, Governor of Missouri as the candidate for Vice President. The platform declared for general amnesty in the South, local self government and the abolition of all military authority as superseding civil law. A great deal of corruption had crept into the civil service, which was denounced and declaration was made against a second term for any President of the United States.

The Republican convention assembled in Philadelphia, June 5, 1872, and renominated General Grant with Henry Wilson, of Massachusetts, as the second place on the ticket. The platform favored civil service reform and perfect equality in the enjoyment of all civil, political, and public rights throughout the country. It sustained the President's Southern policy, though insisting that State governments should be allowed to act independently, so far as practicable.

The Democratic convention met in Baltimore, July 9, 1872, and accepted the platform and candidates of the *Come-outers*. This was not done immediately and the discussion at the convention dragged on for days.

"Mister, Speaker. The great state of South Carolina wishes to be heard on the proposal to support Horace Greeley for President."

"The delegate from South Carolina is recognized."

"Mister Speaker, members of the convention, some of you know me. My name is, Robert Caldwell. A member of the Caldwell family has attended every Democratic Convention since the Whigs. What has the world come to? The Republicans have nominated a life long Democrat, General Grant, for their ticket. While, we consider nominating a life-long opponent of everything we Democrats stand for. I propose that we reconvene the convention to consider an alternative to what some of you are willing to support. Let us come together in Louisville, Kentucky, on September 3, 1872, and nominate two men for the Democrat Ballot to be printed in October."

The convention was moved and two names were selected for the ballot in November. Charles O'Conner and Jason Caldwell. Neither campaigned for the office since the time was so short before the election. The election was a landslide victory for President Grant despite the efforts of Greeley in the campaign. Greeley carried only 6 states, all southern, while Grant received the votes of 31 states, and 286 of the 366 electoral votes cast. Grant's victory had a majority of 760,000 popular vote. O'Conner and Caldwell carried the State of Maryland, with an overwhelming vote cast from the Annapolis area of the State.

111
The Naval Academy
1872-73

The third year of teaching at the Academy (1872-73) began with the sad news that Rachael Mason's father had died suddenly in Arlington, Virginia. Sam moved his family into the house with Rachael's mother and he faced a major decision in his life. He did not want to commute from Arlington to Annapolis and be away from his family for long periods of time. He and I talked on the telephone between his office in the basement of the Army Navy Building and the new Naval Institute Building at the Academy or at my home office.

"Admiral, I do not think we will ever move our family to Annapolis."

"I accept that, Sam. You are still an employee of CI, would you like to work for Monty Blair in DC?"

"No, Sir. I think I will accept the President's offer to rejoin the USMC. I will work for Major Tom Schneider here in the Army Navy Building."

"Major, I thought Tom was a Colonel? How is Tom? I have not heard from him in a long time."

"He and Beth are fine, Admiral. They will always be a marine family. His rank was reduced after the war, just like everyone else that stayed in the service. My rank would not be Major either as the President promised two years ago. The best I could hope for would a warrant officer or Master Gunnery Sergeant. Tom asked about Jerome Lewis, the other day. How is he?"

"We see Jerome and his family whenever we vacation in Bermuda, usually Christmas and Easter breaks. I have not taught summers and we go to Seneca Hill or Virginia City every summer now. My life is set into a comfortable rut. I envy you starting a new life experience, Sam."

"You do?"

"Yes, I do. I have always enjoyed the challenges that face us when we have an exciting career."

"Your present career is not exciting or challenging, Admiral?"

"Being a paper pusher was never what I enjoyed, Sam. The Superintendent of the Naval Institute is mostly an honorary thing that I do part-time. Oh, did I tell you James has been accepted here at Annapolis?"

"He will make a fine officer, Sir."

"Sam, take as much time as you need in the basement there. As far as I am concerned we can keep that office open forever. You can collect documents from the Navy and review them for possible storage in the Institute. It looks like Grant will be elected again and the job there will be secure for the next four years, at least."

"Thank you, Sir. I will talk to Rachael and explain the two options. I enjoy collecting and going through the documents here, Sir. I will let you know."

"Goodbye, Sam."

"Goodbye, Sir."

112

Grant Challenges USDF
March 1873

In his second inaugural address, President Grant took a firm stand in favor of the newly freed slaves' civil rights. He insisted that no federal executive control would be exercised in the South which would not be exercised in the North. He pledged himself to do all he could to restore good feeling between the sections. And as a start to that end he was calling for the abolishment of the United States Development Foundation which he claimed had been providing funds for only the recovery of the states back into the Union or the development of territories to qualify to become states. Now that all the southern states were readmitted, he reasoned that funding should be made available to all the states within the Union or none at all.

When the inaugural address was printed in the papers, the White House received several angry letters. The first was from Greenville, Tennessee, the office of USDF presently directed by Andrew Johnson, the 17th President of the United States. In Andrew's normally blunt language, he asked President Grant if he understood the aim and purpose of the foundation.

"It seems odd to me that you would criticize a member of your own administration for his philanthropy. You would be better served to examine your own house and rid the scandals that have become common place during your first four years in office. Caldwell International is beyond reproach and its CEO is doing you a favor by being the Superintendent of the Naval Institute. I cannot think of a better way to drive him from the service of his country than by your stupid appraisal of USDF. If it was not your appraisal, then it is time to fire the one who made it."

The second letter was more to the point. It was from the combined territorial governors of the United States. "Have you lost your mind? As governors we depend upon the funding from USDF to complete the applications required for statehood. The federal government is good at giving us a list of mandates that must be met, but without any funding what-so-ever to meet these mandates. If USDF is abolished, we hereby resign our appointments as territorial governors."

The third letter was from the Democratic Party headquarters, Washington City. "Before you abolish USDF, try looking hard at the following:

1. Credit Mobilier of America Scandal
2. Oakes Ames Bribery of America Congressmen
3. Pinchback Scandal of federal representatives
4. Rioting in New Orleans
5. Civil War in Arkansas

These are real problems that need addressing and you are attacking a non-governmental foundation that is funding what you are incapable of recognizing."

Hundreds of letters poured into the White House and President Grant called his cabinet together and asked, "Who here knows what the Credit Mobilier of America is?"

"Mr. President, I have the background on that for you." His then Attorney-General, one of five who served in his White House, handed him a stack of papers for him to read.

"Boil this down for me, I do not want to read a book."

"Yes, Sir. The Credit Mobilier of America was founded in 1859 as the 'Pennsylvania Fiscal Agency.' In March, 1865, under its new name it made a contract with the Union Pacific Railroad. T. C. Durant was the head of Credit Mobilier. Mr. Durant devised a system whereby he double billed the railroad and the company nearly failed. He sold the company to Oakes Ames, a Republican representative from the State of Massachusetts. In order to get the railroad built on time, Ames distributed 30,000 shares of stock, worth 9 million dollars as bribes among his fellow Republicans in Congress, both the house and senate."

"Oh, my God. What did we do about that?"

"Nothing, Sir. It came to our attention during the campaign for re-election. We believed that the exposure of the scandal would greatly strengthen the canvas of votes for Greeley. Horace was already pointing out the Tammany Organization Scandal and the Tweed frauds."

"Well, you thought wrong, Mr. Ackerman, I want your resignation on my desk by the end of today."

"As you wish, Mr. President."

"I wish I could find a competent Attorney-general."

His cabinet rose to leave the room. "I am not done here yet, gentlemen. What about this colored supporter of the Republican Governor Warmouth of Louisiana, a Mr. Hunchback."

"Pinchback, Sir." Said Hamilton Fish.

"Well, what the hell happened? How did it involve federal employees?"

"Federal election watchers in Louisiana declared that Pinchback's election as President of the Louisiana State Senate was illegal. A Democrat, Carter, was elected speaker of the house in Louisiana. Warmouth was arrested for state fraud of federal funds. His Lieutenant Governor, Dunn, died. Carter tried to take the Governor's chair and was also arrested by state officials for conspiracy to commit fraud of state funds."

"My God, what is wrong with these people?"

"It looks worse than it is, Mr. President."

"But these were Republicans! It reflects on all of us. I wish I had never mentioned USDF in my inaugural address, I already fired that dumb son-of-bitch who put it in."

"I know, Mr. President, but the riots in New Orleans have been stopped and the Arkansas State problem is not really a civil war."

"Have people died?"

"Yes, Mr. President."

"Then it was a civil war to them and their families, I am surrounded by idiots!" And the purging of the cabinet began a new round. The President came to the Naval Academy and met with Jason Caldwell and gave him his assurance that nothing would be done to encourage anything against the fine work being done by President Johnson and the USDF.

113

History of Naval Engagement
First Course 402

As promised to Sam Mason, Naval History 402 was written and approved by the commandant of midshipman for the fall semester of 1873. The first part of the course would be taught on campus and the second part at sea. I was diagraming a classic battle fought September 5, 1781 between the French (De Grasse) and the British (Graves) off Cape Henry. I had drawn the outline of the Chesapeake, with the York and James Rivers. "De Grasse had his fleet split between himself about here in the middle of the Chesapeake," as I drew a circle without looking and said, "Admiral De Barras was down here off Cape Henry," I drew another smaller circle. "There were French Frigates here outside Yorktown blocking Cornwallis. Everything was fine until the British fleet was sighted coming out of the North East from New York." I looked up and President Grant had tiptoed into the back of the lecture hall and found a seat. I dropped my chalk into the board tray, turned and bellowed, "Officer on deck!"

The senior class was so surprised that they leaped to their feet and faced forward at attention. They probably thought the Commandant of the Midshipmen or Superintendent Hagood was in the room. "Today, class we have a real treat. The Commander-in-chief of the United States Armed Forces is in our classroom. He even outranks Admiral Hagood. May I present, the President of the United States. Mr. President, if you would be so kind as to take the front of the class, and tell us about your naval engagements with Admiral Foote on the Mississippi, Ohio and Tennessee Rivers." I waited for the President to walk down the aisle, shook his hand and sat in one of the front seats.

"Thank you, Admiral Caldwell, I suppose this is a history class and the actions from the Civil War are now history, so here goes. I was a colonel from an Illinois volunteer regiment when the war broke out. I was stuck in Missouri and later the Cairo, Illinois, area to oversee the Ohio, Cumberland and Tennessee River Basins. I would still be a colonel stuck in Cairo, if it was not for Admiral Caldwell here. He has probably not told you much of what he did in the Civil War. He was the supreme commander for the western theater of war. I got a letter from the war department that changed my life.

You will be receiving orders from this department identical to those suggested by Admiral Caldwell, his message to us is set forth for you to read and understand. You are to prepare for Commodore Foote and his flotilla and follow the order of attack as planned by Admiral Caldwell.

Edwin Stanton
Secretary of War

"As your instructor here today was writing us, Foote and I were advancing on Fort Donelson with his iron clads, gun boats and towed boats full of marines. Fort Donelson was not a quickly constructed pile of dirt and the stone walls stayed intact while the iron clads could not make any penetration. The cannon fire from the fort put the Essex out of the fight with 42 killed. In sharp fighting, Foote's marine force was driven backward as I watched through my field glasses. I ordered a counterattack by my army forces, this caught the Confederate defenders out in the open and sent them reeling back into the fort. These Confederate forces were led by General Gideon Pillow and when he reported what had happened to the fort commander, John Floyd, he was shaken. I knew Pillow was a political appointee and Foote knew that an arrest warrant waited for Floyd. As Foote and I discussed how to take the fort with our combination of forces, two things happened. Nathan Forrest, a Confederate cavalry officer ordered his men to mount and break through the lines to protect the supply depot at Nashville. During this action, both Floyd and Pillow deserted in the face of the enemy to save themselves. Command now rested with Simon Buckner. He decided to request the terms of surrender from the combined Union forces.

I replied with the following, which was to make me famous: Sir: Yours of February 16, 1862, proposing armistice and appointment of commissioners to settle terms of the capitulation, is received. No terms other than Unconditional Surrender can be accepted. I propose to move immediately upon your works. This was in my orders from Admiral Caldwell and I did not think anything of the unconditional surrender demand. The fall of Fort Donselson was front page news and the reporters decided that my initials stood for, Unconditional Surrender. General Buckner was quoted as saying the initials stood for, Unchivalrous and Sanctimonious.

"The reason I came to Annapolis today is to make a public apology to my former commander, Admiral Caldwell, sitting in the front row of this lecture hall. I did not check my facts before opening my mouth again, and it got me in trouble with a man that I admire and have admired over the years. As the Superintendent of the Naval Institute here in Anapolis, Admiral Caldwell, reports directly to the President of the United States. He is not dependent upon funds from the Academy, the Department of the Navy or even the War Department. His funding comes directly from the Congress through my budget process. I want to assure all you Midshipmen who have worked so hard and long at collecting documents and placing them here in the Institute, that your efforts are appreciated. And as long as I am your commander-in-chief, the Naval Academy will always have the support from the White House that it deserves."

President Grant walked back down the aisle to a standing ovation from the members of my class. I was still sitting in my seat and did not hear the lecture hall door close. I rose from my seat and said, "Thank you, Mr. President, for today's lecture on the history of naval engagements."

"He is gone Sir, a student beside me said in my ear."

"Then why are they still clapping?"

"The clapping is not for him, Sir."

114

James Jason Caldwell
Naval Academy Plebe

September 1873, saw a new crop of fourth class cadets arrive at Annapolis, Maryland. One plebe was already living at the academy his address was #2 Admiral's row and he was the son of the Superintendent of the Naval Institute. He was excited about his appointment to the academy and had moved into the fourth class barracks as described by the cadet hand book pages 14-22. He was not to leave the barracks for any reason without the permission of an upperclassman. He needed permission to attend classes, walk to mess, shower and shave, and even permission to relieve himself in the head. All this went out the window when a plebe saw the President of the United States walk across the Academy grounds. They poured from the barracks onto the lawns without permission. The upperclassmen were too busy gaping at the security detail and the President to care. They began following the President en mass as he walked towards Wise Hall.

"That is where my dad teaches his naval history classes," James said to his roommate. "Why would the President be on the Academy Grounds?"

"He is probably here to see your dad, JJ." His roommate replied.

"No, they would be meeting at the house or at the Institute if President Grant were here to see him. It is someone else." They continued along with the mass of plebes, cadets and Midshipmen until a security agent held up his hand and asked them to stop.

"The President is going to attend a Naval History class this morning in Wise Hall. He will be inside about an hour and if you would like to wait to talk to him after he is through, you are welcome to do so. This many cadets cannot occupy the first floor of Wise Hall. So come back if you like and the President will shake your hand and find out how you like attending the United States Naval Academy."

By this time the Midshipmen had recovered and began herding the plebes back towards their barracks. "You heard what the officer said. Go about your business. You plebes left without permission, drop and give us twenty. Now double time back to rooms or where ever you should be at seven bells, move it, move it.

"Permission to go to class?" JJ Caldwell had grabbed his books and was trying to get back on the parade grounds.

"Permission granted."

James began a brisk pace for the classrooms directly across from Admiral's row. He watched for upperclassmen and when no one noticed, he cut across the street and into #2.

"Mom, Mom. President Grant is on the grounds. He went to see someone in Wise Hall. Is Dad still here? He will want to know."

"James, calm down. The President stopped here first, but I had to tell him that your father is teaching in Wise Hall."

"The President came to see Dad?"

"Yes, your father reports directly to the President."

"Wow. Dad must be in some kind of trouble. What is Dad's classroom number?"

"James, you can not just walk into your Dad's classroom. You have to have permission."

"Got it. I will be right back."

James ran out the rear door of #2 and crossed along the rear to #1, his Uncle Ben's house. He knocked until a steward answered the door. James did not wait for the steward to ask a question, he said. "The President of the United States is on the grounds, is the Superintendent aware of this?"

"Wait here, cadet, I will see if the Superintendent is aware of the President's arrival."

Admiral, Ben Hagood, out of uniform, came rushing to the back door. "JJ, is this some kind of prank?"

"No, Sir. I saw President Grant go into Wise Hall."

"Come inside, JJ, I do not want an upperclassman to see you at the rear of my house. Let me finish dressing and we will walk over to Wise."

In a few minutes, the Superintendent of the Naval Academy and Plebe Caldwell walked past the Presidential security and into Wise Hall. They pulled the door to 147 open quietly and tiptoed into the back of the lecture hall. In front of the class, was the President telling the seniors, "The rest of my story can be found in the Naval Institute Building here on campus. Look for messages sent to: Edwin Stanton from Commander Western Naval Theater, subject, end of naval campaign to free Mississippi and Tennessee River Basins. In one of these messages you will find a recommendation from Admiral Caldwell for my promotion from one star to three stars - an almost unheard of thing, even in war time war is in its simplest terms.'"

"The reason I came to Annapolis today is to make a public apology to my former commander. I did not check my facts before opening my mouth again, and it got me in trouble with a man that I admire and have admired over the years. As the Superintendent of the Naval Institute here in Annapolis, Admiral Caldwell, reports directly to the President of the United States. He is not dependent upon funds from the Academy, the Department of the Navy or even the War Department. His funding comes directly from the Congress. I want to assure all you Midshipmen who have worked so hard and long at collecting documents and placing them here in the Institute, that your efforts are appreciated. And as long as I am your commander-in-chief, the Naval Academy will always have the support from the White House that it deserves."

President Grant walked back up the aisle towards Superintendent Hagood and James Caldwell. As he passed he said, "Superintendent Hagood, JJ, nice to see you both this morning." He did not stop walking until he had picked up his security detail in the hallway and made his way out onto the steps of Wise Hall. Here he stopped and raised his hands above his head and said in a clear voice, "Cadets and Midshipmen line up, I want to shake the hands of the future United States Naval Officer Corps." He moved slowly along the line, shaking hands and asking questions. He answered questions when he could, laughed with the cadets and joked about coming to Annapolis to escape the "madhouse, called the White House." He was making his way towards a waiting carriage, opened the door himself and sat down to be driven to the train station.

Three people stood watching from the top of the steps to Wise Hall, two Admirals and a first year cadet ,called JJ.

"JJ, what are you doing out of barracks without permission?" His dad asked.

"He has the permission of the Superintendent, Admiral Caldwell. I would have missed the whole thing if JJ had not shown some initiative and come to my house."

"You went to Admiral Hagood's house?"

"Yes, Sir. I went to our house first, but you were not home."

"JJ, you can not come to Admiral's row every time you want to, you have to have permission. That is how the system works. You have ten demerits to work off before tomorrow. Dismissed, Plebe."

"Aye, aye. Sir."

James mixed in with the group of plebes that had talked to the President and disappeared across the lawns of the Academy.

"What am I going to do with him, Ben. He thinks he runs the place."

"Scary thought, he is going to be running the place before we know it, Jason. These young men are not like those of us who showed up in '37. They are a new breed, determined to do better than those that came before them. Some will die young in the service to their country, I pray JJ, is not one of them. He is so much like you, Jason. If I had a son, I would want him to be just like James."

"Thank you, Ben." Was all I could manage to say.

Ben and I walked across the street towards #1 and #2. I carried my briefcase full of unfinished notes for that day's lecture. "I enjoy teaching more than I thought I would, Ben"

"We will be here until Grant finishes his term, after that, the new president will select replacements, that is how the Navy works, Jason."

"I have tried to finish my Navy Career a number of times, first after James Buchanan left office, second after Abraham Lincoln died, third after Andrew Johnson left office. Maybe I can get away after US Grant leaves, who knows?"

"Maybe the new guy will ask you to be Secretary of the Navy."

"If you are the new guy, Ben, I will gladly be your secretary! Are you still on for the lecture of the Battle of Mobile for tomorrow? You were the one in command, I think the Midshipmen will appreciate your observations."

"I will be there!"

The next day Ben Hagood was in rare form.

"Let me begin my lecture of the history of naval engagements by saying, the Battle of Mobile was ordered by Jefferson Davis. Upon hearing the news of the CSS victory from Charleston, Davis said ...."

"The second half of this course is spent at sea, Admiral Caldwell will command a squadron of five ships from this period of naval history. And those lucky enough to be assigned to my squadron, will hunt down and destroy the Caldwell flotilla according to the tactics learned in your third year of study, primarily 303 Naval Tactics. Gentlemen, you are the first class ever at the Naval Academy to be engaged in this sort of training. I did not get training of this sort and neither did Admiral Caldwell. We learned it from Admiral Farragut at the battles of New Orleans and Mobile."

115

Johnstone Lodge
Summer 1874

The Caldwells were headed to the horse ranch in Nevada as soon as the academic term was over May 31, 1874. This year James again would not travel with them, he was scheduled to take his second summer cruise. It had been two years since James had visited Nevada and three summers since the building of Johnstone Lodge had begun. It was finished. Jason had used his old mailing list from when he was the National Affairs advisor for Presidents Buchanan and Lincoln to make a select mailing of the Johnstone Lodge Grand Opening. The response had been slow at first and then a funny thing happened, JP Morgan wanted to buy his own penthouse suite. Once this was announced that the named suite "Morgan" had just sold for two million dollars, the feeding frenzy started. Soon nearly all the suites were sold. Transportation to get to Nevada was still by train, it still took more than a week unless you were coming from California. John Nesbitt Jr. came the most often, his family was the closest. The rich and the powerful could rub elbows with each other except for the Caldwells, they still lived in the modest ranch house designed by Corene Wilson nearly ten years ago. Ruth still rode her horses and her little sister, Carol, still worked summers at the newly constructed second level finishing school for young girls called Johnstone Academy. The first three graduates would be ready next spring and then a steady stream of young women would be making applications to colleges throughout the west.

Louise had talked Jason into saddling two horses so they could ride the trails around the ranch. Jason was a sailor. His first choice of travel was by ship, it was still the fastest way to get from point A to point B across any body of water. When land travel was required he consented to a train that had sleepers, dining cars, a club car for drinks and a private family sized compartment. For shorter land travel, he preferred a large four or six horse drawn carriage. A single horse with a saddle was at the bottom of the list.

Here he was, on horse back, riding towards Johnstone. He and Louise were not on the road, which any sane person would use, no, they were going across country and he was sure that in a matter of an hour, they would be hopelessly lost. Louise was chatting away.

"Do you know that we do not get enough exercise, Jason. Ruth and Corene take this ride nearly every day while we push papers around a desk."

"Do you know where we are going, Louise?"

"Yes, Ruth told me exactly which trails to take, relax and follow my horse and stop complaining, will you?"

"I am not complaining. Oh, my, look at that Louise!" We had come out of a small stand of pines and a clear vista opened before us. Across the valley stood the Johnstone Lodge. Its ten storied edifice looked like a castle in Europe built into the mountain side. The gray-white stone shone in the sunlight as clouds cast shadows and they passed across it face like frowns on the face of a mountain giant. The windows bounced the sunlight off the surrounding ponderosa pines which looked like two giant hands opened in prayer before the almighty. As our gazes traveled from the penthouses down to the ground floor we could just make out the arrival of a carriage from the railroad delivering our guests for a week or more stay. Rooms and suites were not rented by the night at Johnstone Lodge.

The carriage disgorged its passengers and a doorman helped the new arrivals into the giant entrance which contained a large stone fireplace and leather covered casual furniture to rest their weary bones upon. The carriage continued on around the entrance to either leave the 6,400 acre property to make a return run to the train station or to return to the stables, we could not see from our vantage point.

"How many employees are there now at Johnstone Lodge, Jason?"

"I have no idea. We can check with Corene, she has all the data on Johnstone Lodge in her files. I do know that over a hundred families have moved into Johnstone in the last four months, I would think that most of them work at the lodge. We under estimated the number of moderate income new houses to build in Virginia City. They are all sold and requests for more are keeping DD and his crews busy. We need to buy residential tracts of land here in Johnstone and do the same thing. It is a never ending process."

"What is? The building of houses or what to do with the income generated from silver in Nevada and oil in Pennsylvania?"

"Yes, and yes. A nice problem to have, by the way."

"Jason?"

"Yes, Louise."

"Did you ever think you would be this rich?"

"I have been as rich as I ever will be the day I met you."

"Oh, Jason! You silver tongued devil, no wonder you make money. I brought a blanket and picnic with us. Do you want to eat now?"

"Yes, Ma'am!"

"Help me with the saddle bags, then. Jason, when you say buy a tract of land, what does that mean."

"A continuous flow of acres without breaks in between. For example, three farms could be for sale but they are not adjacent. That would not be worth trying to develop."

"Okay, I understand that. Before we were married and you came to Western Utah Territory where we stand now, what did you look for?"

"I did not come to Nevada. That was CI employees who were former members of my 'rapid response' unit. Matthew James and Herman Schussler stood on a spot near hear and made an offer to purchase the ten square miles across the valley that we see now."

"Herman 'the German' was a member of your 'rapid response' unit?"

"No, he was not. I think of him as a member because he was a member of corps of engineers working out of the Army Navy Building when I met him about the same time. Have I ever told you what I know about Herman?"

"No, tell me."

"Herman was born in Prussia and educated in Switzerland, or maybe the other way around. Did you know he has a doctor of engineering degree?"

"From Switzerland?"

"Yes, he has a very bright mind, Louise. He designed what he calls 'Lifts' at each end of the lodge. You have seen them, they look like giant cages with folding gates across them. That is how we moved most the heavy items from the ground floor to the upper floors. Each room, or suite, has cast iron steam radiators. Herman designed a steam plant as one of the out buildings that DD was telling us about three years ago. He designed a spur line to come into the property through a mountain tunnel unseen from the general public. We ship things by freight train into the lodge thanks to Herman. He also designed the water system that we gave to Matthew James and Connie."

"Did he design the saw mills that we gave DD and Corene?"

"Yes, he did."

"What have we given Herman and his wife, I do not know her name."

"Her name is, Gertrude. And no we have not given them anything except salary and profit shares from the water recovery and silver recovery mills that Herman designed."

"What is the cash flow from these recovery operations, Jason?"

"Considerable, you are now looking at what paid for the construction of that magnificent piece of architecture across the valley."

"Oh, my, God. Jason, we have to do something for Herman and Gertrude, the lodge cost millions to construct, equip, furnish and insure."

"What did you have in mind?"

"What do you think the water recovery mills and property that they sit on are worth"

"Close to a million."

"Done, have the CI lawyers draw up the deed of transfer in the names of Herman and Gertrude Schussler."

"Yes, Ma'am."

"How many children do they have? I have met Avis and her husband and their child, Frederick and his wife and child ....."

"Herman has 13 children and grandchildren, Louise."

116
Battle of the Superintendents
Atlantic Ocean

It was time for the classroom theory to be put to the test. Ben and I had been looking forward to this part of the course entitled, "History of Naval Engagements". It was two weeks before the summer cruises began between Annapolis and Bermuda and I left for summer vacation in Nevada. The entire Caldwell flotilla had been brought up from St. George with minimum crews, except for a few special sailors. John Butler had talked Robert Whitehall into taking a two week vacation with the "Annapolis Boys" as he called us. They had visited with Samuel Clemens who was staying at the Caldwell Inn trying to finish his next book and he said he would not miss it. He had always wanted to be something else besides a Mississippi River boat Captain and he asked Captain Jacob and the other Caldwell Shipping and Trading sea captains if they would mind if he were the honorary fleet Admiral. They chuckled and said they would be interested in seeing how that could be done. The USS *Nelson* and *Somerset* were rigged with six main sails which made them brigantines. The USS *Jersey* and *Spitfire* were fully operational, antique Brigs with ten sails and ordinance from the Civil War. The USS *Congress, Philadelphia, Cold Harbor* and *Providence* were fully armed Snows. A Snow could carry considerable more sails that a Brig or Brigantine. With all twenty-two sails set, this made the *Cold Harbor* the fastest ship in the flotilla. The USS *New Haven* and *Trumbull* were Ketches from the Mexican Campaign. Normally, these were the fastest ships because of their shallow draft and sail to weight ratios.

These ten ships and invited guests would form an historical fleet. The fleet would be under the command of Admiral Mark Twain. The first squadron would be Ben Hagood's and the second squadron would be mine. The first week was spent in practicing the various formations that we had studied in class. Ten sailing vessels in a line was a pretty picture right out of a history book. Each of the ship's captains were very familiar with his ships handling and the minimum crews were responsible for teaching the Midshipmen from Annapolis the science and art of sailing. The squadrons each had 1 Ketch, 1 Brig, 1 Brigantine and 2 Snows. I divided my squadron into two sections, a Brigantine and Snow in one section and a Brig, Snow and Ketch in the other. We really needed twelve ships so that we could have three sections but there were no other fully armed sailing vessels that either Ben or I knew of for purchase on the east coast.

Midshipmen were placed throughout the fleet and given various tasks to complete during the first week. The fun began when Mark Twain called everyone together and said he was changing the rules slightly for the following week. He understood that normally one squadron hunted the other and a pitched battle resulted until the referees declared a winner by attrition. In other words, the referees counted the paint smears on the vessels, sails and people to declare a winner. He thought that was rather outdated and needed to be improved upon.

"As the fleet Admiral of this exercise, I suggest that we have a blocking fleet that seals St. George Harbor. The runners will try to escape the blockade. Scoring will be done as usual."

"I object," Said Admiral Hagood to Admiral Twain, "Admiral Caldwell has an intimate knowledge of the St. George Harbor and his blocking fleet will have a tremendous advantage."

"Who said Admiral Caldwell will have the blocking fleet? I am assigning you the task of blocking the harbor since you were in command of this all along the eastern seaboard during the war. You will have 8 of the ships for the blocking exercise. Admiral Caldwell, you will have a pair of ships of your choosing from the ten available. After you have picked your pair and sailed into St. George Harbor you have five days to run the blockade. Good luck, gentlemen, shake hands and let us get this second week of instruction under way."

I returned to the *Cold Harbor* and visited with Captain Jacob. "I will not win this year. It is impossible to run a blockade of 8 ships with 2 when they know you are trying to escape."

"Maybe not Captain, which two ships is Mark giving you?

"My choice, why?"

"Remember, you still have access to everything inside the St. George Harbor including extra sets of sails. You are not trying to get in, you are trying to get out. You need to select one of the ships that can pickup and deliver the Bushnell Turtles, cans of white paint, excuse me, bombs to blowup Hagood's fleet! And anything else you can think of to score points with the referees should be added."

"In time of war, yes, anything goes. This is a classroom application. What would I be teaching my students if I do not follow the lessons taught? No, I must chose two ships and the obvious choice are the two Ketches, they are shallow draft and faster than the others in the fleet. That is why I will select the two oldest Snows to make Ben wonder what my strategy for escape may be."

"What is your strategy by picking the two oldest ships, Captain? Speed is critical in outrunning a blockade."

"If we try to escape at night, yes. We should have black sails and silent, swift running. Therefore, we should go at high noon with white sails and what appear to be slow ships."

"I do not follow, Captain."

"We have to make the blockade think of something else and pay no attention to us."

"You only have five days, Captain. You can not disguise your ships to look like something else."

"The purpose is to run past the blockade and not get our ships sunk in the process. What we need is assistance from our friends on the west end."

"You would ask the Royal Navy for help?"

"No, I would make the blockade think I was asking for and getting help from the Royal Naval Dockyards."

"How are we going to do that?"

"I am going to use the telephone and the ferry boats."

"The telephone and ferry boats?"

"Yes. During the summer, the ferries run every two hours between St. George and the west end. I want Ben's lookouts to see several of your officers and my Midshipmen making daily trips back and forth between St. George Harbor and the west end the first four days. If Ben pulls one of his ships away from the blockade, say, one of the fast Ketches, he will get a report that we are delivering and receiving packages from the British."

"That will drive him crazy, Captain. What do you need the telephone for?"

"It sure will! I will use the telephone to let the Admiral in charge of the Dockyards in on our deception and ask for his cooperation to do nothing to come to our assistance on the last day when we take the *Cold Harbor* and the *Providence* past the blockade."

"The *Cold harbor* and the *Providence*, they are oldest of the fleet."

"Yes, but not the slowest, necessarily. We will not use full sail, only enough for steerage and forward movement. We must creep up on the blocking fleet in broad daylight and sink eight ships in a period of a few minutes, or make them think they are going to be sunk."

"Ben will check for mines, torpedeos and anything else on a daily basis, usually early in the morning to make sure nothing unusual has been attached during the night. But will he think to check at noon when Fort St. Catherine begins to shell his fleet?"

"The British will never go along with that, Captain."

"Yes, they will if the smoke from the cannons appears to be coming from St. Catherine's and the splashes that are coming near his ships seem to be real cannon projectiles instead of paint for the referees to count."

"So, you do mean to use the Bushnell Turtles."

"Yes, but only to set the splash charges the night before. I do not think we can get close enough to any of Ben's ships to paint them at night. He will have lookouts posted all night watching the hulls. I wonder if he will have lookouts for anything setting real charges in the dark of night?"

"So who is going to operate the turtles that you have in the repair yards? You do not have a week."

"It will have to be cadets. Would you be willing to take four or five cadets and show them how they work? This must be done carefully because when the first charge explodes, Ben will pull his fleet back from what he thinks the cannon range is from Fort St. Catherine. At that moment we run up all the sails that we would normally use, then add a driver, ringtail, top sail and main from the Jigger Mast which we raise inside the harbor. We hope that Ben or one of his captains does not spot the added mast until it is too late. If there is no wind on the fifth and final day, then the blockade holds and Ben wins. But if there is wind that day, we turn for the open sea and stay ahead of him until the time runs out. All we have to do is stay out of cannon range."

"Captain Jason, I must congratulate on a master plan for running a blockade in broad daylight. It is like old times having you back on the *Cold Harbor*, you will always be the true captain of this ship whenever you are on board, Jason, you know that."

"I will never sail her like you do, Earl. Earl Jacobs will always be the captain of a Caldwell ship as long as he wants to sail the oceans with cargo to faraway ports. I wish I was younger to go with you."

"You are young at heart. Now go ashore and do not let the other two Admirals hear you telephone the Royal Naval Dockyards."

I took a tender with Admiral Hagood and Twain into St. George Harbor and we tied up on Water Street docks. "I have selected the *Cold Harbor* and the *Providence* for my try to run the blockade. Each day I will test the wind inside the harbor, when we have enough wind to fill the sails, I will attempt my run to freedom. If the wind fails me, then you win, Ben."

"I expected you to want the two Ketches, *New Haven* and *Trumbull*."

"You can use them to run down the two Snows as we leave the harbor, Ben. I will have my cadets try to sink the Ketches if you are foolish enough to send two against two. Remember, I have use of everything inside the harbor."

"Yes, I know. I have already set the night watch guards with orders to paint the Bushnell Turtles when they appear."

"I have already considered that and have told all my cadets that painting the hulls of your ships, at night, is not part of what we have taught them this semester. They are to paint only during daylight hours using ordinary naval ordinance. You have my word on that."

By this time, we had walked up the hill to Caldwell Place and I excused myself to make a telephone call. Mark and Ben went into the dining room.

"Operator, connect me with the Royal Naval Dockyards, please."

"One moment, Caldwell Place."

"Lieutenant Styles, may I help you?"

"Yes, Lieutenant, I am Jason Caldwell calling. I own and operate Caldwell Inn over in St. George. I am a dual British and American citizen and I am calling using the British side."

"Yes, Admiral. I know who you are, John Butler is a friend of yours, is he not?"

"Yes, he is. He lives here with his wife, Sally."

"Tell him Clyde Styles said 'hello'. Now, what can the British Navy do for their American cousins?"

"When I wear my Admiral's hat, I sometimes teach at the American Naval Academy in Annapolis, Maryland. There are ten tall sailing vessels off shore this week practicing sailing formations learned in a history class that I teach. Maybe someone has reported seeing them to you."

"Yes, Sir. You are presently off Fort St. Catherine, we can see you from there. We have daily reports by telephone from the fort on the activities."

"You have? Good, do you think any of your training cadets would like to participate this coming week?"

"Participate?"

"Yes, are there any sailing ships left in the dockyards or has the British Navy switched completely to steam powered vessels?"

"We have some older sail and single steam boiler vessels. We could not fire the boiler and I guess they would then be considered sail only."

"Excellent, on June 6 th, 5 days from now here is what I would like your cadets to do........"

"I think that would be an excellent training exercise for us. I am not the commander here, however. I will present this to my Admiral and present it in a favorable light. I think he will agree with you and I. Do you think I could grab the train over to St. George, early on June 6 th and join you on the *Cold Harbor*?"

"I think that would be an excellent idea, Clyde! Why not come a day or two early and I will put you up in the Inn and we can visit and fine tune our plan."

"I say, that is a bloody good idea! Can I call you later today or early tomorrow, Jason?"

"Call me every day at various times, I am spreading the seeds of confusion among the ships of the blocking fleet. I will be sending some of my officers and cadets by ferry boat each day with tightly wrapped empty boxes for you to store for a day, you can send back a couple of empty boxes, clearly marked, *property Royal Naval Dockyards.*"

"Admiral, no wonder, we never fare well against you Yanks. Too much diversion!"

He was laughing as I disconnected. I searched for either Ben or Mark to see if they overheard my conversation. They were both out alongside the pool enjoying a cool drink. "I will need a few things from town, I am catching the train into Hamilton, either of you want to come along?"

"No, you go ahead, Jason, it is going to be a long five days sitting outside the harbor waiting to sink your two runners."

"Tonight may be the last night you get much rest, Ben." I said with a smile.

June 2, 1874, was a listless day with little or no wind inside the harbor. I had Captain Jacob leave the docks at about 11 o'clock and creep toward the harbor entrance. The wind picked up and we set some sail and moved a couple of hundred yards out of the harbor entrance and turned for Fort St. Catherine. The blocking fleet moved upwind and turned to stop us before we reached the fort. We did an about face and returned to the harbor. June 3 rd, Ralph Emerson, the captain of the *Providence* did the same thing. The wind was a little stronger. On June 4 th, only seven ships were in the blockade formation, the *New Haven* was gone, probably following the ferry to the dockyards. On June 5 th, only six ships were in the blockade formation, the *New Haven* and *Trumbull* were both missing, probably following both the east and west bound ferries or on patrol outside the dockyards.

That night the cadets who had been practicing with the turtles made their way out of the harbor. A Bushnell Turtle is normally used for underwater repairs of Caldwell Shipping vessels. Tonight it would be used to create a major diversion. Tonight they would be dropping timed charges in front of Fort St. Catherine, these were real charges and they should go off just slightly after smoke was released from the walls of the Fort by Royal Navy Cadets. In order for this to happen we had to set the timers and alert the cadets up at the fort. We had several float targets attached so that if one was hit with a rifle shot then the timers of all the charges would begin to trigger timed explosions to simulate splashes from the fort.

About sunrise on June 6 th, seven sailing ships, vintage 1850 pulled away from the Royal Naval Dockyards and began a short sail to Fort St. Catherine. The *New Haven* on patrol outside the dockyards set every inch of sail and sped toward the blocking fleet on the east end of the islands. They arrived in plenty of time to report to Ben Hagood that seven ships had left the dockyards headed for the east end. Ben read the signals as the signal man was writing them down.

"Jason has tipped his hand. He is going to use the seven ships as a screen to run by us early this morning. Well that is a clear violation of the rules set down by Admiral Twain. Signal the flag ship and report this to Twain."

While this was being done the British fleet rounded the headland of the fort in echelon formation and came to anchor. The morning passed and nothing happened. At about noon the *Cold Harbor* and *Providence* came to the harbor entrance with minimum yards of sail for steerage, but with jigger masts raised in place.

"He is waiting for the British to move forward to set up the screen. Then he will release maximum sail and dart behind them. Look he raised the jigger mast, a good plan, but he will be disqualified by Twain."

As he finished speaking a rifle barked from the top of the *Cold Harbor*. A puff of smoke appeared from the fort and a huge splash appeared off to the right side of the USS *Spitfire* about a hundred yards away.

"What the hell does the fort think they are doing? This is a commercial harbor." Just then a second splash appeared but without the puff of smoke, they were out of order. Now splashes appeared everywhere all at once.

"What a cheap trick. Making us believe that the fort is firing on us. Well, it will not work. Signal the fleet to form a double inverted column and we will seal the front and rear of the British line and capture Jason Caldwell before he can release any sail whatsoever."

The two Snows came slowly out of the harbor and did not try to go beneath the fort as they had practiced for the last four days. As Ben Hagood's ships made an excellent change of formation to trap the British line, the two Snows released twenty-two sails and headed out to sea in a south-easterly direction. Ben saw his mistake too late.

117

Naval History 201
September 1874

This September would begin my fourth year of teaching at the Naval Academy. The last three years had flown by and in my annual review with the Commandant of Midshipmen he commented that I had never taught the second course in naval history.

"It is time that you teach each of the courses in the history department, Jason. This is probably the hardest course to teach in the curriculum, it deals with the 'Great Commanders Series'. The course is about US Navy formation under General George Washington and includes all the dead heros of the service. Can you make this interesting for the Midshipmen, Jason?"

"I served under David Farragut in the Mexican War and he served with me in the Civil War. I would like to start the series with this genuine hero of the United States Navy."

"I would start with Washington and John Paul Jones, if I were you Jason, but certainly David Farragut was the most famous of the American naval officers. I know you were close, can you tell me the day that you will tell your students about him, I would like to sit quietly in the back of the hall. Do not bellow out, 'Officer on deck', like you did with President Grant."

"I had no idea why Grant came into the lecture hall, Fred, that was the first thing that came into my head."

"Well, you know me. And you know why I am there, I never met David Farragut, our paths never crossed. I feel like I have missed something. Okay?"

"Okay, come the second meeting."

I walked into the second meeting of Naval History 201 held in Wise Hall to begin my description of the man I knew as, David Glasgow Farragut. "Good morning class, please do not jump to your feet when the Commandant walks into the back of class today. Someone complained that I let you out a few minutes early from class yesterday because it was the introduction meeting. He will be here to make sure we all stay the full hour."

There were groans from the third year students as the Commandant of Midshipmen, Naval Academy, September 1874, walked into the back of the lecture hall. And the well meaning students shouted, "Officer on deck."

Instead of siting in the back of the class, Fred Hampton, marched to the front of the hall and bellowed, "As you were." He then turned to me and shouted, "Admiral Caldwell, I understand that you were a 'wet behind the ears' graduate of West Point when you first met Admiral David Farragut. Is that correct?"

"Yes, Sir, Admiral Hampton."

"I have just been over to the Naval Institute to read every scrap of paper that I can find on that man." He pulled a large stack of paper from his tunic. "Do you have a couple of chairs back of that curtain behind you, Admiral?"

"Yes, I do. I will go and get them." The class was still standing and I heard Fred Hampton, bellow. "Be seated, y'all."

I returned dragging two captain's chairs with high backs and arm rests. Fred sat in one and I sat in the other facing each other. He began. "I found in the personnel records that David Farragut was born in 1801 in a place called Campbell's Station. Where is that, exactly?"

"I think it is near Knoxville, Tennessee, if I am not mistaken."

"So that makes him one of us, a good old southern boy! I was born in Texas, 1834. Where were you born, Admiral Caldwell?"

"On a plantation near Beaufort, 1817."

"That makes you 57? What was David Farragut doing at age 57? Do you know?"

"Yes, Sir. I helped him celebrate his birthday on July 5, 1858, aboard the USS Brooklyn."

"You served aboard the Brooklyn?"

"No, I came over from the Army Navy Building when he was in Potomac Dockyards."

"Damn, that must have been exciting?"

"No, actually I was going through a very tragic period in my life when I lost someone close to me."

The students moved forward on their seats, this was interesting. One of them raised his hand and said, "Permission to speak, Admiral?"

"Which Admiral?" Fred Hampton said, smiling.

"Caldwell, Sir."

"Go ahead, John, what was your question?"

"You know the names of your students already?"

"No, John has been with me before. Midshipman Williams, meet our guest interviewer today, Admiral Hampton, from Texas. You probably know him better as, the Commandant!"

There were giggles now from the Midshipmen and John Williams continued. "Admiral Caldwell, you served under David Farragut, the most famous American naval officer?"

"Yes, David Farragut has sailed every one of the oceans and seas on the globe. I was lucky enough to be with him for tours in most of them. I am glad I missed the Arctic and Antarctica though!"

"Maybe you should begin at the beginning of your story, Admiral Caldwell, while we listen, care to take the podium?" Admiral Hampton was smiling.

I gathered my notes and walked to the podium and said, "Commandant Hampton, thank you for helping me introduce the first lecture of Naval History 201. Midshipmen, welcome back to another session of 201. Please interrupt me with questions when things are not plain. This is a personal story about a man about my father's age who taught me most of what I know about life in the Navy. Admiral Farragut has been gone nearly four years now and I miss him every day.

I looked at my pocket watch and we were two minutes past the hour. Not a midshipman had moved from the edge of his seat. "Tomorrow, we will continue with the career of Admiral David Farragut, the first Admiral in the United States Navy to have a special rank provided for him above that of a four star." I heard a single pair of hands beginning to clap behind me. It was Commandant Hampton. I had forgotten that he was seated there, I was so into my story. The Midshipmen rose and joined their Commandant.

118
History of Naval Ordnance
Spring 1875

The cover of the 1848 United States Naval Ordnance Handbook that David Farragut wrote and that I edited was tacked to my classroom door. Each student who entered should have seen it. I had learned with very young men to trust nothing. "Welcome back to another history course at the Academy gentlemen. This is Naval History 302. If you think you are somewhere else, now is a good time to get there!" Two Midshipmen looked surprised and hurried from the classroom to find where they were supposed to be.

"The word 'ordnance' is now commonly understood to mean all cannon or heavy guns requiring a support or mounting of some form. The navy has two types of ordnance. That which is used on ships and that used by the marines which is taken from ships to be used in a land battle. Since the time that ships went to war at sea, ordnance has been there. Fire has always been a great fear aboard any ship, so the first weapon used in ancient times were fire arrows fired from one ship onto another. A bow and an arrow, is not ordnance. When barges floated on the Nile, fire arrows were used. Soon barges stayed away from each other and ways to get a fire arrow longer distances were invented. These, gentlemen, were the first use of ordnance. Some clever Egyptian, figured out if a child could design a sling shot to kill a small bird with a stone, he could use a bigger one to deliver either fire arrows or large stones against an enemy barge. These large sling shots were called 'catapults'. We would probably still be throwing stones at each other if the Chinese had not invented, and perfected, gun powder!

With gun powder came the invention of the cannon. At the beginning of the fourteenth century, cannons were used alongside catapults on ships of war. While cannons made a lot of noise, they had less actual effect on the enemy because the first cannons were wide mouthed bowls, like an apothecary's mortar. A stone was placed in the bowl and it was projected with little velocity towards the enemy. Gunnery mates preferred the use of catapults for longer distance and accuracy because catapults could be aimed, mortars could not. The modern mortar that we have on ships today has little resemblance to early cannons, only the name has stuck. The ordnance of this period had no trunnions and many did not even carriages. Some were mounted on blocks of timber to which they were lashed with no movement for aiming. Later improvements in shape were made, the bore being cylindrical with a narrow powder chamber. This made the effect of the powder gas more concentrated, the walls of the ordnance stronger and the projectile always in the same position.

The fifteenth century witnessed use of cannon and many changes. The improvements in shape continued and there was constant striving to increase size. Mortars were made as large as 18 tons and fired stones as heavy as 900 pounds. Most naval ordnance in this century were forged or cast of iron in one piece. Look on page 158 of your handbook for diagrams that indicate how early blast furnaces prepared molten iron. Page 161 shows how the molten metal was poured into molds to produce the raw shape of the cannon. The steps in the manufacture of a cannon are complete when the cannon is bored inside its barrel.

Framed carriages were made, some having the gun lashed to a hinged beam which could be altered in elevation. France made marked improvements from 1461, to 1483, in the manufacture of cannons. Trunnions were introduced, stone projectiles became obsolete and were replaced with cast iron projectiles shown on page 155. Notice that everyone assumes only round shot, called cannon balls, were used. That is not true. When ships fired at ships in battle, cannon balls were a waste of time. Chain shot was used instead, it could cut a mast in to. Bar shot was popular because it tumbled during flight and tore giant holes in ship hulls. If the ordnance was used against ground troops, as was common in the last war, grapeshot was used. Notice that the grapeshots was not just poured into the cannon. It was always in a cloth bag for loading and came apart during flight. More Confederate ground troops died on the battle field from grapeshot than any other projectile, it was deadly. Notice that other bagged projectiles were used, langrape was used to bring down the sails of opposing ships. Crossbar shot and expanding bar shot were also used against ship's riggings.

At the beginning of the sixteenth century, ordnance was generally of cast iron and as the pieces became larger, they were too heavy to use by Navy Marines in the field, so brass was introduced. Ordnance of the middle sixteenth century had handles and cascabels, you can find examples of these on page 167 of your handbook. As you read the handbook, you will see that ordnance became very ornamented and given individual names as well as complicated class designations, depending upon the size and proportion of length to caliber. During this century the field-carriage limber was introduced. Case shot and explosive shells were also introduced, but as the fuses for these had to be lighted before insertion in the barrel, many accidents happened. War veterans of this era came home without a hand. On page 171, you will see how these were made. The shells were hollow with gun powder inside the round shot. In the fifteen hundreds, ordnance was sometimes made of extreme length, for instance, 58 Calibers. It was mistakenly thought that the range increased with the length of the barrel without limit.

To increase mobility, Gustavus Adolphus brought forth his 'leather cannon' of thin copper wound with leather for strength, and afterwards, he introduced an iron 4-pounder weighing only 650 pounds. Adolphus also introduced the method of inserting the powder charge in a packet, or cartridge. This avoided the danger and loss of time due to ladling it into the gun from a powder barrel.

In 1747, the French made the important discovery that, if the earth tamping about a shell were omitted, the discharge would ignite the shell fuse. This expedited loading, removed the danger of shell missfire and increased its use. Around 1767, a Frenchman by the name of Gribeauval had his guns cast solid instead of hollow and then turned them to exact inside dimensions. This reduced clearance between shell and barrel, with the result of no loss of power, in spite of reduced barrel length and weight.

Near the end of the of the eighteenth century, carronades became popular, these are pictured on page 189. At sea, they were used more, than by marines in the field, because at close quarters their heavy projectiles with low velocity were very effective. Early in the nineteenth century, Colonel Bomford of the United States, invented the columbiad, which was an ordnance of considerable length and it was very effective in the War of 1812. It could fire at high velocities and low elevation either shot or shell. In 1856, Admiral Dahlgren of the USN, modified a British gun to perform as a ship mounted piece of ordnance, which was heavy at the breech and light at the muzzle.

Please read carefully, everything I have outlined for you in your handbooks. For tomorrow, please read the sections covering the Rodman Cast Iron Guns, Chamber's 1849 patent, Blakely's 1855, patent and Sir Armstrong of England's hydraulic pieces of ordnance."

I stopped talking and looked around the room. "How many of you have taken a course from me before?"

Several hands went up. "It is my custom to stop ten to fifteen minutes early on each lecture and tell you a story from my own experiences with the topic at hand. Close your notebooks and enjoy the following:

In October, 1857, I was on a field mission for Naval Intelligence traveling through Utah Territory with a modified Dahlgren, model 1440 Naval Deck Gun. The Dahlgren was mounted on a Butterfield Overland Mail Service wagon. The Butterfield Overland Mail Service had built way stations for the US mail to be carried from St. Joseph, Missouri to Sacramento in just ten days! The postmaster had arranged for transportation from a place called Hebron Station in South Eastern Nebraska Territory. My written orders were ....

119

Johnstone Lodge
Summer 1875

A full year away from the operations of the Johnstone Lodge proved to be instructional. So did the fact that we checked in as guests for a month instead of opening the ranch house and staying there. We wanted to get a first hand impression of what the guests got for their hundred dollars a night! We were shown to the Morgan suite on the ninth floor.

"I thought the Morgan suite was a penthouse suite?" Louise asked as we stepped off the lift.

"It is Madam. Mr. Morgan wanted you to get the full effect of what he paid for." The bellman opened the double doors to 901 and they swung open revealing a huge foyer with a center staircase directly ahead and rooms off to either side. "I shall place the bags in the bedrooms upstairs you each have a separate room. Miss Ruth, you are in the first one to the right, Miss Carol you are in the first one to the left. Admiral, you and Mrs. Caldwell are in the master. And if your son comes this month, he shall be the fourth."

We stood dumb founded at what JP had done to the place. When we furnished the lodge a year ago, we selected western motif. Lots of tanned leathers, braided rugs, earth tones and Russian antiques from California. He had removed everything and repainted every surface an egg shell white. He and his wife must have bought everything for sale in Northern Mexico because the place looked like it belonged in Monterey.

"It is absolutely beautiful, Jason. It must be nice to have the Morgan's kind of money!"

"Look, Louise, JP has left us a note."

"Read it to me, I want to see the upstairs!" and she was off with me bringing up the rear trying to read his hand writing.

"Someone is ringing the door chimes, Jason. Can you get it?"

I walked down the stairs and pulled open the door. Gertrude and Herman were standing there, smiling from ear to ear. "Captain, welcome back to Nevada. It is so good to see you again. Where are your children? Is Louise upstairs? And Gertrude was off climbing the stairs humming a German Lullaby. "Where are my three beautiful girls from the German State of Pennsylvania?"

"Herman, it is good to be back in Nevada. How are things at the mill?"

"Could be better, could be worse. You know business, Jason. I never worried about financial matters when you owned the mill. Oh, I have something for you." He reached into his pocket and withdrew a small leather box. "That is the first ounce of silver recovered from the mill after it became operational so many years ago. I kept it as a memento of the successful design for the recovery process. I would like you to have it."

"Oh, Herman. This is special to you, I cannot take this."

"What is special is the trust that you placed in me so many years ago, Jason. I have become a very wealthy man, long before you gave me the mill. My patents alone, have made me the most successful mining engineer in the west. The annual salary and profit sharing with CI are most generous. What I have just given you, is a symbol of my admiration for you."

"Thank you, Herman. CI in the west has been successful because of your efforts, not mine. The people who I sent out here in '58 are still here doing a fantastic job for me. Just look at this hotel! Your engineering has made it a masterpiece."

"I thought you were crazy when you came to me and asked me to design the steam plant and mechanical systems for this building – I truly enjoyed it. The tunnel for the train was just like a mining engineering problem."

"Herman, where are my manners? Come into the living room here and let me see if we have any schnaps."

We found it in a liquor cabinet in the corner of the room. I grabbed two aperitif glasses and poured two small schnaps.

"What is that wonderful peppermint smell?" Louise, Gertrude and the two girls were standing behind us. I had not heard them enter the room. "Pour us one of those will you, Jason?"

I reached for four more glasses, filled them and placed them on one of JP's silver serving trays. "Allow me, Madams." I passed the tray to Gertrude, Louise, Ruth and Carol. We all found seats and began a conversation. Carol was not used to liquor of any type and said, "This smells really good, but it burns all the way down!"

Louise laughed and said, "You must sip it darling, not swallow it, whole."

"Yes, if you are going to live in Pennsylvania Dutch country, you are going to have to learn how to enjoy your schnaps." Gertrude added. "Ask the Admiral why we came over here the minute we knew you had arrived." I looked confused and Herman said in German, "Tell, not ask."

Gertrude repeated herself, "Yes, tell him why we are here so early before their bags are even run up the pole." I began to laugh and soon everyone including Gertrude was giggling.

"My English is better than your German, Admiral Jason, so you just catch it."

"Watch it, I corrected her."

"Watch what?"

"Never mind. Why are you and Herman here, Gertrude?"

"We have grandchildren that go to school here in Johnstone."

"Yes."

"The girls have just finished a year at the Johnstone Academy and they just loved it. We have a grandson that will be ready for second levels next year and his parents will have to send him to Virginia City or Carson City."

"Yes, that is why Jason and I helped Karen Peters get started with a second level here in Johnstone."

"I know, I know. But you see boys are not accepted by Mrs. Peters. Herman and I have plenty of money and we would like to do what you and Jason did, for girls."

"You want to start a second level, for boys?"

"Yes, how do we start? Can we rent the place where the girls started on Orchard Street, do you think? Where do we get the head master and teachers?"

"Let me give you the address of a friend of mine." I said. "He lives in Council Bluffs and is on the board of visitors for Iowa Normal College in Cedar Falls. He found teachers for the elementary school here a number of years ago." I got up and found a pencil and paper.

"You need to talk to Carol, here. She helped Karen Peters set up the whole operation. That is what Carol wants to do after she graduates from college." Louise added.

"If you like, Mrs. Schussler, I can get you a copy of most of the paper work that has to filled out for the State of Nevada." Carol was smiling because she knew that a new summer job was about to open for her.

"Oh, dear girl, that would be so kind of you." Gertrude was relieved.

"You need to get the announcement of openings in the Cedar Falls papers and into the placement office, it is already summer and I doubt anything will happen until midyear." I said.

120
Naval Academy
Fall 1875

I returned from Nevada refreshed and determined to continue my teaching career on a high note. Sam and Rachael had sold their house in Arlington after her mother died and all of paper work was sorted in the basement of the Army Navy building. They lived close to the Naval Academy and I had turned the operations of the Naval Institute building over to Sam. When the election of next year was over, I would recommend to the new president that he consider Sam for the Superintendent's chair at Annapolis. Sam was no longer an employee of CI, he was older and his salary with the federal government was nearly equal to mine and he could devote his entire career to the Navy. President Grant had asked him to return to the United States Marine Corps, as a major. He wore his new uniform with pride and taught several courses at the Naval Academy in addition to his operation of the Naval Institute. He loved his summer cruises and looked forward to them each year. He worked summers and I tried to relax on the ranch in Nevada.

I was fifty-eight years old, this past June, and I would be sixty when James graduated, sixty-two when Ruth graduated from Harvard and sixty-five when Carol graduated from Columbia. Louise and I would retire from government service when James graduated from Annapolis, so that we could spend more time with the two girls. One would be in Boston, the other New York but we would be free to visit whenever we wanted.

I opened my old notebook and turned the pages of my old notes for Naval History 101 and checked my watch again to make sure I would not be late for class. There it was, the first course that I had taught in September, 1870. I had an academic aide, my first six months in Annapolis. His name was Mr. Merrill Edwards. He and I began to review the course syllabus for fourth year, newly entered, cadets to the Naval Academy. It was dry and boring. I remembered asking him, "What can be changed and what must remain intact so that cadets will be able to move on into History 201, Mr. Edwards?"

"Jason, what are you doing, your class is about to start and you are sitting here in the den, day dreaming?"

I shot a look at my watch and she was right. I scooped up my notes and tore out the front door and ran to the Wise Hall across the street this time.

I found the classroom less than a minute before the class was to start and opened the door to hear nothing, just silence. The room was nearly empty. Before the class sounded, however, the room began to fill.

I walked to the lectern and placed my briefcase on a small table beside it. And I began my favorite lecture, "This is Naval History 101. Anyone who thinks they are somewhere else should take this opportunity to get to their proper class."

"I was a member of the United States Navy for thirty years and I am proud of that, but I am not a member of that service today and you do not have to give me the military courtesy of saluting or standing in my presence. Is that clear?" There was no response from the class. I opened my brief case and took out my list of topics which I had penciled on a small piece of paper and my pocket watch so I would not go over the hour with them. I started with the first topic which was the outline for the course.

"This first course is a history of the world's navies, how they were formed; what rivers, seas and oceans that they sailed and why. The course will end when we are still the 13 British Colonies. For those of you who thought you would learn all about the US Navy, you will. Because, the USN is based largely on what the British established for us as a pattern. The British stole from the Spanish, who stole from the Dutch, who stole from the countries inside the Mediterranean. So, I guess you can say, that navies are composed of a bunch of thieves."

Just like 1870, not a chuckle, not a smile anywhere on the faces of the fifty-five cadets. I am still not reaching them, I thought. "Gentlemen, it is okay to smile at my jokes. Not only were there thieves serving in the British Navy, there were also convicted murderers, rapists, and men who were escaping debtor's prison and imprisonment by the Queen's courts. Many times the ranks could not be filled by volunteers and those escaping judgements. Sometimes the British had to kidnap their own citizens and citizens of other countries to fill the ranks. This is a true story that I was involved in when I was a Captain...............................

121
Naval History 404
Spring 1876

The last history course that I taught at the Naval Academy turned out to be the most interesting. JJ and I had managed to avoid each other during his time at Annapolis, as far as instructor and student were concerned. This was a required course for graduation and I was the only one teaching it. As I looked out over the lecture hall, I found his face among the sea of others and I smiled and began the introduction to the course.

"This could be called, the history of the war ship just as well as 'The Old Man's Memories 404.' Do not look so shocked, gentlemen, I have ears and I hear what Midshipmen and Ensigns talk about. This is my last opportunity to teach a course at the Naval Institute. This November, we will all go to the polls and select a new President of the United States and a new boss for the Naval Institute and probably the Superintendent of the Naval Academy. Presidents have a habit of doing that every four or eight years. The only way I will be standing here next year, will be if President Grant is elected to a third term, and I doubt he will run again. The Commandant and I have become great friends and I will miss not seeing him. I hope he remains at the Academy as the Commandant of Midshipmen or even Superintendent. Admiral Hagood and I entered the Navy on the same day, at the same place and we have been friends ever since. I retired from active duty in June, 1867, and my son will enter as an officer ten years later, if he passes this course!"

There was a restless shifting of seats and I said, "But you did not come here today to listen to me go down memory lane. This summer you will take your final required cruise on a war ship bound for a transatlantic port. This course will help prepare you for that. You will be on a current battle ship of the line, not a sailing vessel, but many of the things, you will find the same. The curvature of the earth has not changed in millions of years, for example. The function of a war ship has always been, to bring to bear, on the enemy, as large an offensive armament as possible, no matter in what century the war ship was used. The naval architects are the ones who design our war ships and over the centuries they used the materials available to them. Today's ships are constructed of iron and steel, yesterday's ships were constructed of specially selected trees from which ship timbers were cut. One of the reasons England wanted to hold on to her American colonies, was the abundance of 'live oak' trees available along our southern coasts. Men searched our forests, looking for particular shaped trees to harvest. They selected tall straight trunks from which to cut stern posts and masts. They looked for gently curved trunks from which to cut futtocks, cat heads and wing knees. Severely curved limbs and upper trunks were ideal for knees, channel wales and water ways. These terms are still used in ship building today!"

There was less shifting in the seats but the students were still not in tune with me. I shifted gears and said, "On your cruise this summer you will serve aboard a ship that has been designed by the finest naval architects in the world. It has undergone extensive sea trials and is as safe as we know how to make it. Did you ever wonder how designs are tested? How did we get to the ships that we use today? How many years does it take to make a complete modification in the war ships of the United States?" Butts began to slide forward. I had their attention now.

"Without your understanding of where we came from in this navy, it will be harder to advance and produce modern ships of the line for combat in the twentieth century. Yes, that is right, this is 1876, almost '77, and the navy must think ahead to when it might fight its next war. Will it be before the turn of the century? If not, what will the rest of the world put upon the seas to face us in 1901 or 1915? By 1915 we could be involved in a world wide conflict if transportation continues to advance at such a rapid rate. The world becomes smaller, time wise, when you can ride a train across our country in a few days, when it used to take months making the same trip ten years ago! What if this summer you are on a high speed ship and you sail from New York to South Hampton in less than a week! The size of the Atlantic Ocean just got 75% smaller for you than it did for me in my graduation cruise! The French and the Germans have used lighter than air ships for many years as observation platforms to direct land and sea battles. Both countries are building air ships that are propelled through the air instead of a hot air balloon. You fill them once and tie them to the round for use over and over again without refilling the air supply inside the giant envelope. If future improvements on design of these ships continue, than you will be able to fly from Germany to England in a matter of hours!

So in the Navy, we study our past to improve our future. You already have studied the ordnance used in the past to the present, so we can skip that in this course. You have already studied the use of ships in war time formations, so we can skip that. This course deals only with ships of war. A frigate for instance is not a ship of war. Have they been used in wars? Absolutely, but they are no longer being built by us or the other great navies of the world. They were invented to be used in the Mediterranean in the fourteenth and fifteenth centuries. They were a narrow fast-sailing vessel, fitted to be propelled by oars during 'calms', which happen often on the Mediterranean. The first frigate to be built in England was the *Constant Warwick*. It was built with 26 cannon and increased to 42 in 1677. The *Constant Warwick* was so fast that the English fleet could not keep up with it on routine cruises and the Warwick became a scout vessel. A fleet moves at the speed of the slowest ship within its squadrons, not the fastest.

What then, is an historical War Ship? It was a large vessel with three or more masts, of which three were square-rigged. We have already covered how ships were propelled in the Naval History 101 course, remember, we started with oars and ended with steam engine propulsion. Before the application of steam to marine propulsion, the largest war ships rarely exceeded 200 feet in length and the proportion of length to beam was usually not far from 4 to 1. The bows were bluff and are shown in your texts in page 89, and the stern hardly less so, particularly in line-of-battle ships. You may want to review your notes from the course on, Tactics and Signals, that you took from me. The full bows and relatively great widths, while they reduced the speed, gave great handiness or maneuvering ability; a most necessary requisite in battle and in narrow channels or crowded harbors. The advent of steam changed the conditions materially. Sailing vessels were no longer used as fighting ships of war. Since 1850, clippers have replaced frigates. Men no longer climb the masts and walk the yardarms to set the sail. Yardarms are raised by a steam engine. Steam is used to operate the steering on all ships in the US Navy.

Please, remember, that the sailing ship was a development of the galley, and it was not until the eighteenth century that it attained a form and character suitable to ocean navigation under all conditions of weather. The earlier types were often profusely ornamented and carefully made, but clumsy, slow and unseaworthy in rough weather. The sterns, and sometimes the bows, were built high in the air. These were gradually reduced in height until they took final shape in the poop and topgallant forecastle so common in steamers of the present day. The reform in design of the rigging and sails was simultaneous with the improvement in the hull of war ships. The poorly set and absurdly placed sails of the eighteenth century gave way to what we see today. We have metal masts and yards, not wooden ones. We have metal cables, not hemp ropes. This has given us choices for ship rigging. A sail powdered war ship was a ship-rig, of course, but now we have bark-rig, barkentine-rig, sloop-rig, yawl-rig, cutter-rig, and cat-rig. You, gentlemen, have a lot more information to carry around in your heads than I had to.

I notice the hour is almost gone again and those of you who have taken a course from me, are ready to close your notes and listen to a story of my experiences with ships of war."

I closed my notes, walked up on the small stage behind the lectern and sat down in one of the captain's chairs that were often sitting there. "Those of you in the way back, come down and sit in the space between the stage and the first row of seats. I am going to try to light this cigar that Admiral Hagood gave me and hope that it does not explode in my face."

I waited a few minutes and I began. "This is a true story that happened to me in, 1853...

The bell rang and the midshipmen left except for JJ.

"Dad is that true about Washington being so dangerous?"

"The crime rate in our nation's capital is greater than any other city. When you are stationed there, James, and you will be. Consider it a battle zone, if not a war zone and it will help you survive."

"Is that why you and Mom never let us kids live in Washington and you rode back and forth on a train. We only saw you on weekends."

"I know that was bad for you, James. I am sorry about that. You were too small to remember the White House, you lived there with us until Uncle James retired. Baby Ruth came to live with us there also, but she can not remember it, either."

"Why did you adopt Ruth and I, when you could have your own, like Carol?"

"James, it is not that simple. Your mother and I did not meet until it was almost too late for her to conceive. We tried everyday for a year, we were both exhausted and we found you, covered with chicken pox, waiting for a mother and father to show up. One look at you and we knew we had a son for life. I hope you feel the same way?"

"I do, Dad. You and Mom have been my parents since I was born, it just took a little while for us to find each other."

"That is exactly how we feel, James."

"I have to get to another class, Dad. I am glad that we had this talk." We started to walk up the aisle and we saw Louise sitting in the back row.

"Mom. How long have you been here?"

"Just got here, saw you two had your heads together and I did not want to bother you."

"I am late for my next class, got to run." He bent down and gave his mother a kiss and was off.

"Jason?"

"Yes, Louise."

"Thank you for telling James what you did about finding him waiting for us. That was beautiful."

"Your hearing is very good, for an old lady, you know that, Louise?"

"It is above average, just like how we found each other at age 38 standing in a receiving line at the White House."

"You changed and saved my life, Louise. I will never forget that."

"Where do you want to eat lunch, Admiral? I am buying."

"Number 2, Admiral's row, on the back porch, just the two of us."

"Deal."

122
Summer Cruise
1876

JJ's last summer cruise was a transatlantic adventure that consumed the entire summer break. In 1873, the year JJ was accepted to the Naval Academy, the course of study for cadet Midshipmen was extended to six years, the last two years to be spent at sea. This was an attempt to fill the officer ranks of the United States Navy. Ships and ordnance were no use without the seamen to sail and fight them. What sort of officers and seamen were they, who maned the fleets of the post Civil War? They were graduates of the Naval Academy, regular Navy career officers and enlisted seamen, and Navy reserve. JJ's captain on this cruise was a member of the Navy reserve and reported only during the summer. Some reserve officers, like Sam Mason, had just recently returned to active duty and he was on this cruise as a Marine Major in command of the 189 marines that came aboard the USS *Monongahela* at Norfolk, Virginia.

The purpose of the cruise was, of course, to give experience to the cadets at Annapolis but it also allowed the USS *Castor*, *Monongahela* and *Nispsic* to complete their crews and make ports of calls in Europe. Both the English and American navies were perennially short of men, but with this difference, American war ships lacking crews stayed in port, while English ships had to go to sea. The safety of Britain depended on it.

The three ships partaking of the US Naval Academy summer cruise of 1876 were:

USS *Nispic*, a 1375-ton Adams class gunboat, was the last vessel built at the Potomac Dock Yards prior to the Civil War. At the close of the war she was rebuilt one and one half her original size and was now ready for sea trials. James Jason Caldwell, was assigned as her gunnery officer.

USS *Monongahela*, a 2078-ton steam sloop built at the Philadelphia Navy Yard in January, 1863. She participated in the Gulf of Mexico fleet under Farragut, was in the battles of New Orleans and Mobile Bay. She had just returned from assignment in the western and southern Atlantic. She would be the home to Sam Mason and his marines for the summer cruise of 1876.

USS *Castor*, a 2100 ton Canonicus class monitor built in Jersey City Ship Yards in 1864. She was famous for her two battles at Fort Fisher in North

Carolina. The first destroyed the fort and the second sealed off the port of Wilmington. She was involved in the capture of Richmond in 1865. She remained out of commission until 1869, when she was recommissioned as the USS *Mahopac.*

The US Navy had decided to send these three vessels on a transatlantic cruise to the European ports of: South Hampton, England; Copenhagen, Denmark; Oslo, Norway; Stockholm, Sweden; Helsinki, Finland; St. Petersburg and Tallin, Russia; Danzig, Prussia and then back to South Hampton. In order to get to South Hampton, the three ships needed to complete their crews. They cruised from three different locations. The *Monongahela* was stationed in Norfolk and would load Sam's marines and head for Annapolis straight up the Chesapeake. The *Nipsic* would begin her sea trials from Potomac Dock yards, sail down the Potomac and then north up the Chesapeake to Annapolis. The *Castor* was stationed on the James River basin and she, too, would steam straight north to Annapolis. The three ships arrived in Annapolis on June 7, 1876. All officers and hands were given 24 hours shore leave and on the morning of June 9, 1876, they left Annapolis and sailed south back down the Chesapeake and into the Atlantic Ocean. JJ had spent many hours aboard ships inside the Chesapeake and across the middle Atlantic to Bermuda and back to Annapolis. He was fairly comfortable with the Nispic, she was, after all, classified as a 'gun boat' and he was the ordnance officer in charge of every gun on board.

They had smooth sailing to Philadelphia, two short days, then left for Yarmouth, Nova Scotia. The temperatures dropped fifteen degrees during the five day sail. They were given 24 hours leave again, but JJ was assigned to ship duty because during the rougher water of the North Atlantic some gun mounts needed adjustment and realignment. June 17th was the day they were to begin heading across the North Atlantic to England in one giant leap.

Shore leave was granted in Copenhagen and several hundred American sailors descended upon the city. The Danes may be the most playful people in Europe. Even the capital has a "look" about it; coppery green towers alongside gingerbread houses, inlets and millponds surrounded by willows, dozens of bicycles along cobblestone streets. The Danish Vikings were once the scourge of Europe. They raided and held large areas of England, France and Spain. But then they discovered that they could also use their knowledge of the sea to trade peacefully and they prospered. Built as it is on the narrowest point of the Kattegat Straight between Sweden and Denmark, the settlement was ideal for trade and water travel.

In 1801, the coast of Denmark had been the location for a great sea battle and the sea ports were used to seeing Baltic navies from Russia, Finland, Prussia, Sweden and even Norway sail into its harbors. Copenhagen was not used to 189 drunken marines, however, and they began to be arrested and returned to the *Monongahela*. Admiral Hagood had seen enough, he ordered Major Mason to round up the few marines still left in port and set sail for Ganzig, Prussia. The *Castor* and the *Nispic* followed in two days. JJ had never been farther east than Bermuda and he wanted to see as much of Copenhagen as he could in two days. He decided to visit the palaces. Amalienborg palace is the official royal residence during most of year and was not open for him to tour. He found Christianborg palace and it was the Danish Parliament. It had been the King's palace until it burned down in 1794 and when it was restored, the King decided to have it be the home of the Danish Parliament. Rosenborg Palace was next on his list and he found it to be the home of the crown jewels. JJ found that some of the most delightful buildings in the city were visible from the waterfront. The canal district never stopped being busy night or day. The Church of Our Savior had a unique tower with an outside spiral stairway leading to the top of the green pinnacle. His eyes feasted on his surroundings. The tower of the Borsen, the world's oldest active stock exchange, was even more intriguing because it was built to look like three green dragons, their tails twisted together to form the spire. At night he ate with some of his shipmates at the Tivoli Gardens. He hated to leave after just two days.

Prussia was not Denmark. The Danes spoke fluent English. The Prussians spoke only German. There were exactly seven Americans who spoke German and they were used as interpreters for small groups of well behaved sailors who toured the city. JJ found Danzig to be one of the most beautiful cities in the Baltic. It is ideally located where the Vistula River empties into the Baltic and is the main seaport for the export of goods from Poland. Amber, salt, furs and every type of agricultural and manufactured product passed through St. Mary's gate in Ganzig on its way to Scandinavia and the Baltic States. St. Mary's street passed through the gates and led to the largest church in Prussia, The Church of our Lady. It is also the largest brick church in the world having been built between 1343 and 1502. Its nave holds 25,000 worshipers. Next to the church stood the spired Royal Chapel, the only Baroque church in Danzig. Elsewhere in the city were two grain mills built by the Teutonic Knights. The 17th century was the golden age for building and architecture in Danzig. Flemish, Dutch and Italian craftsmen were paid to do their finest artistry on public buildings.

Two days later they docked in Tallinn, Russia. Again, there were no English speaking natives and no Americans with Estonian language skills. The seven German speaking interpreters sought out those Estonians who also spoke German and in this manner they toured Katherine the Great's summer palace and the city of Tallinn. The city of Tallinn rises dramatically above its port, proud of being the best preserved medieval city in Northern Europe. The city was also founded by Teutonic Knights, that is why the town center looked like a town of German origin. The oldest parts visible to JJ were the corner towers, including the one nicknamed Pikk Herman.

"That looks a little bit like 'Herman the German' who works for my father." JJ said to a shipmate.

The upper town was the preserve of the Bishop and the Knights, but the lower town was the heart of the commercial district and the town's wealth. They visited St. Nicholas, St. Olav and Holy Ghost Churches. These were built by each foreign ruler of Tallinn; Prussia, Sweden and Russia.

The next day they docked in St. Petersburg as the midnight sun was just beginning to catch the gold on the spires and domes throughout the city. By design, it was to be the world's most beautiful city, and the capital of its largest empire. Peter the Great, Czar of all Russia, had commanded that a "window to the west" be built to replace the old capital, Moscow. He hired the best Italian, French and German architects to design palaces and buildings in the baroque style. JJ and his friends admired the Admiralty building which Czar Peter had placed in the geographic center of the city. The soaring gold spire was a symbol of his new navy and merchant marine fleets. Lost American sailors used the spire as a landmark to travel around the city. His wife, Katherine I, succeeded him and continued the construction of the city. She was succeeded by her two daughters Czarina Elizabeth and Katherine II. The city gained its most beautiful buildings after Peter's death.

It was not until they docked in South Hampton that JJ learned of this father's knighthood.

123

South Hampton
1876

My last summer as the Superintendent of the Naval Institute was spent in Nevada at the ranch house in Virginia City. I received a cablegram from Nevelle Napier in London informing me that he was meeting James's ship, the *Nispic,* in South Hampton. He would meet with Admiral Hagood and request his permission to have JJ leave his ship long enough to travel with him to London.

The Queen was about to announce the latest peers of the realm. One of those to be knighted was Jason Edwin Caldwell, of St. George, Bermuda. And since he was in Nevada, half way around the world, and his son was in South Hampton, Lord Napier reasoned that a knighthood could be bestowed upon the son, for the father. I was speechless.

When the USNA cruise arrived in South Hampton, England, they were paid a courtesy call from Lord Napier. He asked for permission to come aboard the *Nispic* and introduced himself to Captain Evans. He asked to see Ensign Caldwell so he could deliver a missive from Admiral Hagood. The Captain of the *Nispic* sent for Ensign Caldwell. JJ appeared in a few minutes and saluted the captain and then the Admiral. Captain Evans said, "Sit down for a minute, Ensign, Admiral Napier has orders for you from Admiral Hagood."

"So you are Jason's son, I have heard a lot about you. Your father talks about you, nonstop. He says you live and breathe US Navy from sun up until sun down."

"I watched my father for the last twenty-one years. I learned everything about what the Navy was between 1833 to 1876. He was my history instructor at the Academy. I remember my father talking about how much he admired you when he returned the *Resolute* to you."

"Your father is a remarkable man, James, please give him this letter when you see him. It is the official invitation to London. The Queen has recognized the fact that Jason Caldwell is a dual national and wishes to reward his 40 years of service to the US Navy and the Bermuda Crown Colony."

"Thank you, Lord Napier."

"And here are your orders for the next few days, from Admiral Hagood. You are to accompany me to London for the knighthood to be bestowed upon your father. You will kneel before the Queen and accept on his behalf."

"Knighthood?"

"Yes, the next time I see your father, I can address him as Sir Jason Caldwell, Knight of the Realm, Protector of Bermuda.

124

Nominating Conventions
1876

The National Republican Convention met in Cincinnati, June 14th. President Grant polled his friends and closest advisors to see if any of them would put his name in nomination for a third term. They all recommended that he wait until 1880 to run for a third term, so that he would not hold the exalted office longer than George Washington for continuous years (8). They urged him to support his vice president, Henry Wilson of Massachusetts for the nomination. His advisors, however, planned to support the speaker of the house, James Blaine for the Republican candidate in November, 1876.

James Gillespie Blaine was an eminent American statesman and political leader. His great grandfather, Ephraim Blaine (1741-1804) was a signer of the Declaration of Independence. James was a red blooded American patriot, born in Brownsville, Pennsylvania, on January 31, 1830. He graduated from Washington College, Pennsylvania, in 1847. He was a school teacher and newspaper editor until 1858, when he was elected to the state legislature, became speaker of the state house and chairman of the state Republican Party. In 1862, he was elected to the US House of Representatives, where he served for seven terms, three of those as speaker. He lost the speakership when the Democrats regained control of the US House in 1875. In 1876, the Democrats made a vigorous effort to include him in the various railroad scandals. This culminated in the highly dramatic incident of June 5, 1876, when he produced ,on the floor of the House, the "mulligan letters" which gave him his vindication. The Republicans went to the national convention the next week with the disturbance hanging over their heads.

The party was hopelessly split and a caucus was held to see who might support James Blaine or Henry Wilson. A suggestion was to run Blaine as president and Wilson as vice president, but Wilson's supporters said he was already past the second chair and deserved the first place nomination. A second ballot was taken with little change in the rank order.

Horace Maynard withdrew from consideration and released his votes. On the third ballot a change began to form. William Evarts withdrew from consideration and released his votes. On the forth ballot, no change occurred, and a second caucus was held. The top two candidates proposed that they be nominated as first and second places on the ticket, but agreement was not reached. Outside the caucus, Grant's people proposed that his name now be brought forward. Blaine delegates became concerned and caucused with Hayes delegates to reach a compromise. On the fourth ,ballot the votes were closer. Schuyler Colfax withdrew from consideration and released his votes. It was now a three way race for first place on the ticket. On the seventh ballot, Hayes received 355 votes and the nomination for president. Little was known about Rutherford Birchard Hayes outside of Ohio, except he was a good governor, had a fine record as a soldier, and his name had never been connected with a railroad scandal.

The Democratic National Convention met at St. Louis, two weeks later and on the second ballot nominated Samuel J. Tilden of New York. He was a native of New York, born in 1814. He was an able lawyer and had done great service to the cause of reform, when governor of New York in 1875. During the campaign of 1876, Tilden drew huge crowds, while Hayes never managed to excite the people who came to meet the candidate and hear him speak. The newspapers followed and reported the ground swell of support for the New York governor and the lack of support for the Ohio governor.

The Washington Post had the following headline after the election for President, 1876.

DEMOCRATS WIN CLEAR VICTORY

	States	Popular Vote	Electoral Vote
Tilden	17	1,866,352	180
Hayes	11	1,045,703	120
Grant	0	389,581	0

The campaign had been comparatively quiet, but it ended in an excitement that threatened revolution. The newspapers, like the Washington Post, reported Tilden a clear winner in both popular vote and electoral votes. It was expected that the result would be close, but for several days a final count was not available, this placed the official results in doubt – so much so, indeed, that the belief gained ground that the vote was undergoing manipulation. There was no doubt that Tilden had carried New York, his home state. He also carried New Jersey by a large popular vote. Indiana and Connecticut voted nearly total Democratic tickets. With the aid of the Democratic south, Tilden totaled 180 electoral votes. The returning election boards of Louisiana, Florida and South Carolina began to throw out the votes of heavily Democratic districts on the grounds of voter fraud and black intimidation.

It took several days before enough changes were made to award the electoral votes from Florida, Louisiana and South Carolina to Rutherford B. Hayes, Hayes now had 161 to Tilden's 160.

Rutherford Birchard Hayes was now the certified winner and he wasted little time in leaving Ohio and boarding a train for Washington. He stepped off the train in Washington, caught a cab to the White House and met with the President.

"Mr. President elect, welcome to Washington and the White House." Said a relieved President Grant.

"Thank you, Mr. President, but I was not elected and I should not be called the President elect. The Republican Party bought and paid for the electoral votes. I am ashamed to call myself a Republican. The Democrats may still lodge a complaint with the Supreme Court. The proof of bribes paid and received is a matter of record."

"Yes, Rutherford, that is certainly true. Republicans paid bribes to whom?"

"What do you mean, to whom?"

"They bought votes because the Democrats sold them! All I ever asked my cabinet officers was to be honest. Most were a bunch of thieves, liars and dandies with their hands out ready to take any offer from anyone. My Secretary of War was impeached for God's Sake."

"How can I avoid the revolving door of the cabinet members, Ulysses? I will not tolerate misconduct, I will replace them at the same rate that you did."

"Find honest men and women to serve, Rutherford."

"Women?"

"Yes, Andrew Johnson fired Lincoln's personal secretary and replaced him with a woman. You should have at least 1 woman, 1 colored, 1 American Indian, 1 Confederate, 1 Democrat, 1 Independent and the rest honest Republicans. I would try very hard to represent every section of the population. There are over 100,000 American Indians presently living on government reservations in this country plus probably another 200,000 roaming free.

"Good, I was considering David McKakey, of Tennessee for Post Master General but he is a former Confederate."

"Excellent choice, I know David. He is honest and will serve you well. Who else are you considering?"

"I am considering either Pinchback from Louisiana or Shurman of Ohio, both black men, as Secretary of the Treasury."

"I would ask Shurman first, Pinchback is a hothead!" "That only leaves the Attorney-General slot. Try to find an honest attorney in this town! I tried five different people in that position, Rutherford, I do not think it can be done!" They were both relaxed and chuckling at this point.

"I feel better, Ulysses, if this meeting did not go well, I was considering resigning and handing it over to the Vice President."

"Oh, My God, no. You stick in there, Rutherford, I will give you every assistance that I can. I will gladly tell you all the stupid mistakes that I made in the first year of office and you can avoid all of those. It is my fault, Rutherford, I did not want to think that fellow officers would suddenly make money the number one object in their lives. If I had it to do over, I would have ignored anyone who had served in the military."

"Ulysses, you did not create the morals that those men exhibited. I have an idea. We need to forward every piece of dirty laundry that we have to the newspapers concerning every Senator or Representative or Justice before we submit any cabinet member nominations. Let the rotten apples be fully aired to the public. Then, I will submit a list of names to the newspapers that I intend to send to the Senate. I will then include a statement that I do not expect any of these names to be confirmed because they are totally honest men and women above reproach and would not function with the majority of the dishonest members of the present Senate."

During the next month, the newspapers had a field day, exposure after exposure appeared and warrants for arrests were issued in the home districts of US Senators and Representatives and one Justice of the Supreme Court. The list of cabinet members nominated by the incoming President was published in the major newspapers: Postmaster General was David McKakey of Tennessee. Secretary Treasury was John Shurman of Ohio. Secretary Interior was George Crow, Tama Indian Reservation. Secretary War was Carl Schurz of Missouri via Prussia. Attorney General was Mrs. C. E. Devens of Massachusetts. Secretary Navy was Benjamin Hagood of Georgia. Secretary of State was William Evarts of New York.

125
Graduation Day
June 1877

The graduation of the United States Naval Academy in June, 1877, was held at Annapolis, Maryland. I was more nervous that JJ. He had come to Admiral's row to have his mother help him with his new uniform. He would receive his college diploma today and his commission after he had completed his sea trials. Things had really changed in forty years. I graduated in 1837 from a single military academy which held both branches, the Army and Navy. They had separate campuses now and had very separate missions to perform. New Navy Cadets were taken by train to Annapolis for a summer cruise to see if they were qualified to become seagoing officers in the USN (United States Navy). A, soon to be graduate of the US Naval Academy, left his parent's house and found his place in line to march in with the rest of the graduation class of 1877. He sat with his fellow officers and searched the spectators for his mother and father, Ruth and Carol Caldwell. They should be sitting next to his uncle and aunt. He could not find them among the crowd, but he knew they were there. He had welcomed his aunt and uncle the day before. They had come all the way from Beaufort, South Carolina, on one of his father's packet ships out of Port Royal, South Carolina. It was not until he walked across the platform and received his bachelor's degree that he heard a rebel yell from his Uncle Robert and located where they were sitting.

"Does this sound familiar to you, Robert? You and Carol asked me the same thing forty years ago. Listen to what JJ is telling his sisters."

"I began as a Midshipman, Ensign and Lieutenant JG."

"And you are a Lieutenant now? Did you skip over the Ensign and JG grades?" Carol asked.

"No, I worked hard and earned them, little sister. My instructors have recommended that I go directly to the Naval War College at Newport, Rhode Island."

"Will you write to me?"

"Yes, Carol."

"Oh, my, God. Jason, I do remember. JJ is not going to the Naval War College, is he?"

"The apple does not fall far from the tree, brother. I tried to talk him out of the San Francisco part of it."

Robert looked at me and a sad smile came across his face. He nodded his head and gave me a huge hug. "What are you two doing over there?" Mariann asked.

"Just remembering something that happened forty years ago on this very spot. Mom, Dad, Carol and I were standing talking to Jason. Now, only he and I are alive to see JJ follow in his father's footsteps. It is kind of sad, that is all."

"Where are we going to eat?" I asked.

"I want Chesapeake crab!" Mariann had decided for us. She began walking towards the waterfront in search of a restaurant. The rest of us trailed along after her, like a bunch of ducklings following their mother to the water.

Epilogue

It was June 29th and after dinner each evening, I had talked about my life experiences from a Plebe at West Point to Admiral in the United States Navy. I was celebrating my 60th birthday, and the party had lasted three days. After my retirement from teaching at the Naval Academy, we moved to Seneca Hill, Pennsylvania, and had a giant, retirement, graduation and birthday party with family and friends. For a week people had arrived in Oil City by train. The first to arrive was Monty Blair with the news that Bell's air cooled telephone lines had been successfully strung and tested in Boston, he left the first night to get back to Boston. Sam and Rachael Mason had come up from Annapolis and had moved into their old living quarters for the week, they were called away by one of their children. They returned to the Naval Academy. My brother, Robert, and his wife, Mariann, had come for our son's graduation and they came north with us to Pennsylvania. Robert's twin daughters, Karen and Sharon, were both married, one lived in Virginia and the other in Maryland with their families. Robert left after the second day to stop in Maryland and Virginia on the way back home.

Our son, James, known as JJ, had graduated from the Naval Academy on June 2nd and was scheduled to begin his two year tour of sea duty, shortly. He left to report to the Philadelphia shipyards after three days. His sister, Ruth, was home from Harvard with the "nice young man" she had met, a Mr. Theodore Roosevelt. She told her mother that it was not serious, but I had seen them mooning over each other and they left to return to New York City and the Roosevelt's Park Avenue apartment. Carol had finished her last year of preparatory school before entering Columbia University. She left with the Peters when they continued their trip to Pittsburgh.

The hotel rooms in Franklin, Oil City and as far away as Titusville were left by our guests over the three days since their arrival. There was a definite pecking order to who left first. You could not ask the President of the United States, his Secretary of the Navy or the Commandant of the Marine Corps to stay an entire week. I had become one of President Hayes' closest confidants. We had bounced ideas off of each other by telephone since March 4th. He stayed in the house one night and was called back to Washington. His Secretary of the Navy, Ben Hagood, and the Marine Commandant, Chris Merryweather had the same emergency and they left with him,

Mark twain listened to every word of my nightly monologs, then announced that he would be leaving with the others back to Bermuda on the Cold Harbor. Jerome Lewis and his family were called back to Louisville because of a large murder case. Jerome was retired from the navy and was now the Chief of Police for Louisville.

Brigadier General Tom Schneider and his wife, Beth, checked out of the Oil City Hotel and moved into the spaces left by Sam Mason and settled in for the week. Won Sing still followed the President of Seneca Oil around, making fun of him at every turn. The president was Peter Clivestone, who had dropped his British accent, and left Seneca Hill long enough to study for a degree in business administration from Penn College. He would remind Won Sing that his father never liked him and he was a terrible cook. Won would bow low and reply, "Most honorable president of world's smallest oil company, you wery good person at hart. But Admiral will fire your ass, if he ever hear you say that about honorable father."

The train for Nevada left the fourth day before I had a chance to finish my life's story. Louise was a former first lady in the White House and a departure this size did not affect her. She was the commanding general of the "house on the hill" between Oil City and Titusville, Pennsylvania. It was built while we both worked in the White House under the Buchanan Administration and it had over a 135 rooms, because that is what Louise wanted.

"You are the chairman of Caldwell International, Jason. You will be entertaining US Presidents and foreign heads of state. We need something as impressive as my 'brother's house'".

"You mean, The White House?" I was stunned.

"That is exactly what I mean. You are an Admiral in the United States Navy and you are the National Affairs Advisor to the President of the United States."

And so the building began and it became a corporate headquarters for the company I had founded many years before in Port Royal, South Carolina, called Caldwell Shipping and Trading. Today, June 29, 1877, the house was nearly empty. Every bedroom was no longer taken. Louise had hired more household staff for the week. The evening meals were not unlike those she organized in the White House. The main table held all the Admirals and Generals in the house, now only Tom and me. Empty chairs were now where President Hayes, a former brigadier general, and now the commander-in-chief, and Mrs. Hayes had sat. Admiral Ben Hagood and his side kick, General Chris Merryweather, had been next to the Chief of Police and his wife from Louisville Kentucky. Next to them, Colonel Sam Mason, Superintendent of the Naval Institute, and his wife from Annapolis, Maryland had been sitting. They had been seated next to General John Butler and his wife, Sally from Bermuda. The tables forming the dining hall were nearly empty. The tables had had a theme to them, the rapid response marines and their families were grouped together and some of them stayed because Tom Schneider had asked them to. The Nevada group of tables was now empty. The original Caldwell Shipping group was headed by Captain Jacobs and his family and they stayed. The original Caldwell Trading and Banking group was headed by Robert Whitehall and his family and they stayed also. The ATT table was half full. And so the dining room that fourth evening looked like a little lonesome.

After dinner, Louise said, "Welcome everyone to our home for the final installment of Jason's story. I have asked Jason to write a book about his adventures. It involves everyone who was invited to this house. As I warned you three nights ago, Jason, is a talker and he may not be finished after this party. He has decided to tell his story in three parts entitled; Calm Before the Storm, Death Before Dishonor and Lull After the Storm. The Woolfall Book Company of St. Paul, Minnesota, has agreed to publish it. You are all invited back next year, for one day, June 26th to have Jason sign a copy for you. Jason, you have the floor." Louise sat back down on her dining room chair and I stood.

"Thank you everyone for coming to this special celebration. My voice is about gone, so this will be a very short chat. Did I ever tell you about how I met Louise in Ostend, Belgium and later visited her in London?"

Acknowledgments

The publication of this sixth book by Authorhouse required many hands. My thanks, as always, to the following:

Acquisitions editor, Cindi Henson, in Indianapolis -

Copy editor, Connie Ryan. Thankfully, one of us knows where a comma goes -

Cover design team in Bloomington -

Courtney, Scott, Angela, Jamie and Adrienne for their wise counsel and zealous representation.

Alexandra Wallace for her many hours of emails and telephone conversations with me with the past two books.

LaVergne, TN USA
03 March 2010
174780LV00002B/32/P